NIGHT OVER WATER
&
A DANGEROUS FORTUNE

Also by Ken Follett

THE MODIGLIANI SCANDAL
PAPER MONEY
EYE OF THE NEEDLE
TRIPLE
THE KEY TO REBECCA
THE MAN FROM ST PETERSBURG
ON WINGS OF EAGLES
LIE DOWN WITH LIONS
THE PILLARS OF THE EARTH
A DANGEROUS FORTUNE
A PLACE CALLED FREEDOM
THE THIRD TWIN
THE HAMMER OF EDEN
CODE TO ZERO

KEN FOLLETT was only twenty-seven when he wrote the award-winning novel *Eye of the Needle*, which became an international bestseller. He has since written several equally successful novels, including, most recently, *Code to Zero*. He is also author of the non-fiction bestseller *On Wings of Eagles*. He lives with his family in London and Hertfordshire.

Visit the Ken Follett website at http://www.ken-follett.com

KEN FOLLETT

NIGHT OVER WATER
&
A DANGEROUS FORTUNE

PAN BOOKS

Night Over Water first published 1991
by Macmillan and first published by Pan Books 1992
A Dangerous Fortune first published 1993
by Macmillan and first published by Pan Books 1995

This omnibus edition published 2002 by Pan Books
an imprint of Pan Macmillan Ltd
Pan Macmillan, 20 New Wharf Road, London N1 9RR
Basingstoke and Oxford
Associated companies throughout the world
www.panmacmillan.com

ISBN 0 330 41819 X

1 3 5 7 9 8 6 4 2

A CIP catalogue record for this book is available from
the British Library.

Typeset by SetSystems Ltd, Saffron Walden, Essex
Printed and bound in Great Britain by
Mackays of Chatham plc, Chatham, Kent

NIGHT OVER WATER

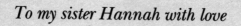

To my sister Hannah with love

PASSENGER DECK PLAN
PAN AMERICAN AIRWAYS SUPER-CLASS

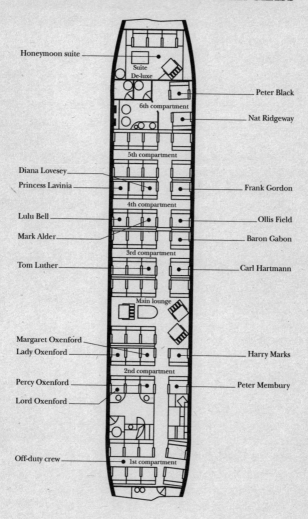

Honeymoon suite

Suite
De-luxe

Peter Black

6th compartment

Nat Ridgeway

5th compartment

Diana Lovesey

Princess Lavinia

Frank Gordon

4th compartment

Lulu Bell

Ollis Field

Mark Alder

Baron Gabon

3rd compartment

Tom Luther

Carl Hartmann

Main lounge

Margaret Oxenford

Lady Oxenford

Harry Marks

2nd compartment

Percy Oxenford

Peter Membury

Lord Oxenford

Off-duty crew

1st compartment

AUTHOR'S NOTE

The first air passenger service between the USA and Europe was started by Pan American in the summer of 1939. It lasted only a few weeks: the service was curtailed when Hitler invaded Poland.

This novel is the story of an imaginary last flight, taking place a few days after war was declared. The flight, the passengers and the crew are all fictional. However, the plane itself is real.

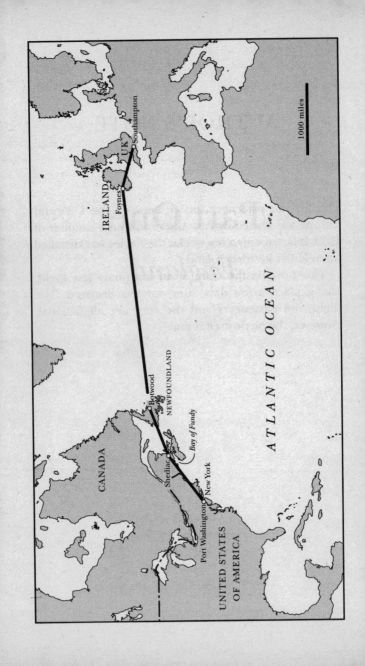

Part One

England

CHAPTER ONE

IT WAS the most romantic plane ever made.

Standing on the dock at Southampton, at half-past twelve on the day war was declared, Tom Luther peered into the sky, waiting for the plane with a heart full of eagerness and dread. Under his breath he hummed a few bars of Beethoven over and over again: the first movement of the 'Emperor' concerto, a stirring tune, appropriately warlike.

There was a crowd of sightseers around him: aircraft enthusiasts with binoculars, small boys and curiosity seekers. Luther reckoned this must be the ninth time the Pan American Clipper had landed on Southampton Water, but the novelty had not worn off. The plane was so fascinating, so enchanting, that people flocked to look at it even on the day their country went to war. Beside the same dock were two magnificent ocean liners, towering over people's heads, but the floating hotels had lost their magic: everyone was looking at the sky.

However, while they waited they were all talking about the war in their English accents. The children were excited by the prospect; the men spoke knowingly in low tones about tanks and artillery; the women just looked grim. Luther was an American, and he hoped his country would stay out of the war: it was none of their business. Besides, one thing you could say for the Nazis, they were tough on Communism.

Luther was a businessman, manufacturing wool cloth, and he had had a lot of trouble with reds in his mills at one time. He had been at their mercy: they had almost ruined him. He still felt bitter about it. His father's menswear store had been run into the ground by Jews setting up in competition, and then Luther Woolens was threatened by the Commies – most of whom were Jews! Then Luther had met Ray Patriarca, and his life had changed. Patriarca's people knew what to do about Communists. There were some accidents. One hothead got his hand caught in a loom. A union recruiter was killed in a hit-and-run. Two men who complained about breaches of the safety regulations got into a fight in a bar and finished up in hospital. A woman troublemaker dropped her lawsuit against the company after her house burned down. It only took a few weeks. Since then there had been no unrest. Patriarca knew what Hitler knew: the way to deal with Communists was to crush them like cockroaches. Luther stamped his foot, still humming Beethoven.

A launch put out from the Imperial Airways flying-boat dock, across the estuary at Hythe, and made several passes along the splashdown zone, checking for floating debris. An eager murmur went up from the crowd: the plane must be approaching.

The first to spot it was a small boy with large new boots. He had no binoculars, but his eleven-year-old eyesight was better than lenses. 'Here it comes!' he shrilled. 'Here comes the Clipper!' He pointed south-west. Everyone looked that way. At first Luther could see only a vague shape that might have been a bird, but soon its outline resolved and a buzz of excitement spread through the crowd as people told one another that the boy was right.

Everyone called it the Clipper, but technically it was a Boeing B-314. Pan American had commissioned Boeing to build a plane capable of carrying passengers across the Atlantic Ocean in total luxury, and this was the result: enormous, majestic, unbelievably powerful, an airborne palace. The airline had taken delivery of six and ordered another six. In comfort and elegance they were equal to the fabulous ocean liners which docked at Southampton, but the ships took four or five days to cross the Atlantic whereas the Clipper could make the trip in twenty-five to thirty hours.

It looked like a winged whale, Luther thought as the plane came closer. It had a big blunt whale-like snout, a massive body, and a tapering rear which culminated in twin high-mounted tailfins. The huge engines were built into the wings. Below the wings was a pair of stubby sea-wings which served to stabilize the aircraft when it was in the water. The bottom of the plane had a sharp knife-edge like the hull of a fast ship.

Soon Luther could make out the big rectangular windows, in two irregular rows marking upper and lower decks. He had come to England on the Clipper exactly a week earlier, so he was familiar with its lay-out. The upper deck comprised the flight cabin and baggage holds and the lower was the passenger deck. Instead of seat rows, the passenger deck had a series of lounges with davenport couches. At mealtimes the main lounge became the dining room, and at night the couches were converted into beds.

Everything was done to insulate the passengers from the world and the weather outside the windows. There were thick carpets, soft lighting, velvet fabrics, soothing colours and deep upholstery. The heavy soundproofing reduced the roar of the mighty engines to a distant, reassuring hum. The Captain was calmly authoritative, the crew clean-cut and smart in their Pan American uniforms, the stewards ever-attentive. Every need was catered for: there was constant food and drink; whatever you wanted appeared as if by magic, just when you wanted it – curtained bunks at bedtime, fresh strawberries at breakfast. The world outside started to appear unreal, like a film projected on to the windows, and the interior of the aircraft seemed like the whole universe.

Such comfort did not come cheap. The round trip fare was $675, half the price of a small house. The passengers were royalty, movie stars, chairmen of large corporations and presidents of small countries.

Tom Luther was none of those things. He was rich, but he had worked hard for his money and he would not normally have squandered it on luxury. However, he had needed to familiarize himself with the plane. He had been asked to do a dangerous job for a powerful man – very powerful indeed. He would not be paid for his work, but to be owed a favour by such a man was better than money.

The whole thing might yet be called off: Luther was waiting for a message giving him the final go-ahead. Half the time he was eager to get on with it; the other half, he hoped he would not have to do it.

The plane came down at an angle, its tail lower than its nose. It was quite close now, and Luther was struck again by its tremendous size. He knew that it was 109 feet long, and 152 feet from one wing tip to the other, but the measurements were just numbers until you actually saw the goddamn thing floating through the air.

For a moment it looked as if it was not flying but falling, and would crash into the sea like a dropped stone and sink to the bottom. Then it seemed to hang in the air, just above the surface, as if suspended on a string, for a long moment of suspense. At last it touched the water, skipping the surface, splashing across the tops of the waves like a stone thrown skimwise, sending up small explosions of foam. But there was very little swell in the sheltered estuary, and a moment later, with an explosion of spray like the smoke from a bomb, the hull plunged into the water.

It cleaved the surface, ploughing a white furrow in the green, sending twin curves of spray high in the air on either side: Luther thought of a mallard coming down on a lake with spread wings and folded feet. The hull sank lower, enlarging the sail-shaped curtains of spray that flew up to left and right; then it began to tilt forward. The spray increased as the plane levelled out, submerging more and more of its belly. Then at last its nose was down. Its speed slowed suddenly, the spray

7

diminished to a wash, and the aircraft sailed the sea like the ship it was, as calmly as if it had never dared to reach for the sky.

Luther realized he had been holding his breath, and let it out in a long relieved sigh. He started humming again.

The plane taxied towards its berth, where Luther had disembarked a week ago. The dock was a specially designed raft with twin piers. In a few minutes, ropes would be attached to stanchions at the front and rear of the plane and it would be winched in, backwards, to its parking slot between the piers. Then the privileged passengers would emerge, stepping from the door on to the broad surface of the sea-wing, then on to the raft, and from there up a gangway to dry land.

Luther turned away, then stopped suddenly. Standing at his shoulder was someone he had not seen before: a man of about his own height, dressed in a dark grey suit and a bowler hat, like a clerk on his way to the office. Luther was about to pass on, then he looked again. The face beneath the bowler hat was not that of a clerk. The man had a high forehead, bright blue eyes, a long jaw and a thin, cruel mouth. He was older than Luther, about forty, but he was broad-shouldered and seemed fit. He looked handsome and dangerous. He stared into Luther's eyes.

Luther stopped humming.

The man said, 'I am Henry Faber.'

'Tom Luther.'

'I have a message for you.'

Luther's heart skipped a beat. He tried to hide his

excitement, and spoke in the same clipped tones as the other man. 'Good. Go ahead.'

'The man you're so interested in will be on this plane on Wednesday when it leaves for New York.'

'You're sure?'

The man looked hard at Luther and did not answer.

Luther nodded grimly. So the job was on. At least the suspense was over. 'Thank you,' he said.

'There's more.'

'I'm listening.'

'The second part of the message is: Don't let us down.'

Luther took a deep breath. 'Tell them not to worry,' he said, with more confidence than he really felt. 'The guy may leave Southampton, but he'll never reach New York.'

Imperial Airways had a flying-boat facility just across the estuary from Southampton docks. Imperial's mechanics serviced the Clipper, supervised by the Pan American flight engineer. On this trip the engineer was Eddie Deakin.

It was a big job, but they had three days. After discharging its passengers at Berth 108, the Clipper taxied across to Hythe. There, in the water, it was manoeuvred on to a dolly, then it was winched up a slipway and towed, looking like a whale balanced on a baby carriage, into the enormous green hangar.

The transatlantic flight was a punishing task for the engines. On the longest leg, from Newfoundland to

Ireland, the plane was in the air for nine hours and on the return journey, against head winds, the same route took sixteen and a half. Hour after hour the fuel flowed, the plugs sparked, the fourteen cylinders in each enormous engine pumped tirelessly up and down, and the fifteen-foot propellers chopped through clouds and rain and gales.

For Eddie that was the romance of engineering. It was wonderful, it was amazing that men could make engines that would work perfectly and precisely, hour after hour. There were so many things that might have gone wrong, so many moving parts that had to be precision-made and meticulously fitted together so that they would not snap, slip, get blocked or simply wear out while they carried a forty-one-ton airplane over thousands of miles.

By Wednesday morning the Clipper would be ready to do it again.

CHAPTER TWO

T HE DAY war broke out was a lovely late-summer Sunday, mild and sunny.

A few minutes before the news was broadcast on the wireless, Margaret Oxenford was outside the sprawling brick mansion that was her family home, perspiring gently in a hat and coat, and fuming because she was forced to go to church. On the far side of the village the single bell in the church tower tolled a monotonous note.

Margaret hated church, but her father would not let her miss the service, even though she was nineteen and old enough to make up her own mind about religion. A year or so ago she had summoned up the nerve to tell him that she did not want to go, but he had refused to listen. Margaret had said, 'Don't you think it's hypocritical for me to go to church when I don't believe in God?' Father had replied, 'Don't be ridiculous.' Defeated and angry, she had told her mother that when she was of age she would never go to church again. Mother had said, 'That will be up to your husband, dear.' As far as they were concerned the argument was over, but Margaret had seethed with resentment every Sunday morning since then.

Her sister and brother came out of the house. Elizabeth was twenty-one. She was tall and clumsy and not very pretty. Once upon a time the two sisters had known everything about one another. As girls they had been together constantly for years, for they never went to school, but got a haphazard education at home from governesses and tutors. They had always shared one another's secrets. But lately they had grown apart. In adolescence, Elizabeth had embraced their parents' rigid traditional values: she was ultra-conservative, fervently royalist, blind to new ideas and hostile to change. Margaret had taken the opposite path. She was a feminist and a socialist, interested in jazz music, cubist painting and free verse. Elizabeth felt Margaret was disloyal to her family in adopting radical ideas. Margaret was irritated by her sister's foolishness, but she was also sad that they were no longer intimate friends. She did not have many intimate friends.

Percy was fourteen. He was neither for nor against radical ideas, but he was naturally mischievous, and he empathized with Margaret's rebelliousness. Fellow-sufferers under their father's tyranny; they gave one another sympathy and support, and Margaret loved him dearly.

Mother and Father came out a moment later. Father was wearing a hideous orange-and-green tie. He was practically colour-blind, but Mother had probably bought it for him. Mother had red hair and sea-green eyes and pale, creamy skin, and she looked radiant in colours like orange and green. But Father had black

hair going grey and a flushed complexion; on him the
tie looked like a warning against something dangerous.

Elizabeth resembled Father, with dark hair and
irregular features. Margaret had Mother's colouring:
she would have liked a scarf in the silk of Father's tie.
Percy was changing so rapidly that no one could tell
whom he would eventually take after.

They walked down the long drive to the little village
outside the gates. Father owned most of the houses and
all the farmland for miles around. He had done
nothing to earn such wealth: a series of marriages in
the early nineteenth century had united the three most
important landowning families in the county, and the
resulting huge estate had been handed down intact
from generation to generation.

They walked along the village street and across the
green to the grey stone church. They entered in
procession: Father and Mother first; Margaret behind
with Elizabeth; and Percy bringing up the rear. The
villagers in the congregation touched their forelocks as
the Oxenfords made their way down the aisle to the
family pew. The wealthier farmers, all of whom rented
their land from Father, inclined their heads in polite
bows; and the middle classes, Dr Rowan and Colonel
Smythe and Sir Alfred, nodded respectfully. This
ludicrous feudal ritual made Margaret cringe with
embarrassment every time it happened. All men were
supposed to be equal before God, weren't they? She
wanted to shout out, 'My father is no better than any of
you, and a lot worse than most!' One of these days

13

perhaps she would have the courage. If she made a scene in church she might never have to go back. But she was too scared of what Father would do.

Just as they were entering their pew, with all eyes on them, Percy said in a loud stage whisper, 'Nice tie, Father.' Margaret suppressed a laugh and was seized by a fit of the giggles. She and Percy sat down quickly and hid their faces, pretending to pray, until the fit passed. After that Margaret felt better.

The vicar preached a sermon about the Prodigal Son. Margaret thought the silly old duffer might have chosen a topic more relevant to what was on everyone's mind: the likelihood of war. The Prime Minister had sent Hitler an ultimatum, which the Führer had ignored, and a declaration of war was expected at any moment.

Margaret dreaded war. A boy she loved had died in the Spanish Civil War. It was just over a year ago, but she still cried sometimes at night. To her, war meant that thousands more girls would know the grief she had suffered. The thought was almost unbearable.

And yet another part of her wanted war. For years she had felt strongly about Britain's cowardice during the Spanish war. Her country had stood by and watched while the elected socialist government was overthrown by a gang of bullies armed by Hitler and Mussolini. Hundreds of idealistic young men from all over Europe had gone to Spain to fight for democracy. But they lacked weapons, and the democratic governments of the world had refused to supply them, so the young men had lost their lives, and people such as Margaret had felt angry and helpless and ashamed. If Britain would now take a stand against the Fascists she could begin to feel proud of her country again.

There was another reason why her heart leaped at the prospect of war. It would surely mean the end of the narrow, suffocating life she lived with her parents. She was bored, cramped and frustrated by their unvarying rituals and their pointless social life. She longed to escape and have a life of her own, but it seemed impossible: she was under age, she had no money, and there was no kind of work that she was fit for. But, she thought eagerly, surely everything would be different in wartime?

She had read with fascination how in the last war women had put on trousers and gone to work in factories. Nowadays there were female branches of the army, navy and air force. Margaret dreamed of volunteering for the Auxiliary Territorial Service, the women's army. One of the few practical skills she possessed was that she could drive. Father's chauffeur, Digby, had taught her on the Rolls, and Ian, the boy who died, had let her ride his motorcycle. She could even handle a motor boat, for Father kept a small yacht at Nice. The ATS needed ambulance drivers and dispatch riders. She saw herself in uniform, wearing a helmet, astride a motorcycle, carrying urgent reports from one battlefield to another at top speed, with a photograph of Ian in the breast pocket of her khaki jacket. She felt sure she could be brave, given the chance.

War was actually declared during the service, they

found out later. There was even an air-raid warning at twenty-eight minutes past eleven, in the middle of the sermon, but it did not reach their village, and anyway it was a false alarm. So the Oxenford family walked home from church unaware that they were at war with Germany.

Percy wanted to take a gun and go after rabbits. They could all shoot: it was a family pastime, almost an obsession. But of course Father turned down Percy's request, for it was not done to shoot on Sundays. Percy was disappointed, but he would obey. Although he was full of devilment, he was not yet man enough to defy Father openly.

Margaret loved her brother's impishness. He was the only ray of sunshine in the gloom of her life. She often wished that she could mock Father as Percy did, and laugh behind his back, but she got too cross to joke about it.

At home they were astonished to find a barefoot parlourmaid watering flowers in the hall. Father did not recognize her. 'Who are you?' he said abruptly.

Mother said in her soft American voice, 'Her name is Jenkins, she started this week.'

The girl dropped a curtsy.

Father went on, 'And where the devil are her shoes?'

An expression of suspicion crossed the girl's face and she shot an accusing look at Percy. 'Please, your lordship, it was young Lord Isley.' Percy was the Earl of Isley. 'He told me parlourmaids must go barefoot on Sunday out of respect.'

Mother sighed and Father gave an exasperated

grunt. Margaret could not help giggling. This was Percy's favourite trick: telling new servants of imaginary house rules. He could say ridiculous things with a dead straight face, and the family had such a reputation for eccentricity that people would believe anything of them.

Percy often made Margaret laugh, but now she was sorry for the poor parlourmaid, standing barefoot in the hall and feeling foolish.

'Go and put your shoes on,' Mother said.

Margaret added, 'And never believe Lord Isley.'

They took off their hats and went into the morning room. Margaret pulled Percy's hair and hissed, 'That was a mean thing to do.' Percy just grinned: he was incorrigible. He had once told the vicar that Father had died of a heart attack in the night, and the whole village went into mourning before they found out it was not true.

Father turned on the wireless, and it was then that they heard the news: Britain had declared war on Germany.

Margaret felt a kind of savage glee rising in her breast, like the excitement of driving too fast or climbing to the top of a tall tree. There was no longer any point in agonizing over it: there would be tragedy and bereavement, pain and grief, but now these things could not be avoided, the die was cast and the only thing to do was fight. The thought made her heart beat faster. Everything would be different. Social conventions would be abandoned, women would join in the struggle, class barriers would break down, everyone would work together. She could taste the air of freedom already. And they would be at war with the Fascists, the very people who had killed poor Ian and thousands more fine young men. Margaret did not believe she was a vindictive person, but when she thought about fighting the Nazis she felt vengeful. The feeling was unfamiliar, frightening and thrilling.

Father was furious. He was already portly and red-faced, and when he got angry he always looked as if he might burst. 'Damn Chamberlain!' he said. 'Damn and blast the wretched man!'

'Algernon, please,' Mother said, reproving him for his intemperate language.

Father had been one of the founders of the British Union of Fascists. He had been a different person then: not just younger, but slimmer, more handsome, and less irritable. He had charmed people and won their loyalty. He had written a controversial book called *Mongrel Men: The Threat of Racial Pollution*, about how civilization had gone downhill since white people started to interbreed with Jews, Asians, Orientals and even Negroes. He had corresponded with Adolf Hitler, who he thought to be the greatest statesman since Napoleon. There had been big house parties here every weekend, with politicians, foreign statesmen sometimes, and – on one unforgettable occasion – the King. The discussions went on far into the night, the butler bringing up more brandy from the cellar while the footmen yawned in the hall. All through the Depression, Father had waited for the country to call him to its rescue in its hour of need, and ask him to be

Prime Minister in a government of national reconstruction. But the call never came. The weekend parties got fewer and smaller; the more distinguished guests found ways to dissociate themselves publicly from the British Union of Fascists; and Father became a bitter, disappointed man. His charm went with his confidence. His good looks were ruined by resentment, boredom and drink. His intellect had never been real: Margaret had read his book and had been shocked to find that it was not just wrong, but foolish.

In recent years his platform had shrunk to one obsessive idea: that Britain and Germany should unite against the Soviet Union. He had advocated this in magazine articles and letters to the newspapers, and on the increasingly rare occasions when he was invited to speak at political meetings and university debating societies. He held on to the idea defiantly as events in Europe made his policy more and more unrealistic. With the declaration of war between Britain and Germany his hopes were finally dashed and Margaret found in her heart a little pity for him among all her other tumultuous emotions.

'Britain and Germany will wipe one another out and leave Europe to be dominated by atheistical Communism!' he said.

The reference to atheism reminded Margaret of being forced to go to church, and she said, 'I don't mind, I'm an atheist.'

Mother said, 'You can't be, dear, you're Church of England.'

Margaret could not help laughing. Elizabeth, who

was close to tears, said, 'How can you laugh? It's a tragedy!'

Elizabeth was a great admirer of the Nazis. She spoke German – they both did, thanks to a German governess who had lasted longer than most – and she had been to Berlin several times and twice dined with the Führer himself. Margaret suspected the Nazis were snobs who liked to bask in the approval of an English aristocrat.

Now Margaret turned to Elizabeth and said, 'It's time we stood up to those bullies.'

'They aren't bullies,' Elizabeth spoke indignantly. 'They're proud, strong, pure-bred Aryans, and it's a tragedy that our country is at war with them. Father's right – the white people will wipe each other out and the world will be left to the mongrels and the Jews.'

Margaret had no patience with this kind of drivel. 'There's nothing wrong with Jews!' she said hotly.

Father held a finger up in the air. 'There's nothing wrong with the Jew – *in his place*.'

'Which is under the heel of the jackboot, in your – your Fascist system.' She had been on the point of saying 'your filthy system' but she suddenly became scared and bit back the insult: it was dangerous to make Father too angry.

Elizabeth said, 'And in your Bolshevik system the Jews rule the roost!'

'I'm not a Bolshevik, I'm a socialist.'

Percy imitated Mother's accent. 'You can't be, dear, you're Church of England.'

Margaret laughed despite herself, and once again her laughter infuriated her sister. Elizabeth said bitterly, 'You just want to destroy everything that's fine and pure, and then laugh about it afterwards.'

That was hardly worth a response but Margaret still wanted to make her point. She turned to Father and said, 'Well, I agree with you about Neville Chamberlain, anyway. He's made our military position far worse by letting the Fascists take over Spain. Now the enemy is in the west as well as the east.'

'Chamberlain did not let the Fascists take over Spain,' Father said. 'Britain made a non-intervention pact with Germany, Italy and France. All we did was keep our word.'

This was completely hypocritical, and he knew it. Margaret felt herself flush with indignation. 'We kept our word while the Italians and the Germans broke theirs!' she protested. 'So the Fascists got guns and the democrats got nothing . . . but heroes.'

There was a moment of embarrassed silence.

Mother said, 'I'm truly sorry that Ian died, dear, but he was a very bad influence on you.'

Suddenly Margaret wanted to cry.

Ian Rochdale was the best thing that ever happened to her, and the pain of his death could still make her gasp.

For years she had been dancing at hunt balls with empty-headed young members of the squirearchy, boys who had nothing on their minds but drinking and hunting, and she had despaired of ever meeting a man of her own age who interested her. Ian had come into her life like the light of reason and since he died she had been living in the dark.

He had been in his final year at Oxford. Margaret would have loved to go to university, but there was no possibility of her qualifying: she had never gone to school. However, she had read widely – there was nothing else to do! – and she was thrilled to find someone like herself, who liked talking about ideas. He was the only man who could explain things to her without condescension. Ian was the most clear-thinking person she had ever come across; he had endless patience in discussion and he was quite without intellectual vanity – he never pretended to understand when he did not. She adored him from the very start.

For a long time she did not think of it as love. But one day he confessed, awkwardly and with great embarrassment, uncharacteristically struggling to find the right words, finally saying, 'I think I must have fallen in love with you – will it spoil everything?' And then she realized joyfully that she too was in love.

He changed her life. It was as if she had moved to another country, where everything was different: the landscape, the weather, the people, the food. She enjoyed everything. The constraints and irritations of living with her parents came to seem minor.

Even after he joined the International Brigade and went to Spain to fight for the elected socialist government against the Fascist rebels, he continued to light up her life. She was proud of him because he had the courage of his convictions and was ready to risk death for the cause he believed in. Sometimes she would get a letter from him. Once he sent a poem. Then came the note that said he was dead, blown to bits by a direct hit from a shell, and Margaret felt that her life had come to an end.

'A bad influence,' she echoed bitterly. 'Yes. He taught me to question dogma, to disbelieve lies, to hate ignorance and to despise hypocrisy. As a result, I'm hardly fit for civilized society.'

Father, Mother and Elizabeth all started talking at once, then stopped because none of them could be heard, and Percy spoke into the sudden silence. 'Talking of Jews,' he said, 'I came across a curious picture in the cellar, in one of those old suitcases from Stamford.' Stamford, Connecticut, was where Mother's family lived. Percy took from his shirt pocket a creased and faded sepia photograph. 'I did have a great-grandmother called Ruth Glencarry, didn't I?'

Mother answered, 'Yes – she was my mother's mother. Why, dear, what have you found?'

Percy gave the photograph to Father and the others crowded around to look at it. It showed a street scene in an American city, probably New York, about seventy years ago. In the foreground was a Jewish man of about thirty with a black beard, dressed in rough working-men's clothes and a hat. He stood by a handcart bearing a grinding-wheel. The cart was clearly lettered with the words 'Reuben Fishbein – Grinder'. Beside the man stood a girl about ten years old in a shabby cotton dress and heavy boots.

Father asked, 'What is this, Percy? Who are these wretched people?'

'Turn it over,' said Percy.

Father turned the picture over. On the back was written: 'Ruthie Glencarry, née Fishbein, aged 10.'

Margaret looked at Father. He was utterly horrified.

Percy went on, 'Interesting that Mother's grand-father should marry the daughter of an itinerant Jewish knife-grinder, but they say America's like that.'

'This is impossible!' Father said, but his voice was shaky and Margaret guessed that he thought it was all too possible.

Percy went on blithely, 'Anyway, Jewishness descends through the female, so as my mother's mother was Jewish, that makes me a Jew.'

Father had gone quite pale. Mother looked mysti-fied, a slight frown creasing her brow.

Percy said, 'I do hope the Germans don't win this war. I shan't be allowed to go to the cinema and Mother will have to sew yellow stars on all her ball-gowns.'

This was sounding too good to be true. Margaret peered intently at the words written on the back of the picture, and the truth dawned. 'Percy!' she said delight-edly. 'That's *your* handwriting!'

'No, it's not!' said Percy.

But everyone could see that it was. Margaret laughed gleefully. Percy had found this old picture of a little Jewish girl somewhere and had faked the inscription on the back to fool Father. Father had fallen for it, too, and no wonder: it must be the ultimate nightmare of every racist to find that he has mixed ancestry. Serve him right.

Father said,'Bah!' and threw the picture down on a table.

Mother said, 'Percy, really,' in an aggrieved voice. They might have said more, but at that moment the door opened and Bates, the bad-tempered butler, said, 'Luncheon is served, my lady.'

They left the morning room and crossed the hall to the small dining room. There would be overdone roast beef, as always on Sundays. Mother would have a salad: she never ate cooked food, believing that the heat destroyed the goodness.

Father said grace and they sat down. Bates offered Mother the smoked salmon. Smoked, pickled or otherwise preserved foods were all right, according to her theory.

'Of course, there's only one thing to be done,' Mother said as she helped herself from the proffered plate. She spoke in the offhand tone of one who merely draws attention to the obvious. 'We must all go and live in America until this silly war is over.'

There was a moment of shocked silence.

Margaret, horrified, burst out, 'No!'

Mother said, 'Now, I think we've had quite enough squabbling for one day. Please let us have lunch in peace and harmony.'

'No!' Margaret repeated. She was almost speechless with outrage. 'You – you can't do this, it's – it's—' She wanted to rail and storm at them, to accuse them of treason and cowardice, to shout her contempt and defiance out loud, but the words would not come, and all she could say was, 'It's not fair!'

25

Even that was too much. Father said, 'If you can't hold your tongue you'd better leave us.'

Margaret put her napkin to her mouth to choke down a sob, pushed her chair back, stood up and fled the room.

They had been planning this for months, of course.

Percy came to Margaret's room after lunch and told her the details. The house was to be closed up, the furniture covered with dust sheets and the servants dismissed. The estate would be left in the hands of Father's business manager, who would collect the rents. The money would pile up in the bank: it could not be sent to America because of wartime exchange control rules. The horses would be sold, the blankets moth-balled, the silver locked away.

Elizabeth, Margaret and Percy were to pack one suitcase each: the rest of their belongings would be forwarded by a removal company. Father had booked tickets for all of them on the Pan American Clipper and they were to leave on Wednesday.

Percy was wild with excitement. He had flown once or twice before, but the Clipper was different. The plane was huge and opulent: the newspapers had been full of it when the service was inaugurated just a few weeks ago. The flight to New York took twenty-nine hours, and everyone went to bed at night over the Atlantic Ocean.

It was disgustingly appropriate, Margaret thought, that they should depart in cosseted luxury, when they were leaving their countrymen to deprivation, hardship and war.

Percy left to pack his case and Margaret lay on her bed, staring at the ceiling, bitterly disappointed, boiling with rage, crying with frustration, powerless to do anything about her fate.

She stayed in her room until bedtime.

On Monday morning, while she was still in bed, Mother came to her room. Margaret sat up and gave her a hostile stare. Mother sat at the dressing-table and looked at Margaret in the mirror. 'Please don't make trouble with your father over this,' she said.

Margaret realized that her mother was nervous. In other circumstances this might have caused Margaret to soften her tone but she was too upset to sympathize. 'It's so cowardly!' she burst out.

Mother paled. 'We're not being cowardly.'

'But to run away from your country when a war begins!'

'We have no choice. We have to go.'

Margaret was perplexed. 'Why?'

Mother turned from the mirror and looked directly at her. 'Otherwise they will put your father in prison.'

Margaret was taken completely by surprise. 'How can they do that? It's not a crime to be a Fascist.'

'They have Emergency Powers. Does it matter? A sympathizer in the Home Office warned us. Father will be arrested if he's still in Britain at the end of the week.'

Margaret could hardly believe that they wanted to put her father in jail like a thief. She felt foolish: she had not thought about how much difference war would make to everyday life.

'But they won't let us take any money with us,' Mother said bitterly. 'So much for the British sense of fair play.'

Money was the last thing Margaret cared about right now. Her whole life was in the balance. She felt a sudden access of bravery, and she made up her mind to tell her mother the truth. Before she had time to lose her nerve, she took a deep breath and said, 'Mother, I don't want to go with you.'

Mother displayed no surprise. Perhaps she had even expected something like this. In the mild, vague tone she used when trying to avoid an argument, she said, 'You have to come, dear.'

'They're not going to put *me* in jail. I can live with Aunt Martha, or even Cousin Catherine. Won't you talk to Father?'

Suddenly Mother looked uncharacteristically fierce. I gave birth to you in pain and suffering, and I'm not going to let you risk your life while I can prevent it.'

For a moment Margaret was taken aback by her mother's naked emotion. Then she protested, 'I ought to have a say in it – it's my life!'

Mother sighed and reverted to her normal languorous manner. 'It makes no difference what you and I think. Your father won't let you stay behind, whatever we say.'

Her passivity annoyed Margaret, and she resolved to take action. 'I shall ask him directly.'

'I wish you wouldn't,' Mother said, and now there was a pleading note in her voice. 'This is awfully hard for him as it is. He loves England, you know. In any other circumstances he'd be telephoning to the War Office trying to get a job. It's breaking his heart.'

'What about my heart?'

'It's not the same for you. You're young, your life is in front of you. For him this is the end of all hope.'

'It's not my fault he's a Fascist,' Margaret retorted harshly.

Mother stood up. 'I hoped you'd be kinder,' she said quietly, and she went out.

Margaret felt guilty and indignant at the same time. It was so unfair! Her father had been pouring scorn on her opinions ever since she had had any, and now that events had proved him wrong she was being asked to sympathize.

She sighed. Her mother was beautiful, eccentric and vague. She had been born rich and determined. Her eccentricities were the result of a strong will with no education to help her discriminate between sense and nonsense. The vagueness was a strong woman's way of coping with masculine dominance: she was not allowed to confront her husband, so the only way she could escape his control was by pretending not to understand him. Margaret loved her mother and regarded her peculiarities with a fond tolerance – but she was determined not to be like her, despite their physical resemblance. If others refused to educate her she would jolly well teach herself; and she would rather be an old spinster than marry some pig who thought he had the right to boss her around like an underhouse parlourmaid.

Sometimes she longed for a different kind of relationship with her mother. She wanted to confide in her, gain her sympathy, ask her advice. They could be allies, struggling together for freedom against a world that wanted to treat them as ornaments. But Mother had given up that struggle long ago, and she wanted Margaret to do the same. It was not going to happen. Margaret was going to be herself: she was absolutely set on it. But how?

All day Monday she felt unable to eat. She drank endless cups of tea while the servants went about the business of closing up the house. On Tuesday, when Mother realized that Margaret was not going to pack, she told the new maid, Jenkins, to do it for her. Of course, Jenkins did not know what to pack, and Margaret had to help her; so in the end Mother got her way, as she so often did.

Margaret said to the girl, 'It's bad luck for you that we decided to close up the house the week after you started work here.'

'There'll be no shortage of work now, m'lady,' Jenkins said. 'Our dad says there's no unemployment in wartime.'

'What will you do – work in a factory?'

'I'm going to join up. It said on the wireless that seventeen thousand women joined the ATS yesterday. There's queues outside every town hall in the country – I seen a picture in the paper.'

'Lucky you,' Margaret said despondently. 'The only thing I'll be queuing for is a plane to America.'

'You've got to do what the Marquess wants,' Jenkins said.

'What does your dad say about you joining up?'

'I shan't tell him – just do it.'

'But what if he takes you back?'

'He can't do that. I'm eighteen. Once you've signed on, that's it. Provided you're old enough there's nothing your parents can do about it.'

Margaret was startled. 'Are you sure?'

'Course. Everyone knows.'

'I didn't,' Margaret said thoughtfully.

Jenkins took Margaret's case down to the hall. They would be leaving very early on Wednesday morning. Seeing the cases lined up, Margaret realized that she was going to spend the war in Connecticut unless she did something other than sulk. Despite Mother's plea not to make a fuss, she had to confront her father.

The very thought made her feel shaky. She went back to her room to steel her nerves and consider what she might say. She would have to be calm. Tears would not move him and anger would only provoke his scorn. She should appear sensible, responsible, mature. She should not be argumentative, for that would enrage him, and then he would frighten her so much that she would be unable to go on.

How should she begin? 'I think I have a right to say something about my own future.'

No, that was no good. He would reply, 'I am responsible for you so I must decide.'

31

Perhaps she should begin, 'May I talk to you about going to America?'

He would probably say, 'There is nothing to discuss.'

Her opening had to be so inoffensive that even he would not be able to rebuff it. She decided she would try, 'Can I ask you something?' He would have to agree to that.

Then what? How could she approach the subject without provoking one of his dreadful rages? She might say, 'You were in the army in the last war, weren't you?' She knew he had seen action in France. Then she would ask, 'Was Mother involved?' She knew the answer to this, too: Mother had been a volunteer nurse in London, caring for wounded American officers. Finally she would end, 'You both served your countries, so I know you'll understand why I want to do the same.' Now surely that was irresistible.

If only he would concede the principle, she could deal with his other objections, she felt. She could live with relatives until she joined up, which would be a matter of days. She was nineteen: many girls of that age had been working full time for six years. She was old enough to get married, drive a car, and go to jail. There was no reason why she should not be allowed to stay in England.

That made sense. Now all she needed was courage.

Father would be in his study with his business manager. Margaret left her room. On the landing outside her bedroom door she suddenly felt weak with fear. It infuriated him to be opposed. His rages were terrible and his punishments cruel. When she was eleven she had been made to stand in the corner of his study, facing the wall, for an entire day after being rude to a house-guest; he had taken away her teddy bear as a punishment for bed-wetting at the age of seven; once, in a fury, he had thrown a cat out of an upstairs window. What would he do now when she told him she wanted to stay in England and fight against the Nazis?

She forced herself to go down the stairs, but as she approached his study her fears grew. She visualized him getting angry, his face reddening and his eyes bulging, and she felt terrified. She tried to calm her racing pulse by asking herself whether there was really anything to be afraid of. He could no longer break her heart by taking away her teddy bear. But she knew deep down that he could still find ways of making her wish she were dead.

As she stood outside the study door, trembling, the housekeeper rustled across the hall in her black silk dress. Mrs Allen ruled the female staff of the household strictly, but she had always been indulgent towards the children. She was fond of the family and was upset that they were leaving: it was the end of a way of life for her. She gave Margaret a tearful smile.

Looking at her, Margaret was struck by a heart-stopping notion.

An entire plan of escape came full-blown into her head. She would borrow money from Mrs Allen, leave the house now, catch the four fifty-five train to London, stay overnight at her cousin Catherine's flat, and join the ATS first thing in the morning. By the time Father caught up with her it would be too late.

It was so simple and daring that she could hardly believe it might be possible. But before she could think twice about it she found herself saying, 'Oh, Mrs Allen, would you give me some money? I've got to do some last-minute shopping and I don't want to disturb Father, he's so busy.'

Mrs Allen did not hesitate. 'Of course, my lady. How much do you need?'

Margaret did not know what the train fare to London was: she had never bought her own ticket. Guessing wildly, she said, 'Oh, a pound should be enough.' She was thinking: Am I really doing this?

Mrs Allen took two ten-shilling notes from her purse. She would probably have handed over her life savings if asked.

Margaret took the money with trembling fingers. This could be my ticket to freedom, she thought and, frightened as she was, a small flame of joyful hope flickered in her breast.

Mrs Allen, thinking she was upset about emigrating, squeezed her hand. 'This is a sad day, Lady Margaret,' she said. 'A sad day for us all.' Shaking her grey head dismally she disappeared into the back of the house.

Margaret looked around frenziedly. No one was in sight. Her heart was fluttering like a trapped bird and her breath came in shallow gasps. She knew that if she hesitated she would lose her nerve. She did not dare wait long enough to put on a coat. Clutching the money in her hand she walked out of the front door.

The station was two miles away in the next village. At every step along the road Margaret expected to hear

Father's Rolls-Royce purring up behind her. But how could he know what she had done? It was unlikely that anyone would notice her absence before dinner time and if they did they would assume she had gone shopping as she had told Mrs Allen. All the same, she was in a constant fever of apprehension.

She got to the station in plenty of time, bought her ticket – she had more than enough money – and sat in the ladies' waiting room watching the hands of the big clock on the wall.

The train was late.

Four fifty-five came around, then five o'clock, then five past five. By this time Margaret was so frightened that she felt like giving up and returning home just to escape the tension.

The train came in at fourteen minutes past five, and still Father had not come.

Margaret boarded with her heart in her mouth.

She stood at the window, staring at the ticket barrier, expecting to see him arrive at the last minute to catch her.

At last the train moved.

She could hardly believe that she was getting away.

The train picked up speed and the first faint tremors of elation stirred in her heart. A few seconds later it was out of the station. Margaret watched the village recede, and her heart filled with triumph. She had done it – she had escaped!

Suddenly she felt weak-kneed. She looked around for a seat, and realized for the first time that the train was full. Every seat was taken, even in this first-class carriage, and there were soldiers sitting on the floor. She remained standing.

Her euphoria did not diminish even though the journey was, by normal standards, something of a nightmare. More people crowded into the carriages at each station. The train was delayed for three hours outside Reading. All the light bulbs had been removed because of the blackout, so after nightfall the train was in total darkness, except for the occasional flash of the guard's torch as he patrolled, picking his way over passengers sitting and lying on the floor. When Margaret could stand no longer she too sat on the floor. This sort of thing did not matter any more, she told herself. Her dress would get filthy but tomorrow she would be in uniform. Everything was different: there was a war on.

Margaret wondered whether Father might have learned she was missing, found out that she caught the train, and driven at top speed to London to intercept her at Paddington station. It was unlikely, but possible, and her heart filled with dread as the train pulled into the station.

However, when at last she got off he was nowhere to be seen, and she felt another thrill of triumph. He was not omnipotent after all! She managed to find a taxi in the cavernous gloom of the station. It took her to Bayswater using only its sidelights. The driver used a torch to light her to the apartment building in which Catherine had a flat.

The building's windows were all blacked out, but the hall was a blaze of light. The porter had gone off duty

– it was now almost midnight – but Margaret knew her way. She went up the stairs and rang the bell.

There was no reply.

Her heart sank.

She rang again, but she knew it was pointless: the flat was small and the bell was loud. Catherine was not there.

It was hardly surprising: Catherine lived with her parents in Kent, and used the flat as a *pied-à-terre*. London social life had come to a halt, of course, so Catherine would have no reason to be here. Margaret had not thought of that.

She was not dashed, but she was disappointed. She had been looking forward to sitting down with Catherine, drinking cocoa and sharing with her the details of her great adventure. However, that would have to wait. She considered what she should do next. She had several relatives in London, but if she went to them they would telephone Father. Catherine would have been a willing co-conspirator, but she could not trust any of her other relations.

Then she remembered that Aunt Martha did not have a telephone.

She was a great-aunt, in fact; a fractious spinster of about seventy. She lived less than a mile away. She would be fast asleep by now, and it would make her furious to be wakened, but that could not be helped. The important thing was that she would have no way of alerting Father to Margaret's whereabouts.

Margaret went back down the stairs and out into the street – to find herself in total darkness.

The blackout was quite scary. She stood outside the door and looked around, her eyes wide open and staring, seeing nothing. It gave her a queer feeling in her tummy, like being dizzy.

She closed her eyes and pictured the familiar street scene as it ought to be. Behind her was Ovington House where Catherine lived. Normally there would be lights in several windows and a splash of brilliance from the lamp over the door. On the corner to her left was a small church whose portico was always floodlit. The pavement was lined with lamp-posts, each of which should cast a little circle of light, and the road should be lit by the headlamps of buses, taxis and cars.

She opened her eyes again, and saw nothing.

It was unnerving. For a moment she imagined that there was nothing around her: the street had disappeared and she was in limbo, falling through a void. She felt suddenly seasick. Then she pulled herself together and visualized the route to Aunt Martha's house.

I head east from here, she thought, and go left at the second turning, and Aunt Martha's place is at the end of that block. It should be easy enough, even in the dark.

She longed for some relief: a lighted taxi, a full moon, or a helpful policeman. After a moment her wish was granted: a car came creeping along, its faint sidelights like the eyes of a cat in the heavy gloom, and suddenly she could see the line of the kerb all the way to the street corner.

She began to walk.

The car passed on, its red rear lights receding into the dark distance. Margaret thought she was still three or four steps from the corner when she stumbled down the kerb. She crossed the road and found the opposite pavement without falling over it. That encouraged her and she walked on more confidently.

Suddenly something hard smacked into her face with agonizing violence.

She cried out in pain and sudden fear. For a moment she was in a blind panic and wanted to turn and run. With an effort she calmed herself. Her hand went to her cheek and rubbed where it hurt. What on earth had happened? What was there to hit her at face level in the middle of the pavement? She reached out with both hands. She felt something almost immediately, and jerked her hands back fearfully; then she gritted her teeth and reached out again. She was touching something cold and hard and round, like an oversize pie dish floating in mid-air. Exploring it further, she felt a round column with a rectangular hole and an out-jutting top. When she realized what it was she laughed despite her sore face. She had been attacked by a pillar-box.

She felt her way round it, then walked on with both arms stretched out in front of her.

After a while she stumbled down another kerb. Regaining her balance, she felt relieved: she had reached Aunt Martha's street. She turned left.

It occurred to her that Aunt Martha might not hear the doorbell. She lived alone: there was no one else to answer. If that happened, Margaret would have to make

39

her way back to Catherine's building and sleep in the corridor. She could cope with sleeping on the floor, but she dreaded another walk through the blackout. Perhaps she would simply curl up on Aunt Martha's doorstep and wait for daylight.

Aunt Martha's small house was at the far end of a long block. Margaret walked slowly. The city was dark but not silent. She could hear the occasional car in the distance. Dogs barked as she passed their doors and a pair of cats howled oblivious of her. Once she heard the tinkling music of a late party. A little farther on she picked up the muffled shouts of a domestic row behind the blackout curtains. She found herself longing to be inside a house with lamps and a fireplace and a teapot.

The block seemed longer than Margaret remembered. However, she could not possibly have gone wrong: she had turned left at the second cross-street. Nevertheless, the suspicion that she was lost grew relentlessly. Her sense of time failed her: had she been walking along this block for five minutes, twenty minutes, two hours or all night? Suddenly she was not even sure whether there were any houses near by. She could be in the middle of Hyde Park, having wandered through the entrance by blind chance. She began to feel that there were creatures all around her in the darkness, watching her with cat-like night vision, waiting for her to stumble into them so they could grab her. A scream started low in her throat and she pushed it back.

She made herself think. Where could she have gone

wrong? She knew there was a cross-street when she stumbled down a kerb. But, she now recalled, as well as the main cross-streets there were little alleys and mews. She might have turned down one of those. By now she could have walked a mile or more in the wrong direction.

She tried to recall the heady feeling of excitement and triumph she had felt on the train, but it had gone, and now she just felt alone and afraid.

She decided to stop and stand quite still. No harm could come to her like that.

She stayed still for a long time: after a while she could not tell how long. Now she was afraid to move: fear had paralysed her. She thought she would stand upright until she fainted with exhaustion, or until morning.

Then a car appeared.

Its dim sidelights gave very little illumination, but by comparison with the previous pitch blackness it seemed like daylight. She saw that she was, indeed, standing in the middle of the road, and she scurried to the pavement to get out of the way of the car. She was in a square that seemed vaguely familiar. The car passed her and turned a corner, and she hurried after it, hoping to see a landmark that would tell her where she was. Reaching the corner, she saw the car at the far end of a short, narrow street of small shops, one of which was a milliner's patronized by Mother, and she realized she was just a few yards from Marble Arch.

She could have wept with relief.

At the next corner she waited for another car to light up the way ahead; then she walked on into Mayfair.

A few minutes later she stood outside Claridge's Hotel. The building was blacked out, of course, but she was able to locate the door, and she wondered whether to go in.

She did not think she had enough money to pay for a room, but her recollection was that people did not pay their hotel bill until they left. She could take a room for two nights, go out tomorrow as if she expected to return later, join the ATS, then phone the hotel and tell them to send the bill to Father's lawyer.

She took a deep breath and pushed open the door.

Like most public buildings that were open at night, the hotel had rigged up a double door, like an air-lock, so that people could go in and out without the interior lights showing on the outside. Margaret let the outer door close behind her, then went through the second door and into the grateful light of the hotel foyer. She felt a tremendous surge of relief. This was normality: the nightmare was over.

A young night porter was dozing at the desk. Margaret coughed, and he woke up, startled and confused. Margaret said, 'I need a room.'

'At this time of night?' the man blurted.

'I got caught in the blackout,' Margaret explained. 'Now I can't get home.'

The man began to gather his wits. 'No luggage?'

'No,' Margaret said guiltily. Then she was struck by

a thought, and added, 'Of course not – I didn't *plan* to get stranded.'

He looked at her rather strangely. Surely, Margaret thought, he could not refuse her? He swallowed, rubbed his face, and pretended to consult a book. What was the matter with the man? Making up his mind, he closed the book and said, 'We're full.'

'Oh, come on, you must have *something*—'

'You've had a fight with your old man, haven't you?' he said with a wink.

Margaret could hardly believe this was happening. 'I can't get home,' she repeated, as the man had obviously failed to understand her the first time.

'I can't help that,' he said. With a sudden access of wit he added, 'Blame Hitler.'

He was rather young. 'Where is your supervisor?' she said.

He looked offended. 'I'm in charge until six o'clock.'

Margaret looked around. 'I'll just have to sit in the lounge until morning,' she said wearily.

'You can't do that!' the porter said, looking scared. 'A young girl alone, with no luggage, spending the night in the lounge? It's more than my job's worth.'

'I'm not a *young girl*,' she said angrily. 'I'm Lady Margaret Oxenford.' She hated to use her title but she was desperate.

However, it did no good. The porter gave her a hard, insolent look, and said, 'Oh, yeah?'

Margaret was about to shout at him when she caught sight of her reflection in the glass of the door, and realized she had a black eye. On top of that her hands were filthy and her dress was torn. She recalled that she had bumped into a pillar-box and sat on the floor of a train. No wonder the porter would not give her a room. She said desperately, 'But you can't turn me out into the blackout!'

'I can't do anything else!' the porter said.

Margaret wondered how he would react if she simply sat down and refused to move. That was what she felt like doing: she was bone tired and weak with strain. But she had been through so much that she had no energy left for a confrontation. Besides, it was late and they were alone: there was no telling what the man might do if she gave him an excuse to lay hands on her.

Wearily, she turned her back on him and went out, bitterly disappointed, into the night.

Even as she walked away from the hotel she wished she had put up more of a fight. Why was it that her intentions were always so much more fierce than her actions? Now that she had given in, she was angry enough to defy the porter. She was almost ready to turn back. But she kept on walking: it seemed easier.

She had nowhere to go. She would not be able to find Catherine's building again; she had never succeeded in finding Aunt Martha's house; she could not trust any other relatives and she was too dirty to get a hotel room.

She would just have to wander around until it got light. The weather was fine: there was no rain and the night air was only slightly chilly. If she kept moving she would not even feel cold. She could see where she was going now: there were plenty of traffic lights in the West End, and a car passed every minute or two. She could hear music and noise from the nightclubs, and now and again she would see people of her own class, the women in gorgeous gowns and the men wearing white-tie-and-tails, arriving home in their chauffeur-driven cars after a late party. In one street, rather curiously, she saw three other solitary women: one standing in a doorway, one leaning on a lamp-post and one sitting in a car. They were all smoking and apparently waiting for people. She wondered if they were what Mother called Fallen Women.

She began to feel tired. She was still wearing the light indoor shoes she had had on when she made her escape from home. On impulse she sat down on a doorstep, took off her shoes, and rubbed her aching feet.

Looking up, she could make out the vague shape of the buildings on the other side of the street. Was it getting light at last? Perhaps she would find a workman's café that opened early. She could order breakfast and wait there until the recruiting offices opened. She had eaten next to nothing for two days, and the thought of bacon and eggs made her mouth water.

Suddenly there was a white face hovering in the air in front of her. She let out a little cry of fright. The face came closer and she saw a youngish man in evening dress. He said, 'Hello, beautiful.'

Margaret scrambled to her feet quickly. She hated

drunks – they were so undignified. 'Please go away,' she said. She tried to sound firm but there was a tremor in her voice.

He staggered closer. 'Give us a kiss, then.'

'Certainly not!' she said, horrified. She took a step back, stumbled, and dropped her shoes. Somehow the loss of her shoes made her feel helplessly vulnerable. She turned around and bent down to grope for them. He chuckled fruitily, then to her horror she felt his hand between her thighs, fumbling with painful clumsiness. She straightened up instantly, without finding her shoes, and stepped away from him. Turning to face him, she shouted, 'Get away from me!'

He laughed again and said, 'That's right, go on, I like a bit of resistance.' With surprising agility he grabbed her by the shoulders and pulled her to him. His alcoholic breath blew over her face in a nauseating fog and suddenly he was kissing her mouth.

It was unspeakably disgusting, and she felt quite sick, but his embrace was so strong that she could hardly breathe, let alone protest. She squirmed ineffectually while he slobbered over her. Then he took one hand from her shoulder to grasp her breast. He squeezed brutally hard and she gasped with pain. But because he had let go of her shoulder she was mercifully able to half-turn away from him and start to scream.

She screamed loud and long.

She could vaguely hear him saying, in a worried voice, 'All right, all right, don't take on so, I didn't mean any harm,' but she was too scared to be reasoned

with and she just carried on screaming. Faces material-
ized out of the darkness: a passer-by in workman's
clothes, a Fallen Woman with cigarette and handbag,
and a head at a window in the house behind them. The
drunk vanished into the night, and Margaret stopped
screaming and began to cry. Then there was the sound
of running boots, the narrow beam of a masked flashlight, and a policeman's helmet.

The policeman shone his light on Margaret's face.

The woman muttered, 'She ain't one of us, Steve.'

The policeman called Steve said, 'What's your name,
girl?'

'Margaret Oxenford.'

The man in work clothes said, 'A toff took her for a
tart, that's what happened.' Satisfied, he went off.

The policeman said, 'Would that be *Lady* Margaret
Oxenford?'

Margaret sniffed miserably and nodded.

The woman said, 'I told you she weren't one of us.'
With that she drew on her cigarette, dropped the end,
trod on it and disappeared.

The policeman said, 'You come with me, my Lady,
you'll be all right now.'

Margaret wiped her face with her sleeve. The policeman offered her his arm. She took it. He shone his
torch on the pavement in front of her and they began
to walk.

After a moment Margaret shuddered and said, 'That
frightful man.'

The policeman was briskly unsympathetic. 'Can't

really blame him,' he said cheerfully. 'This is the most notorious street in London. It's a fair assumption that a girl alone here at this hour is a Lady of the Night.'

Margaret supposed he was right, although it seemed rather unfair.

The familiar blue lamp of a police station appeared in the morning twilight. The policeman said, 'You have a nice cup of tea and you'll feel better.'

They went inside. Two policemen stood behind a counter, one middle-aged and stocky and the other young and thin. On each side of the hall was a plain wooden bench up against the wall. There was only one other person in the hall: a pale woman with her hair in a scarf and house slippers on her feet, sitting on one of the benches, waiting with tired patience.

Margaret's rescuer directed her to the opposite bench, saying. 'Sit yourself down there for a minute.' Margaret did as she was told. The constable went up to the desk and spoke to the older man. 'Sarge, that's Lady Margaret Oxenford. Had a run-in with a drunk in Bolting Lane.'

'I suppose he thought she was on the game.'

Margaret was struck by the variety of euphemisms for prostitution. People seemed to have a horror of calling it what it was and had to refer to it obliquely. She herself had known about it only in the vaguest possible way, indeed she had not really believed it went on, until tonight. But there had been nothing vague about the intentions of the young man in evening dress.

The sergeant looked over at Margaret in an

48

interested way, then said something in a low voice that she could not hear. Steve nodded and disappeared into the back of the building.

Margaret realized she had left her shoes on that doorstep. Now there were holes in the feet of her stockings. She began to worry: she could hardly turn up at the recruiting station in this state. Perhaps she could go back for her shoes in daylight. But they might no longer be there. And she badly needed a wash and a clean dress, too. It would be heartbreaking to be turned down for the ATS after all this. But where could she go to tidy herself? By morning even Aunt Martha's house would not be safe: Father might turn up there, searching for her. Surely, she thought with anguish, her whole plan was not going to fall apart because of a pair of shoes?

Her policeman came back with tea in a thick earthenware mug. It was weak and had too much sugar in it, but Margaret sipped it gratefully. It restored her resolve. She *could* overcome her problems. She would leave as soon as she had finished her tea. She would go to a poor district and find a shop selling cheap clothes – she still had a few shillings. She would buy a dress, a pair of sandals and a set of clean underwear. She would go to a public bathhouse and wash and change. Then she would be ready for the army.

While she was elaborating this plan, there was a noise outside the door and a group of young men burst in. They were well dressed, some in evening clothes and others in lounge suits. After a moment

Margaret realized they were dragging with them an unwilling companion. One of the men started to shout at the sergeant behind the counter.

The sergeant interrupted him. 'All right, all right, quieten down!' he said in a commanding voice. 'You're not on the rugby field now, you know – this is a police station.' The noise muted somewhat, but not enough for the sergeant. 'If you don't behave yourselves I'll clap the lot of you in the bleedin' cells,' he shouted. 'Now bloody well SHUT UP!'

They became quiet and released their prisoner, who stood there looking sulky. The sergeant pointed at one of the men, a dark-haired fellow of about Margaret's age. 'Right – you. Tell me what all the fuss is about.'

The young man pointed at the prisoner. 'This blighter took my sister to a restaurant then sneaked off without paying!' he said indignantly. He spoke with an upper-class accent, and his face was vaguely familiar to Margaret. She hoped he would not recognize her: it would be too humiliating for people to know that she had had to be rescued by a policeman after running away from home.

A younger man in a striped suit added, 'His name's Harry Marks and he ought to be locked up.'

Margaret looked with interest at Harry Marks. He was a strikingly handsome man of twenty-two or twenty-three, with blond hair and regular features. Although he was rather rumpled, he wore his double-breasted dinner jacket with easy elegance. He looked around contemptuously and said, 'These fellows are drunk.'

The young man in the striped suit burst out, 'We

may be drunk but he's a cad – and a thief. Look what we found in his pocket.' He threw something down on the counter. 'These cufflinks were stolen earlier in the evening from Sir Simon Monkford.'

'All right,' said the sergeant. 'So you're accusing him of obtaining a pecuniary advantage by deception – that's not paying his restaurant bill – *and* of stealing. Anything else?'

The wearer of the striped suit laughed scornfully and said, 'Isn't that enough for you?'

The sergeant pointed his pencil at him. 'You remember where you bloody well are, son. You may have been born with a silver spoon in your mouth but this is a police station and if you don't speak politely you'll spend the rest of the night in a bleedin' cell.'

The young man looked foolish and said no more.

The sergeant turned his attention back to the first speaker. 'Now, can you supply all the details of both accusations? I need the name and address of the restaurant, your sister's name and address, plus the name and address of the party that owns the cufflinks.'

'Yes, I can give you all that. The restaurant—'

'Good. You stay here.' He pointed at the accused man. 'You sit down.' He waved his hand at the crowd of young men. 'The rest of you can go home.'

They all looked rather nonplussed. Their great adventure had ended in anticlimax. For a moment none of them moved.

The sergeant said, 'Go on, bugger off, the lot of you!'

Margaret had never heard so much swearing in one day.

The young men moved off, muttering. The boy in the striped suit said, 'You bring a thief to justice and you get treated as if you were a criminal yourself!' But he was passing through the door before he finished the sentence.

The sergeant began to question the dark-haired boy, making notes. Harry Marks stood beside him for a moment, then turned away impatiently. He spotted Margaret, threw her a sunny grin, and sat down next to her. He said, 'All right, girl? What you doing here, then, this time o' night?'

Margaret was bewildered. He was quite transformed. His haughty manner and refined speech had gone, and he spoke with the same accent as the sergeant. For a moment she was too surprised to reply.

Harry threw an appraising glance at the doorway, as if he might be thinking of making a dash for it; then he looked back at the desk and saw the younger police-man, who had not yet said a word, staring at him watchfully. He seemed to give up the idea of escape. He turned back to Margaret. 'Who give you that black eye – your old man?'

Margaret found her voice and said, 'I got lost in the blackout and bumped into a pillar-box.'

It was his turn to be surprised. He had taken her for a working-class girl. Now, hearing her accent, he realized his mistake. Without a blink he reverted to his former persona. 'I say, what jolly bad luck!'

Margaret was fascinated. Which was his real self? He smelled of cologne. His hair was well cut, if a fraction

52

too long. He wore a midnight-blue evening suit in the fashion set by Edward VIII, with silk socks and patent-leather shoes. His jewellery was very good: diamond studs in his shirt-front with matching cufflinks, a gold wristwatch with a black crocodile strap, and a signet ring on the little finger of his left hand. His hands were large and strong-looking, but his fingernails were perfectly clean.

In a low voice she said, 'Did you really leave the restaurant without paying?'

He looked at her appraisingly, then seemed to reach a decision. 'Actually, I did,' he said in a conspiratorial tone.

'But why?'

'Because, if I'd listened for one more minute to Rebecca Maugham-Flint talking about her blasted horses, I should have been unable to resist the urge to take her by the throat and strangle her.'

Margaret giggled. She knew Rebecca Maugham-Flint, who was a large, plain girl, the daughter of a general, with her father's hearty manner and parade-ground voice. 'I can just imagine it,' she said. It would be hard to think of a more unsuitable dinner companion for the attractive Mr Marks.

Constable Steve appeared and picked up her empty mug. 'Feeling better, Lady Margaret?'

Out of the corner of her eye she saw Harry Marks react to her title. 'Much better, thank you,' she said. For a moment she had forgotten her own troubles in talking to Harry, but now she remembered all she had to do. 'You've been so kind,' she went on. 'Now I'm going to leave you to get on with more important things.'

'No need for you to rush off,' the constable said. 'Your father, the Marquess, is on his way to fetch you.'

Margaret's heart stopped. How could this be? She had been so convinced that she was safe – she had underestimated her father! Now she was as frightened as she had been walking along the road to the railway station. He was after her, on his way here at this very minute! She felt shaky. 'How does he know where I am?' she said in a high, strained voice.

The young policeman looked proud. 'Your description was circulated late yesterday evening, and I read it when I come on duty. I never recognized you in the blackout, but I remembered the name. The instruction is to inform the Marquess immediately. As soon as I brought you in here, I rung him up on the telephone.'

Margaret stood up, her heart fluttering wildly. 'I shan't wait for him,' she said. 'It's light now.'

The policeman looked anxious. 'Just a minute,' he said nervously. He turned to the desk. 'Sarge, the lady doesn't want to wait for her father.'

Harry Marks said to Margaret, 'They can't make you stay – running away from home isn't a crime at your age. If you want to go, just walk out.'

Margaret was terrified that they would find some excuse to detain her.

The sergeant got off his seat and came around the counter. 'He's quite right,' the sergeant said. 'You can go any time you like.'

'Oh, thank you,' Margaret said gratefully.

The sergeant smiled. 'But you've got no shoes, and there's holes in your stockings. If you must leave before your father gets here, at least let us call a taxi.'

Margaret thought for a moment. They had phoned Father as soon as she arrived at the police station, but that was less than an hour ago. Father could not possibly get here for another hour or more. 'All right,' she said to the kindly sergeant. 'Thank you.'

He opened a door off the hall. 'You'll be more comfortable in here, while you wait for the taxi.' He switched on the light.

Margaret would have preferred to stay and talk to the fascinating Harry Marks, but she did not want to refuse the sergeant's kindness, especially after he had given in to her. 'Thank you,' she said again.

As she walked to the door she heard Harry say, 'More fool you.'

She stepped into the little room. There were some cheap chairs and a bench, a naked bulb hanging from the ceiling, and a barred window. She could not imagine why the sergeant thought this more comfortable than the hallway. She turned to tell him so.

The door closed in her face. A presentiment of ruin filled her heart with dread. She lunged at the door and grabbed the handle. As she did so her sudden fear was confirmed and she heard a key turn in the lock. She rattled the handle furiously. The door would not open.

She slumped in despair with her head against the wood.

From outside she heard a low laugh, then Harry's voice, muffled but comprehensible, saying, 'You bastard.'

The sergeant's voice was now anything but kindly. 'You shut your hole,' he said crudely.

'You've got no right, you know that.'

'Her father's a bloody marquess, and that's all the right I need.'

No more was said.

Margaret realized bitterly that she had lost. Her great escape had failed. She had been betrayed by the very people she thought were helping her. For a little while she had been free, but now it was over. She would not be joining the ATS today, she thought miserably, she would be boarding the Pan American Clipper and flying to New York, running away from the war. After all she had been through her fate was unchanged. It seemed so desperately unfair.

After a long moment she turned from the door and walked the few steps to the window. She could see an empty yard and a brick wall. She stood there, defeated and helpless, looking through the bars at the brightening daylight, waiting for her father.

Eddie Deakin gave the Pan American Clipper a final once-over. The four Wright Cyclone 1500-horsepower engines gleamed with oil. Each engine was as high as a man. All fifty-six spark plugs had been replaced. On impulse, Eddie took a feeler from his overalls pocket and slid it into an engine mount between the rubber and the metal to test the bond. The pounding vibration of the long flight put a terrific strain on the adhesive.

But Eddie's feeler would not go in even a quarter of an inch. The mounts were holding.

He closed the hatch and climbed down the ladder. While the plane was being eased back into the water he would change out of his overalls, get cleaned up, and put on his black Pan American flight uniform.

The sun was shining as he left the dock and strolled up the hill towards the hotel where the crew stayed during the layover. He was proud of the plane and the job he did. The Clipper crews were an élite, the best men the airline had, for the new transatlantic service was the most prestigious route. All his life he would be able to say he had flown the Atlantic in the early days.

However, he was planning to give it up soon. He was thirty years old, he had been married for a year, and Carol-Ann was pregnant. Flying was all right for a single man but he was not going to spend his life away from his wife and children. He had been saving money and he had almost enough to start a business. He had an option on a site near Bangor, Maine, that would make a perfect airfield. He would service planes and sell fuel, and eventually have an aircraft for charter. Secretly he dreamed that one day he might have an airline of his own, like the pioneering Juan Trippe, founder of Pan American.

He entered the grounds of the Langdown Lawn Hotel. It was a piece of luck for Pan American crew that there was such a pleasant hotel a mile or so from the Imperial Airways complex. The place was a typical English country house, run by a gracious couple who charmed everyone and served tea on the lawn on sunny afternoons.

He went inside. In the hall he ran into his assistant engineer, Desmond Finn – known, inevitably, as Mickey. Mickey reminded Eddie of the Jimmy Olsen character in the Superman comics: he was a happy-go-lucky type with a big toothy grin and a propensity to hero-worship Eddie, who found such adoration embarrassing. He was speaking into the telephone and now, when he saw Eddie, he said, 'Oh, wait, you're lucky, he just walked in.' He handed the earpiece to Eddie and said, 'A phone call for you.' Then he went upstairs, politely leaving Eddie alone.

Eddie spoke into the phone. 'Hello?'

'Is this Edward Deakin?'

Eddie frowned. The voice was unfamiliar, and nobody called him Edward. He said, 'Yes, I'm Eddie Deakin. Who are you?'

'Wait, I have your wife on the line.'

Eddie's heart lurched. Why was Carol-Ann calling him from the States? Something was wrong.

A moment later he heard her voice. 'Eddie?'

'Hi, honey, what's up?'

She burst into tears.

A whole series of awful explanations came to mind: the house had burned down, someone had died, she had hurt herself in some kind of accident, she had suffered a miscarriage—

'Carol-Ann, calm down, are you all right?'

She spoke through sobs. 'I'm – not – hurt—'

'What, then?' he said fearfully. 'What's happened? Try to tell me, babe.'

'These men – came to the house.'

Eddie went cold with dread. 'What men? What did they do?'

'They made me get into a car.'

'Jesus God, who are they?' The anger was like a pain in his chest and he had to fight for breath. 'Did they hurt you?'

'I'm all right . . . but Eddie, I'm so scared.'

He did not know what to say next. Too many questions came to his lips. Men had gone to his house and forced Carol-Ann to get into a car! What was happening? Finally he said, 'But why?'

'They won't tell me.'

'What did they say?'

'Eddie, you have to do what they want, that's all I know.'

Even in his anger and fear, Eddie heard Pop say *Never sign a blank cheque.* All the same he did not hesitate. 'I'll do it, but what—'

'Promise!'

'I promise!'

'Thank God.'

'When did this happen?'

'A couple of hours ago.'

'Where are you now?'

'We're in a house not far—' Her speech turned into a shocked cry.

'Carol-Ann! What's happening? Are you okay?'

There was no response. Furious, frightened and impotent, Eddie squeezed the phone until his knuckles turned white.

Then the original male voice returned. 'Listen to me very carefully, Edward.'

'No, you listen to me, shitheel,' Eddie raged. 'If you hurt her I'll kill you, I swear to God, I'll track you down if it takes as long as I live and when I find you, you punk, I'll tear your head off your neck with my hands, now do you read me loud and clear?'

There was a moment's hesitation, as if the man at the other end of the line had not expected such a tirade. Then he said, 'Don't act tough, you're too far away.' He sounded a little shook, but he was right: Eddie could do nothing. The man went on: 'Just pay attention.'

Eddie held his tongue with an effort.

'You'll get your instructions on the plane from a man called Tom Luther.'

On the plane! What did that mean? Would this Tom Luther be a passenger, or what? Eddie said, 'But what do you want me to do?'

'Shut up. Luther will tell you. And you'd better follow his orders to the letter if you want to see your wife again.'

'How do I know—'

'And one more thing. Don't call the police. It won't do you any good. But if you do call them, I'll fuck her just to be mean.'

'You bastard, I'll—'

The line went dead.

CHAPTER THREE

HARRY MARKS was the luckiest man alive.

His mother had always told him he was lucky. Although his father had been killed in the Great War, he was lucky to have a strong and capable mother to bring him up. She cleaned offices for a living, and all through the slump she had never been out of work. They lived in a tenement in Battersea, with a cold-water tap on each landing and outside toilets, but they were surrounded by good neighbours, people who helped one another through times of trouble. Harry had a knack of escaping from trouble. When boys were being thrashed at school, the teacher's cane would break just before he got to Harry. Harry could fall under a horse and cart and have them pass over him without touching him.

It was his love of jewellery that had made him a thief.

As an adolescent he had loved to walk along the opulent shopping streets of the West End and look in the windows of jewellers' shops. He was enraptured by the diamonds and precious stones glinting on dark velvet pads under the bright display lights. He liked them for their beauty, but also because they symbolized a kind of life he had read about in books, a life of spacious country houses with broad green lawns, where pretty girls with names like Lady Penelope and Jessica Chumley played tennis all afternoon and came in panting for tea.

He had been apprenticed to a jeweller, but he had been bored and restless, and he left after six months. Mending broken watch straps and enlarging wedding rings for overweight wives had no glamour. But he had learned to tell a ruby from a red garnet, a natural pearl from a cultured one, and a modern brilliant-cut diamond from a nineteenth-century old mine cut. He had also discovered the difference between an appropriate setting and an ugly one, a graceful design and a tasteless piece of ostentation; and the ability to discriminate had further inflamed his lust for beautiful jewellery and his longing for the style of life that went with it.

He eventually found a way to satisfy both desires by making use of girls such as Rebecca Maugham-Flint.

. He had met Rebecca at Ascot. He often picked up rich girls at race meetings. The open air and the crowds made it possible for him to hover between two groups of young racegoers in such a way that everyone thought he was part of the other group. Rebecca was a tall girl with a big nose, dreadfully dressed in a ruched jersey frock and a Robin Hood hat with a feather in it. None of the young men around her paid any attention to her, and she was pathetically grateful to Harry for talking to her.

He had not pursued the acquaintanceship right away, for it was best not to seem eager. But when he ran into her a month later, at an art gallery, she greeted him like an old friend and introduced him to her mother.

Girls such as Rebecca were not supposed to go unchaperoned to cinemas and restaurants with boys, of course; only shop-girls and factory workers did that. So they would always pretend to their parents that they were going out in a crowd and, to make it look right, they would generally begin the evening at a cocktail party. Afterwards they could discreetly go off in pairs. This suited Harry ideally: since he was not officially 'courting' Rebecca, her parents saw no need to look closely into his background, and they never questioned the vague stories he told of a country house in Yorkshire, a minor public school in Scotland, an invalid mother living in the South of France and a prospective commission in the Royal Air Force.

Vague stories were common in upper-class society, he had found. They were told by young men who did not want to admit to being desperately poor, or having parents who were hopeless drunks, or coming from families which had disgraced themselves by scandal. No one troubled to pin a fellow down until he showed signs of a serious attachment to a well-bred girl.

In this indefinite way Harry had been going around with Rebecca for three weeks. She had got him invited to a weekend house-party in Kent, where he had played cricket and stolen money from the hosts, who had been too embarrassed to report the theft for fear of offending their guests. She had also taken him to several balls where he had picked pockets and emptied purses. In addition, when calling at her parents' house he had taken small sums of money, some silver cutlery and three interesting Victorian brooches which her mother had not yet missed.

There was nothing immoral in what he did, in his opinion. The people from whom he stole did not deserve their wealth. Most of them had never done a day's work in their lives. Those few who had to have some kind of job used their public-school connections to get overpaid sinecures: they were diplomats, chairmen of companies, judges, or Conservative MPs. Stealing from them was like killing Nazis: a service to the public, not a crime.

He had been doing this for two years, and he knew it could not go on for ever. The world of upper-class English society was large but limited, and eventually someone would find him out. The war had come at a time when he was ready to look for a different way of life.

However, he was not going to join the army as a regular soldier. Bad food, itchy clothes, bullying and military discipline were not for him, and he looked sickly in olive drab. Air Force blue matched his eyes, however, and he could easily see himself as a pilot. So he was going to be an officer in the RAF. He had not yet figured out how, but he would manage it: he was lucky that way.

In the meantime he decided to use Rebecca to get inside one more wealthy home before dropping her.

They began the evening at a reception in the Belgravia home of Sir Simon Monkford, a rich publisher.

Harry spent some time with the Honourable Lydia

Moss, overweight daughter of a Scottish earl. Awkward and lonely, she was just the kind of girl who was most vulnerable to his charm, and he enchanted her for twenty minutes more or less out of habit. Then he talked to Rebecca for a while, to keep her sweet. After that he judged the time was right to make his move.

He excused himself and left the room. The party was going on in the large double drawing room on the first floor. As he crossed the landing and slipped up the stairs he felt the thrilling rush of adrenalin that always came to him when he was about to do a job. The knowledge that he was going to steal from his hosts, and risk being caught red-handed and shown up as a fraud, filled him with fear and excitement.

He reached the next floor and followed the corridor to the front of the house. The farthest door probably led to the master bedroom suite, he thought. He opened it and saw a large bedroom with flowered curtains and a pink bedspread. He was about to step inside when another door opened and a challenging voice called out, 'I say!'

Harry turned around, his tension drawing tighter. He saw a man of about his own age step into the corridor and look curiously at him.

As always, the right words came to him when he needed them. 'Ah, is it in there?' he said.

'What?'

'Is that the lav?'

The young man's face cleared. 'Oh, I see. You want the green door at the other end of the corridor.'

'Thanks awfully.'

'Not at all.'

Harry went along the corridor. 'Lovely house,' he remarked.

'Isn't it.' The man descended the staircase and disappeared.

Harry allowed himself a pleased grin. People could be so gullible.

He retraced his steps and went into the pink bedroom. As usual, there was a suite of rooms. The colour scheme indicated that this was Lady Monkford's room. A rapid survey revealed a small dressing room off to one side, also decorated in pink; an adjoining, smaller bedroom, with green leather chairs and striped wallpaper; and a gentleman's dressing room off that. Upper-class couples often slept separately, Harry had learned. He had not yet decided whether that was because they were less randy than the working class, or because they felt obliged to make use of all the many rooms in their vast houses.

Sir Simon's dressing room was furnished with a heavy mahogany wardrobe and matching chest. Harry opened the top drawer of the chest. There, inside a small leather jewel box, was an assortment of studs, collar stiffeners and cufflinks, not neatly arranged but tumbled about haphazardly. Most of them were rather ordinary, but Harry's discriminating eye lit on a charming pair of gold cufflinks with small rubies inset. He put them in his pocket. Next to the jewel box was a soft leather wallet containing about fifty pounds in five-pound notes. Harry took twenty pounds and felt pleased with himself. Easy, he thought. It would take most people two months' hard work in a dirty factory to earn twenty pounds.

He never stole everything. Taking just a few items created a doubt. People thought they might have mislaid the jewellery or made a mistake about how much was in the wallet, so they hesitated to report the theft.

He closed the drawer and moved into Lady Monkford's bedroom. He was tempted to get out now with the useful haul he had already made, but he decided to risk a few minutes more. Women generally had better jewellery than their husbands. Lady Monkford might have sapphires. Harry loved sapphires.

It was a fine evening, and a window was open wide. Harry glanced through it and saw a small balcony with a wrought-iron balustrade. He went quickly into the dressing room and sat at the dressing-table. He opened all the drawers and found several boxes and trays of jewellery. He began to go through them rapidly, listening warily for the sound of the door opening.

Lady Monkford did not have good taste. She was a pretty woman who had struck Harry as rather ineffectual, and she – or her husband – chose showy, rather cheap jewellery. Her pearls were ill-matched, her brooches big and ugly, her earrings clumsy and her bracelets flashy. He was disappointed.

He was hesitating over an almost-attractive pendant when he heard the bedroom door open.

He froze, stomach in a knot, thinking fast.

The only door out of the dressing room led to the bedroom. There was a small window, but it was firmly closed and he probably could not open it quickly or silently enough. He wondered if he had time to hide in the wardrobe.

From where he stood he could not quite see the bedroom door. He heard it close again, then there was a feminine cough and light footsteps on the carpet. He leaned towards the mirror and found he could see into the bedroom. Lady Monkford had come in and she was heading for the dressing room. There was not even time to close the drawers.

His breath came fast. He was taut with fear, but he had been in spots like this before. He paused for one more moment, forcing himself to breathe evenly, calming his mind. Then he moved.

He stood up, stepped quickly through the door into the bedroom, and said, 'I say!'

Lady Monkford was brought up short in the middle of the room. She put her hand to her mouth and let out a tiny scream.

A flowered curtain flapped in the breeze from the open window, and Harry was inspired.

'I say,' he repeated, deliberately sounding a bit stupefied. 'I've just seen someone jump out of your window.'

She found her voice. 'What on earth do you mean?' she said. 'And what are you doing in my bedroom?'

Acting the part, Harry strode to the window and looked out. 'Gone already!' he said.

'Please explain yourself!'

Harry took a deep breath, as if marshalling his thoughts. Lady Monkford was about forty, a fluttery woman in a green silk dress. If he kept his nerve he could deal with her. He smiled winningly, assumed the persona of a hearty, rugby-playing, overgrown schoolboy – a type that must be familiar to her – and began to pull the wool over her eyes.

'It's the oddest thing I ever saw,' he said. 'I was in the corridor when a strange-looking cove peeped out of this room. He caught my eye and ducked back in again. I knew it was your bedroom, because I had looked in here myself when I was hunting for the bathroom. I wondered what the chap was up to – he didn't look like one of your servants and he certainly wasn't a guest. So I came along to ask him. When I opened the door he jumped out of the window.' Then, to account for the still-open drawers of the dressing-table, he added, 'I've just looked into your dressing room, and I'm afraid there's no doubt he was after your jewellery.'

That was brilliant, he said admiringly to himself. I should be on the bleedin' wireless.

She put her hand to her forehead. 'Oh, what a dreadful thing,' she said weakly.

'You'd better sit down,' Harry said solicitously. He helped her to a small pink chair.

'To think!' she said. 'If you hadn't chased him off, he would have been here when I walked in! I'm afraid I shall faint.' She grasped Harry's hand and held it tightly. 'I'm so grateful to you.'

Harry smothered a grin. He had got away with it again.

He thought ahead for a moment. He did not want

her to make too much fuss. Ideally he would like her to keep the whole thing to herself. 'Look, don't tell Rebecca what's happened, will you?' he said as a first step. 'She's got a nervous disposition and something like this could lay her low for weeks.'

'Me, too,' said Lady Monkford. 'Weeks!' She was too upset to reflect that the muscular, hearty Rebecca was hardly the type to have a nervous disposition.

'You'll probably have to call the police, and so on, but it will spoil the party,' he went on.

'Oh dear – that would be too dreadful. Do we *have* to call them?'

'Well . . .' Harry concealed his satisfaction. 'It rather depends on what the blighter stole. Why don't you have a quick look?'

'Oh, goodness, yes, I'd better.'

Harry squeezed her hand for encouragement then helped her up. They went into the dressing room. She gasped when she saw all the drawers open. Harry handed her to her chair. She sat down and started looking through her jewellery. After a moment she said, 'I don't think he can have taken much.'

'Perhaps I surprised him before he got started,' Harry said.

She continued sorting through the necklaces, bracelets and brooches. 'I think you must have,' she said. 'How wonderful you are.'

'If you haven't lost anything, you don't really have to tell anyone.'

'Except Sir Simon, of course,' she said.

'Of course,' Harry said, although he had hoped otherwise. 'You could tell him after the party's over. That way at least you won't spoil his evening.'

'What a good idea,' she said gratefully.

This was very satisfactory. Harry was immensely relieved. He decided to quit while he was so far ahead. 'I'd better go down,' he said. 'I'll leave you to catch your breath.' He bent swiftly and kissed her cheek. She was taken by surprise, and she blushed. He whispered in her ear, 'I think you're terribly brave.' With that he went out.

Middle-aged women were even easier than their daughters, he thought. In the empty corridor he caught sight of himself in a mirror. He stopped to adjust his bow tie and grinned triumphantly at his reflection. 'You are a devil, Harold,' he murmured.

The party was coming to an end. When Harry re-entered the drawing room, Rebecca said irritably, 'Where have you been?'

'Talking to our hostess,' he replied. 'Sorry. Shall we take our leave?'

He walked out of the house with his host's cufflinks and twenty pounds in his pocket.

They got a cab in Belgrave Square and rode to a restaurant in Piccadilly. Harry loved good restaurants: he got a deep sense of well-being from the crisp napkins, the polished glasses, the menus in French and the deferential waiters. His father had never seen the inside of such a place. His mother might have, if she had come in to clean it. He ordered a bottle of champagne, consulting the list carefully and choosing a vintage he knew to be good but not rare, so that the price was not too high.

When he first started taking girls to restaurants he had made a few mistakes, but he was a quick learner. One useful trick had been to leave the menu unopened, and say, 'I'd like a sole, have you got any?' The waiter would open the menu and show him where it said *Sole meunière, Les goujons de sole avec sauce tartare*, and *Sole grillée*, and then, seeing him hesitate, would probably say, 'The goujons are very nice, sir.' Harry soon learned the French for all the basic dishes. He also noticed that people who frequently ate in such places quite often asked the waiter what a particular dish was: wealthy English people did not necessarily understand French. Thereafter he made a point of asking for the translation of one dish every time he ate in a fancy restaurant, and now he could read a menu better than most rich boys of his age. Wine was no problem, either. Sommeliers were normally pleased to be asked for a recommendation, and they did not expect a young man to be familiar with all the châteaux and communes and the different vintages. The trick, in restaurants as in life, was to appear at ease, especially when you were not.

The champagne he chose was good, but there was something wrong with his mood tonight, and he soon figured out that the problem was Rebecca. He kept thinking how delightful it would be to bring a *pretty* girl to a place like this. He always went out with unattractive girls: plain girls, fat girls, spotty girls, silly girls. They were easy to get acquainted with and then, once they had fallen for him, they were eager to take him at face value, reluctant to question him in case they should lose him. As a strategy for getting inside wealthy homes it was matchless. The snag was that he spent all his time with girls he did not like. One day, perhaps . . .

Rebecca was sullen tonight. She was discontented about something. Perhaps after seeing Harry regularly for three weeks she was wondering why he still had not attempted to 'go too far', by which she would mean touching her breasts. The truth was he could not pretend to lust after her. He could charm her, romance her, make her laugh, and make her love him, but he could not desire her. On one excruciating occasion he had found himself in a hay loft with a skinny, depressed girl set on losing her virginity, and he had tried to force himself; but his body had refused to co-operate, and he still squirmed with embarrassment every time he thought of it.

His sexual experience, such as it was, was mostly with girls of his own class, and none of those relationships had lasted. He had had just one deeply satisfying love affair. At the age of eighteen he had been shamelessly picked up in Bond Street by an older woman, the bored wife of a busy solicitor, and they had been lovers for two years. He had learned a lot from Marjorie – about making love, which she taught him enthusiastically; about upper-class manners, which he picked up surreptitiously; and about poetry, which they read and discussed in bed together. Harry had been deeply fond of her. She ended the affair instantly and brutally when her husband found out that she had a lover (he never knew who). Since then Harry had seen them both several times: the woman always looked at him as if he were not there. Harry found this cruel. She had meant a lot to him, and she had seemed to care for him. Was she strong-willed, or just heartless? He would probably never know.

The champagne and the good food were not lifting Harry's spirits or Rebecca's. He began to feel restless. He had been planning to drop her gently after tonight, but suddenly he could not bear the thought of spending even the rest of this evening with her. He wished he had not wasted money on dinner for her. He looked at her grumpy face, bare of make-up and squashed beneath a silly little hat with a feather, and he began to hate her.

When they had finished dessert he ordered coffee and went to the lavatory. The cloakroom was right next to the men's room, near the exit door, and not visible from their table. Harry was seized by an irresistible impulse. He collected his hat, tipped the cloakroom attendant, and slipped out of the restaurant.

It was a mild night. The blackout made it very dark, but Harry knew the West End well, and there were traffic lights to navigate by, plus the sparing glow of car sidelights. He felt as if he had been let out of school. He had got rid of Rebecca, saved himself seven or eight pounds and given himself a night off, all at one inspired stroke.

The theatres, cinemas and dance halls had been closed by the government, 'until the scale of the

German attack upon Britain has been judged', they said. But nightclubs always operated on the fringe of the law and there were still plenty open if you knew where to look. Soon Harry was making himself comfortable at a table in a cellar in Soho, sipping whisky and listening to a first-rate American jazz band and toying with the idea of making a play for the cigarette girl.

He was still thinking about it when Rebecca's brother came in.

The following morning he sat in a cell in the basement underneath the courthouse, depressed and remorseful, waiting to be taken before the magistrates. He was in deep trouble.

Walking out of the restaurant like that had been bloody silly. Rebecca was not the type to swallow her pride and pay the bill quietly. She had made a fuss, the manager had called the police, her family had been dragged in . . . It was just the kind of furore Harry was normally so careful to avoid. Even so he would have got away with it, had it not been for the incredible bad luck of running into Rebecca's brother a couple of hours later.

He was in a large cell with fifteen or twenty other prisoners who would be brought before the Bench this morning. There were no windows, and the room was full of cigarette smoke. Harry would not be tried today: this would be a preliminary hearing.

He would eventually be convicted, of course. The evidence against him was indisputable. The head waiter

would corroborate Rebecca's complaint, and Sir Simon
Monkford would identify the cufflinks as his.

But it was worse than that. Harry had been interviewed by an inspector from the Criminal Investigation
Department. The man had been wearing the detective's
uniform of serviceable serge suit, plain white shirt and
black tie, waistcoat with no watch chain, and highly
polished, well-worn boots. He was an experienced
policeman with a sharp mind and a wary manner. He
had said, 'For the last two or three years we've been
getting odd reports, from wealthy houses, of *lost* jewellery. Not *stolen*, of course. Just missing. Bracelets,
earrings, pendants, shirt studs ... The losers are quite
sure the stuff can't have been stolen, because the only
people who had the opportunity to take it would have
been their guests. The only reason they report it is that
they want to claim it if it turns up somewhere.'

Harry had kept his mouth shut tight throughout the
entire interview, but inside he was feeling sick. He had
been sure that his career had gone entirely unnoticed
until now. He was shocked to learn the opposite: they
had been on to him for some time.

The detective opened a fat file. 'The Earl of Dorset,
a Georgian silver bonbonnière and a lacquered snuff
box, also Georgian. Mrs Harry Jaspers, a pearl bracelet
with ruby clasp by Tiffany's. The Contessa di Malvoli,
an art-deco diamond pendant on a silver chain. This
man has good taste.' The detective looked pointedly at
the diamond studs in Harry's dress shirt.

Harry realized the file must contain details of dozens
of crimes committed by him. He knew also that he

would eventually be convicted of at least some. This shrewd detective had put together all the basic facts: he could easily gather witnesses to say that Harry had been at each location at the time of the theft. Sooner or later they would search his lodgings and his mother's house. Most of the jewellery had been fenced, but he had kept a few pieces: the shirt studs the detective had noticed had been taken from a sleeping drunk at a ball in Grosvenor Square, and his mother had a brooch he had deftly plucked from the bosom of a countess at a wedding reception in a Surrey garden. And then how would he answer when they asked him what he lived on?

He was headed for a long stretch in jail. And when he got out he would be conscripted into the army, which was more or less the same thing. The thought made his blood run cold.

He steadfastly refused to say a word, even when the detective took him by the lapels of his dinner jacket and slammed him against the wall; but silence would not save him. The law had time on its side.

Harry had only one chance of freedom. He would have to persuade the magistrates to give him bail, then disappear. Suddenly he yearned for freedom as if he had been in jail for years instead of hours.

Disappearing would not be simple, but the alternative made him shiver.

In robbing the rich he had grown accustomed to their style of living. He got up late, drank coffee from a china cup, wore beautiful clothes and ate in expensive restaurants. He still enjoyed returning to his roots, drinking in the pub with old mates or taking his ma to the Odeon. But the thought of prison was unbearable: the dirty clothes, the horrible food, the total lack of privacy, and, worst of all, the grinding boredom of a totally pointless existence.

With a shudder of loathing he concentrated his mind on the problem of getting bail.

The police would oppose bail, of course, but the magistrates would make the decision. Harry had never appeared in court before, but in the streets from which he came people knew these things just as they knew who was eligible for a council house and how to sweep chimneys. Bail was automatically refused only in murder trials. Otherwise it was up to the discretion of the magistrates. Normally they did what the police asked, but not always. Sometimes they could be talked round, by a clever lawyer or by a defendant with a sob story about a sick child. Sometimes, if the police prosecutor was a little too arrogant, they would give bail just to assert their independence. He would have to put up some money, probably twenty-five or fifty pounds. This was no problem. He had plenty of money. He had been allowed to make a phone call, and he had rung the newsagent's shop on the corner of the street where his ma lived and asked Bernie, the proprietor, to send one of the paper-boys to fetch ma to the phone. When finally she got there he told her where to find his money.

'They'll give me bail, Ma,' Harry said cockily.

'I know, son,' his mother said. 'You've always been lucky.'

But if not . . .

I've got out of awkward situations before, he told himself cheerily.

But not this awkward.

A warder shouted out, 'Marks!'

Harry stood up. He had not planned what he would say: he was a spur-of-the-moment improviser. But for once he wished he had something prepared. Let's get it over with, he thought edgily. He buttoned his jacket, adjusted his bow tie and straightened the square of white linen in his breast pocket. He rubbed his chin and wished he had been allowed to shave. At the last minute the germ of a story appeared in his mind, and he took the cufflinks out of his shirt and pocketed them.

The gate was opened and he stepped outside.

He was led up a concrete staircase and emerged in the dock in the middle of the courtroom. In front of him were the lawyers' seats, all empty, the magistrates' clerk, a qualified lawyer, behind his desk, and the Bench, with three non-professional magistrates.

Harry thought, Christ, I hope the bastards let me go.

In the press gallery, to one side, was a young reporter with a notebook. Harry turned round and looked towards the back of the court. There in the public seats he spotted Ma, in her best coat and a new hat. She tapped her pocket significantly: Harry took that to mean that she had the money for his bail. He saw to his horror that she was wearing the brooch he had stolen from the Countess of Eyer.

He faced front and grasped the rail to keep his

hands from trembling. The prosecutor, a bald police inspector with a big nose, was saying, 'Number three on your list, your worships. Theft of twenty pounds in money and a pair of gold cufflinks worth fifteen guineas, the property of Sir Simon Monkford, and obtaining a pecuniary advantage by deception at the Saint Raphael restaurant in Piccadilly. The police are requesting a remand in custody because we are investigating further offences involving large sums of money.'

Harry was studying the magistrates warily. On one side was an old codger with white sideburns and a stiff collar, and on the other a military type in a regimental tie. They both looked down their noses at him, and he guessed they believed that everyone who appeared before them must be guilty of something. He felt hopeless. Then he told himself that stupid prejudice could quickly be turned into equally foolish credulity. Better they should not be too clever, if he was going to pull the wool over their eyes. The chairman, in the middle, was the only one who really counted. He was a middle-aged man with a grey moustache, grey suit and a world-weary air which suggested that in his time he had heard more tall stories and plausible excuses than he cared to remember. He would be the one to watch, Harry thought anxiously.

The chairman now said to Harry, 'Are you asking for bail?'

Harry pretended to be confused. 'Oh! Goodness gracious! I think so. Yes – yes, I am.'

All three magistrates sat up and began to take notice when they heard his upper-class accent. Harry enjoyed the effect. He was proud of his ability to confound people's social expectations. The reaction of the Bench gave him heart. I can fool them, he thought. I bet I can.

The chairman said, 'Well, what have you got to say for yourself?'

Harry was listening carefully to the chairman's accent, trying to place his social class precisely. He decided the man was educated middle class: a pharmacist, perhaps, or a bank manager. He would be shrewd, but he would be in the habit of deferring to the upper classes.

Harry put on an expression of embarrassment, and adopted the tone of a schoolboy addressing a headmaster. 'I'm afraid there's been the most frightful muddle, sir,' he began. The interest of the magistrates went up another notch, and they shifted in their seats and leaned forward interestedly. This was not going to be a run-of-the-mill case, they could see, and they were grateful for some relief from the usual tedium. Harry went on, 'To tell you the truth, some of the fellows drank too much port at the Carlton Club yesterday, and that was really the cause of it all.' He paused, as if that might be all he had to say, and looked expectantly at the Bench.

The military magistrate said: 'The Carlton Club!' His expression said it was not often that members of that august institution appeared before the Bench.

Harry wondered if he had gone too far. Perhaps they would refuse to believe that he was a member. He hurried on, 'It's dreadfully embarrassing, but I shall go round and apologize *immediately* to all concerned and get the whole thing straightened out without delay . . .' He pretended to remember suddenly that he was wearing evening dress. 'That is, as soon as I've changed.'

The old codger said, 'Are you saying you didn't *intend* to take twenty pounds and a pair of cufflinks?'

His tone was incredulous, but nevertheless it was a good sign that they were asking questions. It meant they were not dismissing his story out of hand. If they had not believed a word of what he was saying they would not have bothered to challenge him on the details. His heart lifted: perhaps he would be freed!

He said, 'I did borrow the cufflinks – I had come out without my own.' He held up his arms to show the unfastened cuffs of his dress shirt sticking out from the sleeves of his jacket. His cufflinks were in his pocket.

The old codger asked, 'And what about the twenty pounds?'

That was a more difficult question, Harry realized anxiously. No plausible excuse came to mind. You might forget your cufflinks and casually borrow someone else's, but borrowing money without permission was the same as stealing. He was on the edge of panic when inspiration rescued him once again. 'I do think Sir Simon might have been mistaken about how much there was in his wallet originally.' Harry lowered his voice, as if to say something to the magistrates that the common people in the court ought not to hear. 'He is frightfully rich, sir.'

The chairman said, 'He didn't get rich by forgetting

how much money he had.' There was a ripple of laughter from the people in the court. A sense of humour might have been an encouraging sign, but the chairman did not crack a smile: he had not intended to be funny. He's a bank manager, Harry thought; money's no joking matter. The magistrate went on, 'And why did you not pay your bill at the restaurant?'

'I say, I am most awfully sorry about that. I had the most appalling row with – with my dining partner.' Harry ostentatiously refrained from saying who he was dining with: it was bad form, among public-school boys, to bandy a woman's name about, and the magistrates would know that. 'I'm afraid I sort of stormed out, completely forgetting about the bill.'

The chairman looked over the top of his spectacles and fixed Harry with a hard stare. Harry felt he had gone wrong somewhere. His heart sank. What had he said? It occurred to him that he had displayed a casual attitude towards a debt. This was normal among the upper classes but a deadly sin to a bank manager. Panic seized him and he felt he was about to lose everything by a small error of judgement. Quickly he blurted out, 'Fearfully irresponsible of me, sir, and I shall go round there this lunchtime and settle up, of course. That is, if you let me go.'

He could not tell whether the chairman was mollified or not. 'So you're telling me that when you have made your explanations the charges against you are likely to be dropped?'

Harry decided he ought to guard against appearing to have a glib answer to every question. He hung his head and looked foolish. 'I suppose it would serve me bally well right if people refused to drop the charges.'

'It probably would,' the chairman said sternly.

You pompous old fart, Harry thought, but he knew that this kind of thing, though humiliating, was good for his case. The more they scolded him, the less likely they were to send him back to jail.

'Is there anything else you would like to say?' the chairman asked.

In a low voice Harry replied, 'Only that I'm most frightfully ashamed of myself, sir.'

'Hm.' The chairman grunted sceptically, but the military man nodded approvingly.

The three magistrates conferred in murmurs for a while. After a while Harry realized he was holding his breath, and forced himself to let it out. It was unbearable that his whole future should be in the hands of these old duffers. He wished they would hurry up and make up their minds; then when they all nodded in unison he wished they would postpone the awful moment.

The chairman looked up. 'I hope a night in the cells has taught you a lesson,' he said.

Oh, God, I think he's going to let me go, Harry thought. He swallowed and said, 'Absolutely, sir. I never want to go back there again, ever.'

'Make sure of it.'

There was another pause, then the chairman looked away from Harry and addressed the court. 'I'm not saying we believe everything we've heard, but we don't think this is a case for a custodial remand.'

A wave of relief washed over Harry, and his legs went weak.

The chairman said, 'Remanded for seven days. Bail in the sum of fifty pounds.'

Harry was free.

He saw the streets with new eyes, as if he had been in prison for a year instead of a few hours. London was getting ready for war. Dozens of huge silver balloons floated high in the skies to obstruct German planes. Shops and public buildings were surrounded by sandbags to protect them from bomb damage. There were new air-raid shelters in the parks and everyone carried a gas-mask. People felt they might be wiped out at any minute, and this caused them to drop their reserve and converse amiably with total strangers.

Harry had no memory of the Great War – he had been two years old when it ended. As a little boy he had thought 'the War' was a place, for everyone said to him, 'Your father was killed in the War,' like they said, 'Go and play in the Park, don't fall in the River, Ma's going to the Pub.' Later, when he was old enough to understand what he had lost, any mention of the War was painful to him. With Marjorie, the solicitor's wife who had been his lover for two years, he had read the poetry of the Great War and for a while he had called himself a pacifist. Then he had seen the Blackshirts marching in London and the scared faces of the old Jews as they watched, and he had decided some wars might be worth fighting. In the last few years he had been disgusted at the way the British government turned a blind eye to what was happening in Germany, just because they hoped Hitler would destroy the Soviet Union. But now that war had actually broken out, he thought only of all the small boys who would live, as he had, with a hole in their lives where a father should be.

But the bombers had not yet come, and it was another sunny day.

Harry decided not to go to his lodgings. The police would be furious about his getting bail and they would want to re-arrest him at the first opportunity. He had better lie low for a while. But how long would he have to keep looking back over his shoulder? Could he evade the police for ever? And if not, what would he do?

He got on the bus with his ma. He would go to her place in Battersea for the moment.

Ma looked sad. She knew how he made his living, although they had never talked about it. Now she said thoughtfully, 'I could never give you nothing.'

'You gave me everything, Ma,' he protested.

'No, I didn't, otherwise why would you need to steal?'

He did not have an answer to that.

When they got off the bus he went into the corner newsagent's, thanked Bernie for calling Ma to the phone earlier and bought the *Daily Express*. The headline said POLES BOMB BERLIN. As he came out he saw a bobby cycling along the road, and he felt a moment of foolish panic. He almost turned and ran before he got himself under control and remembered they always sent two people to arrest you.

I can't live like this, he thought.

They went to Ma's building and climbed the stone staircase to the fourth floor. Ma put the kettle on and said, 'I've pressed your blue suit – you can change into that.' She still took care of his clothes, sewing on buttons and darning his silk socks. Harry went into the bedroom, dragged his case from under the bed and counted his money.

After two years of thieving he had two hundred and forty-seven pounds. I must have pinched four times that much, he thought. I wonder what I spent the rest on?

He also had an American passport.

He flicked through it thoughtfully. He remembered finding it in a bureau at the home of a diplomat in Kensington. He had noticed that the owner's name was Harold and the picture looked a little like himself, so he had pocketed it.

America, he thought.

He could do an American accent. In fact, he knew something most British people did not – that there were several different American accents, some of which were posher than others. Take the word *Boston*. People from Boston would say *Baston*. People from New York would say *Bawston*. The more English you sounded, the more upper class you were in America – and there were millions of rich American girls just waiting to be romanced.

Whereas in this country there was nothing for him but jail and the army.

He had a passport and a pocketful of money. He had a clean suit in his mother's wardrobe and he could buy a few shirts and a suitcase. He was seventy-five miles from Southampton.

He could be gone today.

It was like a dream.

His mother woke him up by calling from the kitchen, 'Harry, d'you want a bacon sandwich?'

'Yes, please.'

He went into the kitchen and sat at the table. She put a sandwich in front of him but he did not pick it up. 'Let's go to America, Ma,' he said.

She burst out laughing. 'Me? America? I should cocoa!'

'I mean it. I'm going.'

She became solemn. 'It's not for me, son. I'm too old to emigrate.'

'But there's going to be a war.'

'I've lived here through one war, and a general strike and a slump.' She looked around at the tiny kitchen. 'It ain't much but it's what I know.'

Harry had not really expected her to agree, but now that she had said it he felt despondent. His mother was all he had.

She said, 'What'll you do there, anyway?'

'Are you worried about me thieving?'

'It always ends up the same way, thieving. I never heard of a tea-leaf that wasn't collared sooner or later.'

A tea-leaf was a thief, in rhyming slang. Harry said, 'I'd like to join the air force and learn to fly.'

'Would you be allowed?'

'Over there they don't care if you're working class, so long as you've got the brains.'

She looked more cheerful then. She sat down and sipped her tea while Harry ate his bacon sandwich. When he had finished he took out his money and counted out fifty pounds.

'What's that for?' she said. It was as much money as she earned in two years of cleaning offices.

'It'll come in handy,' he said. 'Take it, Ma. I want you to have it.'

She took the money. 'You're really going, then.'

'I'm going to borrow Sid Brennan's motorbike and drive to Southampton today and get a ship.'

She reached across the little table and took his hand. 'Good luck to you, son.'

He squeezed her hand gently. 'I'll send you more money from America.'

'No need, unless you've got it to spare. I'd rather you send me a letter now and again, so I know how you're going on.'

'Yeah. I'll write.'

Her eyes filled with tears. 'Come back and see your old ma one day, won't you?'

He squeezed her hand. 'Course I will, Ma. I'll be back.'

Harry looked at himself in the barber's mirror. The blue suit which had cost him thirteen pounds in Savile Row, fitted beautifully and went well with his blue eyes. The soft collar of his new shirt looked American. The barber brushed the padded shoulders of the double-breasted jacket, and Harry tipped him and left.

He went up the marble staircase from the basement and emerged in the ornate lobby of the South-Western Hotel. It was thronged with people. This was the departure point for most transatlantic crossings, and thousands of people were trying to leave England.

Harry had discovered how many when he tried to get a berth on a liner. All the ships were booked up for weeks ahead. Some of the shipping lines had closed their offices rather than waste staff time turning people away. For a while it had looked impossible. He had been ready to give up, and start thinking of another plan, when a travel agent had mentioned the Pan American Clipper.

He had read about the Clipper in the newspapers. The service had started in the summer. You could fly to New York in less than thirty hours, instead of four or five days on a ship. But a one-way ticket cost ninety pounds. Ninety pounds! You could almost buy a new car for that.

Harry had spent the money. It was mad, but now that he had made up his mind to go he would pay any price to get out of the country. And the plane was seductively luxurious: it would be champagne all the way to New York. This was the kind of insane extravagance that Harry loved.

He was no longer jumping every time he saw a copper: there was no way the Southampton police could know about him. However, he had never flown before, and now he was feeling nervous about that.

He checked his wristwatch, a Patek Philippe stolen

from a royal equerry. He had time for a quick cup of coffee to settle his stomach. He went into the lounge.

While he was sipping his coffee a stunningly beautiful woman walked in. She was a perfect blonde, and she wore a wasp-waisted dress of cream silk with orange-red polka dots. She was in her early thirties, about ten years older than Harry, but that did not stop him smiling when he caught her eye.

She sat at the next table, sideways-on to Harry, and he studied the way the spotted silk clung to her bosom and draped her knees. She had cream shoes and a straw hat, and she put a small handbag on the table.

After a moment she was joined by a man in a blazer. Hearing them speak, Harry discovered that she was English but he was American. Harry listened carefully, brushing up his accent. Her name was Diana; the man was Mark. He saw the man touch her arm. She leaned closer. They were in love and saw no one but each other: the room might have been empty.

Harry felt a pang of envy.

He looked away. He still felt queasy. He was about to fly all the way across the Atlantic. It seemed a long way to go with no land beneath. He had never understood the principle of air travel, anyway: the propellers went round and round, so how come the plane went up?

While he listened to Mark and Diana, he practised looking nonchalant. He did not want the other passengers on the Clipper to know he was nervous. I'm Harry Vandenpost, he thought, a well-off young American returning home because of the war in Europe.

Pronounced Yurrup. I don't have a job, just now, but I suppose I'll have to settle down to something soon. My father has investments. My mother, God rest her soul, was English and I went to school over there. I didn't go to university – never did like swotting. (Did Americans say 'swotting'? He was not sure.) I've spent so much time in England that I've picked up some of the local lingo. I've flown a few times, sure, but this is my first flight across the Atlantic Ocean, you bet. I'm *really* looking forward to it!

By the time he finished his coffee he was hardly scared at all.

Eddie Deakin hung up. He looked around the hall: it was empty. No one had overheard. He stared at the phone that had plunged him into horror, hating it, as if he might end the nightmare by smashing the instrument. Then he slowly turned away.

Who were they? Where had they taken Carol-Ann? Why had they kidnapped her? What could they possibly want from him? The questions buzzed in his head like flies in a jar. He tried to think. He forced himself to concentrate on one question at a time.

Who *were* they? Could they be simple lunatics? No. They were too well organized: crazy people might manage a kidnap, but it had taken careful planning to find out where Eddie would be immediately after the snatch and get him on the phone with Carol-Ann at the right moment. They were rational people, then, but they were prepared to break the law. They might be anarchists of some kind, but most likely he was dealing with gangsters.

Where had they taken Carol-Ann? She had said she was in a house. It might belong to one of the kidnappers, but more likely they had taken over or rented an empty house in a lonely spot. Carol-Ann had said it had happened a couple of hours ago, so the house could not be more than sixty or seventy miles from Bangor.

Why had they kidnapped her? They wanted something from him, something he would not give voluntarily, something he would not do for money – something, he guessed, that he would want to refuse them. But what? He had no money, he knew no secrets, and no one was in his power.

It had to be something to do with the Clipper.

He would get his instructions on the plane, they had said, from a man called Tom Luther. Might Luther be working for someone who wanted details of the construction and operation of the plane? Another airline, perhaps, or a foreign country? It was possible. The Germans or the Japanese might be hoping to build a copy to use as a bomber. But there had to be easier ways for them to get blueprints. Hundreds of people, maybe thousands, could supply such information: Pan American employees, Boeing employees, even the Imperial Airways mechanics who serviced the engines here at Hythe. Kidnapping was not necessary. Hell, enough technical details had been published in the magazines.

Might someone want to steal the plane? It was hard to imagine.

The likeliest explanation was that they wanted Eddie to co-operate in smuggling something, or somebody, into the United States.

Well, that was as much as he knew or could guess. What was he going to do?

He was a law-abiding citizen and the victim of a crime, and he wanted with all his heart to call the police.

But he was terrified.

He had never been so scared in his life. As a boy he had been frightened of Pop and the Devil, but since then nothing had really petrified him. Now he was helpless and rigid with fear. He felt paralysed: for a moment he could not even move from where he stood.

He thought of the police.

He was in goddamn England, there was no point in talking to their bicycling local cops. But he could try to put a telephone call through to the county sheriff back home, or the Maine State Police, or even the FBI, and get them to start searching for an isolated house that had recently been rented by a man—

Don't call the police, it won't do you any good, the voice on the phone had said. *But if you do call them, I'll fuck her just to be mean.*

Eddie believed him. There had been a note of longing in the spiteful voice, as if the man was half hoping for an excuse to rape her. With her rounded belly and swollen breasts she had a lush, ripe look that—

He clenched his fist, but there was nothing to punch but the wall. With a groan of despair he stumbled out through the front door. Not looking where he was going, he crossed the lawn. He came to a stand of trees, stopped and leaned his forehead against the furrowed bark of an oak.

Eddie was a simple man. He had been born in a farmhouse a few miles out of Bangor. His father was a poor farmer, with a few acres of potato fields, some chickens, a cow and a vegetable patch. New England was a bad place to be poor: the winters were long and bitterly cold. Mom and Pop believed that everything was the will of God. Even when Eddie's baby sister caught pneumonia and died, Pop said God had a purpose in it, 'too deep for us to comprehend'. In those days Eddie daydreamed about finding buried treasure in the woods: a brass-bound pirate's chest full of gold and precious gems like in the stories. In his fantasy he took a gold coin into Bangor and bought big soft beds, a truckload of firewood, pretty china for his mother, sheepskin coats for all the family, thick steaks and an icebox full of ice cream and a pineapple. The dismal, ramshackle farmhouse was transformed into a place of warmth, comfort and happiness.

He never found buried treasure, but he got education, walking the six miles to school every day. He liked it because the schoolroom was warmer than his home, and Mrs Maple liked him because he always asked how things worked.

Years later it was Mrs Maple who wrote to the congressman who got Eddie a chance to take the entrance examination for Annapolis.

He thought the Naval Academy was paradise. There were blankets and good clothes and all the food you could eat: he had never imagined such plenty. The tough physical regime was easy to him; the bullshit was no worse than he had listened to in chapel all his life; and the 'hazing' was petty harassment by comparison with the beatings his father handed out.

It was at Annapolis that he first became aware of how he appeared to other people. He learned that he was earnest, dogged, inflexible and hard-working. Even though he was skinny, bullies rarely picked on him: there was a look in his eye that scared them off. People liked him because they could rely on him to do what he promised, but nobody ever cried on his shoulder.

He was surprised to be praised as a hard worker. Both Pop and Mrs Maple had taught him that you could get what you wanted by working for it, and Eddie had never conceived of any other way. All the same the compliment pleased him. His father's highest term of praise had been to call someone a 'driver', the Maine dialect word for a hard worker.

He was commissioned an ensign and assigned to aviation training on flying boats. Annapolis had been comfortable, by comparison with his home, but the US Navy was positively luxurious. He was able to send money home to his parents, for them to fix the farm-house roof and buy a new stove.

He had been four years in the Navy when Mom died, and Pop went just five months later. Their few acres were absorbed into the neighbouring farm, but Eddie was able to buy the house and the woodland for a song. He resigned from the Navy and got a well-paid job with Pan American Airways System.

In between flights he worked on the old house, installing plumbing and electricity and a water heater, doing the work himself and paying for the materials out of his engineer's wages. He got electric heaters for the bedrooms, a radio and even a telephone. Then he found Carol-Ann. Soon, he had thought, the house would be filled with the laughter of children, and then his dream would have come true.

Instead it had turned into a nightmare.

CHAPTER FOUR

T HE FIRST words Mark Alder said to Diana Lovesey were, 'My goodness, you're the nicest thing I've seen all day.'

People said that sort of thing to her all the time. She was pretty and vivacious, and she loved to dress well. That night she was wearing a long turquoise dress with little lapels, a shirred bodice and short sleeves gathered at the elbow, and she knew she looked wonderful.

She was at the Midland Hotel in Manchester, attending a dinner-dance. She was not sure whether it was the Chamber of Commerce, the Freemasons' ladies' night, or the Red Cross fund-raiser: the same people were at all such functions. She had danced with most of her husband Mervyn's business associates, who had held her too close and trodden on her toes, and all of their wives had glared daggers at her. It was strange, Diana thought, that when a man made a bit of a fool of himself over a pretty girl, his wife always hated the girl for it, not the man. It was not as if Diana had designs on any of their pompous, whisky-soaked husbands.

She had scandalized them all and embarrassed her husband by teaching the deputy mayor to jitterbug.

Now, feeling the need of a break, she had slipped into the hotel bar on the pretence of buying cigarettes.

He was there alone, sipping a small cognac, and he looked up at her as though she had brought sunshine into the room. He was a small, neat man with a boyish smile and an American accent. His remark seemed spontaneous and he had a charming manner, so she smiled radiantly at him, but she did not speak. She bought cigarettes and drank a glass of iced water, then returned to the dance.

He must have asked the barman who she was, and found her address somehow, for the next day she got a note from him, on Midland Hotel writing paper.

Actually, it was a poem.

It began:

> Fixed in my heart, the picture of your smile
> Engraven, ever present to mind's eye
> Not pain, nor years, nor sorrow can defile

It made her cry.

She cried because of everything she had hoped for and never achieved. She cried because she lived in a grimy industrial city with a husband who hated to take holidays. She cried because the poem was the only gracious, romantic thing that had happened to her for five years. And she cried because she was no longer in love with Mervyn.

After that it happened very quickly.

The next day was Sunday. She went into town on the Monday. Normally she would have gone first to Boots to change her book at the Circulating Library, then bought a combined lunch-and-matinée ticket for two shillings and sixpence at the Paramount Cinema in Oxford Street. After the film she would have walked around Lewis's department store and Finnigan's, and bought ribbons, or napkins, or gifts for her sister's children. She might have gone to one of the little shops in the Shambles to buy some exotic cheese or special ham for Mervyn. Then she would have taken the train back to Altrincham, the suburb where she lived, in time to get the supper.

This time, she had coffee in the bar of the Midland Hotel, lunch in the German restaurant in the basement of the Midland Hotel, and afternoon tea in the lounge of the Midland Hotel. But she did not see the charming man with the American accent.

She went home feeling heartsick. That was ridiculous, she told herself. She had met him for less than a minute and had never said a word to him! He had seemed to symbolize everything she felt was missing from her life. But if she saw him again she would surely discover that he was boorish, insane, diseased, smelly, or all of those things.

She got off the train and walked along the street of large suburban villas where she lived. As she approached her own home, she was shocked and flustered to see him walking towards her, looking at her house with a pretence of idle curiosity.

She flushed scarlet and her heart raced. He, too, was startled. He stopped, but she carried on walking. Then, as she passed him, she said, 'Meet me in the Central Library tomorrow morning!'

She did not expect him to reply, but – she would learn later – he had a quick, humorous mind and he immediately said, 'What section?'

It was a big library, although not so big that two people could lose one another for long; but she said the first thing that came into her mind. 'Biology.' And he laughed.

She entered her house with that laugh in her ears: a warm, relaxed, delighted laugh, the laugh of a man who loved life and felt good about himself.

The house was empty. Mrs Rollins, who did the housework, had already left and Mervyn was not home yet. Diana sat in the modern hygienic kitchen and thought old-fashioned unhygienic thoughts about her humorous American poet.

The next morning she found him sitting at a table under a notice that read SILENCE. When she said, 'Hello,' he put a finger to his lips, pointed to a chair, and wrote her a note.

It said: *I love your hat.*

She had a little hat like an upturned flower-pot with a brim, and she wore it tilted all the way over to one side so that it almost covered her left eye: it was the current fashion, although few women in Manchester had the nerve for it.

She took a little pen from her bag and wrote underneath: *It wouldn't suit you.*

But my geraniums would look perfect in it, he wrote.

She giggled, and he said, 'Shhh!'

Diana thought, Is he mad, or just funny?

She wrote, *I love your poem.*

Then he wrote, *I love you.*

Mad, she thought, but tears came to her eyes. She wrote, *I don't even know your name!*

He gave her a business card. His name was Mark Alder, and he lived in Los Angeles.

California!

They went for early lunch to a VEM restaurant – Vegetables, Eggs and Milk – because she could be sure she would not run into her husband there: wild horses could not have dragged him into a vegetarian restaurant. Then, as it was Tuesday, there was a midday concert at the Houldsworth Hall in Deansgate, with the city's famous Hallé Orchestra and its new conductor, Malcolm Sargent. Diana felt proud that her city could offer such a cultural treat to a visitor.

That day she learned that Mark was a writer of comedy scripts for radio shows. She had never heard of the people he wrote for, but he said they were famous: Jack Benny, Fred Allen, Amos 'n' Andy. He also owned a radio station. He wore a cashmere blazer. He was on an extended holiday, tracing his roots: his family had come originally from Liverpool, the port city a few miles west of Manchester. He was not much taller than Diana, and about her age, with hazel eyes and a few freckles.

And he was pure delight.

He was intelligent, funny and charming. His manners were nice, his fingernails were clean and his clothes were neat. He liked Mozart but he knew about Louis Armstrong. Most of all, he liked Diana.

It was a peculiar thing how few men actually liked women, she thought. The men she knew would fawn on her, try to paw her, suggest discreet assignations when Mervyn's back was turned, and sometimes, when they got maudlin drunk, declare their love for her. But they didn't really like her: their conversation was all banter, they never listened to her and they knew nothing about her. Mark was quite different, as she found out during the following days and weeks.

The day after they met in the library, he rented a car and drove her to the coast where they ate sandwiches on a breezy beach and kissed in the shelter of the dunes.

He had a suite at the Midland, but they could not meet there because Diana was too well known: if she had been seen going upstairs after lunch the news would have been all around town by teatime. However, Mark's inventive mind produced a solution. They drove to the seaside town of Lytham St Anne's, taking a suitcase, and checked into a hotel as Mr and Mrs Alder. They had lunch, then went to bed.

Making love with Mark was such fun.

The first time, he made a pantomime of trying to undress in complete silence, and she was laughing too much to feel shy as she took off her clothes. She did not worry about whether he would like her: he obviously adored her. She was not nervous because he was so nice.

They spent the afternoon in bed, and then checked out, saying they had changed their minds about staying. Mark paid in full for the night so that there was no bad feeling. He dropped her at a station one stop down the line from Altrincham and she arrived home by train just as if she had spent the afternoon in Manchester.

They did this all the blissful summer.

He was supposed to go back to the States at the beginning of August to work on a new show but he stayed and wrote a series of sketches about an American on holiday in Britain, sending his scripts over every week by the new airmail service operated by Pan American.

Despite this reminder that time was running out for them, Diana managed not to think about the future much. Of course Mark would go home one day, but he would still be here tomorrow and that was as far ahead as she cared to look. It was like the war: everyone knew it would be awful, but nobody could tell when it would start, and until it happened there was nothing to do but carry on and try to have a good time.

The day after war broke out he told her he was going home.

She was sitting up in bed with the covers pulled up just under her bust, so that her breasts showed: Mark loved her to sit like that. He thought her breasts were wonderful, although she felt they were too large.

They were having a serious conversation. Britain had declared war on Germany, and even happy lovers had to talk about it. Diana had been following the grisly conflict in China all year, and the thought of war in Europe filled her with dread. Like the Fascists in Spain, the Japanese did not scruple to drop bombs on women and children; and the carnage in Chungking and Ichang had been sickening.

She asked Mark the question that was on everyone's lips. 'What do you think will happen?'

For once he did not have a funny answer. 'I think it's going to be awful,' he said solemnly. 'I believe Europe will be devastated. Maybe this country will survive, being an island. I hope so.'

'Oh,' Diana said. Suddenly, she was frightened. British people were not saying things like that. The newspapers were full of fighting talk, and Mervyn was positively looking forward to war. But Mark was an outsider, and his judgement, delivered in that relaxed American voice, sounded worryingly realistic. Would bombs be dropped on Manchester?

She remembered something Mervyn had said, and repeated it. 'America will have to come into the war sooner or later.'

Mark shocked her by saying, 'Christ, I hope not. This is a European squabble, nothing to do with us. I can just about see why Britain declared war, but I'm damned if I want to see Americans die defending fucking Poland.'

She had never heard him swear like this. Sometimes he whispered obscenities in her ear while they were making love, but that was different. Now he seemed angry. She thought perhaps he was a little frightened.

She knew Mervyn was frightened: in him it came out as reckless optimism. Mark's fear showed as isolationism and cursing.

She was dismayed by his attitude, but she could see his point of view: Why *should* Americans go to war for Poland, or even for Europe? 'But what about me?' she said. She tried for a note of levity. 'You wouldn't like me to be raped by blond Nazis in gleaming jackboots, would you?' It wasn't very funny and she regretted it immediately.

That was when he took an envelope out of his suitcase and handed it to her.

She pulled out a ticket and looked at it. Suddenly she was terrified. 'You're going home!' she cried. It was like the end of the world.

Looking solemn, he said simply, 'There are two tickets.'

She felt as if her heart would stop. 'Two tickets,' she repeated tonelessly. She was disoriented and strangely frightened.

He sat on the bed beside her and took her hand. She knew what he was going to say, and she was at the same time thrilled and terrified.

'Come home with me, Diana,' he said. 'Fly to New York with me. Then come to Reno and get divorced. Then let's go to California and be married. I love you.'

Fly. She could hardly imagine flying across the Atlantic Ocean: such things belonged in fairy tales.

To New York. New York was a dream of skyscrapers and nightclubs, gangsters and millionaires, fashionable heiresses and enormous cars.

And get divorced. And be free of Mervyn!

Then let's go to California. Where movies were made, and oranges grew on trees, and the sun shone every day.

And be married. And have Mark all the time, every day, every night.

She was unable to speak.

Mark said, 'We could have babies.'

She wanted to cry.

'Ask me again,' she whispered.

He said, 'I love you, will you marry me, and have my children?'

'Oh, yes,' she said, and she felt as if she were already flying. 'Yes, yes, yes!'

She had to tell Mervyn that night.

It was Monday. On Tuesday she would have to travel to Southampton with Mark. The Clipper left on Wednesday at 2 p.m.

She was floating on air when she arrived home on Monday afternoon but as soon as she entered the house her euphoria evaporated.

How was she going to tell him?

It was a nice house: a big new villa, white with a red roof. It had four bedrooms, three of which were almost never used, a nice modern bathroom and a kitchen with all the latest gadgets. Now that she was leaving it, she looked at it with nostalgic fondness: it had been her home for five years.

She prepared Mervyn's meals herself. Mrs Rollins

did the cleaning and laundry and if Diana had not cooked she would have had nothing to do. Besides, Mervyn was a working-class boy at heart and he liked his wife to put his meal on the table when he came home. He even called the meal 'tea', and he would drink tea with it, although it was always something substantial – sausages or steak or a meat pie. For Mervyn, 'dinner' was served in hotels. At home you had tea.

What would she say?

Today he would have cold beef, left over from Sunday's roast. Diana put on an apron and began to slice potatoes for frying. When she thought of how angry Mervyn was going to be her hands shook, and she cut her finger with the vegetable knife.

She tried to get a grip on herself as she washed the wound under the cold tap, dried it with a towel and wrapped a bandage round it. What am I afraid of? she asked herself. He won't kill me. He can't stop me: I'm over twenty-one and it's a free country.

The thought did not calm her nerves.

She set the table and washed a lettuce. Although Mervyn worked hard, he almost always came home at the same time. He would say, 'What's the point of being the boss if I have to stop at work when everyone else goes home?' He was an engineer and had a factory that made all kinds of rotors, from small fans for cooling systems to huge screws for ocean liners. Mervyn had always been successful – he was a good businessman – but he hit the jackpot when he started manufacturing propellers for aircraft. Flying was his hobby and he had his own small plane, a Tiger Moth, at an airfield outside town. When the government started to build up the Air Force, two or three years ago, very few people knew how to make curved rotors with mathematical precision but Mervyn was one of those few. Since then, business had boomed.

Diana was his second wife. The first had left him, seven years ago, and run off with another man, taking their two children. Mervyn had divorced her as quickly as he could and had proposed to Diana as soon as the divorce came through. Diana was then twenty-eight and he was thirty-eight. He was attractive, masculine and prosperous, and he worshipped her. His wedding present to her had been a diamond necklace.

A few weeks ago, on their fifth wedding anniversary, he had given her a sewing machine.

Looking back, she could see that the sewing machine had been the last straw. She had been hoping for a car of her own: she could drive and Mervyn could afford it. When she saw the sewing machine she felt she had come to the end of her tether. They had been together for five years and he had not noticed that she never sewed.

She knew that Mervyn loved her, but he did not *see* her. In his vision there was just a person marked 'wife'. She was pretty, she performed her social role adequately, she put his food on the table, and she was always willing in bed. What else should a wife be? He never consulted her about anything. Since she was neither a businessman nor an engineer, it never occurred to him that she had a brain. He talked to the men at his factory more seriously than he talked to her. In his world, men wanted cars and wives wanted sewing machines.

And yet he was very clever. The son of a lathe operator, he had gone to Manchester Grammar School and had studied physics at Manchester University. He had had the opportunity to go on to Cambridge and take his master's degree, but he was not the academic type and he found a job in the design department of a large engineering company. He still followed developments in physics and would talk endlessly to his father – but never to Diana, of course – about atoms and radiation and nuclear fission.

Unfortunately, Diana did not understand physics anyway. She knew a lot about music and literature and a little about history but Mervyn was not much interested in culture, although he liked films and dance music. So they had nothing to talk about.

It might have been different if they had had children. But Mervyn already had two children by his first wife and he did not want any more. Diana had been willing to love them, but she had never been given the chance: their mother had poisoned their minds against Diana, pretending that she had caused the break-up of the marriage. Diana's sister in Liverpool had cute little twin girls with pigtails and Diana lavished all her maternal affection on them.

She was going to miss the twins.

Mervyn enjoyed an energetic social life with the city's leading businessmen and politicians, and for a while Diana enjoyed being his hostess. She had always loved beautiful clothes and she wore them well. But there had to be more to life than that.

For a while she had played the role of the nonconformist of Manchester society – smoking cigars, dressing extravagantly, talking about free love and Communism. She had enjoyed shocking the matrons, but Manchester was not a highly conservative place, and Mervyn and his friends were Liberals, so she had not caused much of a stir.

She was discontented, but she wondered whether she had the right. Most women thought her lucky: she had a sober, reliable, generous husband, a lovely home, and crowds of friends. She told herself she ought to be happy. But she was not – and then Mark came along.

She heard Mervyn's car pull up outside. It was such a familiar noise but tonight it sounded ominous, like the growl of a dangerous beast.

She put the frying-pan on the gas stove with a shaking hand.

Mervyn came into the kitchen.

He was breathtakingly handsome. There was grey in his dark hair now, but it only made him look more distinguished. He was tall and had not got fat like most of his friends. He had no vanity but Diana made him wear well-cut dark suits and expensive white shirts, because she liked him to look as successful as he was.

She was terrified he would see the guilt on her face and demand to know what was the matter.

He kissed her mouth. Full of shame, she kissed him back. Sometimes he would embrace her and press his hand into the cleft of her buttocks, and they would

111

become passionate, so that they had to hurry to the bedroom and leave the food to burn. But that did not happen much any more, and today was no exception, thank God.

He took off his jacket, waistcoat, tie and collar, and rolled up his sleeves; then he washed his hands and face at the kitchen sink. He had broad shoulders and strong arms.

He had not sensed that anything was wrong. He would not, of course: he did not *see* her, she was just there, like the kitchen table. She had no need to worry. He would not know anything until she told him.

I won't tell him yet, she thought.

While the potatoes were frying she buttered the bread and made a pot of tea. She was still shaky, but she hid it. Mervyn read the *Manchester Evening News* and hardly looked at her.

'I've got a bloody troublemaker at the works,' he said as she put the plate in front of him.

I couldn't care less, Diana thought hysterically. I'm nothing to do with you any more.

Then why have I cooked your tea?

'He's a Londoner, from Battersea, and I think he's a Communist. Anyway, he's asking for higher rates for working on the new jig borer. It's not unreasonable, really, but I've priced the job based on the old rates, so he'll have to put up with it.'

Diana screwed up her nerve and said, 'I've got something to tell you.' Then she wished fervently that she could take the words back, but it was too late.

'What did you do to your finger?' he asked, noticing the little bandage.

This commonplace question deflated her. 'Nothing,' she said, slumping into her chair. 'I cut it slicing potatoes.' She picked up her knife and fork.

Mervyn ate heartily. 'I should be more careful who I take on but the trouble is, good toolmakers are hard to come by nowadays.'

She was not expected to respond when he talked about his business. If she made a suggestion, he would give her an irritated look as if she had spoken out of turn. She was there to listen.

While he talked about the new jig borer and the Battersea Communist she remembered their wedding day. Her mother had been alive then. They had got married in Manchester, and the reception had been held at the Midland Hotel. Mervyn in morning dress had been the handsomest man in England. Diana had thought it was for ever. The idea that the marriage might not last had not crossed her mind. She had never met a divorced person before Mervyn. Recalling how she felt then, she wanted to cry.

She also knew that Mervyn would be shattered by her leaving. He had no idea of what was in her mind. The fact that his first wife had left him in exactly the same way made it worse. He was going to be distraught. But first he would be furious.

He finished his beef and poured himself another cup of tea. 'You haven't eaten much,' he said. In fact she had not eaten anything.

'I had a big lunch,' she replied.

'Where did you go?'

The innocent question threw her into a panic. She had eaten sandwiches in bed with Mark at a hotel in Blackpool, and she could not think of a plausible lie. The names of the principal restaurants in Manchester came to mind, but it was possible that Mervyn had had lunch in one of those. After a painful pause she said, 'The Waldorf Café.' There were several Waldorf Cafés – it was a chain of inexpensive restaurants where you could get steak and chips for one shilling and ninepence.

Mervyn did not ask her which one.

She picked up the plates and stood up. Her knees felt so weak she was afraid she would fall down, but she made it to the sink. 'Do you want a sweet?' she asked him.

'Yes, please.'

She went to the pantry and found a can of pears and some condensed milk. She opened the tins and brought his dessert to the table.

Watching him eat canned pears, she was swamped by a sense of the horror of what she was about to do. It seemed unforgivably destructive. Like the coming war, it would smash everything. The life that she and Mervyn had created together in this house, in this city, would be ruined.

She suddenly realized she could not do it.

Mervyn put down his spoon and looked at his fob watch. 'Half-past seven – let's tune in to the news.'

'I can't do it,' Diana said aloud.

'What?'

'I can't do it,' she said again. She would call the whole thing off. She would go and see Mark now and tell him she had changed her mind, she was not going to run away with him after all.

'Why can't you listen to the wireless?' Mervyn asked impatiently.

Diana stared at him. She was tempted to tell him the whole truth, but she did not have the nerve for that either. 'I have to go out,' she said. She cast about frantically for an excuse. 'Doris Williams is in hospital and I ought to visit her.'

'Who's Doris Williams, for heaven's sake?'

There was no such person. 'You have met her,' Diana said, improvising wildly. 'She's had an operation.'

'I don't remember her,' he said, but he was not suspicious: he had a bad memory for casual acquaintances.

Diana was inspired to say, 'Do you want to come with me?'

'Good God, no!' he said, as she had known he would.

'I'll drive myself, then.'

'Don't go too fast in the blackout.' He got up and went through to the sitting room where the wireless was.

Diana stared after him for a moment. He'll never know how close I came to leaving him, she thought with a kind of sadness.

She put on a hat and went out with her coat over her arm. The car started first time, thank God.

115

She steered out of the drive and turned towards Manchester.

The journey was a nightmare. She was in a desperate rush, but she had to crawl along because her headlights were masked and she could see only a few yards in front – and besides, her vision was blurred because she could not stop crying. If she had not known the road well she would probably have crashed.

The distance was less than ten miles but it took her more than an hour.

When she finally stopped the car outside the Midland she was exhausted. She sat still for a minute, trying to compose herself. She took out her compact and powdered her face to hide the signs of tears.

Mark would be broken-hearted, she knew, but he could bear it. He would soon come to look back on this as a summer romance. It was less cruel to end a short, passionate love affair than to break up a five-year marriage. She and Mark would always look back on the summer of 1939 fondly—

She burst into tears again.

It was no use sitting here thinking about it, she decided after a while. She had to go in and get it over with. She repaired her make-up again and got out of the car.

She walked through the lobby of the hotel and went up the staircase without stopping at the desk. She knew Mark's room number. It was, of course, quite scandalous for a woman alone to go to a single man's hotel room, but she had to take the risk. The alternative would have been to see Mark in the lounge or the bar, and it was unthinkable to give him this kind of news in a public place. She did not look around her, so she did not know whether she had been seen by anyone she knew.

She tapped on his door, praying that he would be there. What if he had decided to go out to a restaurant, or to see a film? There was no reply, and she knocked again, harder. How could he go to the cinema at a time like this?

Then she heard his voice. 'Hello?'

She knocked again and said, 'It's me!'

She heard rapid footsteps. The door was flung open and Mark stood there, looking startled. He smiled happily, drew her inside, closed the door, and embraced her.

Now she felt as disloyal to him as she had to Mervyn earlier. She kissed him guiltily, and the familiar warmth of desire glowed in her veins; but she pulled away and said, 'I can't go with you.'

He paled. 'Don't say that.'

She looked around the suite. He was packing. The wardrobe and drawers were open, his cases were on the floor and everywhere there were folded shirts, tidy piles of underwear and shoes in bags. He was so neat. 'I can't go,' she repeated.

He took her hand and drew her into the bedroom. They sat on the bed. He looked distraught. 'You don't mean this,' he said.

'Mervyn loves me, and we've been together for five years. I can't do this to him.'

'What about me?'

She looked at him. He was wearing a dusty-pink sweater and a bow tie, blue-grey flannel trousers and cordovan shoes. He looked good enough to eat. 'You both love me,' she said. 'But he's my husband.'

'We both love you, but I *like* you,' Mark said.

'Don't you think he likes me?'

'I don't think he even knows you. Listen. I'm thirty-five years old, I've been in love before, I once had an affair that lasted six years. I've never been married but I've been around. I *know* this is right. Nothing has ever felt so right to me. You're beautiful, you're funny, you're unorthodox, you're bright, and you love to make love. I'm cute, I'm funny, I'm unorthodox, I'm bright, and I want to make love to you right now—'

'No,' she said, but she did not mean it.

He drew her to him gently and they kissed.

'We're so right for each other,' he murmured. 'Remember writing notes to one another underneath the SILENCE sign? You understood the game, right away, without explanations. Other women think I'm nuts, but you like me this way.'

It was true, she thought, and when she did odd things, like smoking a pipe, or going out with no panties on, or attending Fascist meetings and sounding the fire alarm, Mervyn became annoyed, whereas Mark laughed delightedly.

He stroked her hair, then her cheek. Slowly her panic subsided and she began to feel soothed. She laid her head on his shoulder and let her lips brush the soft skin of his neck. She felt his fingertips on her leg, beneath her dress, stroking the inside of her thigh where her stockings ended. This was not what was supposed to happen, she thought weakly.

He pushed her gently backwards on the bed, and her hat fell off. 'This isn't right,' she said feebly. He kissed her mouth, nibbling her lips gently with his own. She felt his fingers through the fine silk of her panties, and she shuddered with pleasure. After a moment his hand slid inside.

He knew just what to do.

One day early in the summer, as they lay naked in a hotel bedroom with the sound of the waves coming through the open window, he had said, 'Show me what you do when you touch yourself.'

She had been embarrassed, and pretended not to understand. 'What do you mean?'

'You know. When you touch yourself. Show me. Then I'll know what you like.'

'I don't touch myself,' she lied.

'Well ... when you were a girl, before you were married – you must have done it then, everyone does. Show me what you used to do.'

She was about to refuse, then she thought how sexy it would be. 'You want me to stimulate myself – down there – while you watch?' she said, and her voice was thick with desire.

He grinned wickedly and nodded.

'You mean ... all the way?'

'All the way.'

'I couldn't,' she said, but she did.

Now his fingertips touched her knowingly, in exactly the right places, with the same familiar motion and just the right pressure. She closed her eyes and gave herself up to the sensation.

After a while she began to moan softly and raise and lower her hips rhythmically. She felt his warm breath on her face as he leaned closer to her. Then, just as she was losing control, he said urgently, 'Look at me.'

She opened her eyes. He continued to caress her in exactly the same way, just a little faster. 'Don't close your eyes,' he said. Looking into his eyes while he did that was shockingly intimate, a kind of hyper-nakedness. It was as if he could see everything and know everything about her, and she felt an exhilarating freedom because she had nothing left to hide. The climax came, and she forced herself to hold his gaze while her hips jerked and she grimaced and gasped with the spasms of pleasure that shook her body, and he smiled down at her all the while and said, 'I love you, Diana, I love you so much.'

When it was over she grabbed him and held him, panting and shaking with emotion, feeling that she never wanted to let go. She would have wept, but she had no tears left.

She never did tell Mervyn.

Mark's inventive mind came up with the solution, and she rehearsed it as she drove home, calm and collected and quietly determined.

Mervyn was in his pyjamas and dressing-gown, smoking a cigarette and listening to music on the wireless. 'That were a bloody long visit,' he said mildly.

Only a little nervous, Diana said, 'I had to drive terribly slowly.' She swallowed, took a deep breath, and said, 'I'm going away tomorrow.'

He was faintly surprised. 'Where to?'

'I'd like to visit Thea and see the twins. I want to make sure she's all right, and there's no telling when I'll get another chance – the trains are already becoming irregular and petrol rationing starts next week.'

He nodded assent. 'Aye, you're right. Better go now while you can.'

'I'll go up and pack a case.'

'Pack one for me, will you?'

For an awful moment she thought he wanted to go with her. 'What for?' she said, aghast.

'I'll not sleep in an empty house,' he said. 'I'll stop at the Reform Club tomorrow night. You'll be back Wednesday?'

'Yes, Wednesday,' she lied.

'All right.'

She went upstairs. As she put his underwear and socks into a small suitcase, she thought, It's the last time I'll ever do this for him. She folded a white shirt and picked out a silver-grey tie: sombre colours suited his dark hair and brown eyes. She was relieved that he had accepted her story, but she also felt frustrated, as if there were something she had left undone. Although she was terrified of confronting him, she also wanted to explain why she was leaving him. She needed to tell him that he had let her down, he had become overbearing and thoughtless, he no longer cherished her as he once had. But now she never would say those things to him, and she felt oddly disappointed.

She closed his case and began to put make-up and toiletries into her sponge bag. It seemed a funny way to end five years of marriage, packing socks and tooth-paste and cold cream.

After a while he came upstairs. The packing was all done and she was in her least attractive nightdress, sitting in front of her dressing-table mirror, taking off her make-up. He came up behind her and grasped her breasts.

Oh, no, she thought, not tonight, please!

Although she was horrified, her body responded immediately and she blushed guiltily. Mervyn's fingers squeezed her swelling nipples and she drew in her breath in a small gasp of pleasure and despair. He took her hands and drew her up. She followed helplessly as he led her to the bed. He turned out the light and they lay down in pitch blackness. He mounted her immedi-ately and made love to her with a kind of furious desperation, almost as if he knew she was going away from him and there was nothing he could do about it. Her body betrayed her and she thrilled with pleasure and shame. She realized with mortification that she would have reached orgasm with two men in two hours, and she tried to stop herself, but she could not.

When she came, she cried.

Fortunately, Mervyn did not notice.

*

Sitting in the elegant lounge of the South-Western Hotel on Wednesday morning, waiting for a taxi to take her and Mark to Berth 108 in Southampton Docks to board the Pan American Clipper, she felt triumphant and free.

Everyone in the room was either looking at her or trying not to look at her. She was getting a particularly hard stare from a handsome man in a blue suit who must be ten years younger than she was. But she was used to that. It always happened when she looked good, and today she was stunning. Her cream and red spotted silk dress was fresh, summery and striking. Her cream shoes were right and the straw hat finished off the outfit perfectly. Her lipstick and nail varnish were orange-red like the spots on the dress. She had thought about red shoes but decided they would look tarty.

She loved travelling: packing and unpacking her clothes, meeting new people, being pampered and cosseted and plied with champagne and food, and seeing new places. She was nervous about flying but crossing the Atlantic was the most glamorous voyage of all, for at the other end was America. She could hardly wait to get there. She had a film-goer's picture of what it was like: she saw herself in an art-deco apartment, all windows and mirrors, a uniformed maid helping her put on a white fur coat, and a long black car in the street outside with its engine running and a coloured chauffeur waiting to take her to a nightclub, where she would order a martini, very dry, and dance to a jazz band that had Bing Crosby as its singer. That was a fantasy, she knew, but she could hardly wait to discover the reality.

She felt ambivalent about leaving Britain just as the war was starting. It seemed a cowardly thing to do, yet she was thrilled to be going.

She knew a lot of Jewish people. Manchester had a big Jewish community; they had planted a thousand trees in Nazareth. Diana's Jewish friends watched the progress of events in Europe with horror and dread. It was not just the Jews, either: the Fascists hated the coloureds, and the gypsies, and the queers, and anyone else who disagreed with Fascism. Diana had an uncle who was queer and he had always been kind to her and treated her like a daughter.

She was too old to join up, but she probably ought to stay in Manchester and do voluntary work, winding bandages for the Red Cross . . .

That was a fantasy, even more unlikely than dancing to Bing Crosby. She was not the type to wind bandages. Austerity and uniforms did not suit her.

But none of that was truly important. The only thing that counted was that she was in love. She would go where Mark was. She would have followed him into the heart of a battlefield if necessary. They were going to get married and have children. He was going home, and she was going with him.

She would miss her twin nieces. She wondered how long it would be before she would see them. They might be grown up next time, wearing perfume and brassières instead of ankle socks and pigtails.

But she might have little girls of her own . . .

She was thrilled about travelling on the Pan American Clipper. She had read all about it in the *Manchester Guardian*, never dreaming that one day she would actually fly in it. To get to New York in little more than a day seemed like a miracle.

She had written Mervyn a note. It did not say any of the things she wanted to tell him, did not explain how he had slowly and inexorably lost her love through carelessness and indifference, did not even say that Mark was wonderful. *Dear Mervyn*, she had written, *I am leaving you. I feel you have become cold towards me, and I have fallen in love with someone else. By the time you read this we will be in America. I am sorry to hurt you but it is partly your fault.* She could not think of an appropriate way to sign off – she could not write 'yours' or 'with love' – so she just put, *Diana*.

At first she had intended to leave the note in the house on the kitchen table. Then she had become obsessed by the possibility that he would change his plans, and instead of staying at his club on Tuesday night he would go home, find the note, and make some kind of trouble for her and Mark before they were out of the country. So in the end she had mailed it to him at the factory where it would arrive today.

She looked at her wristwatch (a present from Mervyn, who liked her to be punctual). She knew his routine: he spent most of the morning on the factory floor, then towards midday he would go up to his office and look through the mail before going to lunch. She had marked the envelope 'Personal' so that his secretary would not open it. It would be lying on his desk in a pile of invoices, orders, letters and memos. He would be reading it about now. The thought made her guilty and sad, but also relieved that she was two hundred miles away.

'Our taxi's here,' Mark said.

She felt a little nervous. Across the Atlantic in a plane!

'Time to go,' he said.

She suppressed her anxiety. She put down her coffee cup, stood up, and gave him her brightest smile. 'Yes,' she said happily. 'Time to fly.'

Eddie had always been shy with girls.

He had graduated from Annapolis a virgin. When he was stationed at Pearl Harbor he had gone with prostitutes, and that experience had left him with a sense of self-disgust. After leaving the Navy he had been a loner, driving to a bar a few miles away any time he felt the need of companionship. Carol-Ann was a ground hostess working for the airline at Port Washington, the New York terminal for flying boats. She was a suntanned blonde with eyes of Pan American blue, and Eddie would never have dared to ask her for a date. But one day in the canteen a young radio operator gave him two tickets to *Life with Father* on Broadway, and when he said he did not have anyone to take, the radioman turned to the next table and asked Carol-Ann if she wanted to go.

'Ayuh,' she said, and Eddie realized she was from his part of the world.

He later learned that at that time she had been desperately lonely. She was a country girl, and the sophisticated ways of New Yorkers made her anxious and tense. She was a sensual person, but she did not know what to do when men took liberties, so in her embarrassment she rebuffed advances indignantly. Her nervousness got her the reputation of an ice queen and she was not often asked out.

But Eddie knew nothing of this at the time. He felt like a king with her on his arm. He took her to dinner, then back to her apartment in a taxi. On the doorstep he thanked her for a nice evening and screwed up his courage to kiss her cheek, whereupon she burst into tears and said he was the first decent man she had met in New York. Before he knew what he was saying he had asked her for another date.

He fell in love with her on that second date. They went to Coney Island on a hot Friday in July, and she wore white slacks and a sky-blue blouse. He realized, to his astonishment, that she was actually proud to be seen walking alongside him. They ate ice cream, rode a roller-coaster called the Cyclone, bought silly hats, held hands, and revealed trivial intimate secrets. When he took her home Eddie told her frankly that he had never been this happy in his entire life, and she astonished him again by saying she hadn't either.

Soon he was neglecting the farmhouse and spending all his leave in New York, sleeping on the couch of a surprised but encouraging fellow engineer. Carol-Ann took him to Bristol, New Hampshire, to meet her parents, two small, thin, middle-aged people, poor and

127

hard-working. They reminded him of his own parents, but without the unforgiving religion. They could hardly believe they had produced a daughter so beautiful and Eddie understood how they felt, for he could hardly believe such a girl could have fallen in love with him.

He thought of how much he loved her as he stood in the grounds of the Langdown Lawn Hotel, staring at the bark of the oak tree. He was in a nightmare, one of those hellish dreams in which you start by feeling safe and happy but you think, in a fit of idle speculation, of the worst thing that could occur and suddenly it is actually happening, the worst thing in the world is actually, unstoppably, terrifyingly happening, and there is nothing you can do about it.

What made it even more terrible was that they had quarrelled just before he left home, and had parted without making it up.

She had been sitting on the couch, wearing a denim work shirt that belonged to him and not much else, her long sun-tanned legs stretched out in front, her fine fair hair lying across her shoulders like a shawl. She was reading a magazine. Her breasts were normally quite small but lately they had swollen. He felt an urge to touch them, and he thought, Why not? So he slid his hand inside the shirt and touched her nipple. She looked up at him and smiled lovingly, then went on with her reading.

He kissed the top of her head then sat down next to her. She had astonished him right from the start. They were both shy at first, but soon after they returned from their honeymoon holiday and started living together here in the old farmhouse, she had become wildly uninhibited.

First, she wanted to make love with the light on. Eddie felt awkward about it, but he consented, and he kind of liked it although he felt bashful. Then he noticed that she did not lock the door when she took a bath. After that he felt foolish about locking the door himself, so he did the same as her, and one day she just walked in with no clothes on and got right in the tub with him! Eddie had never felt so embarrassed in his life. No woman had seen him naked since he was about four years old. He got an enormous hard-on just watching Carol-Ann wash her underarms, and he covered his dick with a flannel until she laughed him out of it.

She started walking around the farmhouse in various states of undress. The way she was now, this was nothing, she was practically overdressed by her standards, you could only just see a little white triangle of cotton at the top of her legs where the shirt did not quite cover her panties. She was normally much worse. He would be making coffee in the kitchen and she would come in wearing nothing but her underwear and start toasting muffins; or he would be shaving and she would appear in her panties, with no brassière, and just brush her teeth like that; or she would come into the bedroom stark naked with his breakfast on a tray. He wondered if she was 'oversexed' – he had heard people use that term. But he also liked her to be this way. He liked it a lot. He had never dreamed he would have a beautiful wife who would walk around his house undressed. He felt so lucky.

Living with her for a year had changed him. He had gotten so uninhibited that he would walk naked from the bedroom to the bathroom; sometimes he did not even put on his pyjamas before getting into bed; once he even took her here in the living room, right on that couch.

He still wondered whether there was something psychologically abnormal about this kind of behaviour, but he had decided that it did not matter: he and Carol-Ann could do anything they liked. When he accepted that, he felt like a bird let out of a cage. It was incredible; it was wonderful; it was like being in heaven.

He sat beside her, saying nothing, just enjoying being with her and smelling the mild breeze coming in from the woods through the open windows. His bag was packed and in a few minutes he was leaving for Port Washington. Carol-Ann had left Pan American – she could not live in Maine and work in New York – and she had taken a job in a store in Bangor. Eddie wanted to talk to her about that before he left.

Carol-Ann looked up from *Life* magazine and said, 'What?'

'I didn't say anything.'

'But you're going to, aren't you?'

He grinned. 'How did you know?'

'Eddie, you know I can hear when your brain is working. What is it?'

He put his big, blunt hand on her belly and felt the slight swelling there. 'I want you to quit your job.'

'It's too early—'

'It's okay. We can afford it. And I want you to take real good care of yourself.'

'I'll take care of myself. I'll quit work when I need to.'

He felt hurt. 'I thought you'd be pleased. Why do you want to carry on?'

'Because we need the money and I have to have something to do.'

'I told you, we can afford it.'

'I'd get bored.'

'Most wives don't work.'

She raised her voice. 'Eddie, why are you trying to tie me down?'

He did not want to tie her down and the suggestion infuriated him. He said, 'Why are you so determined to go against me?'

'I'm not going against you! I just don't want to sit here like a lumper's helper!'

'Don't you have stuff to do?'

'What?'

'Knit baby clothes, make preserves, take naps—'

She was scornful. 'Oh, for heaven's sake—'

'What's wrong with that, for Christ's sake?' he said crossly.

'There'll be plenty of time for all that when the baby comes. I'd like to enjoy my last few weeks of freedom.'

Eddie felt humiliated but he was not sure how it had

happened. He wanted to get out of there. He looked at his watch. 'I've got a train to catch.'

Carol-Ann looked sad. 'Don't be angry,' she said in a conciliatory tone.

But he was angry. 'I guess I just don't understand you,' he said with irritation.

'I hate to be fenced in.'

'I was trying to be nice.' He stood up and went into the kitchen where his uniform jacket hung on a peg. He felt foolish and wrong-footed. He had set out to do something generous and she saw it as an imposition.

She brought his suitcase from the bedroom and handed it to him when he had his jacket on. She turned up her face and he kissed her briefly.

'Don't go out the door mad at me,' she said.

But he did.

And now he stood in a garden in a foreign country, thousands of miles from her, with a heart as heavy as lead, wondering if he would ever see his Carol-Ann again.

CHAPTER FIVE

FOR THE first time in her life, Nancy Lenehan was putting on weight.

She stood in her suite at the Adelphi Hotel in Liverpool, beside a pile of luggage that was waiting to be taken on board the SS *Oriania*, and gazed, horrified, into the mirror.

She was neither beautiful nor plain, but she had regular features – a straight nose, straight dark hair and a neat chin – and she looked attractive when she dressed carefully, which was most of the time. Today she was wearing a featherweight flannel suit by Paquin, in cerise, with a grey silk blouse. The jacket was fashionably tight-waisted, and it was this that had revealed to her that she was gaining weight. When she fastened the buttons of the jacket, a slight but unmistakable crease appeared, and the lower buttons pulled against the buttonholes.

There was only one explanation for this. The waist of the jacket was smaller than the waist of Mrs Lenehan.

It was probably a result of having lunched and dined at all the best restaurants in Paris throughout August. She sighed. She would diet for the entire transatlantic crossing. When she reached New York she would have her figure back.

She had never had to diet before. The prospect did not trouble her: although she liked good food, she was not greedy. What really worried her was that she suspected it was a sign of age.

Today was her fortieth birthday.

She had always been slender, and she looked good in expensive tailored clothes. She had hated the draped, low-slung fashions of the twenties and rejoiced when waists came back into fashion. She spent a lot of time and money shopping and she enjoyed it. Sometimes she used the excuse that she had to look right because she was in the fashion business, but in truth she did it for pleasure.

Her father had started a shoe factory in Brockton, Massachusetts, outside Boston, in 1899, the year Nancy was born. He had high-class shoes sent over from London and made cheap copies; then he made a selling point out of his plagiarism. His advertisements showed a twenty-nine-dollar London shoe next to a ten-dollar Black's copy and asked, 'Can you tell the difference?' He worked hard and did well, and during the Great War he won the first of the military contracts that were still a staple of the business.

In the twenties he built up a chain of stores, mostly in New England, selling only his shoes. When the depression hit he reduced the number of styles from a thousand to fifty and introduced a standard price of six dollars sixty for every pair of shoes regardless of style.

His audacity paid off, and while everyone else was going broke, Black's profits increased.

He used to say that it cost as much to make bad shoes as good ones, and there was no reason why working people should be poorly shod. At a time when poor folk were buying shoes with cardboard soles that wore out in a few days, Black's boots were cheap and long-lasting. Pa was proud of this, and so was Nancy. For her, the good boots the family made justified the grand Back Bay house they lived in, the big Packard with the chauffeur, their parties and their pretty clothes and their servants. She was not like some of the rich kids, who took inherited wealth for granted.

She wished she could say the same for her brother.

Peter was thirty-eight. When Pa died, five years ago, he left Peter and Nancy equal shares in the company, forty per cent each. Pa's sister, Aunt Tilly, got ten per cent, and the remaining ten went to Danny Riley, his disreputable old lawyer.

Nancy had always assumed she would take over when Pa died. Pa had always favoured her over Peter. A woman running a company was unusual, but not unknown, especially in the clothing industry.

Pa had a deputy, Nat Ridgeway, an able lieutenant who made it clear that he thought he was the best man for the job of chairman of Black's Boots.

But Peter wanted it too, and he was the son. Nancy had always felt guilty about being Pa's favourite. Peter would be humiliated and bitterly disappointed if he did not inherit his father's mantle. Nancy did not have the heart to deal with such a crushing blow so she agreed that Peter should take over. Between them, she and her brother owned eighty per cent of the stock, so when they were in agreement they got their way.

Nat Ridgeway resigned and went to work for General Textiles in New York. He was a loss to the business, but in another way he was a loss to Nancy. Just before Pa died Nat and Nancy had started dating.

Nancy had not dated anyone since her husband Sean died – she had not wanted to – but Nat had picked his time perfectly, for after five years she was beginning to feel that her life was all work and no fun and she was ready for a little romance. They had enjoyed a few quiet dinners and a theatre visit or two, and she had kissed him goodnight, quite warmly. But that was as far as it had gone when the crisis hit, and when Nat left Black's the romance ended too, leaving Nancy feeling cheated.

Since then, he had done spectacularly well at General Textiles, and he was now president of the company. He had also got married, to a pretty blonde woman ten years younger than Nancy.

By contrast, Peter had done badly. The truth was that he was not up to the job. In the five years during which he had been in charge the business had gone steeply downhill. The stores were no longer making a profit, just breaking even. Peter had opened a swanky shoe store on Fifth Avenue in New York, selling expensive fashion shoes for ladies, which took all his time and attention – but it lost money.

Only the factory, which Nancy managed, was making

money. In the mid-thirties, as America came out of the depression, she had started making cheap open-toed sandals for women, and it had turned out to be an immensely popular line. She was convinced that in women's shoes the future lay in light, colourful products that were cheap enough to throw away.

She could sell double the number of shoes she was making, if she had the manufacturing capacity. But her profits were swallowed up by Peter's losses and there was nothing left for expansion.

Nancy knew what had to be done to save the business.

The chain of stores would have to be sold, perhaps to their managers, to raise cash. The money from the sale would be used to modernize the factory and switch to the conveyor-belt style of production, which was being introduced in all the more progressive shoe-manufacturing plants. Peter would have to hand over the reins to her, and confine himself to running his New York store, working within strict cost controls.

She was willing for him to retain the title of chairman and the prestige that went with it, and she would continue to subsidize his store from the factory's profits, within limits; but he would have to give up all real power.

She had put these proposals in a written report, for Peter's eyes only. He had promised to think about it. Nancy had told him, as gently as she could, that the decline of the company could not be allowed to continue, and that if he did not agree to her plan she would have to go over his head to the board – which would inevitably mean that he would be sacked and she would become chairman. She hoped fervently that he would see sense. If he were to provoke a crisis, it was sure to end with a humiliating defeat for him and a family split that might never be repaired.

So far he had not taken offence. He seemed calm and thoughtful, and remained friendly. They decided to go to Paris together. Peter bought fashion shoes for his store, and Nancy shopped for herself at the couturiers and kept an eye on Peter's expenditure. Nancy had loved Europe, Paris especially, and she had been looking forward to London. Then war was declared.

They decided to return to the States immediately – but so did everyone else, of course, and they had terrible trouble getting passage. In the end Nancy got tickets on a ship leaving from Liverpool. After a long journey from Paris by train and ferry they had arrived here yesterday, and they were due to embark today.

She was unnerved by England's war preparations. Yesterday afternoon a bellhop had come to her room and installed an elaborate light-proof screen over the window. All windows had to be completely blacked out every evening, so that the city would not be visible from the air at night. The window panes were criss-crossed with adhesive tape so that splinters of glass would not fly when the city was bombed. There were stacks of sandbags at the front of the hotel and an underground air-raid shelter at the back.

Her terrible fear was that America would get into the war and her sons Liam and Hugh would be conscripted. She remembered Pa saying, when Hitler first came to power, that the Nazis would stop Germany going Communist, and that was the last time she had thought about Hitler. She had too much to do to worry about Europe. She was not interested in international politics, the balance of power, or the rise of Fascism: such abstractions seemed foolish when set against the lives of her sons. The Poles, the Austrians, the Jews and the Slavs would have to take care of themselves. Her job was to take care of Liam and Hugh.

Not that they needed much taking care of. Nancy had married young and had her children right away, so the boys were grown up. Liam was married and living in Houston, and Hugh was in his final year at Yale. He was not studying as hard as he should, and she had been disturbed to learn that he had bought a fast sports car, but he was well past the age of listening to his mother's advice. So, as she could not keep them out of the army, there was not much to draw her home.

She knew that war would be good for business. There would be an economic boom in America, and people would have more money to buy shoes. Whether the USA got into the war or not, the military was bound to be expanded, and that meant increased orders on her government contracts. All in all, she guessed her sales would double and perhaps treble over the next two or three years – another reason for modernizing her factory.

However, all that paled into insignificance beside the glaring, awful possibility that her own sons would be conscripted, to fight and be wounded and perhaps to die in agony on a battlefield.

A porter came for her bags and interrupted her morbid thoughts. She asked the man whether Peter had yet dispatched his luggage. In a thick local accent she could hardly understand he told her that Peter had sent his bags to the ship last night.

She went along to his room to see whether he was ready to leave. When she knocked, the door was opened by a maid, who told her in the same guttural accent that he had left yesterday.

Nancy was puzzled. The two of them had checked in together yesterday evening. Nancy had decided to have dinner in her room and get an early night, and Peter had said he would do the same. If he had changed his mind, where had he gone? Where had he spent the night? And where was he now?

She went down to the lobby to phone, but she was not sure whom to call. Neither she nor Peter knew anybody in England. Liverpool was just across the water from Dublin: could Peter have gone to Ireland, to see the country where the Black family came from? It had been part of their original plan. But Peter would know he could not get back from there in time for the departure of the ship.

On impulse, she asked the operator for Aunt Tilly's number.

Calling America from Europe was a chancy business. There were not enough lines, and sometimes you could wait a long time. If you were lucky you might get through in a few minutes but the sound quality was generally bad and you had to shout.

It was a few minutes before 7 a.m. in Boston, but

140

Aunt Tilly would be up. Like many older people she slept little and woke early. She was very alert.

The lines were not busy at the moment – perhaps because it was too early for businessmen in the States to be at their desks – and after only five minutes the phone in the booth rang. Nancy picked it up to hear the familiar American ringing tone in her ear. She pictured Aunt Tilly in her silk dressing-gown and fur slippers, padding across the gleaming wood floor of her kitchen to the black telephone in the hall.

'Hello?'

'Aunt Tilly, this is Nancy.'

'My goodness, child, are you all right?'

'I'm fine. They've declared war but the shooting hasn't started yet, at least not in England. Have you heard from the boys?'

'They're both fine. I had a postcard from Liam in Palm Beach, he says Jacqueline is even more beautiful with a suntan. Hugh took me for a ride in his new car, which is very pretty.'

'Does he drive it very fast?'

'He seemed quite careful to me, and he refused a cocktail because he says people shouldn't drive powerful automobiles when they've been drinking.'

'That makes me feel better.'

'Happy birthday, dear! What are you doing in England?'

'I'm in Liverpool, about to take ship for New York, but I've lost Peter. I don't suppose you've heard from him, have you?'

'Why, my dear, of course I have. He's called a board

meeting for the day after tomorrow, first thing in the morning.'

Nancy was mystified. 'You mean Friday morning?'

'Yes, dear, Friday is the day after tomorrow,' Tilly said with a touch of pique. Her tone of voice implied, 'I'm not so old that I don't know what day of the week it is.'

Nancy was baffled. What was the point of calling a board meeting when neither she nor Peter would be there? The only other directors were Tilly and Danny Riley, and they would never decide anything on their own.

This had the marks of a plot. Was Peter up to something?

'What's on the agenda, Aunt?'

'I was just looking it over.' Aunt Tilly read aloud. 'To approve the sale of Black's Boots, Inc., to General Textiles, Inc., on the terms negotiated by the chairman.'

'Good God!' Nancy was so shocked that she felt faint. Peter was selling the company behind her back!

For a moment she was too stunned to speak. Then, with an effort, she said in a shaky voice, 'Would you mind reading that to me again, Aunt?'

Aunt Tilly repeated it.

Nancy suddenly felt cold. How had Peter managed to do this beneath her eyes? When had he negotiated the deal? He must have been working on it surreptitiously ever since she gave him her secret report. While pretending to consider her proposals he had in fact been plotting against her.

She had always known that Peter was weak, but she would never have suspected him of such shameful treachery.

'Are you there, Nancy?'

Nancy swallowed. 'Yes, I'm here. Just dumbstruck. Peter has kept this from me.'

'Really? That's not fair, is it?'

'He obviously wants it passed while I'm away . . . but he won't be at the meeting, either. We're taking ship today – we won't be home for five days.' And yet, she thought, Peter has disappeared . . .

'Isn't there an airplane now?'

'The Clipper!' Nancy remembered: it had been in all the papers. You could fly across the Atlantic in a day. Was that what Peter was doing?

'That's right, the Clipper,' said Tilly. 'Danny Riley says Peter's coming back on the Clipper and he'll be here in time for the board meeting.'

Nancy was finding it hard to take in the shameless way her brother had lied to her. He had travelled all the way to Liverpool with her, to make her think he was taking the ship. He must have left again, the moment they parted company in the hotel corridor, and driven overnight to Southampton in time for the plane. How could he have spent all that time with her, talking and eating together, discussing the forthcoming voyage, when all along he was scheming to do her down?

Aunt Tilly said, 'Why don't you come on the Clipper too?'

Was it too late? Peter must have planned this carefully.

He would have known she would make some enquiries when she discovered he was not going on the ship, and he would try to make sure that she was not able to catch up with him. But timing was not Peter's strength and he might have left a gap.

She hardly dared to hope.

'I'm going to try,' Nancy said with sudden determination. 'Goodbye.' She hung up.

She thought for a moment. Peter had left yesterday evening and must have travelled overnight. The Clipper must be scheduled to leave Southampton today and arrive in New York tomorrow, in time for Peter to get to Boston for the meeting on Friday. But what time did the Clipper take off? And could Nancy get to Southampton by then?

With her heart in her mouth, she went to the desk and asked the head porter what time the Pan American Clipper took off from Southampton.

'You've missed it, madam,' he said.

'Just check the time, please,' she said, trying to keep the note of impatience out of her voice.

He took out a timetable and opened it. 'Two o'clock.'

She checked her watch: it was just noon.

The porter said, 'You couldn't get to Southampton in time even if you had a private aeroplane standing by.'

'Are there any airplanes?' she persisted.

His face took on the tolerant expression of a hotel employee humouring a foolish foreigner. 'There's an airfield about ten miles from here. Generally you can find a pilot to take you anywhere, for a price. But you've got to get to the field, find the pilot, make the journey, land somewhere near Southampton, then get from that airfield to the docks. It can't be done in two hours, believe me.'

She turned away from him in frustration.

Getting mad was no use in business, she had learned long ago. When things went wrong you had to find a way to put them right. I can't get to Boston in time, she thought, so maybe I can stop the sale by remote control.

She returned to the phone booth. It was just after seven o'clock in Boston. Her lawyer, Patrick McBride, would be at home. She gave the operator his number.

Mac was the man her brother should have been. When Sean died he stepped in and took care of everything: the inquest, the funeral, the will, and Nancy's personal finances. He was marvellous with the boys, taking them to ball games, turning up to see them in school plays, and advising them on college and careers. At different times he had talked to each of them about the facts of life. When Pa died, Mac counselled Nancy against letting Peter become chairman; she went against his advice, and now events had proved that Mac had been right. She knew that he was more or less in love with her. It was not a dangerous attachment: Mac was a devout Catholic and faithful to his plain, dumpy, loyal wife. Nancy was very fond of him but he was not the kind of man she could ever fall in love with: he was a soft, round, mild-mannered type with a bald dome, and she was always attracted to strong-willed men with plenty of hair: men such as Nat Ridgeway.

While she waited for the connection, she had time

to reflect on the irony of her situation. Peter's co-conspirator against her was Nat Ridgeway, her father's one-time deputy and her old flame. Nat had left the company – and Nancy – because he could not be boss; and now, from his position as president of General Textiles, he was trying again to take control of Black's Boots.

She knew Nat had been in Paris for the collections, although she had not run into him. But Peter must have held meetings with him and closed the deal there, while pretending to be innocently buying shoes. Nancy had not suspected anything. When she thought how easily she had been deceived she felt furious with Peter and Nat – and most of all with herself.

The phone in the booth rang and she picked it up: she was lucky with connections today.

Mac answered with his mouth full of breakfast. 'Hmm?'

'Mac, it's Nancy.'

He swallowed rapidly. 'Thank God you called, I've been searching Europe for you. Peter is trying to—'

'I know, I just heard,' she interrupted. 'What are the terms of the deal?'

'One share in General Textiles, plus twenty-seven cents cash, for five shares in Black's.'

'Jesus, that's a giveaway!'

'On your profits it's not so low—'

'But our asset value is much higher!'

'Hey, I'm not fighting you,' he said mildly.

'Sorry, Mac, I'm just angry.'

'I understand.'

She could hear his children squabbling in the background. He had five, all girls. She could also hear a radio playing and a kettle whistling.

After a moment he went on, 'I agree that the offer is too low. It reflects the current profit level, yes, but it ignores asset value and future potential.'

'You can say that again.'

'There's something else, too.'

'Tell me.'

'Peter will be retained to run the Black's operation for five years following the takeover. But there's no job for you.'

Nancy closed her eyes. This was the cruellest blow of all. She felt sick. Lazy, dumb Peter, whom she had sheltered and covered for, would remain; she, who had kept the business afloat, would be thrown out. 'How could he do this to me?' she said. 'He's my brother!'

'I'm really sorry, Nan.'

'Thanks.'

'I never trusted Peter.'

'My father spent his life building up this business,' she cried. 'Peter can't be allowed to destroy it.'

'What do you want me to do?'

'Can we stop it?'

'If you could get here for the board meeting I believe you could persuade your aunt and Danny Riley to turn it down—'

'I can't get there, that's my problem. Can't you persuade them?'

'I might, but it would do no good – Peter outvotes them. They only have ten per cent each and he has forty.'

'Can't you vote my stock on my behalf?'

'I don't have your proxy.'

'Can I vote by phone?'

'Interesting idea ... I think it would be up to the board, and Peter would use his majority to rule it out.'

There was a silence while they both racked their brains.

In the pause she remembered her manners, and said, 'How's the family?'

'Unwashed, undressed and unruly, right now. And Betty's pregnant.'

For a moment she forgot her troubles. 'No kidding!' She had thought they had stopped having children: the youngest was now five. 'After all this time!'

'I thought I'd found out what was causing it.'

Nancy laughed. 'Hey, congratulations!'

'Thanks, although Betty's a little ... ambivalent about it.'

'Why? She's younger than I am.'

'But six is a lot of kids.'

'You can afford it.'

'Yes ... Are you sure you can't make that plane?'

Nancy sighed. 'I'm in Liverpool. Southampton is two hundred miles away and the plane takes off in less than two hours. It's impossible.'

'Liverpool? That's not far from Ireland.'

'Spare me the travelogue—'

'But the Clipper touches down in Ireland.'

Nancy's heart skipped a beat. 'Are you sure?'

'I read it in the newspaper.'

This changed everything, she realized with a surge of hope. She might be able to make the plane after all! 'Where does it come down – Dublin?'

'No, some place on the west coast, I forget the name. But you might still make it.'

'I'll check it out and call you later. Bye.'

'Hey, Nancy?

'What?'

'Happy Birthday.'

She smiled at the wall. 'Mac . . . you're great.'

'Good luck.'

'Goodbye.' She hung up and went back to the desk. The head porter gave her a condescending smile. She resisted the temptation to put him in his place: that would make him even more unhelpful. 'I believe the Clipper touches down in Ireland,' she said, forcing herself to sound friendly.

'That's correct, madam. At Foynes, in the Shannon estuary.'

She wanted to say, 'So why didn't you tell me that before, you pompous little prick?' Instead she smiled and said, 'What time?'

He reached for his timetable. 'It's scheduled to land at three thirty and take off again at four thirty.'

'Can I get there by then?'

His tolerant smile vanished and he looked at her with more respect. 'I never thought of that,' he said. 'It's a two-hour flight in a small aeroplane. If you can find a pilot you can do it.'

Her tension went up a notch. This was beginning to look seriously possible. 'Get me a taxi to take me to that airfield right away, would you?'

He snapped his fingers at a bellhop. 'Taxi for the lady!' He turned back to Nancy. 'What about your trunks?' They were now stacked in the lobby. 'You won't get that lot in a small plane.'

'Send them to the ship, please.'

'Very good.'

'Bring my bill as quick as you can.'

'Right away.'

Nancy retrieved her small overnight case from the stack of luggage. In it she had her essential toiletries, make-up and a change of underwear. She opened a suitcase and found a clean blouse for tomorrow morning, in plain navy blue silk, and a nightdress and bathrobe. Over her arm she had a light-grey cashmere coat which she had intended to wear on deck if the wind was cold. She decided to keep it with her now: she might need it to keep warm in the plane.

She closed up her bags.

'Your bill, Mrs Lenehan.'

She scribbled a cheque and handed it over with a tip.

'Very kind of you, Mrs Lenehan. The taxi is waiting.'

She hurried outside and climbed into a cramped little British car. The porter put her overnight case on the seat beside her and gave instructions to the driver. Nancy added, 'And go as fast as you can!'

The car went infuriatingly slowly through the city

centre. She tapped the toe of her grey suede shoe impatiently. The delay was caused by men painting white lines down the middle of the road, on the kerbs and around roadside trees. She wondered irritably what their purpose was, then she figured out that the lines were to help motorists in the blackout.

The taxi picked up speed as it wound through the suburbs and headed into the country. Here she saw no preparations for war. The Germans would not bomb fields, unless by accident. She kept looking at her watch. It was already twelve thirty. If she found an aeroplane, and a pilot, and persuaded him to take her, and negotiated a fee, all without delay, she might take off by one o'clock. Two hours' flight, the porter had said. She would land at three. Then, of course, she would have to find her way from the airfield to Foynes. But that should not be too great a distance. She might well arrive with time to spare. Would there be a car to take her to the dockside? She tried to calm herself. There was no point in worrying that far ahead.

It occurred to her that the Clipper might be full: all the ships were.

She put the thought out of her mind.

She was about to ask her driver how much farther they had to go when, to her grateful relief, he abruptly turned off the road and steered through an open gate into a field. As the car bumped over the grass Nancy saw ahead of her a small hangar. All around it, small brightly coloured planes were tethered to the green turf, like a collection of butterflies on a velvet cloth.

There was no shortage of aircraft, she noted with satisfaction. But she needed a pilot too, and there seemed to be no one about.

The driver took her up to the big door of the hangar.

'Wait for me, please,' she said as she jumped out. She did not want to get stranded.

She hurried into the hangar. There were three planes inside but no people. She went out into the sunshine again. Surely the place could not be unattended, she thought anxiously. There had to be *someone* around, otherwise the door would be locked. She walked around the hangar to the back, and there at last she saw three men standing by a plane.

The aircraft itself was ravishing. It was painted canary yellow all over, with little yellow wheels that made Nancy think of toy cars. It was a biplane, its upper and lower wings joined by wires and struts, and it had a single engine in the nose. It sat there with its propeller in the air and its tail on the ground like a puppy begging to be taken for a walk.

It was being fuelled. A man in oily blue overalls and a cloth cap was standing on a stepladder pouring petrol from a can into a bulge on the wing over the front seat. On the ground was a tall, good-looking man of about Nancy's age wearing a flying helmet and a leather jacket. He was deep in conversation with a man in a tweed suit.

Nancy coughed and said, 'Excuse me.'

The two men glanced at her but the tall man continued speaking and they both looked away again.

It was not a good start.

Nancy said, 'I'm sorry to bother you. I want to charter a plane.'

The tall man interrupted his conversation to say, 'Can't help you.'

'It's an emergency,' Nancy said.

'I'm not a bloody taxi driver,' the man said, and turned away again.

Nancy was angered sufficiently to say, 'Why do you have to be so rude?'

That got his attention. He turned an interested, quizzical look at her, and she noticed that he had arched black eyebrows. 'I didn't intend to be rude,' he said mildly. 'But my plane isn't for hire, and nor am I.'

Desperately, she said, 'Please don't be offended, but if it's a matter of money, I'll pay a high price . . .'

He was offended: his expression froze and he turned away.

Nancy observed that there was a chalk-striped dark-grey suit under the leather jacket, and the man's black Oxford shoes were the genuine article, not inexpensive imitations such as Nancy made. He was obviously a wealthy businessman who flew his own plane for pleasure.

'Is there anybody else, then?' she said.

The mechanic looked up from the fuel tank and shook his head. 'Nobody about today,' he said.

The tall man said to his companion, 'I'm not in business to lose money. You tell Seward that what he's getting paid is the rate for the job.'

'The trouble is, he has a point, you know,' said the one in the tweed suit.

'I know that. Say we'll negotiate a higher rate for the next job.'

'That may not satisfy him.'

'In that case he can get his cards and bugger off.'

Nancy wanted to scream with frustration. Here was a perfectly good plane and a pilot, and nothing she said would make them take her where she needed to go. Close to tears, she said, 'I just *have* to get to Foynes!'

The tall man turned round again. 'Did you say Foynes?'

'Yes.'

'Why?'

At least she had succeeded in engaging him in conversation. 'I'm trying to catch up with the Pan American Clipper.'

'That's funny,' he said. 'So am I.'

Her hopes lifted again. 'Oh, my God,' she said. 'You're going to Foynes?'

'Aye.' He looked grim. 'I'm chasing my wife.'

It was an odd thing to say, she noticed, even though she was so wrought up: a man who would confess to that was either very weak or very self-assured. She looked at his plane. There appeared to be two cockpits, one behind the other. 'Are there two seats in your plane?' she asked with trepidation.

He looked her up and down. 'Aye,' he said. 'Two seats.'

'*Please* take me with you.'

He hesitated, then shrugged. 'Why not?'

She wanted to faint with relief. 'Oh, thank God,' she said. 'I'm so grateful.'

'Don't mention it.' He stuck out a big hand. 'Mervyn Lovesey. How do you do.'

She shook hands. 'Nancy Lenehan,' she replied. 'Am I pleased to meet you.'

Eddie needed to talk to someone.

It would have to be someone he could trust absolutely, someone who could keep it secret.

The only person he discussed this kind of thing with was Carol-Ann. She was his confidante. He would not even have discussed it with Pop when Pop was alive: he never liked to show weakness to his father. Was there anyone he could trust?

He considered Captain Baker. Marvin Baker was just the kind of pilot that passengers liked: good-looking, square-jawed, confident and assertive. Eddie respected him and liked him, too. But Baker's loyalty was to the plane and the safety of the passengers, and he was a stickler for the rules. He would insist on going straight to the police with this story. He was no use.

Anyone else?

Yes. There was Steve Appleby.

Steve was a lumberjack's son from Oregon, a tall boy with muscles as hard as wood, a Catholic from a dirt-poor family. They had been midshipmen together at Annapolis. They had become friends on their first day, in the vast white mess hall. While the other plebs were bitching about the chow, Eddie cleaned his plate.

Looking up, he saw that there was one other cadet poor enough to think this was great food: Steve. Their eyes had met and they understood one another perfectly.

They had been pals through the academy, then later they were both stationed at Pearl Harbor. When Steve married Nella, Eddie was best man, and last year Steve did the same service for Eddie. Steve was still in the Navy, stationed at the shipyard in Portsmouth, New Hampshire. They saw each other infrequently now but it did not matter, for theirs was a friendship that would survive long periods with no contact. They would not write letters unless they had something specific to say. When they both happened to be in New York they would have dinner or go to a ball game and would be as close as if they had parted company only the day before. Eddie would have trusted Steve with his soul.

Steve was also a great fixer. A weekend pass, a bottle of hooch, a pair of tickets for the big game – he could get them when no one else could.

Eddie decided to try to get in touch with him.

He felt a little better having made some kind of decision. He hurried back into the hotel.

He went to the little office and gave the number of the naval base to the hotel's proprietress, then he returned to his room. She would fetch him when the call came through.

He took off his overalls. He did not want to be in the tub when she came, so he scrubbed his hands and washed his face in the bedroom, then put on a clean white shirt and his uniform pants. The routine activity calmed him a little but he was feverishly impatient. He did not know what Steve would say but it would be a tremendous relief to share the problem.

He was knotting his tie when the proprietress knocked at the door, but he ran down the stairs and picked up the phone. He was connected with the switchboard operator at the base.

He said, 'Would you put me through to Steve Appleby, please?'

'Lieutenant Appleby cannot be reached by telephone at this time,' he said. Eddie's heart sank. She added, 'May I give him a message?'

Eddie was bitterly disappointed. He knew Steve would not have been able to wave a wand and rescue Carol-Ann, but at least they could have talked, and maybe some ideas would have come out of the discussion.

He said, 'Miss, this is an emergency. Where the hell is he?'

'May I ask who is calling, sir?'

'This is Eddie Deakin.'

She dropped her formal tone immediately. 'Oh, hi, Eddie! You were his best man, weren't you? I'm Laura Gross, we met.' She lowered her voice conspiratorially. 'Unofficially, Steve spent last night off the base.'

Eddie groaned inwardly. Steve was doing something he shouldn't – at just the wrong time. 'When do you expect him?'

'He should have been back before daybreak but he didn't show up.'

Worse yet – Steve was not just absent but possibly in trouble too.

The operator said, 'I could put you through to Nella, she's in the typing pool.'

'Okay, thanks.' He could not confide in Nella, of course, but he could find out a little more about where Steve might be. He tapped his foot restlessly while he waited for the connection. He could picture Nella: she was a warm-hearted, round-faced girl with long curly hair.

At last he heard her voice. 'Hello?'

'Nella, this is Eddie Deakin.'

'Hello, Eddie, where are you?'

'I'm calling from England. Nella, where's Steve?'

'Calling from England! My goodness! Steve is, uh, out of touch right now.' She sounded uneasy as she added, 'Is something wrong?'

'Ayuh. When do you think Steve will be back?'

'Some time this morning, maybe in an hour or so. Eddie, you sound really shook. What is it? Are you in some kind of trouble?'

'Maybe Steve could phone me here if he gets back in time.' He gave her the phone number of Langdown Lawn.

She repeated it. 'Eddie, won't you please tell me what's goin' on?'

'I can't. Just get him to call. I'll be here for another hour. After that I have to go to the plane – we fly back to New York today.'

'Whatever you say,' Nella said doubtfully. 'How's Carol-Ann?'

'I have to go now,' he said. 'Goodbye, Nella.' He hung up without waiting for her reply. He knew he was being discourteous but he was too upset to care. His insides felt tied in knots.

He did not know what to do next so he climbed the stairs and went to his room. He left the door ajar, so that he would hear the ring of the phone from the hall, and sat down on the edge of the single bed. He felt close to tears for the first time since he was a child. He buried his head in his hands and whispered, 'What am I going to do?'

He recalled the Lindbergh kidnapping. It had been in all the papers when he was at Annapolis, seven years ago. The child had been killed. 'Oh, God, keep Carol-Ann safe,' he prayed.

He did not often pray nowadays. Prayer had never done his parents any good. He believed in helping himself. He shook his head. This was no time to revert to religion. He had to think it out and do something.

The people who had kidnapped Carol-Ann wanted Eddie on the plane, that much was clear. Maybe that was a reason not to go. But if he stayed away he would never meet Tom Luther and find out what they wanted. He might frustrate their plans but he would lose any slight chance of gaining control of the situation.

He stood up and opened his small suitcase. He could not think of anything but Carol-Ann, but he automatically stowed his shaving kit, his pyjamas and his laundry. He brushed his hair absently and packed the brushes.

As he was sitting down again, the phone rang.

He was out of the room in two strides. He hurried down the stairs, but someone got to the phone before him. Crossing the hall, he heard the proprietress say, 'October the fourth? Just let me see whether we have a vacancy.'

Crestfallen, he turned back. He told himself there was nothing Steve could do anyway. Nobody could do anything. Someone had kidnapped Carol-Ann and Eddie was just going to have to do whatever they wanted, then he would get her back. No one could release him from the bind he was in.

With a heavy heart he recalled again that they had quarrelled the last time he saw her. He would never forgive himself for that. He wished with all his soul that he had bitten his tongue instead. What the hell had they been arguing about, anyway? He swore he would not fight with her ever again, if only he could have her back safe.

Why wouldn't that goddamn phone ring?

There was a tap on the door and Mickey came in, wearing his flight uniform and carrying his suitcase. 'Ready to go?' he said cheerfully.

Eddie felt panicky. 'It can't be time already!'

'Sure is!'

'Shit . . .'

'What's the matter, you like it so much here? You want to stay and fight the Germans?'

Eddie had to give Steve a few more minutes. 'You honk on ahead,' he said to Mickey. 'I'll catch you up.'

Mickey looked a little hurt that Eddie did not want to go with him. He shrugged, said, 'See you later,' and went out.

Where the hell was Steve Appleby?

He sat and stared at the wallpaper for the next fifteen minutes.

At last he picked up his case and went slowly down the stairs, staring at the phone as if it were a rattlesnake poised to strike. He stopped in the hall, waiting for it to ring.

Captain Baker came down and looked at Eddie in surprise. 'You're running late,' he said. 'You'd better come in the taxi with me.' The Captain had the privilege of a taxi to the hangar.

'I'm waiting for a telephone call,' Eddie said.

The ghost of a frown shadowed the Captain's brow. 'Well, you can't wait any longer. Let's go!'

Eddie did not move for a moment. Then he realized this was stupid. Steve was not going to call, and Eddie had to be on the plane if he was going to do anything. He forced himself to pick up his case and walk out through the door.

The taxi was waiting and they got in.

Eddie knew he had been almost insubordinate. He did not want to offend Baker, who was a good captain and had always treated Eddie decently. 'I'm sorry about that,' he said. 'I was expecting a call from the States.'

The Captain smiled forgivingly. 'Hell, you'll be there tomorrow!' he said cheerfully.

'Right,' Eddie said grimly.

He was on his own.

Part Two

*Southampton to
Foynes*

CHAPTER SIX

As THE train rolled south through the pine woods of Surrey towards Southampton, Margaret Oxenford's sister Elizabeth made a shocking announcement.

The Oxenford family were in a special carriage reserved for Pan American Clipper passengers. Margaret was standing at the end of the carriage, alone, staring out of the window. Her mood swung wildly between black despair and rising excitement. She was angry and miserable to be abandoning her country in its hour of need, but she could not help feeling thrilled at the prospect of flying to America.

Her sister Elizabeth detached herself from the family group and came up to her, looking solemn. After a moment's hesitation she said, 'I love you, Margaret.'

Margaret was touched. Over the last few years, since they had been old enough to understand the battle of ideas raging throughout the world, they had taken violently opposite points of view and because of that they had become estranged. But she had missed being close to her sister, and the estrangement made her sad. It would be wonderful if they could be real pals again. 'I love you, too,' she said, and she hugged Elizabeth hard.

After a moment Elizabeth said, 'I'm not coming to America.'

Margaret gasped with astonishment. 'How can you not?'

'I shall simply tell Mother and Father that I'm not going. I'm twenty-one – they can't force me.'

Margaret was not sure she was right about that, but she let it pass for the moment: she had too many other questions. 'Where will you go?'

'To Germany.'

'But, Elizabeth!' Margaret said, horrified. 'You'll get killed!'

Elizabeth looked defiant. 'It's not only socialists who are willing to die for a cause, you know.'

'But for Nazism!'

'It's not just for Fascism,' Elizabeth said, and there was an odd light in her eyes. 'It's for all the thorough-bred white people who are in danger of being swamped by niggers and half-breeds. It's for the human race.'

Margaret was revolted. It was bad enough to be losing her sister – but to lose her to such a wicked cause! However, Margaret did not want to go over the bitter old political argument now: she was more con-cerned about her sister's safety. She said, 'What will you live on?'

'I've got my own money.'

Margaret remembered that they both inherited money from their grandfather at the age of twenty-one. It was not much, but it might be enough to live on.

She thought of something else. 'But your luggage is checked through to New York.'

'Those cases are full of old tablecloths. I packed another set of bags and sent them ahead on Monday.'

Margaret was astonished. Elizabeth had arranged everything perfectly and carried out her scheme in total secrecy. Bitterly, Margaret reflected how impetuous and ill-thought-out her own escape attempt had been by comparison. While I was brooding and refusing to eat, she thought, Elizabeth was booking passage and sending her luggage on ahead. Of course, Elizabeth was the right side of twenty-one and Margaret the wrong, but that had not counted as much as careful planning and cool execution. Margaret felt ashamed that her sister, who was so stupid and wrong about politics, had behaved so much more intelligently.

Suddenly it struck her how she would miss Elizabeth. Although they were no longer great friends, Elizabeth was always around. Mostly they argued, quarrelled, and mocked one another's ideas, but Margaret would miss that, too. And they still supported one another in distress. Elizabeth always suffered bad period pains and Margaret would tuck her up in bed and bring her a cup of hot chocolate and *Picture Post* magazine. Elizabeth had been deeply sorry when Ian died, even though she disapproved of him, and she had been a comfort to Margaret. Tearfully, Margaret said, 'I shall miss you dreadfully.'

'Don't make a fuss,' Elizabeth said anxiously. 'I don't want them to know yet.'

Margaret composed herself. 'When will you tell them?'

'At the last minute. Can you act normally until then?'

'All right.' She forced a bright smile. 'I shall be as horrible as ever to you.'

'Oh, Margaret!' Elizabeth was on the point of tears. She swallowed and said, 'Go and talk to them while I calm down.'

Margaret squeezed her sister's hand, then returned to her seat.

Mother was leafing through *Vogue* magazine and reading occasional paragraphs to Father, oblivious of his complete lack of interest. 'Lace is being worn,' she quoted, adding, 'I haven't noticed, have you?' The fact that she got no reply did not discourage her in the least. 'White is glamour colour number one. Well, I don't like it. White makes me look kind of bilious.'

Father was wearing an unbearably smug expression. He was pleased with himself, Margaret knew, for reasserting his parental authority and crushing her rebellion. But he did not know that his elder daughter had planted a time-bomb.

Would Elizabeth have the pluck to go through with this? It was one thing to tell Margaret and quite another to tell Father. Elizabeth might lose her nerve at the last minute. Margaret herself had planned a confrontation with him but had ducked it in the end.

Even if Elizabeth went ahead and told Father it was not certain that she would escape. She might be twenty-one and have her own money but he was fearfully strong-willed and quite ruthless about getting his own way. If he could think of some means of stopping Elizabeth he would, Margaret felt sure. He might not mind her joining the Fascist side, in principle, but he would be furious that she was refusing to go along with his plans for the family.

Margaret had been in many such fights with Father. He had been furious when she learned to drive without his permission, and when he found out she had gone to hear a speech by Marie Stopes, the controversial pioneer of contraception, he had been apoplectic. But on those occasions she had succeeded only by going behind his back. She had never won in a direct conflict. He had refused to let her go on a camping holiday, at the age of sixteen, with her cousin Catherine and several of Catherine's friends, even though the whole thing was supervised by a vicar and his wife. Father had objected because there would be boys as well as girls. Their biggest battle had been over going to school. She had begged and pleaded, screamed and sobbed and sulked, and he had been stonily implacable. 'School is wasted on girls,' he had said. 'They only grow up and get married.'

But he could not go on bullying and bossing his children for ever, could he?

Margaret felt restless. She stood up and walked along the carriage; just for something to do. Most of the other Clipper passengers seemed to share her dual mood, half excited and half depressed. When they all joined the train at Waterloo station there had been a good deal of lively conversation and laughter. They had checked their baggage at Waterloo: there had been a fuss about Mother's steamer trunk, which exceeded the weight limit many times over, but she had blithely ignored everything the Pan American staff said and eventually the trunk had been accepted. A young man in uniform had taken their tickets and ushered them into their special carriage. Then, as they left London behind, the passengers had become quiet, as if privately saying goodbye to a country they might never see again.

There was a world-famous American film star among the passengers, which partly accounted for the undertone of excitement. Her name was Lulu Bell. Percy was sitting with her now, talking to her as if he had known her all his life. Margaret herself had wanted to speak to her, but she had not had the cheek just to go up and engage her in conversation. Percy was bolder.

In the flesh Lulu Bell looked older than on the screen. Margaret guessed she was in her late thirties, although she still played débutantes and newlyweds. All the same she was pretty. Small and lively, she made Margaret think of a little bird, a sparrow or a wren.

Margaret smiled at her, and Lulu said, 'Your kid brother has been keeping me entertained.'

'I hope he's being polite,' Margaret replied.

'Oh, sure. He's telling me all about your great-grandmother, Ruthie Fishbein.' Lulu's voice became solemn, as if she were speaking of tragic heroism. 'She must have been a *wonderful* woman.'

Margaret was embarrassed. It was wicked of Percy to tell lies to total strangers. What on earth had he said to this poor woman? Feeling flustered, she smiled vaguely – a trick she had learned from Mother – and passed on.

Percy had always been mischievous, but lately he

seemed to be getting bolder. He was growing taller, his voice was getting deeper, and his practical jokes were verging on dangerous. He was still afraid of Father, and would only go against parental authority if Margaret backed him up, but she had an idea that the day was coming when Percy would rebel openly. How would Father deal with that? Could he bully a boy as easily as he had bullied his girls? Margaret was not sure it would be quite the same.

At the far end of the carriage was a mysterious figure who seemed vaguely familiar to Margaret. A tall, intense-looking man with burning eyes, he stood out in this well-dressed, well-fed crowd because he was as thin as death and wore a shabby suit of thick, coarse cloth. His hair was cut painfully short like a prisoner's. He seemed worried and tense.

She looked at him now and he caught her eye. Suddenly she remembered him. They had never met but she had seen his photograph in the newspapers: he was Carl Hartmann, the German socialist and scientist. Deciding to be bold like her brother, Margaret sat down opposite him and introduced herself. A long-time opponent of Hitler, Hartmann had become a hero to young people such as Margaret for his bravery. Then he had disappeared about a year ago, and everyone had feared the worst. Margaret assumed he had escaped from Germany. He looked like a man who had been through hell.

'The whole world has been wondering what happened to you,' Margaret said to him.

He replied in heavily accented but correct English. 'I was placed under house arrest but permitted to continue with my scientific work.'

'And then?'

'I have escaped,' he said simply. He introduced the man beside him. 'Do you know my friend Baron Gabon?'

Margaret had heard of him. Philippe Gabon was a French banker who used his vast wealth to promote Jewish causes such as Zionism, which made him unpopular with the British government. He spent much of his time travelling the world trying to persuade countries to admit Jewish refugees from the Nazis. He was a small, rather plump man with a neat beard, wearing a stylish black suit with a dove-grey waistcoat and a silver tie. Margaret guessed he was paying for Hartmann's ticket. She shook his hand and returned her attention to Hartmann.

'Your escape hasn't been reported in the newspapers,' she said.

Baron Gabon said, 'We have tried to keep it quiet until Carl is safely out of Europe.'

That was ominous, Margaret thought. It sounded as if the Nazis might still be after him. 'What are you going to do in America?' she asked.

'I am going to Princeton, to work in the physics department there,' Hartmann replied. A bitter expression came over his face. 'I did not want to leave my country. But if I had stayed, my work might have contributed to a Nazi victory.'

Margaret did not know anything about his work, just

that he was a scientist. It was his politics that interested her. 'Your courage has been an inspiration to so many people,' she said. She was thinking of Ian, who had translated Hartmann's speeches, in the days when Hartmann had been allowed to make speeches.

Her praise seemed to make him uncomfortable. 'I wish I could have continued,' he said. 'I regret having given up.'

Baron Gabon interjected, 'You haven't given up, Carl. Don't accuse yourself. You did the only thing you could.'

Hartmann nodded, and Margaret could see that in his head he knew Gabon was right, but in his heart he felt he had let his country down. She would have liked to say something comforting but she did not know what. Her dilemma was resolved by the Pan American escort, who came by saying, 'Our luncheon is ready in the next car. Please take your seats.'

Margaret stood up and said, 'It's such an honour to know you. I hope we can talk some more.'

'I'm sure we will,' Hartmann said, and for the first time he smiled. 'We're going three thousand miles together.'

She moved into the restaurant car and sat down with her family. Mother and Father sat on one side of the table, and the three children were squeezed together on the other, Percy between Margaret and Elizabeth. Margaret looked sideways at Elizabeth. When would she drop her bombshell?

The waiter poured water and Father ordered a bottle of hock. Elizabeth was silent, looking out of the window.

Margaret waited in suspense. Mother sensed the tension and said, 'What's up with you girls?'

Margaret said nothing. Elizabeth said, 'I've got something important to tell you.'

The waiter came with cream of mushroom soup. Elizabeth paused while he served them. Mother asked for a salad.

When he had gone, Mother said, 'What is it, dear?'

Margaret held her breath.

Elizabeth said, 'I've decided not to go to America.'

'What the devil are you talking about?' Father said irritably. 'Of course you're going – we're on the way!'

'No, I shan't be flying with you,' Elizabeth persisted calmly. Margaret watched her closely. Elizabeth's voice was level but her long, rather plain face was white with tension and Margaret's heart went out to her.

Mother said, 'Don't be silly, Elizabeth, Father's bought you a ticket.'

Percy said, 'Perhaps we can get a refund.'

'Be quiet, foolish boy,' said Father.

Elizabeth said, 'If you try to force me, I shall refuse to go on board the aeroplane. I think you'll find that the airline will not permit you to carry me aboard kicking and screaming.'

How clever Elizabeth had been, Margaret thought. She had caught Father at a vulnerable moment. He could not take her aboard by force and he could not stay behind to deal with the problem because the authorities were about to arrest him as a Fascist.

But Father was not beaten yet. He now understood that she was serious. He put down his spoon. 'What on earth do you suppose you would do if you stayed behind?' he said scathingly. 'Join the army, as your feeble-minded sister proposed to do?'

Margaret flushed with anger at being called feeble-minded, but she bit her tongue and said nothing, waiting for Elizabeth to crush him.

Elizabeth said, 'I shall go to Germany.'

For a moment Father was shocked into silence.

Mother said, 'Darling, don't you think you're taking all this too far?'

Percy spoke in an accurate imitation of Father. 'This is what happens when girls are allowed to discuss politics,' he said pompously. 'I blame that Marie Stopes—'

'Shut up, Percy,' said Margaret, digging him in the ribs.

They were silent while the waiter cleared away their untouched soup. She's done it, Margaret thought. She actually had the guts to come out and say it. Now, will she get away with it?

Margaret could see that Father was already disconcerted. It had been easy for him to scorn Margaret for wanting to stay behind and fight against the Fascists but it was harder to deride Elizabeth because she was on his side.

However, moral doubt never troubled him for very long and when the waiter went away he said, 'I absolutely forbid it.' His tone was conclusive, as if that ended the discussion.

Margaret looked at Elizabeth. How would she respond? He wasn't even bothering to argue with her.

With surprising gentleness, Elizabeth said, 'I'm afraid you can't forbid it, Father dear. I'm twenty-one years old and I can do as I please.'

'Not while you're dependent on me,' he said.

'Then I may have to do without your support,' she said. 'I have a small income of my own.'

Father drank some hock very quickly and said, 'I shan't permit it and that's that.'

It sounded hollow. Margaret began to believe that Elizabeth might really get away with it. She did not know whether to feel delighted at the prospect of Elizabeth defeating Father, or revolted that she was going to join the Nazis.

They were served Dover sole. Only Percy ate. Elizabeth was pale with fright but there was a look of determination about her mouth. Margaret could not help admiring her fortitude, even though she despised her mission.

Percy said, 'If you're not coming to America, why did you get on the train?'

'I've booked passage on a ship from Southampton.'

'You can't get a ship to Germany from this country,' Father said triumphantly.

Margaret was appalled. Of course you couldn't. Had Elizabeth slipped up? Would her entire plan founder on this detail?

Elizabeth was unruffled. 'I'm taking a ship to Lisbon,' she said calmly. 'I've wired money to a bank there and I have a reservation at an hotel.'

'You deceitful child!' Father said furiously. His voice was loud and a man at the next table looked round.

Elizabeth went on as if he had not spoken. 'Once I'm there I'll be able to find a ship going to Germany.'

Mother said, 'And then?'

'I have friends in Berlin, Mother, you know that.'

Mother sighed. 'Yes, dear.' She looked very sad, and Margaret saw she had now accepted that Elizabeth would go.

Father said loudly, 'I have friends in Berlin, too.'

Several people at adjoining tables looked up, and Mother said, 'Hush, dear. We can all hear you just fine.'

Father went on more quietly, 'I have friends in Berlin who will send you packing the moment you arrive.'

Margaret's hand went to her mouth. Of course, Father could get the Germans to expel Elizabeth: in a Fascist country the government could do anything. Would Elizabeth's escape end with some wretched bureaucrat in a passport control booth shaking his head woodenly and refusing her an entry permit?

'They won't do that,' said Elizabeth.

'We shall see,' said Father, and to Margaret's ear he sounded unsure of himself.

'They'll welcome me, Father,' Elizabeth said, and the note of weariness in her voice somehow made her sound more convincing. 'They'll send out a press release to tell the world that I've escaped from England and joined their side, just the way the wretched British newspapers publicize the defection of prominent German Jews.'

Percy said, 'I hope they don't find out about Grandma Fishbein.'

Elizabeth was armoured against Father's attack but

177

Percy's cruel humour slipped under her guard. 'Shut up, you horrible boy!' she said, and she began to cry.

Once again the waiter took away their untouched plates. The next course was lamb cutlets with vegetables. The waiter poured wine. Mother took a sip, a rare sign that she was upset.

Father began to eat, attacking the meat with his knife and fork and chewing furiously. Margaret studied his angry face, and was surprised to detect a trace of bewilderment beneath the mask of rage. It was odd to see him shaken: his arrogance normally weathered every crisis. Studying his expression, she began to realize that his whole world was falling apart. This war was the end of his hopes: he had wanted the British people to embrace Fascism under his leadership, but instead they had declared war on Fascism and exiled him.

In truth, they had rejected him in the mid-thirties, but until now he had been able to turn a blind eye to that, and pretend to himself that one day they would come to him in their hour of need. That was why he was so awful, she supposed: he was living a lie. His crusading zeal had developed into obsessive mania, his confidence had degenerated into bluster and, having failed to become the dictator of Britain, he had been reduced to tyrannizing his children. But now he could no longer ignore the truth. He was leaving his country and might never be allowed to return.

On top of all that, at the moment when his political hopes were unmistakably turning to dust, his children were rebelling too. Percy was pretending to be Jewish,

Margaret had tried to run away and now even Elizabeth, his one remaining follower, was defying him.

Margaret had thought she would be grateful for any crack in his armour, but instead she felt uneasy. His unvarying despotism had been a constant in her life, and she was disconcerted by the thought that he might crumble. Like an oppressed nation faced with the prospect of revolution, she felt suddenly insecure.

She tried to eat but she could hardly swallow. Mother pushed a tomato around her plate for a while, then put her fork down. Suddenly she said, 'Is there a boy you like in Berlin, Elizabeth?'

'No,' Elizabeth said. Margaret believed her, but all the same Mother's question had been perceptive. Margaret knew that the appeal of Germany to Elizabeth was not purely ideological. There was something about the tall, blond soldiers, in their immaculate uniforms and gleaming jackboots, that thrilled Elizabeth at a deeper level. And whereas in London society Elizabeth was thought of as a rather plain, ordinary girl from an eccentric family, in Berlin she was something special: an English aristocrat, the daughter of a pioneering Fascist, a foreigner who admired German Nazism. Her defection at the outbreak of war would make her famous there: she would be lionized. She would probably fall in love with a young officer, or an up-and-coming Party official, and they would marry and have blond children who would grow up speaking German.

Mother said, 'What you're doing is so dangerous, dear. Father and I are only worried about your safety.'

Margaret wondered whether Father really was

concerned for Elizabeth's safety. Mother was, certainly, but Father was angry mainly at being disobeyed. Perhaps underneath his fury there was also a vestige of tenderness. He had not always been harsh: Margaret could remember moments of kindliness and even fun, in the old days. The thought made her sad.

Elizabeth said, 'I know it's dangerous, Mother, but my future is at stake in this war. I don't want to live in a world dominated by Jewish financiers and grubby little Communist trade unionists.'

'What absolute twaddle!' Margaret said, but no one was listening.

'Then come with us,' Mother said to Elizabeth. 'America is a good place.'

'Wall Street is run by Jews—'

'I do believe that's exaggerated,' Mother said firmly, avoiding Father's eye. 'There are too many Jews and other unsavoury types in American business, it's true, but they're far outnumbered by decent people. Remember that your grandfather owned a bank.'

Percy said, 'Incredible that we went from knife-grinding to banking in just two generations.' Nobody took any notice.

Mother went on, 'I agree with your views, dear, you know that, but believing in something doesn't mean you have to die for it. No cause is worth that.'

Margaret was shocked. Mother was implying that the Fascist cause was not worth dying for, which amounted almost to blasphemy in Father's eyes. She had never known Mother to go against him like this. Elizabeth was surprised, too, Margaret could see. They both looked at Father. He reddened slightly and grunted disapprovingly, but the outburst they were expecting did not come. And that was the most shocking thing of all.

Coffee was served and Margaret saw that they had reached the outskirts of Southampton. They would arrive at the station in a few minutes. Would Elizabeth really do it?

The train slowed down.

Elizabeth said to the waiter, 'I'm leaving the train at the main station. Would you please bring my suitcase from the other carriage? It's a red leather bag and the name is Lady Elizabeth Oxenford.'

'Certainly, m'Lady,' he said.

Red-brick suburban houses marched past the carriage windows like ranks of soldiers. Margaret was watching Father. He said nothing but his face was taut as a balloon with suppressed rage. Mother put a hand on his knee and said, 'Please don't make a scene, dear.' He did not reply.

The train pulled into the station.

Elizabeth was sitting by the window. She caught Margaret's eye. Margaret and Percy got up and let her out, then sat down again.

Father stood up.

The other passengers sensed the tension and looked at the little tableau: Elizabeth and Father facing one another in the aisle as the train came to a halt.

It struck Margaret once again that Elizabeth had chosen her moment well. It would be difficult for Father to use force in these circumstances: if he tried he might even be restrained by other passengers. Nevertheless she felt sick with fear.

Father's face was flushed and his eyes bulged. He was breathing hard through his nose. Elizabeth was shaking, but her mouth was set firm.

Father said, 'If you get off this train now, I never want to see you again.'

'Don't say that!' Margaret cried, but she was too late. It had been said, and he would never take it back.

Mother began to cry.

Elizabeth just said, 'Goodbye.'

Margaret stood up and threw her arms round her sister. 'Good luck!' she whispered.

'You, too,' Elizabeth said, hugging her back.

Elizabeth kissed Percy's cheek, then leaned awkwardly across the table and kissed Mother's face, which was wet with tears. Finally she looked at Father again and said in a trembling voice, 'Will you shake hands?'

His face was a mask of hate. He said, 'My daughter is dead.'

Mother gave a cry of distress.

The carriage was very quiet, as if everyone knew that a family drama was reaching its tragic conclusion.

Elizabeth turned and walked away.

Margaret wished she could pick her father up and shake him until his teeth rattled. His needless obstinacy made her livid. Why the hell couldn't he just give in for once? Elizabeth was an adult: she wasn't obliged to obey her parents for the rest of her life! Father had no right to banish her. In his rage he had split the family, pointlessly and vindictively. At that moment Margaret hated him. As he stood there, looking furious and belligerent, she wanted to tell him that he was mean and unjust and stupid but, as always with Father, she bit her lip and said nothing.

Elizabeth walked past the carriage window, carrying her red suitcase. She looked at them all, smiled tearfully, and gave a small, hesitant wave with her free hand. Mother began to sob quietly. Percy and Margaret waved back. Father looked away. Then Elizabeth passed out of sight.

Father sat down and Margaret followed suit.

A whistle blew and the train moved off.

They saw Elizabeth again, waiting in line at the exit. She glanced up as their carriage went by. This time there was no smile or wave: she just looked sad and grim.

The train picked up speed, and she was lost from view.

'Family life is a wonderful thing,' Percy said, and although he was being sarcastic, there was no humour in his voice, just bitterness.

Margaret wondered whether she would ever see her sister again.

Mother was dabbing at her eyes with a little linen handkerchief but she was unable to stop crying. It was rare for her to lose her composure. Margaret could not remember seeing her cry ever before. Percy looked shaken. Margaret was depressed by Elizabeth's foolish attachment to such an evil cause but she could not help also feeling a sense of exultation. Elizabeth had done it: she had defied Father and got away with it! She had stood up to him, defeated him, and escaped from him.

If Elizabeth could do it, so could Margaret.

She smelled the sea. The train entered the docks and ran along the waterfront, moving slowly past sheds, cranes and ocean liners. Despite her grief at parting with her sister, Margaret began to feel the thrill of anticipation.

The train stopped behind a building marked 'Imperial House'. It was an ultra-modern structure that looked a bit like a ship: its corners were rounded and the upper storey had a wide veranda like a deck, with a white rail all around.

With the other passengers, the Oxenfords retrieved their overnight bags and got off the train. While their checked baggage was being transferred from the train to the plane, they all went into Imperial House to complete the departure formalities.

Margaret felt dazed. The world around her was changing too rapidly. She had left her home, her country was at war, she had lost her sister, and she was about to fly to America. She wished she could stop the clock for a while and try to take it all in.

Father explained that Elizabeth would not be joining them, and a Pan American official said, 'That's all right – there's someone waiting here hoping to buy an unused ticket. I'll take care of it.'

Margaret noticed Professor Hartmann standing in a corner, smoking a cigarette, looking around him with nervous, wary glances. He seemed jumpy and impatient. People like my sister have made him like this, Margaret thought. Fascists have persecuted him and turned him into a nervous wreck. I don't blame him for being in a hurry to get out of Europe.

They could not see the plane from the waiting room, so Percy went off to find a better vantage point. He came back full of information. 'Take-off will be on schedule at two o'clock,' he said. Margaret felt a shiver of apprehension. He went on, 'It should take us an hour and a half to get to our first stop, which is Foynes. Ireland is on summer time, like Britain, so we should arrive there at half-past three. We wait there an hour while they refuel and finalize the flight plan, and take off again at half-past four.'

Margaret noticed that there were new faces here, people who had not been on the train. Some passengers must have come directly to Southampton this morning, or perhaps stayed overnight at a local hotel. As she thought this, a strikingly beautiful woman arrived in a taxi. She was a blonde in her thirties, and she wore a stunning dress, cream silk with red spots. She was accompanied by a rather ordinary, smiling man in a cashmere blazer. Everyone stared at them: they looked so happy and attractive.

A few minutes later the plane was ready for boarding.

They went out through the front doors of Imperial House directly on to the quay. The Clipper was moored there, rising and falling gently on the water, the sun gleaming off its silver sides.

It was *huge*.

Margaret had never seen a plane even half this size. It was as high as a house and as long as two tennis courts. A big American flag was painted on its whale-like snout. The wings were high, level with the very top of the fuselage. Four enormous engines were built into the wings, and the propellers looked about fifteen feet across.

How could such a thing *fly*?

'Is it very light?' she wondered aloud.

Percy heard her. 'Forty-one tons,' he said promptly.

It would be like taking to the air in a house.

They came to the edge of the quay. A gangplank led down to a floating dock. Mother trod gingerly, hanging on tight to the rail: she looked almost doddery, as if she had aged twenty years. Father had both their bags – Mother never carried anything, it was one of her foibles.

From the floating dock, a shorter gangplank took them on to what looked like a stubby secondary wing, half submerged in the water. 'Hydrostabilizer,' Percy said knowledgeably. 'Also known as a sea-wing. Prevents the plane from tipping sideways in the water.' The surface of the sea-wing was slightly curved: Margaret felt as if she might slip but she did not. Now she was in the shadow of the huge wing above her head. She would have liked to touch one of the vast propeller blades but she would not have been able to reach it.

There was a doorway in the fuselage just under the word AMERICAN in PAN AMERICAN AIRWAYS SYSTEM. Margaret ducked her head and stepped through the door.

There were three steps down to the floor of the plane.

Margaret found herself in a room about twelve feet square with a luxurious terracotta carpet, beige walls and blue chairs with a gay pattern of stars on the upholstery. There were dome lights in the ceiling and large square windows with venetian blinds. The walls and ceiling were straight, instead of curving with the fuselage: it was more like entering a house than boarding a plane.

Two doorways led from this room. Some passengers were directed towards the rear of the plane. Looking that way, Margaret could see that there was a series of lounges, all luxuriously carpeted and decorated in soft tans and greens. But the Oxenfords were seated forward. A small, rather plump steward in a white jacket introduced himself as Nicky and showed them into the next compartment.

This was a little smaller than the other room, and was decorated in a different colour scheme: turquoise carpet, pale green walls, and beige upholstery. To Margaret's right were two large three-seater divans, facing one another, with a small table between them under the window. To her left, on the other side of the aisle, was another pair of divans, these a little smaller, seating two.

Nicky directed them to the larger seats on the right. Father and Mother sat by the window, and Margaret and Percy next to the aisle, leaving two empty seats between them, and four empty seats on the other side of the aisle. Margaret wondered who would be sitting with them. The beautiful woman in the spotted dress would be interesting. So would Lulu Bell, especially if she wanted to talk about Grandma Fishbein! Best of all would be Carl Hartmann.

She could feel the plane moving up and down with

the slight rise and fall of the water. The movement was not much, just enough to remind her that she was at sea. The plane was like a magic carpet, she decided. It was impossible to grasp how mere engines could make it fly, much easier to believe that it would be borne through the air by the power of an ancient enchantment.

Percy stood up. 'I'm going to look around,' he said.

'Stay here,' Father said. 'You'll get in everyone's way if you start running around.'

Percy sat down promptly. Father had not lost all his authority.

Mother powdered her nose. She had stopped crying. She must be feeling better, Margaret decided.

She heard an American voice say, 'I'd really rather sit facing forward.' She looked up. Nicky the steward was showing a man to a seat on the other side of the compartment. Margaret could not tell who it was – he had his back to her. He had blond hair and wore a blue suit.

The steward said, 'No problem, Mr Vandenpost, take the opposite seat.'

The man turned around. Margaret looked at him with curiosity, and their eyes met.

She was astonished to recognize him.

He was not American and his name was not Mr Vandenpost.

His blue eyes flashed her a warning but he was too late.

'Good grief!' she blurted out. 'It's Harry Marks!'

CHAPTER SEVEN

MOMENTS SUCH as this brought out the best in Harry Marks.

Jumping bail, travelling on a stolen passport, using a false name, and pretending to be American, he had the incredibly bad luck to run into a girl who knew he was a thief, had heard him speak in different accents, and loudly called him by his real name.

For an instant he was possessed by blind panic.

A horrid vision of all he was running from appeared before his eyes: a trial, prison, and then the wretched life of a squaddie in the British Army.

Then he remembered that he was lucky, and he smiled.

The girl looked totally bewildered. He waited for her name to come back to him.

Margaret. Lady Margaret Oxenford.

She stared at him in amazement, too surprised to say anything, while he waited for inspiration.

'Harry Vandenpost is the name,' he said. 'But my memory is better than yours, I'll bet. You're Margaret Oxenford, aren't you? How are you?'

'I'm fine,' she said dazedly. She was more confused than he. She would let him take charge of the situation.

He put out his hand as if to shake and she extended her own, and in that moment inspiration came to him. Instead of shaking her hand, at the last moment he bent over it with an old-fashioned bow; and when his head was close to hers he said in a low voice, 'Pretend you never saw me in a police station and I'll do the same for you.'

He stood upright and looked into her eyes. They were an unusual shade of dark green, he noticed; quite beautiful.

For a moment she remained flustered. Then her face cleared, and she grinned broadly. She had cottoned on and was pleased and intrigued by the little conspiracy he was proposing. 'Of course, how silly of me, Harry Vandenpost,' she said.

Harry relaxed gratefully. Luckiest man in the world, he thought.

With a mischievous little frown Margaret added, 'By the way, where *did* we meet?'

Harry fielded that one easily. 'Was it at Pippa Matchingham's ball?'

'No, I didn't go.'

Harry knew very little about Margaret. Did she live in London right through the social 'season' or hide away in the countryside? Did she hunt, shoot, support charities, campaign for women's rights, paint watercolours, or carry out agricultural experiments on her father's farm? He decided to name one of the big events of the season. 'I'm sure we met at Ascot, then.'

'Yes, of course we did,' she said.

He allowed himself a little smile of satisfaction. He had turned her into a co-conspirator already.

She went on, 'But I don't think you've met my people. Mother, may I present Mr Vandenpost, from . . .'

'Pennsylvania,' Harry said rashly. He regretted it immediately. Where the hell was Pennsylvania? He had no idea.

'My mother, Lady Oxenford, my father, the Marquess. And this is my brother, Lord Isley.'

Harry had heard of them all, of course: they were a famous family. He shook hands all round with a hearty, over-friendly manner which the Oxenfords would think typically American.

Lord Oxenford looked like what he was: an overfed, bad-tempered old Fascist. He wore a brown tweed suit with a waistcoat that was about to pop its buttons and he had not taken off his brown trilby hat.

Harry spoke to Lady Oxenford. 'I'm thrilled to meet you, ma'am. I'm interested in antique jewellery, and I've heard you have one of the finest collections in the world.'

'Why, thank you,' she said. 'It is a particular interest of mine.'

He was shocked to hear her American accent. What he knew about her came from his careful reading of society magazines. He had thought she was British. But now he vaguely remembered some gossip about the Oxenfords. The Marquess, like many aristocrats with vast country estates, had almost gone bankrupt after the war because of the world slump in agricultural prices. Some had sold their estates and gone to live in Nice or Florence where their dwindling fortunes bought a higher standard of living. But Algernon Oxenford had married the heiress to an American bank and it was her money that had enabled him to continue to live in the style of his ancestors.

All of which simply meant that Harry's act was going to have to fool a genuine American. It had to be faultless, and he would have to keep it up for the next thirty hours.

He decided to be charming to her. He guessed she was not averse to compliments, especially from good-looking young men. He looked closely at the brooch pinned to the bosom of her burnt-orange travelling suit. It was made of emeralds, sapphires, rubies and diamonds in the form of a butterfly landing on a wild rose spray. It was extraordinarily realistic. He decided it was French from about 1880 and took a guess as to the maker. 'Is your brooch by Oscar Massin?'

'You're quite right.'

'It's very fine.'

'Thank you again.'

She was rather beautiful. He could understand why Oxenford had married her, but it was harder to see why she had fallen for him. Perhaps he had been more attractive twenty-five years ago.

'I think I know the Philadelphia Vandenposts,' she said.

Harry thought, Blimey, I hope not. However, she sounded rather vague.

'My family are the Glencarrys of Stamford, Connecticut,' she added.

'Indeed!' said Harry, pretending to be impressed. He was still thinking about Philadelphia. Had he said he came from Philadelphia, or Pennsylvania? He could not remember. Maybe they were the same place. They seemed to go together. Philadelphia, Pennsylvania. Stamford, Connecticut. He remembered that when you asked Americans where they came from they always gave two answers. Houston, Texas; San Francisco, California. Yeah.

The boy said, 'My name's Percy.'

'Harry,' said Harry, glad to be back on familiar ground. Percy's was a courtesy title, for the heir to use until his father died, whereupon he would become the Marquess of Oxenford. Most of these people were ludicrously proud of their stupid titles. Harry had once been introduced to a snot-nosed three-year-old as Baron Portrail. However, Percy seemed all right. He was courteously letting Harry know that he did not want to be addressed formally.

Harry sat down. He was facing forward, so Margaret was next to him across the narrow aisle, and he would be able to talk to her without the others hearing. The plane was as quiet as a church. Everyone was rather awestruck.

He tried to relax. It was going to be a tense trip. Margaret knew his true identity, and that created a big new risk. Even though she had accepted his subterfuge, she could change her mind, or let something slip by accident. Harry could not afford to arouse misgivings.

He could get through US Immigration if no searching questions were asked, but if something happened to make them suspicious, and they decided to check up on him, they would quickly find out that he was using a stolen passport and it would be all over.

Another passenger was brought to the seat opposite Harry. He was quite tall, with a bowler hat and a dark grey suit which had once been all right but was now past its best. Something about him struck Harry, who watched the man taking off his overcoat and settling in his seat. He had stout, well-worn black shoes, heavy-weight wool socks, and a wine-coloured waistcoat under his double-breasted jacket. His dark blue tie looked as if it had been tied in the same place every day for ten years.

If I didn't know the price of a ticket on this flying palace, Harry thought, I'd swear blind that man was a copper.

It was not too late to stand up and get off the plane.

No one would stop him. He could simply walk away and disappear.

But he had paid ninety pounds!

Besides, it might be weeks before he could get another transatlantic passage and while he was waiting he might be re-arrested.

He thought again about going on the run in England, and once again dismissed the idea. It would be difficult, in wartime, with every busybody on the look-out for foreign spies; but, more importantly, life as a fugitive would be unbearable – living in cheap boarding-houses, avoiding policemen, always on the move.

The man opposite him, if he were a policeman, was certainly not after Harry, of course – otherwise he would not be sitting down and making himself comfortable for the flight. Harry could not imagine what the man was doing, but for the moment he put that out of his mind and concentrated on his own predicament. Margaret was the danger factor. What could he do to protect himself?

She had entered into his subterfuge in a spirit of fun. As things stood he could not rely on her to keep it up. But he could improve his chances by getting close to her. If he could win her affection, she might begin to feel a sense of loyalty to him, and then she would take his charade more seriously and be careful not to betray him.

Getting to know Margaret Oxenford would not be an unpleasant duty. He studied her out of the corner of his eye. She had the same pale autumnal colouring as her mother: red hair, cream skin with a few freckles, and those fascinating dark green eyes. He could not tell what her figure was like, but she had slender calves and narrow feet. She wore a rather plain camel-coloured lightweight coat over a red-brown dress. Although her clothes looked expensive she did not have her mother's sense of style: that might come as she grew older and more confident. She wore no interesting jewellery, just a plain single strand of pearls around her neck. She had neat, regular features and a determined chin. She was not his usual type – he always picked girls with a weakness, because they were so much easier to romance. Margaret was too good-looking to be a pushover. However, she seemed to like him and that was a start. He made up his mind to win her heart.

The steward, Nicky, came into the compartment. He was a small, plump, effeminate man in his middle twenties, and Harry thought he was probably a queer. A lot of waiters were like that, he had noticed. Nicky handed out a typewritten sheet with the names of the passengers and crew on today's flight.

Harry studied it with interest. He knew of Baron Philippe Gabon, the wealthy Zionist. The next name, Professor Carl Hartmann, also rang a bell. He had not heard of Princess Lavinia Bazarov, but her name suggested a Russian who had fled from the Communists and her presence on this plane presumably meant she had got at least part of her wealth out of the country. He had most certainly heard of Lulu Bell, the film star. Only a week ago he had taken Rebecca Maugham-Flint to see her in *A Spy in Paris* at the Gaumont in Shaftesbury Avenue. She had played a plucky girl, as usual. Harry was very curious to meet her.

Percy, who sat facing the rear and could see into the next compartment, said, 'They've closed the door.'

Harry began to feel nervous again.

For the first time he noticed that the plane was rising and falling gently on the water.

There was a rumble, like the gunfire of a distant battle. Harry anxiously looked out of the window. As he watched, the noise increased, and a propeller began to turn. The engines were being started. He heard the third and the fourth give voice. Although the noise was muffled by heavy sound-proofing, the vibration of the mighty motors could be felt and Harry's apprehension increased.

On the floating dock a seaman cast off the flying boat's moorings. Harry had a foolish feeling of inevitable doom as the ropes tying him to the land were carelessly dropped into the sea.

He was embarrassed about being afraid and did not want anyone else to know how he felt, so he took out a newspaper, opened it, and sat back with his legs crossed.

Margaret touched his knee. She did not need to raise her voice to be heard: the soundproofing was amazing. 'I'm scared, too,' she said.

Harry was mortified. He thought he had succeeded in appearing calm.

The plane moved. He grabbed the arm of his chair, holding on tight; then he forced himself to let go. Of course she could tell he was scared. He was probably as white as the newspaper he was pretending to read.

She was sitting with her knees pressed close together and her hands clasped tightly in her lap. She seemed apprehensive and excited at the same time, as if she were about to take a roller-coaster ride. Her flushed cheeks, wide eyes and slightly open mouth made her look sexy. Harry wondered again what her body was like under that coat.

He looked at the others. The man opposite him was calmly fastening his safety belt. Margaret's parents were gazing out of the windows. Lady Oxenford appeared unperturbed, but Lord Oxenford kept clearing his

throat noisily, a sure sign of tension. Young Percy was
so thrilled he could hardly sit still, but he did not seem
in the least frightened.

Harry stared at his paper but he could not read a
word, so he lowered it and looked out of the window
instead. The mighty aircraft was taxiing majestically out
into Southampton Water. He could see the ocean liners
in a row along the dockside. They were already some
distance away and there were several smaller craft
between him and the land. Can't get off now, he
thought.

The water became choppy as the aircraft moved into
the middle of the estuary. Harry was not normally
seasick but now he felt distinctly uncomfortable as the
Clipper began to ride the waves. The compartment
looked like a room in a house but the motion reminded
him that he was sailing in a boat, a fragile craft of thin
aluminium.

The plane reached the middle of the estuary, slowed,
and began to swing round. It rocked with the breeze,
and Harry realized it was turning into the wind for
take-off. Then it seemed to pause, hesitating, pitching
a little with the wind and rolling with the slight swell, as
if it were a monstrous animal sniffing the air with its
enormous snout. The suspense was almost too much: it
took an effort of will for Harry to restrain himself from
leaping out of his seat and yelling to be let off.

Suddenly there was a terrific roar, like a fearsome
storm breaking out, as the four huge engines were
pushed to full power. Harry let out a cry of shock but it
was drowned. The aircraft seemed to settle a little in

the water, as if it were sinking under the strain, but a moment later it surged forward.

It picked up speed rapidly, like a fast boat, except that no boat this big could accelerate so quickly. White water sped past the windows. The Clipper still pitched and rolled with the movement of the sea. Harry wanted to close his eyes but he was afraid to. He felt panicky. I'm going to die, he thought hysterically.

The Clipper went faster and faster. Harry had never travelled at such a pace across water: no speedboat could reach this velocity. They were doing fifty, sixty, seventy miles an hour. Spray flew past the window, hazing his view. We're going to sink, explode, or crash, Harry thought.

There was a new vibration, like being in a car driving over ruts. What was it? Harry felt sure that something was terribly wrong, and the plane was about to break up. It occurred to him that it had begun to rise and the vibration was caused by its bumping across the waves like a speedboat. Was that normal?

Suddenly the water seemed to exert less drag. Peering through the spray, Harry saw that the surface of the estuary appeared to have tilted, and he realized that the plane's nose must be up, although he had not felt the change. He was terrified and wanted to throw up. He swallowed hard.

The vibration changed. Instead of bumping across ruts they seemed to be jumping from wave to wave, like a stone skimming the surface. The engines screamed and the propellers thrashed the air. It might be impossible, Harry thought; maybe such a huge machine could not take to the air after all; perhaps it could only ride the waves like an overweight dolphin. Then, suddenly, he sensed that the plane had been set free. It surged forward and up, and he felt the restraining water fall away underneath him. The view from the window cleared as the spray was left behind, and he saw the water receding below as the plane went up. Gorblimey, we're flying, he thought; this huge great palace is actually bloody flying!

Now that he was in the air his fear dropped away and was replaced by a tremendous feeling of exhilaration. It was as if he were personally responsible for the fact that the plane had succeeded in taking off. He wanted to cheer. Looking around, he saw that everyone else was smiling with relief. Becoming conscious of other people again, he discovered he was wet with sweat. He took out a white linen handkerchief, surreptitiously wiped his face and quickly stuffed it back into his pocket.

The plane continued to rise. Harry saw the south coast of England disappear beneath the stubby lower sea-wings, then he looked ahead and saw the Isle of Wight. After a while the plane levelled out and the roar of the engines was suddenly reduced to a low hum.

Nicky the steward reappeared in his white jacket and black tie. He did not have to raise his voice, now that the engines had been throttled back. He said, 'Would you care for a cocktail, Mr Vandenpost?'

That's exactly what I would care for, Harry thought. 'Large Scotch,' he said immediately. Then he remembered he was supposed to be American. 'On the rocks,' he added in the correct accent.

Nicky took orders from the Oxenfords and then disappeared through the forward doorway.

Harry drummed his fingers restlessly on the arm of the seat. The carpet, the soundproofing, the soft seats and the soothing colours made him feel as if he was in a padded cell, comfortable but trapped. After a moment he unbuckled his safety belt and got up.

He went forward, the way the steward had gone, and stepped through the doorway. On his left was the galley, a tiny kitchen gleaming with stainless steel, where the steward was making the drinks. On his right was a door marked 'Men's Retiring Room' which he assumed was the carsey. I must remember to call it the john, he thought. Next to the john was a staircase spiralling up, presumably to the flight deck. Beyond was another passenger compartment, decorated in different colours, and occupied by uniformed flight crew. For a moment Harry wondered what they were doing there, then he realized that on a flight lasting almost thirty hours crew members would have to take rests and be replaced.

He walked back along the plane, passing the galley and going through his compartment and the larger compartment by which they had boarded. Beyond that, towards the rear of the plane, were three more passenger compartments, decorated in alternating colour schemes, turquoise carpet and pale green walls or terracotta carpet with beige walls. There were steps up between the compartments, for the hull of the plane was curved, and the floor rose towards the rear. As he passed through he gave several friendly nods in the vague direction of the other passengers, as a wealthy and self-confident young American might do.

The fourth compartment had two small couches on one side, and on the other the Ladies' Powder Room – another fancy name for a carsey, no doubt. Beside the door to the ladies' room, a ladder on the wall led up to a trapdoor in the ceiling. The aisle, which ran the length of the plane, ended at a door. This must be the famous honeymoon suite that had caused so much press comment. Harry tried the door: it was locked.

Strolling back the length of the plane, he took another look at his fellow passengers.

He guessed that the man in smart French clothes was Baron Gabon. With him was a nervous fellow with no socks on. That was very peculiar. Perhaps he was Professor Hartmann. He wore a really terrible suit and looked half-starved.

Harry recognized Lulu Bell but was shocked to find that she looked about forty: he had imagined she was the age she appeared in her films, which was about nineteen. She was wearing a lot of good quality modern jewellery: rectangular earrings, big bracelets and a rock crystal brooch, probably by Boucheron.

He saw again the beautiful blonde he had noticed in the coffee lounge of the South-Western Hotel. She had taken off her straw hat. She had blue eyes and clear skin. She was laughing at something her companion was saying. She was obviously in love with him, even though he was not strikingly good-looking. But women like a man who makes them laugh, Harry thought.

The old duck with the Fabergé pendant in rose diamonds was presumably the Princess Lavinia. She wore a frozen expression of distaste, like a Baptist in a nightclub.

The larger compartment through which they had boarded had been empty during take-off but now, Harry observed, it was in use as a communal lounge. Four or five people had moved into it, including the tall man who had been seated opposite Harry. Some of the men were playing cards, and it crossed Harry's mind that a professional gambler might make a lot of money on a trip such as this.

He returned to his seat and the steward brought him his Scotch. 'The plane seems half empty,' Harry said.

Nicky shook his head. 'We're full up.'

Harry looked around. 'But there are four spare seats in this compartment, and all the others are the same.'

'Sure, this compartment seats ten on a daytime flight. But it only sleeps six. You'll see why when we make up the bunks after dinner. Meanwhile, enjoy the space.'

Harry sipped his drink. The steward was perfectly polite and efficient but not as obsequious as, say, a waiter in a London hotel. Harry wondered whether American waiters had a different attitude. He hoped so. On his expeditions into the strange world of London's high society, he had always found it a bit degrading to be bowed and scraped to and called 'sir' every time he turned round.

It was time to further his friendship with Margaret Oxenford, who was sipping a glass of champagne and leafing through a magazine. He had flirted with dozens of girls of her age and social station, and he went into his routine automatically. 'Do you live in London?'

'We've got a house in Eaton Square, but we spend most of our time in the country,' she said. 'Our place is in Berkshire. Father also has a shooting lodge in Scotland.' Her tone was rather too matter-of-fact, as if she found the question boring and wanted to dispose of it as quickly as possible.

'Do you hunt?' Harry said. This was a standard conversational ploy: most rich people did, and they loved to talk about it.

'Not much,' she said. 'We shoot more.'

'Do *you* shoot?' he asked in surprise: it was not considered a ladylike pursuit.

'When they let me.'

'I suppose you have lots of admirers.'

She turned to face him and lowered her voice. 'Why are you asking me all these stupid questions?'

Harry was floored. He hardly knew what to say. He had asked dozens of girls the same questions and none of them had reacted this way. 'Are they stupid?' he fumbled.

'You don't care where I live or whether I hunt.'

'But that's what people talk about in high society.'

'But you're not in high society,' she said bluntly.

'Stone the crows!' he exclaimed in his natural accent. 'You don't beat about the bush, do you?'

She laughed. 'That's better.'

'I can't keep changing my accent, I'll get confused.'

'All right. I'll put up with your American accent if you promise not to make silly small talk.'

'Thanks, honey,' he said, reverting to the role of Harry Vandenpost. She's no pushover, he was thinking. She was a girl who knew her own mind, all right. But that made her a lot more interesting.

'You're very good at it,' she was saying. 'I would never have guessed you were faking it. I suppose it's part of your *modus operandi*.'

They always baffled him when they spoke Latin. 'I guess it is,' he said without having the faintest idea what she meant. He would have to change the subject. He wondered what was the way to her heart. It was clear that he could not flirt with her the way he had with all the others. Perhaps she was the psychic type, interested in seances and necromancy. 'Do you believe in ghosts?' he tried.

That drew another sharp response. 'What do you take me for?' she said crossly. 'And why do you have to change the subject?'

He would have laughed it off with any other girl, but for some reason Margaret got to him. 'Because I don't speak Latin,' he snapped.

'What on earth are you talking about?'

'I don't understand words like *modus andy*.'

She looked mystified and irritated for a moment, then her face cleared and she repeated the phrase. '*Modus operandi*.'

'I never stayed at school long enough to learn that stuff,' he said.

The effect on her was quite startling. She flushed with shame and said, 'I'm most dreadfully sorry. How rude of me.'

He was surprised by the turnaround. A lot of them seemed to feel it was their duty to stuff their education down a man's throat. He was glad that Margaret had better manners than most of her kind. He smiled at her and said, 'All forgiven.'

She surprised him yet again by saying, 'I know how it feels, because I've never had a proper education either.'

'With all your money?' he said incredulously.

She nodded. 'We never went to school, you see.'

Harry was amazed. For respectable working-class Londoners it was shameful not to send your children to school, almost as bad as having the police round or being turned out by the bailiffs. Most children had to take a day off when their boots were at the mender's, for they did not have a spare pair, and mothers were embarrassed enough about that. 'But children have to go to school – it's the law!' said Harry.

'We had these stupid governesses. That's why I can't go to university – no qualifications.' She looked sad. 'I think I should have liked university.'

'It's unbelievable. I thought rich people could do anything they liked.'

'Not with my father.'

'What about the kid?' Harry nodded at Percy.

'Oh, he's at Eton, of course,' she said bitterly. 'It's different for boys.'

Harry considered. 'Does that mean,' he said diffidently, 'that you don't agree with your father in other things – politics, for instance?'

'I certainly don't,' she said fiercely. 'I'm a socialist.'

This, Harry thought, could be the key to her. 'I used to belong to the Communist Party,' he said. It was true: he had joined when he was sixteen and left after three weeks. He waited for her reaction before deciding how much to tell her.

She immediately became animated. 'Why did you leave?'

The truth was that political meetings bored him stiff, but it might be a mistake to say so. 'It's hard to put into words, exactly,' he prevaricated.

He should have known that would not wash with her. 'You must know why you left,' she said impatiently.

'I guess it was too much like Sunday School.'

She laughed at that. 'I know just what you mean.'

'Anyway, I reckon I've done more than the Commies in the way of returning wealth to the workers who produced it.'

'How is that?'

'Well, I liberate cash from Mayfair and take it to Battersea.'

'You mean you only rob the rich?'

'There's no point in robbing the poor, they haven't got any money.'

She laughed again. 'But surely you don't give away your ill-gotten gains, like Robin Hood?'

He considered what to tell her. Would she believe him if he pretended he robbed the rich to give to the poor? Although she was intelligent, she was also naïve –

but, he decided, not that naïve. 'I'm not a charity,' he said with a shrug. 'But I do help people sometimes.'

'This is amazing,' she said. Her eyes sparkled with interest and animation, and she looked quite ravishing. 'I suppose I knew there were people like you, but it's just extraordinary to actually meet you and talk to you.'

Don't overdo it, girl, Harry thought. He was nervous of women who became too enthusiastic about him: they were liable to feel outraged when they found out he was human. 'I'm not that special,' he said. 'I just come from a world you've never seen.'

She gave him a look that said she thought he *was* special.

This had gone far enough, he decided. It was time to change the subject. 'You're embarrassing me,' he said bashfully.

'I'm sorry,' she said quickly. She thought for a moment then added, 'Why are you going to America?'

'To get away from Rebecca Maugham-Flint.'

She laughed. 'No, seriously.'

She was like a terrier when she got hold of something, he thought: she wouldn't let go. She was impossible to control, which made her dangerous. 'I had to leave to stay out of jail,' he said.

'What will you do when you get there?'

'I thought I might join the Canadian Air Force. I'd like to learn to fly.'

'How exciting.'

'What about you? Why are you going to America?'

'We're running away,' she said disgustedly.

'What do you mean?'

'You know that my father is a Fascist?'

Harry nodded. 'I've read about him in the papers.'

'Well, he thinks the Nazis are wonderful and he doesn't want to fight against them. Besides, the government would put him in jail if he stayed.'

'So you're going to live in America?'

'My mother's family come from Connecticut.'

'And how long will you be there?'

'My parents are going to stay at least for the duration of the war. They may never come back.'

'But you don't want to go?'

'Certainly not,' she said forcefully. 'I want to stay and fight. Fascism is the most frightful wickedness and this war is dreadfully important, and I want to do my bit.' She started to talk about the Spanish Civil War but Harry was only half listening. He had been struck by a thought so shocking that his heart was beating faster and he had to make an effort to keep a normal expression on his face.

When people flee a country at the outbreak of war, they do not leave their valuables behind.

It was quite simple. Peasants would drive their livestock before them as they ran from invading armies. Jews fled from the Nazis with gold coins sewn inside their coats. After 1917, Russian aristocrats such as Princess Lavinia arrived in all the capitals of Europe clutching their Fabergé eggs.

Lord Oxenford must have considered the possibility that he would never return. Moreover, the government had brought in exchange controls to prevent the British upper classes from transferring all their money abroad.

The Oxenfords knew they might never again see what they left behind. It was certain they had brought whatever assets they could carry.

It was a little risky, of course, carrying a fortune in jewellery in your luggage. But what would be less risky? Mailing it? Sending it by courier? Leaving it behind, possibly to be confiscated by a vengeful government, looted by an invading army, or even 'liberated' in a post-war revolution?

No. The Oxenfords would have their jewellery with them.

In particular, they would be carrying the Delhi Suite.

The very thought of it took his breath away.

The Delhi Suite was the centrepiece of Lady Oxenford's famous collection of antique jewellery. Made of rubies and diamonds in gold settings, it consisted of a necklace with matching earrings and a bracelet. The rubies were Burmese, the most precious kind, and huge: they had been brought to England in the eighteenth century by the general Robert Clive, known as Clive of India, and set by the Crown jewellers.

The Delhi Suite was said to be worth a quarter of a million pounds – more money than a man could ever spend.

And it was almost certainly on this plane.

No professional thief would steal while travelling on a ship or plane: the list of suspects was too short. Furthermore, Harry was impersonating an American, travelling on a false passport, jumping bail and sitting opposite a policeman. It would be madness to try to get his hands on the suite, and he felt shaky just at the thought of the risks involved.

On the other hand, he would never have another chance like this. And suddenly he needed those jewels the way a drowning man gasps for air.

He would not be able to sell the suite for a quarter of a million, of course. But he would get about a tenth of its value, say twenty-five thousand pounds, which was more than a hundred thousand dollars.

In either currency it was enough for him to live on for the rest of his life.

The thought of that much money made his mouth water – but the jewellery itself was irresistible. Harry had seen pictures of it. The graduated stones of the necklace were perfectly matched; the diamonds set off the rubies like teardrops on a baby's cheek; and the smaller pieces, the earrings and the bracelet, were perfectly proportioned. The whole ensemble, on the neck, ears and wrist of a beautiful woman, would be utterly ravishing.

Harry knew he would never again be this close to such a masterpiece. Never.

He had to steal it.

The risks were appalling – but then, he had always been lucky.

'I don't believe you're listening to me,' Margaret said.

Harry grinned. 'I'm sorry. Something you said sent me into a daydream.'

'I know,' she said. 'From the look on your face, you were dreaming about someone you love.'

CHAPTER EIGHT

Nancy Lenehan waited in a fever of impatience while Mervyn Lovesey's pretty yellow aeroplane was readied for take-off. He was giving last-minute instructions to the man in the tweed suit, who seemed to be the foreman of a factory he owned. Nancy gathered that he had union trouble and a strike was threatened.

When he had finished he turned to Nancy and said, 'I employ seventeen toolmakers and every one of them's a ruddy individualist.'

'What do you make?' she asked.

'Fans,' he replied. He pointed at the plane. 'Aircraft propellers, screws for ships, that kind of thing. Anything that has complex curves. But the engineering is the easy part. It's the human factor that gives me grief.' He smiled condescendingly and added, 'Still, you're not interested in industrial problems.'

'But I am,' she said. 'I run a factory too.'

He was taken aback. 'What kind?'

'I make five thousand seven hundred pairs of shoes a day.'

He was impressed, but he also seemed to feel he had been trumped, for he said, 'Good for you,' in a tone that mixed mockery with admiration. Nancy guessed that his business was much smaller than hers.

'Maybe I ought to say I *used* to make shoes,' she said, and the taste of bile was in her mouth as she admitted it. 'My brother is trying to sell the business out from under my feet. That', she added with an anxious look at the plane, 'is why I have to catch the Clipper.'

'You will,' he said confidently. 'My Tiger Moth will get us there with an hour to spare.'

She hoped with all her heart that he was right.

The mechanic jumped down from the plane. 'All set, Mr Lovesey.'

Lovesey looked at Nancy. 'Fetch her a helmet,' he said to the mechanic. 'She can't fly in that bloody silly little hat.'

Nancy was taken aback by the sudden reversion to his previous offhand manner. Clearly, he was happy enough to talk to her while there was nothing else to do but as soon as something important cropped up he lost interest. She was not used to such a casual attitude from men. Although not the seductive type, she was attractive enough to catch a man's eye and she carried a certain authority. Men patronized her often enough, but they rarely treated her with Lovesey's insouciance. However, she was not going to protest. She would put up with a lot worse than rudeness for the chance of catching up with her treacherous brother.

She was mightily curious about his marriage. 'I'm chasing my wife,' he had said, a surprisingly candid admission. She could see why a woman would run away from him. He was terribly good-looking, but he was also

213

self-absorbed and insensitive. That was why it was so odd that he was running after his wife. He seemed the type who would be too proud. Nancy would have guessed he would say, 'Let her go to hell.' Perhaps she had misjudged him.

She wondered what the wife was like. Would she be pretty? Sexy? Selfish and spoilt? A frightened mouse? Nancy would find out soon – if they could catch up with the Clipper.

The mechanic brought her a helmet and she put it on. Lovesey climbed aboard, shouting over his shoulder, 'Give her a leg up, will you?'

The mechanic, more courteous than his master, helped her put on her coat, saying, 'It's chilly up there, even when the sun shines.' Then he hoisted her up and she clambered into the back seat. He passed her overnight case to her and she stowed it under her feet.

As the engine turned over she realized, with a shiver of nervousness, that she was about to take to the air with a total stranger.

For all she knew, Mervyn Lovesey might be a completely incompetent pilot, inadequately trained, with a poorly maintained plane. He could even be a white slaver, intent on selling her into a Turkish brothel. No, she was too old for that. But she had no reason to trust him. All she knew was that he was an Englishman with an aeroplane.

Nancy had flown three times before but always in larger planes with enclosed cabins. She had never experienced an old-fashioned biplane. It was like taking off in an open-top car. They sped down the runway with the roar of the engine in their ears and the wind buffeting their helmets.

The passenger aircraft Nancy had flown in seemed to ease gently into the air, but this went up with a jump, like a racehorse taking a fence. Then Lovesey banked so steeply that Nancy held on tight, terrified she would fall out despite her safety belt. Did he even have a pilot's licence?

He straightened up and the little plane climbed rapidly. Its flight seemed more comprehensible, less miraculous, than that of a big passenger aircraft. She could see the wings and breathe the wind and hear the howl of the little engine, and she could *feel* how it stayed aloft, feel the propeller pumping air and the wind lifting the broad fabric wings, the way you could feel a kite riding the wind when you held its string. There was no such sensation in an enclosed plane.

However, being in touch with the little plane's struggle to fly also gave her an uneasy sensation in the pit of her stomach. The wings were only flimsy things of wood and canvas; the propeller could get stuck, or break, or fall off; the helpful wind might change faithlessly and turn against them; there might be fog, or lightning, or hailstorms.

But all that seemed unlikely as the plane rose into the sunshine and turned its nose bravely towards Ireland. Nancy felt as if she were riding on the back of a big yellow dragonfly. It was scary but exhilarating, like a fairground ride.

They soon left the coast of England behind. She allowed herself a small moment of triumph as they headed west over the water. Peter would be boarding the Clipper soon and, as he did so, would congratulate himself on having outwitted his clever older sister. But his jubilation would be premature, she thought with angry satisfaction. He had not got the best of her yet. He would get a tremendous shock when he saw her arrive in Foynes. She could hardly wait to see the look on his face.

She still had a fight ahead, of course, even after she had caught up with Peter. She would not defeat him just by appearing at the board meeting. She would have to convince Aunt Tilly and Danny Riley that they would do better to hold on to their shares and stick with her.

She wanted to expose Peter's vicious behaviour to them all, so that they would know how he had lied to his sister and plotted against her; she wanted to crush him and mortify him by showing them all what a snake he was. But a moment's reflection told her that was not the smart thing to do. If she let her fury and resentment show, they would think she was opposing the merger for purely emotional reasons. She had to talk coolly and calmly about the prospects for the future, and act as if her disagreement with Peter was merely a business matter. They all knew she was a better manager than her brother.

Anyway, her argument made simple sense. The price they were being offered for their shares was based on Black's profits, which were low because of Peter's bad management. Nancy guessed they could make more by closing down the company and selling off all the shops.

But best of all would be to restructure the company according to her plan and make it profitable again.

There was another reason for waiting: the war. War was good for business in general and especially for companies such as Black's that supplied to the military. The US might not get into the war but there was sure to be a precautionary build-up. So profits were set to rise anyway. No doubt that was why Nat Ridgeway wanted to buy the company.

She brooded over the situation as they crossed the Irish Sea, blocking out her speech in her head. She rehearsed key lines and phrases, speaking them out loud, confident that the wind would whip the words away before they could reach the helmeted ears of Mervyn Lovesey a yard in front of her.

She became so absorbed in her speech that she hardly noticed the first time the engine faltered.

'The war in Europe will double this company's value in twelve months,' she was saying. 'If the US gets into the war, the price will double again—'

The second time it happened Nancy snapped out of her reverie. The continuous high roar altered momentarily, like the sound of a tap with air trapped in the pipe. It recovered to normal, then changed again and settled into a different note, a ragged, altogether feebler sound that unnerved her.

The plane began to lose height.

'What's going on?' she yelled at the top of her voice, but there was no response. Either he could not hear her or he was too busy to reply.

217

The engine note changed again, mounting higher, as if he had stepped on the gas, and the plane levelled out.

Nancy was agitated. What was happening? Was the problem serious or not? She wished she could just see his face, but it remained resolutely turned forward.

The engine sound was no longer constant. Sometimes it seemed to recover to its previous full-throated roar; then it would quaver again and become uneven. Scared, Nancy peered forward, trying to discern some change in the spin of the propeller, but she could see none. However, each time the engine stuttered the plane lost a little height.

She could not stand the tension any longer. She unbuckled her safety belt, leaned forward, and tapped Lovesey's shoulder. He turned his head to one side and she shouted in his ear, 'What's wrong?'

'Don't know!' he yelled back.

She was too frightened to accept that. 'What's happening?' she persisted.

'Engine's missing on one cylinder, I think.'

'Well, how many cylinders has it got?'

'Four.'

The plane suddenly lurched lower. Nancy hastily sat back and buckled up. She was a car driver and had a notion that a car could keep going with one cylinder missing. However, her Cadillac had twelve. Could a plane fly on three out of four cylinders? The uncertainty was torture.

They were losing height steadily now. Nancy guessed the plane could fly on three cylinders, but not for long.

How soon would they fall into the sea? She gazed into the distance and, to her relief, saw land ahead. Unable to restrain herself, she undid her belt and spoke to Lovesey again. 'Can we reach the land?'

'Don't know!' he shouted.

'You don't know anything!' she yelled. Fear turned her shout into a scream. She forced herself to be calm again. 'What's your best estimate?'

'Shut your mouth and let me concentrate!'

She sat back again. I may die now, she thought, and once again she fought down the panic and made herself think calmly. It's lucky I raised my boys before this happened, she told herself. It will be hard for them, especially after losing their father in a car crash. But they're men, big and strong, and they'll never lack for money. They'll be okay.

I wish I'd had another lover. It's been . . . how long? Ten years! No wonder I'm getting used to it. I might as well be a nun. I should have gone to bed with Nat Ridgeway: he would have been nice.

She had had a couple of dates with a new man, just before leaving for Europe, an unmarried accountant of about her own age, but she did not wish she had gone to bed with him. He was kind but weak, like too many of the men she met. They saw her as strong and they wanted her to take care of them. But I want someone to take care of me! she thought.

If I survive this I'm going to make damn sure I have one more lover before I die.

Peter would win now. That was a damn shame. The business was all that was left of their father and now it would be absorbed and disappear into the amorphous mass of General Textiles. Pa had worked hard all his life to build that company and Peter had destroyed it in five idle, selfish years.

Sometimes she still missed her father. He had been such a clever man. When there was a problem, whether it was a major business crisis such as the depression or a little family matter like one of the boys doing poorly at school, Pa would come up with a positive, hopeful way of dealing with it. He had been very good with mechanical things, and the people who manufactured the big machines used in shoemaking would often consult him before finalizing a design. Nancy understood the production process perfectly well, but her expertise was in predicting what styles the market wanted, and since she took over the factory they had made more profit from women's shoes than men's. She never felt overshadowed by her father, the way Peter did; she just missed him.

Suddenly the thought that she would die seemed ridiculous and unreal. It would be like the curtain coming down before the play ended, when the leading actor was in the middle of a speech: that was simply not how things happened. For a while she felt irrationally cheerful, confident that she would live.

The plane continued to lose height, but the coast of Ireland came rapidly nearer. Soon she could see emerald fields and brown bogs. This is where the Black family originated, she thought with a little thrill.

Immediately in front of her, Mervyn Lovesey's head and shoulders began to move, as if he was struggling with the controls. Nancy's mood switched again, and she started to pray. She had been raised Catholic but she had not gone to mass since Sean was killed; in fact, the last time she had been inside a church had been his funeral. She did not really know whether she was a believer or not, but now she prayed hard, figuring that she had nothing to lose, anyway. She said the Our Father, then she asked God to save her so that she could be around for Hugh at least until he got married and settled down; and so that she might see her grandchildren; and because she wanted to turn the business around and continue to employ all those men and women and make good shoes for ordinary people; and because she wanted a little happiness for herself. Her life, she felt suddenly, had been all work for too long.

She could see the white tops of the waves now. The blur of the approaching coastline resolved into surf, beach, cliff and green field. She wondered, with a shiver of fear, whether she would be able to swim to shore if the plane came down in the water. She thought of herself as a strong swimmer but stroking happily up and down a pool was very different from surviving in the turbulent sea. The water would be bone-chillingly cold. What was the word used when people died of cold? Exposure. 'Mrs Lenehan's plane came down in the Irish Sea and she died of exposure', the Boston *Globe* would say. She shivered inside her cashmere coat.

If the plane crashed she probably would not live to feel the temperature of the water. She wondered how fast it was travelling. It cruised at about ninety miles per hour, Lovesey had told her, but it was losing speed now. Say it was down to fifty. Sean had crashed at fifty and he had died. No, there was no point in speculating how far she could swim.

The shore came nearer. Perhaps her prayers had been answered, she thought. Perhaps the plane would make landfall after all. There had been no further deterioration in the engine sound: it went on at the same high, ragged roar, with an angry tone, like the vengeful buzzing of a wounded wasp. Now she began to worry about where they would land if they did make it. Could a plane come down on a sandy beach? What about a pebble beach? A plane could land in a field, if it were not too rough, but what about a peat bog?

She would know only too soon.

The coast was now about a quarter of a mile away. She could see that the shoreline was rocky and the surf heavy. The beach looked awfully uneven, she saw with a sinking heart: it was littered with jagged boulders. There was a low cliff rising to a stretch of moorland with a few grazing sheep. She studied the moorland. It looked smooth, with no hedges and few trees. Perhaps the plane could land there. She did not know whether to hope for that or try to prepare herself for death.

The yellow plane struggled bravely on, still losing height. The salty smell of the sea reached Nancy's nose. It would surely be better to come down on the water, she thought fearfully, than to try to land on that beach. Those sharp stones would tear the flimsy little plane to pieces – and her, too.

She hoped she would die quickly.

When the shore was a hundred yards away she saw that the plane was not going to hit the beach: it was still too high. Lovesey was obviously aiming at the clifftop pasture. But would he get there? They now seemed almost on a level with the cliff top, and they were still losing height. They were going to smash into the cliff. She wanted to close her eyes but she did not dare. Instead she stared hypnotically at the cliff rushing at her.

The engine howled like a sick animal. The wind blew sea spray into Nancy's face. The sheep on the cliff were scattering in all directions as the plane zoomed at them. Nancy gripped the rim of the cockpit so hard her hands hurt. She seemed to be flying straight at the very lip of the cliff. It came at her in a rush. We're going to hit it, she thought; this is the end. Then a gust of wind lifted the plane a fraction, and she thought they were clear. But it dropped again. The cliff edge was going to knock the little yellow wheels off their struts, she thought. Then, with the cliff a split second away, she closed her eyes and screamed.

For a moment nothing happened.

Then there was a bump, and Nancy was thrown forward hard against her seat belt. For an instant she thought she was going to die. Then she felt the plane rise again. She stopped screaming and opened her eyes.

They were in the air still, just two or three feet above the clifftop grass. The plane bumped down again, and this time it stayed down. Nancy was shaken mercilessly as it juddered over the uneven ground. She saw that they were headed for a patch of bramble and they could yet crash. Then Lovesey did something and the plane turned, avoiding the hazard. The shaking eased; they were slowing down. Nancy could hardly believe she was still alive. The plane came unsteadily to a halt.

Relief shook her like a fit. She could not stop trembling. For a moment she let herself shudder. Then she felt hysteria coming on and took a grip on herself. 'It's over,' she said aloud. 'It's over, it's over, I'm all right.'

In front of her, Lovesey got up and climbed out of his seat with a toolbox in his hand. Without looking at her, he jumped down and walked round to the front of the aircraft where he opened the hood and peered in at the engine.

He might have asked me if I'm all right, Nancy thought.

In an odd way, Lovesey's rudeness calmed her. She looked around. The sheep had returned to their grazing as if nothing had happened. Now that the engine was silent, she could hear the waves exploding on the beach. The sun was shining, but she could feel a cold, damp wind on her cheek.

She sat still for a moment, then, when she was sure her legs would hold her, she stood up and clambered out of the aircraft. She stood on Irish soil for the first time in her life and felt moved almost to tears. This is where we came from, she thought, all those years ago. Oppressed by the British, persecuted by the Protestants, starved by potato blight, we crowded into wooden ships and sailed away from our homeland to a new world.

And a very Irish way this is to come back, she thought with a grin. I almost died landing here.

That was enough sentiment. She was alive, so could she still catch the Clipper? She looked at her wristwatch. It was two-fifteen. The Clipper had just taken off from Southampton. She could get to Foynes in time, if this plane could be made to fly, and if she could summon up the nerve to get back into it.

She walked around to the front of the plane. Lovesey was using a big spanner to loosen a nut. Nancy said, 'Can you fix it?'

He did not look up. 'Don't know.'

'What's the problem?'

'Don't know.'

Clearly he had reverted to his taciturn mood. Exasperated, Nancy said, 'I thought you were supposed to be an engineer.'

That stung him. He looked at her and said, 'I studied mathematics and physics. My speciality is wind resistance of complex curves. I'm not a bloody motor mechanic!'

'Then maybe we should fetch a motor mechanic.'

'You won't find one in bloody Ireland. This country is still in the Stone Age.'

'Only because the people have been trodden down by the brutal British for so many centuries!'

He withdrew his head from the engine and stood upright. 'How the hell did we get on to politics?'

'You haven't even asked me if I'm all right.'

'I can see you're all right.'

'You nearly killed me!'

'I saved your life.'

The man was impossible.

She looked around the horizon. About a quarter of a mile away was a line of hedge or wall that might border a road, and a little farther she could see several low thatched roofs in a cluster. Maybe she could get a car and drive to Foynes. 'Where are we?' she said. 'And don't tell me you don't know!'

He grinned. It was the second or third time he had surprised her by not being as bad-tempered as he seemed. 'I think we're a few miles outside Dublin.'

She decided she was not going to stand there and watch him fiddle with the engine. 'I'm going to get help.'

He looked at her feet. 'You won't get far in those shoes.'

I'll show him something, she thought angrily. She lifted her skirt and quickly unfastened her stockings. He stared at her, shocked, and blushed crimson. She rolled her stockings down and took them off along with her shoes. She enjoyed discomposing him. Tucking her shoes into the pockets of her coat, she said, 'I shan't be long,' and walked off barefoot.

When her back was turned and she was a few yards away she permitted herself a broad grin. He had been completely nonplussed. It served him right for being so goddamn condescending.

The pleasure of having bested him soon wore off. Her feet rapidly became wet, cold and filthy dirty. The cottages were farther away than she had thought. She did not even know what she was going to do when she got there. She guessed she would try to get a ride into Dublin. Lovesey was probably right about the scarcity of motor mechanics in Ireland.

It took her twenty minutes to reach the first house. Behind it she found a small woman in clogs digging in a vegetable garden. Nancy called out, 'Hello.'

The woman looked up and gave a cry of fright.

Nancy said, 'There's something wrong with my airplane.'

The woman stared at her as if she had come from outer space.

Nancy realized that she must be a somewhat unusual sight, in a cashmere coat and bare feet. Indeed, a creature from outer space would be hardly less surprising, to a peasant woman digging her garden, than a woman in an aeroplane. The woman reached out a tentative hand and touched Nancy's coat. Nancy was embarrassed: the woman was treating her like a goddess.

'I'm Irish,' Nancy said, in an effort to make herself seem more human.

The woman smiled and shook her head, as if to say, 'You can't fool me.'

'I need a ride to Dublin,' Nancy said.

That made sense to the woman, and she spoke at last. 'Oh, yes, you do!' she said. Clearly she felt that apparitions such as Nancy belonged in the big city.

Nancy was relieved to hear her use English: she had

been afraid the woman might speak only Gaelic. 'How far is it?'

'You could get there in an hour and a half, if you had a decent pony,' the woman said in a musical lilt.

That was no good. In two hours the Clipper was due to take off from Foynes, on the other side of the country. 'Does anyone around here have an automobile?'

'No '

'Damn.'

'But the smith has a motorcycle.' She pronounced it 'motor sickle'.

'That'll do!' In Dublin she might get a car to take her to Foynes. She was not sure how far Foynes was, or how long it would take to get there, but she felt she had to try. 'Where's the smith?'

'I'll take you.' The woman stuck her spade in the ground.

Nancy followed her round the house. The road was just a mud track, Nancy saw with a sinking heart: a motorcycle could not go much faster than a pony on such a surface.

Another snag occurred to her as they walked through the hamlet. A motorcycle would take only one passenger. She had been planning to go back to the downed plane and pick up Lovesey, if she could get a car. But only one of them could be taken on a bike – unless the owner would sell it, in which case Lovesey could drive and Nancy could ride. Then, she thought excitedly, they could drive all the way to Foynes.

They walked to the last house and approached a lean-to workshop at the side. Nancy's high hopes were dashed instantly: the motorcycle was in pieces all over the earth floor and the blacksmith was working on it. 'Oh, hell,' Nancy said.

The woman spoke to the smith in Gaelic. He looked at Nancy with a trace of amusement. He was very young, with the Irish black hair and blue eyes, and he had a bushy moustache. He nodded, then said to Nancy, 'Where's your aeroplane?'

'About half a mile away.'

'Maybe I should take a look.'

'Do you know anything about planes?' she said sceptically.

He shrugged. 'Engines are engines.'

If he could take a motorcycle to pieces he might be able to fix an aero-engine.

The smith went on, 'However, it sounds to me as if I might be too late.'

Nancy frowned, then she heard what he had noticed: the sound of an airplane. Could it be the Tiger Moth? She ran outside and looked up into the sky. Sure enough, the little yellow plane was flying low over the hamlet.

Lovesey had fixed it – and he had taken off without waiting for her!

She gazed up unbelievingly. How could he do this to her? He even had her overnight case!

The plane swooped low over the hamlet, as if to mock her. She shook her fist at it. Lovesey waved to her and then climbed away.

She watched the plane recede. The smith and the peasant woman were standing beside her. 'He's leaving without you,' the smith said.

'He's a heartless fiend.'

'Is it your husband?'

'Certainly not!'

'Just as well, I suppose.'

Nancy felt sick. Two men had betrayed her today. Was there something wrong with her? she wondered.

She thought she might as well give up. She could not catch the Clipper now. Peter would sell the company to Nat Ridgeway and that would be the end of it.

The plane banked and turned. Lovesey was setting course for Foynes, she presumed. He would catch up with his runaway wife. Nancy hoped she would refuse to go back to him.

Unexpectedly, the plane kept on turning. When it was pointing towards the hamlet it straightened up. What was he doing now?

It came in along the line of the mud road, losing height. Why was he coming back? As the plane approached, Nancy began to wonder whether he was going to land. Was the engine faltering again?

The little plane touched down on the mud road and bounced along towards the three people outside the blacksmith's house.

Nancy almost fainted with relief. He had come back for her!

The plane juddered to a halt. Mervyn shouted something she could not make out. 'What?' she yelled.

Impatiently, he beckoned to her. She ran up to the

plane. He leaned towards her and shouted, 'What are you waiting for? Get in!'

She looked at her watch. It was a quarter to three. They could still make it to Foynes in time. Her spirits bounded with optimism again. I'm not finished yet! she thought.

The young blacksmith came up with a twinkle in his eye and shouted, 'Let me help you up.' He made a step with his linked hands. She put her muddy bare foot on it and he boosted her up. She scrambled into her seat.

The plane pulled away immediately.

A few seconds later they were in the air.

CHAPTER NINE

MERVYN LOVESEY'S wife was very happy.

Diana had been frightened when the Clipper took off, but now she felt nothing but elation.

She had not flown before. Mervyn had never invited her to go up in his little plane, even though she had spent days painting it a lovely bright yellow for him. She discovered that, once you got over the nervousness, it was a terrific thrill to be this high in the air in something like a first-class hotel with wings, looking down on England's pastures and cornfields, roads and railways, houses and churches and factories. She felt free. She was free. She had left Mervyn and run away with Mark.

Last night, at the South-Western Hotel in Southampton, they had registered as Mr and Mrs Alder and had spent their first whole night together. They had made love, then gone to sleep, then woken up in the morning and made love again. It seemed such a luxury, after three months of short afternoons and snatched kisses.

Flying the Clipper was like living in a movie. The décor was opulent, the people were elegant, the two stewards were quietly efficient, everything happened on cue as if it were scripted, and there were famous faces everywhere. There was Baron Gabon, the wealthy Zionist, always in intense discussion with his haggard companion. The Marquess of Oxenford, the famous Fascist, was on board with his beautiful wife. Princess Lavinia Bazarov, one of the pillars of Paris society, was in Diana's compartment in the window seat of Diana's divan.

Opposite the princess, in the other window seat on this side, was the movie star Lulu Bell. Diana had seen her in lots of films: *My Cousin Jake, Torment, The Secret Life, Helen of Troy* and many others had come to the Paramount Cinema in Oxford Street, Manchester. But the biggest surprise was that Mark knew her. As they were settling into their seats, a strident American voice had called out, 'Mark! Mark Alder! Is that really you?' and Diana had turned round to see a small blonde woman like a canary swooping on him.

It turned out they had worked together on a radio show in Chicago years ago, before Lulu was a big star. Mark had introduced Diana, and Lulu had been very sweet, saying how beautiful Diana was and how lucky Mark had been to find her. But naturally she was more interested in Mark, and the two of them had been chatting ever since take-off, reminiscing about the old days when they were young and short of money and lived in flophouses and stayed up all night drinking bootleg liquor.

Diana was surprised that Lulu was so short. In her films she seemed taller. Also younger. And in real life you could see that her hair was not naturally blonde, as

Diana's was, but dyed. However, she did have the chirpy, pushy personality she displayed in most of the movies. She was the centre of attention even now. Although she was talking to Mark, everyone was looking at her: Princess Lavinia in the corner, Diana opposite Mark, and the two men on the other side of the aisle.

She was telling a story about a radio broadcast during which one of the actors had left, thinking his part was over, when in fact he had one line to speak right at the end. 'So I said my line, which was: "Who ate the Easter cake?" And everybody looked around – but George had disappeared! And there was a *long* silence.' She paused for dramatic effect. Diana smiled. What on earth *did* people do when things went wrong during radio shows? She listened to the radio a lot but she could not remember anything like this happening. Lulu resumed. 'So I said my line again: "Who ate the Easter cake?" Then I went like this.' She lowered her chin and spoke in an astonishingly convincing gruff male voice. '"I think it must have been the cat."'

Everyone laughed.

'And that was the end of the show,' she finished.

Diana remembered a broadcast during which an announcer had been so shocked at something that he said, 'Jesus H. Christ!' in astonishment. 'I heard an announcer swear once,' she said.

She was about to tell the story, but Mark said, 'Oh, that happens all the time,' and turned back to Lulu, saying, 'Remember when Max Gifford said Babe Ruth had clean balls, and then couldn't stop laughing?'

Both Mark and Lulu giggled helplessly over that and

Diana smiled, but she was beginning to feel left out. She reflected that she was rather spoilt: for three months, while Mark had been alone in a strange town, she had had his undivided attention. Obviously that could not go on for ever. She would have to get used to sharing him with other people from now on. However, she did not have to play the part of audience. She turned to Princess Lavinia, sitting on her right, and said, 'Do you listen to the wireless, Princess?'

The old Russian woman looked down her thin, beaked nose and replied, 'I find it slightly vulgar.'

Diana had met sniffy old ladies before, and they did not intimidate her. 'How surprising,' she said. 'Only last night we tuned in to some Beethoven quintets.'

'German music is so mechanical,' the Princess returned.

There would be no pleasing her, Diana decided. She had once belonged to the most idle and privileged class the world had ever seen and she wanted everyone to know it, so she pretended that everything she was offered was not as good as what she had once been used to. She was going to be a bore.

The steward assigned to the rear half of the aircraft, whose name was Davy, arrived to take orders for cocktails. He was a small, neat, charming young man with fair hair, and he walked the carpeted aisle with a bouncy step. Diana asked for a dry martini. She did not know what it was, but she remembered from the movies that it was a chic drink in America.

She studied the two men on the other side of the compartment. They were both looking out of the windows. Nearest her was a handsome young man in a rather flashy suit. He was broad-shouldered, like an athlete, and wore several rings. His dark colouring led Diana to wonder whether he was South American. Opposite him was a man who looked rather out of place. His suit was too big and his shirt collar was worn. He did not look as if he could afford the price of a Clipper ticket. He was also as bald as a light bulb. The two men did not speak or look at one another but Diana was sure they were together.

She wondered what Mervyn was doing right now. He had almost certainly read her note. He might be crying, she thought guiltily. No, that was not like him. He was more likely to be raging. But who would he rage at? His poor employees, perhaps. She wished her note had been kinder, or at least more enlightening, but she had been too distraught to do better. He would probably phone her sister Thea, she guessed. He would think Thea might know where she had gone. Well, Thea didn't. She would be shocked. What would she tell the twins? The thought upset Diana.

Davy came back with their drinks. Mark raised his glass to Lulu, and then to Diana – almost as an afterthought, she reflected sourly. She tasted her martini and nearly spat it out. 'Ugh!' she said. 'It tastes like neat gin!'

Everyone laughed at her. 'It is mostly gin, honey,' said Mark. 'Haven't you had a martini before?'

Diana felt humiliated. She had not known what she was ordering, like a schoolgirl in a bar. All these cosmopolitan people now thought she was an ignorant provincial.

Davy said, 'Let me bring you something else, ma'am.'

'A glass of champagne, then,' she said sulkily.

'Right away.'

Diana spoke crossly to Mark. 'I haven't had a martini before. I just thought I'd try it. There's nothing wrong with that, is there?'

'Of course not, honey,' he said, and patted her knee.

Princess Lavinia said, 'This brandy is disgusting, young man. Bring me some tea instead.'

'Right away, Your Highness.'

Diana decided to go to the ladies' room. She stood up, said 'Excuse me,' and went out through the arched doorway that led rearwards.

She passed through another passenger compartment just like the one she had left, then found herself at the back of the plane. On one side was a small compartment with just two people in it, and on the other side a door marked 'Ladies' Powder Room'. She went in.

The powder room cheered her up. It really was very pretty. There was a neat dressing-table with two stools upholstered in turquoise leather, and the walls were covered with beige fabric. Diana sat down to repair her make-up. Mark called it rewriting her face. Paper tissues and cold cream were laid out neatly in front of her.

But when she looked at herself she saw an unhappy woman. Lulu Bell had come like a cloud blocking the sun. She had taken Mark's attention away and made him treat Diana like a slight inconvenience. Of course,

Lulu was nearer to Mark's age: he was thirty-nine and she had to be past forty. Diana was only thirty-four. Did Mark know how old Lulu was? Men could be stupid about things like that.

The real trouble was that Lulu and Mark had so much in common: both in show business, both American, both veterans of the early days of radio. Diana had not done anything like that. If you wanted to be harsh, you could say that she had not done anything except be a socialite in a provincial city.

Would it always be this way with Mark? She was going to his country. From now on he would know everything, but all would be unfamiliar to her. They would be mixing with his friends, for she had none in America. How many more times would she be laughed at for not knowing what everyone else knew, like the fact that a dry martini tasted of nothing but cold gin?

She wondered how much she would miss the comfortable, predictable world she had left behind, the world of charity balls and Masonic dinners at Manchester hotels where she knew all the people and all the drinks and all the menus, too. It was dull, but it was safe.

She shook her head, making her hair fluff out prettily. She was not going to think like that. I was bored to distraction in that world, she thought; I longed for adventure and excitement; and now that I've got it, I'm going to enjoy it.

She decided to make a determined effort to win back Mark's attention. What could she do? She did not want to confront him directly and tell him she resented his behaviour. That seemed weak. Maybe a taste of his own medicine would do the trick. She could talk to someone else the way he was talking to Lulu. That might make him sit up and take notice. Who would it be? The handsome boy across the aisle would do just fine. He was younger than Mark, and bigger. That ought to make Mark jealous as hell.

She dabbed perfume behind her ears and between her breasts, then left the powder room. She swung her hips a little more than was necessary as she walked along the plane, and she took pleasure in the lustful stares of the men and the admiring or envious looks of the women. I'm the most beautiful woman on the plane and Lulu Bell knows it, she thought.

When she reached her compartment she did not take her seat, but turned to the left-hand side and looked out of the window over the shoulder of the young man in the striped suit. He gave her a good-to-see-you smile.

She smiled back and said, 'Isn't this wonderful?'

'Ain't it just?' he said; but she noticed he threw a wary glance at the man opposite, as if he expected a reprimand. It was almost as if the other man was his chaperon.

Diana said, 'Are you two together?'

The bald man answered curtly. 'You could say we're associates.' Then he seemed to remember his manners, and held out his hand, saying, 'Ollis Field.'

'Diana Lovesey.' She shook his hand reluctantly. He had dirty fingernails. She turned back to the younger man.

'Frank Gordon,' he said.

Both men were American, but all resemblance ended there. Frank Gordon was smartly dressed, with a pin through his collar and a silk handkerchief in his breast pocket. He smelled of cologne and his curly hair was lightly oiled. 'What part is this, that we're flying over – is this still England?' he asked.

Diana leaned over him and looked out of the window, letting him smell her perfume. 'I think that must be Devon,' she said, although she really did not know.

'What part are you from?' he said.

She sat down beside him. 'Manchester,' she said. She glanced over at Mark, caught his startled look, and returned her attention to Frank. 'That's in the north-west.'

Opposite, Ollis Field lit a cigarette with a disapproving air. Diana crossed her legs.

Frank said, 'My family come from Italy.'

The Italian government was Fascist. Diana said candidly, 'Do you think Italy will enter the war?'

Frank shook his head. 'Italian people don't want war.'

'I don't suppose anybody wants war.'

'So why does it happen?'

She found him difficult to make out. He obviously had money but he seemed uneducated. Most men were eager to explain things to her, to show off their knowledge, whether or not she wanted it. This one had no such impulse. She looked over at his companion and said, 'What do you think, Mr Field?'

'No opinion,' he said grumpily.

She turned back to the younger man. 'Perhaps war is the only way Fascist leaders can keep their people under control.'

She looked at Mark again, and was disappointed to see that once again he was deep in conversation with Lulu, and they were giggling together like school-children. She felt let down. What was the matter with him? Mervyn would have been ready to punch Frank's nose by now.

She looked back at Frank. The words on her lips were, 'Tell me all about yourself,' but suddenly she could not face the boredom of listening to his reply and she said nothing. At that point Davy brought her champagne and a plate of caviar on toast. She took the opportunity to return to her seat, feeling despondent.

She listened resentfully to Mark and Lulu for a while, then her thoughts drifted away. She was silly to get upset about Lulu. Mark was committed to her, Diana. He was just enjoying talking about old times. There was no point in Diana's worrying about America: the decision had been taken, the die was cast, Mervyn had read her note. It was stupid to start having second thoughts on account of a forty-five-year-old bottle-blonde such as Lulu. She would soon learn American ways, their drinks, their radio shows and their manners. Before long she would have more friends than Mark: she was like that, she attracted people to her.

She began to look forward to the long flight across the Atlantic. She had thought, when she read about the Clipper in the *Manchester Guardian*, that it sounded like

the most romantic journey in the world. From Ireland
to Newfoundland was almost two thousand miles, and
it took for ever, something like seventeen hours. There
was time to have dinner, and go to bed, and sleep all
night and get up again, before the plane landed. The
idea of wearing the nightclothes that she had worn
with Mervyn had seemed wrong but she had not had
time to shop for the trip. Fortunately she had a beautiful *café-au-lait* silk robe and salmon-pink pyjamas which
she had never worn. There were no double beds, not
even in the honeymoon suite – Mark had checked –
but his bunk would be over hers. It was thrilling,
and at the same time frightening, to think of going to
bed high over the ocean and flying on, hour after
hour, hundreds of miles from land. She wondered if
she would be able to sleep. The engines would work
just as well whether she was awake or not, but all the
same she would worry that they might stop while she
slept.

Glancing out of the window she saw that they were
now over water. It must be the Irish Sea. People said a
flying boat could not come down in the open sea
because of the waves, but it seemed to Diana that it
surely had a better chance than a land plane.

They flew into clouds and she could see nothing.
After a while the plane began to shake. Passengers
looked at one another and smiled nervously, and the
steward went around asking everyone to fasten their
safety belts. Diana felt anxious with no land in sight.
Princess Lavinia was gripping the arm of her seat hard,
but Mark and Lulu carried on talking as if nothing was

happening. Frank Gordon and Ollis Field appeared calm but both lit cigarettes and drew hard on them.

Just as Mark was saying, 'What the hell happened to Muriel Fairfield?' there was a thud and the plane seemed to fall. Diana felt as if her stomach came up into her throat. In another compartment, a passenger screamed. But then the aircraft righted itself, almost as if it had landed.

Lulu answered, 'Muriel married a millionaire.'

'No kidding!' said Mark. 'But she was so ugly.'

Diana said, 'Mark, I'm scared!'

He turned to her. 'It was only an air pocket, honey. It's normal.'

'But it felt as if we were going to crash!'

'We won't. It happens all the time.'

He turned back to Lulu. For a moment Lulu gazed at Diana, expecting her to say something but Diana looked away, furious with Mark.

Mark went on, 'How did Muriel get a millionaire?'

Lulu paused. 'I don't know, but now they live in Hollywood and he puts money into movies.'

'Unbelievable!'

Unbelievable was right, Diana thought. As soon as she could get Mark on his own she was going to give him a piece of her mind.

His lack of sympathy made her feel more scared. By nightfall they would be over the Atlantic Ocean, rather than the Irish Sea. How would she feel then? She imagined the Atlantic as a vast, featureless blank, cold and deadly for thousands of miles. The only things you ever saw, according to the *Manchester Guardian*, were icebergs. If there had been some islands to relieve the seascape Diana might have felt less jittery. It was the complete blankness of the picture that was so frightening: nothing but the plane and the moon and the heaving sea. In a funny way it was like her anxiety about going to America: in her head she knew it was not dangerous, but the scenery was strange and there was not one single familiar landmark.

She was getting jumpy. She tried to think of other things. She was looking forward to the seven-course dinner, for she enjoyed long, elegant meals. Climbing into bunk beds would be childishly thrilling, like going to sleep in a tent in the garden. And the dizzying towers of New York were waiting for her on the other side. But the excitement of a journey into the unknown had now turned to fear. She drained her glass and ordered more champagne, but it failed to calm her. She longed for the feel of firm ground under her feet again. She shivered, thinking how cold the sea must be. Nothing she did could take her mind off her fear. If she had been alone, she would have hidden her face in her hands and shut her eyes tight. She stared malevolently at Mark and Lulu, who were chatting cheerfully, oblivious to her torment. She was even tempted to make a scene, to burst into tears or have hysterics, but she swallowed hard and stayed calm. Soon the plane would come down at Foynes and she could get off and walk around on dry land.

But then she would have to board again for the long transatlantic flight.

Somehow she could not bear that idea.

I can hardly get through an hour like this, she thought. How can I do it all night? It will kill me.

But what else can I do?

Of course, no one was going to force her to get back on the plane at Foynes.

And if no one forced her, she did not think she could do it.

But what would I do?

I know what I'd do.

I would telephone Mervyn.

She could hardly believe that her bright dream should collapse like this; but she knew it was going to happen.

Mark was being eaten alive in front of her eyes by an older woman with dyed hair and too much make-up, and Diana was going to telephone Mervyn and say, 'I'm sorry, I made a mistake, I want to come home.'

She knew he would forgive her. Feeling so sure of his reaction made her a little ashamed. She had wounded him, but he would still take her in his arms and be happy that she had returned.

But I don't want that, she thought miserably. I want to go to America and marry Mark and live in California. I love him.

No, that was a foolish dream. She was Mrs Mervyn Lovesey of Manchester, sister of Thea and Auntie Diana to the twins, the not-very-dangerous rebel of Manchester society. She would never live in a house with palm trees in the garden and a swimming pool. She was married to a loyal, grumpy man who was more interested in his business than in her. Most of the women she knew were in exactly the same situation, so it must be normal. They were all disappointed, but they were better off than the one or two who had married wastrels and drunks, so they commiserated with each other, agreed that it could be worse, and spent their husband's hard-earned money in department stores and hairdressing salons. But they never went to California.

The plane plunged into emptiness again, then righted itself as before. Diana had to concentrate hard not to throw up. But for some reason she was no longer scared. She knew what the future held. She felt safe.

She just wanted to cry.

CHAPTER TEN

FLIGHT ENGINEER Eddie Deakin thought of the Clipper as a giant soap bubble, beautiful and fragile, which he must carry carefully across the sea, while the people inside made merry, oblivious of how thin was the film between them and the howling night.

The journey was more hazardous than they knew, for the technology of the aircraft was new and the night sky over the Atlantic was uncharted territory, full of unexpected dangers. Nevertheless, Eddie always felt, proudly, that the skill of the Captain, the dedication of the crew and the reliability of American engineering would take them safely home.

On this journey, however, he was sick with fear.

There was a Tom Luther on the passenger list. Eddie had kept looking out of the flight deck windows as the passengers boarded, wondering which of them was responsible for kidnapping Carol-Ann, but of course he could not tell – they were just the usual crowd of well-dressed, well-fed tycoons and movie stars and aristocrats.

For a while, preparing for take-off, he had been able to turn his mind away from tormenting thoughts of Carol-Ann and concentrate on the task in hand:

checking his instruments, priming the four massive radial engines, warming them up, adjusting the fuel mixture and the cowl flaps, and governing engine speeds during taxiing. But once the plane reached its cruising altitude there was less for him to do. He had to synchronize engine speeds, regulate the engine temperature, and adjust the fuel mixture; then his job consisted mainly of monitoring the engines to check that they were performing smoothly. And his mind started wandering again.

He had a desperate, irrational need to know what Carol-Ann was wearing. He would feel just a little less bad if he could picture her in her sheepskin coat, buttoned and belted, and wet-weather boots, not because she might be cold – it was only September – but so that the shape of her body would be disguised. However, it was more likely she would have on the lavender-coloured sleeveless dress he loved so much, which showed off her lush figure. She was going to be locked up with a bunch of brutes for the next twenty-four hours and the thought of what might happen if they started drinking was agony to him.

What the hell did they want from him?

He hoped the rest of the crew would not notice the state he was in. Fortunately they were all concentrating on their own tasks and they were not crammed together as closely as in most aircraft. The flight deck of the Boeing B-314 was very large. The spacious cockpit was only part of it. Captain Baker and co-pilot Johnny Dott sat on raised seats side by side at their controls, with a gap between them leading to a trapdoor which gave access to the bow compartment in the nose of the plane. Heavy curtains could be drawn behind the pilots at night, so that the light from the rest of the cabin would not diminish their night vision.

That section alone was bigger than most flight decks, but the rest of the Clipper's flight cabin was even more generous. Most of the port side, on the left as you faced forward, was taken up by the seven-foot-long chart table, at which navigator Jack Ashford now stood, bending over his maps. Aft of that was a small conference table, at which the Captain could sit when he was not actually flying the plane. Beside the table was an oval hatch leading to the crawlway inside the wing, a special feature of the Clipper, from which the engines could be reached during flight so that Eddie could do simple maintenance or repairs, such as fixing an oil leak, without the plane having to come down.

On the starboard, right-hand side, immediately behind the co-pilot's seat was the staircase leading down to the passenger deck. Then came the radio operator's station, where Ben Thompson sat facing forward. Behind Ben sat Eddie. He faced sideways, looking at a wall of dials and a bank of levers. A little to his right was the oval hatch leading to the starboard wing crawlway. At the back of the flight deck, a doorway led to the cargo holds.

The whole thing was twenty-one feet long and nine feet wide, with full headroom throughout. Carpeted, soundproofed, and decorated with soft green wall

fabric and brown leather seats, it was the most unbelievably luxurious flight deck ever made: when Eddie first
saw it he thought it was some kind of joke.

Now, however, he saw only the bent backs and
concentrated frowns of his crew-mates, and judged,
with relief, that they had not noticed that he was beside
himself with fear.

Desperate to understand why this nightmare was
happening to him, he wanted to give the unknown Mr
Luther an early opportunity to present himself. After
take-off he hunted around for an excuse to pass
through the passenger cabin. He could not think of a
good reason, so he made do with a bad one. He stood
up, mumbled to the navigator, 'Just going to check the
rudder trim control cables,' and went quickly down the
stairs. If anyone should ask him why he took it into his
head to perform that check at that moment he would
just say, 'Hunch.'

He walked slowly through the passenger cabin. Nicky
and Davy were serving cocktails and snacks. The passengers were relaxing and conversing in several
languages. There was already a card game in progress
in the main lounge. Eddie saw some familiar faces but
he was too distracted to figure out who the famous
people were. He made eye contact with several passengers, hoping that one would reveal himself to be Tom
Luther, but no one spoke to him.

He reached the back of the plane and climbed a
wall-mounted ladder beside the door to the ladies'
powder room. This led to a hatch in the ceiling which
gave access to the empty space in the tail. He could

have reached the same place by remaining on the upper deck and going back through the baggage holds.

He checked the rudder control cables in a perfunctory way then closed the hatch and descended the ladder. A boy of fourteen or fifteen was standing there watching him with lively curiosity. Eddie forced himself to smile. Encouraged, the boy said, 'Can I see the flight deck?'

'Sure you can,' Eddie said automatically. He did not want to be bothered right now, but on this of all planes the crew had to be charming to the passengers, and anyway the distraction might take his mind off Carol-Ann briefly.

'Super, thanks!'

'Honk back to your seat for a minute and I'll pick you up.'

A puzzled look passed briefly over the boy's face, then he nodded and hurried away. 'Honk back' was a New England expression, Eddie remembered: it was not familiar to New Yorkers, let alone Europeans.

Eddie walked even more slowly back along the aisle, waiting for someone to approach him, but no one did and he had to assume the man would wait for a more discreet opportunity. He could have asked the stewards where Mr Luther was seated, but they would naturally wonder why he wanted to know, and he was reluctant to arouse their curiosity.

The boy was in No. 2 compartment, near the front, with his family. Eddie said, 'Okay, kid, come on up,' and smiled at the parents. They nodded rather frostily at him. A girl with long red hair – the boy's sister, maybe – gave him a grateful smile and his heart missed a beat: she was beautiful when she smiled.

'What's your name?' he asked the boy as they went up the spiral staircase.

'Percy Oxenford.'

'I'm Eddie Deakin, the flight engineer.'

They reached the top of the stairs. 'Most flight decks ain't as nice as this,' Eddie said, forcing himself to be cheerful.

'What are they like usually?'

'Bare and cold and noisy. And they have sharp projections that stick into you every time you turn around.'

'What does an engineer do?'

'I take care of the engines – keep them drivin' all the way to America.'

'What are all those levers and dials for?'

'Let's see . . . These levers here control the propeller speed, the engine temperature and the fuel mixture. There's one complete set for each of the four engines.' This was all a bit vague, he realized, and the boy was quite bright. He made an effort to be more informative. 'Here, sit in my chair,' he said. Percy sat down eagerly. 'Look at this dial. It shows that the temperature of number two engine, at its head, is two hundred and five degrees Centigrade. That's a little too close to the maximum permissible, which is two hundred and thirty-two degrees while cruising. So we'll cool it down.'

'How do you do that?'

'Take that lever in your hand and pull it down a

fraction . . . that's just enough. Now you've opened the cowl flap an inch more to let in extra cold air, and in a few moments you'll see that temperature drop. Have you studied much physics?'

'I go to an old-fashioned school,' Percy said. 'We do a lot of Latin and Greek but they're not very keen on science.'

It seemed to Eddie that Latin and Greek were not going to help Britain win the war, but he kept the thought to himself.

Percy asked, 'What do the rest of them do?'

'Well, now, the most important person is the naviga-tor: that's Jack Ashford, standing at the chart table.' Jack, a dark-haired, blue-chinned man with regular features, looked up and gave a friendly smile. Eddie went on, 'He has to figure out where we are, which can be difficult in the middle of the Atlantic. He has an observation dome, back there between the cargo holds, and he takes sightings on the stars with his sextant.'

Jack said, 'Actually, it's a bubble octant.'

'What's that?'

Jack showed Percy the instrument. 'The bubble is just to tell you when the octant is level. You identify a star then look at it through the mirror, and adjust the angle of the mirror until the star appears to be on the horizon. You read off the angle of the mirror here, and look it up in the book of tables, and that gives you your position on the earth's surface.'

'It sounds simple,' Percy said.

'It is in theory,' Jack said with a laugh. 'One of the

problems on this route is that we can be flying through cloud for the whole journey, so I never get to see a star.'

'But surely, if you know where you started and you keep heading in the same direction, you can't go wrong.'

'That's called dead reckoning. But you *can* go wrong, because the wind blows you sideways.'

'Can't you guess how much?'

'We can do better than guess. There's a little trap-door in the wing, and I drop a flare in the water and watch it carefully as we fly away from it. If it stays in line with the tail of the plane we're not drifting, but if it seems to move to one side or the other, that shows me our drift.'

'It sounds a bit rough-and-ready.'

Jack laughed again. 'It is. If I'm unlucky, and I don't get a look at the stars all the way across the ocean, and I make a wrong estimate of our drift, we can end up a hundred miles or more off course.'

'And then what happens?'

'We find out about it as soon as we come within range of a beacon, or a radio station, and we set about correcting our course.'

Eddie watched as curiosity and understanding showed on the boyish, intelligent face. One day, he thought, I'll explain things to my own child. That made him think of Carol-Ann, and the reminder hurt like a pain in his heart. If only the faceless Mr Luther would make himself known Eddie would feel better. When he knew what was wanted of him he would at least under-stand why this awful thing was happening.

Percy said, 'May I see inside the wing?'

'Sure.' Eddie opened the hatch to the starboard wing. The roar of the huge engines immediately sounded much louder, and there was a smell of hot oil. Inside the wing was a low passage with a crawlway like a narrow plank. Behind each of the two engines was a mechanic's station with room for a man to stand upright, just about. Pan American's interior decorators had not got into this space, and it was a utilitarian world of struts and rivets, cables and pipes. 'That's what most flight decks are like,' Eddie shouted.

'May I go inside?'

Eddie shook his head and closed the door. 'No passengers beyond this point, I'm sorry.'

Jack said, 'I'll show you my observation dome.' He took Percy through the door at the back of the flight deck, and Eddie checked the dials he had been ignor-ing for the past few minutes. All was well.

The radioman, Ben Thompson, sang out the con-ditions at Foynes. 'Westerly wind, twenty-two knots, choppy sea.'

A moment later, on Eddie's board, the light over the word 'Cruising' winked out and the light over 'Landing' came on. He scanned his temperature dials and reported, 'Engines okay for landing.' The check was necessary because the high-compression motors could be damaged by too abrupt throttling back.

Eddie opened the door to the rear of the plane.

There was a narrow passage with cargo holds either side, and a dome, above the passage, reached by a ladder. Percy was standing on the ladder looking through the octant. Beyond the cargo holds was a space which was supposed to be for crew beds, but it had never been furnished: off-duty crew used No. I compartment. At the back of that area was a hatch leading to the tail space where the control cables ran. Eddie called, 'Landing, Jack.'

Jack said, 'Time to get back to your seat, young man.'

Eddie had a feeling that Percy was too good to be true. Although the boy did as he was told, there was a mischievous glint in his eye. However, for the moment he was on his best behaviour and he went obediently forward to the staircase and down to the passenger deck.

The engine note changed and the plane began to lose height. The crew went automatically into the smoothly co-ordinated landing routine. Eddie wished he could tell the others what was happening to him. He felt desperately lonely. These were his friends and colleagues; they trusted one another; they had flown the Atlantic together; he wanted to explain his plight and ask their advice. But it was too risky.

He stood up for a moment to look out of the window. He could see a small town which he guessed was Limerick. Outside the town, on the north bank of the Shannon estuary, a large new airport was being constructed, for land planes and seaplanes. Until it was finished the flying boats were coming down on the south side of the estuary, in the lee of a small island, off the village of Foynes.

Their course was north-west, so Captain Baker had to turn the plane through forty-five degrees to land into the westerly wind. A launch from the village would be patrolling the landing zone to check for large floating debris that might damage the aircraft. The refuelling boat would be standing by, loaded with fifty-gallon drums, and there would be a crowd of sightseers on the shore, come to watch the miracle of a ship that could fly.

Ben Thompson was talking into his radio micro-phone. At any distance greater than a few miles he had to use Morse code, but now he was close enough for voice radio. Eddie could not distinguish the words but he could tell from the calm, relaxed tone of voice that all was well.

They lost height steadily. Eddie watched his dials vigilantly, making occasional adjustments. One of his most important tasks was to synchronize engine speeds, a job that became more demanding when the pilot made frequent throttle changes.

Landing in a calm sea could be almost impercept-ible. In ideal conditions the hull of the Clipper went into the water like a spoon into cream. Eddie, concen-trating on his instrument panel, often was not aware that the plane had touched down until it had been in the water for several seconds. However, today the sea was choppy – which was as bad as it got in any of the places where the Clipper came down on this route.

The lowest point of the hull, which was called the

step, touched first, and there was a light thud-thud-thud as it clipped the tops of the waves. That lasted only a second or two, then the huge aircraft eased down another few inches and cleaved the surface. Eddie found it much smoother than coming down in a land plane, when there was always a perceptible bump, and sometimes several. Very little spray reached the windows of the flight deck, which was on the upper level. The pilot throttled right down and the aircraft slowed immediately. The plane was a boat again.

Eddie looked out of the windows again as they taxied to their mooring. On one side was the island, low and bare: he saw a small white house and a few sheep. On the other side was the mainland. He could see a sizeable concrete jetty with a large fishing-boat tied up to its side, several big oil storage tanks, and a straggle of grey houses. This was Foynes.

Unlike Southampton, Foynes did not have a purpose-built jetty for flying boats, so the Clipper would moor in the estuary and the people would be landed by launch. Mooring was the engineer's responsibility.

Eddie went forward, knelt between the two pilots' seats and opened the hatch leading to the bow compartment. He descended the ladder into the empty space. Stepping into the nose of the plane, he opened a hatch and stuck out his head. The air was fresh and salty, and he took a deep breath.

A launch came alongside. One of the hands waved to Eddie. The man was holding a rope attached to a buoy. He threw the rope into the water.

There was a collapsible capstan on the nose of the

flying boat. Eddie lifted it and locked it into position, then he took a boat-hook from inside and used it to pick up the rope that was floating in the water. He attached the rope to the capstan, and the aircraft was moored. Looking up to the windscreen behind him, he gave Captain Baker the thumbs-up sign.

Another launch was already coming alongside to take the passengers and crew off the plane.

Eddie closed the hatch and returned to the flight deck. Captain Baker and Ben, the radioman, were still at their stations, but the co-pilot, Johnny, was leaning on the chart table chatting to Jack. Eddie sat at his station and closed down the engines. When everything was shipshape he put on his black uniform jacket and white cap. The crew went down the stairs, passed through No. 2 passenger compartment, went into the lounge and stepped out on to the sea-wing. From there they boarded the launch. Eddie's deputy, Mickey Finn, remained behind to supervise the refuelling.

The sun was shining but there was a cool, salty breeze. Eddie surveyed the passengers on the launch, wondering yet again which one was Tom Luther. He recognized a woman's face, and realized with a faint shock that he had seen her making love to a French count in a movie called *A Spy in Paris*: she was the film star Lulu Bell. She was chatting animatedly to a guy in a blazer. Could he be Tom Luther? With them was a beautiful woman in a spotted dress who looked miserable. There were several other familiar faces but most of the passengers were anonymous men in suits and hats and rich women in furs.

If Luther did not make his move soon, Eddie would seek him out and to hell with discretion, he decided. He could not stand the waiting.

The launch puttered away from the Clipper towards the land. Eddie stared across the water, thinking of his wife. He kept picturing the scene as the men burst into the house. Carol-Ann might have been eating eggs, or making coffee, or getting dressed for work. What if she had been in the bathtub? Eddie loved to look at her in the tub. She would pin up her hair, showing her long neck, and lie in the water languidly sponging her suntanned limbs. She liked him to sit on the edge and talk to her. Until he met her, he had thought this kind of thing only happened in erotic daydreams. But now the picture was blighted by three coarse men in fedoras who burst in and grabbed her—

The thought of her fear and shock as they seized her maddened Eddie almost beyond endurance. He felt his head spinning and he had to concentrate to stay upright in the launch. It was his utter helplessness that made the predicament so agonizing. She was in desperate trouble and there was nothing he could do, nothing. He found he was clenching his fists spasmodically, and forced himself to stop.

The launch reached the shore and tied up to a floating pontoon connected by a gangway to the dock. The crew helped the passengers disembark then followed them up the gangway. They were directed to the customs shed.

The formalities were brief. The passengers drifted into the little village. Across the road from the harbour was a former inn which had been almost entirely taken over by airline personnel, and the crew headed for that.

Eddie was the last to leave, and as he came out of the customs shed he was approached by a passenger who said, 'Are you the engineer?'

Eddie tensed. The passenger was a man of about thirty-five, shorter than he but stocky and muscular. He wore a pale grey suit, a tie with a stickpin and a grey felt hat. Eddie said, 'Yes, I'm Eddie Deakin.'

'My name is Tom Luther.'

A red haze blurred Eddie's vision and his rage boiled over in an instant. He grabbed Luther by the lapels, swung him around, and banged him against the wall of the customs shed. 'What have you done to Carol-Ann?' he spat. Luther was taken completely by surprise: he had expected a frightened, compliant victim. Eddie shook him until his teeth rattled. 'You Christless son of a whore, where is my wife?'

Luther recovered quickly from the shock. The stunned look left his face. He broke Eddie's hold with a swift, powerful move and threw a punch. Eddie dodged it and hit him in the stomach twice. Luther expelled air like a cushion and doubled up. He was strong but out of condition. Eddie grabbed him by the throat and started to squeeze.

Luther stared at him out of terrified eyes.

After a moment Eddie realized he was killing the man.

He eased his grip, then let go completely. Luther slumped against the wall, gasping for air, his hand on his bruised neck.

The Irish customs officer looked out of the shed. He must have heard the thump as Eddie threw Luther against the wall. 'What happened?'

Luther stood upright with an effort. 'I stumbled, but I'm okay,' he managed.

The customs man bent down and picked up Luther's hat. He gave a curious look as he handed it over but he said no more and went back inside.

Eddie looked around. No one else had observed the scuffle. The passengers and crew had disappeared round the other side of the little railway station.

Luther put his hat on. In a hoarse voice he said, 'If you mess this up we'll both be killed as well as your damn wife, you imbecile.'

The reference to Carol-Ann maddened Eddie all over again and he drew back his fist to hit Luther, but Luther raised a protective arm and said, 'Calm down, will you? You won't get her back that way. Don't you understand that you need me?'

Eddie understood that perfectly well: he had simply lost his reason for a few moments. He took a step back and studied the man. Luther was well spoken and expensively dressed. He had a bristly blond moustache and pale eyes full of hate. Eddie had no regrets about punching him. He had needed to hit something and Luther was an appropriate target. Now he said, 'What do you want from me, you pile of shit?'

Luther put his hand inside his suit jacket. It crossed Eddie's mind that there might be a gun in there, but Luther took out a postcard and handed it over.

Eddie looked at it. It was a picture of Bangor, Maine. 'What the hell does this mean?'

Luther said, 'Turn over.'

On the other side was written: '44.70N, 67.00W'.

'What are these numbers – map co-ordinates?' Eddie asked.

'Yes. That's where you have to bring the plane down.'

Eddie stared at him. 'Bring the plane down?' he repeated stupidly.

'Yes.'

'That's what you want from me – that's what this is all about?'

'Bring the plane down right there.'

'But why?'

'Because you want your pretty wife back.'

'Where is this location?'

'Off the coast of Maine.'

People often assumed a seaplane could splash down anywhere, but in fact it needed very calm waters. For safety, Pan American would not allow a touchdown in waves more than three feet high. If the plane came down in a heavy sea it would break up. Eddie said, 'You can't land a flying boat in the open sea—'

'We know that. This is a sheltered place.'

'That doesn't mean—'

'Just check it out. You can come down there. I made sure of it.'

He sounded so confident that Eddie sensed he really had made sure. But there were other snags. 'How am I supposed to bring the plane down? I'm not the Captain.'

'I've looked into this very carefully. The Captain could bring the plane down in theory, but what excuse would he have? You're the engineer, you can make something go wrong.'

'You want me to crash the plane?'

'You'd better not – I'm going to be on board. Just have something go wrong so the Captain is forced to make an unscheduled splashdown.' He touched the postcard with a manicured finger. 'Right there.'

The engineer *could* create a problem that would force the plane down, no doubt about that; but an emergency was difficult to control and Eddie could not immediately see how to arrange an unscheduled splashdown at such a precise location. 'It just ain't that easy—'

'I know it's not easy, Deakin. But I know it can be done. I checked.'

Who had he checked with? Who was he? 'Who the hell are you, anyway?'

'Don't ask.'

Eddie had started out threatening this man but somehow the tables had turned and now he felt intimidated. Luther was part of a ruthless team that had planned this carefully. They had picked out Eddie to be their tool; they had kidnapped Carol-Ann; they had him in their power.

He put the postcard in the pocket of his uniform jacket and turned away.

'So you'll do it?' Luther said anxiously.

Eddie turned back and gave him a cold stare. He held Luther's eyes for a long moment, then walked away without speaking.

He was acting tough but in truth he was floored. Why were they doing this? At one point he had speculated that the Germans wanted to steal a Boeing B-314 to copy it, but that far-fetched theory was now washed out completely, for the Germans would want to steal the plane in Europe, not Maine.

The fact that they were so precise about the location at which they wanted the Clipper to come down was a clue. It suggested there would be a boat waiting there. But what for? Did Luther want to smuggle something or somebody into the United States – a suitcase full of opium, a bazooka, a Communist agitator or a Nazi spy? The person or thing would have to be pretty damned important to be worth all this trouble.

At least he knew why they had picked on him. If you wanted to bring the Clipper down, the engineer was your man. The navigator could not do it, nor could the radio operator, and a pilot would need the co-operation of his co-pilot; but an engineer, all on his own, could stop the engines.

Luther must have got a list of Clipper engineers out of Pan American. That would not be too difficult: someone could have broken into the offices one night, or just bribed a secretary. Why Eddie? For some reason Luther decided on this particular flight and got hold of the roster. Then he asked himself how to make Eddie Deakin co-operate and came up with the answer: kidnap his wife.

It would break Eddie's heart to help these gangsters. He hated crooks. Too greedy to live like regular people and too lazy to earn a buck, they cheated and stole from hard-working citizens and lived high on the hog. While others broke their backs ploughing and reaping, or worked eighteen hours a day to build up a business, or dug for coal under the ground, or sweated all day in a steelworks, the gangsters went around in fancy suits and big cars and did nothing but bully people and beat them up and scare them to death. The electric chair was too good for them.

His father had felt the same. He remembered what Pop had said about bullies at school: 'Those guys are mean, all right, but they ain't smart.' Tom Luther was mean, but was he smart? 'It's tough to fight those guys, but it ain't so hard to fool 'em,' Pop had said. But Tom Luther would not be easy to fool. He had thought up an elaborate plan and so far it seemed to be working perfectly.

Eddie would have done almost anything for a chance to fool Luther. But Luther had Carol-Ann. Anything Eddie did to foul up Luther's scheme might lead them to hurt her. He could not fight them *or* fool them: he just had to try to do what they wanted. Seething with frustration, he left the harbour and crossed the single road that led through the village of Foynes.

The air terminal was a former inn with a central yard. Since the village had become an important flying-boat airport, the building had been almost entirely taken over by Pan American, although there was still a bar, called Mrs Walsh's pub, in a small room with its own street door. Eddie went upstairs to the Operations Room, where Captain Marvin Baker and First Officer Johnny Dott were in conference with the Pan American station chief. Here, amid the coffee cups and ashtrays and the piles of radio messages and weather reports, they would take the final decision whether to make the long transatlantic crossing.

The crucial factor was the strength of the wind. The westward trip was a constant battle against the prevailing wind. Pilots would change altitude constantly in a search for the most favourable conditions, a game known as 'hunting the wind'. The lightest winds were generally found at lower altitudes, but below a certain point the plane would be in danger of colliding with a ship or, more likely, an iceberg. Strong winds required more fuel and sometimes the forecast winds were so strong that the Clipper simply could not carry enough to last the two thousand miles to Newfoundland. Then the flight would have to be postponed and the passengers taken to a hotel to wait until the weather improved.

But if that should happen today, what would become of Carol-Ann?

Eddie took a preliminary glance at the weather reports. The winds were strong and there was a storm in mid-Atlantic. He knew that the plane was full. Therefore there would have to be a careful calculation before the flight could get the go-ahead. The thought ratcheted up his anxiety: he could not bear to be stuck in Ireland while Carol-Ann was in the hands of those bastards on the other side of the ocean. Would they feed her? Did she have somewhere to lie down? Was she warm enough, wherever they were holding her?

He went to the Atlantic chart on the wall and checked the map reference Luther had given him. The spot had been quite well chosen. It was close to the Canadian border, a mile or two off shore, in a channel between the coast and a large island, in the Bay of Fundy. Someone who knew a little about flying boats would think it an ideal place to come down. It was not ideal – the ports used by the Clippers were even more sheltered – but it would be calmer than the open sea and the Clipper would probably be able to splash down there without great risk. Eddie was somewhat relieved: at least that part of the scheme might be made to work. He realized he had a big investment in the success of Luther's plan. The thought left a sour taste in his mouth.

He was still worried about just how he would bring the plane down. He could fake engine trouble, but the Clipper could fly on three engines and there was an assistant engineer, Mickey Finn, who could not be fooled for very long. He racked his brains but did not come up with a solution.

Plotting to do this to Captain Baker and the others made him feel like the worst kind of heel. He was betraying people who trusted him. But he had no choice.

Now an even greater hazard occurred to him. Tom Luther might not keep his promise. Why should he? He was a crook! Eddie might bring the plane down and still not get Carol-Ann back.

The navigator, Jack, came in with some more

weather reports, and shot a peculiar look at Eddie. Eddie realized that no one had spoken to him since he came into the room. They seemed to be tiptoeing around him: had they noticed how preoccupied he was? He had to make more effort to behave normally. 'Try not to get lost this trip, Jack,' he said, repeating an old joke. He was not much of an actor, and the gag seemed forced to him, but they laughed and the atmosphere eased.

Captain Baker looked at the fresh weather reports and said, 'This storm is getting worse.'

Jack nodded. 'It's going to be what Eddie would call a honker.'

They always ribbed him about his New England dialect. He managed to grin, and said, 'Or a baster.'

Baker said, 'I'm going to fly around it.'

Together, Baker and Johnny Dott produced a flight plan to Botwood, in Newfoundland, skirting the edge of the storm and avoiding the worst of the head winds. When they had finished, Eddie sat down with the weather forecasts and began his calculations.

For each sector of the trip he had predictions of the wind direction and force at one thousand feet, four thousand, eight thousand and twelve thousand. Knowing the cruising air-speed of the plane and the wind force, Eddie could calculate the ground speed. That gave him a flight time for each sector at the most favourable altitude. Then he would use printed tables to find the fuel consumption over that time with the current payload of the Clipper. He would plot the fuel requirement stage by stage, on a graph which the crew called the Howgozit Curve, work out the total and add a safety margin.

When he completed his calculations he saw to his consternation that the amount of fuel required to get them to Newfoundland was more than the Clipper could carry.

For a moment he did nothing.

The shortfall was terribly small: just a few pounds of payload too much, a few gallons of gas too little. And Carol-Ann was waiting somewhere, scared to death.

He should now tell Captain Baker that take-off would have to be postponed until the weather improved, unless he was willing to fly through the heart of the storm.

But the gap was so small.

Could he lie?

There was a safety margin built in, anyhow. If things went badly the plane could fly through the storm instead of going around it.

He hated the thought of deceiving his captain. He had always been aware that the lives of the passengers depended on him, and he was proud of his meticulous accuracy.

On the other hand, his decision was not irrevocable. Every hour during the trip he had to compare actual fuel consumption with the projection on the Howgozit Curve. If they burned more than anticipated they simply had to turn back.

He might be found out, and that would be the end of his career, but what did that matter when the lives of his wife and his unborn baby were at stake?

He worked through the calculation again, but this time, when checking the tables, he made two deliberate errors, taking fuel consumption for the lower payload in the next column of figures. Now the result came inside the safety margin.

Still he hesitated. Lying did not come easily to him, even in this appalling predicament.

Finally Captain Baker got impatient and looked over Eddie's shoulder, saying, 'Snap it up, Ed – do we go or stay?'

Eddie showed him the doctored result on the pad and kept his eyes down, not wanting to look Baker in the eye. He cleared his throat nervously, then did his best to speak in a firm, confident voice.

He said: 'It's close, Captain – but we go.'

Part Three

*Foynes to
mid-Atlantic*

CHAPTER ELEVEN

DIANA LOVESEY stepped on to the dock at Foynes and felt pathetically grateful for the feeling of solid ground under her feet.

She was sad but calm. She had made her decision: she was not going to get back on the Clipper, she was not going to fly to America and she was not going to marry Mark Alder.

Her knees seemed wobbly, and for a moment she was afraid she might fall, but the sensation passed and she walked along the dock to the customs shed.

She put her arm through Mark's. She would tell him as soon as they were alone. It would break his heart, she thought with a stab of grief: he loved her very much. But it was too late to think of that now.

Most of the passengers had disembarked. The exceptions were the odd couple sitting near Diana, handsome Frank Gordon and bald Ollis Field, who had stayed on board. Lulu Bell had not stopped chatting to Mark. Diana ignored her. She no longer felt angry with Lulu. The woman was intrusive and overbearing, but she had enabled Diana to see her true situation.

They passed through customs and left the dock. They found themselves at the western end of a

275

one-street village. A herd of cows was being driven through it and they had to wait for them to pass.

Diana heard Princess Lavinia say loudly, 'Why have I been brought to this *farm?*'

Davy, the little steward, replied in a soothing voice, 'I'll take you into the terminal building, Your Highness.' He pointed across the road to a large building like an old inn with ivy growing up the walls. 'There's a very comfortable bar, called Mrs Walsh's pub, where they sell excellent Irish whiskey.'

When the cows had gone, several of the passengers followed Davy to Mrs Walsh's pub. Diana said to Mark, 'Let's walk through the village.' She wanted to get him on his own as soon as possible. He smiled and agreed. However, some other passengers had the same idea, Lulu among them, and it was a small crowd that strolled along the main street of Foynes.

There was a railway station, a post office and a church, then two rows of grey stone houses with slate roofs. Some of the houses had shop fronts. There were several pony carts parked along the street but only one motorized truck. The villagers, dressed in tweeds and homespun, stared at the visitors in silk and furs, and Diana felt as if she was in a procession. Foynes had not yet got used to being a stopover for the world's wealthy and privileged élite.

She was hoping that the party would split up, but they stayed together in a knot, like explorers afraid of getting lost. She began to feel trapped. Time was passing. They went by another bar, and she suddenly said to Mark, 'Let's go in there.'

Lulu immediately said, 'What a great idea – there's nothing to see in Foynes.'

Diana had had quite enough of Lulu. 'I'd really like to talk to Mark alone,' she said crossly.

Mark was embarrassed. 'Honey!' he protested.

'Don't worry!' Lulu said immediately. 'We'll walk on and leave you lovers alone. There'll be another bar, if I know anything at all about Ireland!' Her tone was gay, but her eyes were cold.

Mark said, 'I'm sorry, Lulu—'

'Don't be!' she said brightly.

Diana did not like Mark apologizing for her. She turned on her heel and went into the building, leaving him to follow at his leisure.

The place was dim and cool. There was a high bar, with bottles and barrels racked behind it. In front were a few wooden tables and chairs on a plank floor. Two old men sitting in the corner stared up at Diana. She was wearing an orange-red silk coat over her spotted dress. She felt like a princess in a pawnshop.

A small woman in an apron appeared behind the bar. Diana said, 'May I have a brandy, please?' She wanted some Dutch courage. She sat down at a small table.

Mark came in – probably having apologized some more to Lulu, Diana thought sourly. He sat beside her and said, 'What was all that about?'

'I've had enough of Lulu,' Diana said.

'Why did you have to be so rude?'

'I wasn't rude. I simply said I wanted to talk to you alone.'

'Couldn't you have found a more tactful way of saying so?'

'I think she's probably oblivious to hints.'

He looked annoyed and defensive. 'Well, you're wrong. She's actually a sensitive person, although she seems brash.'

'It doesn't matter, anyway.'

'How can it not matter? You've just offended one of my oldest friends!'

The barmaid brought Diana's brandy. She drank some quickly to steel her nerve. Mark ordered a glass of Guinness. Diana said, 'It doesn't matter because I've changed my mind about this whole thing, and I'm not coming to America with you.'

He went pale. 'You can't mean that.'

'I've been thinking. I don't want to go. I'm going back to Mervyn – if he'll have me.' But she felt sure he would.

'You don't love him. You told me that. And I know it's true.'

'What do you know? You've never been married.' He looked hurt and she softened. She put her hand on his knee. 'You're right, I don't love Mervyn the way I love you.' She felt ashamed of herself, and took her hand away. 'But it's no good.'

'I've been paying too much attention to Lulu,' Mark said penitently. 'I'm sorry, honey. I apologize. I guess I got wrapped up in her because it's so long since I last saw her. I've been ignoring you. This is our big adventure, and I forgot that for an hour. Please forgive me.'

He was sweet when he felt he had been wrong: he had a sorrowful expression that looked boyish. Diana forced herself to remember how she had been feeling an hour ago. 'It's not just Lulu,' she said. 'I think I've been foolhardy.'

The barmaid brought Mark's drink but he did not touch it.

Diana went on, 'I've left everything I know – home, husband, friends and country. I'm on a flight across the Atlantic which is dangerous in itself. And I'm going to a strange country where I have no friends, no money, nothing.'

Mark looked distraught. 'Oh, God, I see what I've done. I abandoned you just when you were feeling vulnerable. Baby, I feel such a horse's ass. I promise I'll never do that again.'

Perhaps he would keep such a promise, and perhaps he would not. He was loving, but he was also easy-going. It was not in him to stick to a plan. He was sincere now, but would he remember his vow next time he ran into an old friend? It was his playful attitude to life that had attracted Diana in the first place and now, ironically, she saw that that very attitude made him unreliable. One thing you could say for Mervyn was that he was reliable: good or bad, his habits never changed.

'I don't feel I can rely on you,' she said.

He looked angry. 'When have I ever let you down?'

She could not think of an instance. 'You will, though,' she said.

'Anyway, you *want* to leave all these things behind.

You're unhappy with your husband, your country's at war, and you're bored with your home and your friends – you told me that.'

'Bored, but not frightened.'

'There's nothing to be frightened of. America is like England. People speak the same language, go to the same movies, listen to the same jazz bands. You're going to love it. I'll take care of you, I promise.'

She wished she could believe him.

'And there's another thing,' he went on. 'Children.'

That shaft went home. She did so long to have a baby, and Mervyn was adamant that he would not. Mark would be such a good father, loving and happy and tender. Now she felt confused, and her determination weakened. Maybe she *should* give up everything, after all. What was home and security to her if she could not have a family?

But what if Mark were to abandon her half-way to California? Suppose another Lulu turned up in Reno, just after the divorce, and Mark went off with her? Diana would be stranded with no husband, no children, no money and no home.

She wished now that she had been slower to say yes to him. Instead of throwing her arms around him and agreeing to everything right away, she should have discussed the future carefully and thought of all the snags. She should have asked for some kind of security, even just the price of a ticket home, in case things went wrong. But that might have offended him, and anyway it was going to take more than a ticket to get across the Atlantic once the war started in earnest.

I don't know what I should have done, she thought miserably, but it's too late for regrets. I've made my decision and I won't be talked out of it.

Mark took her hands in his own, and she was too sad to withdraw them. 'You changed your mind once, now change it back,' he said persuasively. 'Come with me, and be my wife, and we'll have children together. We'll live in a house right on the beach, and take our toddlers paddling in the waves. They'll be blond and suntanned, and grow up playing tennis and surfing and riding bicycles. How many kids would you like? Two? Three? Six?'

But her moment of weakness had passed. 'It's no good, Mark,' she said wistfully. 'I'm going back home.'

She could see from his eyes that now he believed her. They looked at one another sadly. For a while neither of them spoke.

Then Mervyn walked in.

Diana could not believe her eyes. She stared at him as if he were a ghost. He could not be here, it was impossible!

'So there you are,' he said in his familiar baritone voice.

Diana was swamped by contrary emotions. She was appalled, thrilled, frightened, relieved, embarrassed and ashamed. She realized her husband was looking at her holding hands with another man. She snatched her hands out of Mark's grasp.

Mark said, 'What is it? What's the matter?'

Mervyn came up to their table and stood with his hands on his hips, staring at them.

Mark said, 'Who the hell is this jerk?'

'Mervyn,' Diana said weakly.

'Christ Jesus!'

Diana said, 'Mervyn . . . how did you get here?'

'Flew,' he said with his customary terseness.

She noticed he was wearing a leather jacket and carrying a helmet. 'But – but how did you know where to find us?'

'Your letter said you were flying to America and there's only one way to do that,' he said with a note of triumph.

She could see that he was pleased with himself for having worked out where she was and intercepted her, somewhat against the odds. She had never imagined he could catch them up in his own plane: it simply had not occurred to her. She found herself weak with gratitude to him for caring enough to chase after her this way.

He sat down opposite them. 'Bring me a large Irish whiskey,' he called to the barmaid.

Mark picked up his beer glass and sipped nervously. Diana looked at him. At first he had seemed intimidated by Mervyn but now he had realized Mervyn was not going to start a fist fight he just looked uneasy. He moved his chair back from the table an inch, as if to distance himself from Diana. Perhaps he, too, felt ashamed at being caught holding hands.

Diana sipped some brandy to give her strength. Mervyn was watching her anxiously. His expression of bewilderment and hurt made her want to throw herself into his arms. He had come all this way without knowing what sort of reception he would get. She reached out and touched his arm reassuringly.

To her surprise, he looked uncomfortable and threw a worried glance at Mark, as if he felt disconcerted at being touched by his wife in front of her lover. His whiskey came and he drank it quickly. Mark looked wounded, and moved his chair closer to the table again.

Diana felt flustered. She had never been in a situation like this. They both loved her. She had been to bed with both of them – and they both knew it. It was unbearably embarrassing. She wanted to comfort them both, but she was afraid to. Feeling defensive she leaned back, putting more space between herself and them. 'Mervyn,' she said, 'I didn't want to hurt you.'

He looked hard at her. 'I believe you,' he said evenly.

'Do you . . . can you understand what happened?'

'I can grasp the broad outlines, simple soul though I am,' he said sarcastically. 'You've run off with your fancy man.' He looked at Mark and leaned towards him aggressively. 'An American, I gather; the weedy type that'll let you have your own way.'

Mark leaned back and said nothing, but stared intently at Mervyn. Mark was not a confronter. He did not look offended, just intrigued. Mervyn had been a major figure in Mark's life although they had never met. All these months Mark must have been consumed with curiosity about the man Diana slept with every night. Now he was finding out and he was fascinated. Mervyn, by contrast, was not the least interested in Mark.

Diana watched the two men. They could hardly have

been more different. Mervyn was tall, aggressive, bitter, nervy; Mark was small, neat, alert, open-minded. The thought occurred to her that Mark would probably use this scene in a comedy script one day.

Her eyes were heavy with tears. She took out a handkerchief and blew her nose. 'I know I've been imprudent,' she said.

'Imprudent!' Mervyn snapped, mocking the inadequacy of the word. 'You've been bloody daft.'

Diana winced. His scorn always cut her to the quick but on this occasion she deserved it.

The barmaid and the two men in the corner were following the conversation with unabashed interest. Mervyn waved to the barmaid and called out, 'Could I have a plate of ham sandwiches, love?'

'With pleasure,' she said politely. Barmaids always liked Mervyn.

Diana said, 'I just ... I've been so miserable lately. I was only looking for a little happiness.'

'Looking for happiness! In America – where you've no friends, no relations, no home ... Where's your sense?'

She was grateful to him for coming, but she wished he would be kinder. She felt Mark's hand on her shoulder. 'Don't listen to him,' he said quietly. 'Why shouldn't you be happy? There's nothing wrong with that.'

She looked fearfully at Mervyn, afraid of offending him further. He might yet reject her. How humiliating it would be if he should spurn her in front of Mark (and, she thought in the back of her mind, while the horrible Lulu Bell was on the scene). He was capable of it: that was the kind of thing he did. She wished now that he had not followed her. It meant he would have to make a spot decision. Given more time, she could have soothed his wounded pride. This was too rushed. She picked up her glass and put it to her lips, then set it down untasted. 'I don't want this,' she said.

Mark said, 'I expect you'd like a cup of tea.'

That was just what she wanted. 'Yes, I'd love it.'

He went to the bar and ordered it.

Mervyn would never have done that: to his way of thinking, tea was got by women. He gave Mark a look of contempt. 'Is that what's wrong with me?' he asked her angrily. 'I don't fetch your tea, is that it? You want me to be housemaid as well as breadwinner?' His sandwiches came but he did not eat any.

Diana did not know how to answer him. 'There's no need for a row,' she said softly.

'No need for a row? When is there need for one, then, if not now? You run off with this little pillock, without saying goodbye, leaving me a silly bloody note . . .' He took a piece of paper out of his jacket pocket and Diana recognized her letter. She blushed scarlet, feeling humiliated. She had shed tears over that note: how could he wave it about in a bar? She moved back from him, feeling resentful.

The tea came and Mark picked up the pot. He looked at Mervyn and said, 'Would you like a cup of tea poured by a little pillock?' The two Irishmen in the corner burst out laughing, but Mervyn glared stonily and said nothing.

Diana began to feel angry with him. 'I may be bloody daft, Mervyn, but I've got a right to be happy.'

He pointed an accusing finger at her. 'You made a vow when you married me and you've no right to leave.'

She felt mad with frustration: he was so completely unyielding, it was like explaining something to a block of wood. Why couldn't he be reasonable? Why did he have to be so damn certain he was always right and everyone else was wrong?

Suddenly she recognized this feeling. She had had it about once a week for five years. During the last few hours, in her panic on the plane, she had forgotten how awful he could be and how unhappy he could make her. Now it all came back like the horror of a remembered nightmare.

Mark said, 'She can do what she likes, Mervyn. You can't make her do a single thing. She's a grown-up. If she wants to go home with you, she will; and if she wants to come to America and marry me, she'll do that.'

Mervyn banged his fist on the table. 'She can't marry you, she's already married to me!'

'She can divorce you.'

'On what grounds?'

'You don't need grounds in Nevada.'

Mervyn turned his angry eyes on Diana. 'You're not going to Nevada. You're coming back to Manchester with me.'

She looked at Mark. He smiled gently at her. 'You don't have to obey anyone,' he said. 'Do what *you* want.'

Mervyn said, 'Get your coat on.'

In his blundering way, Mervyn had given Diana back her sense of proportion. She now saw her fear of the flight and her anxieties about living in America as minor worries by comparison with the all-important question: who did she want to live with? She loved Mark and Mark loved her, and all other considerations were marginal. A tremendous sense of relief came over her as she made her decision and announced it to the two men who loved her. She took a deep breath. 'I'm sorry, Mervyn,' she said. 'I'm going with Mark.'

CHAPTER TWELVE

Nancy Lenehan enjoyed a minute of jubilation as she looked down from Mervyn Lovesey's Tiger Moth and saw the Pan American Clipper floating majestically on the calm water of the Shannon estuary.

The odds had been against her but she had caught up with her brother and foiled at least part of his plan. You've got to get up very early in the morning to outsmart Nancy Lenehan, she thought, in a rare moment of self-congratulation.

Peter was going to have the shock of his life when he saw her.

As the little yellow plane circled and Mervyn searched for a place to land, Nancy began to feel tense about the forthcoming confrontation with her brother. She still found it hard to believe that he had deceived and betrayed her with such complete ruthlessness. How could he? As children they had been bathed together. She had put Band-Aids on his knees, told him how babies were made and always given him a chew of her gum. She had kept his secrets and told him her own. After they grew up she had nursed his ego, never letting him be embarrassed because she was so much smarter even though she was a girl.

All their lives she had taken care of him. And when Pa died she had allowed Peter to become chairman of the company. That had cost her dearly. Not only had she suppressed her own ambition to make way for him: at the same time she had stifled a budding romance; for Nat Ridgeway, Pa's deputy, had resigned when Peter took charge. Whether anything would have come of that romance, she would never know, for Ridgeway had since married.

Her friend and lawyer, 'Mac' McBride, had advised her not to let Peter be chairman, but she had gone against his counsel, and her own best interests, because she knew how wounded Peter would be that people thought he was not fit to fill his father's shoes. When she remembered all she had done for him, and then thought of how he had tried to cheat her and lie to her, she wanted to weep with resentment and rage.

She was desperately impatient to find him, stand in front of him and look into his eyes. She wanted to know how he would act and what he would say to her.

She was also eager to join battle. Her catching up with Peter was only the first step. She had to get on the plane. That might be straightforward but if it was full she would have to try to buy someone else's seat, or use her charm on the Captain, or even bribe her way on board. Then, when she got to Boston, she had to persuade the minority shareholders, her aunt Tilly and her father's old lawyer Danny Riley, that they should refuse to sell their holdings to Nat Ridgeway. She felt she could do that, but Peter would not give up without a fight, and Nat Ridgeway was a formidable opponent.

Mervyn brought down the plane on a farm track at the edge of the little village. In an uncharacteristic display of good manners, he helped Nancy climb down to the ground. As she set foot on Irish soil for the second time she thought of her father, who although he had talked constantly of the old country never actually went there. She felt that was sad. He would have been pleased to know that his children had made it to Ireland. But it would have broken his heart to know how the company that had been his life had been run down by his son. Better that he was not here to see that.

Mervyn roped the plane down. Nancy was relieved to leave it behind. Pretty though it was, it had almost killed her. She still shivered every time she remembered flying towards that cliff. She did not intend to get into a small plane again for the rest of her life.

They walked briskly into the village, following a horse-drawn wagon loaded with potatoes. Nancy could tell that Mervyn, too, was feeling a mixture of triumph and apprehension. Like her, he had been deceived and betrayed and had refused to take it lying down; and like her he got great satisfaction from defying the expectations of those who had plotted against him. But for both of them the real challenge was still ahead.

A single street led through Foynes. Half-way along it they met a group of well-dressed people who could only be Clipper passengers: they looked as if they had wandered on to the wrong set at a film studio. Mervyn approached them and said, 'I'm looking for

Mrs Diana Lovesey – I believe she's a passenger on the Clipper.'

'She sure is!' said one of the women, and Nancy recognized the movie star Lulu Bell. There was a note in her voice that suggested she did not like Mrs Lovesey. Once again Nancy wondered what Mervyn's wife was like. Lulu Bell went on, 'Mrs Lovesey and her . . . companion? . . . went into a bar just along the street here.'

Nancy said, 'Could you direct me to the ticket office?'

'If I ever get cast as a tour guide, I won't need to rehearse!' said Lulu, and the passengers with her laughed. 'The airline building is at the far end of the street, past the railroad station, opposite the harbour.'

Nancy thanked her and walked on. Mervyn had already started and she had to run to catch up with him. However, he stopped suddenly when he caught sight of two men strolling up the street, deep in conversation. Nancy looked curiously at the men, wondering why they had stopped Mervyn in his tracks. One was a silver-haired swell in a black suit with a dove-grey waistcoat, obviously a passenger from the Clipper. The other was a scarecrow of a man, tall and bony with hair so short he almost looked bald and the expression of someone who has just woken up from a nightmare. Mervyn went up to the scarecrow and said, 'You're Professor Hartmann, aren't you?'

The man's reaction was quite shocking. He jumped back a pace and held up his hands defensively, as if he thought he was about to be attacked.

His companion said, 'It's all right, Carl.'

Mervyn said, 'I'd be honoured to shake your hand, sir.'

Hartmann dropped his arms, although he still looked wary. He shook hands.

Nancy was surprised at Mervyn's behaviour. She would have said that Mervyn Lovesey thought nobody in the world was his superior, yet here he was acting like a schoolboy asking a baseball star for his autograph.

Mervyn said, 'I'm glad to see you got out. We feared the worst, you know, when you disappeared. By the way, my name is Mervyn Lovesey.'

Hartmann said, 'This is my friend Baron Gabon, who helped me to escape.'

Mervyn shook hands with Gabon, then said, 'I won't intrude any more. *Bon voyage*, gentlemen.'

Hartmann must be something very special, Nancy thought, to have distracted Mervyn, even for a few moments, from his single-minded pursuit of his wife. As they walked on through the village she said, 'So who's he?'

'Professor Carl Hartmann, the greatest physicist in the world,' Mervyn replied. 'He's been working on splitting the atom. He got into trouble with the Nazis for his political views and everyone thought he was dead.'

'How do you know about him?'

'I did physics at university. I thought of becoming a research scientist, but I haven't the patience for it. I still keep up with developments, though. It so happens there have been some amazing discoveries in the field over the last ten years.'

'Such as?'

'There's an Austrian woman – another refugee from the Nazis, by the way – called Lise Meitner, working in Copenhagen, who managed to break the uranium atom into two smaller atoms, barium and krypton.'

'I thought atoms were indivisible.'

'So did we all until recently. That's what's so amazing. It makes a very big bang when it happens, which is why the military are so interested. If they can control the process they'll be able to make the most destructive bomb ever known.'

Nancy looked back over her shoulder at the frightened, shabby man with the burning gaze. The most destructive bomb ever known, she said to herself, and she shivered. 'I'm surprised they let him walk around unguarded,' she said.

'I'm not sure he is unguarded,' Mervyn said. 'Look at that chap.'

Following the direction of Mervyn's nod, Nancy looked across the street. Another Clipper passenger was idling along on his own: a tall, hefty man in a bowler hat and a grey suit with a wine-red waistcoat. 'Do you think that's his bodyguard?' she said.

Mervyn shrugged. 'The man looks like a copper to me. Hartmann may not know it but I'd say he's got a guardian angel in size twelve boots.'

Nancy had not thought Mervyn was that observant.

'I think this must be the bar,' Mervyn said, switching from the cosmic to the mundane without pausing for breath. He stopped at the door.

'Good luck,' Nancy said. She meant it. In a funny way she had grown to like him, despite his infuriating ways.

He smiled. 'Thanks. Good luck to you, too.'

He went inside and Nancy continued along the street.

At the far end, across the road from the harbour, was an ivy-grown building larger than anything else in the village. Inside, Nancy found a makeshift office and a good-looking young man in a Pan American uniform. He looked at her with a twinkle in his eye, even though he had to be fifteen years her junior.

'I want to buy a ticket to New York,' she told him.

He was surprised and intrigued. 'Is that so! We don't generally sell tickets here – in fact, we don't have any.'

That did not sound like a serious problem. She smiled at him: a smile always helped in overcoming trivial bureaucratic obstacles. 'Well, a ticket is only a piece of paper,' she said. 'If I give you the fare, I guess you'll let me on the plane, won't you?'

He grinned. She figured he would oblige her if he could. 'I guess so,' he said. 'But the plane is full.'

'Hell!' she muttered. She felt crushed. Had she gone through all this for nothing? But she was not yet ready to give up, not by a long way. 'There must be *something*,' she said. 'I don't need a bed. I'll sleep in a seat. Even a crew seat would do.'

'You can't take a crew seat. The only thing vacant is the honeymoon suite.'

'Can I take that?' she said hopefully.

'Why, I don't even know what price to charge—'

'But you could find out, couldn't you?'

'I guess it has to cost at least as much as two regular fares, and that would make it seven hundred and fifty bucks one way, but it could be more.'

She didn't care if it cost seven thousand dollars. 'I'll give you a blank cheque,' she said.

'Boy, you really want to ride this airplane, don't you?'

'I have to be in New York tomorrow. It's ... very important.' She could not find words to express how important it was.

'Let's go ask the Captain,' the boy said. 'This way please, ma'am.'

Nancy followed him, wondering whether she had been wasting her efforts on someone who did not have the authority to make a decision.

He led her to an upstairs office. Six or seven of the Clipper's crew were there in their shirtsleeves, smoking and drinking coffee while they studied charts and weather reports. The young man introduced her to Captain Marvin Baker. When the handsome Captain shook her hand she had the oddest feeling that he was going to take her pulse, and she realized it was because he had a doctor's bedside manner.

The young fellow said, 'Mrs Lenehan needs to get to New York real bad, Captain, and she's willing to pay for the honeymoon suite. Can we take her?'

Nancy waited anxiously for the reply, but the Captain

asked another question. 'Is your husband with you, Mrs Lenehan?'

She fluttered her eyelashes, always a useful move when you were hoping to persuade a man to do something. 'I'm a widow, Captain.'

'I'm sorry. Do you have any baggage?'

'Just this overnight case.'

'We'll be glad to take you to New York, Mrs Lenehan,' he said.

'Thank God,' Nancy said fervently. 'I can't tell you how important it is to me.' For a moment her knees felt weak. She sat in the nearest chair. She was embarrassed about feeling so emotional. To cover up, she rummaged in her handbag and took out her cheque book. With a shaky hand she signed a blank cheque and gave it to the young man.

Now it was time to confront Peter.

'I saw some passengers in the village,' she said. 'Where would the rest of them be?'

'Most are in Mrs Walsh's pub,' the young man said. 'It's a bar in this building. The entrance is around the side.'

She stood up. The shaky spell had passed. 'I'm much obliged to you,' she said.

'Glad to be able to help.'

Nancy went out.

As she closed the door she heard a buzz of comment break out and she knew they were making ribald remarks about an attractive widow who could afford to sign blank cheques.

She went outside. It was a mild afternoon with weak

sunlight and the air was pleasantly damp with the salty taste of the sea. Now she had to look for her faithless brother.

She went around to the side of the building and entered the bar.

It was the kind of place into which she would never normally go: small, dark, roughly furnished, very masculine. Clearly it was originally intended to serve beer to fishermen and farmers, but now it was full of millionaires drinking cocktails. The atmosphere was stuffy and the noise level was high in several languages: there was something of a party atmosphere among the passengers. Was it her imagination, or was there a faintly hysterical note in the laughter? Did the jollification mask anxiety about the long flight over the ocean?

She scanned the faces and spotted Peter.

He did not notice her.

She stared at him for a moment, anger boiling up inside her. She felt her cheeks flush with rage. She had a powerful urge to slap his face. But she suppressed her fury. She would not show him how upset she was. It was always smarter to play it cool.

He was sitting in a corner, and Nat Ridgeway was with him. That was another shock. Nancy had known Nat was in Paris for the collections, but it had not occurred to her that he might fly back with Peter. She wished he were not here. The presence of an old flame just complicated matters. She would just have to forget that she had once kissed him. She put the thought out of her mind.

She pushed through the crowd and went up to their

table. Nat was the first to look up. His face showed shock and guilt, which gave her some satisfaction. Noticing his expression, Peter looked up.

Nancy met his eye.

He went pale and started up out of his chair. 'Good Christ!' he exclaimed. He looked scared to death.

'Why are you so frightened, Peter?' Nancy said contemptuously.

He swallowed hard and sank back into his seat.

Nancy continued, 'You actually paid for a ticket on the SS *Oriana*, knowing you weren't going to use it. You came to Liverpool with me and checked into the Adelphi Hotel, even though you weren't going to stay there. And all because you were afraid to tell me you were taking the Clipper!'

He stared back at her, white-faced and silent.

She had not planned to make a speech but the words just came. 'You slunk out of the hotel yesterday and rushed all the way to Southampton, hoping I wouldn't find out!' She leaned on the table and he shrank away from her. 'What are you so scared of? I'm not going to *bite* you!' As she said the word *bite* he flinched, as if she might really do it.

She had not troubled to lower her voice. The people nearby had gone quiet. Peter looked around with an embarrassed expression. Nancy said, 'I'm not surprised you feel foolish. After all I've done for you! All these years I've protected you, covered up for your stupid mistakes, and let you go on being chairman of the company even though you couldn't organize a church bazaar! After all that, you tried to steal the business from me! How could you do it? Doesn't it make you feel like a *worm?*'

He flushed crimson. 'You've never protected me, you've always looked after yourself,' he protested. 'You always wanted to be boss – but you didn't get the job! I got it, and you've been scheming to take it away from me ever since.'

This was so unjust that Nancy did not know whether to laugh, cry, or spit in his face. 'You idiot, I've been scheming ever since to let you *keep* the chairmanship.'

He pulled some papers from his pocket with a flourish. 'Like this?'

Nancy recognized her report. 'You bet like that,' she said. 'That plan is the only way for you to keep your job.'

'While you take control! I saw through it right away.' He looked defiant. 'That's why I came up with my own plan.'

'Which hasn't worked,' Nancy said triumphantly. 'I've got a seat on the plane and I'm coming back for the board meeting.'

For the first time she turned to Nat Ridgeway and spoke to him. 'I guess you still can't take control of Black's Boots, Nat.'

Peter said, 'Don't be so sure.'

She looked at him. He was petulantly aggressive. Surely he could not have something up his sleeve? He was not that smart. She said, 'You and I own forty per cent each, Peter. Aunt Tilly and Danny Riley hold the balance. They've always followed my lead. They know me and they know you. I make money and you lose it, and they understand that, even if they're polite to you for Pa's sake. They'll vote the way I ask them to.'

'Riley will vote with me,' Peter said obstinately.

There was something in his mulishness that worried her. 'Why would he vote with you when you've practically run the company into the ground?' she said scornfully, but she was not as confident as she made herself sound.

He sensed her anxiety. 'I've got you scared now, haven't I?' he sneered.

Unfortunately he was right. She was beginning to feel worried. He did not look as crushed as he should. She had to find out whether there was anything behind this bluster. 'I guess you're just talking through your hat,' she jeered.

'No, I'm not.'

If she kept taunting him he would feel compelled to prove her wrong, she knew. 'You always pretend to have something up your sleeve but it generally amounts to nothing at all.'

'Riley has promised.'

'And Riley is as trustworthy as a rattlesnake,' she said dismissively.

Peter was stung. 'Not if he gets . . . an incentive.'

So that was it: Danny Riley had been bribed. That bothered Nancy. Danny was nothing if not corruptible. What had Peter offered him? She had to know, so that she could either spoil the bribe or offer more. She said, 'Well, if your plan hinges on Danny Riley's reliability, I guess I don't have anything to worry about!' and she laughed derisively.

'It hinges on Riley's *greed*,' Peter said.

She turned to Nat. 'If I were you I'd be very sceptical about all this.'

'Nat knows it's true.' Peter was smug.

Nat clearly would have preferred to remain silent, but when they both stared at him he gave a reluctant nod of assent.

Peter said, 'He's giving Riley a big chunk of General Textiles work.'

That was a blow, and Nancy's breath caught in her throat. There was nothing Riley would have liked better than to get a foot in the door of a major corporation such as General Textiles. To a small New York law firm it was the opportunity of a lifetime. For a bribe like that Riley would sell his mother.

Peter's shares plus Riley's came to fifty per cent. Nancy's plus Aunt Tilly's also amounted to fifty per cent. With the votes divided equally, the issue would be decided by the casting vote of the chairman – Peter.

Peter could see he had trumped Nancy, and he allowed himself a smile of victory.

Nancy was not yet willing to concede defeat. She pulled out a chair and sat down. She turned her attention to Nat Ridgeway. She had sensed his disapproval all the way through the argument and wondered if he knew that Peter had been working behind her back. She decided to put it to him. 'I suppose you knew Peter was lying to me about this?'

He stared at her, tight-lipped, but she could do that, too, and she simply waited, looking expectant. Finally she outstared him, and he said, 'I didn't ask. Your family quarrels are none of my concern. I'm not a social worker, I'm a businessman.'

But there was a time, she thought, when you held my hand in restaurants and kissed me goodnight; and once you caressed my breasts. She asked, 'Are you an honest businessman?'

'You know I am,' he said stiffly.

'In that case, you won't approve of dishonest methods being used on your behalf.'

He thought for a moment, then said, 'This a take-over, not a tea-party.'

He was going to say more but she jumped in. 'If you're willing to gain by my brother's dishonesty, you're dishonest yourself. You've changed since you worked for my father.' She turned back to Peter before Nat could reply. 'Don't you realize you could get twice the price for your shares if you let me implement my plan for a couple of years?'

'I don't like your plan.'

'Even without restructuring, the company is going to be worth more because of the war. We've always supplied soldiers' boots – think of the extra business if the US gets into the war!'

'The US won't get into this war.'

'Even so, the war in Europe will be good for busi-ness.' She looked at Nat. 'You know that, don't you? That's why you want to buy us out.'

Nat said nothing.

She turned back to Peter. 'But we'd do better to wait. Listen to me. Have I ever been wrong about this sort of thing? Have you ever lost money by following my advice? Have you ever made money by disregarding it?'

'You just don't understand, do you?' Peter said.

Now she could not imagine what was coming. 'What don't I understand?'

'Why I'm merging the company, why I'm doing this.'

'All right, why?'

He stared at her in silence, and she saw the answer in his eyes.

He hated her.

She was shocked rigid. She felt as if she had run headlong into an invisible brick wall. She wanted to disbelieve it, but the grotesque expression of malevolence on his distorted face could not be ignored. There had always been tension between them, natural sibling rivalry, but this, this was awful, weird, pathological. She had never suspected this. Her little brother Peter hated her.

This is what it must be like, she thought, when the man you have been married to for twenty years tells you he's having an affair with his secretary and he doesn't love you any more.

She felt dizzy, as if she had banged her head. It was going to take a while to adjust to this.

Peter was not merely being foolish, or mean, or spiteful. He was actually doing himself harm in order to ruin his sister. That was pure hatred.

He had to be at least a little bit crazy.

She needed to think. She decided to leave this hot, smoky bar and get some air. She stood up and left them without saying goodbye.

As soon as she stepped outside she felt a little better. There was a cool breeze blowing in off the estuary. She crossed the road and walked along the dockside, listening to the seagulls cry.

The Clipper was out in mid-channel. It was bigger than she had imagined: the men refuelling it looked tiny. She found its huge engines and enormous propellers reassuring. She would not feel nervous on this plane, she thought; not after surviving a trip across the Irish Sea in a single-engined Tiger Moth.

But what would she do when she got home? Peter would never be talked out of his plan. There were too many years of hidden anger behind his behaviour. She felt sorry for him in a way: he had been so unhappy all this time. But she was not going to give in to him. There might still be a way to save her birthright.

Danny Riley was the weak link. A man who could be bribed by one side could be bribed by the other. Perhaps Nancy could think of something else to offer him, something that would tempt him to change sides. But that would be tough. Peter's bribe, a chunk of General Textiles' law business, was hard to top.

Maybe she could threaten him. That would be cheaper, too. But how? She could take away some family and personal business from his firm, but that would not amount to much, nothing compared to the new business he would get from General Textiles. What Danny would like best would be straight cash, of course, but her fortune was mostly tied up in Black's Boots. She could lay her hands on a few thousand dollars without much trouble, but Danny would want more, maybe a hundred grand. She could not get hold of that much cash in time.

While she was deep in thought, her name was called. She turned around to see the young Pan American employee waving at her. 'There's a telephone call for you,' he shouted. 'A Mr McBride from Boston.'

She felt suddenly hopeful. Maybe Mac could think of a way out of this. He knew Danny Riley. Both men were like her father, second-generation Irish who spent all their time with other Irishmen and were suspicious of Protestants even if they were Irish. Mac was honest and Danny was not, but otherwise they were alike. Pa had been honest, but he had been willing to turn a blind eye to a little sharp practice, especially if it would help a buddy from the old country.

Pa had saved Danny from ruin once, she recalled as she hurried back along the dock. It was just a few years ago, not long before Pa died. Danny had been losing a big and important case, and in desperation he had approached the judge at their golf club and tried to bribe him. The judge had not been bribable and he had told Danny to retire or be disbarred. Pa had intervened with the judge and persuaded him that it was a momentary lapse. Nancy knew all about it: Pa had confided in her a lot towards the end of his life.

That was Danny: slippery, unreliable, rather foolish, easily swayed. Surely she could win him back to her own side.

But she only had two days.

She went into the building and the young man showed her the phone. She put the earpiece to her ear and picked up the stand. It was good to hear the familiar, affectionate voice of Mac. 'So you caught up with the Clipper,' he said jubilantly. 'Attagirl!'

'I'll be at the board meeting – but the bad news is that Peter says he's got Danny's vote tied up.'

'Do you believe him?'

'Yes. General Textiles is giving Danny a chunk of corporate business.'

Mac's voice became despondent. 'Are you sure it's true?'

'Nat Ridgeway is here with him.'

'That snake!'

Mac had never liked Nat and had hated him when he started dating Nancy. Even though Mac was happily married he was jealous of anyone who showed a romantic interest in Nancy.

'I pity General Textiles, having Danny do their law work,' Mac added.

'I guess they'll give him the low-grade stuff. Mac, is it legal for them to offer him this incentive?'

'Probably not, but the violation would be hard to prove.'

'Then I'm in trouble.'

'I guess so. I'm sorry, Nancy.'

'Thanks, old friend. You warned me not to let Peter be the boss.'

'I sure did.'

That was enough crying over spilt milk, Nancy decided. She adopted a brisker tone. 'Listen, if we were relying on Danny, we'd be worried, right?'

'You bet we would—'

'Worried that he'd change sides, worried that the opposition would make him a better offer. So what do we think his price is?'

'Hmm.' There was silence on the line for a few moments, then Mac said, 'Nothing springs to mind.'

Nancy was thinking about Danny trying to bribe a judge. 'Do you remember that time Pa got Danny out of a hole? It was the Jersey Rubber case.'

'I sure do. No details on the phone, okay?'

'Yes. Can we use that case somehow?'

'I don't see how.'

'To threaten him?'

'With exposure, you mean?'

'Yes.'

'Do we have proof?'

'Not unless there's something in Pa's old papers.'

'You have all those papers, Nancy.'

There were several cartons of Pa's personal records in the cellar of Nancy's house in Boston. 'I've never looked through them.'

'And there's no time for that now.'

'But we could pretend,' she said thoughtfully.

'I'm not following you.'

'I'm just thinking aloud. Bear with me for a minute. We could pretend to Danny that there is something, or might be something, in Pa's old papers, something that would bring that whole business out into the open.'

'I don't see how that—'

'No, listen to me, Mac, this is an idea.' Nancy's voice

307

rose with excitement as she began to see possibilities. 'Suppose the Bar Association, or whoever it is, decided to open an inquiry into the Jersey Rubber case.'

'Why would they do that?'

'Someone could tell them it was fishy.'

'All right, what then?'

Nancy began to feel she might have the makings of a workable plan. 'Suppose they heard that there was crucial evidence among Pa's stuff.'

'They would ask you if they could examine the papers.'

'Would it be up to me whether I let them?'

'In a simple Bar inquiry, yes. If there was a criminal inquiry you could be subpoenaed, and then of course you'd have no choice.'

A scheme was forming in Nancy's mind faster than she could explain it aloud. She hardly dared to hope that it might work. 'Listen, I want you to call Danny,' she said urgently. 'Ask him the following question—'

'Let me pick up a pencil. Okay, go ahead.'

'Ask him this. If there were a Bar inquiry into the Jersey Rubber case, would he want me to hand over Pa's papers?'

Mac was puzzled. 'You think he'll say no.'

'I think he'll panic, Mac! He'll be scared to death. He doesn't know what's there – notes, diaries, letters, could be anything.'

'I'm beginning to see how this could work,' Mac said, and Nancy could hear the hope creeping into his voice. 'Danny would think you have something he wants . . .'

'He'll ask me to protect him, as Pa did. He'll ask me to refuse the Bar permission to look at the papers. And I'll agree – on condition he votes with me against the merger with General Textiles.'

'Wait a minute. Don't open the champagne yet. Danny may be venal but he's not stupid. Won't he suspect that we've cooked this whole thing up to pressure him?'

'Of course he will,' Nancy said. 'But he won't be sure. And he won't have long to think about it.'

'Yeah. And right now it's our only chance.'

'Want to give it a try?'

'Okay.'

Nancy was feeling much better: full of hope and the will to win. 'Call me at our next stop.'

'Where's that?'

'Botwood, Newfoundland. We should be there in seventeen hours.'

'Do they have phones there?'

'They must, if there's an airport. You should book the call in advance.'

'Okay. Enjoy the flight.'

'Bye, Mac.'

She put the earpiece on the hook. Her spirits were high. There was no telling whether Danny would fall for it but she felt immensely cheered just to have a ploy.

It was twenty past four, time to board the plane. She left the room and passed through another office in which Mervyn Lovesey was speaking on another telephone. He put out his hand to stop her as she went by. Through the window she could see the passengers on the dockside boarding the launch, but she paused for a moment. He said into the phone, 'I can't be bothered with that now. Give the buggers the rate they're asking for and get on with the job.'

She was surprised. She recalled that there had been some kind of industrial dispute at his factory. It sounded as if he was giving in, which did not seem characteristic of him.

The person he was talking to seemed to be surprised too, for after a moment Mervyn said, 'Yes, I do bloody well mean it, I'm too busy to argue with toolmakers. Goodbye!' He hung up the earpiece. 'I've been looking for you,' he said to Nancy.

'Were you successful?' she asked him. 'Did you persuade your wife to come back?'

'No. But I didn't put it to her right.'

'That's too bad. Is she out there now?'

He looked through the window. 'That's her in the red coat.'

Nancy saw a blonde woman in her early thirties. 'Mervyn, she's beautiful!' she said. Somehow she had imagined Mervyn's wife as a tougher, less cute type, Bette Davis rather than Lana Turner. 'I can see why you don't want to lose her.' The woman was holding on to the arm of a man in a blue blazer, presumably the boyfriend. He was not nearly as handsome as Mervyn. He was a little below average height and his hair was beginning to recede. But he had a pleasant, easy-going look about him. Nancy could see instantly that the woman had gone for Mervyn's opposite. She felt sympathy for Mervyn. 'I'm sorry, Mervyn,' she said.

'I haven't given up,' Mervyn said. 'I'm coming to New York.'

Nancy smiled. This was more like Mervyn. 'Why not?' she said. 'She looks like the kind of woman a man might chase all the way across the Atlantic.'

'The thing is, it's up to you,' he said. 'The plane is full.'

'Of course. So how can you come? Why is it up to me?'

'You own the only remaining seat. You've taken the honeymoon suite. It seats two. I'm asking you to sell me the spare seat.'

She laughed. 'Mervyn, I can't share a honeymoon suite with a man. I'm a respectable widow, not a chorus girl!'

'You owe me a favour,' he said insistently.

'I owe you a favour, not my reputation!'

His handsome face took on an obstinate expression. 'You didn't think about your reputation when you wanted to fly across the Irish Sea with me.'

'That didn't involve our spending the night together!' She wished she could help him: there was something touching about his determination to get his beautiful wife back. 'I'm sorry, I really am,' she said. 'But I can't be involved in a public scandal at my age.'

'Listen. I've enquired about this honeymoon suite, and it's not that much different from the rest of the plane. There's two separate bunk beds. If we leave the door open at night we'll be in exactly the same situation as two total strangers who happen to be allocated adjoining bunks.'

'But think what people would say!'

'Who are you worried about? You've no husband to get offended, and your parents aren't alive. Who cares what you do?'

He could be extremely blunt when he wanted something, she thought. 'I've got two sons in their early twenties,' she protested.

'They'll think it's a lark, I bet.'

They probably would, she thought ruefully. 'I'm also worried about the whole of Boston society. Something like this would be sure to get around.'

'Look. You were desperate when you came to me on that airfield. You were in trouble and I saved your bacon. Now I'm desperate – you can see that, can't you?'

'Yes, I can.'

'I'm in trouble and I'm appealing to you. This is my last chance to save my marriage. You can do it. I saved you and you can save me. All it will cost you is a whiff of scandal. That never killed anybody. Please, Nancy.'

She thought about that 'whiff' of scandal. Did it really matter if a widow was faintly indiscreet on her fortieth birthday? It would not kill her, as he said, and it probably would not even damage her reputation. The matrons of Beacon Hill would think her 'fast', but people of her own age would probably admire her nerve. It's not as if I'm supposed to be a virgin, she thought.

She looked at his hurt, stubborn face and her heart went out to him. To hell with Boston society, she thought; this is a man in pain. He helped me when I needed it. Without him I wouldn't be here. He's right. I owe him.

'Will you help me, Nancy?' he begged. 'Please?'

Nancy took a deep breath. 'Hell, yes,' she said.

CHAPTER THIRTEEN

H ARRY MARKS'S last sight of Europe was a white lighthouse, standing proud on the north bank of the mouth of the Shannon, while the Atlantic Ocean angrily lashed the foot of the cliff below. A few minutes later there was no land in sight: whichever way he looked he saw nothing but the endless sea.

When I get to America I'm going to be rich, he thought.

Being this close to the famous Delhi Suite was so tantalizing as to be almost sexy. Somewhere on this plane, no more than a few yards from where he sat, was a fortune in jewellery. His fingers itched to touch it.

A million dollars in gems would be worth at least a hundred thousand from a fence. I could buy a nice flat and a car, he thought, or maybe a house in the country with a tennis court. Or perhaps I should invest it and live on the interest. I'd be a toff with a private income!

But first he had to get hold of the stuff.

Lady Oxenford was not wearing the jewellery, therefore it had to be in one of two places: the cabin baggage, right here in the compartment, or the checked baggage in the hold. If it were mine I'd keep it really close, Harry thought. I'd have it in my cabin bag. I'd be scared to let it out of my sight. But there was no telling how her mind worked.

He would check her cabin bag first. He could see it, under her seat, an expensive burgundy leather case with brass corners. He wondered how he might get inside it. Perhaps there would be a chance during the night when everyone was asleep.

He would find a way. It would be risky: thieving was a dangerous game. But somehow he always got away with it, even when things went wrong. Look at me, he thought; yesterday I was caught red-handed, with stolen cufflinks in my trousers pocket; I spent last night in jail and now here I am going to New York on the Pan American Clipper. Lucky? It's not the word!

He had once heard a joke about a man who jumped out of a tenth-floor window, and falling past the fifth floor was heard to say, 'So far, so good.' But that was not him.

The steward, Nicky, brought the dinner menu and offered him a cocktail. He did not need a drink but he ordered a glass of champagne just because it seemed like the right thing to do. This is the life, Harry boy, he said to himself. His elation at being on the world's most luxurious plane vied with his anxiety about flying across the ocean, but as the champagne took effect, elation won out.

He was surprised to see that the menu was in English. Did the Americans not know that posh menus were supposed to be in French? Perhaps they were just too sensible to print menus in a foreign language. Harry had a feeling he was going to like America.

The dining room seated only fourteen so dinner would be served in three sittings, the steward explained. 'Would you like to dine at six, seven thirty, or nine o'clock, Mr Vandenpost?'

This might be his chance, Harry realized. If the Oxenfords ate earlier or later than he, he might be left alone in the compartment. But which sitting would they choose? Harry mentally cursed the steward for starting with him. A British steward would automatically have spoken to the titled people first, but this democratic American was probably going by seat numbers. He would have to guess which the Oxenfords would choose. 'Let me see,' he said to gain time. Rich people ate their meals late, in his experience. A labourer might have breakfast at seven, dinner at noon and tea at five, but a lord would breakfast at nine, have lunch at two and dine at eight thirty. The Oxenfords would eat late so Harry picked the first sitting. 'I'm kinda hungry,' he said. 'I'll eat at six.'

The steward turned to the Oxenfords, and Harry held his breath.

Lord Oxenford said, 'Nine o'clock, I think.'

Harry suppressed a smile of satisfaction.

But Lady Oxenford said, 'That's too long for Percy to wait – let's make it earlier.'

All right, Harry thought uneasily, but not too early, for heaven's sake.

Lord Oxenford said, 'Seven thirty, then.'

Harry felt a little glow of pleasure. He was one step nearer the Delhi Suite.

Now the steward turned to the passenger opposite

Harry, the guy in the wine-red waistcoat who looked like a policeman. His name was Clive Membury, he had told them. Say seven thirty, Harry thought, and leave me alone in the compartment. But to his disappointment Membury was not hungry, and chose nine o'clock.

What a nuisance, Harry thought. Now Membury would be here while the Oxenfords were eating. Maybe he would step out for a few minutes: he was a restless type, always up and down. But if he would not go of his own accord Harry would have to find a way to get rid of him. That would have been easy if they had not been on a plane: Harry would have told him he was wanted in another room, or there was a telephone call for him, or there was a naked woman in the street outside. Here it might be harder.

The steward said, 'Mr Vandenpost, the engineer and the navigator will join you at your table, if that's agreeable.'

'Sure is,' Harry said. He would enjoy talking to some of the crew.

Lord Oxenford ordered another whisky. There was a man that had a thirst, as the Irish would say. His wife was pale and quiet. She had a book in her lap but she never turned a page. She looked depressed.

Young Percy went forward to talk to the off-duty crew, and Margaret came and sat next to Harry. He caught a breath of her scent and identified it as Tosca. She had taken off her coat, and he was able to see that she had her mother's figure: she was quite tall, with square shoulders and a deep bust, and long legs. Her clothes, good quality but plain, did not do her justice: Harry could imagine her in a long evening dress with a plunging neckline, her red hair up and her long white neck graced by drop earrings in carved emeralds by Louis Cartier in his Indian period ... She would be stunning. Obviously that was not how she saw herself. She was embarrassed about being a wealthy aristocrat so she dressed like a vicar's wife.

She was a formidable girl and Harry was a little intimidated by her, but he could also see her vulnerable side, and he found that endearing. He thought: Never mind endearing, Harry boy – just remember that she's a danger to you and you need to cultivate her.

He asked her if she had flown before. 'Only to Paris with Mother,' she said.

Only to Paris with Mother, he thought wonderingly. His mother would never see Paris or fly in a plane. 'What was it like?' he asked. 'To be so privileged?'

'I hated those trips to Paris,' she said. 'I had to have tea with boring English people when I wanted to go to smoky restaurants that had Negro bands.'

'My ma used to take me to Margate,' Harry said. 'I used to paddle in the sea, and we had ice cream and fish and chips.'

As the words came out he remembered that he was supposed to lie about this, and he felt panicky. He should be mumbling something vague about boarding school and a remote country house, as he normally did when forced to talk about his childhood to upper-class girls. But Margaret knew his secret, and no one else could hear what he was saying above the hum of the

Clipper's engines. All the same, as he found himself spilling out the truth he felt as if he had jumped out of the plane and was waiting for his parachute to open.

'We never went to the seaside,' Margaret said wistfully. 'Only the common people went paddling in the sea. My sister and I used to envy the poor children. They could do anything they liked.'

Harry was amused. Here was further proof that he had been born lucky: the wealthy children, driving in big black cars, wearing coats with velvet collars and eating meat every day, had envied him his barefoot freedom and his fish and chips.

'I remember the smells,' she went on. 'The smell outside a pie shop door at lunchtime, the smell of the oiled machinery as you go past a fairground, the cosy smell of beer and tobacco that comes out when a pub door opens on a winter evening. People always seemed to be having such fun in those places. I've never been in a pub.'

'You haven't missed much,' said Harry, who did not like pubs. 'The food is better at the Ritz.'

'We each prefer the other's way of life,' she mused.

'But I've tried both,' Harry pointed out. 'I *know* which is best.'

She looked thoughtful for a minute, then asked, 'What are you going to do with your life?'

It was a peculiar question. 'Enjoy myself,' Harry said.

'No, but really.'

'What do you mean, "really"?'

'Everyone wants to enjoy themselves. What will you *do*?'

'What I do now.' Impulsively, Harry decided to tell her something he had never revealed before. 'Did you ever read *The Amateur Cracksman*, by Hornung?' She shook her head. 'It's about a gentleman thief called Raffles, who smokes Turkish cigarettes and wears beautiful clothes and gets invited to people's houses and steals their jewellery. I want to be like him.'

'Oh, come on, don't be silly,' she said brusquely.

He was a little hurt. She could be brutally direct when she thought you were talking nonsense. But this was not nonsense, this was his dream. Now that he had opened his heart to her, he felt the need to convince her that he was telling the truth. 'It's not silly,' he snapped.

'But you can't be a thief all your life,' she said. 'You'll end up growing old in jail. Even Robin Hood got married and settled down eventually. What would you *really* like?'

Harry normally answered this question with a shopping list: a flat, a car, girls, parties, Savile Row suits and fine jewels. But he knew she would pour scorn on that. He resented her attitude; but all the same it was true that his ambitions were not quite so materialistic. He very much wanted her to believe in his dreams. 'I'd like to live in a big country house with ivy growing up the walls,' he said.

He stopped. Suddenly he felt emotional. He was embarrassed, but for some reason he wanted very badly to tell her this. 'A house in the country with a tennis court and stables, and rhododendrons all up the drive,' he went on. He could see it in his mind, and it seemed like the safest, most comfortable place in the world. 'I'd walk around the grounds in brown boots and a tweed suit, talking to the gardeners and the stable boys, and they'd all think I was a real gent. I'd have all my money in rock-solid investments and never spend half the income. I'd give garden parties in the summer, with strawberries and cream. And five daughters all as pretty as their mother.'

'Five!' she laughed. 'You'd better marry someone strong!' But she became serious immediately. 'It's a lovely dream,' she said. 'I hope it comes true.'

He felt very close to her, as if he could ask her anything. 'What about you?' he said. 'Have you got a dream?'

'I want to be in the war,' she said. 'I'm going to join the ATS.'

It still seemed funny to talk about women joining the army, but of course it was common now. 'What would you do?'

'Drive. They need women to be dispatch riders and ambulance drivers.'

'It will be dangerous.'

'I know. I don't care. I just want to be in the fight. This is our last chance to stop Fascism.' Her jaw was set firm and there was a reckless look in her eye, and Harry thought she was terribly brave.

He said, 'You seem very determined.'

'I had a . . . friend who was killed by the Fascists in Spain, and I want to finish the work he began.' She looked sad.

On impulse, Harry asked, 'Did you love him?'

She nodded.

He could see that she was close to tears. He touched her arm in sympathy. 'Do you still love him?'

'I always will, a little bit.' Her voice dropped to a whisper. 'His name was Ian.'

Harry felt a lump in his throat. He wanted to take her in his arms and comfort her, and he would have done so had it not been for her red-faced father sitting on the far side of the compartment drinking whisky and reading *The Times*. He had to be content with giving her hand a quick, discreet squeeze. She smiled gratefully, seeming to understand.

The steward said, 'Dinner is served, Mr Vandenpost.'

Harry was surprised that it was six o'clock already. He was sorry to break off his conversation with Margaret.

She read his mind. 'We've got lots more time to talk,' she said. 'We're going to be together for the next twenty-four hours.'

'Right.' He smiled. He touched her hand again. 'See you later,' he murmured.

He had started out befriending her in order to manipulate her, he remembered. He had ended up telling her all his secrets. She had a way of overturning his plans that was kind of worrying. Worst of all was that he liked it.

He went into the next compartment. He was a little startled to see that it had been completely transformed, from a lounge into a dining room. There were three tables each for four people, plus two smaller serving-tables. It was set out like a good restaurant, with linen tablecloths and napkins, and bone china crockery, white with the blue Pan American symbol. He noticed that the walls in this area were papered with a design showing a map of the world and the same winged Pan American symbol.

The steward showed him to a seat opposite a short, thickset man in a pale grey suit that Harry rather envied. His tie was fixed with a pin that had a large, genuine pearl. Harry introduced himself, and the man stuck out a hand and said, 'Tom Luther.' Harry saw that his cufflinks matched the tiepin. Here was a man who spent money on jewellery.

Harry sat down and unfolded his napkin. Luther had an American accent with something else at the bottom of it, some European intonation. 'Where are you from, Tom?' Harry said, probing.

'Providence, Rhode Island. You?'

'Philadelphia.' Harry wished to hell he knew where Philadelphia was. 'But I've lived all over. My father was in insurance.'

Luther nodded politely, not much interested. That suited Harry. He did not want to be questioned about his background: it was too easy to slip up.

The two crew members arrived and introduced themselves. Eddie Deakin, the engineer, was a broad-shouldered, sandy-haired type with a pleasant face: Harry got the impression he would have liked to undo his tie and take off his uniform jacket. Jack Ashford, the navigator, was dark-haired and blue-chinned, a regular, precise man who looked as if he had been born in a uniform.

As soon as they sat down, Harry sensed hostility

between Eddie the engineer and Luther the passenger. That was interesting.

The dinner started with shrimp cocktail. The two crew members drank Coke. Harry had a glass of hock and Tom Luther ordered a martini.

Harry was still thinking about Margaret Oxenford and the boyfriend killed in Spain. He looked out of the window, wondering how much she still felt for the boy. A year was a long time, especially at her age.

Jack Ashford followed his look and said, 'We're lucky with the weather, so far.'

Harry noticed that the sky was clear and the sun was shining on the wings. 'What's it usually like?' he said.

'Sometimes it rains all the way from Ireland to Newfoundland,' Jack said. 'We get hail, snow, ice, thunder and lightning.'

Harry remembered something he had read. 'Isn't ice dangerous?'

'We plan our route to avoid freezing conditions. But in any event the plane is fitted with rubber de-icing boots.'

'Boots?'

'Just rubber covers that fit over the wings and tail where they tend to ice up.'

'So what's the forecast for the rest of the trip?'

Jack hesitated momentarily, and Harry saw that he wished he had not mentioned the weather. 'There's a storm in the Atlantic,' he said.

'Bad?'

'In the centre it's bad, but we'll only touch the skirt of it, I expect.' He sounded only half convinced.

Tom Luther asked, 'What's it like in a storm?' He was smiling, showing his teeth, but Harry saw fear in his pale blue eyes.

'It gets a little bumpy,' Jack said.

He did not elaborate, but the engineer, Eddie, spoke up. Looking directly at Tom Luther, he said, 'It's kind of like trying to ride an unbroken horse.'

Luther blanched. Jack frowned at Eddie, plainly disapproving of his tactlessness.

The next course was turtle soup. Both stewards were serving now, Nicky and Davy. Nicky was fat and Davy was small. In Harry's estimation they were both homosexual – or 'musical', as the Noël Coward set would say. Harry liked their informal efficiency.

The engineer seemed preoccupied. Harry studied him covertly. He did not look the sulky type: he had an open, good-natured face. In an attempt to draw him out, Harry said, 'Who's flying the plane while you're eating dinner, Eddie?'

'The assistant engineer, Mickey Finn, is doing my job,' Eddie said. He spoke pleasantly enough, although he did not smile. 'We carry a crew of nine, not counting the two stewards. All except the Captain work alternate four-hour shifts. Jack and I have been on duty since we took off from Southampton at two o'clock, so we stood down at six, a few minutes ago.'

'What about the Captain?' Tom Luther said worriedly. 'Does he take pills to stay awake?'

'He naps when he can,' Eddie said. 'He'll probably take a long break when we pass the point of no return.'

'So we'll be flying through the sky and the Captain

will be asleep?' Luther said, and his voice was a little too loud.

'Sure,' said Eddie with a grin.

Luther was looking terrified. Harry tried to steer the conversation into calmer waters. 'What's the point of no return?'

'We monitor our fuel reserves constantly. When we don't have enough fuel to get back to Foynes, we've passed the point of no return.' Eddie spoke brusquely, and Harry now had no doubt the engineer was trying to scare Tom Luther.

The navigator broke in, trying to be reassuring. 'Right now we have enough fuel to reach our destination or return home.'

Luther said, 'But what if you don't have enough to get there or get back?'

Eddie leaned across the table and grinned humourlessly at Luther. 'Trust me, Mr Luther,' he said.

'It would never happen,' the navigator said hastily. 'We'd turn back for Foynes before we reached that point. And for extra safety, we make the calculations based on three engines instead of four, just in case something should go wrong with one engine.'

Jack was trying to restore Luther's confidence, but of course talk of engines going wrong only made the man more frightened. He tried to drink some soup but his hand was shaking and he spilled it on his tie.

Eddie sank back into silence, apparently satisfied. Jack tried to make small talk, and Harry did his best to help out, but there was an awkward atmosphere. Harry wondered what the hell was going on between Eddie and Luther.

The dining room filled up rapidly. The beautiful woman in the spotted dress came to sit at the next table with her blue-blazered escort. Harry had found out that their names were Diana Lovesey and Mark Alder. Margaret should dress like Mrs Lovesey, Harry thought: she could look even better. However, Mrs Lovesey did not look happy – in fact she looked as miserable as sin.

The service was fast and the food was good. The main course was *filet mignon* with asparagus hollandaise and mashed potatoes. The steak was about twice as big as would have been served in an English restaurant. Harry did not eat it all and he refused another glass of wine. He wanted to be alert. He was going to steal the Delhi Suite. The thought thrilled him but also made him apprehensive. It would be the biggest job of his career, and it could be the last, if he so chose. It could buy him that ivy-grown country house with a tennis court.

After the steak they served a salad, which surprised Harry. Salad was not often served in fancy restaurants in London, and certainly not as a separate course following the main dish.

Peach melba, coffee and *petits fours* came in rapid succession. Eddie the engineer seemed to realize he was being unsociable and made an effort to converse. 'May I ask what's the purpose of your trip, Mr Vandenpost?'

'I guess I want to stay out of the way of Hitler,' Harry said. 'At least until America gets into the war.'

'You think that will happen?' Eddie asked sceptically.

'It did last time.'

Tom Luther said, 'We have no quarrel with the Nazis. They're against Communism and so are we.'

Jack nodded in agreement.

Harry was taken aback. In England everyone thought America would come into the war. But around this table there was no such assumption. Perhaps the British were kidding themselves, he thought pessimistically. Maybe there was no help to be had from America. That would be bad news for Ma, back in London.

Eddie said, 'I think we may have to fight the Nazis.' There was an angry note in his voice. 'They're like gangsters,' he said, looking directly at Luther. 'In the end, people of that type just have to be exterminated, like rats.'

Jack stood up abruptly, looking worried. 'If we're through, Eddie, we'd better get a little rest,' he said firmly.

Eddie looked startled at this sudden demand, but after a moment he nodded assent and the two crew members took their leave.

Harry said, 'That engineer was kind of rude.'

'Was he?' said Luther. 'I didn't notice.'

You bloody liar, Harry thought. He practically called you a gangster!

Luther ordered a brandy. Harry wondered if he really was a gangster. The ones Harry knew in London were much more showy, with multiple rings and fur coats and two-tone shoes. Luther looked more like a self-made millionaire businessman, a meat packer or shipbuilder, something industrial. On impulse Harry asked him, 'What do you do for a living, Tom?'

'I'm a businessman in Rhode Island.'

It was not an encouraging reply, and a few moments later Harry stood up, gave a polite nod and left.

When he re-entered his compartment, Lord Oxenford said abruptly, 'Dinner any good?'

Harry had enjoyed it thoroughly, but upper-class people were never too enthusiastic about food. 'Not bad,' he said neutrally. 'And there's a drinkable hock.'

Oxenford grunted and went back to his newspaper. There's no one as rude as a rude lord, Harry thought.

Margaret smiled and looked pleased to see him. 'What was it like, really?' she said in a conspiratorial murmur.

'Delicious,' he replied, and they both laughed.

Margaret looked different when she laughed. In repose she was pale and unremarkable, but now her cheeks turned pink and she opened her mouth, showing two rows of even teeth, and tossed her hair; and she let out a throaty chuckle that Harry found sexy. He wanted to reach across the narrow aisle and touch her. He was about to do so when he caught the eye of Clive Membury, sitting opposite him, and for some reason that made him resist the impulse.

'There's a storm over the Atlantic,' he told her.

'Does that mean we'll have a rough ride?'

'Yes. They'll try to fly around the edge of it, but all the same it's going to be bumpy.'

It was hard to talk to her because the stewards were constantly passing along the aisle between them, carrying food to the dining room and returning with trays of dirty crockery. Harry was impressed that just two men were able to do the cooking and serving for so many diners.

He picked up a copy of *Life* magazine that Margaret had discarded and began to leaf through it while he waited impatiently for the Oxenfords to go to dinner. He had not brought any books or magazines: he was not much of a reader. He liked to see what was in the newspaper, but for entertainment he preferred the radio and the cinema.

At last the Oxenfords were called for dinner, and Harry was left alone with Clive Membury. The man had sat in the main lounge, playing cards, on the first leg of the trip, but now that the lounge had become the dining room he had settled in his seat. Perhaps he'll go to the carsey, Harry thought; and perhaps I'd better start calling it the john before I get caught out.

He wondered again whether Membury was a policeman, and if so what he was doing on the Pan American Clipper. If he was following a suspect, the crime would have to be a major one for the British police force to fork out for a Clipper ticket. But perhaps he was one of those people who save up for years and years to take some dream trip, a cruise down the Nile or a ride on the Orient Express. He might be an aircraft fanatic who just wanted to make the great transatlantic flight. If so I hope he's enjoying it, Harry thought. Ninety quid is a hell of a lot of money for a copper.

Patience was not Harry's strong point, and when after half an hour Membury had not moved, he decided to take matters into his own hands. 'Have you seen the flight deck, Mr Membury?' he asked.

'No—'

'Apparently it's really something. They say it's as big as the entire interior of a Douglas DC-3, and that's a pretty big airplane.'

'Goodness.' Membury was only politely interested. He was not an aircraft enthusiast, then.

'We ought to go look at it.' Harry stopped Nicky, who was going by with a tureen of turtle soup. 'Can passengers visit the flight deck?'

'Yes, sir, and welcome!'

'Is now a good time?'

'It's a very good time, Mr Vandenpost. We're not landing or taking off, the crew aren't changing watches, and the weather is calm. You couldn't pick a better moment.'

Harry had been hoping he would say that. He stood up and looked expectantly at Membury. 'Shall we?'

Membury looked as if he was about to refuse. He was not the type to be easily bullied. On the other hand, it might seem churlish to refuse to go and see the flight deck; and perhaps Membury would not want to seem disagreeable. After a moment's hesitation, he got to his feet, saying, 'By all means.'

Harry led him forward, past the kitchen and the men's room, and turned right, mounting the twisting staircase. At the top he emerged on to the flight deck. Membury was right behind him.

Harry looked around. It was nothing like his picture of the cockpit of an aeroplane. Clean, quiet and comfortable, it looked more like an office in a modern building. Harry's dinner companions, the navigator and the engineer, were not present, of course, as they were off duty; this was the alternative shift. However, the Captain was here, sitting behind a small table at the rear of the cabin. He looked up, smiled pleasantly, and said, 'Good evening, gentlemen. Would you like to look around?'

'Sure would,' said Harry. 'But I got to get my camera. Is it okay to take a picture?'

'You bet.'

'I'll be right back.'

He hurried down the stairs, pleased with himself but tense too. He had got Membury out of the way for a while, but his search would have to be very quick.

He returned to the compartment. One steward was in the galley and the other in the dining room. He would have liked to wait until both were busy serving at tables, so that he could feel confident they would not pass through the compartment for a few minutes, but he did not have time. He would just have to take a chance on being interrupted.

He pulled Lady Oxenford's bag out from under her seat. It was too big and heavy for a cabin bag, but she probably did not carry it herself. He put it on the seat and opened it. It was not locked: that was a bad sign – even she was not likely to be so innocent as to leave priceless jewellery in an unlocked case.

All the same he rummaged through it quickly, watching out of the corner of his eye in case anyone should walk in. There was scent and make-up, a silver brush-and-comb set, a chestnut-coloured dressing-gown, a nightdress, dainty slippers, peach-coloured silk underwear, stockings, a sponge bag containing a tooth-brush and the usual toiletries, and a book of Blake's poems – but no jewels.

Harry cursed silently. He had felt this was the likeliest place it would be. Now he began to doubt his whole theory.

The search had taken about twenty seconds.

He closed the case quickly and put it back under the seat.

He wondered whether she had asked her husband to carry the jewels.

He looked at the bag under Lord Oxenford's seat. The stewards were still busy. He decided to push his luck.

He pulled out Oxenford's bag. It was like a carpet-bag, but leather. It was fastened with a zip at the top and the zip had a little padlock. Harry carried a penknife with him for moments such as this. He used the knife to snap the padlock, then unzipped the bag.

As he was rifling through the contents, the little steward, Davy, came through, carrying a tray of drinks from the galley. Harry looked up at him and smiled; Davy looked at the bag. Harry held his breath and kept his frozen smile. The steward passed on into the dining room. He had naturally assumed the bag was Harry's own.

Harry breathed again. He was a master at disarming suspicion, but every time he did it he was scared to death.

Oxenford's bag contained the masculine equivalent of what his wife was carrying: shaving tackle, hair oil, striped pyjamas, flannel underwear and a biography of Napoleon. Harry zipped it up and replaced the padlock. Oxenford would find it broken and wonder how it had happened. If he was suspicious he would check to see whether anything was missing. Finding everything in place, he would imagine the lock had been faulty.

Harry put the bag back in its place.

He had got away with it, but he was no nearer the Delhi Suite.

It was unlikely the children were carrying the jewels but, recklessly, he decided to go through their luggage.

If Lord Oxenford had decided to be sly and put his wife's jewellery in his children's luggage, he would be more likely to pick Percy, who would be thrilled by the conspiracy, than Margaret, who was disposed to defy her father.

Harry picked up Percy's canvas hold-all and put it on the seat just where he had placed Oxenford's bag, hoping that if Davy the steward passed through again he would think it was the same bag.

Percy's things were so neatly packed that Harry was sure a servant had done it. No normal fourteen-year-old boy would fold his pyjamas and wrap them in tissue paper. His sponge bag contained a new toothbrush and a fresh tube of toothpaste. There was a pocket chess set, a small bundle of comics, and a packet of chocolate biscuits – put there, Harry imagined, by a fond cook or housemaid. Harry looked inside the chess set, riffled through the comics and broke open the biscuit packet, but he found no jewels.

As he was replacing the bag, a passenger walked through on the way to the men's room. Harry ignored him.

He could not believe Lady Oxenford had left the Delhi Suite behind, in a country that might be invaded and conquered within a few weeks. But she was not wearing it, or carrying it, as far as he could tell. If it was not in Margaret's bag, it had to be in the checked baggage. That would be tough to get at. Could you get into the hold while the plane was in the air? The alternative might be to follow the Oxenfords to their hotel in New York . . .

The Captain and Clive Membury would be wondering how he could take so long to fetch his camera.

He picked up Margaret's bag. It looked like a birthday present: a small, round-cornered case made of soft cream leather with beautiful brass fittings. When he opened it he smelled her perfume, Tosca. He found a cotton nightdress with a pattern of small flowers, and tried to picture her in it. It was too girlish for her. Her underwear was plain white cotton. He wondered whether she was a virgin. There was a small framed photograph of a boy about twenty-one, a handsome fellow with longish dark hair and black eyebrows, wearing a college gown and a mortar-board hat: the boy who died in Spain, presumably. Had she slept with him? Harry rather thought she might have, despite her schoolgirl underpants. She was reading a novel by D. H. Lawrence. I bet her mother doesn't know about that, Harry thought. There was a little stack of linen handkerchiefs embroidered 'M.O.'. They smelled of Tosca.

The jewels were not here. Damn it to hell.

Harry decided to take one of the scented handkerchiefs as a souvenir; and just as he picked it up, Davy the steward passed through carrying a tray stacked high with soup bowls.

He glanced at Harry and then stopped, frowning. Margaret's bag looked quite different from Lord Oxenford's, of course. It was plain that Harry could not be the owner of both bags; therefore he had to be looking in other people's.

Davy stared at him for a moment, obviously suspicious but also frightened of accusing a passenger. Eventually he stammered, 'Sir, is that your case?'

Harry showed him the little handkerchief. 'Would I blow my nose in this?' He closed the case and replaced it.

Davy still looked worried. Harry said, 'She asked me to fetch it. The things we do . . .'

Davy's expression changed and he looked embarrassed. 'I'm sorry, sir, but I hope you understand—'

'I'm happy you're on your toes,' Harry said. 'Keep up the good work.' He patted Davy's shoulder. Now he had to give the damn handkerchief to Margaret in order to lend credence to his story. He stepped into the dining room.

She was at a table with her parents and her brother. He held out the handkerchief to her, saying, 'You dropped this.'

She was surprised. 'Did I? Thank you!'

'You bet.' He got out fast. Would Davy check his story by asking her whether she had told Harry to fetch her a clean handkerchief? He doubted it.

He went back through his compartment, passed the galley where Davy was stacking the dirty dishes, and climbed the spiral staircase. How the hell was he going to get into the baggage hold? He did not even know where it was: he had not watched the luggage being loaded. But there had to be a way.

Captain Baker was explaining to Clive Membury how they navigated across the featureless ocean. 'Most of the time we're out of range of the radio beacons, so the stars provide our best guide – when we can see them.'

Membury looked up at Harry. 'No camera?' he said sharply.

Definitely a copper, Harry thought. 'I forgot to load it with film,' he said. 'Dumb, huh?' He looked around. 'How can you see the stars from in here?'

'Oh, the navigator just steps outside for a moment,' the Captain said straight-faced. Then he grinned. 'Just kidding. There's an observatory. I'll show you.' He opened a door at the rear end of the flight deck and stepped through. Harry followed and found himself in a narrow passage. The Captain pointed up. 'This is the observation dome.' Harry looked up without much interest: his mind was still on Lady Oxenford's jewellery. There was a glazed bubble in the roof, and a folding ladder hung on a hook to one side. 'He just climbs up there with his octant any time there's a break in the cloud. This is also the baggage loading hatch.'

Harry was suddenly attentive. 'The baggage comes in through the roof?' he said.

'Sure. Right here.'

'And then where is it stowed?'

The Captain pointed to the two doors either side of the narrow passage. 'In the baggage holds.'

Harry could hardly believe his luck. 'So all the bags are right here, behind those doors?'

'Yes, sir.'

Harry tried one of the doors. It was not locked. He looked inside. There were the suitcases and trunks of the passengers, carefully stacked and roped to the struts so they would not move in flight.

Somewhere in there was the Delhi Suite, and a life of luxury for Harry Marks.

Clive Membury was looking over Harry's shoulder. 'Fascinating,' he murmured.

'You can say that again,' said Harry.

CHAPTER FOURTEEN

MARGARET WAS in high spirits. She kept forgetting that she did not want to go to America. She could hardly believe she had made friends with a real thief! Ordinarily, if someone had said to her, 'I'm a thief,' she would not have believed him; but in Harry's case she knew it was true because she had met him in a police station and seen him accused.

She had always been fascinated by people who lived outside the ordered social world: criminals, Bohemians, anarchists, prostitutes and tramps. They seemed so free. Of course, they might not be free to order champagne or fly to New York or send their children to university – she was not so naïve as to overlook the restrictions of being an outcast. But people such as Harry never had to do anything just because they were ordered to, and that seemed wonderful to her. She dreamed of being a guerrilla fighter, living in the hills, wearing trousers and carrying a rifle, stealing food and sleeping under the stars and never having her clothes ironed.

She never met people like that; or if she met them she did not recognize them for what they were – had she not sat on a doorstep in 'the most notorious street in London' without realizing she would be taken for a prostitute? How long ago that seemed, although it was only last night.

Getting to know Harry was the most interesting thing that had happened to her for ages. He represented everything she had ever longed for. He could do anything he liked! This morning he had decided to go to America and this afternoon he was on his way. If he wanted to dance all night and sleep all day he just did. He ate and drank what he liked, when he felt like it, at the Ritz or in a pub or on board the Pan American Clipper. He could join the Communist Party and then leave it without explaining himself to anyone. When he needed money he just took some from people who had more than they deserved. He was a complete free spirit!

She longed to know more about him, and resented the time she had to waste having dinner without him.

There were three tables of four in the dining room. Baron Gabon and Carl Hartmann were at the next table to the Oxenfords. Father had thrown a dirty look at them when they came in, presumably because they were Jewish. Sharing their table were Ollis Field and Frank Gordon. Frank Gordon was a boy a bit older than Harry, a handsome devil, though with something of a brutal look to his mouth, and Ollis Field was a washed-out-looking older man, completely bald. These two had attracted some comment by remaining on board the plane when everyone else had disembarked at Foynes.

At the third table were Lulu Bell and Princess Lavinia, who was loudly complaining that there was too much salt in the sauce on the shrimp cocktail. With them were two people who had joined the plane at Foynes, Mr Lovesey and Mrs Lenehan. Percy said the new people were sharing the honeymoon suite although they were not married. Margaret was surprised that Pan American allowed that. Perhaps they were bending the rules because so many people were desperate to get to America.

Percy sat down to dinner wearing a black Jewish skull-cap. Margaret giggled. Where on earth had he got that? Father snatched it off his head, growling furiously, 'Foolish boy!'

Mother's face had the glazed look it had shown ever since she stopped crying over Elizabeth. She said vaguely, 'It seems awfully early to be dining.'

'It's half-past seven,' Father said.

'Why isn't it getting dark?'

Percy answered, 'It is, back in England. But we're three hundred miles off the Irish coast. We're chasing the sun.'

'But it will get dark eventually.'

'About nine o'clock, I should think,' Percy said.

'Good,' Mother said.

'Do you realize that if we went fast enough, we would keep up with the sun and it would never get dark?' said Percy.

Father said condescendingly, 'I don't think there's any chance men will ever build planes that fast.'

The steward, Nicky, brought their first course. 'Not for me, thank you,' Percy said. 'Shrimps aren't kosher.'

The steward shot him a startled look but said nothing. Father went red.

Margaret hastily changed the subject. 'When do we reach the next stop, Percy?' He always knew such things.

'Journey time to Botwood is sixteen and a half hours,' he said. 'We should arrive at nine a.m. British Summer Time.'

'But what will the time be there?'

'Newfoundland Standard Time is three and a half hours behind Greenwich Mean Time.'

'Three and a *half*?' Margaret was surprised. 'I didn't know there were places that took odd half-hours.'

Percy went on, 'And Botwood is on Daylight Saving, like Britain, so the local time when we land will be five thirty in the morning.'

'I shan't be able to wake up,' Mother said tiredly.

'Yes, you will,' Percy said impatiently. 'You'll *feel* as if it's nine o'clock.'

Mother murmured, 'Boys are so good at technical things.'

She irritated Margaret when she pretended to be stupid. She believed it was not feminine to understand technicalities. 'Men don't like girls to be too clever, dear,' she had said to Margaret, more than once. Margaret no longer argued with her but she did not believe it. Only stupid men felt that way, in her opinion. Clever men liked clever girls.

She became conscious of slightly raised voices at the next table. Baron Gabon and Carl Hartmann were arguing, while their dinner companions looked on in bemused silence. Margaret had noticed that Gabon and Hartmann had been deep in discussion every time she looked at them. Perhaps it was not surprising: if you were talking to one of the greatest brains in the world you wouldn't make small talk. She heard the word 'Palestine'. They must be discussing Zionism. She shot a nervous glance at Father. He too had heard, and was looking bad-tempered. Before he could say anything Margaret said, 'We're going to fly through a storm. It could get bumpy.'

'How do you know?' Percy said. There was a jealous note in his voice: he was the expert on flight details, not Margaret.

'Harry told me.'

'And how would *he* know?'

'He dined with the engineer and the navigator.'

'I'm not scared,' Percy said, in a tone which suggested that he was.

It had not occurred to Margaret to worry about the storm. It might be uncomfortable, but surely there was no real danger?

Father drained his glass and asked the steward irritably for more wine. Was he frightened of the storm? He was drinking even more than usual, she had observed. His face was flushed and his pale eyes seemed to stare. Was he nervous? Perhaps he was still upset over Elizabeth.

Mother said, 'Margaret, you should talk more to that quiet Mr Membury.'

Margaret was surprised. 'Why? He seems to want to be left alone.'

'I expect he's just shy.'

It was not like Mother to take pity on shy people,

especially if they were, like Mr Membury, unmistakably middle-class. 'Out with it, Mother,' said Margaret. 'What do you mean?'

'I just don't want you to spend the entire flight talking to Mr Vandenpost.'

That was exactly what Margaret *was* going to do. 'Why on earth shouldn't I?' she said.

'Well, he's your age, you know, and you don't want to give him ideas.'

'I might rather like to give him ideas. He's frightfully good-looking.'

'No, dear,' she said firmly. 'There's something about him that isn't quite *quite.*' She meant he was not upper class. Like many foreigners who married into the aristocracy, Mother was even more snobbish than the English.

So she had not been completely taken in by Harry's impersonation of a wealthy young American. Her social antennae were infallible. 'But you said you knew the Philadelphia Vandenposts,' Margaret said.

'I do, but now that I think about it I'm sure he's not from that family.'

'I may cultivate him just to punish you for being such a snob, Mother.'

'It's not snobbery, dear, it's breeding. Snobbery is vulgar.'

Margaret gave up. The armour of Mother's superiority was impenetrable. It was useless to reason with her. But Margaret had no intention of obeying her. Harry was far too interesting.

Percy said, 'I wonder what Mr Membury is? I like his

red waistcoat. He doesn't look like a regular transatlantic traveller.'

Mother remarked, 'I expect he's some kind of functionary.'

That was just what he looked like, Margaret thought. Mother had the sharpest eye for that sort of thing.

Father said, 'He probably works for the airline.'

'More like a civil servant, I should say,' Mother said.

The stewards brought the main course. Mother refused the *filet mignon*. 'I never eat cooked food,' she told Nicky. 'Just bring me some celery and caviar.'

From the next table Margaret heard Baron Gabon say, 'We must have a land of our own – there's no other solution!'

Carl Hartmann replied, 'But you've admitted that it will have to be a militarized state—'

'For defence against hostile neighbours!'

'And you concede that it will have to discriminate against Arabs in favour of Jews – but militarism and racism combined make Fascism, which is what you're supposed to be fighting against!'

'Hush, not so loud,' Gabon said, and they lowered their voices.

In normal circumstances Margaret would have been interested in the argument: she had discussed it with Ian. Socialists were divided about Palestine: some said it was an opportunity to create an ideal state; others that it belonged to the people who lived there and could not be 'given' to the Jews any more than Ireland, or Hong Kong, or Texas. The fact that so many socialists were Jewish only complicated the issue.

However, now she just wished Gabon and Hartmann would calm down so that Father would not hear.

Unfortunately it was not to be. They were arguing about something close to their hearts. Hartmann raised his voice again and said, 'I don't want to live in a racist state!'

Father said loudly, 'I didn't know we were travelling with a pack of Jews.'

'Oy, vey,' said Percy.

Margaret looked at her father in dismay. There had been a time when his political philosophy had made a kind of sense. When millions of able-bodied men were unemployed and starving, it had seemed courageous to say that both capitalism and socialism had failed and that democracy did the ordinary man no good. There had been something appealing about the idea of an all-powerful State directing industry under the leadership of a benevolent dictator. But those high ideals and bold policies had now degenerated into this mindless bigotry. She had thought of Father when she found a copy of *Hamlet* in the library at home and read the line, 'O, what a noble mind is here o'erthrown!'

She did not think the two men had heard Father's crass remark, for he had his back to them and they were absorbed in the debate. To get Father off the subject she said brightly, 'What time should we all go to bed?'

Percy said, 'I'd like to go early.' That was unusual, but of course he was looking forward to the novelty of sleeping on a plane.

Mother said, 'We'll go at the usual time.'

'But in what time zone?' Percy said. 'Shall I go at ten thirty British Summer Time, or ten thirty Newfoundland Daylight Saving Time?'

'America is racist!' Baron Gabon exclaimed. 'So is France – England – the Soviet Union – all racist states!'

Father exclaimed, 'For God's sake!'

Margaret said, 'Half-past nine would suit me fine.'

Percy noticed the rhyme. 'I'll be more dead than alive by ten-oh-five,' he countered.

It was a game they had played as children. Mother joined in. 'You won't see me again after quarter to ten.'

'Show me your tattoo at a quarter to.'

'I'll be the last at twenty past.'

'Your turn, Father,' said Percy.

There was a moment of silence. Father had played the game with them, in the old days, before he became bitter and disappointed. For an instant his face softened, and Margaret thought he would join in.

Then Carl Hartmann said, 'So why set up yet another racist state?'

That did it. Father turned round, red-faced and spluttering. Before anybody could do anything to stop him he burst out, 'You Jewboys had better keep your voices down.'

Hartmann and Gabon stared at him in astonishment.

Margaret felt her face flush bright red. Father had spoken loudly enough for everyone to hear, and the room had gone completely quiet. She wanted the floor to open up and swallow her. She was mortified that people should look at her and know she was the daughter of the coarse, drunken fool sitting opposite

347

her. She caught the eye of Nicky, and saw by his face that he felt sorry for her; and that made her feel worse.

Baron Gabon turned pale. For a moment it seemed that he would say something in return, but then he changed his mind and looked away. Hartmann gave a twisted grin, and the thought flashed through Margaret's mind that to him, coming from Nazi Germany, this sort of thing probably seemed mild.

Father had not finished. 'This is a first class compartment,' he added.

Margaret was watching Baron Gabon. In an attempt to ignore Father, he picked up his spoon, but his hand was shaking and he spilled soup on his dove-grey waistcoat. He gave up and put the spoon down.

This visible sign of his distress touched Margaret's heart. She felt fiercely angry with her father. She turned to him and for once she had the courage to tell him what she thought. She said furiously, 'You have just grossly insulted two of the most distinguished men in Europe!'

He said, 'Two of the most distinguished *Jews* in Europe.'

Percy said, 'Remember Granny Fishbein.'

Father rounded on him. Wagging a finger he said, 'You're to stop that nonsense, do you hear me?'

'I need to go to the lavatory,' Percy said, getting up. 'I feel sick.' He left the room.

Margaret realized that both Percy and she had stood up to Father, and he had not been able to do anything about it. That had to be some kind of milestone.

Father lowered his voice and spoke to Margaret.

'Remember that these are the people who have driven us out of our home!' he hissed. Then he raised his voice again. 'If they want to travel with us they ought to learn manners.'

'That's enough!' said a new voice.

Margaret looked across the room. The speaker was Mervyn Lovesey, the man who had got on at Foynes. He was standing up. The stewards, Nicky and Davy, stood frozen still, looking scared. Lovesey came across the dining room and leaned on the Oxenfords' table, looking dangerous. He was a tall, authoritative man in his forties with thick greying hair, black eyebrows and chiselled features. He wore an expensive suit but spoke with a Lancashire accent. 'I'll thank you to keep those views to yourself,' he said in a quietly threatening tone.

Father said, 'None of your damn business—'

'But it is,' said Lovesey.

Margaret saw Nicky leave hastily, and guessed he was going to summon help from the flight deck.

Lovesey went on, 'You wouldn't know anything about this, but Professor Hartmann is the leading physicist in the world.'

'I don't care what he is—'

'No, you wouldn't. But I do. And I find your opinions as offensive as a bad smell.'

'I shall say what I please,' Father said, and he made to get up.

Lovesey held him down with a strong hand on his shoulder. 'We're at war with people like you.'

Father said weakly, 'Clear off, will you?'

'I'll clear off if you'll shut up.'

'I shall call the Captain—'

'No need,' said a new voice, and Captain Baker appeared, looking calmly authoritative in his uniform cap. 'I'm here. Mr Lovesey, may I ask you to return to your seat? I'd be much obliged to you.'

'Aye, I'll sit down,' said Lovesey. 'But I'll not listen in silence while the most eminent scientist in Europe is told to keep his voice down and called a Jewboy by this drunken oaf.'

'Please, Mr Lovesey.'

Lovesey returned to his seat.

The Captain turned to Father. 'Lord Oxenford, perhaps you were misheard. I'm sure you would not call another passenger the word mentioned by Mr Lovesey.'

Margaret prayed that Father would accept this way out, but to her dismay he became more belligerent. 'I called him a Jewboy because that's what he is!' he blustered.

'Father, stop it!' she cried.

The Captain said to Father, 'I must ask you not to use such terms while you're on board my aircraft.'

Father was scornful. 'Is he ashamed of being a Jewboy?'

Margaret could see that Captain Baker was getting angry. 'This is an American airplane, sir, and we have American standards of behaviour. I insist that you stop insulting other passengers, and I warn you that I am empowered to have you arrested and confined to prison by the local police at our next port of call. You should be aware that in such cases, rare though they are, the airline always presses charges.'

Father was shaken by the threat of imprisonment. For a moment he was silenced. Margaret felt deeply humiliated. Although she had tried to stop her father, and protested against his behaviour, nevertheless she felt ashamed. His oafishness reflected on her: she was his daughter. She buried her face in her hands. She could not take any more.

She heard Father say, 'I shall return to my compartment.' She looked up. He was getting to his feet. He turned to Mother. 'My dear?'

Mother stood up, Father holding her chair. Margaret felt that all eyes were on her.

Harry suddenly appeared out of nowhere. He rested his hands lightly on the back of Margaret's chair. 'Lady Margaret,' he said with a little bow. She stood up, and he drew back the chair. She felt deeply grateful for this gesture of support.

Mother walked away from the table, her face expressionless, her head held high. Father followed her.

Harry gave Margaret his arm. It was only a little thing, but it meant a great deal to her. Although she was blushing furiously, she felt able to walk out of the room with dignity.

A buzz of conversation broke out behind her as she passed into the compartment.

Harry handed her to her seat.

'That was so gracious of you,' she said with feeling. 'I don't know how to thank you.'

'I could hear the row from in here,' he said quietly. 'I knew you'd be feeling bad.'

'I've never been so humiliated,' she said abjectly.

But Father had not yet finished. 'They'll be sorry one day, the damn fools!' he said. Mother sat in her corner and stared blankly at him. 'They're going to lose this war, you mark my words.'

Margaret said, 'No more, Father, please.' Fortunately only Harry was present to hear the tirade continue: Mr Membury had disappeared.

Father ignored her. 'The German army will sweep across England like a tidal wave!' he said. 'And then what do you think will happen? Hitler will install a Fascist government, of course.' Suddenly there was an odd light in his eye. My God, he looks crazy, Margaret thought; my father is going insane. He lowered his voice, and his face took on a crafty expression. 'An *English* Fascist government, of course. And he will need an English Fascist to lead it!'

'Oh, my God,' said Margaret. She saw what he was thinking and it made her despair.

Father thought Hitler was going to make him dictator of Britain.

He thought Britain would be conquered, and Hitler would call him back from exile to be the leader of a puppet government.

'And when there's a Fascist Prime Minister in London – *then* they'll dance to a different tune!' Father said triumphantly, as if he had won some argument.

Harry was staring at Father in astonishment. 'Do you imagine . . . do you expect Hitler to ask *you* . . .?'

'Who knows?' Father said. 'It would have to be someone who bore no taint of the defeated administration. If called upon ... my duty to my country ... fresh start, no recriminations ...'

Harry looked too shocked to say anything.

Margaret was in despair. She had to get away from Father. She could not take any more. She shuddered when she recalled the ignominious upshot of her last attempt to run away, but she should not let one failure discourage her. She had to try again.

It would be different this time. She would learn by Elizabeth's example. She would think carefully and plan ahead. She would make sure she had money, friends and a place to sleep. This time she would make it work.

Percy emerged from the men's room, having missed most of the drama. However, he appeared to have been in a drama of his own: his face was flushed and he looked excited. 'Guess what!' he said to the compartment in general. 'I just saw Mr Membury in the washroom – he had his jacket undone and he was tucking his shirt into his trousers – and he's got a shoulder holster under his jacket – and there's a gun in it!'

CHAPTER FIFTEEN

T HE CLIPPER was approaching the point of no
return.

Eddie Deakin, distracted, nervy, unrested, went back
on duty at 10 p.m., British time. By this hour the sun
had raced ahead, leaving the aircraft in darkness. The
weather had changed too. Rain lashed the windows,
cloud obscured the stars, and inconstant winds buffeted the mighty plane disrespectfully, shaking up the
passengers.

The weather was generally worse at low altitudes, but
despite this Captain Baker was flying close to sea level.
He was 'hunting the wind', searching for the altitude at
which the westerly head wind was least strong.

Eddie was worried because he knew the plane was
low on fuel. He sat down at his station and began
to calculate the distance the plane could travel on
what remained in the tanks. Because the weather was
a little worse than forecast, the engines must have
burned more fuel than anticipated. If there was not
sufficient left to carry the plane to Newfoundland, it
would have to turn back before it reached the point of
no return.

And then what would happen to Carol-Ann?

Tom Luther was nothing if not a careful planner and he must have considered the possibility that the Clipper would be delayed. He had to have some way of contacting his cronies to confirm or alter the time of the rendezvous.

But if the plane turned back, Carol-Ann would remain in the hands of the kidnappers for at least another twenty-four hours.

Eddie had sat in the forward compartment, fidgeting restlessly and looking out of the window at nothing at all, for most of his off-duty shift. He had not even tried to sleep, knowing it would be hopeless. Images of Carol-Ann had tormented him constantly: Carol-Ann in tears, or tied up, or bruised; Carol-Ann frightened, pleading, hysterical, desperate. Every five minutes he wanted to put his fist through the fuselage, and he had fought constantly against the impulse to run up the stairs and ask his replacement, Mickey Finn, about the fuel consumption.

It was because he was so distracted that he had allowed himself to needle Tom Luther in the dining room. His behaviour had been very dumb. A piece of real bad luck had put them at the same table. Afterwards, the navigator, Jack Ashford, had lectured Eddie, and he saw how stupid he had been. Now Jack knew something was going on between Eddie and Luther. Eddie had refused to enlighten Jack further, and Jack had accepted that – for now. Eddie had mentally vowed to be more careful. If Captain Baker should even suspect that his engineer was being blackmailed he would abort the flight, and then Eddie would be powerless to help Carol-Ann. Now he had that to worry about as well.

Eddie's attitude to Tom Luther had been forgotten, during the second dinner sitting, in the excitement of the near-fight between Mervyn Lovesey and Lord Oxenford. Eddie had not witnessed it – he had been in the forward compartment, worrying – but the stewards had told him all about it soon afterwards. Oxenford seemed to Eddie to be a brute who needed to be brought down a peg or two, and that was what Captain Baker had done. Eddie felt sorry for the boy, Percy, being raised by such a father.

The third sitting would be coming to an end in a few minutes, and then things would start to go quiet on the passenger deck. The older ones would go to bed. The majority would sit for a couple of hours, riding the bumps, too excited or nervous to feel sleepy; then, one by one, they would succumb to nature's timetable and retire to bed. A few diehards would start a card game in the main lounge, and they would continue drinking, but it would be the quiet, steady kind of all-night drinking that rarely led to trouble.

Eddie anxiously plotted the plane's fuel consumption on the Howgozit Curve. The red line which showed actual consumption was consistently above the pencil line of his forecast. That was almost inevitable, since he had faked his forecast. But the difference was greater than he had expected because of the weather.

He got more worried as he worked out the plane's effective range with the remaining fuel. When he made the calculation on the basis of three engines – which he was obliged to do by the safety rules – he found that there was not enough fuel to take them to Newfoundland.

He should have told the Captain immediately, but he did not.

The shortfall was very small: with four engines there would be enough fuel. Furthermore, the situation might change in the next couple of hours. The winds might be lighter than forecast so that the plane used less fuel than anticipated, and there would be more left for the rest of the journey. And finally, if the worst came to the worst, they could change their route and fly through the heart of the storm, thereby shortening the distance. The passengers would just have to suffer the bumps.

On his left the radio operator, Ben Thompson, was transcribing a Morse code message, his bald head bent over his console. Hoping it would be a forecast of better weather, Eddie stood behind him and read over his shoulder.

The message astonished and mystified him.

It was from the FBI, addressed to someone called Ollis Field. It read:

THE BUREAU HAS RECEIVED INFORMATION THAT ASSOCIATES OF KNOWN CRIMINALS MAY BE ON YOUR FLIGHT. TAKE EXTRA PRECAUTIONS WITH THE PRISONER.

What did it mean? And did it have something to do with the kidnapping of Carol-Ann? For a moment Eddie's head spun with the possibilities.

Ben tore the page off his pad and said, 'Captain! You'd better take a look at this.'

Jack Ashford glanced up from his chart table, alerted by the urgent note in the radioman's voice. Eddie took the message from Ben, showed it to Jack for a moment, then passed it to Captain Baker, who was eating steak and mashed potatoes from a tray at the conference table at the rear of the cabin.

The Captain's face darkened as he read. 'I don't like the look of this,' he said. 'Ollis Field must be an FBI agent.'

'Is he a passenger?' Eddie asked.

'Yes. I thought there was something strange about him. Drab character, not a typical Clipper passenger. He stayed on board during the stopover at Foynes.'

Eddie had not noticed him, but the navigator had. 'I think I know who you mean,' said Jack, scratching his blue chin. 'Bald guy. There's a younger fellow with him, kind of flashily dressed. They seem like an odd couple.'

The Captain said, 'The kid must be the prisoner. I think his name is Frank Gordon.'

Eddie's mind was working fast. 'That's why they stayed on board at Foynes: the FBI man doesn't want to give his prisoner a chance to escape.'

The Captain nodded grimly. 'Gordon must have been extradited from Britain – and you don't get extradition orders for shoplifters. The guy must be a dangerous criminal. And they put him on my plane without telling me!'

The radio operator said, 'I wonder what he did.'

'Frank Gordon,' Jack mused. 'It rings a bell. Wait a minute – I bet he's Frankie Gordino!'

Eddie remembered reading about Gordino in the newspapers. He was an enforcer for a New England gang. The particular crime he was wanted for involved a Boston nightclub owner who refused to pay protection money. Gordino had bust into the club, shot the owner in the stomach, raped the man's girlfriend, then torched the club. The guy died but the girl escaped the fire and identified Gordino from pictures.

'We'll soon find out if it's him,' said Baker. 'Eddie, do me a favour, go and ask this Ollis Field to come up here.'

'Sure thing.' Eddie put on his cap and uniform jacket and went down the stairs, turning this new development over in his mind. He was sure there was some connection between Frankie Gordino and the people who had Carol-Ann, and he tried frantically to figure it out, without success.

He looked into the galley, where a steward was filling a coffee jug from the massive fifty-gallon urn. 'Davy,' he said. 'Where's Mr Ollis Field?'

'Compartment number four, port side, facing the rear,' the steward said.

Eddie walked along the aisle, keeping his balance on the unsteady floor with a practised gait. He noticed the Oxenford family looking subdued in No. 2 compartment. In the dining room the last sitting was just about finished, the after-dinner coffee spilling into the saucers as the gathering storm buffeted the plane. He went through No. 3 then up a step to No. 4.

In the rear-facing seat on the port side was a bald man of about forty, looking sleepy, smoking a cigarette and staring through the window at the darkness outside. This was not Eddie's picture of an FBI agent: he could not see this man with a gun in his hand bursting into a room full of bootleggers.

Opposite Field was a younger man, much better dressed, with the build of a retired athlete who is putting on weight. That would have to be Gordino. He had the puffy, sulky face of a spoilt child. Would he shoot a man in the stomach? Eddie wondered. Yes, I think he would.

Eddie spoke to the older man. 'Mr Field?'

'Yes.'

'The Captain would like a word, if you can spare him a moment.'

A slight frown crossed Field's face, followed by a look of resignation. He had guessed that his secret was out, and he was irritated, but his look implied that in the long run it was all the same to him. 'Of course,' he said. He crushed out his cigarette in the wall-mounted ashtray, unfastened his seat belt, and stood up.

'Follow me, please,' Eddie said.

On the way back, passing through No. 3 compartment, Eddie saw Tom Luther, and their eyes met. In that instant Eddie had a flash of inspiration.

Tom Luther's mission was to rescue Frankie Gordino.

He was so struck by the explanation that he stopped, and Ollis Field bumped into his back.

Luther stared at him with a panicky look in his eyes,

obviously afraid Eddie was going to do something that would give the game away.

'Pardon me,' Eddie said to Field, and he walked on.

Everything was becoming clear. Frankie Gordino had been forced to flee the States, but the FBI had tracked him down in Britain and got him extradited. They had decided to fly him back, and somehow his partners in crime had found out about it. They were going to try to get Gordino off the plane before it reached the United States.

That was where Eddie came in. He would bring the Clipper down in the sea off the Maine coast. There would be a fast boat waiting. Gordino would be taken off the Clipper and would speed away in the boat. A few minutes later he would go ashore at some sheltered inlet, possibly on the Canadian side of the border. A car would be waiting to whisk him into hiding. He would have escaped justice – thanks to Eddie Deakin.

As he led Field up the spiral staircase to the flight deck, Eddie felt relieved that at last he understood what was going on, and horrified that in order to save his wife he had to help a murderer go free.

'Captain, this is Mr Field,' he said.

Captain Baker had put on his uniform jacket and was seated behind the conference table with the radio message in his hand. His dinner tray had been taken away. His cap covered his blond hair, and gave him an air of authority. He looked up at Field but did not ask him to sit down. 'I've received a message for you – from the FBI,' he said.

Field held out his hand for the paper, but Baker did not give it to him.

'Are you an agent of the FBI?' the Captain asked.

'Yes.'

'And are you on Bureau business right now?'

'Yes, I am.'

'What is that business, Mr Field?'

'I don't think you need to know that, Captain. Please give me the message. You did say it was addressed to me, not to you.'

'I'm the Captain of this vessel, and it's my judgement that I do need to know what business you're on. Don't argue with me, Mr Field, just do as I say.'

Eddie studied Field. He was a pale, tired man with a bald head and watery blue eyes. He was tall and had once been powerfully built, but he was now round-shouldered and slack-looking. Eddie guessed him to be arrogant rather than brave and this was confirmed when Field immediately caved in under pressure from the Captain.

'I'm escorting an extradited prisoner back to the United States for trial,' he said. 'His name is Frank Gordon.'

'Also known as Frankie Gordino?'

'That's right.'

'I want you to know, mister, that I object to your bringing a dangerous criminal on board my airplane without telling me.'

'If you know the man's real name, you probably also know what he does for a living. He works for Raymond Patriarca, who is responsible for armed robberies,

extortion, loansharking, illegal gambling and prostitution from Rhode Island to Maine. Ray Patriarca has
been declared Public Enemy Number One by the
Providence Board of Public Safety. Gordino is what we
call an enforcer: he terrorizes, tortures and murders
people on Patriarca's orders. We couldn't warn you
about him for security reasons.'

'Your security is shit, Field.' Baker was really angry:
Eddie had never known him to swear at a passenger.
'The Patriarca gang knows all about it.' He handed
over the radio message.

Field read it and turned grey. 'How the *hell* did they
find out?' he muttered.

'I have to ask which passengers are the "associates of
known criminals",' said the Captain. 'Do you recognize
anyone on board?'

'Of course not,' Field said irritably. 'If I had, I would
have alerted the Bureau already.'

'If we can identify the people I'll put them off the
plane at the next stop.'

Eddie thought, I know who they are – Tom Luther
and me.

Field said, 'Radio the agency with a complete list of
passengers and crew. They'll run a check on every
name.'

A shiver of anxiety ran through Eddie. Was there
any risk that Tom Luther would be exposed by this
check? That could ruin everything. Was he a known
criminal? Was Tom Luther his real name? If he was
using a false name he needed a forged passport too –
but that might not be a problem if he was in league

with big-time racketeers. Surely he would have taken that precaution? Everything else he had done had been well organized.

Captain Baker bristled. 'I don't think we need to worry about the crew.'

Field shrugged. 'Please yourself. The Bureau will get the names from Pan American in a minute.'

Field was a tactless man, Eddie reflected. Did FBI agents get advice on how to be unpleasant from J. Edgar Hoover?

The Captain picked up the passenger manifest and crew list from his table and handed it to the radio operator. 'Send that right away, Ben,' he said. He paused, then added, 'Include the crew.'

Ben Thompson sat at his console and began to tap out the message in Morse.

'One more thing,' the Captain said to Field. 'I'll have to relieve you of your weapon.'

That was smart, Eddie thought. It had not even occurred to him that Field might be armed – but he had to be, if he was escorting a dangerous criminal.

Field said, 'I object—'

'Passengers are not allowed to carry firearms. There are no exceptions to this rule. Hand over your gun.'

'If I refuse?'

'Mr Deakin and Mr Ashford will take it from you anyway.'

Eddie was surprised by this announcement, but he played the part and moved threateningly closer to Field. Jack did the same.

Baker continued, 'And if you oblige me to use force,

I will have you put off the plane at our next stop, and I will not permit you to re-board.'

Eddie was impressed at how the Captain maintained his superiority despite the fact that his antagonist was armed. This was not how it happened in the movies, where the man with the gun was able to boss everyone else around.

What would Field do? The FBI would not approve of his giving up his gun, but on the other hand it would surely be worse to get thrown off the plane.

Field said, 'I'm escorting a dangerous prisoner – I need to be armed.'

Eddie saw something out of the corner of his eye. The door at the rear of the cabin, that led to the observation dome and the cargo holds, was ajar, and behind it something moved.

Captain Baker said, 'Take his gun, Eddie.'

Eddie reached inside Field's jacket. The man did not move. Eddie found the shoulder holster, unbuttoned the flap and withdrew the gun. Field looked ahead stonily.

Then Eddie stepped to the rear of the cabin and threw open the door.

Young Percy Oxenford stood there.

Eddie was relieved. He had half imagined that some of Gordino's gang would be waiting there with machine-guns.

Captain Baker stared at Percy and said, 'Where did you come from?'

'There's a ladder next to the ladies' powder room,' Percy said. 'It leads up into the tail of the plane.' That was where Eddie had inspected the rudder trim control cables. 'You can crawl along from there. It comes out by the baggage holds.'

Eddie was still holding Ollis Field's gun. He put it in the navigator's chart drawer.

Captain Baker said to Percy, 'Go back to your seat, please, young man, and don't leave the passenger cabin at any time during the remainder of the flight.' Percy turned to go back the way he had come. 'Not that way,' Baker snapped. 'Down the stairs.'

Looking a little scared, Percy hurried through the cabin and scuttled off down the stairs.

'How long had he been there, Eddie?' said the Captain.

'I don't know. I guess he probably heard the whole thing.'

'There goes our hope of keeping this from the passengers.' For a moment Baker looked weary, and Eddie had a flash of insight into the weight of responsibility the Captain carried. Then Baker became brisk again. 'You may return to your seat, Mr Field. Thank you for your co-operation.' Ollis Field turned around and left without speaking. 'Let's get back to work, men,' the Captain finished.

The crew returned to their stations. Eddie checked his dials automatically, although his mind was in turmoil. He observed that the fuel tanks in the wings, which fed the engines, were getting low, and he proceeded to transfer fuel from the main tanks, which were located in the hydrostabilizers or sea-wings. But his thoughts were on Frankie Gordino. Gordino had shot a man and raped a woman and burned down a nightclub, but he had been caught and would be punished for his horrible crimes – except that Eddie Deakin was going to save him. Thanks to Eddie, that girl would see her rapist get away scot-free.

Worse still, Gordino would almost certainly kill again. He was probably no good for anything else. So a day would come when Eddie would read in the papers of some ghastly crime – it might be a revenge murder, the victim tortured and mutilated before being finished off, or perhaps a building torched with women and children burned to death inside, or a girl held down and raped by three different men – and the police would link it with Ray Patriarca's gang, and Eddie would think, Was that Gordino? Am I responsible for that? Did those people suffer and die because I helped Gordino escape?

How many murders would he have on his conscience if he went ahead with this?

But he had no choice. Carol-Ann was in the hands of Ray Patriarca. Every time he thought of it he felt cold sweat dampen his temples. He had to protect her, and the only way he could do that was to co-operate with Tom Luther.

He looked at his watch: it was midnight.

Jack Ashford gave him the plane's current position, as best he could estimate it: he had not yet been able to shoot a star. Ben Thompson produced the latest weather forecasts: the storm was a bad one. Eddie read off a new set of figures from the fuel tanks and began to update his calculations. Perhaps this would resolve his dilemma:

if they did not have enough fuel to reach Newfoundland they would have to turn back, and that would be the end of it. But the thought was no consolation to him. He was no fatalist: he had to *do* something.

Captain Baker sang out, 'How goes it, Eddie?'

'Not quite done,' he replied.

'Look sharp – we must be close to the point of no return.'

Eddie felt a bead of sweat drip down his cheek. He wiped it away with a quick, surreptitious movement.

He finished the arithmetic.

The remaining fuel was not enough.

For a moment he said nothing.

He bent over his scratch pad and his tables, pretending he had not yet finished. The situation was worse than it had been at the start of his shift. Now there was not enough fuel to finish the journey, on the route the Captain had chosen, even on four engines: the safety margin had disappeared. The only way they could make it was to shorten the journey by flying through the storm instead of skirting it; and even then, if they should lose an engine they would be finished.

All these passengers would die, and I would too; and then what would happen to Carol-Ann?

'Come on, Eddie,' said the Captain. 'What's it to be? On to Botwood or back to Foynes?'

Eddie gritted his teeth. He could not bear the thought of leaving Carol-Ann with the kidnappers for another day. He would rather risk everything.

'Are you prepared to change course, and fly through the storm?' he said.

'Do we have to?'

'Either that, or turn back.' Eddie held his breath.

'Damn,' said the Captain. They all hated turning back halfway across the Atlantic: it was such a let-down.

Eddie waited for the Captain's decision.

'Heck with it,' said Captain Baker. 'We'll fly through the storm.'

Part Four

Mid-Atlantic to Botwood

CHAPTER SIXTEEN

DIANA LOVESEY was furious with her husband, Mervyn, for boarding the Clipper at Foynes. She was, first of all, painfully embarrassed by his pursuit of her, and afraid people would think the whole situation highly comical. More importantly, she did not want the opportunity to change her mind which he was giving her. She had made her decision, but Mervyn had refused to accept it as final, and somehow that cast doubt on her determination. Now she would have to make the decision again and again, as he would keep asking her to reconsider. Finally, he had completely spoiled her pleasure in the flight. It was supposed to be the trip of a lifetime, a romantic journey with her lover. But the exhilarating sense of freedom she had felt as they took off from Southampton had gone for good. She got no pleasure from the flight, the luxurious plane, the elegant company or the gourmet food. She was afraid to touch Mark, to kiss his cheek or stroke his arm or hold his hand, in case Mervyn should happen to pass through the compartment at that moment and see what she was doing. She was not sure where Mervyn was sitting, but she expected to see him at every moment.

Mark was completely flattened by this development. After Diana turned Mervyn down at Foynes, Mark had been elated, affectionate and optimistic, talking about California and making jokes and kissing her at every opportunity, quite his usual self. Then he had watched in horror as his rival had stepped on board the plane. Now he was like a punctured balloon. He sat silently beside her, leafing disconsolately through magazines without reading a word. She could understand his feeling depressed. Once already she had changed her mind about running away with him: with Mervyn on board, how could he be sure she would not change it again?

To make matters worse, the weather had become stormy, and the plane bumped like a car crossing a field. Every now and again a passenger would pass through the compartment on the way to the bathroom, looking green. People said it was forecast to get worse. Diana was glad now that she had been feeling too upset to eat much at dinner.

She wished she knew where Mervyn was sitting. Perhaps if she did she would stop expecting him to materialize at any moment. She decided to go to the ladies' room and look for him on the way.

She was in No. 4 compartment. She took a quick look into No. 3, the next one forward, but Mervyn was not there. Turning back, she walked aft, holding on to anything she could grab as the plane bucked and swayed. She passed through No. 5 and established that he was not there either. That was the last big compartment. Most of No. 6 was taken up by the ladies' powder

room, on the starboard side, leaving room for only two
people on the port side. These seats were occupied by
two businessmen. They were not very attractive seats,
Diana thought: fancy paying all that money and then
sitting outside the ladies' toilet for the whole flight!
Beyond No. 6 there was nothing but the honeymoon
suite. Mervyn must be seated farther forward, then, in
No. 1 or 2, unless he was in the main lounge, playing
cards.

She went into the powder room. There were two
stools in front of the mirror, one already occupied by a
woman Diana had not yet spoken to. As Diana closed
the door behind her, the plane plunged again and she
almost lost her balance. She staggered in and fell into
the vacant seat.

'Are you all right?' the other woman said.

'Yes, thanks. I hate it when the plane does this.'

'So do I. But someone said it's going to get worse.
There's a big storm ahead.'

The turbulence eased, and Diana opened her handbag and started to brush her hair.

'You're Mrs Lovesey, aren't you?' the woman said.

'Yes. Call me Diana.'

'I'm Nancy Lenehan.' The woman hesitated, looking
awkward, then went on, 'I got on the plane at Foynes. I
came over from Liverpool with your ... with Mr
Lovesey.'

'Oh!' Diana felt her face go pink. 'I didn't know he
had a companion.'

'He helped me out of a jam. I needed to catch the
plane, but I was stuck in Liverpool with no way of

getting to Southampton in time, so I just drove out to the airfield and begged a ride.'

'I'm glad for you,' Diana said. 'But it's frightfully embarrassing for me.'

'I don't see why *you* should be embarrassed. It must be nice to have two men desperately in love with you. I don't even have one.'

Diana looked at her in the mirror. She was attractive rather than beautiful, with regular features and dark hair, and she wore a very smart red suit with a grey silk blouse. She had a brisk, confident air. Mervyn *would* give you a lift, Diana thought; you're just his type. 'Was he polite to you?' she asked.

'Not very,' Nancy said with a rueful smile.

'I'm sorry. His manners aren't his strong point.' Diana took out her lipstick.

'I was just grateful for the ride.' Nancy blew her nose delicately on a tissue. Diana noticed that she wore a wedding ring. 'He is a little abrupt,' Nancy went on. 'But I think he's a nice man. I had dinner with him, too. He makes me laugh. And he's terribly handsome.'

'He is a nice man,' Diana found herself saying. 'But he's as arrogant as a duchess and he's got no patience at all. I drive him up the wall because I hesitate and change my mind and don't always say what I mean.'

Nancy ran a comb through her hair. It was thick and dark, and Diana wondered whether she dyed it to conceal grey streaks. Nancy said, 'He seems willing to go a long way to get you back.'

'That's just pride,' Diana said. 'It's because another man has taken me away. Mervyn's competitive. If I'd left him and gone to live at my sister's house he wouldn't have cared tuppence.'

Nancy laughed. 'It sounds as if he has no chance of getting you back.'

'None whatsoever.' Suddenly Diana did not want to talk to Nancy Lenehan any longer. She felt unaccountably hostile. She put away her make-up and her comb and stood up. She smiled to cover her sudden feeling of dislike, saying, 'Let's see if I can cakewalk back to my seat.'

'Good luck!'

As she left the powder room, Lulu Bell and Princess Lavinia came in, carrying their overnight cases. When she got back to the compartment, Davy the steward was converting their seat into a double bunk. Diana was intrigued to see how an ordinary-looking divan seat could be made into two beds. She sat down and watched.

First he took off all the cushions and pulled the armrests out of their slots. Reaching over the seat frame, he pulled down two flaps in the wall at chest level to reveal hooks. Bending over the seat, he unfastened a strap and lifted out a flat frame. He hung this from the wall hooks to form the base of the upper bunk. The outward side slotted into a hole in the side wall. Diana was just thinking that it did not look very strong when Davy picked up two stout-looking struts and attached them to both upper and lower frames to form bedposts. Now the structure looked more sturdy.

He replaced the seat cushions on the lower bed and used the back cushions as a mattress for the upper one.

He took pale blue sheets and blankets from under the seat and made up the beds with fast, practised movements.

The bunks looked comfortable but rather public. However, Davy broke out a dark blue curtain, complete with hooks and hung it from a moulding on the ceiling which Diana had thought was merely decorative. He attached the curtain to the bunk frames with press-studs, making a tight fit. He left a triangular opening, like the entrance to a tent, for the sleeper to climb inside. Finally he unfolded a little stepladder and placed it convenient to the upper bunk.

He turned to Diana and Mark with a faintly pleased look, as if he had performed a magic trick. 'Just let me know when you're ready and I'll make up your side,' he said.

'Doesn't it get stuffy in there?' Diana asked him.

'Each bunk has its own ventilator,' he replied. 'If you look just above your head you can see yours.' Diana looked up and saw a grille with an open/closed lever. 'You've also got your own window, electric light, clothes hanger and shelf; and if you need anything else, press this button to call me.'

While he had been working, the two passengers on the port side, handsome Frank Gordon and bald Ollis Field, had picked up their overnight bags and trooped off to the men's room; now Davy began to make up the bunk on that side. The arrangement was slightly differ-ent over there. The aisle was not in the centre of the plane, but nearer to the port side, so on that side there was only one pair of bunks, placed lengthwise rather than across the width of the plane.

Princess Lavinia returned in a floor-length navy blue *peignoir* trimmed with blue lace, and a matching turban. Her face was a mask of frozen dignity: obviously she found it painfully uncomfortable to appear in public in her nightclothes. She looked at the bunk in horror. 'I shall *die* of claustrophobia,' she moaned. No one took any notice. She stepped out of little silk slippers and climbed into the lower bunk. Without saying goodnight, she pulled the curtain shut and fastened it tight.

A moment later Lulu Bell appeared in a rather flimsy pink chiffon ensemble that did little to conceal her charms. She had been stiffly polite with Diana and Mark since Foynes, but now she seemed to have suddenly forgotten her pique. She sat down beside them on the divan and said, 'You'll never guess what I just heard about our companions!' She jerked a thumb at the seats vacated by Field and Gordon.

Mark looked nervously at Diana and said, 'What did you hear, Lulu?'

'Mr Field is an FBI man!'

That was not so startling, Diana thought. An FBI agent was only a policeman.

Lulu went on, 'And what's more, Frank Gordon is a prisoner!'

Mark asked sceptically, 'Who told you this?'

'Everyone's talking about it in the ladies' room.'

'That doesn't make it true, Lulu.'

'I knew you wouldn't believe me!' she said. 'That kid overheard a row between Field and the Captain of the plane. The Captain was mad as hell because the FBI didn't warn Pan American that they had a dangerous prisoner on board. There was a real set-to and in the end the crew took away Mr Field's gun!'

Diana recalled thinking that Field seemed like Gordon's chaperon. 'What do they say Frank did?'

'He's a mobster. He shot a guy and raped a girl and torched a nightclub.'

Diana found that hard to believe. She had talked to the man herself! He was not very refined, it was true, but he was handsome and nicely dressed, and he had flirted with her politely. She could see him as a confidence trickster or a tax dodger, and she could imagine his being involved in illegal gambling, say; but it did not seem possible that he had deliberately killed people. Lulu was an excitable person who would believe anything.

Mark said, 'It's kinda hard to credit.'

'I give up,' Lulu said with a deprecating wave of her hand. 'You guys have no sense of adventure.' She stood up. 'I'm going to bed. If he starts raping people, wake me up.' She climbed the little step-ladder and crawled into the top bunk. She pulled the curtains, then looked out again and spoke to Diana. 'Honey, I understand why you got ticked off at me back there in Ireland. I been thinking about it, and I figure I asked for what I got. I was kind of all over Mark. Dumb, I know. I'm ready to forget it as soon as you are. Goodnight.'

It was close enough to an apology, and Diana did

not have the heart to reject it. 'Goodnight, Lulu,' she said.

Lulu closed the curtain.

Mark said, 'It was my fault as much as hers. I'm sorry, baby.'

By way of reply, Diana kissed him.

Suddenly she felt comfortable and at ease with him again. Her whole body relaxed and she slumped back on the seat, still kissing him. She was conscious that her right breast was pressing up against his chest. It was nice to be getting physical with him again. The tip of his tongue touched her lips and she parted them a fraction to let him in. He began to breathe harder. This was going a bit too far, Diana thought. She opened her eyes – and saw Mervyn.

He was passing through the compartment, going forward, and he might not have noticed her, but he turned and glanced over his shoulder and froze, almost in mid-stride. His face paled with shock.

Diana knew him so well that she could read his mind. Although he had been told that she was in love with Mark, he was too downright stubborn to accept it, so it came as a blow to him to see her actually kissing someone else, almost as bad as if he had had no warning.

His brow darkened and his black eyebrows contracted in an angry frown. For a split second Diana thought he was going to start a fight. Then he turned away and walked on.

Mark said, 'What's the matter?' He had not seen Mervyn – he had been too busy kissing Diana.

She decided not to tell him. 'Someone might see,' she murmured.

Reluctantly he drew away from her.

She was relieved for a moment, then she began to feel angry. Mervyn had no right to follow her across the world and frown at her every time she kissed Mark. Marriage was not slavery: she had left him, and he had to accept that. Mark lit a cigarette. Diana felt the need to confront Mervyn. She wanted to tell him to get out of her life.

She stood up. 'I'm going to see what's happening in the lounge,' she said. 'You stay there and smoke.' She left without waiting for a reply.

She had established that Mervyn was not seated to the rear, so she went forward. The turbulence had eased enough for her to walk without holding on. Mervyn was not in No. 3 compartment. In the main lounge the card-players were settling down to a long game, their seat belts fastened, clouds of smoke around them and bottles of whisky on the tables. She went into No. 2. The Oxenford family took up one side of that compartment. Everyone on the plane knew that Lord Oxenford had insulted Carl Hartmann, the scientist, and that Mervyn Lovesey had sprung to his defence. Mervyn had his good points: she had never denied that.

Next she came to the kitchen. Nicky, the fat steward, was washing dishes at a tremendous pace while his colleague was making beds farther back. The men's room door was opposite the kitchen. After that was the staircase to the flight deck, and beyond that, in the nose of the plane, No. 1 compartment. She assumed

Mervyn had to be there, but in fact it was occupied by off-duty flight crew.

She went up the stairs to the flight cabin. It was as luxurious as the passenger deck, she noticed. However, the crew all looked terrifically busy, and one of them said to her, 'We'd love to show you around at another time, ma'am, but while we're flying through this bad weather we have to ask you to remain seated and fasten your safety belt.'

Mervyn had to be in the men's room, then, she thought as she went down the stairs. She still had not found out where he was sitting.

When she reached the foot of the staircase she bumped into Mark. She gave a guilty start. 'What are you doing?' she said.

'I was wondering that about you,' he said, and there was something unpleasant in his tone of voice.

'I was just looking around.'

'Looking for Mervyn?' he said accusingly.

'Mark, why are you angry with me?'

'Because you're sneaking off to see him.'

Nicky interrupted them. 'Folks, would you return to your seats, please? We're getting a smooth ride for the moment but it's not going to last.'

They made their way back to their compartment. Diana felt foolish. She had been following Mervyn and Mark had been following her. It seemed silly.

They sat down. Before they could continue their conversation, Ollis Field and Frank Gordon followed them in. Frank wore a yellow silk dressing-gown with a dragon on the back, Field a grubby old woollen one.

Frank took off his dressing-gown to reveal red pyjamas with white piping. He stepped out of his carpet-slippers and climbed the little ladder to the top bunk.

Then, to Diana's horror, Field took a pair of gleaming silvery handcuffs from the pocket of his brown robe. He said something to Frank in a low voice. Diana could not hear the reply, but she could tell that Frank was protesting. However, Field insisted, and in the end Frank offered one wrist. Field clapped one cuff on him and attached the other to the frame of the bunk. Then he drew the curtain on Frank and fastened the press-studs.

It was true, then; Frank *was* a prisoner.

Mark said, 'Well, shit.'

Diana whispered, 'I still don't believe he's a *murderer*.'

'I hope not!' Mark said. 'We would have been safer paying fifty bucks and travelling steerage in a tramp steamer!'

'I wish he hadn't put the handcuffs on. I don't know how that boy can sleep chained to his bed. He won't even be able to roll over!'

'You're soft-hearted,' Mark said, giving her a hug. 'The man is probably a rapist and you're feeling sorry for him because he might not be able to sleep.'

She put her head on his shoulder. He stroked her hair. He had been mad at her a couple of minutes ago but that seemed to have passed. 'Mark,' she said. 'Do you think two people can get into one of these bunks?'

'Are you frightened, honey?'

'No.'

He gave her a puzzled look, then he understood and

grinned. I guess you could get two in – though not side by side . . .'

'Not side by side?'

'It looks too narrow.'

'Well . . .' She lowered her voice. 'One of us will have to get on top.'

He murmured into her ear, 'Would you like to get on top?'

She giggled. 'I think I might.'

'I'll have to consider that,' he said thickly. 'What do you weigh?'

'Eight stone and two breasts.'

'Shall we get changed?'

She took off her hat and put it down on the seat beside her. Mark pulled their cases from under the seat. His was a well-used cordovan Gladstone bag, hers a small hard-sided tan leather case with her initials in gold lettering.

Diana stood up.

'Be quick,' Mark said. He kissed her.

She gave him a swift hug, and as he pressed against her she felt his erection. 'Goodness,' she said. In a whisper she added, 'Can you keep it like that until you get back?'

'I don't think so. Not unless I pee out the window.' She laughed. He added, 'But I'll show you a quick way to make it hard again.'

'I can't wait,' she whispered.

Mark picked up his case and went out, going forward towards the men's room. As he left the compartment he passed Mervyn coming the other way. They looked at one another like cats across a fence, but they did not speak.

Diana was startled to see Mervyn dressed in a coarse flannel nightshirt with broad brown stripes. 'What on *earth* have you got on?' she said incredulously.

'Go on, laugh,' he said. 'It was all I could find in Foynes. The local shop has never heard of silk pyjamas – they didn't know whether I was queer or just daft.'

'Well, your friend Mrs Lenehan won't fancy you in that get-up.' Now why did I say that? Diana wondered.

'I don't suppose she'd fancy me in anything,' Mervyn said crossly, and he passed on out of the compartment.

The steward came in. Diana said, 'Oh, Davy, would you make up our beds now, please?'

'Right away, ma'am.'

'Thank you.' She picked up her case and went out.

As she passed through No. 5 compartment it occurred to her to wonder where Mervyn was sleeping. None of these bunks was made up yet, nor any in No. 6, and yet he had disappeared. It dawned on Diana that he must be in the honeymoon suite. An instant later she realized that she had not seen Mrs Lenehan seated anywhere when she walked the length of the plane a few moments earlier. She stood outside the ladies' room, with her bag in her hand, frozen still with surprise. It was outrageous. Mervyn and Mrs Lenehan must be sharing the honeymoon suite!

Surely the airline would not allow it. Perhaps Mrs Lenehan had already gone to bed, and was out of sight in a curtained bunk in a forward compartment.

Diana had to know.

She stepped to the door of the honeymoon suite and hesitated.

Then she turned the handle and opened the door.

The suite was about the same size as a regular compartment, and had a terracotta carpet, beige walls and the blue upholstery with the pattern of stars that was also in the main lounge. At the rear of the room was a pair of bunks. On one side was a couch and a coffee table, and on the other a stool, a dressing-table and a mirror. There were two windows on each side.

Mervyn stood in the middle of the room, startled by her sudden appearance. Mrs Lenehan was not present, but her grey cashmere coat was draped over the couch.

Diana slammed the door behind her and said, 'How could you do this to me?'

'Do what?'

It was a good question, she thought in the back of her mind. What was she so angry about? 'Everyone will know that you're spending the night with her!'

'I had no choice,' he protested. 'There were no other seats left.'

'Don't you know how people will laugh at us? It's bad enough your following me like this!'

'Why would I care? Everyone laughs at a chap whose wife runs off with another fellow.'

'But this is making it worse! You should have accepted the situation and made the best of it.'

'You ought to know me better than that.'

'I do – that's why I tried to prevent you following me.'

He shrugged. 'Well, you failed. You're not clever enough to outwit me.'

'And you're not clever enough to know when to give in gracefully!'

'I've never pretended to be graceful.'

'And what kind of tramp is she? She's married – I saw her ring!'

'She's a widow. Anyway, what right have you got to be so damn superior? You're married, and you're spending the night with your fancy man.'

'At least we'll be in separate bunks in a public compartment, not tucked away in a cosy little bridal suite,' she said, suppressing a guilty pang as she recalled how she had planned to share a bunk with Mark.

'But I'm not having an affair with Mrs Lenehan,' he said in an exasperated tone. 'Whereas you've been dropping your drawers for that playboy all bloody summer, haven't you?'

'Don't be so vulgar,' she hissed, but she felt somehow he was right. That was exactly what she had been doing: whipping her panties off as quick as she could every time she got near Mark. He was right.

'If it's vulgar to say it, it must be worse to do it,' he said.

'At least I was discreet – I didn't flaunt it and humiliate you.'

'I'm not so sure about that. I'll probably find I was the only person in Manchester who didn't know what you were up to. Adulterers are never as discreet as they think.'

'Don't call me that!' she protested. It made her feel ashamed.

'Why not? It's what you are.'

'It sounds vile,' she said, looking away.

'Be thankful we don't stone adulteresses like they did in the Bible.'

'It's a horrible word.'

'You should be ashamed of the deed, not the word.'

'You're so bloody righteous,' she said wearily. 'You've never done anything wrong, have you?'

'I've always done right by you!' he said angrily.

She became thoroughly exasperated with him. 'Two wives have run away from you but you've always been the innocent party. Will it ever occur to you to wonder where *you* might be going wrong?'

That got to him. He grabbed her, holding her arms above the elbow, and shook her. 'I gave you everything you wanted!'

'But you don't care how I feel about things,' she shouted. 'You never did. That's why I left you.' She put her hands on his chest to push him away – and at that moment the door opened and Mark came in.

He stood there in his pyjamas, staring at the two of them, and said, 'What the hell is this, Diana? Are you planning to spend the night in the honeymoon suite?'

She pushed Mervyn away and he let her go. 'No, I'm not,' she said to Mark. 'This is Mrs Lenehan's accommodation – Mervyn's sharing it.'

Mark laughed scornfully. 'That's rich!' he said. 'I have to put this in a script some time!'

'It's not funny!' she protested.

'But it is!' he said. 'This guy comes chasing his wife like a lunatic, then what does he do, he shacks up with a girl he meets on the way!'

Diana resented his attitude and found herself unwillingly defending Mervyn. 'They're not shacked up,' she said impatiently. 'These were the only seats left.'

'You should be glad,' Mark said. 'If he falls for her maybe he'll stop chasing you.'

'Can't you see I'm upset?'

'Sure, but I don't understand why,' he said. 'You don't love Mervyn any more. Sometimes you talk as if you hate him. You've left him. So why do you care who he sleeps with?'

'I don't know, but I do! I feel humiliated!'

Mark was too cross to be sympathetic. 'A few hours ago you decided to go back to Mervyn. Then he annoyed you and you changed your mind. Now you're mad at him for sleeping with someone else.'

'I'm not sleeping with her,' Mervyn put in.

Mark ignored him. 'Are you sure you're not still in love with Mervyn?' he said angrily to Diana.

'That's a horrible thing to say to me!'

'I know, but is it true?'

'No, it isn't true, and I hate you for thinking it might be.' She was in tears now.

'Then prove it to me. Forget about him and where he sleeps.'

'I was never any good at tests!' she shouted. 'Stop being so bloody logical! This is not the Debating Society!'

'No, it's not!' said a new voice. The three of them turned around and saw Nancy Lenehan in the door, looking very attractive in a bright blue silk robe. 'In fact,' she said, 'I believe this is my suite. What the hell is going on?'

CHAPTER SEVENTEEN

MARGARET OXENFORD was angry and ashamed. She felt sure the other passengers were staring at her, thinking about the dreadful scene in the dining room, and assuming that she shared her father's horrible attitudes. She was afraid to look anyone in the eye.

Harry Marks had rescued the shreds of her dignity. It had been clever of him, and so gracious, to step in and hold her chair like that, then offer her his arm as she walked out: a small gesture, almost silly, but for her it had made a world of difference.

Still, it was only a vestige of her self-respect that she had retained, and she boiled with resentment towards Father for putting her in such a shameful position.

There was a cold silence in the compartment for two hours after dinner. When the weather started to get rough, Mother and Father retired to change into their nightclothes. Then Percy surprised Margaret by saying, 'Let's apologize.'

Her first thought was that this would involve further embarrassment and humiliation. 'I don't think I've got the courage,' she said.

'We'll just go up to Baron Gabon and Professor Hartmann and say we're sorry Father was so rude.'

The idea of somehow mitigating her father's offence was very tempting. It would make her feel a lot better. 'Father would be furious, of course,' she said.

'He doesn't have to know. But I don't care if he is angry. I think he's going round the bend. I'm not even afraid of him any more.'

Margaret wondered whether that was true. As a small boy Percy had often said he was not afraid when in fact he was terrified. But he was not a small boy any more.

She was actually a little worried by the thought that Percy might no longer be under Father's control. Only Father could restrain Percy. With no rein on his mischief, what might he do?

'Come on,' Percy said. 'Let's do it now. They're in number three compartment – I checked.'

Still Margaret hesitated. She cringed at the thought of walking up to the men Father had insulted so. It could cause them more pain. They might prefer to forget the whole thing as quickly as possible. But they might also be wondering how many other passengers secretly agreed with Father. Surely it was more important to make a stand against racial prejudice?

Margaret decided to do it. She had often been faint-hearted and she had usually regretted it. She stood up, steadying herself by holding on to the arm of her seat, for the plane was bucking every few moments. 'All right,' she said. 'Let's apologize.'

She was trembling a little with apprehension but her shakiness was masked by the unsteadiness of the plane.

She led the way through the main lounge into No. 3 compartment.

Gabon and Hartmann were on the port side, facing each other. Hartmann was absorbed in reading, his long thin body in a curve, his close-cropped head bent, his arched nose pointing at a page of mathematical calculations. Gabon was doing nothing, apparently bored, and he saw them first. When Margaret stopped beside him and held on to the back of his seat for support, he stiffened and looked hostile.

Margaret said quickly, 'We've come to apologize.'

'I'm surprised you are so bold,' Gabon said. He spoke English perfectly, with only the trace of a French accent.

It was not the reaction Margaret had hoped for, but she ploughed on regardless. 'I'm most dreadfully sorry about what happened, and my brother feels the same way. I admire Professor Hartmann so much, I told him earlier.'

Hartmann had looked up from his book, and now he nodded agreement. But Gabon was still angry. 'It's too easy for people like you to be sorry,' he said. Margaret stared at the floor and wished she had not come. 'Germany is full of polite, wealthy people who are "most dreadfully sorry" for what is happening there,' Gabon went on. 'But what do they do? What do *you* do?'

Margaret felt her face flush crimson. She did not know what to do or say.

'Hush, Philippe,' Hartmann said softly. 'Can't you

see that they're young?' He looked at Margaret. 'I accept your apology, and thank you.'

'Oh dear,' she said. 'Have I made everything worse?'

'Not at all,' Hartmann said. 'You have made it a little better, and I'm grateful to you. My friend the Baron is terribly upset, but he will see it my way eventually, I think.'

'We'd better go,' Margaret said wretchedly.

Hartmann nodded.

She turned away.

Percy said, 'I'm terribly sorry.' He followed her out.

They staggered back to their compartment. Davy was making up the bunks. Harry had disappeared, presumably to the men's room. Margaret decided to get ready for bed. She picked up her overnight case and made her way to the ladies' room to change. Mother was just coming out, looking stunning in her chestnut-coloured dressing-gown. 'Goodnight, dear,' she said. Margaret passed her without speaking.

In the crowded ladies' room she changed quickly into her cotton nightdress and towelling bathrobe. Her night-clothes seemed dowdy among the brightly coloured silks and cashmeres of the other women, but she hardly cared. Apologizing had brought her no relief in the end because Baron Gabon's remarks had rung true. It *was* too easy to say sorry and do nothing about the problem.

When she returned to her compartment, Father and Mother were in bed behind closed curtains, and a muffled snore came from Father's bunk. Her own bed was not ready, so she had to sit in the lounge.

She knew very well that there was only one way out of her predicament. She *had* to leave her parents and live on her own. She was now more determined than ever to do so; but she was no nearer to solving the practical problems of money, work and accommodation.

Mrs Lenehan, the attractive woman who had joined the plane at Foynes, came and sat beside her, wearing a bright blue robe over a black négligé. 'I came to ask for a brandy, but the stewards seem so busy,' she said. She did not seem very disappointed. She waved a hand to indicate all the passengers. 'This is like a pyjama party, or a midnight feast in the dormitory – everyone wandering around *en déshabille*. Don't you agree?'

Margaret had never been to a pyjama party or slept in a dormitory, so she just said, 'It's very strange. It makes us all seem like one family.'

Mrs Lenehan fastened her seat belt: she was in a mood to chat. 'It's not possible to be formal when you're in your nightclothes, I guess. Even Frankie Gordino looked cute in his red p.j.s, didn't he?'

At first Margaret was not sure who she meant; then she remembered that Percy had overheard an angry exchange between the Captain and an FBI agent. 'Is that the prisoner?'

'Yes.'

'Aren't you afraid of him?'

'I guess not. He won't do me any harm.'

'But people are saying he's a murderer, and worse than that.'

'There will always be crime in the slums. Take

Gordino away and somebody else will do the killing. I'd leave him there. Gambling and prostitution have been going on since God was a boy, and if there has to be crime it might as well be organized.'

This was a rather shocking speech. Perhaps something about the atmosphere of the plane led people to be unusually candid. Margaret also guessed that Mrs Lenehan would not have talked like this in mixed company: women were always more down-to-earth when there were no men around. Whatever the reason, Margaret was fascinated. 'Wouldn't it be better for crime to be *dis*organized?' she said.

'Certainly not. Organized, it's contained. The gangs each have their own territory and they stay there. They don't rub people out on Fifth Avenue and they don't demand protection money from the Harvard Club, so why bother them?'

Margaret could not let this pass. 'What about the poor people who waste their money gambling? What about the wretched girls who ruin their health?'

'It's not that I don't care about them,' Mrs Lenehan said. Margaret looked carefully at her face, wondering whether she was sincere. 'Listen,' she went on. 'I make shoes.' Margaret must have looked surprised, for Mrs Lenehan added, 'That's what I do for a living, I own a shoe factory. My men's shoes are cheap, and they last for five or ten years. If you want to you can buy even cheaper shoes, but they're no good – they have cardboard soles that last about ten days. And, believe it or not, some people buy the cardboard ones! Now, I figure I've done my duty by making good shoes. If people are dumb enough to buy bad shoes there's nothing I can do about it. And if people are dumb enough to spend their money gambling when they can't afford to buy a steak for supper, that's not my problem either.'

'Have you ever been poor yourself?' Margaret asked.

Mrs Lenehan laughed. 'Smart question. No, I haven't, so maybe I shouldn't shoot off my mouth. My grandfather made boots by hand and my father opened the factory that I now run. I don't know anything about life in the slums. Do you?'

'Not much, but I think there are reasons why people gamble and steal and sell their bodies. They aren't just stupid. They're victims of a cruel system.'

'I suppose you're some kind of Communist.' Mrs Lenehan said this without hostility.

'Socialist,' Margaret said.

'That's good,' she said surprisingly. 'You may change your mind later – everyone's notions alter as they get older – but if you don't have ideals to start with, what is there to improve? I'm not cynical. I think we should learn from experience but hold on to our ideals. Why am I preaching at you like this? Maybe because today is my fortieth birthday.'

'Many happy returns.' Margaret normally resented people who said she would change her mind when she was older: it was a condescending thing to say, and often said when they had lost an argument but would not admit it. However, Mrs Lenehan was different. 'What are your ideals?' Margaret asked her.

'I just want to make good shoes.' She gave a self-deprecating smile. 'Not much of an ideal, I guess, but it's important to me. I have a nice life. I live in a beautiful home, my sons have everything they need, I spend a fortune on clothes. Why do I have all this? Because I make good shoes. If I made cardboard shoes I'd feel like a thief. I'd be as bad as Frankie.'

'A rather socialist point of view,' Margaret said with a smile.

'I just adopted my father's ideals, really,' Mrs Lenehan said reflectively. 'Where do your ideals come from? Not your father, I know.'

Margaret blushed. 'You heard about the scene at dinner.'

'I was there.'

'I've got to get away from my parents.'

'What's keeping you?'

'I'm only nineteen.'

Mrs Lenehan was mildly scornful. 'So what? People run away from home at ten!'

'I did try,' Margaret said. 'I got into trouble and the police picked me up.'

'You give in pretty easy.'

Margaret wanted Mrs Lenehan to understand that it was not from lack of courage that she had failed. 'I've no money and no skills. I've never had a proper education. I don't know how I'd make a living.'

'Honey, you're on your way to America. Most people arrived there with a lot less than you, and some of them are millionaires now. You can read and write English, you're personable, intelligent, pretty . . . You could get a job easily. I'd hire you.'

Margaret's heart seemed to turn over. She had been beginning to feel resentful of Mrs Lenehan's unsympathetic attitude. Now she realized she was being given an opportunity. 'Would you?' she said. 'Would you hire me?'

'Sure.'

'As what?'

Mrs Lenehan thought for a moment. 'I'd put you in the sales office – licking stamps, going for coffee, answering the phone, being nice to customers. If you made yourself useful you'd soon be promoted to assistant sales manager.'

'What does that involve?'

'It means doing the same things for more money.'

To Margaret it seemed like an impossible dream. 'Oh, my goodness, a real job in a real office,' she said longingly.

Mrs Lenehan laughed. 'Most people think of it as drudgery!'

'To me it would be such an adventure.'

'At first, maybe.'

'Do you really mean it?' Margaret said solemnly. 'If I come to your office in a week's time, will you give me a job?'

Mrs Lenehan looked startled. 'My God, you're deadly serious, aren't you?' she said. 'I kind of thought we were talking theoretically.'

Margaret's heart sank. 'Then you won't give me a job?' she said plaintively. 'All this was just talk?'

'I'd like to hire you, but there's a snag. In a week's time I may not have a job myself.'

Margaret wanted to cry. 'What do you mean?'

'My brother is trying to take the company away from me.'

'How can he do that?'

'It's complicated, and he may not succeed. I'm fighting him off, but I can't be sure how it will end.'

Margaret could hardly believe that this chance had been snatched away from her after only a few moments. 'You must win!' she said fiercely.

Before Mrs Lenehan could reply, Harry appeared, looking like a sunrise in red pyjamas and a sky-blue robe. The sight of him made Margaret feel calmer. He sat down and Margaret introduced him. 'Mrs Lenehan came to get a brandy but the stewards are busy,' she added.

Harry looked surprised. 'They may be busy, but they can still serve drinks.' He stood up and put his head into the next compartment. 'Davy, just bring a cognac for Mrs Lenehan right away, would you please?'

Margaret heard the steward say, 'Sure thing, Mr Vandenpost!' Harry had a way of getting people to do what he wanted.

He sat down again. 'I couldn't help noticing your earrings, Mrs Lenehan,' he said. 'They're absolutely beautiful.'

'Thank you,' she said with a smile. She seemed pleased by the compliment.

Margaret looked more closely. Each earring was a single large pearl inside a latticework of gold wire and diamond chips. They were quietly elegant. She wished she had on some exquisite jewellery to excite Harry's interest.

'Did you get them in the States?' Harry asked.

'Yes, they're from Paul Flato.'

Harry nodded. 'But I think they were designed by Fulco di Verdura.'

'I wouldn't know,' Mrs Lenehan said. 'Jewellery is an unusual interest for a young man,' she added perceptively.

Margaret wanted to say, 'He's mainly interested in stealing it, so watch out!' But she was impressed by his expertise. He always noticed the finest pieces, and often knew who had designed them.

Davy brought Mrs Lenehan's brandy. He seemed able to walk without staggering, despite the tossing of the plane.

She took it and stood up. 'I'm going to get some sleep.'

'Good luck,' Margaret said, thinking of Mrs Lenehan's battle with her brother. If she won it she would hire Margaret, she had promised.

'Thanks. Goodnight.'

As Mrs Lenehan staggered off towards the rear of the plane, Harry said a little jealously, 'What were you talking about?'

Margaret hesitated to tell him about Nancy offering her a job. She was thrilled about it, but there was a snag, so she could not ask Harry to rejoice with her. She decided to hug it to herself a little longer. 'We started off talking about Frankie Gordino,' she said. 'Nancy believes that people like him should be left alone. All they do is organize things like gambling and ... prostitution ... which do no harm except to people who choose to take part in them.' She felt herself blush faintly: she had never spoken the word 'prostitution' aloud before.

Harry looked thoughtful. 'Not all prostitutes are volunteers,' he said after a minute. 'Some are forced into it. You've heard of white slavery.'

'Is that what it means?' Margaret had seen the phrase in newspapers, but had vaguely imagined that girls were kidnapped and sent off to be chambermaids in Istanbul. How silly she had been.

Harry said, 'There's not as much of it as the papers make out. There's only one white slaver in London – his name's Benny the Malt, he's from Malta.'

Margaret was riveted. To think all this was going on under her nose! 'It might have happened to me!'

'It could have, that night you ran away from home,' Harry said. 'That's just the kind of situation Benny can work with. A young girl on her own, with no money and nowhere to sleep. He'd have given you a nice dinner and offered you a job with a dance troupe leaving for Paris in the morning, and you'd think he was your salvation. The dance troupe would turn out to be a strip show, but you wouldn't find that out until you were stuck in Paris with no money and no way of getting home, so you'd stand in the back row and wiggle as best you could.' Margaret put herself in that situation and realized that she would probably do exactly that. 'Then one night they'd ask you to "be nice" to a drunk stockbroker from the audience, and if you refused they'd hold you down for him.' Margaret closed her eyes, revolted and scared to think what might have happened to her. 'Next day you might walk out, but where would you go? You might have a few francs, but it wouldn't be enough to get you home. And you'd start thinking about what you were going to tell your family when you arrived. The truth? Never. So you'd drift back to your lodgings with the other girls, who at least would be friendly and understanding. And then you'd start to think that if you've done it once you can do it again, and the next stockbroker would be a little easier. Before you know it you're looking forward to the tips the clients leave on the nightstand in the morning.'

Margaret shuddered. 'That's the most horrible thing I've ever heard.'

'It's why I don't think Frankie Gordino should be left alone.'

They were both quiet for a minute or two, then Harry said meditatively, 'I wonder what the connection is between Frankie Gordino and Clive Membury.'

'Is there one?'

'Well, Percy says Membury's got a gun. I'd already guessed he might be a copper.'

'Really? How?'

'That red waistcoat. A copper would think it was just the thing to make him look like a playboy.'

'Perhaps he's helping to guard Frankie Gordino.'

Harry looked dubious. 'Why? Gordino's an American villain on his way to an American jail. He's out of British territory and in the custody of the FBI. I can't think why Scotland Yard would send someone to help guard him, especially given the cost of a Clipper ticket.'

Margaret lowered her voice. 'Could he be following you?'

'To America?' Harry said sceptically. 'On the Clipper? With a gun? For a pair of cufflinks?'

'Can you think of another explanation?'

'No.'

'Anyway, perhaps all the fuss about Gordino will take people's minds off my father's appalling behaviour at dinner.'

'Why do you think he let rip like that?' Harry said curiously.

'I don't know. He wasn't always like this. I remember him being quite reasonable when I was younger.'

'I've run into a few Fascists,' Harry said. 'They're normally frightened people.'

'Is that so?' Margaret found the idea surprising and rather implausible. 'They seem so aggressive.'

'I know. But inside they're terrified. That's why they like marching up and down and wearing uniforms – they feel safe when they're part of a gang. That's why they don't like democracy – too uncertain. They feel happier in a dictatorship where you know what's going to happen next and the government can't be turned out all of a sudden.'

This made a lot of sense to Margaret and she nodded thoughtfully. 'I remember, even before he got so bitter, he would get unreasonably angry about Communists, or Zionists, or trade unions, or Fenians, or fifth columnists – there was always someone about to bring the country to its knees. Come to think of it, it was never very likely that Zionists would bring England to its knees, was it?'

Harry smiled. 'Fascists are always angry, too. They're often people who are disappointed in life for some reason.'

'That applies to Father as well. When my grandfather died and Father inherited the estate, he found it was bankrupt. He was broke until he married Mother. Then he stood for Parliament and never got in. Now he's been thrown out of his country.' She suddenly felt she understood her father better. Harry was surprisingly perceptive. 'Where did you learn all this?' she said. 'You're not much older than I am.'

He shrugged. 'Battersea is a very political place. Biggest Communist Party branch in London, I believe.'

Understanding her father's emotions better, she felt a little less ashamed of what had happened. There was still no excuse for him, of course, but all the same it was comforting to think of him as a disappointed and frightened man rather than a deranged and vindictive one. How clever Harry Marks was. She wished she could have his help in escaping from her family. She wondered whether he would still want to see her after they got to America. 'Do you know where you're going to live now?' she said.

'I suppose I'll get lodgings in New York,' he said. 'I've got some money and I can soon find more.'

He made it sound so easy. Probably it *was* easier for men. A woman needed protection. 'Nancy Lenehan offered me a job,' she said impulsively. 'But she may not be able to keep her promise because her brother is trying to take the company away from her.'

He looked at her then looked away again with an uncharacteristically diffident expression on his face, as if he were a little unsure of himself for once. 'You know, if you want, I wouldn't mind, I mean, giving you a hand.'

It was what she had been hoping to hear. 'Would you, really?' she said.

He seemed to think there was not much he could do. 'I could help you look for a room.'

The relief was tremendous. 'That would be wonderful,' she said. 'I've never looked for lodgings, I don't know where to begin.'

'You look in the paper,' he said.

'What paper?'

'The newspaper.'

'Newspapers tell you about lodgings?'

'They have advertisements.'

'They don't advertise lodgings in *The Times*.' It was the only newspaper Father took.

'The evening papers are best.'

She felt foolish, not knowing such a simple thing. 'I really need a friend to help me.'

'I guess I can protect you from the American equivalent of Benny the Malt, at least.'

'I feel so happy,' Margaret said. 'First Mrs Lenehan, then you. I know I can make a life for myself if I have friends. I'm so grateful to you, I don't know what to say.'

Davy came into the main lounge. Margaret realized the plane had been flying smoothly for the past five or ten minutes. Davy said, 'Look out of the port windows, everyone. You'll see something in a few seconds.'

Margaret looked out. Harry unfastened his belt and came closer to look over her shoulder. The plane tilted to port. After a moment Margaret saw that they were flying low over a big passenger liner, all lit up like Piccadilly Circus. Someone said, 'They must have put the lights on for us: they normally sail without lights since war was declared – they're afraid of submarines.' Margaret was very conscious of Harry's closeness to her, and she did not mind in the least. The crew of the Clipper must have talked by radio with the crew of the ship, for the ship's passengers had all come out on deck and stood there looking up at the plane and waving. They were so close that Margaret could see their clothes: the men wore white dinner jackets and the women long gowns. The ship was moving fast, its pointed bows knifing effortlessly through the huge waves, and the plane passed it quite slowly. It was a special moment: Margaret felt enchanted. She glanced at Harry and they smiled at one another, sharing the magic. He rested his right hand on her waist, on the side shielded by his body where no one could see it. His touch was feather-light yet she felt it like a burn. It made her hot and confused but she did not want him to take his hand away. After a while the ship receded, and its lights were dimmed, then extinguished altogether. The Clipper passengers returned to their seats and Harry moved back.

More people drifted off to bed and now only the card-players were left in the main lounge with Margaret and Harry. Margaret was bashful and did not know what to do with herself. She felt so awkward that she found herself saying, 'It's getting late. We'd better go to bed.' Why did I say that? she thought. I don't *want* to go to bed!

Harry looked disappointed. 'I guess I'll make a move in a minute.'

Margaret stood up. 'Thank you so much for your offer of help,' she said.

'Not at all,' he said.

Why are we being so formal? Margaret wondered. I don't want to say goodnight like this. 'Sleep well,' she said.

'You too.'

She turned away, then back. 'You do mean it, about helping me, don't you? You won't let me down?'

His face softened and he gave her a look which was almost loving. 'I won't let you down, Margaret, I promise.'

Suddenly she felt terribly fond of him. On impulse, without thinking about it, she bent down and kissed him. It was a fleeting brush of her lips on his but she felt desire like an electric shock when they touched. She straightened up immediately, startled by what she had done and the way she felt. For an instant they stared into one another's eyes. Then she stepped into the next compartment.

She felt weak-kneed. Looking around, she saw that Mr Membury had taken the top bunk on the port side, leaving the lower one free for Harry. Percy had also taken a top bunk. She got into the one below Percy's and fastened the curtain.

I kissed him, she thought, and it was nice.

She slid under the covers and turned off the little light. It was just like being in a tent and she felt quite cosy. She could see out of the window but there was nothing to look at: just clouds and rain. All the same it was exciting. It reminded her of times when she and Elizabeth had been allowed to pitch a tent in the grounds and sleep out on warm summer nights when they were little girls. She had always felt she would never go to sleep, it was so exciting; but the next thing she knew it would be light, and Cook would be tapping on the canvas and handing in a tray of tea and toast.

She wondered where Elizabeth was now.

Just as she was thinking that, there was a soft tap on her curtain.

At first she thought she had imagined it because she was thinking of Cook. Then it came again, a sound like a fingernail, tap, tap, tap. She hesitated, then lifted herself, leaning on her elbow, and pulled the sheet up around her throat.

Tap, tap, tap.

She opened the curtain a fraction and saw Harry.

'What is it?' she hissed, although she thought she knew.

'I want to kiss you again,' he whispered.

She was both pleased and horrified. 'Don't be silly!'

'Please.'

'Go away.'

'No one will see.'

It was an outrageous request, but she was sorely tempted. She remembered the electric tingle of the first kiss and wanted another. Almost involuntarily, she opened the curtain a little more. He put his head through and gave her a pleading look. It was irresistible. She kissed his mouth. He smelled of toothpaste. She intended a quick kiss like the last one, but he had other ideas. He nibbled her lower lip. She found it exciting. She instinctively opened her mouth a fraction, and she felt his tongue brush her lips drily. Ian had never done that. It was a weird sensation, but nice. Feeling depraved, she put out her own tongue to meet his. He began to breathe heavily. Suddenly Percy moved in the bunk over her head, reminding her of where she was. She felt panicked: how could she do this? She was publicly kissing a man she hardly knew! If Father should see there would be hell to pay! She broke away, panting. Harry pushed his head in farther, wanting to kiss her again, but she shoved him away.

'Let me in,' he said.

'Don't be ridiculous!' she hissed.

'Please.'

This was impossible. She was not even tempted: she was scared. 'No, no, no,' she said.

He looked crestfallen.

She softened. 'You're the nicest man I've met for a long time, perhaps ever, but you're not that nice,' she said. 'Go to bed.'

Harry realized she meant it. He gave a rueful half-smile. He seemed about to speak, but Margaret closed the curtain before he could.

She listened intently and thought she heard a soft footfall as he went away.

She turned off the light and lay back, breathing hard. Oh, my God, she thought, that was dreamy. She smiled in the dark, reliving the kiss. She had really wanted to go farther. She caressed herself gently as she thought about it.

Her mind went back to her first lover, Monica, a cousin who had come to stay the summer Margaret was thirteen. Monica was sixteen, blonde and pretty, and seemed to know everything, and Margaret adored her from the beginning.

She lived in France, and perhaps because of that, or perhaps just because her parents were more easy-going than Margaret's, Monica naturally walked around naked in the bedrooms and bathroom of the children's wing. Margaret had never seen a grown-up naked, and she had been fascinated by Monica's big breasts and the bush of honey-coloured hair between her legs: she herself had only a small bust and a little downy hair, at that age.

But Monica had seduced Elizabeth first – ugly, bossy Elizabeth, who had spots on her chin! Margaret had heard them murmuring and kissing in the night, and she had been by turns mystified, angry, jealous and finally envious. She saw that Monica became very fond of Elizabeth. She felt hurt and excluded by the little glances that went between them and the apparently accidental touch of hands as they walked in the woods or sat at tea.

Then, one day when Elizabeth went to London with Mother for some reason, Margaret came on Monica in the bath. She was lying in the hot water with her eyes closed, touching herself between the legs. She heard Margaret, and blinked, but she did not stop, and Margaret watched, scared but fascinated, while she masturbated to a climax.

That night Monica came to Margaret's bed instead of Elizabeth's; but Elizabeth threw a tantrum and threatened to tell all, so in the end they shared her, like wife and mistress in a jealous triangle. Margaret felt guilty and deceitful all summer, but the intense affection and the new-found physical delight was too wonderful to give up, and it ended only when Monica went back to France in September.

After Monica, going to bed with Ian had been a rude shock. He had been awkward and clumsy and Margaret discovered that a young man such as he knew next to nothing about women's bodies, so naturally he could not give her pleasure as Monica had. She soon got over the initial disappointment, however, and Ian loved her so desperately that his passion made up for his inexperience.

Thinking of Ian made her want to cry, as always. She wished with all her heart that she had made love to him more willingly and oftener. She had been very resistant at first, although she longed for it as badly as he did, and he had pleaded with her for months before finally she gave in. After the first time, although she wanted to do it again, she had made difficulties. She had been unwilling to make love in her bedroom in case someone should find the door locked and wonder why; she had been frightened of doing it in the open air, even though she knew lots of hiding-places in the woods around their home; and she had been uncomfortable about using his friends' flats for fear she would get a bad reputation. Behind it all had been the terror of what Father would do if ever he found out.

Torn apart by conflicting desire and anxiety, she had always made love furtively, hurriedly and guiltily, and they had managed it only three times before he went to Spain. Of course, she had blithely imagined that they had all the time in the world ahead of them. Then he had been killed, and with the news came the dreadful realization that she would never touch his body again; and she had cried so hard that she thought her heart would burst. She had thought they would spend the rest of their lives learning how to make one another happy, but she never saw him again.

Now she wished she had given herself to him freely, right from the start, and made love recklessly at every opportunity. Her fears seemed so trivial now that he was buried on a dusty hillside in Catalonia.

Suddenly it occurred to her that she might be making the same mistake again, right now.

She wanted Harry Marks. Her body ached for him. He was the only man who had made her feel this way since Ian. But she had turned him down. Why? Because she was afraid. Because she was on a plane, and the bunks were small, and someone might hear, and her father was close by, and she was terrified of being caught.

Was she being foolishly faint-hearted again?

What if the plane should crash? They were on a pioneering transatlantic flight. Right now they were half-way between Europe and America, hundreds of miles from land in any direction: if something should go wrong they would all die in minutes. And her last thought would be regret that she had never made love to Harry Marks.

The plane was not going to crash, but even so this might be her last chance. She had no idea what was going to happen when they got to America. She planned to join the armed forces as soon as she possibly could, and Harry had spoken about becoming a pilot in the Canadian Air Force. He might die fighting, like Ian. What did her reputation matter, who could worry about parental anger, when life could be so short? She almost wished she had let Harry in.

Would he try again? She thought not. She had given him a very firm no. Any boy who ignored that kind of rejection would have to be a complete pest. Harry had been persistent, flatteringly so, but he was not mulish. He would not ask her again tonight.

What a fool I am, she thought. He might be here now: all I had to say was yes. She hugged herself, imagining that Harry was hugging her, and in her mind she put out a tentative hand and stroked his naked hip. There would be curly blond hair on his thighs, she thought.

She decided to get up and go to the ladies' room.

Perhaps Harry would get up at the same time, by lucky chance; or he might call the steward for a drink, or something. She put her arms into her dressing-gown, unfastened her curtains and sat up. Harry's bunk was tightly curtained. She slid her feet into her slippers and stood up.

Almost everyone had gone to bed now. She peeped into the galley: it was empty. Of course, the stewards needed sleep too. They were probably dozing in No. 1 compartment with the off-duty crew. Going in the opposite direction, she passed through the lounge and saw the diehards, all men, still playing poker. There was a whisky bottle on the table and they were helping themselves. She continued towards the back, weaving from side to side as the plane lurched. The floor rose towards the tail, and there were steps between the compartments. Two or three people sat up reading, with the curtains drawn back, but most bunks were closed and silent.

The ladies' powder room was empty. Margaret sat in front of the mirror and looked at herself. It struck her as odd that a man should find this woman desirable. Her face was rather ordinary, her skin very pale, her eyes an odd shade of green. Her hair was her only good feature, she sometimes thought: it was long and straight, and the colour was a glowing bronze. Men often noticed her hair.

What would Harry have thought of her body, if she had let him in? He might be revolted by big breasts: they might make him think of motherhood or cows' udders or something. She had heard that men liked small, neat breasts, the same shape as the little glasses champagne was served in at parties. You couldn't get one of mine into a champagne glass, she thought ruefully.

She would have liked to be petite, like the models in *Vogue* magazine, but instead she looked like a Spanish dancer. Whenever she put on a ball-gown she had to wear a corset underneath it otherwise her bust wobbled uncontrollably. But Ian had loved her body. He said model girls looked like dolls. 'You're a real woman,' he had said one afternoon, in a snatched moment in the old nursery wing, kissing her neck and stroking both her breasts at the same time with his hands under her cashmere sweater. She had liked her breasts then.

The plane entered a bad patch of turbulence, and she had to hold on to the edge of the dressing-table to avoid being thrown off the stool. Before I die, she thought morbidly, I'd like to have my breasts stroked again.

When the plane steadied she went back to her compartment. All the bunks were still tightly buttoned up. She stood there for a moment, willing Harry to open his curtain, but he did not. She looked along the aisle, up and down the length of the plane. No one stirred.

All her life she had been faint-hearted.

But she had never wanted anything this much.

She shook Harry's curtain.

For a moment nothing happened. She had no plan: she did not know what she was going to do or say.

There was no sound from inside. She shook the curtain again.

A moment later Harry looked out.

They stared at one another in silence: he startled, she tongue-tied.

Then she heard a sound behind her.

Looking over her shoulder, she saw movement behind her father's curtain. A hand grasped it from inside. He was about to get up and go to the bathroom.

Without another thought, Margaret pushed Harry back on to his bed and clambered in with him.

As she closed the curtain behind her she saw Father emerge from his bunk. By a miracle, he did not see her, thank God!

She knelt at the foot of the bunk and looked at Harry. He was sitting at the other end with his knees under his chin, staring at her in the dim light that filtered through the curtain. He looked like a child who had seen Santa Claus come down the chimney: he could hardly believe his good fortune. He opened his mouth to speak, and Margaret silenced him with a finger on his lips.

Suddenly she realized she had left her slippers behind when she jumped in.

They were embroidered with her initials, so anyone could tell whose they were; and they were lying on the floor beside Harry's, just like shoes outside a hotel bedroom, so that everyone would know she was sleeping with him.

Only a couple of seconds had passed. She peeped out. Father was climbing down the step-ladder from his bunk, and his back was to her. She reached out between the curtains. If he should turn around now she was finished. She scrabbled for the slippers and found them. She picked them up just as Father put his bare feet on the airline carpet. She whipped them inside and closed the curtain a split second before he turned his head.

She should have been scared, but instead she felt thrilled.

She did not have a clear idea of what she wanted to happen now. She just knew she wanted to be with Harry. The prospect of spending the night lying in her own bunk wishing he were there had become intolerable. But she was not going to give herself to him. She would like to – very much – but there were all sorts of practical problems, not the least of which was Mr Membury, fast asleep a few inches above them.

In the next moment she realized that, unlike her, Harry knew exactly what he wanted.

He leaned forward, put his hand behind her head, pulled her to him and kissed her lips.

After a momentary hesitation she abandoned all thought of resistance and gave herself up to the sensation.

She had been thinking about it for so long that she felt as if she had already been making love to him for hours. But this was real: there was a strong hand on her neck, a real mouth kissing hers, a real person mingling his breath with her own. It was a slow, tender kiss, gentle and tentative, and she was aware of every small detail: his fingers moving in her hair, the roughness of his shaved chin, his warm breath on her soft cheek, his moving mouth, his teeth nibbling her lips, and finally his exploring tongue pressing between her lips and seeking her own. Yielding to an irresistible impulse, she opened her mouth wide.

After a moment they broke apart, panting. Harry's gaze dropped to her bosom. Looking down, she saw that her dressing-gown had fallen open and her nipples were pressing against the cotton of her nightdress. Harry gazed as if hypnotized. Moving in slow motion, he reached out with one hand and lightly brushed her left breast with his fingers, stroking the sensitive tip through the fine fabric, causing her to gasp with pleasure.

Suddenly clothing seemed intolerable. She shrugged off her dressing-gown quickly. She grasped the hem of her nightdress, then hesitated. A warning voice in the back of her mind said, 'After this, there's no turning back,' and she thought, Good! and pulled her nightdress over her head and knelt in front of him naked.

She felt vulnerable and shy, but somehow the anxiety heightened her excitement. Harry's eyes roamed over her body and she saw in his face both adoration and desire. Twisting in the cramped space, he got on his knees and leaned forward, bringing his head down to her bosom. She felt a moment of uncertainty: what was he going to do? His lips brushed the tops of her breasts, first one then the other. She felt his hand beneath her left breast, first stroking, then weighing, then squeezing softly. His lips tracked down until they came to her nipple. He nibbled gently. Her nipple was so taut it felt as if it would burst. Then he began to suck, and she groaned with delight.

After a while she wanted him to do the same to the other one, but she was too shy to ask. However, perhaps he sensed her desire, for he did what she wanted a moment later. She stroked the bristly hair at the back of his head, then, yielding to an impulse, she pressed his head to her breast. He sucked harder in response.

She wanted to explore his body. When he paused, she pushed him away and undid the buttons of his pyjama jacket. Both of them were breathing like sprinters but neither spoke for fear of being heard. He shrugged out of his jacket. There was no hair on his chest. She wanted him to be completely naked, as she was. She found the drawstring of his pyjama trousers and, feeling wanton, pulled it undone.

He looked hesitant and a little startled, giving Margaret the uneasy feeling that she might be bolder than other girls in his experience; but she felt she had to continue what she had begun. She pushed him back until he was lying down with his head on the pillow, then grasped the waistband of his trousers and tugged. He raised his hips.

There was a thatch of dark-blond hair at the base of his belly. She drew the red cotton down farther, and then gasped as his penis sprang free, sticking up like a flagpole. She stared at it, fascinated. The skin was stretched taut over the veins and the end was swollen like a blue tulip. He lay still, sensing that this was what she wanted; but her looking at it seemed to inflame him, and she heard his breathing become hoarse. She felt impelled, by curiosity and some other emotion, to touch it. Her hand was drawn forward irresistibly. He gave a low groan as he saw what she was about to do. She hesitated at the last instant. Her pale hand wavered next to the dark penis. He made a sound like a whimper. Then, with a sigh, she grasped it, her slender fingers wrapping around the thick shaft. The skin was hot to her touch, and soft, but when she squeezed slightly – making him gasp – she found it was hard as a bone underneath. She glanced at him. His face was flushed with desire and he was breathing hard through his mouth. She longed to please him. Shifting her grip, she began to rub his penis in a motion she had learned from Ian: gripping firmly to push down, then easing her grasp for the upward stroke.

The effect took her by surprise. He moaned, closed his eyes tight, and pressed his knees together; and then, as she pressed down a second time, he jerked convulsively, his face screwed up in a grimace, and white semen spurted from the end of his penis. Astonished and mesmerized, Margaret continued the action, and with each downstroke more came out. She herself was possessed by lust: her breasts felt heavy, her throat was dry, and she could feel moisture trickling down the inside of her thigh. At last, at the fifth or sixth stroke, it ended. His thighs relaxed, his face became smooth, and his head slumped sideways on the pillow.

Margaret lay down beside him.

He looked ashamed. 'I'm sorry,' he whispered.

'Don't be sorry,' she replied. 'It was amazing. I've never done that. I feel wonderful.'

He was surprised. 'Did you enjoy it?'

She was too abashed to say yes aloud, so she just nodded.

He said, 'But I didn't. I mean, you didn't . . .'

She said nothing. There was something he could do for her, but she was afraid to ask.

He rolled on to his side so that they faced one another in the narrow bunk. He said, 'In a few minutes, maybe . . .'

I can't wait a few minutes, she thought. Why shouldn't I ask him to do for me what I did for him? She found his hand and squeezed it. Still she could not say what she wanted. She closed her eyes, then drew his hand to her groin. Her mouth was next to his ear, and she whispered, 'Be gentle.'

He got the idea. His hand moved, exploring. She was wet, dripping wet. His fingers slid easily between her lips. She put her arms around his neck and hugged him hard. His finger moved inside her. She wanted to say 'Not there, higher!' and as if reading her thoughts he drew his finger out and slid it up to the most sensitive place. She was instantly transfixed. Her body was racked with spasms of pleasure. She shuddered convulsively, and to stop herself crying out she sank her teeth into the flesh of Harry's upper arm and bit. He froze, but she rubbed herself against his hand and the sensations continued unabated.

When at last the pleasure eased, Harry moved his finger again, and she was abruptly shaken by another climax as intense as the first.

Then finally the spot became too sensitive, and she pushed his hand away.

After a moment Harry eased away from her and rubbed his arm where she had bitten him.

Breathlessly, she panted, 'I'm sorry – did it hurt?'

'Yes, it bloody did,' he whispered, and they both began to giggle. Trying not to laugh aloud made it worse, and for a minute or two they were both helpless with suppressed laughter.

When they calmed down he said, 'Your body is wonderful – wonderful.'

'So is yours,' she said fervently.

He did not believe her. 'No, I mean it,' he said.

'So do I!' She would never forget his swollen penis standing up from the thatch of golden hair. She ran her hand over his stomach, searching for it, and found it lying across his thigh like a hose pipe, neither stiff nor shrivelled. The skin was silky. She felt she would like to kiss it, and was shocked by her own depravity.

Instead she kissed his arm where she had bitten him. Even in the near-dark she could see the marks her teeth had made. He was going to have a bad bruise. 'I'm sorry,' she whispered, too low for him to hear. She felt quite sad that she had damaged his perfect flesh after his body had given her such joy. She kissed the bruise again.

They were limp with exhaustion and pleasure, and they both drifted into a light doze. Margaret seemed to hear the drone of the engines all through her sleep, as if she were dreaming of planes. Once she heard footsteps pass through the compartment and return a few minutes later, but she was too contented to be curious about what they meant.

For a while the motion of the plane was smooth, and she fell into a real sleep.

She woke with a shock. Was it daytime? Had everyone got up? Would they all see her climbing out of Harry's bunk? Her heart raced.

'What is it?' he whispered.

'What's the time?'

'It's the middle of the night.'

He was right. There was no movement outside, the cabin lights were dim, and there was no sign of daylight at the window. She could sneak out in safety. 'I must go back to my own bunk, right now, before we're discovered,' she said frantically. She began looking for her slippers and could not find them.

Harry put a hand on her shoulder. 'Calm down,' he whispered. 'We've got hours.'

'But I'm worried that Father—' She stopped herself. Why was she so worried? She took a deep breath and looked at Harry. When their eyes met in the semi-darkness, she remembered what had happened before they went to sleep, and she could tell he was thinking the same thing. They smiled at one another, a knowing, intimate, lovers' smile.

Suddenly she was not so worried. She did not need to go yet. She wanted to stay here, so she would. There was plenty of time.

Harry moved against her, and she felt his stiffening penis. 'Don't go yet,' he said.

She sighed happily. 'All right, not yet,' she said, and she began to kiss him.

CHAPTER EIGHTEEN

EDDIE DEAKIN had himself under rigid control, but he was a boiling kettle with the lid jammed on, a volcano waiting to blow. He sweated constantly, his guts ached, and he could hardly sit still. He was managing to do his job, but only just.

He was due to go off duty at 2 a.m., British time. As the end of his shift approached he faked one more set of fuel figures. Earlier he had understated the plane's consumption to give the impression that there was just enough fuel to complete the journey, so that the Captain would not turn back. Now he overstated, to compensate, so that when his replacement, Mickey Finn, came on duty and read the fuel gauges there would be no discrepancy. The Howgozit Curve would show fuel consumption fluctuating wildly, and Mickey would wonder why; but Eddie would explain it as due to the stormy weather. Anyway, Mickey was the least of his worries. His deep anxiety, the one that held his heart in the cold grip of fear, was that the plane would run out of fuel before it reached Newfoundland.

It did not have the regulation minimum. The regulations left a safety margin, of course; but safety margins were there for a reason. This flight no longer had an extra reserve of fuel for emergencies such as engine failure. If something went wrong it would plunge into the stormy Atlantic Ocean. It could not splash down safely in mid-ocean: it would sink within a few minutes. There would be no survivors.

Mickey came up to the flight cabin a few minutes before two, looking fresh and young and eager. 'We're running very low,' Eddie said right away. 'I've told the Captain.'

Mickey nodded noncommittally and picked up the flashlight. His first duty on taking over was to make a visual inspection of all four engines.

Eddie left him to it and went down to the passenger deck. The first officer, Johnny Dott, the navigator, Jack Ashford, and the radio operator, Ben Thompson, followed him down the stairs as their replacements arrived. Jack went to the galley to make a sandwich. The thought of food nauseated Eddie: he got a cup of coffee and went to sit in No. 1 compartment.

When he was not working he had nothing to take his mind off the thought of Carol-Ann in the hands of her kidnappers.

It was just after 9 p.m. in Maine now. It would be dark. Carol-Ann would be weary and dispirited at best. She tended to fall asleep much earlier since she got pregnant. Would they give her somewhere to lie down? She would not sleep tonight, but perhaps she could rest her body. Eddie just hoped that the thought of bedtime did not put ideas into the heads of the hoodlums who were guarding her . . .

Before his coffee was cold the storm hit in earnest.

The ride had been bumpy for several hours, but now it became really rough. It was like being on a ship in a storm. The huge aircraft was like a boat on the waves, rising slowly then dropping fast, hitting the trough with a thump and then climbing again, rolling and tossing from side to side as the winds caught it. Eddie sat on a bunk and braced himself with his feet on the corner-post. The passengers began to wake up, ring for stewards, and rush to the bathroom. The two stewards, Nicky and Davy, who had been dozing in No. 1 compartment with the off-duty crew, buttoned their collars and put on their jackets, then hurried off to answer the bells.

After a while Eddie went to the galley for more coffee. As he got there, the door of the men's room opened and Tom Luther came out, looking pale and sweaty. Eddie stared at him contemptuously. He felt an urge to take the man by the throat, but he fought it down.

'Is this normal?' Luther said in a scared voice.

Eddie felt not a shred of sympathy. 'No, this is not normal,' he replied. 'We ought to fly around the storm, but we don't have enough fuel.'

'Why not?'

'We're running out.'

Luther was scared. 'But you told us you would turn back before the point of no return!'

Eddie was more worried than Luther, but he took grim satisfaction in the other man's distress. 'We should have turned back, but I faked the figures. I have a special reason for wanting to complete this flight on schedule, remember?'

'You crazy bastard!' Luther said despairingly. 'Are you trying to kill us all?'

'I'd rather take the chance of killing you than leave my wife with your friends.'

'But if we all die that won't help your wife!'

'I know.' Eddie was taking a dreadful risk, but he could not bear the thought of leaving Carol-Ann with the kidnappers for another day. 'Maybe I am crazy,' he said to Luther.

Luther looked ill. 'But this plane can land on the sea, right?'

'Wrong. We can only splash down on calm water. If we went down in mid-Atlantic in a storm like this, the plane would break up in seconds.'

'Oh, God,' Luther moaned. 'I should never have got on this plane.'

'You should never have messed with my wife, you bastard,' Eddie said through his teeth.

The plane lurched crazily, and Luther turned and staggered back into the bathroom.

Eddie stepped through No. 2 compartment and into the lounge. The card-players were strapped into their seats and hanging on tight. Glasses, cards and a bottle rolled around the carpet as the aircraft swayed and shook. Eddie looked along the aisle. After the initial panic the passengers were calming down. Most had returned to their bunks and strapped themselves in, realizing that was the best way to ride the bumps. They lay with their curtains open, some looking cheerfully resigned to the discomfort, others clearly scared to death. Everything that was not tied down had fallen to the floor and the carpet was a litter of books, spectacles, dressing-gowns, false teeth, change, cufflinks and all the other things people kept beside their beds at night. The rich and the glamorous of the world suddenly looked very human, and Eddie suffered an agonizing stab of conscience. Were all these people going to die because of him?

He returned to his seat and strapped himself in. There was nothing he could do now about the fuel consumption, and the only way he could help Carol-Ann was make sure the emergency splashdown went according to plan.

As the plane shuddered on through the night, he tried to suppress his seething anger and run over his scenario.

He would be on duty when they took off from Shediac, the last port before New York. He would immediately begin to jettison fuel. The gauges would show this, of course. Mickey Finn might notice the loss, if he should come up to the flight deck for any reason; but by that time, twenty-four hours after leaving South-ampton, off-duty crew were not interested in anything but sleep. And it was not likely that any other crew member would look at the fuel gauges, especially on the short leg of the flight when fuel consumption was no longer critical. He loathed the thought of deceiving his colleagues, and for a moment his rage boiled up again. He balled his fists, but there was nothing to hit. He tried to concentrate on his plan.

As the plane approached the place where Luther wanted to splash down, Eddie would jettison more fuel, judging it finely so that they would almost have run out when they reached the right area. At that point he would tell the Captain that they were out of fuel and had to come down.

He would have to monitor their route carefully. They did not follow exactly the same course every time: navigation was not that precise. But Luther had selected his rendezvous cleverly. It was clearly the best place within a wide radius for a flying boat to splash down, so that even if they were some miles off course, the Captain was sure to head there in an emergency.

If there was time, the Captain would ask – angrily – how come Eddie had not noticed the dramatic loss of fuel before it became critical. Eddie would have to answer that all the gauges must have got stuck, a wildly unlikely notion. He ground his teeth as he thought of it. His colleagues relied on him to perform the crucial task of monitoring the aircraft's fuel consumption. They trusted him with their lives. They would know he had let them down.

A fast launch would be waiting in the area and would approach the Clipper. The Captain would think they had come to help. He might invite them aboard, but failing that Eddie would open the door to them. Then the gangsters would overpower the FBI man, Ollis Field, and rescue Frankie Gordino.

They would have to be quick. The radio operator would have sent out a Mayday before the plane touched water, and the Clipper was big enough to be seen from some distance, so other vessels would approach before too long. There was even a chance the Coast Guard might be quick enough to interfere with the rescue. That could ruin it for Luther's gang, Eddie thought; and for a moment he felt hopeful – then he remembered that he wanted Luther to succeed, not fail.

He just could not get into the habit of hoping that the criminals would get what they wanted. He racked his brains constantly for some way of foiling Luther's plan, but everything he came up with had the same snag: Carol-Ann. If Luther did not get Gordino, Eddie would not get Carol-Ann.

He had tried to think of some way to ensure that Gordino would get caught twenty-four hours later, when Carol-Ann was safe; but it was impossible. Gordino would be far away by then. The only alternative was to persuade Luther to surrender Carol-Ann earlier, and he had more sense than to agree to that. The trouble was, Eddie had nothing with which to threaten Luther. Luther had Carol-Ann, and Eddie had . . .

Well, he thought suddenly, I've got Gordino.

Wait a minute.

They've got Carol-Ann, and I can't get her back without co-operating with them. But Gordino is on this plane, and they can't get him back unless they co-operate with me. Maybe they don't hold all the cards.

He wondered whether there was a way for him to take charge, seize the initiative.

He stared blindly at the opposite wall, holding on tight, lost in thought.

There was a way.

Why should they get Gordino first? An exchange of hostages should be simultaneous.

He fought down surging hope and forced himself to think coolly.

How would the exchange work? They would have to bring Carol-Ann to the Clipper on the launch that would take Gordino away.

Why not? *Why the hell not?*

He wondered frantically whether it could be arranged in time. He had calculated that she was being held no more than sixty or seventy miles from their home, which in turn was about seventy miles from the location of the emergency splashdown. At worst, then, she was four hours' drive away. Was that too much?

Suppose Tom Luther agreed. His first chance to call his men would come at the next stop, Botwood, where the Clipper was due at 9 a.m. British time. After that the plane went on to Shediac. The unscheduled splashdown would take place an hour out of Shediac, at about 4 p.m. British time, seven hours later. The gang could get Carol-Ann there with a couple of hours to spare.

Eddie could hardly contain his excitement as he contemplated the prospect of getting Carol-Ann back earlier. It also occurred to him that it might give him a chance, albeit slender, of doing something to spoil Luther's rescue. And that might redeem him in the eyes of the rest of the crew. They might forgive his treachery to them if they saw him catch a bunch of murdering gangsters.

Once again he told himself not to raise his hopes. All this was only an idea. Luther probably would not buy the deal. Eddie could threaten not to bring the plane down unless they met his terms; but they might see that as an empty threat. They would reckon that Eddie would do anything to save his wife, and they would be right. They were only trying to save a buddy. Eddie was more desperate, and that made him weaker, he thought; and he plunged once more into despair.

But still he would be presenting Luther with a problem, creating a doubt and a worry in the man's mind. Luther might not believe Eddie's threat, but how could he be sure? It would take guts to call Eddie's bluff, and Luther was not a brave man, at least not right now.

Anyway, he thought, what do I have to lose?

He would give it a try.

He got up from his bunk.

He thought he probably should plan the whole conversation carefully, preparing his answers to Luther's objections; but he was already screwed up to screaming pitch and he could not sit still and think any longer. He had to do it or go mad.

Holding on to anything he could grab, he picked his way along the rocking, swaying plane to the main lounge.

Luther was one of the passengers who had not gone to bed. He was in a corner of the lounge, drinking whisky, but not joining in the card game. The colour had returned to his face and he appeared to have got over his nausea. He was reading a British magazine, *The Illustrated London News*. Eddie tapped him on the shoulder. He looked up, startled and a little frightened.

When he saw Eddie his face turned hostile. Eddie said, 'The Captain would like a word with you, Mr Luther.'

Luther looked anxious. He sat still for a moment. Eddie beckoned him with a peremptory jerk of the head. Luther put down his magazine, unfastened his seat belt and stood up.

Eddie led him out of the lounge and through No. 2 compartment, but instead of going up to the flight deck he opened the door of the men's room and held it for Luther.

There was a faint smell of vomit. Unfortunately they were not alone: a passenger in pyjamas was washing his hands. Eddie pointed to the lavatory and Luther went inside while Eddie combed his hair and waited. After a few moments the passenger left. Eddie tapped on the lavatory door and Luther came out. 'What the hell is going on?' he asked.

'Shut your mouth and listen up,' Eddie said. He had not planned to be aggressive but Luther just made him mad. 'I know what you're here for, I've figured out your plan, and I'm making a change. When I bring this plane down, Carol-Ann has to be on the boat waiting.'

Luther was scornful. 'You can't make demands.'

Eddie had not expected him to cave in immediately. Now he had to bluff. 'Okay,' he said with as much conviction as he could muster. 'The deal is off.'

Luther looked a little worried, but he said, 'You're full of shit. You want your little wife back. You'll bring down this plane.'

It was the truth, but Eddie shook his head. 'I don't trust you,' he said. 'Why should I? I could do everything you want and you could double-cross me. I'm not going to take that chance. I want a new deal.'

Luther's confidence was not yet shaken. 'No new deal.'

'Okay.' It was time for Eddie to play his trump card. 'Okay, so you go to jail.'

Luther laughed nervously. 'What are you talking about?'

Eddie felt a little more confident: Luther was weakening. 'I'll tell the Captain the whole thing. You'll be taken off the plane at the next stop. The police will be waiting for you. You'll go to jail – in Canada, where your hoodlum friends won't be able to spring you. You'll be charged with kidnapping, piracy – hell, Luther, you may never come out.'

At last Luther was rattled. 'Everything's set up,' he protested. 'It's too late to change the plan.'

'No, it's not,' Eddie said. 'You can call your people from the next stop and tell them what to do. They'll have seven hours to get Carol-Ann on that launch. There's time.'

Luther suddenly caved in. 'Okay, I'll do it.'

Eddie did not believe him: the switch had been too quick. His instinct told him Luther had decided to double-cross him. 'Tell them they have to call me at the last stop, Shediac, and confirm that they've made the arrangements.'

A look of anger passed briefly across Luther's face, and Eddie knew his suspicion had been correct.

Eddie went on, 'And when the launch meets the Clipper, I have to *see* Carol-Ann, on the deck of the boat, before I open the doors, you understand? If I don't see her I'll give the alarm. Ollis Field will grab you before you can open the door, and the Coast Guard will be here before your goons can break in. So you make sure this is done exactly right or you're all dead.'

Luther got his nerve back suddenly. 'You won't do any of this,' he sneered. 'You wouldn't risk your wife's life.'

Eddie tried to foster doubt. 'Are you sure, Luther?'

It was not enough. Luther shook his head decisively. 'You ain't that crazy.'

Eddie knew he had to convince Luther right away. This was the moment of crisis. The word 'crazy' gave him the inspiration he needed. 'I'll show you how crazy I am,' he said. He pushed Luther up against the wall next to the big square window. For a moment the man was too surprised to resist. 'I'll show you just how goddamn crazy I am.' He kicked Luther's legs away with a sudden movement, and the man fell heavily to the floor. At that moment he *felt* crazy. 'You see this window, shitheel?' Eddie took hold of the venetian blind and ripped it from its fastenings. 'I'm crazy enough to throw you out this fucking window, that's how crazy I am.' He jumped up on to the washstand and kicked at the window pane. He was wearing stout boots but the window was made of strong Plexiglass, three-sixteenths of an inch thick. He kicked again, harder, and this time it cracked. One more kick broke it. Shattered glass flew into the room. The plane was travelling at 125 miles per hour, and the icy wind and freezing rain blew in like a hurricane.

Luther was scrambling to his feet, terrified. Eddie jumped back on to the floor and stopped him getting away. Catching the man off balance, he pushed him up against the wall. Rage gave him the strength to overpower Luther, although they were much the same weight. He took Luther by the lapels and shoved the man's head out of the window.

Luther screamed.

The noise of the wind was so loud that the scream was almost inaudible.

Eddie pulled him back in and shouted in his ear, 'I'll throw you out, I swear to God!' He pushed Luther's head out again and lifted him off the floor.

If Luther had not panicked he might have broken free, but he had lost control and was helpless. He screamed again, and Eddie could just make out the words, 'I'll do it, I'll do it, let me go, let me go!'

Eddie felt a powerful urge to push him all the way out; then he realized he was in danger of losing control too. He did not want to kill Luther, he reminded himself; just scare him half to death. He had achieved that already. It was enough.

He lowered Luther to the floor and relaxed his grip.

Luther ran for the door.

Eddie let him go.

I do a pretty good crazy act, Eddie thought, but he knew he had not really been acting.

He leaned against the washstand, catching his breath. The mad rage left him as quickly as it had come. He felt calm, but shocked by his own violence, almost as if someone else had done it.

A moment later a passenger came in.

It was the man who had joined the flight at Foynes, Mervyn Lovesey, a tall guy in a striped nightshirt that looked pretty funny. He was a down-to-earth Englishman of about forty. He looked at the damage and said, 'By heck, what happened here?'

Eddie swallowed. 'A broken window,' he said.

Lovesey gave him a satiric look. 'That much I worked out for myself.'

'It sometimes happens in a storm,' Eddie said. 'These violent winds carry lumps of ice or even stones.'

Lovesey was sceptical. 'Well! I've been flying my own plane for ten years and I never heard that.'

Eddie was right, of course. Windows did sometimes break on trips, but it usually happened when the plane was in harbour, not in mid-Atlantic. For such eventualities they carried aluminium window covers called deadlights, which happened to be stowed right here in the men's room. Eddie opened the locker and pulled one out. 'That's why we carry these,' he said.

Lovesey was convinced at last. 'Fancy that,' he remarked. He went into the cubicle.

Stowed with the deadlights was the screwdriver which was the only tool required to install them. Eddie decided that it would minimize the fuss if he did the job himself. In a few seconds he took off the window frame, unscrewed the remainder of the broken pane, screwed the deadlight in its place, and replaced the frame.

'Very impressive,' said Mervyn Lovesey, coming out of the toilet. Eddie had a feeling he was not completely reassured, all the same. However, he was not likely to do anything about it.

Eddie went out and found Davy making a milk drink in the galley. 'The window's broken in the john,' he told him.

'I'll fix it as soon as I've given the Princess her cocoa.'

'I've installed the deadlight.'

'Gee, thanks, Eddie.'

'But you need to sweep up the glass as soon as you can.'

'Okay.'

Eddie would have liked to offer to sweep up himself, because he had made the mess. That was how his mother had trained him. However, he was in danger of appearing suspiciously over-helpful, and betraying his guilty conscience. So, feeling bad, he left Davy to it.

He had achieved something, anyway. He had scared Luther badly. He now thought Luther would go along with the new plan and have Carol-Ann brought to the rendezvous in the launch. At least he had reason to hope.

His mind returned to his other worry; the plane's fuel reserve. Although it was not yet time for him to go back on duty, he went up to the flight deck to speak to Mickey Finn.

'The curve is all over the place!' Mickey said excitably as soon as Eddie arrived.

But have we got enough? Eddie wondered. However, he maintained a superficial calm. 'Show me.'

'Look – fuel consumption is incredibly high for the

first hour of my shift, then it comes back to normal for the second hour.'

'It was all over the place during my shift, too,' Eddie said, trying to show mild concern where he felt terrible fear. 'I guess the storm makes everything unpredictable.' Then he asked the question that was tormenting him. 'But do we have enough fuel to get home?' He held his breath.

'Yeah, we have enough,' Mickey said.

Eddie's shoulders slumped with relief. Thank God. At least that worry was over.

'But we've got nothing in reserve,' Mickey added. 'I hope to hell we don't lose an engine.'

Eddie could not worry about such a remote possibility: he had too much else on his mind. 'What's the weather forecast? Maybe we're almost through the storm.'

Mickey shook his head. 'Nope,' he said grimly. 'It's about to get an awful lot worse.'

CHAPTER NINETEEN

NANCY LENEHAN found it unsettling to be in bed in a room with a total stranger.

As Mervyn Lovesey had assured her, the 'honeymoon suite' had bunk beds, despite its name. However, he had not been able to wedge the door open permanently, because of the storm: whatever he tried, it kept banging shut, until they both felt it was less embarrassing to leave it closed than to continue fussing about keeping it open.

She had stayed up as long as possible. She was tempted to sit in the main lounge all night, but it had become an unpleasantly masculine place, full of cigarette smoke and whisky fumes and the murmured laughter and cursing of gamblers, and she felt conspicuous there. In the end there was nothing for it but to go to bed.

They put out the light and climbed into their bunks, and Nancy lay down with her eyes closed, but she did not feel in the least sleepy. The glass of brandy which young Harry Marks had got for her had not helped at all: she was as wide awake as if it had been nine o'clock in the morning.

She could tell that Mervyn was awake too. She heard

every move he made in the bunk above her. Unlike the other bunks, those in the honeymoon suite were not curtained, so her only privacy was the darkness.

She lay awake and thought about Margaret Oxenford, so young and naïve, so full of uncertainty and idealism. She sensed great passion beneath Margaret's hesitant surface, and identified with her on that account. Nancy, too, had had battles with her parents; or, at least, with her mother. Ma wanted her to marry a boy from an old Boston family, but at the age of sixteen Nancy fell in love with Sean Lenehan, a medical student whose father was actually a foreman in Pa's own factory, horrors! Ma campaigned against Sean for months, bringing wicked gossip about him and other girls, snubbing his parents viciously, falling ill and retiring to bed only to get up again and harangue her daughter for selfishness and ingratitude. Nancy had suffered under the onslaught but stood firm, and in the end she had married Sean and loved him with all her heart until the day he died.

Margaret might not have Nancy's strength. Perhaps I was a little harsh with her, she thought, saying that if she didn't like her father she should get up and leave home. But she seemed to need someone to tell her to stop whining and grow up. At her age I had two babies!

She had offered practical help, as well as tough-minded advice. She hoped she would be able to fulfil her promise and give Margaret a job.

That all depended on Danny Riley, the old reprobate who held the balance of power in her battle with her brother. Nancy began to worry at the problem all over again. Had Mac, her lawyer, been able to reach Danny? If so, how had Danny received the story about an inquiry into one of his past misdemeanours? Did he suspect that the whole thing had been invented to put pressure on him? Or was he scared out of his wits? She tossed and turned uncomfortably as she reviewed all the unanswered questions. She hoped she could talk to Mac on the phone at the next stop, Botwood in Newfoundland. Perhaps he would be able to relieve the suspense by then.

The plane had been jerking and swaying for some time, making Nancy even more restless and nervous, and after an hour or two the movement got much worse. She had never been frightened in a plane before, but on the other hand she had never experienced such a storm, and she was scared. She held on to the edges of her bunk as the mighty aircraft tossed in the violent winds. She had faced a lot of things alone since her husband died, and now she told herself to be brave and tough it out. But she could not help imagining that the wings would break off or the engines would be destroyed and they all would plunge headlong into the sea; and she became terrified. She screwed her eyes up tight and bit the pillow. Suddenly the plane seemed to go into free fall. She waited for the fall to stop but it went on and on. She could not suppress a whimper of dread. Then at last there was a bump and the plane seemed to right itself.

A moment later she felt Mervyn's hand on her

shoulder. 'It's just a storm,' he said in his flat British accent. 'I've known worse. There's nothing to fear.'

She found his hand and gripped it tightly. He sat on the edge of her bunk and stroked her hair during the moments when the plane was stable. She was still frightened, but it helped to hold hands during the bumpy bits, and she felt a little better.

She did not know how long they stayed like that. Eventually the storm eased. She began to feel self-conscious, and she released Mervyn's hand. She did not know what to say. Mercifully, he stood up and left the room.

Nancy put on the light and got out of bed. She stood up shakily, put on her electric blue silk robe over her black négligé, and sat at the dressing-table. She brushed her hair, which always soothed her. She was embarrassed about having held his hand. At the time she had forgotten about decorum, and had just been grateful for someone to comfort her; but now she felt awkward. She was glad he was sensitive enough to guess at her feelings and leave her alone for a few minutes to collect herself.

He came back with a bottle of brandy and two glasses. He poured drinks and gave one to Nancy. She held the glass in one hand and gripped the edge of the dressing-table with the other: the plane was still bumping a little.

She would have felt worse if he had not been wearing that comical nightshirt. He looked ridiculous, and he knew it, but he behaved with as much dignity as if he were walking around in his double-breasted suit, and somehow that made him funnier. He was obviously a man who was not afraid to appear foolish. She liked him for the way he wore his nightshirt.

She sipped her brandy. The warm liquor immediately made her feel better, and she drank some more.

'An odd thing happened,' he said conversationally. 'As I was going into the men's room, another passenger came out looking scared to death. When I went inside, the window was broken, and the engineer was stood there looking guilty. He gave me a cock-and-bull story about the glass being smashed by a lump of ice in the storm, but it looked to me as if the two of them had had a fight.'

Nancy was grateful to him for talking about something, just so that they did not have to sit there thinking about holding hands. 'Which one is the engineer?' she said.

'A good-looking lad, about my height, fair hair.'

'I know. And which passenger?'

'I don't know his name. Businessman, on his own, in a pale grey suit.' Mervyn got up and poured her some more brandy.

Nancy's robe unfortunately came only just below her knees, and she felt rather undressed with her calves and her bare feet exposed; but once again she reminded herself that Mervyn was in frenzied pursuit of an adored wife, and he had no eyes for anyone else; indeed, he would hardly notice if Nancy were stark naked. His holding her hand had been a friendly gesture from one human being to another, pure and simple. A cynical voice in the back of her mind said that holding hands with someone else's husband was rarely simple and never pure, but she ignored it.

Searching for something to talk about, she said, 'Is your wife still mad at you?'

'She's as cross as a cat with a boil,' Mervyn replied.

Nancy smiled as she recalled the scene she had found in the suite when she returned from getting changed: Mervyn's wife yelling at him, and the boyfriend yelling at her, while Nancy watched from the doorway. Diana and Mark had quietened down immediately and had left, looking rather sheepish, to continue their row elsewhere. Nancy had refrained from commenting at the time, because she did not want Mervyn to think she was laughing at his situation. However, she did not feel inhibited about asking him personal questions: intimacy had been forced on them by circumstances. 'Will she come back to you?'

'There's no telling,' he said. 'That chap she's with ... I think he's a weed, but maybe that's what she wants.'

Nancy nodded. The two men, Mark and Mervyn, could hardly have been more different. Mervyn was tall and imperious, with dark good looks and a blunt manner. Mark was an altogether softer person, with hazel eyes and freckles, who normally wore a mildly amused look on his round face. 'I don't go for the boyish type, but he's attractive in his way,' she said. She was thinking, If Mervyn was my husband, I wouldn't exchange him for Mark; but there's no accounting for taste.

'Aye. At first I thought Diana was just being daft, but now that I've seen him, I'm not so sure.' Mervyn looked thoughtful for a moment, then changed the subject. 'What about you? Will you fight your brother off?'

'I believe I've found his weakness,' she said with grim satisfaction, thinking of Danny Riley. 'I'm working on it.'

He grinned. 'When you look like that, I'd rather have you for a friend than an enemy.'

'It's for my father,' she said. 'I loved him dearly, and the firm is all I have left of him. It's like a memorial to him, but better than that, because it bears the imprint of his personality in every way.'

'What was he like?'

'He was one of those men nobody ever forgets. He was tall, with black hair and a big voice, and you knew the moment you saw him that he was a powerful man. But he knew the name of every man who worked for him, and if their wives were sick, and how their children were getting along in school. He paid for the education of countless sons of factory hands who are now lawyers and accountants: he understood how to win people's loyalty. In that way he was old-fashioned – paternalistic. But he had the best business brain I ever encountered. In the depths of the slump, when factories were closing all over New England, we were taking on men because our sales were going up! He understood the power of advertising before anyone else in the shoe industry, and he used it brilliantly. He was interested in psychology, in what makes people tick. He had the ability to throw a fresh light on any problem you brought to him. I miss him every day. I miss him almost as much as I miss my husband.' She suddenly felt very angry. 'And I *will* not stand by and see his life's work thrown away by my good-for-nothing brother.' She shifted in her seat restlessly, reminded of her anxieties. 'I'm trying to put pressure on a key shareholder, but I won't know how successful I've been until—'

She never finished the sentence. The plane flew into the most severe turbulence yet, and bucked like a wild horse. Nancy dropped her glass and grabbed the edge of the dressing-table with both hands. Mervyn tried to brace himself with his feet, but he could not, and when the plane tilted sideways he rolled on to the floor, knocking the coffee-table aside.

The plane steadied. Nancy reached out a hand to help him up, saying, 'Are you all right?' Then the plane tossed again. She slipped, lost her handhold, and tumbled to the floor on top of him.

After a moment he started to laugh.

She had been afraid she might have hurt him, but she was light and he was a big man. She was lying across him, the two of them making the shape of an X on the terracotta carpet. The plane steadied, and she rolled off and sat up, looking at him. Was he hysterical, or just amused?

'We must look daft,' he said, and recommenced laughing.

His laughter was infectious. For a moment she forgot the accumulated tensions of the last twenty-four hours: the treachery of her brother, the near-crash in Mervyn's small plane, her awkward situation in the honeymoon suite, the ghastly row about Jews in the dining room, the embarrassment of Mervyn's wife's anger, and her fear of the storm. She suddenly realized there was also something highly comical about sitting on the floor in her nightclothes with a strange man in a wildly bucking aircraft. She, too, started to giggle.

The next lurch of the plane threw them against one another. She found herself wrapped in Mervyn's arms, still laughing. They looked at one another.

Suddenly she kissed him.

She surprised herself totally. The thought of kissing him had never even crossed her mind. She was not even sure how much she liked him. It seemed like an impulse that came from nowhere.

He was clearly shocked, but he got over it quickly enough, and kissed her back enthusiastically. There was nothing tentative about his kiss, no slow burn: he was instantly aflame.

After a minute she pulled away from him, gasping. 'What happened?' she said foolishly.

'You kissed me,' he said, looking pleased.

'I didn't mean to.'

'I'm glad you did, though,' he said, and he kissed her again.

She wanted to break away, but his grip was strong and her will was weak. She felt his hand steal inside her robe, and she stiffened: her breasts were so small that she was embarrassed, and afraid he would be disappointed. His large hand closed over her small, round breast, and he groaned deep in his throat. His fingertips found her nipple, and she felt embarrassed all over again: she had had enormous nipples since nursing the boys. Small breasts and big nipples – she felt peculiar, almost deformed; but Mervyn showed no distaste, quite the contrary. He caressed her with surprising gentleness, and she gave herself up to the delicious sensation. It was a long time since she had felt this way.

What am I doing? she thought suddenly. I'm a respectable widow, and here I am rolling on the floor of an airplane with a man I met yesterday! What's come over me? 'Stop!' she said decisively. She pulled away and sat upright. Her négligé had ridden up over her knees. Mervyn stroked her bare thigh. 'Stop,' she said again, pushing his hand away.

'Whatever you say,' he said with obvious reluctance. 'But if you change your mind, I'll be ready.'

She glanced at his lap and saw the bulge in his nightshirt made by his erection. She looked away quickly. 'It was my fault,' she said, still panting from the kiss. 'But it was a mistake. I'm acting like a tease, I know. I'm sorry.'

'Don't apologize,' he said. 'It's the nicest thing that's happened to me for years.'

'But you love your wife, don't you?' she said bluntly.

He winced. 'I thought I did. Now I'm a bit confused, to tell you the truth.'

That was exactly how Nancy felt: confused. After ten years of celibacy she now found herself aching to embrace a man she hardly knew.

But I do know him, she thought; I know him quite well. I've travelled a long way with him and we've shared our troubles. I know he's abrasive, arrogant and proud, but also passionate and loyal and strong. I like him despite his faults. I respect him. He's terribly attractive, even in a brown striped nightshirt. And he held my hand when I was frightened. How nice it would be to have someone to hold my hand any time I was frightened.

As if he had read her mind, he took her hand again. This time he turned it up and kissed her palm. It made her skin tingle. After a few moments he drew her to him and kissed her mouth again.

'Don't do this,' she breathed. 'If we start again we won't be able to stop.'

'I'm just afraid that if we stop now we may never start again,' he murmured, and his voice was thick with desire.

She sensed in him a formidable passion, only just kept under control, and that inflamed her more. She had had too many dates with weak, obliging men who wanted her to give them reassurance and security; men who gave up all too easily when she resisted their demands. Mervyn was going to be insistent, powerfully so. He wanted her, and he wanted her now. She longed to surrender.

She felt his hand on her leg beneath her négligé, his fingertips stroking the soft skin on the inside of her thigh. She closed her eyes and, almost involuntarily, parted her legs a fraction. It was all the invitation he needed. A moment later, his hand found her sex, and she groaned. No one had done this to her since her husband, Sean. That thought suddenly overwhelmed her with sadness. Oh, Sean, I miss you, she thought, I never let myself admit how much I miss you. Her grief was sharper than at any time since the funeral. Tears squeezed between her closed lids and ran down her face. Mervyn kissed her and tasted the tears. 'What is it?' he murmured.

She opened her eyes. Through a blur of tears she saw his face, handsome and troubled; and beyond that her négligé pushed up around her waist, and his hand between her thighs. She took his wrist and moved his hand away gently but firmly. 'Please don't be angry,' she said.

'I won't be angry,' he said softly. 'Tell me.'

'No one has touched me there since Sean died, and it made me think of him.'

'Your husband.'

She nodded.

'How long ago?'

'Ten years.'

'It's a long time.'

'I'm loyal.' She gave a watery smile. 'Like you.'

He sighed. 'You're right. I've been married twice, and this is the first time I've come close to being unfaithful. I was thinking of Diana and that chap.'

'Are we fools?' she said.

'Maybe. We should stop thinking about the past, seize the moment, live for today.'

'Perhaps we should,' she said, and she kissed him again.

The plane bucked as if it had hit something. Their

faces were banged together and the lights flickered. The aircraft tossed and bumped violently. Nancy forgot all about kissing and clung on to Mervyn for stability.

When the turbulence eased a little she saw that his lip was bleeding. 'You bit me,' he said with a rueful grin.

'I'm sorry.'

'I'm glad. I hope there's a scar.'

She hugged him hard, feeling a surge of affection.

They lay together on the floor while the storm raged. In the next pause, Mervyn said, 'Let's try and make it to the bunk – we'll be more comfortable than on this carpet.'

Nancy nodded. Getting up on her hands and knees, she crawled across the floor and scrambled up on to her bunk. Mervyn followed her and lay down beside her. He put his arms around her and she snuggled up to his nightshirt.

Each time the turbulence got worse she held him hard, like a sailor tied to the mast. When it lessened she relaxed, and he stroked her soothingly.

At some point she fell asleep.

She was awakened by a knock at the door and a voice calling, 'Steward!'

She opened her eyes and realized she was lying in Mervyn's arms. 'Oh, Jesus!' she said, panicking. She sat up and looked around frenziedly.

Mervyn put a restraining hand on her shoulder and

called out in a loud and authoritative tone, 'Wait a moment, steward.'

A rather frightened voice replied, 'Okay, sir, take your time.'

Mervyn rolled off the bed, stood up, and pulled the bedclothes over Nancy. She smiled gratefully at him then turned away, pretending to be asleep, so that she would not have to look at the steward.

She heard Mervyn open the door and the steward come in. 'Good morning!' he said cheerfully. The smell of fresh coffee wafted into Nancy's nostrils. 'It's nine thirty in the morning British time, four thirty in the middle of the night in New York, and six o'clock in Newfoundland.'

Mervyn said, 'Did you say it's nine thirty in Britain but six o'clock in Newfoundland?'

'Yes, sir. Newfoundland Standard Time is three and a half hours behind Greenwich Mean Time.'

'I didn't know anyone took half hours. It must make life complicated for the people who write the airline timetables. How long until we splash down?'

'We'll be coming down in thirty minutes, just one hour later than scheduled. The delay is because of the storm.' The steward padded out and the door closed.

Nancy turned over. Mervyn pulled up the Venetian blinds. It was daylight. She watched him pour coffee, and the previous night came back to her in a series of vivid images: Mervyn holding her hand in the storm, the two of them falling on the floor, his hand on her breast, her clinging to him while the plane lurched and swayed, the way he had stroked her to sleep. Holy Jesus, she thought, I like this man a lot.

'How do you take it?' he said.

'Black, no sugar.'

'Same as me.' He handed her a cup.

She sipped it gratefully. She suddenly felt curious to know a hundred different things about Mervyn. Did he play tennis, go to the opera, enjoy shopping? Did he read much? How did he tie his tie? Did he polish his own shoes? As she watched him drinking his coffee she found she could confidently guess a great deal. He probably did play tennis, but he did not read many novels and he definitely would not enjoy shopping. He would be a good poker player and a bad dancer.

'What are you thinking?' he said. 'You're eyeing me as if you're wondering whether I'm a good risk for life insurance.'

She laughed. 'What sort of music do you like?'

'I'm tone deaf,' he said. 'When I was a lad, before the war, ragtime was all the rage in the dance halls. I liked the rhythm, although I was never much of a dancer. What about you?'

'Oh, I danced – had to. Every Saturday morning I went to dancing school in a white frilly dress and white gloves, to learn social dancing with twelve-year-old boys in suits. My mother thought it would give me the *entrée* into the uppermost layer of Boston society. It didn't, of course; but fortunately I didn't care. I was more interested in Pa's factory – much to Ma's despair. Did you fight in the Great War?'

'Aye.' A shadow crossed his face. 'I was at Ypres.' He

pronounced it 'wipers'. 'And I swore I'd never stand by and see another generation of young men sent to die that way. But I didn't expect Hitler.'

She looked at him compassionately. He glanced up. They held each other's eyes, and she knew they were both thinking of how they had kissed and petted in the night. Suddenly she felt embarrassed all over again. She looked away, towards the window, and saw land. That reminded her that when they reached Botwood she was hoping for a phone call that would change her life, one way or the other. 'We're almost there!' she said. She sprang out of bed. 'I must get dressed.'

'Let me go first,' he said. 'It looks better for you.'

'Okay.' She was not sure she had a reputation left to protect, but she did not want to say that. She watched him pick up his suit on its hanger, and the paper bag containing the clean clothes he had bought along with his nightshirt in Foynes: a white shirt, black wool socks and grey cotton underwear. He hesitated at the door, and she guessed he was wondering if he would ever kiss her again. She went to him and lifted her face. 'Thank you for holding me in your arms all night,' she said.

He bent down and kissed her. It was a soft kiss, his closed lips on hers. They held it for a long moment, then separated.

Nancy opened the door for him and he went out.

She sighed as she closed it behind him. I believe I could fall in love with him, she thought.

She wondered if she would ever see that nightshirt again.

She glanced out of the window. The plane was gradually losing height. She had to hurry.

She combed her hair quickly at the dressing-table then took her case into the ladies' room, which was right next door to the honeymoon suite. Lulu Bell and another woman were there, but mercifully not Mervyn's wife. Nancy would have liked a bath, but had to make do with a thorough wash at the basin. She had clean underwear and a fresh blouse, navy instead of grey, to go under her red suit. As she dressed she recalled her morning conversation with Mervyn. The thought of him made her feel happy, but beneath the happiness was a strain of unease. Why was that? Once she had asked herself the question, the answer became obvious. He had said nothing about his wife. Last night he had confessed himself 'confused'. Since then, silence. Did he want Diana back? Did he still love her? He had held Nancy in his arms all night, but that did not wipe out a whole marriage, not necessarily.

And what do I want? she asked herself. Sure, I'd love to see Mervyn again, go on dates with him, probably even have an affair with him; but do I want him to abandon his marriage for me? How can I tell, after one night of unconsummated passion?

She paused in the act of applying lipstick and stared at her face in the mirror. Cut the crap, Nancy, she told herself. You know the truth. You want this man. In ten years he's the first you've really fallen for. You're forty years and one day old and you've met Mr Right. Stop kidding around and start nailing his foot to the floor.

She put on Pink Clover perfume and left the room.

As she stepped out she saw Nat Ridgeway and her brother Peter, who had the seats next to the ladies' room. Nat said, 'Good morning, Nancy.' She remembered instantly how she had felt about this man five years ago. Yes, she thought, I might have fallen in love with him, given time; but there wasn't time. And maybe I was lucky: could be he wanted Black's Boots more than he wanted me. After all, he's still trying to get the company, but for sure he's not still trying to get me. She nodded curtly to him and went into her suite.

The bunks had been dismantled and remade as a divan seat, and Mervyn was sitting there, shaved and dressed in his dark grey suit and white shirt. 'Look out of the window,' he said. 'We're almost there.'

Nancy looked out and saw land. They were flying low over a dense pine forest streaked with silver rivers. As she watched, the trees gave way to water – not the deep, dark water of the Atlantic, but a calm grey estuary. On the far side she could see a harbour and a cluster of wooden buildings crowned by a church.

The plane came down rapidly. Nancy and Mervyn sat on the divan with their seat belts fastened, holding hands. Nancy hardly felt the impact when the hull cleaved the surface of the river, and she was not sure they were down until, a moment later, the windows were obscured by spray.

'Well,' she said, 'I've flown the Atlantic.'

'Aye. There's not many can say that.'

She did not feel very brave. She had spent half the trip worrying about her business and the other half holding hands with someone else's husband. She had only thought about the flight itself when the weather was rough and she was scared stiff. What was she going to tell the boys? They would want all the details. She did not even know how fast the plane flew. She resolved to find out all that sort of thing before they got to New York.

When the plane taxied to a halt, a launch came alongside. Nancy put on her coat and Mervyn his leather flying jacket. About half the passengers had decided to get off the plane and stretch their legs. The rest were still in bed, closed in behind the tightly fastened blue curtains of their bunks.

They passed through the main lounge, stepped out on to the stubby sea-wing, and boarded the launch. The air smelled of the sea and of new timber: there was probably a sawmill near by. Near the Clipper's mooring was a fuel barge marked SHELL AVIATION SERVICE, with men in white overalls waiting to refill the plane's tanks. There were also two quite big freighters in the harbour: the anchorage here must be deep.

Mervyn's wife and her lover were among those who had decided to land, and Diana glared at Nancy as the launch headed for the shore. Nancy was uncomfortable and could not meet her eye, although she had less to feel guilty about than Diana herself: after all, Diana was the one who had actually committed adultery.

They landed via a floating dock, a catwalk and a pier. Despite the early hour, there was a small crowd of sightseers. At the landward end of the pier were the Pan American buildings, one large and two small, all made of wood painted green with red-brown trim. Beside the buildings was a field with a few cows.

The passengers entered the large airline building and showed their passports to a sleepy excise man. Nancy noticed that Newfoundlanders spoke fast with an accent more like Irish than Canadian. There was a waiting room, but it attracted no one, and the passengers all decided to explore the village.

Nancy was impatient to speak to Patrick McBride in Boston. Just as she was about to ask for a phone, her name was called: the building had a voice-hailer system like a ship's. She identified herself to a young man in a Pan American uniform.

'There's a telephone call for you, ma'am,' he said.

Her heart leaped. 'Where's the phone?' she asked, looking around the room.

'In the telegraph office on Wireless Road. It's less than a mile away.'

A mile away! She could hardly contain her impatience. 'Then let's hurry, before the connection is broken! Do you have a car?'

The youngster looked as startled as if she had asked for a space rocket. 'No, ma'am.'

'So we'll walk. Lead the way.'

They left the building, Nancy and Mervyn following the messenger. They went up the hill, following a dirt road with no sidewalk. Loose sheep grazed the verges. Nancy was grateful for comfortable shoes – made by Black's, of course. Would Black's still be her company tomorrow night? Patrick McBride was about to tell her. The delay was unbearable.

In ten minutes or so they reached another small wooden building and went inside. Nancy was shown to a chair in front of a phone. She sat down and picked up the instrument with a shaking hand. 'This is Nancy Lenehan speaking.'

An operator said, 'Hold the line for Boston.'

There was a long pause, then she heard, 'Nancy? Are you there?'

It was not Mac, contrary to what she expected, and she took a moment to recognize the voice. 'Danny Riley!' she exclaimed.

'Nancy, I'm in trouble and you have to help me!'

She gripped the phone harder. It sounded as if her plan had worked. She made her voice calm, almost bored, as if the call was a nuisance. 'What sort of trouble, Danny?'

'People are calling me about that old case!'

This was good news! Mac had put the wind up Danny. His voice was panicky. This was what she wanted. But she pretended not to know what he was talking about. 'What case? What is this?'

'You *know*. I can't talk about it on the phone.'

'If you can't talk about it on the phone, why are you calling me?'

'Nancy! Stop treating me like shit! I need you!'

'Okay, calm down.' He was scared enough: now she had to use his fear to manipulate him. 'Tell me exactly what has happened, leaving out the names and addresses. I think I know what case you're talking about.'

'You have all your pa's old papers, right?'

'Sure, they're in my strong room at home.'

'Some people may ask to look through them.'

Danny was telling Nancy the story she herself had concocted. The ploy had worked perfectly so far. Blithely Nancy said, 'I don't think there's anything you need worry about—'

'How can you be sure?' he interrupted frantically.

'I don't know—'

'Have you been through them all?'

'No, there are too many, but—'

'Nobody *knows* what's in there. You should have burned that stuff years ago.'

'I guess you're right, but I never thought . . . Who wants to see the stuff, anyway?'

'It's a Bar inquiry.'

'Do they have the right?'

'No, but it looks bad if I refuse.'

'And it looks all right if I refuse?'

'You're not a lawyer. They can't pressure you.'

Nancy paused, pretending to hesitate, keeping him in suspense a moment longer. Finally she said, 'Then there's no problem.'

'You'll turn them down?'

'I'll do better than that. I'll burn everything tomorrow.'

'Nancy . . .' He sounded as if he might weep. 'Nancy, you're a true friend.'

She felt a hypocrite as she replied, 'How could I do anything else?'

'I appreciate this, God, I really do. I don't know how to thank you.'

'Well, since you mention it, there is something you could do for me.' She bit her lip. This was the delicate bit. 'You know why I'm flying back in such a rush?'

'I don't know, I've been so worried about this other thing—'

'Peter is trying to sell the company out from under me.'

There was a silence at the other end of the line.

'Danny, are you there?'

'Sure, I'm here. Don't you want to sell the company?'

'No! The price is way too low and there's no job for me in the new set-up – of course I don't want to sell. Peter knows it's a lousy deal but he doesn't care so long as he hurts me.'

'Is it a lousy deal? The company hasn't been doing too well lately.'

'You know why, don't you?'

'I guess . . .'

'Come on, say it. Peter is a lousy manager.'

'Okay . . .'

'Instead of letting him sell the company cheap, why don't we fire him? Let me take over. I can turn it around – you know that. Then, when we're making money, we can think again about selling out – at a much higher price.'

'I don't know.'

'Danny, a war has just started in Europe and that means business is going to boom. We'll be selling shoes faster than we can make them. If we wait two or three years we could sell the company for double, three times the price.'

464

'But the association with Nat Ridgeway would be so useful to my law firm.'

'Forget what's useful – I'm asking you to help me out.'

'I really don't know if it's in your own interests.'

Nancy wanted to say, 'You goddamn liar, it's your interests you're thinking about.' But she bit her tongue and said, 'I know it's the right thing for all of us.'

'Okay, I'll think about it.'

That was not good enough. She was going to have to lay her cards on the table. 'Remember Pa's papers, won't you?' She held her breath.

His voice became lower and he spoke more slowly. 'What are you saying to me?'

'I'm asking you to help me, because I'm helping you. You understand that type of thing, I know.'

'I think I do understand it. Normally it's called blackmail.'

She winced, then she remembered who she was talking to. 'You hypocritical old bastard, you've been doing this sort of thing all your life.'

He laughed. 'You got me there, kid.' But that sparked another thought. 'You didn't *initiate* the damn inquiry yourself, just to have some way of putting pressure on me, did you?'

This was dangerously close to the truth. 'That's what you would have done, I know. But I'm not going to answer any more questions. All you need to know is that if you vote with me tomorrow, you're safe; and if you don't, you're in trouble.' She was bullying him now, and that was the kind of thing he understood; but would he knuckle under, or defy her?

'You can't talk to me like that, I knew you when you wore diapers.'

She softened her tone. 'Isn't that a reason for helping me?'

There was a long pause. Then he said, 'I really don't have a choice, do I?'

'I guess not.'

'Okay,' he said reluctantly. 'I'll support you tomorrow, if you'll take care of that other thing.'

Nancy almost cried with relief. She had done it. She had turned Danny around. Now she would win. Black's Boots was still hers. 'I'm glad, Danny,' she said weakly.

'Your pa said it would be like this.'

The remark came out of nowhere and Nancy did not understand it. 'What do you mean?'

'Your pa. He wanted you and Peter to fight.'

There was a sly note in Danny's voice which made Nancy suspicious. He resented giving in to her, and he wanted to get in a parting shot. She was reluctant to give him that satisfaction but curiosity overcame her caution. 'What the hell are you talking about?'

'He always said the children of rich men were normally bad businessmen because they weren't hungry. He was really worried about it – thought you might throw away everything he'd earned.'

'He never told me he felt that way,' she said suspiciously.

'That's why he set things up so you'd fight one another. He brought you up to take control after his death, but he never put you in place; and he told Peter it would be *his* job to run the company. That way you'd have to fight it out, and the toughest would come out on top.'

'I don't believe this,' Nancy said; but she was not as sure as she sounded. Danny was angry because he had been out-manoeuvred, so he was being nasty to relieve his feelings; but that did not prove he was lying. She felt chilled.

'Believe what you like,' Danny said. 'I'm telling you what your father told me.'

'Pa told Peter he wanted *him* to be chairman?'

'Sure he did. If you don't believe me, ask Peter.'

'If I didn't believe you, I wouldn't believe Peter.'

'Nancy, I first met you when you were two days old,' Danny said, and there was a new, weary note in his voice. 'I've known you all your life and most of mine. You're a good person with a hard streak, like your father. I don't want to fight with you over business, or anything else. I'm sorry I brought this up.'

Now she believed him. He sounded genuinely regretful and that made her think he was sincere. She was shocked by his revelation, and felt weak and a little dizzy. She was silent for a moment, trying to recover her composure.

'I guess I'll see you at the board meeting,' Danny said.

'Okay,' she replied.

'Bye, Nancy.'

'Bye, Danny.' She hung up.

Mervyn said, 'By God, you were brilliant!'

She smiled thinly. 'Thanks.'

He laughed. 'I mean, the way you worked him round

– he never stood a chance! The poor beggar never knew what hit him—'

'Oh, shut up,' she said.

Mervyn looked as if she had slapped him. 'Whatever you say,' he said tightly.

She was sorry right away. 'Forgive me,' she said, touching his arm. 'At the end Danny said something that shocked me.'

'Do you want to tell me about it?' he asked cautiously.

'He says my father set up this fight between me and Peter so that the toughest would end up running the company.'

'Do you believe him?'

'I do, that's the terrible thing. It really rings true. I've never thought about it before but it explains a lot of things about me and my brother.'

He took her hand. 'You're upset.'

'Yeah.' She stroked the sparse black hair on the backs of his fingers. 'I feel like a character in a motion picture, acting out a scenario that was written by someone else. I've been manipulated for years, and I resent it. I'm not even sure I want to win this fight with Peter, now that I know how I was set up.'

He nodded understandingly. 'What would you like to do?'

The answer came to her as soon as he asked the question. 'I'd like to write my own script, that's what I'd like to do.'

CHAPTER TWENTY

HARRY MARKS was so happy he could hardly move.

He lay in bed remembering every moment of the night: the sudden thrill of pleasure when Margaret had kissed him; the anxiety as he worked up the courage to make a pass at her; the disappointment when she turned him down; and the amazement and delight when she had jumped into his bunk like a rabbit diving into its hole.

He cringed as he remembered that he had come the moment she touched him. This always happened to him the first time with a new girl: he had not owned up to that. It was humiliating. One girl had been scornful and mocked him. Mercifully, Margaret had not been disappointed or frustrated. In a funny way she had been aroused by it. Anyway, she had been happy in the end. So had he.

He could hardly believe his luck. He was not clever, he had no money, and he did not come from the right social class. He was a complete fraud and she knew it. What did she see in him? There was no mystery about what attracted *him* to *her*: she was beautiful, lovable, warm-hearted and vulnerable; and if that were not enough she had the body of a goddess. Anyone would have fallen for her. But him? He was not bad-looking, of course, and he knew how to wear clothes, but he had a feeling that sort of thing did not count much with Margaret. However, she was intrigued by him. She found his way of life fascinating, and he knew a lot of stuff that was strange to her, about working-class life in general and the criminal underworld in particular. He guessed that she saw him as a romantic figure, like the Scarlet Pimpernel, or some kind of outlaw, Robin Hood or Billy the Kid, or a pirate. She was extraordinarily grateful to him for holding her chair in the dining room, a trivial thing he had done without even thinking about it, but it meant a lot to her. In fact he was pretty sure that that was the moment when she had really fallen for him. Girls are peculiar, he thought with a mental shrug. Anyway, it no longer mattered what the original attraction had been: once they took their clothes off it was pure chemistry. He would never forget the sight of her white breasts in the dim, filtered light, her nipples so small and pale they were hardly visible; the riot of chestnut hair between her legs; the scattering of freckles at her throat . . .

And now he was going to risk losing it all.

He was going to steal her mother's jewellery.

It was not something a girl could laugh off. Her parents were awful to her, and she probably believed their wealth should be redistributed anyway, but all the same she would be shocked. Robbing someone was like a slap across the face: it might not do much damage, but it angered people out of all proportion. It could be the end of his affair with Margaret.

But the Delhi Suite was here, on this plane, in the baggage hold, just a few steps from where he lay: the most beautiful jewels in the world, worth a fortune, enough for him to live on for the rest of his life.

He longed to hold that necklace in his hands, feast his eyes on the fathomless red of the Burmese rubies, and run his fingertips over the faceted diamonds.

The settings would have to be destroyed, of course, and the suite broken up, as soon as it was fenced. That was a tragedy, but inevitable. The stones would survive, and end up in another suite of jewellery on the skin of some millionaire's wife. And Harry Marks would buy a house.

Yes, that was what he would do with the money. He would buy a country house, somewhere in America, maybe in the area they called New England, wherever that was. He could see it already, with its lawns and trees, the weekend guests in white trousers and straw hats, and his wife coming down the oaken staircase in jodhpurs and riding-boots—

But the wife had Margaret's face.

She had left him at dawn, slipping out through his curtains while there was no one to see. Harry had looked out of the window, thinking of her, while the plane flew over the spruce forests of Newfoundland and splashed down at Botwood. She had said she would stay on board during the stopover, and snatch an hour's sleep; and Harry said he would do the same, although he had no intention of sleeping.

Now he could see, through his window, a straggle of people in overcoats boarding the launch: about half the passengers and most of the crew. Now, while most people on the plane were still asleep, would be his chance of getting into the hold. Luggage locks would not delay him long. In no time at all he could have the Delhi Suite in his hands.

But he was wondering whether Margaret's breasts were not the most precious jewels he would ever hold.

He told himself to come down to earth. She had spent a night with him, but would he ever see her again after they got off the plane? He had heard people talk of 'shipboard romances' as being notoriously ephemeral: seaplane affairs had to be even more fleeting. Margaret was desperate to leave her parents and live independently, but would it ever happen? A lot of rich girls liked the idea of independence, but in practice it was very hard to give up a life of luxury. Margaret was one hundred per cent sincere, Harry knew, but she had no idea how ordinary people lived and when she tried it she was not going to like it.

No, there was no telling what she would do. Jewellery, by contrast, was completely reliable.

It would have been simpler if he had had to make a straight choice. If the Devil came to him and said, 'You can have Margaret or steal the jewels, but not both,' he would choose Margaret. But the reality was more complicated. He might leave the jewels and still lose Margaret. Or he might get both.

All his life he had been a chancer.

He decided to try for both.

He got up.

He stepped into his slippers and pulled on his bathrobe then looked around. The curtains were still drawn over Margaret's bunk and her mother's. The other three were vacant: Percy's, Lord Oxenford's and Mr Membury's. The lounge next door was empty but for a cleaning woman in a headscarf who had presumably come aboard from Botwood and was sleepily emptying the ashtrays. The outside door was open, and cold sea air blew around Harry's bare ankles. In No. 3 compartment, Clive Membury was talking to Baron Gabon. Harry wondered what they were talking about: waistcoats, perhaps? Further back, the stewards were converting bunks back into divan seats. There was a seedy morning-after air about the whole plane.

Harry went forward and climbed the stairs. As usual, he had no plan of action, no prepared excuses, not the faintest idea what he would do if he should be caught. He found that thinking ahead, and figuring out how things might go wrong, got him so anxious that he was unable to go through with it. Even winging it, like this, he found himself suddenly breathless from tension. Calm down, he said to himself; you've done this a hundred times. If it goes wrong you'll make something up, the way you always do.

He reached the flight deck and looked around.

He was in luck. There was no one there. He breathed easier. What a break!

Glancing forward, he saw a low hatch open under the windsceeen between the two pilots' seats. He looked through it into a big empty space in the bows of the aircraft. A door in the fuselage was open and one of the younger crew members was doing something with a rope. Not so good. Harry pulled his head back in before he was spotted.

He passed quickly along the flight cabin and through the door in the back wall. Now he was between the two cargo holds, underneath the loading hatch which also incorporated the navigator's dome. He picked the left-hand hold, went in and closed the door behind him. He was out of sight now, and he guessed the crew would have no reason to look into the hold.

He examined his surroundings. It was like being in a high-class luggage store. Expensive leather cases were stacked all around and roped to the sides. Harry had to find the Oxenfords' baggage quickly. He went to work.

It was not easy. Some cases were stacked with their name tags underneath, some were covered by other cases which were hard to dislodge. There was no heating in the hold and he was cold in his bathrobe. His hands shook and his fingers hurt as he untied the ropes that prevented the cases shifting in flight. He worked systematically, so that he would not miss any or check pieces twice. He re-tied the ropes as best he could. The names were international: Ridgeway, d'Annunzio, Lo, Hartmann, Bazarov – but no Oxenfords. After twenty minutes he had checked every piece, he was shivering, and he had established that the bags he was looking for must be in the other hold. He cursed under his breath.

He tied the last rope and looked around carefully: he had left no evidence of his visit.

Now he would have to go through the same procedure in the other hold. He opened the door and stepped out, and a startled voice cried, 'Shit! Who are you?' It was the officer Harry had seen in the bow compartment, a cheerful, freckled young man in a short-sleeved shirt.

Harry was equally shocked but he covered it up quickly. He smiled, closed the door behind him, and said calmly, 'Harry Vandenpost. Who are you?'

'Mickey Finn, the assistant engineer. Sir, you're not supposed to be here. You gave me a scare. I'm sorry for swearing. But what are you doing?'

'Looking for my suitcase,' Harry said. 'I forgot my razor.'

'Sir, access to checked baggage is not permitted during the journey, under any circumstances.'

'I thought I couldn't do any harm.'

'Well, I'm sorry, but it's not allowed. I could lend you my razor.'

'I appreciate that, but I kind of like my own. If I could just find my case—'

'Boy, I wish I could do what you want, sir, but I really can't. When the Captain comes back aboard you could ask him, but I know he's going to say the same as me.'

Harry realized with a sinking heart that he was going to have to accept defeat, at least for the present. Putting a brave face on it, he smiled, and said as graciously as he could, 'In that case I guess I'll borrow your razor, and thank you kindly.'

Mickey Finn held the door for him and he stepped into the flight cabin and went down the stairs. What rotten luck, he thought angrily. Another few seconds and I would have been there. God knows when I'll get another chance.

Mickey went into No. 1 compartment and returned a moment later with a safety razor, a fresh blade still in its paper wrapper, and shaving soap in a mug. Harry took them and thanked him. Now he had no choice but to shave.

He took his overnight bag into the bathroom, still thinking about those Burmese rubies. Carl Hartmann, the scientist, was there in his undershirt, washing himself vigorously. Harry left his own perfectly good shaving tackle in his case and shaved hurriedly with Mickey's razor. 'Rough night,' he said conversationally.

Hartmann shrugged. 'I've had rougher.'

Harry looked at his bony shoulders. The man was a walking skeleton. 'I bet you have,' Harry said.

They had no more conversation. Hartmann was not talkative, and Harry was preoccupied.

After he had shaved Harry took out a new blue shirt. Unwrapping a new shirt was one of life's small, intense pleasures. He loved the rustle of the tissue paper and the crisp feel of the virgin cotton. He slipped into it deliciously and tied a perfect knot in his wine-coloured silk tie.

When he returned to his compartment he saw that Margaret's curtains were still closed. He imagined her fast asleep, her lovely hair spread across the white pillow, and he smiled to himself. Glancing into the lounge, he saw the stewards setting out a buffet breakfast that made his mouth water, with bowls of strawberries and jugs of cream and orange juice, and cold champagne in dewy silver ice buckets. Those must be hothouse strawberries, he thought, at this time of year.

He stowed his overnight case; then with Mickey Finn's shaving tackle in his hand he went up the stairs to the flight deck to try again.

Mickey was not there, but to Harry's dismay another crew member was sitting at the big chart table doing calculations on a scratch pad. The man looked up, smiled, and said, 'Hi. Can I help you?'

'I'm looking for Mickey, to return his razor.'

'You'll find him in number one, that's the forward-most compartment.'

'Thanks.' Harry hesitated. He had to get past this guy – but how?

'Something else?' the man said pleasantly.

'This flight deck is unbelievable,' Harry said. 'It's like an office.'

'Incredible, isn't it?'

'Do you like flying these planes?'

'I love it. Uh, look, I wish I had time to talk, but I have to finish these calculations and it's going to take me almost until take-off.'

Harry groaned inwardly. That meant the way to the hold would be blocked until it was too late. He could not think of an excuse to go into the hold. Once again he forced himself to conceal his disappointment. 'Sorry,' he said. 'I'll buzz off.'

'Normally we like to talk to passengers, we meet such interesting people. But right now . . .'

'My fault.' Harry racked his brains for another moment, then gave up. He turned and went back down the stairs, cursing to himself.

His luck seemed to be failing him.

He went forward and gave the shaving kit to Mickey, then returned to his compartment. Margaret still had not stirred. Harry went through the lounge and stepped out on to the sea-wing. He took several deep breaths of the cold, damp air. I'm missing the opportunity of a lifetime, he thought angrily. The palms of his hands itched when he pictured the fabulous jewellery just a few feet over his head. But he had not given up yet. There was one more stop, Shediac. That would be his last chance to steal a fortune.

Part Five

Botwood to Shediac

CHAPTER TWENTY-ONE

EDDIE DEAKIN could feel the hostility of his crew-mates as they went ashore in the launch. None of them would meet his eye. They all knew now how close they had come to running out of fuel and crashing into the stormy ocean. Their lives had been in danger. No one yet knew just why it had happened, but fuel was the engineer's responsibility, so Eddie was to blame.

They must have noticed that he had been behaving oddly. He had been preoccupied the whole flight, he had talked scary to Tom Luther during dinner, and a window had inexplicably broken while he was in the men's room. No wonder the others felt he was not one hundred per cent reliable any more. That kind of feeling spread fast in a tightly knit crew whose lives depended on one another.

The knowledge that his mates no longer trusted him was a bitter pill to swallow. He was proud to be considered one of the most solid guys around. To make matters worse, he himself was slow to forgive others' mistakes, and had sometimes been scornful of people whose performance fell off because of personal problems. 'Excuses don't fly,' he sometimes said, a crack which now made him wince every time he thought of it.

He had tried telling himself he did not give a damn. He had to save his wife and he had to do it alone: he could not ask anyone for help and he could not worry about other people's feelings. He had risked their lives, but the gamble had paid off and that was the end of it. It was all perfectly logical, and none of it made any difference. Engineer Deakin, solid as a rock, had turned into Unreliable Eddie, a guy you had to watch in case he screwed up. He hated people like Unreliable Eddie. He hated himself.

A lot of passengers had stayed on board the plane, as always at Botwood: they were glad of the chance to catch some sleep while the plane was still. Ollis Field, the FBI man, and his prisoner, Frankie Gordino, had also stayed on board, of course: they had not disembarked at Foynes either. Tom Luther was in the launch, wearing a topcoat with a fur collar and a dove-grey hat. As they approached the pier, Eddie got next to Luther and murmured, 'Wait for me at the airline building. I'll take you to where the phone is.'

Botwood was a huddle of wooden houses around a deep-water harbour in the landlocked estuary of the Exploits River. Even the millionaires on the Clipper could never find much to buy here. The village had had telephone service only since June. Such few cars as there were drove on the left, for Newfoundland was still under British rule.

They all went into the wooden Pan American building and the crew made their way to the flight room.

Eddie immediately read the weather reports sent by radio from the big new landplane airport thirty-eight miles away at Gander Lake. Then he calculated the fuel requirement for the next leg. Because this hop was so much shorter, the calculation was not so crucial, but all the same the plane never carried a great excess of fuel, because payload was expensive. There was a sour taste in his mouth as he worked out the arithmetic. Would he ever be able to go through these sums again without thinking of this awful day? The question was academic: after what he was about to do, he would never again be engineer on a Clipper.

The Captain might already be wondering whether to trust Eddie's calculations. Eddie needed to do something towards restoring confidence. He decided to show some implicit self-doubt. He went over his figures twice, then handed his work to Captain Baker, saying in a neutral tone, 'I'd appreciate it if someone would check these.'

'Won't hurt,' the Captain said noncommittally, but he looked relieved, as if he had wanted to propose a double-check but had been reluctant to.

'I'm going to get a breath of air,' Eddie said, and he went out.

He found Tom Luther outside the Pan American building, standing with his hands in his pockets, moodily watching the cows in the field. 'I'll take you to the telegraph office,' Eddie said. He led the way up the hill at a brisk pace. Luther lagged behind. 'Set fire, you,' Eddie said. 'I have to get back.' Luther walked faster. He looked like he did not want to make Eddie angry.

Maybe it was not surprising, after Eddie almost threw him out of the plane.

They nodded to two passengers who appeared to be coming back from the telegraph office: Mr Lovesey and Mrs Lenehan, the couple who had got on at Foynes. The guy wore a flying jacket. Distracted though he was, Eddie noticed that they seemed happy together. People always said he and Carol-Ann looked happy together, he recalled, and he felt a stab of pain.

They reached the office and Luther placed the call. He wrote the number he wanted on a piece of paper: he did not want Eddie to hear him say it. They went into a small private room with a phone on a table and a couple of chairs, and waited impatiently for the call to go through. This early in the morning the lines should not be too busy, but there were probably a lot of connections between here and Maine.

Eddie felt confident that Luther would tell his men to bring Carol-Ann to the rendezvous. That was a big step forward: it meant he would be free to act the moment the rescue was over, instead of continuing to worry about his wife. But what exactly could he do? The obvious thing would be to radio the police immediately; but Luther was sure to think of that, and he would probably smash up the Clipper's radio. Nobody would be able to do anything until help turned up. By then Gordino and Luther would be on land, in a car, speeding away – and no one would even know which country they were in, Canada or the USA. Eddie racked his brains for some way to make it easier for the police to trace Gordino, but he could not think of anything.

And if he were to give the warning beforehand, there was a danger the police would blunder in too early and endanger Carol-Ann – the one risk Eddie was not prepared to take. He began to wonder whether he had achieved anything after all.

After a while the phone rang and Luther picked up the earpiece. 'It's me,' he said. 'There's going to be a change of plan. You have to bring the woman on the launch.' There was a pause, then he said, 'The engineer wants it this way, and he says he won't do it any other way, and I believe him, so just bring the woman, okay?' After another pause he looked at Eddie. 'They want to talk to you.'

Eddie's heart sank. So far Luther had acted like the man in charge. Now it sounded as if he might not have the power to order Carol-Ann brought to the rendezvous. Eddie said edgily, 'Are you telling me this is your boss?'

'I'm the boss,' Luther said uneasily. 'But I have partners.'

Clearly the partners did not like the idea of bringing Carol-Ann to the rendezvous. Eddie cursed. Should he give them the chance to talk him out of it? Was there anything at all to be gained by speaking to them? He thought not. They might bring Carol-Ann to the phone and make her scream, to weaken his resolve ... 'Tell them to fuck off,' Eddie said. The phone was on the table and he spoke loudly, hoping they could hear him at the other end of the line.

Luther looked scared. 'You can't talk that way to these people!' he said in a high voice.

Eddie wondered if he should be scared too. Maybe he had misread the situation. If Luther was one of the gangsters, what was he frightened of? But there was no time to reassess the position right now. He had to stick to his plan. 'I just want a yes or no,' he said. 'I don't need to talk to the shitheel.'

'Oh, my God.' Luther picked up the phone and said, 'He won't come to the phone – I told you he was difficult.' There was a pause. 'Yes, good idea. I'll tell him.' He turned to Eddie again and held out the earpiece. 'Your wife is on the line.'

Eddie reached for the phone then pulled his hand back. If he talked to her, he would be putting himself at their mercy. But he was desperate to hear her voice. He summoned up every ounce of will-power, thrust his hands deep into his pockets, and shook his head in silent negation.

Luther stared at him for a moment, then spoke into the phone again. 'He still won't speak! He – Get off the line, cunt. I want to talk to—'

Suddenly Eddie had him by the throat. The phone clattered to the floor. Eddie pressed his thumbs into Luther's thick neck. Luther gasped, 'Stop! Let go! Leave me . . .' His voice was choked off.

The red mist cleared from Eddie's eyes. He eased the pressure but retained his grip. He brought his face close to Luther's, so close that Luther blinked. 'Listen to me,' Eddie said. 'You call my wife Mrs Deakin.'

'Okay, okay!' Luther said hoarsely. 'Let me go, for Christ's sake!'

Eddie let him go.

Luther rubbed his neck, breathing hard, then he grabbed the phone. 'Vincini? He just went for me because I called his wife a – a bad word. Says I have to call her Mrs Deakin. Are you getting it now, or do I have to draw you a picture? He'll do anything!' There was a pause. 'I guess I could handle him, but if people see us fighting, what'll they think? It could blow the whole thing!' He was silent for a while. 'Good. I'll tell him. Listen, we're making the right decision, I know it. Hold on.' He turned to Eddie. 'They'll go along with it. She'll be on the launch.'

Eddie made his face a mask to conceal his tremendous relief.

Luther went on nervously, 'But he says I must tell you that if there are any snags, he's going to shoot her.'

Eddie snatched the phone from his hand. 'Get this, Vincini. One: I have to see her on the deck of your launch before I open the doors of the plane. Two: she has to come on board with you. Three: no matter what snags there might be, if she's hurt I'm going to kill you with my bare hands. Just keep that in your mind, Vincini.' Before the man had time to reply he hung up.

Luther looked dismayed. 'What did you do that for?' He lifted the earpiece and jiggled the cradle. 'Hello? Hello?' He shook his head and hung up. 'Too late.' He looked at Eddie with a mixture of anger and awe. 'You really live dangerously, don't you?'

'Go pay for the call,' Eddie snapped.

Luther reached into his inside pocket and took out a roll of bills. 'Listen,' he said. 'Your getting mad doesn't help anyone. I've given you what you ask. Now we have to work together to make this operation a success for both our sakes. Why don't we just try to get along? We're partners now.'

'Fuck you,' Eddie said, and he went out.

He was angrier than ever as he strode along the road back to the harbour. Luther's remark that they were partners had touched a raw nerve. Eddie had done what he could to protect Carol-Ann, but he was still committed to help free Frankie Gordino, who was a murderer and a rapist. The fact that he was being forced into it should have excused him, and in others' minds perhaps it would, but to him it seemed to make no difference: he knew that if he went through with it he would never hold up his head again.

As he walked down the hill to the bay he looked across the water. The Clipper floated majestically on the calm surface. Eddie's career on Clippers was at an end, he knew. He was mad about that, too. There were also two big freighters at anchor and a few smaller fishing boats; and, to his surprise, he saw a US Navy patrol boat tied up at the dock. He wondered what it was doing here in Newfoundland. Something to do with the war? It reminded him of his days in the Navy. Looking back, that seemed like a golden time, when life was simple. Maybe the past always looked attractive when you were in trouble.

He entered the Pan American building. There in the green and white painted lobby was a man in lieutenant's uniform, presumably off the patrol boat. As Eddie walked in the lieutenant turned around. He was a big, ugly man with small eyes too close together and a wart on his nose. Eddie stared at him in amazement and delight. He could not believe his eyes. 'Steve?' he said. 'Is it really you?'

'Hi, Eddie.'

'How in the hell . . .?' It was Steve Appleby, whom Eddie had tried to call from England: his oldest and best friend, the one man above all others he wanted by his side in a tight spot. He could hardly take it in.

Steve came over and they embraced, hitting each other on the back.

Eddie said, 'You're supposed to be in New Hampshire – what the hell are you doing here?'

'Nella said you sounded frantic when you called.' Steve looked solemn. 'Hell, Eddie, I've never known you seem even a little *shook*. You're always such a rock. I knew you had to be in *bad* trouble.'

'I am. I'm—' Suddenly Eddie was overcome with emotion. For twenty hours he had kept his feelings bottled up and tightly corked, and he was ready to explode. The fact that his best friend had moved heaven and earth to come and help him out touched him deeply. 'I'm in bad trouble,' he confessed. Then tears came to his eyes and his throat seized up so he could not speak. He turned away and went outside.

Steve followed. Eddie led him round the corner of the building and through the big open doorway into the empty boat room, where the launch was normally kept. They would not be seen in here.

Steve spoke to cover his embarrassment. 'I can't

count how many favours I've called in to get here. I've been in the Navy eight years, and a lot of people owe me, but today they all paid me back double, and now I owe them. It's going to take me another eight years just to get back to even!'

Eddie nodded. Steve had a natural aptitude for wheeling and dealing. Eddie wanted to say thank you, but he could not stop the tears.

Steve's tone changed and he said, 'Eddie, what the hell is going on?'

'They've got Carol-Ann,' Eddie managed.

'Who has, for Christ's sake?'

'The Patriarca gang.'

Steve was incredulous. '*Ray* Patriarca? The racketeer?'

'They kidnapped her.'

'God Almighty, why?'

'They want me to bring down the Clipper.'

'What for?'

Eddie wiped his face with his sleeve and brought himself under control. 'There's an FBI agent on board with a prisoner, a hoodlum called Frankie Gordino. I figure Patriarca wants to rescue him. Anyway, a passenger calling himself Tom Luther told me to bring the plane down off the Maine coast. They'll have a fast boat waiting, and Carol-Ann will be on it. We swap Carol-Ann for Gordino, then Gordino disappears.'

Steve nodded. 'And Luther was smart enough to realize that the only possible way to get Eddie Deakin to co-operate was to kidnap his wife.'

'Yeah.'

'The bastards.'

'I want to get these people, Steve. I want to fucking crucify them. I want to nail the bastards up, I swear.'

Steve shook his head. 'But what can you do?'

'I don't know. That's why I called you.'

Steve frowned. 'The danger period for them is from when they come aboard the plane until they get back to their car. Maybe the police could find the car and ambush them.'

Eddie was dubious. 'How would the police recognize it? It will just be a car parked near a beach.'

'It might be worth a try.'

'It's not tight enough, Steve. There's too much to go wrong. And I don't want to call in the police – there's no knowing what they might do to endanger Carol-Ann.'

Steve nodded agreement. 'And the car could be either side of the border, so we'd have to call in the Canadian police as well. Hell, it wouldn't stay secret for five minutes. No, the police are no good. That leaves the Navy or the Coast Guard.'

Eddie felt better just for being able to discuss the dilemma with someone. 'Let's talk Navy.'

'All right. Suppose I could get a patrol boat like this one to intercept the launch after the trade, before Gordino and Luther reach land?'

'That might work,' Eddie said, and he began to feel hopeful. 'But could you do it?' It was next to impossible to get naval vessels to move outside their chain of command.

'I think I can. They're out on exercises anyway,

getting all excited in case the Nazis decided to invade New England after Poland. It's just a question of diverting one. The guy who can do that is Simon Greenbourne's father – remember Simon?'

'Sure I do.' Eddie recalled a wild kid with a crazy sense of humour and a huge thirst for beer. He was always in trouble, but he usually got off lightly because his father was an admiral.

Steve continued, 'Simon went too far one day and set fire to a bar in Pearl City and burned down half a block. It's a long story, but I kept him out of jail and his father is eternally grateful. I think he would do this for me.'

Eddie looked at the vessel Steve had come in. It was an SC-class submarine chaser, twenty years old, with a wooden hull, but it carried a three inch, .23 calibre machine-gun and a depth charge. It would scare the pants off a bunch of citified mobsters in a speedboat. But it was conspicuous. 'They might see the boat beforehand and smell a rat,' he said anxiously.

Steve shook his head. 'These things can hide up creeks. Their draught is less than six feet fully loaded.'

'It's risky, Steve.'

'So they spot a Navy patrol boat. It leaves them alone. What are they going to do – call the whole thing off?'

'They might do something to Carol-Ann.'

Steve seemed about to argue, then he changed his mind. 'That's true,' he said. 'Anything might happen. You're the only one who has the right to say we'll take the risk.'

Eddie knew Steve was not saying what he really felt. 'You think I'm running scared, don't you?' he said testily.

'Yeah. But you're entitled.'

Eddie looked at his watch. 'Christ, I'm due back in the flight room.' He had to make up his mind. Steve had come up with the best plan he could, and now it was up to Eddie to take it or leave it.

Steve said, 'One thing you may not have thought of. They could still be planning to double-cross you.'

'How?'

He shrugged. 'I don't know how, but once they're on board the Clipper it's going to be hard to argue with them. They may decide to take Gordino and Carol-Ann too.'

'Why the hell would they do that?'

'To make sure you don't co-operate too enthusiastically with the police for a while.'

'Shit.' There was another reason, too, Eddie realized. He had yelled at these guys and insulted them. They might well be planning some final pay-off to teach him a lesson.

He was cornered.

He had to go along with Steve's plan now. It was too late to do otherwise.

God forgive me if I'm wrong, he thought.

'All right,' he said. 'Let's do it.'

CHAPTER TWENTY-TWO

MARGARET WOKE up thinking, Today I have to tell Father.

It took her a moment to remember what she had to tell him: that she would not be living with them in Connecticut, she was going to leave the family, find lodgings and get a job.

He was sure to throw a tantrum.

A nauseating sensation of fear and shame came over her. It was a familiar feeling. She got it every time she wanted to defy Father. I'm nineteen years old, she thought; I'm a woman. Last night I made passionate love to a wonderful man. Why am I still scared of my father?

It had been like this as long as she could remember. She had never understood why he was so determined to keep her in a cage. He was the same with Elizabeth, but not with Percy. He seemed to want his daughters to be useless ornaments. He was always worst when they wanted to do something practical, like learn to swim or build a tree house or ride bicycles. He never cared how much they spent on gowns but he would not let them have an account at a bookshop.

It was not simply the prospect of defeat that made

494

her feel sick. It was the way he refused her, the anger and scorn, the mocking jibes and the purple-faced rage.

She had often tried to outwit him by deceit, but that rarely worked: she was so terrified he might hear the scratching of the rescued kitten in the attic, or come across her playing with the 'unsuitable' children from the village, or search her room and find her copy of Elinor Glyn's *The Vicissitudes of Evangeline*, that forbidden delights lost their charm.

She had succeeded in going against his will only with the help of others. Monica had introduced her to sexual pleasure, and he had never been able to take that away from her. Percy showed her how to shoot; Digby the chauffeur taught her to drive. Now perhaps Harry Marks and Nancy Lenehan would help her to become independent.

She already *felt* different. There was a pleasant ache in her muscles, as if she had spent a day at some hard physical work in the fresh air. She lay in her bunk and ran her hands all over her body. For the past six years she had thought of herself as a thing of ungainly bulges and unsightly hair, but now suddenly she liked her body. Harry seemed to think it was wonderful.

From outside her curtained bunk came a few faint noises. People were waking up, she guessed. She peeped out. Nicky, the fat steward, was taking down the opposite bunks, the pair in which Mother and Father had slept, and remaking the divan seat. Harry's and Mr Membury's had already been done. Harry was sitting down, fully dressed, looking out of the window meditatively.

She suddenly felt bashful, and closed the curtain quickly, before he should see her. It was funny: a few hours ago they had been as intimate as two people can possibly be, but now she felt awkward.

She wondered where the others were. Percy would have gone ashore. Father had probably done the same: he generally woke up early. Mother was never very energetic in the morning: she was probably in the ladies' room. Mr Membury was nowhere in sight.

Margaret looked out of the window. It was daylight. The plane was at anchor near a small town in a pine forest. The scene was very still.

She lay back, enjoying the privacy, savouring the memory of the night, recalling the details and storing them away like photographs in an album. She felt as if last night was when she *really* lost her virginity. Previously, with Ian, sexual intercourse had been hurried, difficult, and quick, and she had felt like a guilty child disobediently imitating a grown-up game. Last night she and Harry had been adults taking pleasure in one another's bodies. They had been discreet but not furtive; shy but not embarrassed; uncertain without clumsiness. She had felt like a real woman. I want more of that, she thought; lots more; and she hugged herself, feeling wanton.

She pictured Harry as she had just glimpsed him, sitting by the window in a sky-blue shirt with such a thoughtful look on his handsome face; and suddenly she wanted to kiss him. She sat up, pulled her robe around her shoulders, opened her curtains, and said, 'Good morning, Harry.'

His head jerked round and he looked as if he had been caught doing something wrong. She thought, What were you thinking about? He met her eyes, then smiled. She smiled back, and found that she could not stop. They grinned stupidly at one another for a long minute. Finally Margaret dropped her eyes and stood up.

The steward turned around from fixing Mother's seat and said, 'Good morning, Lady Margaret. Would you care for a cup of coffee?'

'No, thank you, Nicky.' She probably looked a fright, and she was in a hurry to get to a mirror and brush her hair. She felt undressed. She was undressed, whereas Harry had shaved and put on a fresh shirt and looked as bright as a new apple.

However, she still wanted to kiss him.

She stepped into her slippers, remembering how she had indiscreetly left them beside Harry's bunk and retrieved them a split second before Father would have seen them. She put her arms into the sleeves of her robe and saw Harry's eyes drop to her breasts. She did not mind: she *liked* him to look at her breasts. She tied her belt and ran her fingers through her hair.

Nicky finished what he was doing. She hoped he would leave the compartment, so that she could kiss Harry, but instead he asked, 'May I do your bunk now?'

'Of course,' she said, feeling disappointed. She

wondered how long she would have to wait for another chance to kiss Harry. She picked up her bag, shot a regretful look at Harry, then went out.

The other steward, Davy, was laying out a buffet breakfast in the dining room. She stole a strawberry, feeling sinful. She walked the length of the plane. Most of the bunks had now been remade as seats, and a few people were sitting around drinking coffee sleepily. She saw Mr Membury, deep in conversation with Baron Gabon, and wondered what that disparate pair found to talk about so earnestly. Something was missing, and after a moment she realized what: there were no morning newspapers.

She went into the ladies' room. Mother was sitting at the dressing-table. Suddenly Margaret felt dreadfully guilty. How could I have done those things, she thought wildly, with Mother only a couple of steps away? She felt a blush rising to her cheeks. She forced herself to say, 'Good morning, Mother.' To her surprise, her voice sounded quite normal.

'Good morning, dear. You look a little flushed. Did you sleep?'

'Very well,' Margaret said, and she blushed deeper. Then she was inspired, and continued, 'I'm feeling guilty because I stole a strawberry from the breakfast buffet.' She dived into the lavatory to escape. When she came out she ran water into the basin and washed her face vigorously.

She was sorry she had to put on the dress she had been wearing yesterday. She would have liked something fresh. She splashed on extra *eau de toilette*. Harry had told her he liked it. He had even known it was Tosca. He was the first man she had ever met who could identify perfumes.

She took her time brushing her hair. It was her best feature and she needed to make the most of it. I ought to take more trouble over how I look, she thought. She had never cared much until now, but suddenly it seemed to matter. I ought to have dresses that show off my figure, and smart shoes to call attention to my long legs, and colours that look good with red hair and green eyes. The dress she had on was all right: it was a sort of brick red. But it was rather loose and shapeless, and now, looking in the mirror, she wished it had squarer shoulders and a belt at the waist. Mother would never let her wear make-up, of course, so she would have to be satisfied with her pale complexion. At least she had good teeth.

'I'm ready,' she said brightly.

Mother was still in the same position. 'I suppose you're going back to talk to Mr Vandenpost.'

'I suppose I am, since there's no one else there and you're still redecorating your face.'

'Don't be fresh. There's a look of the Jew about him.'

Well, he isn't circumcised, Margaret thought, and she almost said it out of sheer devilment; but instead she started to giggle.

Mother was offended. 'There's nothing to laugh at. I want you to know that I will not permit you to see that young man again after we get off this plane.'

'You'll be happy to know that I don't care tuppence.'

It was true: she was going to leave her parents, so it no longer mattered what they would or would not permit.

Mother threw her a suspicious look. 'Why do I think you're not being quite sincere?'

'Because tyrants can never trust anyone,' Margaret said.

That was quite a good exit line, she thought, and she went to the door; but Mother called her back.

'Don't go away, dear,' Mother said, and her eyes filled with tears.

Did she mean 'Don't leave the room' or 'Don't leave the family'? Could she possibly have guessed what Margaret was planning? She had always had good intuition. Margaret said nothing.

'I've already lost Elizabeth, I couldn't bear to lose you, too.'

'But it's Father's fault!' Margaret burst out, and suddenly she wanted to cry. 'Can't you stop him being so horrid?'

'Don't you think I try?'

Margaret was shocked: Mother had never before admitted that Father might be at fault. 'But I can't help it if he's that way,' she said miserably.

'You could try not to provoke him,' Mother said.

'Give in to him all the time, you mean.'

'Why not? It's only until you're married.'

'If *you* would stand up to him he might not be like this.'

Mother shook her head sadly. 'I can't take your side against him, dear. He's my husband.'

'But he's so wrong!'

'It makes no difference. You'll know that when you're married.'

Margaret felt cornered. 'It's not fair.'

'It's not for long. I'm just asking you to tolerate him a little while longer. As soon as you're twenty-one he'll be different, I promise you, even if you're not married. I know it's hard. But I don't want you to be banished, like poor Elizabeth . . .'

Margaret realized that she would be as upset as Mother if they became estranged. 'I don't want that either, Mother,' she said. She took a step closer to the stool. Mother opened her arms. They embraced awkwardly, Margaret standing and Mother sitting.

'Promise me you won't quarrel with him,' Mother said.

She sounded so sad that Margaret wanted with all her heart to give the promise; but something held her back, and all she would say was, 'I'll try, Mother, I really will.'

Mother let her go and looked at her; and Margaret read bleak resignation in her face. 'Thank you for that, anyway,' Mother said.

There was nothing more to say.

Margaret went out.

Harry stood up when she entered the compartment. She felt so upset that she completely lost all sense of propriety and threw her arms around him. After a moment's startled hesitation he hugged her and kissed the top of her head. She began to feel better right away.

Opening her eyes, she caught an astonished look

from Mr Membury, who was back in his seat. She hardly cared, but she detached herself from Harry and they sat down on the other side of the compartment.

'We've got to make plans,' Harry said. 'This could be our last chance to talk privately.'

Margaret knew that Mother would be back soon, and Father and Percy would return with the other passengers, and after that she and Harry might not be alone again. She was seized by a near-panic as she saw a vision of the two of them parting company at Port Washington and never finding one another again. 'Where can I contact you, tell me quick!' she said.

'I don't know – I don't have anywhere. But don't worry, I'll get in touch with you. What hotel will you be staying at?'

'The Waldorf. Will you telephone me tonight? You must!'

'Calm down, of course I will. I'll call myself Mr Marks.'

Harry's relaxed tone made Margaret see she was being silly . . . and a little selfish, too. She should think of him as well as herself. 'Where will you spend the night?'

'I'll find a cheap hotel.'

She was struck by an idea. 'Would you like to sneak into my room at the Waldorf?'

He grinned. 'Are you serious? You know I would!'

She was happy to have pleased him. 'Normally I'd share with my sister, but now I'll be on my own.'

'Oh, boy. I can't wait.'

She knew how he loved the high life, and she so

wanted to make him happy. What else would he like? 'We'll order scrambled eggs and champagne from room service.'

'I'll want to stay there for ever.'

That brought her back to reality. 'My parents will be moving to my grandfather's place in Connecticut after a few days. Then I'll have to find somewhere to live.'

'We'll look together,' he said. 'Maybe get rooms in the same building, or something.'

'Really?' She was thrilled. They would have rooms in the same building! It was exactly what she wanted. She had been half afraid that he would go over the top and ask her to marry him, and half afraid he would not want to see her again; but this was the ideal: she could stay close to him and get to know him better without making a foolishly hasty commitment. And she would be able to sleep with him. But there was a snag. 'If I work for Nancy Lenehan I'll be in Boston.'

'Maybe I'll go to Boston too.'

'Would you?' She could hardly believe what she was hearing.

'It's as good a place as any. Where is it, anyway?'

'New England.'

'Is that like old England?'

'Well, I've heard that the people are snobbish.'

'It'll be just like home.'

'What sort of rooms will we get?' she said excitedly. 'I mean, how many, and so on?'

He smiled. 'You won't have more than one room, and you'll find it a struggle to pay even for that. If it's anything like the English equivalent, it will have cheap furniture and one window. With luck there might be a gas ring or a hotplate for you to make coffee. You'll share the bathroom with the rest of the house.'

'And the kitchen?'

He shook his head. 'You can't afford a kitchen. Your lunch will be the only hot meal of the day. When you come home you can have a cup of tea and a piece of cake, or you could make toast if you've got an electric fire.'

She knew that he was trying to prepare her for what he saw as unpleasant reality, but she found the whole thing wonderfully romantic. To think of being able to make tea and toast yourself, any time you like, in a little room of your own, with no parents to worry about and no servants to grumble at you ... It sounded heavenly. 'Do the owners of these places generally live there?'

'Sometimes. It's good if they do, because then they keep the place nice – although they poke their noses into your private life, too. But if the owner lives elsewhere, the building often gets run down: broken plumbing, peeling paint, leaking roofs, that sort of thing.'

It dawned on Margaret that she had an awful lot to learn, but nothing Harry said could dismay her: it was all too exhilarating. Before she could ask any more questions, the passengers and crew who had disembarked arrived back, and at the same moment Mother returned from the ladies' room, looking pale but beautiful. Margaret's elation was punctured. Recalling her conversation with Mother, she knew that the thrill of escaping with Harry would be mingled with heartache.

She did not normally eat a lot in the morning, but today she was ravenous. 'I'd like some bacon and eggs,' she said. 'Quite a lot, in fact.' She caught Harry's eye and realized that she was hungry because she had been making love to him all night. She smothered a grin. He read her mind and looked away hastily.

The plane took off a few minutes later. Margaret found it no less exciting even though this was the third time she had experienced it, but she no longer felt afraid.

She mulled over her conversation with Harry. He wanted to go to Boston with her! Although he was so handsome and charming, and must have had lots of chances with girls just like herself, he seemed to have fallen for her in a special way. It was terribly sudden, but he was being very sensible: not making extravagant vows, but ready to do just about anything to stay with her.

That commitment erased all doubt from her mind. Until now she had not allowed herself to think of a future with him, but suddenly she felt completely confident in him. She was going to have everything she wanted: freedom, independence and love.

As soon as the plane levelled out they were invited to help themselves from the breakfast buffet, and Margaret did so with alacrity. They all had strawberries and cream, except for Percy who preferred cornflakes. Father had champagne with his strawberries. Margaret also took hot rolls and butter.

As Margaret was about to return to the compartment she caught the eye of Nancy Lenehan, who was hovering over the hot porridge. Nancy was as trim and smart as ever, with a navy silk blouse in place of the grey one she had worn yesterday. She beckoned to Margaret and said in a low voice, 'I got a very important phone call in Botwood. I'm going to win today. You can take it that you have a job.'

Margaret beamed with pleasure. 'Oh, thank you!'

Nancy put a small white business card on Margaret's bread plate. 'Just call me when you're ready.'

'I will! In just a few days! Thank you!'

Nancy put a finger to her lips and winked.

Margaret returned to her compartment elated. She hoped Father had not seen the business card: she did not want him asking questions. Fortunately he was too intent on his food to notice anything else.

But as she ate, she realized that he had to be told sooner or later. Mother had begged her to avoid a confrontation, but it could not be done. She had tried to sneak away last time, and it had not worked. This time she had to announce openly that she was leaving, so that the world would know. There must be no secret about it, no excuse to call the police. She must make it clear to him that she had a place to go and friends to support her.

And this plane was surely the place to confront him. Elizabeth had done it on a train and that had worked because he had been obliged to behave himself. Later, in their hotel rooms, he could do anything he liked.

When should she tell him? Sooner rather than later:

he would be in his best mood of the day after breakfast, full of champagne and food. Later, as the day wore on and he had a cocktail or two and some wine, he would become more irascible.

Percy stood up and said, 'I'm going to get some more cornflakes.'

'Sit down,' Father said. 'There's bacon coming. You've had enough of that rubbish.' For some reason he was against cornflakes.

'I'm still hungry,' Percy said, and to Margaret's astonishment he went out.

Father was dumbfounded. Percy had never openly defied him. Mother just stared. Everyone waited for Percy to return. He came back with a bowl full of cornflakes. They all watched. He sat down and began to eat.

Father said, 'I told you not to take more of those.'

Percy said, 'It's not your stomach.' He continued to eat.

Father looked as if he was about to get up, but at that moment Nicky came in from the galley and handed him a plate of sausages, bacon and poached eggs. For a second Margaret thought Father might throw the plate at Percy; but he was too hungry. He picked up the knife and fork and said, 'Bring me some English mustard.'

'I'm afraid we don't carry mustard, sir.'

'No mustard?' Father said furiously. 'How can I eat sausages without mustard?'

Nicky looked scared. 'I'm sorry, sir – no one has ever asked before. I'll make sure we have some on the next flight.'

'That's not much use to me now, is it?'

'I guess not. I'm sorry.'

Father grunted and began to eat. He had taken out his anger on the steward, and Percy had got away with it. Margaret was amazed. This had never happened before.

Nicky brought her bacon and eggs and she tucked in heartily. Could it really be that Father was softening at last? The end of his political hopes, the beginning of the war, his exile, and the rebellion of his elder daughter might have combined to crush his ego and weaken his will.

There would never be a better moment to tell him.

She finished her breakfast, waited for the others to finish theirs. Then she waited for the steward to take away the plates; then she waited while Father got more coffee. Finally there was nothing left to wait for.

She moved to the middle seat of the divan, next to Mother and almost opposite Father. She took a deep breath and began. 'I've got something to tell you, Father, and I hope you won't be cross.'

Mother murmured, 'Oh, no . . .'

Father said, 'What now?'

'I'm nineteen years old and I've never done a stroke of work in my life. It's time I began.'

Mother said, 'For heaven's sake, why?'

'I would like to be independent.'

Mother said, 'There are millions of girls working in factories and offices who would give their eyes to be in your position.'

'I know that, Mother.' Margaret also knew that

Mother was arguing to keep Father out of it. However, it would not work for long.

Mother surprised her by capitulating almost immediately. 'Well, I suppose if you're determined to do it, your grandfather may be able to get you a place with someone he knows—'

'I already have a job.'

That took her by surprise. 'In America? How can you?'

Margaret decided not to tell them about Nancy Lenehan: they might talk to her and try to spoil everything. 'It's all arranged,' she said blandly.

'What sort of a job?'

'An assistant in the sales department of a shoe factory.'

'Oh, for goodness' sake, don't be ridiculous.'

Margaret bit her lip. Why did Mother have to be so scornful? 'It's not ridiculous. I'm rather proud of myself. I got a job, all on my own, without help from you or Father or Grandfather, just on my merits.' Perhaps that was not exactly the way it happened but Margaret was becoming defensive.

'Where is this factory?' Mother said.

Father spoke for the first time. 'She can't work in a factory, and that's that.'

Margaret said, 'I'll be working in the sales office, not the factory. And it's in Boston.'

'That settles it, then,' Mother said. 'You'll be living in Stamford, not Boston.'

'No, Mother, I won't. I'll be living in Boston.'

Mother opened her mouth to speak, then closed it

again, understanding at last that she was confronted with something she could not easily dismiss. She was silent for a moment, then she said, 'What are you telling us?'

'Just that I'm going to leave you and go to Boston, and live in lodgings and go to work.'

'Oh, this is too stupid.'

Margaret flared, 'Don't be so *dismissive*.' Mother flinched at her angry tone, and Margaret immediately regretted it. She said more quietly, 'I'm only doing what most girls of my age do.'

'Girls of your age, perhaps, but not girls of your class.'

'Why should that make any difference?'

'Because there's no point in your working at a silly job for five dollars a week and living in an apartment that costs your father a hundred dollars a month.'

'I don't want Father to pay for my apartment.'

'Then where will you live?'

'I've told you, in lodgings.'

'In squalor! But what is the point?'

'I shall save money until I've got enough for a ticket home, then I'll go back and join the ATS.'

Father spoke again. 'You've no idea what you're talking about.'

Margaret was stung. 'What don't I know, Father?'

Mother, trying to interrupt, said, 'No, don't—'

Margaret overrode her. 'I know I shall have to run errands and make coffee and answer the phone in the office. I know I shall live in a single room with a gas ring, and share the bathroom with other lodgers. I

510

know I shan't like being poor – but I shall love being free.'

'You don't know anything,' he said scornfully. 'Free? You? You'll be like a pet rabbit released in a kennel. I'll tell you what you don't know, my girl: you don't know that you've been pampered and spoiled all your life. You've never even been to school—'

The injustice of that brought tears to her eyes and provoked her into a rejoinder. 'I wanted to go to school,' she protested. 'You wouldn't let me!'

He ignored the interruption. 'You've had your clothes washed and your food prepared, you've been chauffeured everywhere you ever wanted to go, you've had children brought to the house to play with you, and you've never given a thought to how all of it was provided—'

'But I have!'

'And now you want to live on your own! You don't know the price of a loaf of bread, do you?'

'I'll soon find out—'

'You don't know how to wash your own underwear. You've never ridden on a bus. You've never slept in a house alone. You don't know how to set an alarm clock, bait a mousetrap, wash dishes, boil an egg – could you boil an egg? Do you know how?'

'Whose fault is it if I don't?' Margaret said tearfully.

He pressed on remorselessly, his face a mask of contempt and anger. 'What use will you be in an office? You can't make the tea – you don't know how! You've never seen a filing cabinet. You've never had to stay in one place from nine in the morning until five in the afternoon. You'll get bored and wander off. You won't last a week.'

He was giving expression to Margaret's own secret worries, and that was why she was getting so upset. In her heart she was terrified that he might be right: she *would* be hopeless at living alone, she *would* get fired from her job. His mercilessly derisive voice confidently predicting that her worst fears would come true was destroying her dream like the sea washing away a sandcastle. She cried openly, tears streaming down her face.

She heard Harry say, 'This is too much—'

'Let him go on,' she said. This was one battle Harry could not fight for her: it was between her and Father.

Red in the face, wagging his finger, speaking more and more loudly, Father raved on. 'Boston isn't like Oxenford village, you know. People don't help one another there. You'll fall ill and get poisoned by half-breed doctors. You'll be robbed by Jew landlords and raped by street niggers. And as for your joining the army . . .!'

'Thousands of girls have joined the ATS,' Margaret said, but her voice was a feeble whisper.

'Not girls like you,' he said. 'Tough girls, perhaps, who are used to getting up early in the morning and scrubbing floors, but not pampered débutantes. And God forbid that you should find yourself in any kind of danger – you'd turn to jelly!'

She remembered how hopeless she had been in the blackout – scared and helpless and panicked – and she burned with shame. He was right, she had turned to jelly. But she would not always be frightened and defenceless. He had done his utmost to make her powerless and dependent, but she was fiercely determined to be her own person, and she kept that flame of hope flickering even as she cringed under his onslaught.

He pointed his finger at her and his eyes bulged so much they looked as if they would burst. 'You won't last a week in an office, and you wouldn't last a day in the ATS,' he said malevolently. 'You're just too soft.' He sat back, looking self-satisfied.

Harry came and sat beside Margaret. Taking out a crisp linen handkerchief, he dabbed her wet cheeks gently.

Father said, 'And as for you, young fellow-me-lad—'

Harry got up out of his seat in a flash and rounded on Father. Margaret gasped, thinking there was going to be a fight. Harry said, 'Don't dare to speak to me that way. I'm not a girl, I'm a grown man, and if you insult me I'll punch your fat head.'

Father subsided into silence.

Harry turned his back on Father and sat down beside Margaret again.

Margaret was upset but in her heart she felt a sense of triumph. She had told him that she was leaving. He had raged and jeered, and he had reduced her to tears, but he had not changed her mind: she was still going to leave.

All the same, he had succeeded in fostering a doubt. She had already been worried that she might not have the courage to go through with her plans, might be paralysed with anxiety at the last minute. He had inflamed that doubt with his mockery and derision. She had never done anything courageous in her entire life: could she manage it now? Yes, I will, she thought. I'm not too soft, and I'll prove it.

He had discouraged her, but he had failed to make her change course. However, he might not have given up yet. She looked over Harry's shoulder. Father was staring out of the window with a malevolent face. Elizabeth had defied him but he had banished her, and she might never see her family again.

What awful revenge was he planning for Margaret?

CHAPTER TWENTY-THREE

Diana Lovesey was thinking mournfully that true love did not last long.

When Mervyn first fell for her, he had delighted in catering to her every desire, the more capricious the better. At a moment's notice he was ready to drive to Blackpool for a stick of rock, take an afternoon off and go to the cinema, or drop everything and fly to Paris. He was happy to visit every shop in Manchester looking for a cashmere scarf in just the right shade of blue-green, leave a concert half-way through because she was bored, or get up at five in the morning and go for breakfast at a working-men's café. But this attitude had not lasted long after the wedding. He rarely denied her anything, but he soon ceased to take pleasure in gratifying her whims. Delight turned to tolerance and then impatience, and sometimes, towards the end, contempt.

Now she was wondering whether her relationship with Mark would follow the same pattern.

All summer he had been her slave, but now, within days of their running away together, they had had a row. On the second night of their elopement they had been so mad at one another that they had slept apart!

In the middle of the night, when the storm broke and the plane bucked and tossed like a wild horse, Diana had been so frightened that she almost swallowed her pride and went to Mark's bunk; but that would have been too humiliating, so she had just lain still, thinking she was going to die. She had hoped he would come to her, but he had been just as proud, and that made her madder still.

This morning they had hardly spoken. She had woken up just as the plane was coming down at Botwood, and when she got up, Mark had already gone ashore. Now they sat opposite one another in the aisle seats of No. 4 compartment, pretending to eat breakfast. Diana toyed with some strawberries and Mark was breaking up a bread roll without eating it.

She was no longer sure why it had made her so angry to learn that Mervyn was sharing the honeymoon suite with Nancy Lenehan. She just thought Mark should have sympathized with her and supported her. Instead, he had questioned her right to feel that way and implied that she must still be in love with Mervyn. How could Mark say that, when she had given up everything to run away with him?

She looked around. On her right, Princess Lavinia and Lulu Bell were carrying on a desultory conversation. Neither had slept at all because of the storm, and both looked exhausted. To her left, across the aisle, the FBI man, Ollis Field, and his prisoner, Frankie Gordino, ate in silence. Gordino's foot was handcuffed to his seat. Everyone seemed tired and rather grumpy. It had been a long night.

Davy the steward came and took away the breakfast plates. Princess Lavinia complained that her poached eggs had been too soft and her bacon overdone. Davy offered coffee. Diana did not take any.

She caught Mark's eye and tried to smile. He glared at her. She said, 'You haven't spoken to me all morning.'

'Because you seem to be more interested in Mervyn than me!' he said.

Suddenly she felt contrite. Maybe he had a right to feel jealous. 'I'm sorry, Mark,' she blurted out. 'You're the only man I'm interested in, truly.'

He reached out and took her hand. 'Do you mean it?'

'Yes, I do. I feel such a fool. I've behaved so badly.'

He stroked the back of her hand. 'You see . . .' He looked into her eyes, and to her surprise she saw that he was close to tears. 'You see, I'm terrified you'll leave me.'

She had not been expecting that. She was quite shocked. It had never occurred to her that he was frightened of losing her.

He went on, 'You're so lovely, so desirable, you could have any man, and it's hard to believe you want me. I'm scared you'll realize your mistake and change your mind.'

She was touched. 'You're the most lovable man in the world, that's why I fell for you.'

'You really don't care for Mervyn?'

She hesitated, only for a moment, but it was enough.

Mark's face changed again, and he said bitterly, 'You do care for him.'

How could she explain? She was no longer in love with Mervyn, but he still had some kind of power over her. 'It's not what you think,' she said desperately.

Mark withdrew his hand. 'Then set me straight. Tell me how it is.'

At that moment Mervyn entered the compartment.

He looked around, located Diana, and said, 'There you are.'

She immediately felt nervous. What did he want? Was he angry? She hoped he would not make a scene.

She looked at Mark. His face was pale and tense. He took a deep breath and said, 'Look here, Lovesey – we don't want another row, so maybe you should just get out of here.'

Mervyn ignored him and spoke to Diana. 'We've got to talk about this.'

She studied him warily. His idea of a conversation could be one-sided: a 'talk' sometimes turned out to be a harangue. However, he did not look aggressive. He was trying to keep his face expressionless, but she had a notion he was feeling sheepish. That made her curious. Cautiously she said, 'I don't want any fuss.'

'No fuss, I promise.'

'All right, then.'

Mervyn sat down beside her. Looking at Mark, he said, 'Would you mind leaving us alone for a few minutes?'

'Hell, yes!' Mark said vociferously.

They both looked at her. She would have to decide. On balance she would have liked to be alone with Mervyn, but if she said that she would hurt Mark, she knew. She hesitated, afraid to side with one or the other. Finally she thought, I've left Mervyn, and I'm with Mark; I should take his side. With her heart pounding, she said, 'Say your piece, Mervyn. If you can't say it in front of Mark, I don't want to hear it.'

He looked shocked. 'All right, all right,' he said irritably; then he composed himself and became mild again. 'I've been thinking about some of the things you said. About me. How I became cold towards you. How miserable you've been.'

He paused. Diana said nothing. This was not like Mervyn. What was coming?

'I want to say that I'm really sorry.'

She was astonished. He meant it, she could tell. What had brought about this change?

He went on, 'I wanted to make you happy. When we were first together, that was all I wanted to do. I never wanted you to be miserable. It's wrong that you should be unhappy. You deserve happiness because you give it. You make people smile just by walking into a room.'

Tears came to her eyes. She knew it was true, people did love to look at her.

'It's a sin to make you sad,' Mervyn said. 'I shan't do it any more.'

Was he going to promise to be good? she wondered with a sudden stab of fear. Would he beg her to come back to him? She did not want him even to ask. 'I'm not coming back to you,' she said anxiously.

He took no notice of that. 'Does Mark make you happy?' he said.

She nodded.

'Will he be good to you?'

'Yes, I know he will.'

Mark said, 'Don't talk about me as if I'm not here!'

Diana reached across and took Mark's hand. 'We love each other,' she said to Mervyn.

'Aye.' For the first time, the hint of a sneer appeared on his face, but it passed quickly. 'Aye, I think you do.'

Was he going soft? This was not like him at all. How much did the widow have to do with the transformation? 'Did Mrs Lenehan tell you to come and speak to me?' Diana said suspiciously.

'No – but she knows what I'm going to say.'

Mark said, 'I wish you'd hurry up and say it.'

Mervyn looked scornful. 'Don't push it, lad – Diana's still my wife.'

Mark stood his ground. 'Forget it,' he said. 'You have no claim on her, so don't try to make one. And don't call me lad, Grandpa.'

Diana said, 'Don't start that. Mervyn, if you've got something to say, come out with it, and stop trying to throw your weight around.'

'All right, all right. It's just this.' He took a deep breath. 'I'm not going to stand in your way. I've asked you to come back to me and you've turned me down. If you think this chap can succeed where I've failed, and make you happy, then good luck to you both. I wish you well.' He paused, and looked from one to the other of them. 'That's it.'

There was a moment's silence. Mark was about to say something, but Diana got in first. 'You bloody hypocrite!' she said. She had seen in a flash what was really going on in Mervyn's mind, and she surprised herself with the fury of her reaction. 'How dare you?' she spat.

He was startled. 'What? Why . . .?'

'What rubbish, saying you won't stand in our way. Don't you condescend to wish us luck, as if you were making some kind of sacrifice. I know you only too damn well, Mervyn Lovesey. The only time you ever give something up is when you don't want it any more!' She could see that everyone in the compartment was listening avidly, but she was too riled to care. 'I know what you're up to. You had it off with that widow last night, didn't you?'

'No!'

'No?' She watched him carefully. She thought he was probably telling the truth. 'It was close, though, wasn't it?' she said; and she could see by his face that she had guessed right this time. 'You've fallen for her, and she likes you, and now you don't want me any more – that's the truth of the matter, isn't it? Now admit it!'

'I'll not admit any such thing—'

'Because you haven't got the courage to be honest. But I know the truth and everyone else on the plane suspects it. I'm disappointed in you, Mervyn. I thought you had more guts.'

'Guts!' That stung him.

'That's right. But instead you had to make up a pitiful story about not standing in our way. Well, you *have* gone soft – soft in the head. I wasn't born yesterday and you can't fool me so easily!'

'All right, all right,' he said, holding up his hands in a defensive gesture. 'I've made a peace offering and you've spurned it. Please yourself.' He stood up. 'From the way you talk, anybody would think I was the one who had run off with a lover.' He went to the doorway. 'Let me know when you get wed. I'll send you a fish slice.' He went out.

'Well!' Diana's blood was still up. 'The nerve of the man!' She looked around at the other passengers. Princess Lavinia looked away haughtily, Lulu Bell grinned, Ollis Field frowned disapprovingly and Frankie Gordino said, 'Attagirl!'

Finally she looked at Mark, wondering what he had thought of Mervyn's performance and her outburst. To her surprise he was grinning broadly. His smile was infectious, and she found herself grinning back. 'What's so funny?' she said with a giggle.

'You were magnificent,' he said. 'I'm proud of you. And I'm pleased.'

'Why pleased?'

'You just stood up to Mervyn for the first time in your life.'

Was that true? She thought it was. 'I suppose I did.'

'You're not scared of him any more, are you?'

She thought about it. 'You're right, I'm not.'

'Do you know what that means?'

'It means I'm not scared of him.'

'It means more than that. It means you don't love him any more.'

'Does it?' she said thoughtfully. She had been telling herself that she stopped loving Mervyn ages ago, but now she looked into her heart and saw that it was not so. All summer, even while she was deceiving him, she had remained in his thrall. He had retained some kind of hold over her, even after she left him, and on the plane she had been full of remorse and had thought of going back to him. But not any longer.

Mark said, 'How would you feel if he went off with the widow?'

Without thinking, she said, 'Why should I care?'

'See?'

She laughed. 'You're right,' she said. 'It's over at last.'

CHAPTER TWENTY-FOUR

As THE Clipper began its descent to Shediac Bay in the St Lawrence Gulf, Harry was having second thoughts about stealing Lady Oxenford's jewels.

His will had been weakened by Margaret. Just to sleep with her in a bed at the Waldorf Hotel, and wake up and order breakfast from room service, was worth more than jewels. But he was also looking forward to going to Boston with her, and living in lodgings; helping her to become independent, and getting to know her really well. Her excitement was infectious, and he shared her thrilled anticipation of their simple life together.

But all that would change if he robbed her mother.

Shediac was the last stop before New York. He had to make up his mind quickly. This would be his last chance to get into the hold.

He wondered again if he could find a way to have Margaret and the jewels both. First of all, would she ever know that he had stolen them? Lady Oxenford would discover the loss when she opened her trunk, presumably at the Waldorf. But no one would know whether the jewels had been taken on the plane, or before, or since. Margaret knew Harry was a thief, so she would certainly suspect him; but if he denied it, would she believe him? She might.

Then what? They would live in poverty in Boston while he had a hundred thousand dollars in the bank! But that would not be for long. She would find some way of returning to England and joining the women's army, and he would go to Canada and become a fighter pilot. The war might last a year or two, maybe longer. When it was over, he would take his money out of the bank and buy that country house; and perhaps Margaret would come and live there with him . . . and then she would want to know where the money had come from.

Whatever happened, sooner or later he would have to tell her.

But later might be better than sooner.

He was going to have to give her some excuse for staying on the plane at Shediac. He could not tell her he felt ill, for then she would want to stay on board with him, and that would spoil everything. He had to make sure she went ashore and left him alone.

He glanced at her across the aisle. At that moment she was fastening her seat belt, pulling her stomach in. In a vivid flash of imagination he saw her sitting there naked, in the same pose, with her bare breasts outlined by the light from the low windows, a tuft of chestnut hair peeping out from between her thighs, and her long legs stretched across the floor. Would he not be a fool, he thought, to risk losing her for the sake of a handful of rubies?

But it was not a handful of rubies, it was the Delhi

Suite, worth a hundred grand, enough to turn Harry into what he had always wanted to be, a gentleman of leisure.

Nevertheless he toyed with the idea of telling her now. 'I'm going to steal your mother's jewels, I hope you don't mind?' She might say, 'Good idea, the old cow never did anything to deserve them.' No, that would not be Margaret's reaction. She thought herself radical, and she believed in redistribution of wealth, but that was all theoretical: she would be shocked to the core if he actually dispossessed her family of some of their riches. She would take it like a body blow, and it would change her feelings about him.

She caught his eye and smiled.

He smiled back, guiltily, then looked out of the window.

The plane was coming down to a horseshoe-shaped bay with a scattering of villages along its edge. Behind the villages was farmland. As they came closer, Harry made out a railway line snaking through farms to a long pier. Close to the pier were moored several vessels of different sizes and a small seaplane. To the east of the pier were miles of sandy beaches, with a few large summer cottages dotted among the dunes. Harry thought how nice it would be to have a summer house on the edge of the beach in a place like this. Well, if that's what I want, that's what I'll have, he said to himself; I'm going to be rich!

The plane splashed down smoothly. Harry felt less tension: he was an experienced air traveller now.

'What time is it, Percy?' he asked.

'Eleven o'clock, local time. We're running an hour late.'

'And how long do we stay here?'

'One hour.'

At Shediac a new method of docking was in operation. The passengers were not landed by launch. Instead, a vessel that looked like a lobster boat came out and towed the plane in. Hawsers were attached to both ends of the plane and it was winched in to a floating dock connected to the pier by a gangway.

This arrangement solved a problem for Harry. At previous stops, where the passengers had been landed by launch, there had been only one chance to go ashore. Harry had consequently been trying to think of some excuse for staying on board throughout this stopover without letting Margaret stay with him. Now, however, he could let Margaret go ashore and tell her he would follow in a few minutes, and she was less likely to insist on staying with him.

A steward opened the door and the passengers started putting on their coats and hats. All the Oxenfords got up. So did Clive Membury, who had hardly spoken a word all through the long flight – except, Harry now recalled, for one rather intense conversation with Baron Gabon. He wondered again what they had been talking about. Impatiently, he brushed the thought aside and concentrated on his own problems. As the Oxenfords were going out, Harry whispered to Margaret, 'I'll catch you up.' Then he went into the men's room.

He combed his hair and washed his hands, just to

have something to do. The window had been broken in the night, somehow, and there was now a solid screen fixed to the frame. He heard the crew come down the stairs from the flight deck and pass the door. He checked his watch and decided to wait another two minutes.

He guessed almost everyone would get off. A lot of them had been too sleepy at Botwood, but by now they wanted to stretch their legs and get some fresh air. Ollis Field and his prisoner would stay on board, as always. It was odd that Membury went ashore, though, if he was supposed to keep an eye on Frankie. Harry was still intrigued by the man in the wine-red waistcoat.

The cleaners would be coming aboard almost immediately. He listened hard: he could hear no sound from the other side of the door. He cracked it an inch and looked out. All was clear. Cautiously, he stepped out.

The kitchen opposite was empty. He glanced into No. 2 compartment: empty. Looking towards the lounge, he saw the back of a woman with a broom. Without further hesitation he went up the staircase.

He trod lightly, not wanting to advertise his approach. At the turn of the stairs he paused and scrutinized as much of the floor of the flight cabin as he could see. No one was there. He was about to go on when a pair of uniformed legs came into view, walking across the carpet away from him. He ducked back around the corner, then peeped out. It was the assistant engineer, Mickey Finn, the one who had caught him last time. The man paused at the engineer's station and turned. Harry pulled his head back again, wondering where the crewman was headed. Would he come down the stairs? Harry listened hard. The footsteps went across the flight deck and became silent. Last time, Harry recalled, he had seen Mickey in the bow compartment, doing something with the anchor. Was the same thing happening now? He had to take a chance on it.

He went on up silently.

As soon as he was high enough he looked forward. His guess appeared to have been right: the hatch was open and Mickey was nowhere to be seen. Harry did not stop to look more closely, but hurried across the flight deck and passed quickly through the door at the rear end into the hold area. He closed the door softly behind him and breathed again.

Last time he had searched the starboard hold. This time he went into the port side.

He knew immediately that he was in luck. In the middle of the hold was a huge steamer trunk in green-and-gold leather with bright brass studs. He felt sure it belonged to Lady Oxenford. He checked the tag: there was no name, but the address was The Manor, Oxenford, Berkshire.

'Bingo,' he said softly.

It was secured by one simple lock which he snapped with the blade of his penknife.

As well as the lock, it had six brass clasps which were fastened without keys. He undid them all.

The trunk was designed to be used as a wardrobe in a stateroom on board a liner. Harry stood it on end and opened it up. It divided into two spacious cupboards. On one side was a hanging rail with dresses and coats, and a small shoe compartment at the bottom. The other contained six drawers.

Harry went through the drawers first. They were made of light wood covered in leather, and were lined with velvet. Lady Oxenford had silk blouses, cashmere sweaters, lace underwear and crocodile belts.

On the other side, the top of the trunk lifted like a lid, and the hanging rail slid out to make it easier to get at the dresses. Harry ran his hands up and down each garment and felt all around the sides of the trunk.

Finally he opened the shoe box. There was nothing in it but shoes.

He was crestfallen. He had been so sure that she would have her jewels with her; but maybe there was a flaw in his reasoning.

It was too soon to give up hope.

His first inclination was to look for the rest of the Oxenford family's luggage, but he thought again. If I were going to transport priceless jewellery in checked baggage, he thought, I would try to conceal them somehow. And it would be easier to make a hiding-place in a big trunk than in a regular suitcase.

He decided to look again.

He started with the hanging compartment. He put one arm inside the trunk and one outside and tried to gauge the thickness of the sides: if they seemed abnormal there might be a hidden compartment. But he found nothing unusual. Turning to the other side, he pulled all the drawers completely out—

And found the hiding-place.

His heart beat faster.

A large manila envelope and a leather wallet were taped to the back of the trunk.

'Amateurs,' he said, shaking his head.

With growing excitement he began detaching the tapes. The first item to come loose was the envelope. It felt as if it contained nothing but a wad of papers, but Harry ripped it open anyway. Inside were about fifty sheets of heavy paper with elaborate printing on one side. It took him a while to figure out what they were, but eventually he decided they were bearer bonds, each worth a hundred thousand dollars.

Fifty of those added up to five million dollars, which was a million pounds.

Harry sat staring at the bonds. A million pounds. It was almost too much to take in.

Harry knew why they were there. The British government had brought in emergency exchange control regulations to stop money leaving the country. Oxenford was smuggling his bonds out, which was a criminal offence, of course.

He's just as much of a crook as I am, Harry thought wryly.

Harry had never stolen bonds. Would he be able to cash them? They were payable to the bearer: that was stated plainly on the front of each certificate. But they were also individually numbered, so that they could be identified. Would Oxenford report them stolen? That might mean admitting he had smuggled them out of England. But he could probably think of a lie to cover that.

It was too dangerous. Harry had no experience in the field. If he tried to cash the bonds he would be caught. Reluctantly, he put them aside.

The other hidden item was a tan leather folder like a man's pocketbook but somewhat larger. Harry detached it.

It looked like a jewellery wallet.

The soft leather was fastened with a zip. He opened it out.

There, lying on the black velvet lining, was the Delhi Suite.

It seemed to glow in the gloom of the baggage hold like stained glass in a cathedral. The profound red of the rubies alternated with the rainbow sparkle of the diamonds. The stones were huge, perfectly matched, and exquisitely cut, each one set on a gold base and surrounded by delicate gold petals. Harry was awestruck.

He picked up the necklace solemnly and let the gems run through his fingers like coloured water. How strange, he thought bemusedly, that something should look so warm and feel so cold. It was the most beautiful piece of jewellery he had ever handled, perhaps the most beautiful ever made.

And it would change his life.

After a minute or two he set down the necklace and

examined the rest of the suite. The bracelet was like the necklace, with alternating rubies and diamonds, although the stones were proportionately smaller. The earrings were particularly dainty: each had a ruby stud with a drop of alternating small diamonds and rubies on a gold chain, each stone on a tiny version of the same gold petal setting.

Harry imagined the suite on Margaret. The red and gold would look stunning on her pale skin. *I'd like to see her wearing nothing but this*, he thought, and the vision gave him an erection.

He was not sure how long he had sat on the floor gazing at the precious stones when he heard someone coming.

The first thought that flashed through his mind was that it was the assistant engineer again; but the footsteps sounded different: intrusive, aggressive, authoritarian . . . official.

Suddenly he was taut with fear, his stomach tight, his teeth clenched, his fists balled.

The steps came rapidly closer. In a sudden frenzy of activity Harry replaced the drawers, threw in the envelope containing the bonds, and closed up the trunk. He was stuffing the Delhi Suite into his pocket when the door to the hold opened.

He ducked behind the trunk.

There was a long moment of silence. He had a dreadful feeling he had not got down fast enough, and the guy had seen him. He heard moderately hard breathing, like that of a fat man who has hurried up stairs. Was the guy going to come right inside and look around, or what? Harry held his breath. The door closed.

Had the man gone? Harry listened hard. He could no longer hear breathing. He stood up slowly and looked out. The man had gone.

He sighed with relief.

But what was going on?

He had a notion those heavy footsteps and hard breathing belonged to a policeman. Or maybe a customs officer? Perhaps this had only been a routine check.

He went to the door and cracked it. He could hear muffled voices from way off in the flight cabin, but there seemed to be no one right outside. He stepped out and stood by the door to the flight cabin. It was ajar, and he could hear two male voices.

'The guy ain't on the plane.'

'He has to be. He didn't get off.'

The accents were a muted American that Harry recognized as Canadian. But who were they talking about?

'Maybe he sneaked off after everyone else.'

'So where has he gone? He's nowhere around.'

Had Frankie Gordino made his escape? Harry wondered.

'Who is he, anyway?'

'They say he's an "associate" of this hoodlum they got on the plane.'

So Gordino himself had not got away, but one of his gang had been on board, had been discovered, and had made his escape. Which of the respectable-looking passengers could it have been?

'It ain't a crime to be an associate, is it?'

'No, but he's travelling on a false passport.'

A chill struck Harry. He was travelling on a false passport himself. Surely they could not be looking for him?

'Well, what do we do now?' he heard.

'Report back to Sergeant Morris.'

After a moment the scary thought dawned on Harry that he *could* be the one they were looking for. If the police had learned, or guessed, that someone on board was going to try to rescue Gordino, they would naturally run a check on the passenger list – and they would soon discover that Harry Vandenpost had reported his passport stolen in London two years ago; and then they would only have to call at his home to learn that he was not on the Pan American Clipper but sitting in the kitchen eating his cornflakes and reading the morning paper, or something. Knowing that Harry was an impostor, they would naturally assume he was the one who was going to try to rescue Gordino.

No, he told himself, don't jump to conclusions. There could be some other explanation.

A third voice joined in the conversation. 'Who are you guys looking for?' It sounded like the assistant engineer, Mickey Finn.

'Guy's using the name of Harry Vandenpost, but he ain't him.'

That settled it. Harry felt stunned with shock. He had been found out. The vision of the country house with the tennis court faded like an ageing photograph, and instead he saw blacked-out London, a court, a prison cell, and then, eventually, an army barracks. This was the worst luck he had ever heard of.

The engineer was saying, 'You know, I found him sneaking around here, while we were at Botwood.'

'Well, he ain't up here now.'

'Are you sure?'

Shut up, Mickey, Harry thought.

'We looked all over.'

'Did you check the mechanics' stations?'

'Where are they?'

'In the wings.'

'Yeah, we looked in the wings.'

'But did you crawl along? There are places to hide in there that you couldn't see from here in the cabin.'

'We better look again.'

These two policemen sounded kind of dumb, Harry thought. He doubted whether their sergeant would trust them very far. If he had any sense he would order one more search of the plane. And next time they would surely look behind the steamer trunk. Where could Harry hide?

There were several little hiding-places, but the crew would know them all. A thorough search was bound to take in the bow compartment, the toilets, the wings, and the shallow void in the tail. Any other place Harry could find would surely be known to the crew.

He was stuck.

Could he leave? He might sneak off the plane and

get away along the beach. It was a slim chance, but better than giving himself up. But even if he could get out of this little village undetected, where could he go? He could talk his way out of anything in a city, but he had a feeling he was an awfully long way from any cities. In the countryside he was a dead loss. He needed crowds, alleyways, railway stations and shops. He had an idea that Canada was a pretty big country, most of it trees.

He would be all right if only he could get to New York.

But where could he hide in the meantime?

He heard the policemen come out of the wings. For safety he ducked back into the hold—

And found himself staring straight at the answer to his problem.

He could hide in Lady Oxenford's trunk.

Could he get inside? He thought so. It was about five feet high and two feet square: if it had been empty you could have got two people into it. It was not empty, of course: he would have to make room in it by taking out some of the clothes. Then what would he do with them? He could not leave them lying around. But he could cram them into his own half-empty suitcase.

He had to hurry.

He crawled over the piled luggage and grabbed his own case. Working feverishly, he opened it and stuffed Lady Oxenford's coats and dresses into it. He had to sit on the lid to close it again.

Now he could get into the trunk. He found he could

close it from the inside easily enough. Would he be able to breathe when it was shut? He would not be inside for long: it might get stuffy but he would live.

Would the cops notice if the clasps were undone? They might. Could he close them from inside? That looked difficult. He studied the problem for a long moment. If he made holes in the trunk near the clasps, he might be able to poke his knife through and manipulate the clasps through the holes. The same holes would bring him air, too.

He took out his penknife. The trunk was made of wood covered with leather. The dark green-brown leather was imprinted with a pattern of gold-coloured flowers. Like all penknives, his had a pointed implement for getting stones out of horses' hooves. He set the point in the middle of one of the flowers and pushed it in. It penetrated the leather easily enough, but the wood was harder. He worked it in and out. The wood was about a quarter of an inch thick, he guessed. It took a minute or two but eventually he got through.

He pulled the point out. Because of the pattern, the hole could hardly be seen.

He got inside the trunk. With relief he found that he could close and open the clasp from inside.

There were two clasps on top and three down the side. He went to work on the top ones first as they were most visible. He had just finished them when he heard footsteps again.

He got inside the trunk and closed it.

Somehow it was not so easy to close the clasps this

time. Standing with his legs bent he found it difficult to manoeuvre. But he managed it at last.

His position was painfully uncomfortable after a couple of minutes. He twisted and turned but got no relief. He would just have to suffer.

His own breathing sounded very loud. Noises from outside were muffled. However, he could hear footsteps outside the hold, probably because there was no carpet there and vibrations were transmitted through the deck. There were now at least three people out there, he guessed. He could not hear doors opening and closing but he suddenly felt a much nearer step and knew someone had come into the hold.

The voice came suddenly from right next to him. 'I don't see how the bastard got away from us.'

Don't look at the side clasps, please, Harry thought fearfully.

There was a knock on the top of the trunk. Harry stopped breathing. Maybe the guy just leaned his elbow on it, he thought.

Someone else spoke from a distance.

'No, he ain't on this plane,' the man replied. 'We've looked everywhere.'

The other party spoke again. Harry's knees hurt. For God's sake, he thought, go and chat somewhere else!

'Oh, we'll catch him all right. He ain't gonna walk a hundred and fifty miles to the border without some-body sees him.'

A hundred and fifty miles! It would take him a week to walk that far. He might hitch a ride, but in this wilderness he would surely be remembered.

There was no speech for a few seconds. At last he heard receding footsteps.

He waited a while, hearing nothing.

He took out his knife and poked it through one of the holes to undo the clasp.

This time it was harder still. His knees hurt so much that he could hardly stand, and would have fallen if there had been room. He became impatient, and poked the blade through the hole again and again. A panicky claustrophobia seized him and he thought, I'm going to suffocate in here! He tried to be calm. After a moment he was able to blank his mind to the pain while he carefully worked the blade through the hole so that it engaged the catch. He pushed the blade. It lifted the brass loop, then slipped. He gritted his teeth and tried again.

This time the catch came undone.

Slowly and painfully he repeated the process with the other catch.

At last he was able to push the two halves of the trunk apart and stand upright. The pain in his knees became excruciating as he straightened his legs, and he almost cried out; then it eased.

What was he going to do?

He could not get off the plane here. He was probably safe until they reached New York, but what then?

He would have to stay in hiding on the plane and then slip out at night.

He might get away with it. He had no alternative, anyway. The world would know that he had stolen Lady Oxenford's jewels. More importantly, Margaret would know. And he would not be around to talk to her about it.

The more he contemplated this possibility, the more he hated it.

He had known that stealing the Delhi Suite put his relationship with Margaret at risk, but he had always imagined that he would be around when she discovered what he had done, so that he could try to make it all right with her. Even so he had still been uncomfortable. Now, however, it might be days before he reached her; and if things went wrong, and he got arrested, it would be years.

He could guess what she would think. He had befriended her, made love to her, and promised to help her find a new home; and it had all been a sham, for he had stolen her mother's jewellery and left her high and dry. She would think the jewels had been all he wanted right from the start. She would be heart-broken, then she would come to hate and despise him.

The idea made him feel sick with misery.

Until this moment he had not fully realized what a difference Margaret had made to him. Her love for him was genuine. Everything else in his life had been faked: his accent, his manners, his clothes – his entire way of life was a disguise. But Margaret had fallen in love with the thief, the working-class boy with no father, the real Harry. It was the best thing that had ever happened to him. If he threw it away, his life would always be what it was now, a matter of pretending and dishonesty. But she had made him want something more. He still hoped for the country house with the tennis courts, but it would not please him unless she were there.

He sighed. Harry boy was not Harry boy any more. Perhaps he was becoming a man.

He opened Lady Oxenford's trunk. He took from his pocket the tan leather wallet containing the Delhi Suite.

He opened the wallet and took out the jewels once again. The rubies glowed like banked fires. I may never see anything like this again, he thought.

He replaced the jewels in their wallet. Then, with a heavy heart, he put the wallet back in Lady Oxenford's trunk.

CHAPTER TWENTY-FIVE

NANCY LENEHAN sat on Shediac's long plank pier, at the shoreward end, outside the air terminal. This was a building like a seaside cottage, with flowers in window-boxes and sunshades over the windows; but a radio mast beside the house and an observation tower rising from its roof gave away its true function.

Mervyn Lovesey sat beside her in another striped canvas deck-chair. The water shushed against the pier in a soothing way, and Nancy closed her eyes. She had not slept much. A faint smile twitched the corners of her mouth as she recalled how she and Mervyn had misbehaved in the night. She was glad she had not gone all the way with him. It would have been too sudden. And now she had something to look forward to.

Shediac was a fishing village and a seaside resort. To the west of the pier was a sunlit bay, on which floated several lobster boats, some cabin cruisers and two planes, the Clipper and a little seaplane. To the east was a wide sandy beach that seemed to go on for miles, and most of the passengers from the Clipper were sitting among the dunes or strolling along the edge of the shore.

The peace of the scene was disturbed by two cars which screeched up the pier and disgorged seven or eight policemen. They went into the flight building in a hurry, and Nancy murmured to Mervyn, 'They looked like they were planning to arrest someone.'

He nodded and said, 'I wonder who?'

'Frankie Gordino, perhaps?'

'They can't – he's already arrested.'

They came out of the building a few moments later. Three went on board the Clipper, two set off along the beach and two followed the road. They looked as if they were searching for someone. When one of the Clipper's crew emerged, Nancy said, 'Who are the cops after?'

The man hesitated, as if he was not sure he should reveal anything; then he shrugged and said, 'The guy's calling himself Harry Vandenpost, but that's not his real name.'

Nancy frowned. 'That was the boy sitting with the Oxenford family.' She had an idea Margaret Oxenford was developing a crush on him.

Mervyn said, 'Aye. Did he get off the plane? I didn't see.'

'I'm not sure.'

'I thought he looked a bit of a wide boy.'

'Really?' Nancy had taken him for a young man from a good family. 'He's got beautiful manners.'

'Exactly.'

Nancy smothered a smile: it seemed characteristic that Mervyn would dislike men with beautiful manners.

'I think Margaret was quite interested in him. I hope she doesn't get hurt.'

'Her parents will be grateful for a narrow escape, I imagine.'

Nancy could not be happy for the parents. She and Mervyn had witnessed the crass behaviour of Lord Oxenford in the dining room of the Clipper. Such people deserved everything they got. However, Nancy felt sorry for Margaret if she had fallen for a bounder.

Mervyn said, 'I'm not normally the impulsive type, Nancy.'

She was suddenly alert.

He went on, 'I met you only a few hours ago, but I feel completely certain that I want to know you for the rest of my life.'

Nancy thought, You can't be *certain*, you idiot! But she was pleased all the same. She said nothing.

'I've been thinking about leaving you in New York and going back to Manchester, and I don't want to do it.'

Nancy smiled. This was just what she wanted him to say. She reached out and touched his hand. 'I'm so glad,' she said.

'Are you?' He leaned forward. 'The trouble is, soon it will be next to impossible to cross the Atlantic, for anyone other than the military.'

She nodded. The problem had occurred to her, too. She had not thought about it very hard, but she felt sure they would be able to find a solution if they were determined enough.

Mervyn went on, 'If we split up now, it may be years, literally, before we can see one another again. I can't accept that.'

'I feel the same.'

Mervyn said, 'So will you come back to England with me?'

Nancy stopped smiling. 'What?'

'Come back with me. Move into a hotel, if you like, or buy a house, or a flat – anything.'

Nancy felt resentment rise up inside her. She gritted her teeth and tried to stay calm. 'You're out of your mind,' she said dismissively. She looked away from him. She was bitterly disappointed.

He looked hurt and puzzled by her reaction. 'What's the matter?'

'I have a home, two sons and a multi-million-dollar business,' she said. 'You're asking me to leave them all to move into a hotel in Manchester?'

'Not if you don't want to!' he said indignantly. 'Live with me, if that's what you want.'

'I'm a respectable widow with a place in society – I'm not going to live like a kept floozie!'

'Look, I think we'll get married, I'm sure we will, but I don't imagine you're ready to commit yourself to that, are you, after just a few hours?'

'That's not the point, Mervyn,' she said, although in a way it was. 'I don't care what arrangements you envisage, I just resent the casual assumption that I'm going to give up everything and follow you to England.'

'But how else could we be together?'

'Why didn't you ask that question, instead of assuming the answer?'

'Because there is only one answer.'

'There are three. I could move to England; you could move to America; or we could both move, to somewhere like Bermuda.'

He was nonplussed. 'But my country is at war. I have to join the fight. I may be too old for active service but the air force is going to need propellers by the thousand, and I know more about making propellers than anyone else in the country. They need me.'

Everything he said seemed to make it worse. 'Why do you assume that my country doesn't need me?' she said. 'I make boots for soldiers, and when the US gets into this war there are going to be a lot more soldiers needing good boots.'

'But I've got a business in Manchester.'

'And I've got a business in Boston – a much bigger one, by the way.'

'It's not the same for a woman!'

'Of course it's the same, you fool!' she yelled.

She regretted the word *fool* right away. A look of stony fury settled on his face: she had offended him mortally. He got up from his chair. She wanted to say something to stop him walking away in a snit, but she could not think of the right words, and a moment later he had gone.

'Damn,' she said bitterly. She was angry with him and furious with herself. She did not want to drive him away – she liked him! Years ago she had learned that nose-to-nose confrontation was not the right approach when dealing with men: they would accept aggression from one another but not from women. In business she had always tempered her combative spirit, softened her tone, and got her way by manipulating people, not quarrelling with them. Now, just for a moment, she had stupidly forgotten all that, and in consequence she had had a fight with the most attractive man she had come across in ten years.

I'm such a fool, she thought; I know he's proud, that's one of the things I like about him, it's part of his strength. He is tough, but he hasn't suppressed all his emotions the way tough men often do. Look at the way he followed that runaway wife half across the world. See how he stood up for the Jews when Lord Oxenford blew his top in the dining room. Remember how he kissed me . . .

The irony of it was that she felt very ready to think about a change in her life.

What Danny Riley had told her about her father had cast a new light over her entire history. She had always assumed that she and Peter quarrelled because he resented her being cleverer. But that kind of sibling rivalry normally faded away in adolescence: her own two boys, having fought like cat and dog for almost twenty years, were now the best of friends and fiercely loyal to one another. By contrast, the hostility between her and Peter had stayed alive into middle age, and she could now see that Pa was responsible.

Pa had told Nancy that she was to be his successor, and Peter would work under her; but he had told Peter the opposite. In consequence, both of them thought they were intended to run the company. But it went back farther than that. Pa had always refused to lay down clear rules or define areas of responsibility, she could now see. He would buy toys they had to share, then refuse to adjudicate the inevitable disputes. When they were old enough to drive he had bought a car for them both to use: they had fought over it for years.

Pa's strategy had worked for Nancy: it had made her strong-willed and smart. But Peter had ended up weak, sly and spiteful. And now the stronger of the two was about to take control of the company, in accordance with Pa's plan.

And that was what disturbed Nancy: it was all *in accordance with Pa's plan.* The knowledge that everything she did had been foreordained by someone else spoiled the taste of victory. Her whole life now seemed like a school assignment set by her father: she had got an 'A', but at forty she was too old to be at school. She had an angry wish to set her own goals and live her own life.

In fact, she had been in just the right mood to have an open-minded discussion with Mervyn about their future together. But he had offended her by assuming that she would drop everything and follow him half across the world, and instead of talking him round she had bawled him out.

She had not expected him to go down on his knees and propose, of course, but . . .

She realized that in her heart she felt he really *should* have proposed. She was not a Bohemian, after all; she was an American woman from a Catholic family, and if a man wanted a commitment from her there was only one kind of commitment he was entitled to ask for, and that was her hand in marriage. If he could not do that he should not ask for anything.

She sighed. It was all very well to be indignant, but she had driven him away. Perhaps the rift would not be permanent. She hoped so with all her heart. Now that she was in danger of losing Mervyn she understood how much she wanted him.

Her thoughts were interrupted by the arrival of another man she had once driven away: Nat Ridgeway.

He stood in front of her, took off his hat politely, and said, 'It seems you've defeated me – again.'

She studied him for a moment. He could never have started a company and built it up as Pa had built Black's Boots: he did not have either the vision or the drive. But he was very good at running a big organization: he was clever, hard-working and tough. 'If it's any consolation, Nat,' said Nancy, 'I know I made a mistake five years ago.'

'A business mistake, or a personal one?' he said, and there was an edge to his voice that betrayed underlying resentment.

'Business,' she said lightly. His departure had ended a romance that had hardly begun: she did not want to talk about that. 'Congratulations on your marriage,' she said. 'I saw a picture of your wife – she's very beautiful.' It was not true: she was attractive at best.

'Thank you,' he said. 'But to revert to business, I'm

rather surprised that you've resorted to blackmail to get what you want.'

'This is a takeover, not a tea-party. You said that to me yesterday.'

'*Touché.*' He hesitated. 'May I sit down?'

Suddenly she was impatient with formality. 'Hell, yes,' she said. 'We worked together for years, and for a few weeks we dated too; you don't have to ask permission to sit down, Nat.'

He smiled. 'Thanks.' He took Mervyn's deck-chair and moved it round so that he could look at her. 'I tried to take over Black's without your help. That was dumb, and I failed. I should have known better.'

'No argument here.' That sounded hostile, she realized. 'And no hard feelings, either.'

'I'm glad you said that – because I still want to buy your company.'

Nancy was taken aback. She saw that she had been in danger of underestimating him. Don't let your guard down! she told herself. 'What did you have in mind?'

'I'm going to try again,' he said. 'Of course, I'll have to make a better offer next time. But more important, I want you on my side – before and after the merger. I want to come to terms with you, and then I want you to become a director of General Textiles and sign a five-year contract.'

She had not expected this, and she did not know how she felt about it. To gain time she asked a question. 'A contract? To do what?'

'To run Black's Boots as a division of General Textiles.'

'I'd lose my independence – I'd be an employee.'

'Depending on how we structure the deal, you might be a shareholder. And while you're making money, you'll have all the independence you want – I don't interfere with profitable divisions. But if you lose money, then yes, you'll forfeit your independence. I fire failures.' He shook his head. 'But you won't fail.'

Nancy's instinct was to turn him down. No matter how he sugared the pill, he still wanted to take the company away from her. But instant refusal was what Pa would have wanted, and she had resolved to stop living her life by her father's programme. However, she had to say something, so she prevaricated. 'I might be interested.'

'That's all I want to know,' he said, standing up. 'Think about it and figure out what kind of deal would make you comfortable. I'm not offering you a blank cheque, but I want you to understand that I'll go a long way to make you happy.' Nancy was faintly bemused: his technique was persuasive. He had learned a lot about negotiating in the last few years. He looked past her, towards the land. 'I think your brother wants to talk to you.'

She looked over her shoulder and saw Peter coming. Nat put on his hat and walked away. This looked like a pincer movement. Nancy stared resentfully at Peter. He had deceived her and betrayed her, and she could hardly bring herself to speak to him. She would have liked to mull over Nat Ridgeway's surprising offer, and think about how it fitted in with her new feelings about her life, but Peter did not give her time. He stood in front of her, put his head on one side in a way that reminded her of his boyhood, and said, 'Can we talk?'

'I doubt it,' she snapped.

'I want to apologize.'

'You're sorry for your treachery now that it's failed.'

'I'd like to make peace.'

Everyone wants to do a deal with me today, she thought sourly. 'How could you possibly make up for what you've done to me?'

'I can't,' he said immediately. 'Never.' He sat down in the chair vacated by Nat. 'When I read your report, I felt such a fool. You were saying I couldn't run the business, I'm not the man my father was, my sister could do it better than me, and I felt so ashamed because in my heart I knew it was true.'

Well, she thought, that's progress.

'It made me mad, Nan, that's the truth.' As children they had called each other Nan and Petey, and his use of the childhood name brought a lump to her throat. 'I don't think I knew what I was doing.'

She shook her head. That was a typical Peter excuse. 'You knew what you were doing.' But she was sad, now, rather than angry.

A group of people stopped near the door to the airline building, chatting. Peter looked irritably at them and said to Nancy, 'Come and walk along the shore with me?'

She sighed. He was, after all, her little brother. She got up.

He gave her a radiant smile.

They walked to the landward end of the pier then

stepped across the railroad track and descended to the beach. Nancy took off her high-heeled shoes and walked along the sand in her stockings. The breeze tossed Peter's fair hair, and she saw, with a little shock, that it was receding from his temples. She wondered why she had not noticed that before, and realized that he combed his hair carefully to conceal it. That made her feel old.

There was nobody near by now, but Peter said no more for a while, and eventually Nancy spoke. 'Danny Riley told me a weird thing. He said Pa deliberately set things up so you and I would fight.'

Peter frowned. 'Why would he do that?'

'To make us tougher.'

Peter laughed harshly. 'Do you believe it?'

'Yes.'

'I guess I do too.'

'I've decided I'm not going to live the rest of my life under Pa's spell.'

He nodded, then said, 'But what does that mean?'

'I don't know, yet. Maybe I'll accept Nat's offer, and merge our company into his.'

'It's not "our" company any more, Nan. It's yours.'

She studied him. Was this genuine? She felt mean, being so suspicious. She decided to give him the benefit of the doubt.

He looked sincere as he went on, 'I'm not cut out for business, so I'm going to leave it to people like you who are good at it.'

'But what will you do?'

'I thought I might buy that house.' They were passing

an attractive white-painted cottage with green shutters. 'I'm going to have lots of time for holidays.'

She felt rather sorry for him. 'It's a pretty house,' she said. 'Is it for sale, though?'

'There's a board on the other side. I was poking around earlier. Come and see.'

They walked around the house. It was locked up, and the shutters were closed, so they could not look into the rooms, but from the outside it was appealing. It had a wide veranda with a hammock. There was a tennis court in the garden. On the far side was a small building without windows, which Nancy guessed was a boat-house. 'You could have a boat,' she said. Peter had always liked sailing.

A side door to the boat-house stood open. Peter went inside. She heard him exclaim, 'Good God!'

She stepped through the doorway and peered into the gloom. 'What is it?' she said anxiously. 'Petey, are you all right?'

Peter appeared beside her and took her arm. For a split second she saw a nasty, triumphant grin on his face, and she knew she had made a terrible mistake. Then he jerked her arm violently, pulling her farther in. She stumbled, cried out, dropped her shoes and handbag, and fell to the dusty floor.

'Peter!' she cried out furiously. She heard him take three rapid steps, then the door banged and she was in darkness. 'Peter?' she called, fearful now. She got to her feet. There was a scraping sound and then a knock as if something was being used to jam the door. She yelled out, 'Peter! Say something!'

There was no reply.

Hysterical fear bubbled up in her throat and she wanted to scream in terror. She put her hand to her mouth and bit the knuckle of her thumb. After a moment the panic began to recede.

Standing there in the dark, blind and disoriented, she realized he had planned this all along: he had found the empty house with its convenient boat-house, lured her here and locked her in, so that she would miss the plane and be unable to vote at the board meeting. His regrets, his apology, his talk of giving up business and his painful honesty had all been faked. He had cynically evoked their childhood to soften her. Once again she had trusted him; once again he had betrayed her. It was enough to make her weep.

She bit her lip and considered her situation. As her eyes became accustomed to the darkness she was able to see a line of light under the door. She walked towards it, holding both hands out in front of her. When she reached the door she felt the wall on both sides of it and found a switch. She turned it and the boat-house was flooded with light. She found the handle of the door and tried, without any real hope, to push it open. It did not budge: he had jammed it well. She put her shoulder to the door and heaved with all her might, but it would not move.

Her elbows and knees hurt where she had fallen, and her stockings were torn. 'You pig,' she said to the absent Peter.

She put on her shoes, picked up her handbag and looked around. Most of the space was taken up by a big sailing boat on a wheeled dolly. Its mast hung in a cradle from the ceiling, and its sails were folded in neat bundles on the deck. At the front of the boat-house was a wide door. Nancy examined it and found, as she expected, that it was securely locked.

The house was set back from the beach a little, but there was a chance that passengers from the Clipper, or even someone else, might meander past. Nancy took a deep breath and shouted at the top of her voice, 'HELP! HELP! HELP!' She decided to yell at one-minute intervals, so that she would not get hoarse.

Both the front and side doors were stout and well-fitting, but she might be able to break them open with a crowbar or something. She looked around. The owner was a neat man: he did not keep his gardening tools in his boat-house. There were no shovels or rakes.

She shouted for help again, then climbed on to the deck of the boat, still looking for a tool. There were several closets on deck but all had been locked shut by the tidy owner. She looked around the place again from up on the deck, but she saw nothing new. 'Damn, damn, damn!' she said aloud.

She sat on the raised centreboard and brooded despondently. It was quite cold in the boat-house, and she was glad of her cashmere coat. She continued to call for help every minute or so but, as time passed, her hopes diminished. The passengers would be back on board the Clipper by now. Soon it would take off, leaving her behind.

It struck her that losing the company might be the least of her worries. Suppose nobody came by this boat-house for a week? She could die here. Panicking, she began to yell loudly and continuously. She could hear a note of hysteria in her own voice, and that scared her even more.

After a while she just got tired, and that calmed her. Peter was wicked but he was not a murderer, he would not leave her to die. He probably intended to place an anonymous call to the Shediac police department and tell them to let her out. But not until after the board meeting, of course. She told herself she was safe, but she still felt deeply uneasy. What if Peter was more wicked than she thought? What if he should forget? What if he should fall ill, or suffer some sort of accident? Who would save her then?

She heard the roar of the Clipper's mighty engines sounding out across the bay. From panic her mood switched to total despair. She had been betrayed and defeated, and she had even lost Mervyn, who would be on board the plane by now, waiting to take off. He might wonder idly what had happened to her, but since her last words to him had been 'You fool!' he probably figured she was through with him.

It had been arrogant of him to assume she would follow him to England, but to be realistic about it, any man would have made the same assumption, and she had been silly to get mad about it. Now they had parted angrily and she would never see him again. She might even die.

The roar of the distant engines rose to a crescendo. The Clipper was taking off. The noise persisted at high volume for a minute or two, then began to fade as, Nancy presumed, the plane climbed into the distant sky. That's it, she thought; I've lost my business and I've lost Mervyn, and I'm probably going to starve to death here. No, she would not starve, she would die of thirst, raving and screaming in agony . . .

She felt a tear on her cheek, and wiped it away with the cuff of her coat. She had to pull herself together. There must be a way out of here. She looked around yet again. She wondered if she could use the mast as a battering ram. She reached up to the sling. No, the mast was much too heavy to be moved by one person. Could she cut through the door somehow? She recalled stories of prisoners in medieval dungeons scratching the stones with their fingernails year after year in a vain attempt to dig a way out. She did not have years, and she would need something stronger than fingernails. She looked in her bag. She had a small ivory comb, a bright red lipstick almost used up, a cheap powder compact the boys had given her for her thirtieth birthday, an embroidered handkerchief, her cheque book, a five-pound note, several fifty-dollar bills, and a small gold pen: nothing she could use. She thought of her clothes. She was wearing a crocodile belt with a gold-plated buckle. It occurred to her that the point of the buckle might be used to gouge away the wood of the door around the lock. It would be a long job; but she had all the time in the world.

She climbed off the boat and located the lock on the big front door. The wood was quite stout, but perhaps she would not need to scratch all the way through: when she had made a deep groove it might then break. She shouted for help again. No one answered.

She took off her belt. Her skirt would not stay up without it, so she took that off, folded it neatly, and draped it over the gunwale of the boat. Although no one could see her, she felt glad she was wearing pretty panties with a lacy trim and a matching garter belt.

She scratched a square mark all around the lock and then began to make it deeper. The metal of her buckle was not very strong, and after a while the prong bent. Nevertheless she carried on, stopping every minute or so to shout. Slowly the mark became a groove. Sawdust trickled out and drifted to the floor.

The wood of the door was soft, perhaps because of the damp air. The work went more quickly and she began to think she might get out soon.

Just as she was becoming hopeful, the prong snapped off.

She picked it up from the floor and tried to continue, but without the buckle the prong on its own was hard to handle. If she dug deep it slipped from her fingers, and if she scratched lightly she made the groove no deeper. After dropping it five or six times she cursed aloud, cried tears of rage, and hammered uselessly on the door with her fists.

A voice called, 'Who's there?'

She shut up and stopped hammering. Had she really heard it? She shouted, 'Hello! Help!'

'Nancy, is that you?'

Her heart leaped. It was a British accent and she recognized the voice. 'Mervyn! Thank God!'

'I've been searching for you. What the devil happened to you?'

'Just let me out, will you?'

The door shook. 'It's locked.'

'Come around the side.'

'On my way.'

Nancy crossed the boat-house, skirting the sailing boat, and went to the side door. She heard him say, 'It's wedged – just a minute . . .' She realized she was standing there in her stockings and underwear, so she pulled her coat around her to cover her nakedness. A moment later the door flew open and she flung herself into Mervyn's arms. 'I thought I was going to die in here!' she said, and to her embarrassment she began to cry.

He hugged her and stroked her hair, saying, 'There, there.'

'Peter locked me in,' she said tearfully.

'I guessed he'd done something sly. That brother of yours is a right bastard, if you ask me.'

Nancy did not care about Peter, she was too glad to see Mervyn. She looked into his eyes through a haze of tears, then kissed his face all over: eyes, cheeks, nose and finally lips. She suddenly felt powerfully aroused. She opened her mouth and kissed him passionately. He put his arms around her and squeezed her tight. She pressed herself against him, hungry for the feel of his body. He ran his hands down her back inside her coat and stopped, startled, when he felt her panties. He drew back and looked at her. Her coat had fallen open. 'What happened to your skirt?'

She laughed. 'I tried to cut through the door with the prong of my belt buckle, and my skirt wouldn't stay up without the belt, so I took it off . . .'

'What a nice surprise,' he said thickly, and he stroked her bottom and her bare thighs. She felt his penis grow erect against her stomach. She reached down and stroked it.

In a moment they were both mad with desire. She wanted to make love now, here, and she knew he felt the same. He covered her small breasts with his big hands, and she gasped. She pulled open the buttons of his fly and reached inside. All the time, in the back of her mind, she was thinking I might have died, I might have died, and the thought made her desperate for satisfaction. She found his penis, squeezed it, and pulled it out. They were both breathing like sprinters now. She stood back and looked down at the big cock in her small white hand. Giving in to an irresistible urge, she bent over and took it in her mouth.

It seemed to fill her up. There was a mossy smell in her nostrils and a salty taste in her mouth. She groaned: she had forgotten how much she liked doing this. She could have gone on for ever, but eventually he drew her head up, moaning, 'Stop, before I burst.'

He bent in front of her and slowly drew her panties down. She felt shy and inflamed at the same time. He kissed her pubic hair. He pulled her panties down to her ankles and she stepped out of them.

He straightened up and embraced her again, and then at last his hand closed over her sex, and a moment later she felt his finger slide easily inside. All the while they kissed wetly, lips and tongues in a frantic tangle, pausing only to gasp for breath. After a while she drew away from him, looked around, and said, 'Where?'

'Put your arms round my neck,' he said.

She reached up and clasped her hands behind his neck. He put his hands under her thighs and lifted her effortlessly off the ground. Her coat swung behind her. As he lowered her, she guided him inside, then wrapped her legs around his waist.

For a moment they were still, and she savoured the feeling she had been without so long, the comforting sense of utter closeness that came from having a man inside her and mingling two bodies so intimately. It was, she now recalled, the best feeling in the world, and she thought she must have been mad to go without it for ten years.

Then she began to move, pulling herself to him and pushing away. She heard him groan deep in his throat, and the thought of the pleasure she was giving him inflamed her more. She felt shameless, making love in this bizarre position with a man she hardly knew. At first she wondered whether he could take her weight; but she was petite and he was a big man. He grasped the globes of her bottom and moved her, lifting her up and down. She closed her eyes and savoured the feeling of his penis going in and out and her clitoris pressing against his belly. She forgot to worry about his strength and concentrated intensely on the sensations in her groin.

After a while she opened her eyes and looked at him. She wanted to tell him that she loved him. Somewhere in the back of her mind a sentinel of common sense told her it was too soon; but all the same she felt it. 'You're very dear,' she whispered to him.

The look in his eyes told her that he understood. He murmured her name and began to move faster.

She closed her eyes again and thought only of the waves of delight emanating from the place where their bodies met. She heard her own voice, as if at a distance, giving small cries of pleasure each time she sank down on him. He was breathing hard, but he held her weight without any sign of strain. Now she sensed him holding back, waiting for her. She thought of the pressure building up inside him with every rise and fall of her hips, and that image pushed her over the top. Her whole body thrilled with pleasure and she cried aloud. She felt him surge and jerk, and she rode him like a bucking horse as the climax shook them both. At last the pleasure eased, Mervyn became still, and she slumped on his chest.

He hugged her hard and said, 'By heck, is it always like that for you?'

She laughed breathlessly. She loved a man who could make her laugh.

Eventually he lowered her to the floor. She stood shakily on her feet, still leaning on him, for a few minutes. Then, reluctantly, she put her clothes back on.

They smiled at one another a lot, but did not speak, as they went out into the mild sunshine and walked slowly along the beach towards the pier.

Nancy was wondering if perhaps it was her destiny to live in England and marry Mervyn. She had lost her battle for control of the company: there was no way she could get to Boston in time for the board meeting, so Peter would outvote Danny Riley and Aunt Tilly, and carry the day. She thought of her boys: they were independent now, she did not need to live her life according to their needs. And she had now discovered that as a lover Mervyn was everything she longed for. She still felt dazed and a little weak after their love-making. But what would I do in England? she thought. I can't be a housewife.

They reached the pier and stood looking over the bay. Nancy wondered how often trains ran from here. She was about to propose making enquiries when she noticed Mervyn staring hard at something in the distance. 'What are you looking at?' she said.

'A Grumman Goose,' he said thoughtfully.

'I don't see any geese.'

He pointed. 'That little seaplane is called a Grumman Goose. It's quite new – they've only been out for a couple of years. They're very fast, faster than the Clipper . . .'

She looked at the seaplane. It was a modern-looking twin-engined monoplane with an enclosed cabin. She realized what he was thinking. In a seaplane she could get to Boston in time for the board meeting. 'Could we charter it?' she asked hesitantly, hardly daring to hope.

'That's what I was thinking.'

'Let's ask!' She hurried along the pier to the airline building, and Mervyn followed, his long stride easily keeping up with her. Her heart was pounding. She might yet save her company. But she kept her elation bottled up: there might be a snag.

They entered the building, and a young man in a Pan American uniform said, 'Hey, you guys missed your plane!'

Without preamble, Nancy said, 'Do you know who the little seaplane belongs to?'

'The Goose? Sure do. A mill owner called Alfred Southborne.'

'Does he ever rent it?'

'Yeah, whenever he can. You want to charter it?'

Nancy's heart leaped. 'Yes!'

'One of the pilots is right here – came to look at the Clipper.' He stepped back and called into an adjoining room. 'Hey, Ned? Someone wants to charter your Goose.'

Ned came out. He was a cheerful man of about thirty in a shirt with epaulettes. He nodded politely and said, 'I'd like to help you folks, but my co-pilot ain't here and the Goose needs a crew of two.'

Nancy's heart sank again.

Mervyn said, 'I'm a pilot.'

Ned looked sceptical. 'Ever flown a seaplane?'

Nancy held her breath.

Mervyn said, 'Yes – the Supermarine.'

Nancy had never heard of a Supermarine, but it must have been a competition plane, for Ned was impressed. 'Do you race?' he asked.

'I did when I was young. Now I just fly for pleasure. I have a Tiger Moth.'

'Well, if you've flown a Supermarine you won't have any trouble being co-pilot on the Goose. And Mr Southborne is away until tomorrow. Where do you want to go?'

'Boston.'

'Cost you a thousand dollars.'

'No problem!' Nancy said excitedly. 'But we need to leave right away.'

The man looked at her in mild surprise: he had assumed the man was in charge. 'We can be gone in a few minutes, ma'am. How would you pay?'

'I can give you a personal cheque, or you can bill my company in Boston, Black's Boots.'

'You work for Black's Boots?'

'I own it.'

'Hey, I'm wearing your shoes!'

She looked down. He had the $6.95 toecapped Oxford in black, size nine. 'How do they feel?' she said automatically.

'Great. They're good shoes. But I guess you know that.'

She smiled. 'Yes,' she said. 'They're good shoes.'

Part Six

*Shediac to the
Bay of Fundy*

CHAPTER TWENTY-SIX

MARGARET WAS frantic with worry as the
Clipper climbed over New Brunswick and
headed for New York. Where was Harry?

The police had found out that he was travelling on a
false passport: that much was common knowledge
among the passengers. She could not imagine how they
had found out, but it was an academic question. More
important was what they would do to him if they caught
him. Presumably he would be sent back to England,
where he would either go to jail for stealing those
wretched cufflinks or be conscripted into the army; and
then how would she ever find him?

As far as she knew, they had not caught him yet. The
last time she saw him, he had gone to the men's room
as she was disembarking at Shediac. Was that the
beginning of some escape plan? Had he known then
that he was in trouble?

The police had searched the plane without finding him, so he must have got off at some point; but
where had he gone? Was he even now walking along a
narrow road through the forest, trying to thumb a lift?
Or had he perhaps talked his way on to a fishing vessel
and left by sea? Whatever he had done, the same

question tortured Margaret: would she ever see him again?

She told herself again and again she must not be discouraged. Losing Harry hurt, but she still had Nancy Lenehan to help her.

Father could not stop her now. He was a failure and an exile, and he had lost his power to coerce her. However, she was still frightened that he might lash out, like a wounded animal at bay, and do something terribly destructive.

As soon as the plane reached cruising height, she unfastened her seat belt and went aft to see Mrs Lenehan.

The stewards were preparing the dining room for lunch as she passed through. Farther back, in No. 4 compartment, Ollis Field and Frank Gordino were sitting side by side, handcuffed together. Margaret went all the way to the rear and knocked on the door of the honeymoon suite. There was no reply. She knocked again, then opened it. It was empty.

Cold fear touched her heart.

Perhaps Nancy was in the ladies' powder room. But, then, where was Mr Lovesey? If he had gone to the flight deck or the men's room, Margaret would have seen him pass through No. 2 compartment. She stood in the doorway, frowning and staring around the suite as if they might be hiding somewhere; but there was nowhere to hide.

Nancy's brother Peter and his companion were sitting right next to the honeymoon suite, across the aisle from the powder room. Margaret said to them, 'Where's Mrs Lenehan?'

Peter replied, 'She decided to leave the flight at Shediac.'

Margaret gasped. 'What?' she said. 'How do you know?'

'She told me.'

'But why?' Margaret said plaintively. 'What made her stay behind?'

He looked offended. 'I guess I don't know,' he said frostily. 'She didn't say. She simply asked me to inform the Captain that she would not be joining the plane for the last leg of the trip.'

Margaret knew it was rude to interrogate him but she had to persist. 'Where did Nancy go?'

He picked up a newspaper from the seat beside him. 'I have no idea,' he said, and began to read.

Margaret was desolate. How could Nancy do this? She knew how much Margaret was relying on her for help. Surely she would not have left the flight without saying anything, or at least leaving some kind of message?

Margaret stared hard at Peter. She thought he had a shifty look. He was a little too touchy about being questioned, too. On impulse she said, 'I don't believe you're telling me the truth.' It was a very insulting thing to say and she held her breath as she waited for his reaction.

He looked up at her, reddening. 'You have inherited your father's bad manners, young lady,' he said. 'Please go away.'

She was crushed. Nothing could be more hateful to her than to be told she was like Father. She turned away without another word, feeling close to tears.

Passing through No. 4 compartment she noticed Diana Lovesey, Mervyn's beautiful wife. Everyone had been riveted by the drama of the runaway wife and the pursuing husband, and amused when Nancy and Mervyn had been obliged to share the honeymoon suite. Now Margaret wondered whether Diana might know what had happened to her husband. It would be embarrassing to ask, of course, but Margaret was too desperate to worry about that. She sat down next to Diana and said, 'Excuse me, but do you know what happened to Mr Lovesey and Mrs Lenehan?'

Diana looked surprised. 'Happened? Aren't they in the honeymoon suite?'

'No – they're not on board.'

'Really?' Diana was obviously shocked and mystified. 'How come? Did they miss the plane?'

'Nancy's brother says they decided not to finish the flight, but I don't think I believe him.'

Diana looked cross. 'Neither of them said anything to me.'

Margaret looked in enquiry at Diana's companion, the mild-mannered Mark. 'They certainly didn't confide in me,' he said.

In a different tone of voice Diana said, 'I hope they're all right.'

Mark said, 'What do you mean, honey?'

'I don't know what I mean. I just hope they're all right.'

Margaret nodded agreement with Diana. 'I don't trust the brother. I think he's dishonest.'

Mark said, 'You may be right, but I guess there's

nothing we can do about it while we're in mid-air. Besides—'

'He's not my concern any more, I know,' Diana said irritably. 'But he was my husband for five years and I'm worried about him.'

'There will probably be a message from him waiting when we get to Port Washington,' Mark said soothingly.

'I hope so,' Diana said.

Davy the steward touched Margaret's arm. 'Lunch is ready, Lady Margaret, and your family are at table.'

'Thank you.' Margaret had no interest in food. However, these two could tell her no more.

As Margaret stood up to leave, Diana said, 'Are you a friend of Mrs Lenehan's?'

'She was going to give me a job,' Margaret said bitterly. She turned away, biting her lip.

Her parents and Percy were already seated in the dining room, and the first course was being served: lobster cocktail made with fresh lobsters from Shediac. Margaret sat down and said automatically, 'I'm so sorry to be late.' Father just glared at her.

She toyed with her food. She felt like laying her head on the table and bursting into tears. Harry and Nancy had both abandoned her without warning. She was back at square one, with no way to support herself and no friends to help her. It was so unfair: she had tried to be like Elizabeth and plan everything, but her careful scheme had fallen apart.

The lobster was taken away and replaced by kidney soup. Margaret took one sip and put down her spoon. She felt tired and irritable. She had a headache and no appetite. The super-luxurious Clipper was beginning to feel like a prison. They had now been *en rôute* for almost twenty-seven hours, and she had had enough. She wanted to get into a real bed, with a soft mattress and lots of pillows, and go to sleep for a week.

The others were also feeling the strain. Mother was pale and tired. Father was hung over, with bloodshot eyes and bad breath. Percy was unsettled and nervy, like someone who has drunk too much strong coffee, and he kept throwing hostile looks at Father. Margaret had a feeling he was going to do something outrageous before long.

For the main course they had a choice: fried sole with cardinal sauce, or fillet steak. She did not want either but she chose the fish. It came with potatoes and Brussels sprouts. She asked Nicky for a glass of white wine.

She thought about the dreary days ahead. She would stay with Mother and Father in the Waldorf, but Harry would not sneak into her room: she would lie in bed alone and long for him. She would have to accompany Mother on shopping trips for clothes. Then they would all go on to Connecticut. Without asking her, they would enrol Margaret in a riding club and a tennis club, and she would be invited to parties. Mother would construct a whole social round for them in no time at all, and before long there would be 'suitable' boys coming for tea or cocktails or bicycle rides. How could she enter into all that when England was at war? The more she thought about it, the more depressed she felt.

For dessert there was apple tart with cream, or ice

cream with chocolate sauce. Margaret ordered ice cream and ate it all.

Father asked for brandy with his coffee, then cleared his throat. He was about to make a speech. Could it be that he would apologize for the frightful scene at dinner yesterday? Impossible.

'Your mother and I have been discussing you,' he began.

'As if I were a disobedient parlourmaid,' Margaret snapped.

Mother said, 'You're a disobedient child.'

'I'm nineteen years old, and I've been menstruating for six years – how could I be a child?'

'Hush!' Mother was shocked. 'The very fact that you can use such words in front of your father shows that you're not yet adult.'

'I give up,' Margaret sighed. 'I can't win.'

Father said, 'Your foolish attitude just confirms everything we've been saying. You can't yet be trusted to lead a normal social life among people of your own class.'

'Thank heaven for that!'

Percy laughed out loud, and Father glared at him, but spoke to Margaret. 'We've been trying to think of somewhere to send you, a place where you will have the minimum opportunity to cause trouble.'

'Did you consider a convent?'

He was not used to her cheeking him, but he controlled his anger with an effort. 'This kind of talk won't make things any better for you.'

'Better? How could things be better for me? My

loving parents are determining my future, with only my best interests at heart. What more could I want?'

To her surprise, her mother shed a tear. 'You're very cruel, Margaret,' she said, wiping it away.

Margaret was touched. The sight of her mother weeping destroyed her resistance. She became meek again. 'What do you want me to do, Mother?'

Father answered the question. 'You're going to live with your aunt Clare. She has a place in Vermont. It's in the mountains, rather remote; there will be nobody near by for you to embarrass.'

Mother added, 'My sister Clare is a wonderful woman. She never married. She's the backbone of the Episcopalian Church in Brattleboro.'

Cold rage gripped Margaret, but she kept herself under control. 'How old is Aunt Clare?' she asked.

'In her fifties.'

'Does she live alone?'

'Apart from the servants, yes.'

Margaret was shaking with anger. 'So this is my punishment for trying to live my own life,' she said in an unsteady voice. 'I'm exiled to the mountains to live alone with a mad spinster aunt. How long do you expect me to stay there?'

'Until you've calmed down,' Father said. 'A year, perhaps.'

'A year!' It seemed a lifetime. But they could not make her stay there. 'Don't be so stupid. I shall go mad, kill myself or run away.'

'You're not to leave without our consent,' Father said. 'And if you do . . .' He hesitated.

Margaret looked at his face. My God, she thought, even he is ashamed of what he's about to say. What on earth can it be?

He pressed his lips together in a determined line, then said, 'If you run away, we will have you certified insane and committed to a lunatic asylum.'

Margaret gasped. She was speechless with horror. She had not imagined him capable of such cruelty. She looked at her mother, but Mother would not meet her eyes.

Percy stood up and flung down his napkin. 'You bloody old fool, you've gone off your rocker,' he said, and he walked out.

If Percy had spoken like that a week ago there would have been hell to pay, but now he was ignored.

Margaret looked again at Father. His expression was guilty, defiant and obstinate. He knew he was doing wrong, but he would not change his mind.

At last she found the words to express what she felt in her heart.

'You've sentenced me to death,' she said.

Mother started to cry quietly.

Suddenly the engine note changed. Everyone heard it and all conversation stopped. There was a lurch, and the plane began to go down.

CHAPTER TWENTY-SEVEN

WHEN BOTH port engines cut out at the same time, Eddie's fate was sealed.

Until that moment he could have changed his mind. The plane would have flown on, no one knowing what he had planned. But now, whatever happened, it would all come out. He would never fly again, except maybe as a passenger: his career was over. He fought down the rage that threatened to possess him. He had to stay cool and get this job done Then he would think about the bastards who had ruined his life.

The plane had to make an emergency splashdown now. The kidnappers would come aboard and rescue Frankie Gordino. After that anything could happen. Would Carol-Ann be safe and unhurt? Would the Navy ambush the gangsters as they headed for shore? Would Eddie go to jail for his part in the whole thing? He was a prisoner of fate. But if he could just hold Carol-Ann in his arms, alive and well, nothing else would matter.

A moment after the engines cut out he heard the voice of Captain Baker in his headphones. 'What the hell is going on?'

Eddie's mouth was dry with tension and he had to swallow twice before he could speak. 'I don't know yet,' he replied; but he did. The engines had stopped because they were getting no fuel: he had cut the supply.

The Clipper had six fuel tanks. The engines were supplied by two small feeder tanks in the wings. Most of the fuel was kept in four large reserve tanks located in the hydrostabilizers, the stubby sea-wings that the passengers stepped on to as they got on and off the plane.

Fuel could be dumped from the reserve tanks, but not by Eddie, because the control was at the second pilot's station. However, Eddie could pump fuel from the reserve tanks up to the wings and back down again. Such transfers were controlled by two large handwheels to the right of the engineer's instrument panel. The plane was now over the Bay of Fundy about five miles from the rendezvous, and in the last few minutes he had drained both the wing tanks. The starboard tank had fuel for a few more miles. The port tank had now run dry, and the port engines had stopped.

It would be a simple matter to pump fuel back up from the reserves, of course. However, while the plane was in Shediac Eddie had come aboard on his own and tampered with the handwheels, moving the dials so that when they said 'Pump' they were in fact off, and when they said 'Off' they were pumping. Now the dials indicated that he was trying to fill the wing tanks when in fact nothing was happening.

He had been using the pumps with the wrong settings for the first part of the flight, of course; and another engineer might have noticed that and wondered what the hell was going on. Eddie had worried every second that the off-duty assistant engineer, Mickey Finn, would come upstairs; but he stayed fast asleep in No. 1 compartment, as Eddie had expected: at this stage of the long flight, off-duty crew always slept.

There had been two nasty moments in Shediac. The first had come when the police announced they had learned the name of Frankie Gordino's accomplice aboard the plane. Eddie assumed they were talking about Luther, and for a while he thought the game was up, and racked his brains for some other way of rescuing Carol-Ann. Then they had named Harry Vandenpost, and Eddie almost jumped for joy. He had no idea why Vandenpost, who appeared to be an amiable young American from a wealthy family, should be travelling with a false passport; but he was grateful to the man for deflecting attention from Luther. The police looked no farther, Luther escaped notice, and the plan could go ahead.

But all this had been too much for Captain Baker. Even while Eddie was still recovering from the scare, Baker had dropped a bombshell. The fact that there really had been an accomplice on board meant that someone was serious about rescuing Gordino, he said, and he wanted Gordino off the plane. That too would have ruined everything for Eddie.

There had been a stand-up row between Baker and Ollis Field, with the FBI man threatening to have the Captain charged with obstruction of justice. In the end Baker had called Pan American in New York and dumped the problem on them; and the airline had decided to let Gordino fly on; and once again Eddie was relieved.

He had got one more piece of good news in Shediac. A cryptic but unmistakable message from Steve Appleby had confirmed that a US Navy cutter would be patrolling the coast where the Clipper was going to come down. It would stay out of sight until the splashdown, then intercept any vessel that made contact with the downed plane.

That made all the difference to Eddie. Knowing the gangsters would be caught afterwards, he could with a clear conscience make sure the plan went off without a hitch.

Now the deed was almost done. The plane was close to the rendezvous and flying on two engines only.

Captain Baker was at Eddie's side in a moment. Eddie said nothing to him at first. With a shaky hand he switched the engine feed so that the starboard wing tank was fuelling all engines, and restarted the port engines. Then he said, 'The port wing tank ran dry and I can't fill it.'

'Why not?' the Captain snapped.

Eddie pointed to the handwheels. Feeling like a traitor, he said, 'I've switched the pumps on but nothing's happening.'

Eddie's instruments did not show either fuel flow or fuel pressure between the reserve tanks and the feeder tanks, but there were four glass sights at the rear of the control cabin for visual checking of the fuel in the pipes. Captain Baker looked at each in turn. 'Nothing!' he said. 'How much is left in the starboard wing tank?'

'It's almost dry – a few miles.'

'How come you've only just noticed?' he said angrily.

'I thought we were pumping,' Eddie said feebly.

It was an inadequate answer and the Captain was furious. 'How could both pumps go at the same time?'

'I don't know – but thank God we have a hand pump.'

Eddie seized the handle next to his table and began to operate the hand pump. This was normally used only when the engineer was draining water from the fuel tanks in flight. He had done this immediately after leaving Shediac, and he had deliberately omitted to reset the F-valve which allowed the water to escape overboard. In consequence, his vigorous pumping action was not filling the wing tanks, but just dumping fuel overboard.

The Captain did not know this, of course, and it was not likely that he would notice the setting on the F-valve; but he could see that no fuel was moving through the sight gauges. 'It's not working!' he said. 'I don't understand how all three pumps could fail at the same time!'

Eddie looked at his dials. 'The starboard wing tank is almost dry,' he said. 'If we don't splash down soon we're going to fall out of the sky.'

'Prepare for emergency splashdown, everybody,' Baker said. He pointed a finger at Eddie. 'I don't like your role in this, Deakin,' he said with ice-cold fury. 'I don't trust you.'

Eddie felt rotten. He had good reason to lie to his

captain, but just the same he hated himself. All his life he had dealt honestly with people, and scorned men who used trickery and deceit. Now he was acting in a way he despised. You'll understand in the end, Captain, he thought; but he wished he could say it.

The Captain turned to the navigator's station and bent over the chart. The navigator, Jack Ashford, shot a puzzled look at Eddie, then put a finger on the chart and said to the Captain, 'We're here.'

The whole plan relied on the Clipper coming down in the channel between the coast and Grand Manan island. The gangsters were betting on that, and so was Eddie. But in emergencies people did strange things. Eddie decided that if Baker irrationally chose another location, he would speak up and point out the advantages of the channel. Baker would be suspicious, but he would have to see the logic of it; and then *he* would be the one behaving oddly if he landed somewhere else.

However, no interference was necessary. After a moment Baker said, 'Here. In this channel. That's. where we'll come down.'

Eddie turned away so that no one could see his expression of triumph. He was another step closer to Carol-Ann.

As they all went through the procedure for emergency splashdown, Eddie looked out of the window and tried to gauge what the sea was like. He saw a small white vessel like a sports fishing boat bobbing on the swell. The surface was choppy. The landing would be rough.

He heard a voice that stopped his heart. 'What's the emergency?' It was Mickey Finn coming up the stairs to investigate.

Eddie stared at him in horror. Mickey would guess in a minute that the F-valve on the hand-pump had not been reset. Eddie had to get rid of him, quickly.

But Captain Baker beat him to it. 'Get out of here, Mickey!' he snapped. 'Off-duty crew must be strapped in during an emergency splashdown, not wandering around the aircraft asking stupid questions!'

Mickey was gone like a shot, and Eddie breathed easy again.

The plane lost height rapidly: Baker wanted to be close to the water in case they ran out of fuel earlier than expected.

They turned west so as not to overfly the island: if they ran out of fuel over land they were all dead. A few moments later they were above the channel.

There was a big swell, about four feet, Eddie estimated. The critical wave height was three feet: above that it was dangerous to land the Clipper. Eddie gritted his teeth. Baker was a good pilot, but it was going to be dicey.

The plane came down fast. Eddie felt the hull touch the top of a high wave. They flew on for a moment or two then it touched again. The second time there was a stronger impact, and his stomach lurched as the huge aircraft bounced up into the air.

Eddie was afraid for his life: this was how flying boats crashed.

Although the plane was airborne now, the impact

had reduced its airspeed, so that it had very little lift; and instead of sliding into the water at a shallow angle, it would come down hard. It was the difference between a smooth racing dive and a painful belly-flop; except that the belly of the plane was made of thin aluminium which could burst like a paper bag.

He froze, waiting for the impact. The plane hit the water with a terrific bang which he felt all the way up his spine. Water covered the windows. Facing sideways as he was, he was thrown to his left, but managed to stay in his seat. The radio operator, who faced forward, banged his head on his microphone. Eddie thought the plane was breaking up. If it dipped a wing that would be the end.

A second passed, then another. The cries of terrified passengers floated up the staircase. The plane lifted again, coming partly out of the water and moving forward with the reduction in drag; then it sank back, and Eddie was thrown sideways again.

But the plane stayed level, and Eddie began to hope they would make it. The windows cleared and he glimpsed the sea. His engines were still roaring: they had not been submerged.

The plane slowed gradually. Second by second Eddie felt safer, until at last the plane was stationary, rising and falling on the waves. In his headphones Eddie heard the Captain say, 'Jesus, that was rougher than I expected,' and the rest of the crew laughed with relief.

Eddie stood up and looked out through all the windows, searching for a boat. The sun was shining but there were rainclouds in the sky. Visibility was fair, but he could not see any other vessels. Perhaps the launch was behind the Clipper, where he could not see it.

He took his seat again and shut down the engines. The radio operator broadcast a Mayday. The Captain said, 'I'd better go and reassure the passengers.' He went down the stairs. The radio operator got a reply, and Eddie hoped it was from the people who were coming for Gordino.

He could not wait to find out. He went forward, opened the hatch in the cockpit, and climbed down the ladder into the bow compartment. The forward hatch opened downward, forming a platform. Eddie stepped outside and stood on it. He had to hold the door frame to keep his balance in the swell. The waves were coming over the sea-wings, and some were high enough to splash his feet as he stood on the platform. The sun was going behind the clouds intermittently, and there was a stiff breeze. He looked carefully at the hull and wings: he could see no damage. The great aircraft appeared to have survived unscathed.

He released the anchor, then stood surveying the sea all around, hunting for a vessel. Where were Luther's buddies? What if something had gone wrong? What if they did not turn up? But then at last he saw a motor launch in the distance. His heart missed a beat. Was this it? And was Carol-Ann on board? Now he worried that it might be some other vessel, coming to look at the downed plane out of curiosity, which would interfere with the plan.

It came in fast, riding up and down the waves. Eddie was supposed to return to his station on the flight deck, having dropped anchor and checked for damage, but he could not move. He stared hypnotically at the launch as it grew larger. It was a big, fast boat with a covered wheelhouse. He knew it was racing at twenty-five or thirty knots, but it seemed painfully slow. There was a group of figures on deck and soon he could count them: four. He noticed that one was much smaller than the others. The group began to look like three men in dark suits and a woman in a blue coat. Carol-Ann had a blue coat.

He thought it was her but he was not sure. The waiting was unbearable. The woman had fair hair and a slight figure, just like her. She was standing apart from the others. All four were at the rail, looking at the Clipper. Then the sun came out from behind a cloud and the woman raised her hand to her face to shield her eyes. Something about the gesture pulled at Eddie's heartstrings, and he knew it was his wife.

'Carol-Ann,' he said aloud.

A surge of excitement seized him, and for a moment he forgot about the perils they both still faced, and gave in to the joy of seeing her again. He raised his arms and waved happily. 'Carol-Ann!' he yelled. 'Carol-Ann!'

She could not hear him, of course, but she could see him. She started with surprise, hesitated as if she was not sure whether it was him, then waved back, timidly at first and then vigorously.

If she could wave like that she must be all right. He felt as weak as a baby with relief and gratitude.

He remembered that it was not over yet. He had

more to do. He gave one more wave then, reluctantly, went back inside.

He emerged on to the flight deck just as the Captain was coming up from the passenger deck. 'Any damage?' Baker said.

'Nothing at all, as far as I can see.'

The Captain turned to the radio operator, who reported, 'Our Mayday has been answered by several ships, but the nearest vessel is a pleasure boat now approaching on the port side. You can probably see her.'

The Captain looked out of the windows and saw the launch. He shook his head. 'She's no use. We have to be towed. Try to raise the Coast Guard.'

'The people on the launch want to come aboard,' the radio operator said.

'Nix to that,' said Baker. Eddie was dismayed. They had to come aboard! 'It's too dangerous,' the Captain went on. 'I don't want a boat tied up to the plane: it could damage the hull. And if we try to transfer people in this swell, someone's sure to fall in the goddamn drink. Tell them we appreciate their offer, but they can't help us.'

Eddie had not anticipated this. He put on an unconcerned look to mask his sudden anxiety. The hell with damage to the plane, Luther's gang were coming aboard! But they would have a hard time without help from the inside.

Even with help, it would be a nightmare to try to board through the normal doors, he realized. The waves were washing over the sea-wings and half-way up the doors: no one could stand on the sea-wing without a rope to hold, and water would pour into the dining room while the door was open. This had not occurred to Eddie before because the Clipper normally landed only on the calmest of seas.

Then how could they board?

They would have to come through the forward hatch in the bow compartment.

The radio operator said, 'I've told them they can't board, Captain, but they don't seem to take any notice.'

Eddie looked out. The launch was circling the plane.

'Just ignore them,' the Captain said.

Eddie stood up and went forward. As he stepped on to the ladder leading down into the bow compartment, Captain Baker snapped, 'Where are you going?'

'I need to check on the anchor,' Eddie said vaguely, and went on without waiting for a reply.

He heard Baker say, 'That guy is *through*.'

I knew that already, he thought with a heavy heart.

He got out on to the platform. The launch was thirty or forty feet from the nose of the Clipper. He could see Carol-Ann standing at the rail. She had on an old dress and flat shoes, just what she would have been wearing for housework. She had thrown on her best coat over her work clothes when they took her. He could see her face now. She looked pale and drained. Eddie felt anger boil deep inside him. I'll get them for this, he thought.

He raised the collapsible capstan, then waved to the launch, pointing to the capstan and miming throwing a rope. He had to do it several times before the men on deck understood. He guessed they were not experienced sailors. They certainly looked out of place on a boat, in their double-breasted suits, holding their fedoras on their heads in the wind. The guy in the wheelhouse, presumably the skipper of the launch, was busy with his controls, trying to keep the boat steady relative to the plane. At last one of the men made a gesture of acknowledgement and picked up a rope.

He was no good at throwing it, and it took four tries before Eddie was able to catch it.

He secured it to the capstan. The men on the launch hauled their craft closer to the plane. The boat, being so much lighter, rose and fell more on the swell. Tying the launch to the plane was going to be difficult and dangerous.

Suddenly he heard Mickey Finn's voice behind him, saying, 'Eddie, what the hell are you doing?'

He turned round. Mickey was in the bow compartment, looking up at him with a concerned expression on his open, freckled face. Eddie yelled, 'Stay right out of this, Mickey! I'm warning you, if you interfere, people are going to get hurt!'

Mickey looked scared. 'Okay, okay, whatever you say.' He retreated towards the flight deck, his face showing that he thought Eddie had gone mad.

Eddie turned back to face the launch. It was quite close now. He looked at the three men. One was very young, no more than eighteen. Another was older but short and thin, with a cigarette dangling from a corner of his mouth. The third, wearing a black suit with a chalk stripe, looked like he was in charge.

They were going to need two ropes, Eddie decided, to hold the launch steady enough. He put his hands to his mouth to make a megaphone and shouted, 'Throw another rope!'

The man in the striped suit picked up a rope in the bow, next to the one they were already using. That was no good: they needed one at each end of the launch, to make a triangle. 'No, not that one,' Eddie called. 'Throw me a stern rope.'

The man got the message.

This time Eddie caught the rope the first time. He took it inside the plane and tied it to a strut.

With a man hauling on each rope the launch came rapidly closer. Suddenly its engines were cut and a man in overalls came out of the wheelhouse and took over the rope work. This guy was obviously a seaman.

Eddie heard another voice from behind him, coming from within the bow compartment. This time it was Captain Baker. He said, 'Deakin, you're disobeying a direct order.'

Eddie ignored him and prayed that he would keep out of the way for a few moments more. The launch was as close as it could come. The skipper wound the ropes around the deck stanchions, leaving just enough slack to allow the boat to rise and fall with the waves. To board the Clipper, the men would have to wait until the swell brought the deck level with the platform, then jump from one to the other. To steady themselves they could hold on to the rope that ran from the stern of the launch to the inside of the bow compartment.

Baker barked, 'Deakin! Get back in here!'

The seaman opened a gate in the rail and the gangster in the striped suit stood ready to jump across. Eddie felt Captain Baker's hand clutch at his jacket from behind. The gangster saw what was happening and reached inside his coat.

Eddie's worst nightmare was that one of his crew-mates would decide to be a hero and get himself killed. He wished he could tell them about the Navy cutter Steve Appleby had sent – but he was afraid that if he did that one of them might accidentally let it out and forewarn the gangsters. So he just had to try and keep the situation under control.

He turned to Baker and yelled, 'Captain! Get out of the way! These bastards have guns!'

Baker looked shocked. He stared at the gangster, then ducked out of sight. Eddie turned round to see the man in the striped suit stuffing a pistol back into his coat pocket. Jesus, I hope I can stop these guys shooting people, he thought fearfully. If someone dies it will be my fault.

The boat was on the crest of a wave, its deck a little above the level of the platform. The gangster grabbed the rope, hesitated, then jumped on to the platform. Eddie caught him, steadying him.

'You Eddie?' the man said.

Eddie recognized the voice – he had heard it over the phone. He recalled the man's name: Vincini. Eddie had insulted him. Now he regretted it, for he needed his co-operation. 'I want to work with you, Vincini,' he said. 'If you want things to go smoothly, with no snags, let me help you.'

Vincini gave him a hard look. 'Okay,' he said after a moment. 'But make one false move and you're dead.' His tone was brisk and businesslike. He showed no sign of resentment: no doubt he had too much on his mind to think about past slights.

'Step inside and wait right there while I bring the others over.'

'Okay.' Vincini turned to the launch. 'Joe – you next. Then Kid. The girl comes last.' He stepped down into the bow compartment.

Looking inside, Eddie saw Captain Baker climbing the ladder that led to the flight deck. Vincini pulled out his gun and said, 'Stay there, you.'

Eddie said, 'Do what he says, Captain, for God's sake, these guys are serious.'

Baker stepped off the ladder and raised his hands in the air.

Eddie turned back. The runty man called Joe was standing at the rail of the launch looking scared to death. 'I can't swim!' he said in a rasping voice.

'You won't have to,' Eddie said. He reached out a hand.

Joe jumped, caught his hand, and half stepped, half fell into the bow compartment.

The young one was last. Having seen the other two make the transfer safely, he was over-confident. 'I can't swim either,' he said with a grin. He jumped too soon, landed on the very edge of the platform, lost his balance, and tipped backwards. Eddie leaned out, holding the rope with his left hand, and grabbed the boy by the waistband of his pants. He pulled him on to the platform.

'Gee, thanks!' the boy said, as if Eddie had merely given him a hand, instead of saving his life.

Now Carol-Ann was standing on the deck of the launch, looking across at the platform with fear on her face. She was not normally timid, but Eddie could tell that Kid's near-disaster had unnerved her. He smiled at her and said, 'Just do what they did, honey. You can make it.'

She nodded and took hold of the rope.

Eddie waited with his heart in his mouth. The swell brought the launch up level with the platform. Carol-Ann hesitated, missed her chance, and looked more fearful. 'Take your time,' Eddie called, making his voice calm to hide his own fear. 'Whenever you're ready.'

The launch went down and rose again. Carol-Ann's face wore an expression of forced resolution, her lips pressed together, her forehead creased in a frown. The launch drifted a foot or two away from the platform, making the gap rather too big. Eddie called, 'Maybe not this time – ' but he was too late. She was so determined to be brave that she had jumped already.

She missed the platform completely.

She let out a scream of terror and swung from the rope, her feet scrabbling in mid-air. Eddie could do nothing as the launch slipped down the slope of the wave and Carol-Ann fell away from the platform. 'Hold tight!' he yelled frantically. 'You'll come up!' He got ready to jump into the sea to save her if she should let go.

But she clung fiercely to the rope as the swell took her down then brought her up again. When she drew level she stretched out one leg towards the platform but it did not reach. Eddie went down on one knee and made a grab for her. He almost overbalanced and fell in the water, but he could not quite touch her leg. The swell took her down again, and she gave a cry of despair.

'Swing!' Eddie yelled. 'Swing to and fro as you come up!'

She heard. He could see her gritting her teeth against the pain in her arms, but she managed to swing backwards and forwards as the swell lifted the launch. Eddie knelt down, reaching out. She came level and swung with all her might. Eddie grabbed and caught her ankle. She had no stockings on. He pulled her closer and got hold of the other ankle, but her feet still did not reach the platform. The launch crested the wave and began to fall. Carol-Ann screamed as she felt herself going down. Eddie still held on to her ankles. Then she let go of the rope.

He held on like grim death. As she fell, he was pulled forward by her weight and almost toppled into the sea; but he was able to flop on to his belly and stay on the platform. Carol-Ann swung upside-down from his hands. In this position he could not lift her, but the sea did the job. The next wave submerged her head but lifted her towards him. He let go of one ankle, freeing his right hand, and got his arm around her waist.

He had her safe. He rested for a moment, saying, 'It's okay, baby, I've got you,' while she choked and spluttered. Then he hauled her up on to the platform.

He held her hand while she turned and stood up, then he helped her inside.

She fell into his arms, sobbing. He pressed her dripping head against his chest. He felt tears come but he forced them back. The three gangsters and Captain Baker were looking at him expectantly, but he ignored them for a few moments more. He held Carol-Ann tightly as she shook violently.

At last he said, 'Are you okay, honey? Did these bastards hurt you?'

She shook her head. 'I'm okay, I guess,' she said through chattering teeth.

He looked up and caught the eye of Captain Baker. Baker looked from him to Carol-Ann and back again, then said, 'Jesus Christ, I'm beginning to understand this . . .'

Vincini said, 'Enough talk, we got work to do.'

Eddie released Carol-Ann. 'Okay. I think we should deal with the crew first, get them calmed down and out of the way. Then I'll take you to the man you want. Is that all right?'

'Yeah, but let's get on with it.'

'Follow me.' Eddie crossed to the ladder and went up it. He came out on to the flight deck first and began speaking right away. In the few seconds before Vincini caught up with him he said, 'Listen, guys, please don't anybody try to be a hero. *It isn't necessary.* I hope you've understood me.' He could not risk more than that hint.

A moment later Carol-Ann, Captain Baker and the three hoodlums came up through the hatch. Eddie went on, 'Everybody keep calm and do what you're told. I don't want any shooting, I don't want anybody to get hurt. The Captain is going to tell you the same thing.' He looked at Baker.

'That's right, men,' Baker said. 'Don't give these people any reason to use their guns.'

Eddie looked at Vincini. 'Okay, let's go. Come with us please, Captain, to calm the passengers. Then Joe and Kid should take the crew to No. 1 compartment.'

Vincini nodded assent.

'Carol-Ann, will you go with the crew, honey?'

'Yes.'

Eddie felt good about that. She would be away from the guns, and she could also explain to his crew-mates why he was helping the gangsters.

He looked at Vincini. 'Do you want to put your gun away? You'll scare the passengers—'

'Fuck you,' said Vincini. 'Let's go.'

Eddie shrugged. It had been worth a try.

He led the way down the stairs to the passenger deck. There was a hubbub of loud talk, some semi-hysterical laughter, and the sound of one woman sobbing. The passengers were all in their seats, and the two stewards were making heroic efforts to look calm and normal.

Eddie went along the plane. The dining room was a mess, with smashed crockery and broken glass all over the floor; although fortunately there was not much spilt food because the meal had been almost over and everyone had been having coffee. People went quiet when they saw Vincini's gun. Behind Vincini, Captain Baker was saying, 'I apologize for this, ladies and gentlemen, but please remain seated and try to keep calm and it will all be over shortly.' He was so smoothly reassuring that Eddie almost felt better himself.

He passed through No. 3 compartment and entered No. 4. Ollis Field and Frankie Gordino were sitting side by side. This is it, Eddie thought; this is where I set free a murderer. He pushed the thought aside, pointed to Gordino, and said to Vincini, 'There's your man.'

Ollis Field stood up. 'This is FBI agent Tommy McArdle,' he said. 'Frankie Gordino crossed the Atlantic on a ship that reached New York yesterday, and he is now in jail in Providence, Rhode Island.'

'Jesus Christ!' Eddie exploded. He was thunderstruck. 'A decoy! I went through all that for a goddamn decoy!' He was not going to free a murderer after all; but he could not feel glad, because he was too scared of what the gangsters might do now. He looked fearfully at Vincini.

Vincini said, 'Hell, we ain't after Frankie. Where's the Kraut?'

Eddie stared at him, flabbergasted. They were not after Gordino? What did it mean? Who was the Kraut?

Tom Luther's voice came from No. 3 compartment. 'He's in here, Vincini. I've got him.' Luther stood in the doorway holding a gun at the head of Carl Hartmann.

Eddie was mystified. Why the hell would the

Patriarca gang want to kidnap Carl Hartmann? 'What do you guys want with a scientist?' he said.

Luther said, 'He's not just a scientist. He's a nuclear physicist.'

'Are you guys Nazis?'

Vincini said, 'Oh, no. We're just doing a job for them. Matter of fact, we're Democrats.' He laughed coarsely.

Luther said coldly, 'I am no Democrat. I am proud to be a member of the Deutsch-Amerikaner Bund.' Eddie had heard of the Bund: it was supposed to be a harmless German-American friendship league, but it was funded by the Nazis. Luther went on, 'These men are just hired hands. I received a personal message from the Führer himself, requesting my help in appre-hending a runaway scientist and returning him to Germany.' He was proud of this honour, Eddie realized: it was the greatest thing that had ever happened to him. 'I paid these people to help me. Now I am going to take Herr Doktor Professor Hartmann back to Germany, where his presence is required by the Third Reich.'

Eddie caught Hartmann's eye. The man looked sick with dread. Eddie was stricken with guilt. Hartmann was going to be taken back to Nazi Germany, and it was Eddie's fault. Eddie said to him, 'They had my wife . . . what could I do?'

Hartmann's face changed immediately. 'I under-stand,' he said. 'We are used to this sort of thing in Germany. They make you betray one loyalty for the sake of another. You had no choice. Don't blame yourself.'

Eddie was astonished that the man could find it in his heart to console *him* at a moment like this.

He caught the eye of Ollis Field. 'But why did you bring a decoy on to the Clipper?' he said. 'Did you *want* the Patriarca gang to hijack the plane?'

'Not at all,' Field said. 'We got information that the gang wanted to *kill* Gordino to stop him squealing. They were going to hit him as soon as he reached America. So we let it out that he was flying on the Clipper, but sent him on ahead by ship. Round about now, the news will be on the radio that Gordino is in jail and the gang will know they've been fooled.'

'Why aren't you guarding Carl Hartmann?'

'We didn't know he was going to be on this flight – nobody told us!'

Was Hartmann completely unprotected? Eddie wondered. Or did he have a bodyguard who had not yet revealed himself?

The little gangster called Joe came into the compartment with his gun in his right hand and an opened bottle of champagne in his left. 'They're quiet as lambs, Vinnie,' he said to Vincini. 'Kid's back there in the dining room, he can cover the whole front part of the plane from there.'

Vincini said to Luther, 'So where's the fuckin' submarine?'

Luther answered, 'It will be here at any moment, I'm sure.'

A submarine! Luther had a rendezvous with a U-boat right here off the coast of Maine! Eddie looked out of the windows, expecting to see it rising from the water like a steel whale, but he saw nothing but waves.

Vincini said, 'Well, we've done our bit, gimme the money.'

Keeping Hartmann covered, Luther stepped back to his seat, picked up a small case, and handed it to Vincini. Vincini opened it. It was packed tight with wads of bills.

Luther said, 'A hundred thousand dollars, all in twenties.'

Vincini said, 'I better check it.' He put his gun away and sat down with the case on his knee.

Luther said, 'It'll take you for ever—'

'What do you think I am, green?' Vincini said in a tone of exaggerated patience. 'I'll check two bundles, then I'll count how many bundles there are. I've done this before.'

Everyone watched Vincini count the money. The passengers in the compartment – Princess Lavinia, Lulu Bell, Mark Alder, Diane Lovesey, Ollis Field and the Frankie Gordino impostor – looked on. Joe recognized Lulu Bell. 'Hey, ain't you in the movies?' he said. Lulu looked away, ignoring him. Joe drank from his bottle, then offered it to Diana Lovesey. She paled and shrank away from him. 'I agree, this stuff is overrated,' Joe said, then he reached out and poured champagne over her cream-and-red spotted dress.

She gave a cry of distress and pushed his hand away. The wet dress clung to her bosom revealingly.

Eddie was appalled. This was the kind of thing that could lead to violence. He said, 'Knock it off, you.'

The man took no notice. 'Great jugs,' he said with a leer. He dropped the bottle and grabbed one of her breasts, squeezing hard.

She screamed.

Her boyfriend, Mark, was struggling with his safety belt, saying, 'Don't touch her, you cheap hood—'

With a surprisingly quick movement, the hoodlum hit him in the mouth with his gun. Blood spurted from Mark's lips.

Eddie said, 'Vincini, for Christ's sake, put a stop to this!'

Vincini said, 'Girl like that, hell, if she ain't had her tits felt by her age, it's about time.'

Joe thrust his hand down the front of Diana's dress. She struggled to avoid his grasp, but she was strapped in her seat.

Mark got his seat belt undone, but as he was rising to his feet the man hit him again. This time the butt of the gun hit the corner of his eye. Joe used his left fist to punch Mark in the stomach, then hit him across the face with the gun a third time. Now blood from his wounds got into Mark's eyes and blinded him. Several women were screaming.

Eddie was appalled. He had been determined to avoid bloodshed. Joe was about to hit Mark again. Eddie could stand it no longer. Taking his life in his hands, he grabbed the little gangster from behind, pinning his arms.

Joe struggled, trying to point his gun at Eddie, but

Eddie held on tight. Joe pulled the trigger. The bang was deafening in the confined space, but the gun was pointing down and the bullet went through the floor.

The first shot had been fired. Eddie had a horrified, scary feeling that he was losing control of the situation. If that happened there could be a bloodbath.

At last Vincini intervened. 'Knock it off, Joe!' he yelled.

The man became still.

Eddie let him go.

Joe gave him a venomous look but said nothing.

Vincini said, 'We can go. The money's all here.'

Eddie saw a ray of hope. If they would leave now at least the bloodshed had been limited. Go, he thought, for God's sake, go!

Vincini went on, 'Bring the cunt with you if you want, Joe. I might prong her myself – I like her better than the engineer's skinny wife.' He stood up.

Diana screamed, 'No, no!'

Joe undid her seat belt and grabbed her by the hair. She struggled with him. Mark got to his feet, trying to wipe the blood from his eyes. Eddie grabbed Mark, restraining him. 'Don't get yourself killed!' he said. Lowering his voice, he said, 'It'll be okay, I promise you!' He wanted to tell Mark that the gang's launch was going to be stopped by a US Navy cutter before they would have time to do anything to Diana, but he was afraid of being overheard by Vincini.

Joe pointed his gun at Mark and said to Diana, 'You come with us or your boyfriend gets it right between the eyes.'

Diana became still and started to sob.

Luther said, 'I'm coming with you, Vincini. My submarine hasn't made it.'

'I knew it wouldn't come,' Vincini said. 'They can't get this close to the USA.'

Vincini did not know anything about submarines. Eddie could guess the real reason why the U-boat had not appeared. The U-boat commander had seen Steve Appleby's Navy cutter patrolling the channel. He was probably now waiting near by, listening to the cutter's radio chatter, hoping it would go away and patrol some other stretch of water.

Luther's decision to flee with the gangsters, instead of waiting for the submarine, raised Eddie's spirits. The gangsters' launch was headed for Steve Appleby's trap, and if Luther and Hartmann were on the launch, Hartmann would be saved. If this whole thing could end with nothing worse than a few stitches in Mark Alder's face, Eddie would rejoice.

'Let's go,' Vincini said. 'Luther first, then the Kraut, then Kid, then me, then the engineer – want you close to me until I get off this crate – then Joe with the blonde. Move!'

Mark Alder began to struggle in Eddie's arms. Vincini said to Ollis Field and the other agent, 'You want to hold this guy down, or you want Joe to shoot him?' They grabbed Mark and held him still.

Eddie filed out behind Vincini. Passengers stared wide-eyed at them as they passed through No. 3 compartment and into the dining room.

As Vincini entered No. 2 compartment, Mr Membury pulled a gun and said, 'Stop!' He aimed directly at Vincini. 'Everybody keep still or I shoot your boss!'

Eddie took one step back to get out of the way.

Vincini went white and said, 'All right, boys, nobody move.'

The one they called Kid swung round and fired twice.

Membury fell.

Vincini yelled furiously at the boy, 'You cocksucker, he might have killed me!'

'Didn't you hear his voice?' Kid replied. 'He's an Englishman.'

'So fuckin' what?' Vincini screamed.

'I seen every movie ever made, and nobody ever gets shot by an Englishman.'

Eddie knelt down beside Membury. The bullets had entered his chest. His blood was the same colour as his waistcoat. 'Who are you?' Eddie said.

'Scotland Yard, Special Branch,' Membury whispered. 'Assigned to protect Hartmann.' So the scientist had not been completely unguarded, Eddie thought. 'Bloody failure,' Membury said hoarsely. His eyes closed and he stopped breathing.

Eddie cursed. He had vowed to get the gangsters off the plane without anyone being killed, and he had come so close to succeeding! Now this brave policeman was dead. 'So unnecessary,' Eddie said aloud.

He heard Vincini say, 'How come you're so sure nobody needs to be a hero?' He looked up. Vincini was staring at him with suspicion and hostility. Jesus Christ, I think he'd like to kill me, Eddie thought. Vincini went on, 'Do you know something the rest of us don't?'

Eddie had no answer, but at that moment the seaman from the launch came rushing down the stairs and into the compartment. 'Hey, Vinnie, I just heard from Willard—'

'I told him not to use that radio except for emergency!'

'This is an emergency – there's a Navy ship going up and down the shore, just like they're looking for someone.'

Eddie's heart stopped. He had not thought of this possibility. The gang had a sentry on shore, keeping watch, with a short-wave radio so he could talk to the launch. Now Vincini knew about the trap.

It was all over, and Eddie had lost.

'You double-crossed me,' Vincini said to Eddie. 'You bastard, I'll kill you for this.'

Eddie caught Captain Baker's eye and saw understanding and a surprised respect in his face.

Vincini pointed his gun at Eddie.

Eddie thought, I did my best, and everyone knows it. I don't care if I die now.

Then Luther said, 'Vincini, listen! Do you hear something?'

They were all silent. Eddie heard the sound of another plane.

Luther looked out of the window. 'It's a seaplane, coming down right near by!'

Vincini lowered his gun. Eddie felt weak at the knees.

Vincini looked out, and Eddie followed his gaze. He saw the Grumman Goose that had been moored at Shediac. As he watched, it splashed down on the long side of a wave and came to rest.

Vincini said, 'So what? If they get in our way we'll shoot the bastards.'

'Don't you see?' Luther said excitedly. 'This is our escape! We can fly over the goddamn Navy and get away!'

Vincini nodded slowly. 'Good thinking. That's what we'll do.'

Eddie realized they were going to get away. His life was saved, but he had failed after all.

CHAPTER TWENTY-EIGHT

NANCY LENEHAN had found the answer to her problem as she flew along the Canadian coast in the chartered seaplane.

She wanted to defeat her brother, but she also wanted to find some way of escaping from the tramlines of her father's plans for her life. She wanted to be with Mervyn, but she was afraid that if she left Black's Boots and went to England she would become a bored housewife like Diana.

Nat Ridgeway had said he was willing to make a higher offer for the company, and give Nancy a job in General Textiles. Thinking about that, she had remembered that General Textiles had several factories in Europe, mostly in Britain; and that Ridgeway was not going to be able to visit them until the war was over, which might be years. So she was going to offer to become the European manager of General Textiles. That way she could be with Mervyn and still be in business.

The solution was remarkably neat. The only snag was that Europe was at war and she might get killed.

She was reflecting on that distant but chilling possibility when Mervyn turned round in his co-pilot's seat and pointed out of the window and down; and she saw the Clipper floating on the sea.

Mervyn tried to raise the Clipper by radio, but he got no response. Nancy forgot about her own troubles as the Goose circled the downed plane. What had happened? Were the people on board all right? The plane appeared undamaged, but there was no sign of life.

Mervyn turned to her and shouted over the roar of the engines, 'We have to go down and see if they need help.'

Nancy nodded vigorously in agreement.

'Strap in and hold tight. It may be a rough splash-down, because of the swell.'

She fastened her safety belt and looked out. The sea was choppy and there were long rollers. The pilot, Ned, brought the seaplane down in a line parallel with the crests of the waves. The hull touched water on the back of a swell, and the seaplane rode the wave like a Hawaiian surf-rider. It was not as rough as Nancy had feared.

There was a motor launch tied up to the Clipper's nose. A man in dungarees and a cap appeared on the deck and beckoned to them. Nancy gathered he wanted the Goose to tie up alongside the launch. The bow door of the Clipper was open, so presumably they would board that way. Nancy could see why: the waves were washing over the sea-wings, so it would be difficult to board through the normal door.

Ned edged the seaplane towards the launch: Nancy could tell it was a tricky manoeuvre in this sea. However, the Goose was a high-winged monoplane, and its wing was well above the superstructure of the launch, so they were able to draw alongside, with the hull of the plane bumping against the row of rubber tyres on the side of the boat. The man on deck tied the plane to his vessel fore and aft.

While Ned shut down the engines of the seaplane, Mervyn came aft, opened the door, and broke out the gangway.

'I ought to stay with my plane,' Ned said to Mervyn. 'You'd better go and find out what's going on.'

'I'm coming too,' said Nancy.

Because the seaplane was roped to the launch, the two vessels rose and fell together on the waves, and the gangway shifted relatively little. Mervyn disembarked first and held out a hand to Nancy.

When they were both on deck, Mervyn said to the man on the launch, 'What happened?'

'They had fuel trouble and had to splash down,' he replied.

'I couldn't get them on the radio.'

The man shrugged. 'You'd better go aboard.'

Getting from the launch to the Clipper involved a little jump, from the deck of the launch on to the platform made by the open bow door. Once again Mervyn went first. Nancy took off her shoes and stuffed them inside her coat, then followed suit. She was a little nervous but in fact it was easy.

In the bow compartment was a young man she did not recognize.

Mervyn said, 'What happened here?'

'Emergency landing,' the young man said. 'We were fishing, saw the whole thing.'

'What's wrong with the radio?'

'Dunno.'

The youngster was not very bright, Nancy decided. Mervyn must have had the same thought, for he said impatiently, 'I'd better speak to the Captain.'

'Go this way – they're all in the dining room.'

The boy was not very sensibly dressed for fishing, in his two-tone shoes and yellow tie, Nancy thought with amusement. She followed Mervyn up the ladder to the flight deck, which was deserted. That explained why Mervyn had been unable to raise the Clipper on the radio. But *why* were they all in the dining room? It was odd that the entire crew should leave the flight deck.

She began to feel uneasy as she went down the stairs to the passenger deck. Mervyn led the way into No. 2 compartment and stopped suddenly.

Looking past him, Nancy saw Mr Membury lying on the floor in a pool of blood. She put her hand to her mouth to stifle a cry of horror.

Mervyn said, 'Dear God, what's been happening here?'

Behind them, the young man in the yellow tie said, 'Keep moving.' His voice had become harsh.

Nancy turned to him and saw that he had a gun in his hand. 'Did you do this?' she said angrily.

'Shut your fuckin' mouth and keep moving!'

They stepped into the dining room.

Three more men with guns were standing in the room. There was a big man in a striped suit who looked as if he might be in charge. A little man with a mean face was standing behind Mervyn's wife, casually fondling her breasts: when Mervyn saw this he let out a curse. The third gunman was a passenger, Mr Luther: he was pointing his gun at another passenger, Professor Hartmann. The Captain and the engineer were also there, looking helpless. Several passengers were seated at tables, but most of the dishes and glassware had fallen to the floor and smashed. Nancy caught a glimpse of Margaret Oxenford, pale and frightened; and in a sudden flash she recalled the conversation in which she had glibly told Margaret that regular people did not need to worry about gangsters because they only operated in the slums. How stupid.

Mr Luther was speaking. 'The gods are on my side, Lovesey. You have arrived in a seaplane just when we need one. You can fly me and Mr Vincini and our associates over the Navy cutter that the treacherous Eddie Deakin has summoned to trap us.'

Mervyn looked hard at him and said nothing.

The man in the striped suit spoke up. 'Let's get moving, before the Navy starts to feel impatient and comes along to investigate. Kid, you take Lovesey. His girlfriend can stay here.'

'Okay, Vinnie.'

Nancy was not sure what was going on, but she knew she did not want to be left behind: if Mervyn was in trouble she would rather be by his side. But no one was asking what she preferred.

The man called Vincini continued giving instructions. 'Luther, you take the Kraut.'

Nancy wondered why they were taking Carl Hartmann. She had assumed this was all something to do with Frankie Gordino, but he was nowhere in sight.

Vincini said, 'Joe, bring the blonde.'

The little man pointed his gun at Diana Lovesey's bosom. 'Let's go,' he said. She did not move.

Nancy was horrified. Why were they kidnapping Diana? She had a dreadful feeling she knew the answer.

Joe poked the barrel of the gun into Diana's soft breast, prodding her hard, and she gasped with pain.

'Wait a minute,' Mervyn said.

They all looked at him.

'All right, I'll fly you out of here, but there's a condition.'

Vincini said, 'Shut up and move. You can't make no fuckin' conditions.'

Mervyn spread his arms wide. 'So shoot me,' he said.

Nancy let out a cry of fear. These were the kind of men who would shoot someone who dared them; didn't Mervyn understand that?

There was a moment of silence, then Luther said, 'What condition?'

Mervyn pointed at Diana. 'She stays.'

Joe, the little man, gave Mervyn a killing look.

Vincini said, 'We don't need you, shithead. There's a whole bunch of Pan American pilots up front – any one of them can fly that seaplane as well as you.'

'And any one of them will make the same condition,' Mervyn said. 'Ask them – if you've got time.'

Nancy realized that the gangsters did not know there was another pilot in the Goose. Not that it made much difference.

Luther said to Joe, 'Leave her behind.'

The little man went red with anger. 'Hell, why—'

'Leave her behind!' Luther shouted. 'I paid you to help me kidnap Hartmann, not rape women!'

Vincini intervened. 'He's right, Joe. You can pick up another cunt later.'

'Okay, okay,' Joe said.

Diana began to cry with relief.

Vincini said, 'We're running out of time, let's get out of here!'

Nancy wondered whether she would ever see Mervyn again.

From outside came the sound of a klaxon. The skipper of the launch was trying to get their attention.

The one they called Kid spoke up from the next room. 'Holy shit, boss, look out the fuckin' window!'

Harry Marks was knocked out when the Clipper splashed down. On the first bounce he fell headlong across the piled suitcases; then, just as he was getting to his hands and knees, the plane flopped into the sea and he was flung against the forward wall. He banged his head and was out cold.

When he came round he wondered what the hell was going on.

He knew they had not arrived at Port Washington: they were only about two hours into a five-hour flight. This was an unscheduled stop, then; and it had seemed like an emergency splashdown.

He sat upright, feeling his injuries. Now he knew

why planes had seat belts. His nose was bleeding, his head hurt like hell, and he was bruised just about everywhere; but nothing was actually broken. He wiped his nose with his handkerchief and considered himself lucky.

There were no windows in the baggage hold, of course, so he had no way of finding out what was going on. He sat still for a while and listened for clues. The engines were shut down, and there was a long period of quiet.

Then he heard a shot.

Firearms meant gangsters, and if there were gangsters on board they were probably after Frankie Gordino. More importantly, gunplay meant confusion and panic, and in those circumstances Harry might be able to get away.

He had to take a look outside.

He opened the door a crack. He saw no one.

He stepped out into the corridor and went forward to the door that led to the flight deck. He stood behind it, listening hard. He heard nothing.

Gently and silently, he eased the door open and peeped through.

The flight deck was deserted.

He stepped over the high threshold, treading softly, and went to the top of the staircase. He could hear men's voices raised in argument, but he could not make out the words.

The cockpit hatch was open. Looking through, he could see daylight in the bow compartment. He went closer and saw that the bow door was open.

He stood up and looked through the window, and saw a motor launch tied up to the nose of the aircraft. There was a man on deck in rubber boots and a cap.

Harry realized he could be very close to escape.

Here was a fast boat that could take him to a lonely spot on the coast. There appeared to be only one man on board. There had to be a way Harry could get rid of him and take the boat.

He heard a footstep right behind him.

He spun around, his heart pounding.

It was Percy Oxenford.

The boy stood in the rear doorway, looking as shocked as Harry felt.

After a moment Percy said, 'Where have you been hiding?'

'Never mind that,' Harry said. 'What's going on down there?'

'Mr Luther is a Nazi who wants to send Professor Hartmann back to Germany. He's hired some gangsters to help him and he gave them a hundred thousand dollars in a briefcase!'

'Blimey,' said Harry, forgetting to do his American accent.

'And they killed Mr Membury. He was a bodyguard from Scotland Yard.'

So that was what he was. 'Is your sister all right?'

'So far. But they want to take Mrs Lovesey with them because she's so pretty – I hope they don't notice Margaret . . .'

'God, what a mess,' said Harry.

'I managed to sneak away and come up through the trapdoor next to the ladies' room.'

'What for?'

'I want Agent Field's gun. I saw Captain Baker confiscate it.' Percy pulled open the drawer under the chart table. Inside was a compact revolver with a short barrel, just the kind of thing an FBI man might carry under his jacket. 'I thought so – it's a Colt Thirty-eight Detective Special,' Percy said. He picked it up, broke it open expertly and spun the cylinder.

Harry shook his head. 'I don't think that's such a great idea. You'll get yourself killed.' He grabbed the boy's wrist, took the gun from him, put it back and closed the drawer.

There was a loud noise from outside. Harry and Percy both looked out of the windows and saw a seaplane circling the Clipper. Who the hell was this? After a moment it started to descend. It splashed down, riding a wave, and taxied towards the Clipper.

'Now what?' said Harry. He turned round. Percy had disappeared. The drawer was open.

And the gun had gone.

'Damn,' Harry said.

He went through the rear door. He dashed past the holds, under the navigator's dome and across a low compartment, then looked through a second door.

Percy was scampering along a crawlway through a space that got lower and narrower as it approached the tail. The plane's structure was bare here, with struts and rivets visible and cables trailing along the floor.

The space was obviously a redundant void above the rear half of the passenger deck. There was light at the far end, and Harry saw Percy drop down through a square hole. He remembered seeing a ladder on the wall next to the ladies' room, with a trapdoor above it.

He could not stop Percy now: it was too late.

He recalled Margaret saying they could all shoot, it was a family obsession; but the boy knew nothing about gangsters. If he got in their way they would gun him down like a dog. Harry liked the boy, but his own feelings did not concern him so much as Margaret's. Harry did not want her to see her brother killed. But what the hell could he do?

He returned to the flight deck and looked out. The seaplane was tying up to the launch. Either the people from the seaplane would come aboard the Clipper, or vice versa: in any event someone would soon be passing through the flight cabin. Harry had to get out of the way for a few moments. He went out through the rear door, leaving it open a crack so he could hear what went on.

Soon someone came up the stairs from the passenger deck and went through to the bow compartment. A few minutes later a number of people, two or three, came back. Harry listened to their footsteps going down the stairs, then came out.

Had they brought help, or reinforcements for the gangsters? Harry was in the dark again.

He went to the top of the stairs. There he hesitated. He decided to risk going part way down to listen.

He went to the bend in the staircase and peeked

around the corner. He could see the little kitchen: it was empty. What would he do now, if the seaman from the launch decided to come aboard the Clipper? I'll hear him coming, Harry thought, and slip into the men's room. He went on down, one slow step at a time, pausing and listening on each step. When he reached the bottom he heard a voice. He recognized Tom Luther's voice, a cultured American accent with a trace of something European underneath. 'The gods are on my side, Lovesey,' he was saying. 'You have arrived in a seaplane just when we need one. You can fly me and Mr Vincini and our associates over the Navy cutter that the treacherous Eddie Deakin has summoned to trap us.'

That answered the question. The seaplane was going to enable Luther and Hartmann to get away.

Harry crept back up the stairs. The thought of poor Hartmann being taken back to the Nazis was heart-breaking; but Harry might have let it happen – he was no hero. However, young Percy Oxenford would do something stupid any moment now, and Harry could not stand aside and let Margaret's brother get himself killed. He had to get in first, create a diversion, somehow put a spoke in the gang's wheel, for her sake.

Looking into the bow compartment, he saw a rope tied to a strut, and he was inspired.

He suddenly saw a way he could create a diversion and maybe get rid of one of the gangsters as well.

First he had to untie the ropes and set the launch adrift.

He went through the hatch and down the ladder.

His heart beat faster. He was scared.

He did not think about what he would say if someone caught him now. He would just make something up, as he always did.

He crossed the compartment. As he had thought, the rope came from the launch.

He reached up to the strut, undid the knot, and dropped the rope on the floor.

Looking out, he saw that there was a second rope running from the bow of the launch to the nose of the Clipper. Damn. He would have to get out on to the platform to reach it, and that meant he might be seen.

But he could not give up now. And he had to hurry. Percy was back there like Daniel in the lions' den.

He stepped up on to the platform. The rope was tied to a capstan sticking up from the nose of the aircraft. He untied it rapidly.

He heard a shout from the launch. 'Hey, you, what are you doing?'

He did not look up. He hoped the guy did not have a gun.

He detached the rope from the capstan and threw it in the sea.

'Hey, you!'

He turned round. The skipper of the launch was standing on deck shouting. He was not armed, thank God. The man picked up his end of the other rope and pulled. The rope snaked out of the bow compartment and fell in the water.

The skipper ducked into the wheelhouse and started his engine.

The next part was more dangerous.

It would only take a few seconds for the gangsters to notice that their launch had come adrift. They would be puzzled and alarmed. One of them would come to investigate and to tie the launch up again. And then—

Harry was too scared to think about what he was going to do then.

He dashed up the ladder and across the flight deck and concealed himself in the cargo area once again.

He knew it was deadly dangerous to fool around like this with gangsters, and he felt cold at the thought of what they would do to him if they caught him.

For a long minute nothing happened. Come on, he thought, hurry up and look out of the window! Your launch is adrift – you have to notice it before I lose my nerve.

At last he heard footsteps again, heavy ones, hurrying, coming up the stairs and through the flight cabin. To his dismay it sounded like two men. He had not anticipated having to deal with two.

When he judged that they must have descended into the bow compartment he looked out. It was all clear. He crossed the cabin and looked through the hatch. Two men with guns in their hands were staring out of the bow door. Even without the guns Harry would have guessed they were crooks by their flashy clothes. One was an ugly little guy with a mean look; the other was very young, about eighteen.

Maybe I should go back and hide, Harry thought.

The skipper was manoeuvring the launch, still with the seaplane tied to its side. The two gangsters would have to tie the launch up to the Clipper again, and they could not do that with guns in their hands. Harry waited for them to put their firearms away.

The skipper shouted something Harry could not make out, and a few moments later the two hoods stuffed the guns into their pockets and stepped out on to the platform.

With his heart in his mouth, Harry went down the ladder into the bow compartment.

The men were trying to catch a rope that the skipper was throwing to them, and all their attention was directed outwards, so they did not see him at first.

He sidled across the compartment.

When he was half-way, the young one caught the rope. The other man, the little one, half turned – and saw Harry. He put his hand in his pocket and got his gun out just as Harry reached him.

Harry felt sure he was about to die.

Desperately, without thinking, he stooped, grabbed the little man's ankle, and heaved.

A shot rang out, but Harry felt nothing.

The man staggered, almost fell, dropped his gun, and seized hold of his buddy for support.

The younger man lost his balance and let go of the rope. For an instant they swayed, clutching at one another. Harry still had hold of the little man's ankle, and he jerked it again.

Both men fell off the platform and plunged into the heaving sea.

Harry let out a whoop of triumph.

They sank below the waves, came up again, and

began to struggle. Harry could tell that neither of them could swim.

'That's for Clive Membury, you bastards!' Harry shouted.

He did not wait to see what became of them. He had to know what happened on the passenger deck. He dashed back across the bow compartment, scrambled up the ladder, emerged into the flight cabin, then tiptoed down the staircase.

On the bottom step he stopped and listened.

Margaret could hear her own heartbeat.

It sounded in her ears like a kettledrum, rhythmic and insistent, and so loud that she fancied other people must be able to hear it too.

She was more frightened than she had ever been in her life. And she was ashamed of her fear.

She had been frightened by the emergency splash-down, the sudden appearance of guns, the bewildering way people such as Frankie Gordino, Mr Luther and the engineer kept changing their roles, and the casual brutality of these stupid thugs in their awful suits; and most of all she was frightened because quiet Mr Membury was lying on the floor dead.

She was too frightened to move, and that made her ashamed.

For years she had been talking about how she wanted to fight Fascism, and now the opportunity had arrived. Right here in front of her, a Fascist was kidnapping Carl Hartmann to take him back to Germany. But she could do nothing about it because she was paralysed by fear.

Perhaps there was nothing she *could* do, anyway; perhaps she would only get herself killed. But she ought to try, and she had always said she was willing to risk her life for the cause and for the memory of Ian.

Her father had been right to pour scorn on her pretensions of bravery, she realized. Her heroism was all in her imagination. Her dream of being a motor-cycle courier on the battlefield was mere fantasy: at the first sound of gunfire she would hide under a hedge. When there was real danger she was completely useless. She sat frozen still while her heart pounded in her ears.

She had not spoken a word while the Clipper splashed down, the gunmen came aboard, and Nancy and Mr Lovesey arrived in the seaplane. She remained silent when the one called Kid saw the launch drifting away, and the one called Vincini sent Kid and Joe to help tie it up again.

But when she saw Kid and Joe drowning she screamed.

She had been staring fixedly out of the window, looking at but not seeing the waves, when the two men drifted into view. Kid was trying to keep afloat, but Joe was on Kid's back, pushing his friend under as he tried to save himself. It was a horrible sight.

When she screamed, Luther rushed to the window and looked out. 'They're in the water!' he yelled hysterically.

Vincini said, 'Who – Kid and Joe?'

'Yes!'

The skipper of the launch threw a rope, but the

drowning men did not see it: Joe was thrashing around in a blind panic and Kid was being held underwater by Joe.

'Do something!' Luther said. He was on the verge of panic himself.

'What?' said Vincini. 'There ain't nothing we can do. Crazy bastards don't have the smarts to save themselves!'

The two men drifted nearer to the sea-wing. If they had kept calm they could have climbed on to it and been saved. But they did not see it.

Kid's head went under and did not come up again.

Joe lost contact with Kid and breathed a lungful of water. Margaret heard one hoarse scream, muffled by the Clipper's soundproofing. Joe's head went under, came up, and went under again for the last time.

Margaret shuddered. They were both dead.

'How did this happen?' Luther said. 'How come they fell in?'

'Maybe they were pushed,' said Vincini.

'Who by?'

'There must be someone else on this fuckin' airplane.'

Margaret thought, Harry!

Was it possible? Could Harry still be on board? Had he hidden somewhere, while the police were searching for him, and come out after the emergency splash-down? Was it Harry who had pushed the two gangsters into the sea?

Then she thought of her brother. Percy had disappeared after the launch tied up to the Clipper and

Margaret had assumed he had gone to the men's room and then decided to stay out of the way. But that was not characteristic. He was more likely to seek out trouble. She knew he had found an unofficial way up to the flight deck. What was he up to now?

Luther said, 'This whole thing is falling apart! What are we going to do?'

'We're leaving on the seaplane, just like we planned – you, me, the Kraut and the money,' said Vincini. 'If anyone gets in the way, put a bullet in his belly. Calm down and let's go.'

Margaret had a dreadful premonition that they would meet Percy on the stairs, and he would be the one to get a bullet in his belly.

Then, just as the three men were leaving the dining room, she heard Percy's voice coming from the back of the plane.

At the top of his voice he shouted, 'Stop right there!'

To Margaret's astonishment he was holding a gun – and pointing it right at Vincini.

It was a short-barrelled revolver, and Margaret guessed immediately that it must be the Colt that had been confiscated from the FBI agent earlier. Now Percy held it in front of him, straight-armed as if he were aiming at a target.

Vincini turned around slowly.

Margaret was proud of Percy even while she was afraid for his life.

The dining room was crowded. Behind Vincini, right

next to where Margaret was sitting, were Luther and Hartmann, Luther holding his gun to Hartmann's head. On the other side of the compartment stood Nancy, Mervyn Lovesey, Diana Lovesey, and the engineer and the Captain. And most of the seats were occupied.

Vincini looked at Percy for a long moment, then said, 'Get out of here, kid.'

'Drop your gun,' Percy said in his cracked adolescent voice.

Vincini moved with surprising speed. He ducked to one side and raised his gun. There was a shot. The bang deafened Margaret: she heard a distant scream and realized it was her own voice. She could not tell who had shot whom. Percy seemed all right. Then Vincini staggered and fell, blood spurting from his chest. He dropped his briefcase and it burst open. Blood splashed the bundles of money.

Percy dropped the gun and stared, horrified, at the man he had shot. He looked as if he was about to burst into tears.

Everyone looked at Luther, the last of the gang, and the one person who still held a gun.

Carl Hartmann made a sudden move, breaking free of Luther's grasp while the man was distracted, and flung himself on the floor. Margaret was terrified Hartmann would be killed; then she thought Luther would shoot Percy; but what actually happened took her completely by surprise.

Luther grabbed *her*.

He pulled her out of her seat and held her in front of himself with his gun at her head, just as he had held Hartmann before.

Everyone froze.

She was too terrified to move, to speak, even to scream. The barrel of the gun dug painfully into her temple. Luther was shaking: he was as frightened as she. In the silence he said, 'Hartmann. Go to the bow door. Go on board the launch. Do as you're told or the girl gets it.'

Suddenly she felt a dreadful calm descend over her. She could see, with hideous clarity, that Luther had been brilliantly cunning. If he had merely pointed his gun at Hartmann, Hartmann might have said, 'Shoot me – I'd rather die than go back to Germany.' But now it was her life at stake. Hartmann might have been prepared to give his own life, but he would not sacrifice a young girl.

Slowly, Hartmann got up from the floor.

Everything was up to her, Margaret understood with icy, fearful logic. She could save Hartmann by sacrificing herself. It's not fair, she thought, I wasn't expecting this, I'm not ready for it, I can't do it!

She caught her father's eye. He looked horrified.

In that awful moment she recalled how he had taunted her, saying she was too soft to fight, she would not last a day in the ATS.

Was he right?

All she had to do was move. Luther might kill her, but the other men would jump on him before he could do anything else, and Hartmann would be saved.

Time passed as slowly as in a nightmare.

I can do it, she thought with the same awful frozen composure.

She took a deep breath and thought, Goodbye, everyone.

Suddenly she heard Harry's voice behind her. 'Mr Luther, I think your submarine has arrived.'

Everyone looked through the windows.

Margaret felt the pressure of the gun barrel at her temple ease a fraction: Luther was momentarily distracted.

She ducked her head and wriggled out of his grasp.

There was a shot, but she felt nothing.

Everyone moved at once.

The engineer, Eddie, flew past her and fell on Luther like a tree.

Margaret saw Harry grab Luther's gun hand and tear the weapon from his grasp.

Luther crashed to the floor with Eddie and Harry on top of him.

Margaret realized she was still alive.

She suddenly felt as weak as a baby, and she sank helplessly into a seat.

Percy dashed to her. She hugged him. Time stood still. She heard herself say, 'Are you all right?'

'I think so,' he said shakily.

'You're so brave!'

'So are you!'

Yes, I was, she thought; I was brave.

All the passengers began to shout at once, then Captain Baker yelled, 'Quiet, everybody, please!'

Margaret looked around.

Luther was still on the floor, face down, pinned and harmless with Eddie and Harry on top of him. The danger from within the aircraft was over. She looked outside. The submarine floated on the water like a great grey shark, its wet steel flanks gleaming in the sunshine.

The Captain said, 'There's a naval cutter nearby and we're going to radio it right away and tell them about the U-boat.' The crew had come through from No. 1 compartment, and now the Captain addressed the radio operator. 'Get on the horn, Ben.'

'The submarine commander may hear our radio message and run for it.'

'All the better,' the Captain growled. 'Our passengers have seen enough danger.'

The radio operator went up the stairs to the flight deck.

Everyone kept looking out at the U-boat. Its hatch stayed shut. Its commander must be waiting to see what would happen.

Captain Baker went on, 'There's one gangster we haven't caught, and I'd like to bring him in: the skipper of the launch. Eddie, go to the bow door and lure him aboard – tell him Vincini wants him.'

Eddie got off Luther and went away.

The Captain spoke to the navigator. 'Jack, collect up all these damn guns and take the ammunition out.' The Captain realized he had cursed, and added, 'Pardon my language, ladies.'

They had heard so much foul language from the

gangsters that Margaret laughed at him apologizing for a 'damn'; and the other passengers nearby laughed too. He was taken aback at first, and then saw the joke, and he smiled.

The laughter was a sign that they were out of danger, and some of the passengers began to relax. Margaret still felt peculiar: she was shivering as if she was freezing cold.

The Captain nudged Luther with the toe of his shoe and spoke to another crewman. 'Johnny, stick this guy in No. 1 compartment and keep a close watch on him.'

Harry got off Luther and one of the crew took the man away.

Harry and Margaret looked at one another.

She had imagined he had abandoned her; she had thought she would never see him again; she had been sure she was about to die. Suddenly it seemed unbearably wonderful that they were both alive and together. He sat down next to her, and she threw herself into his arms. They hugged one another tight.

After a while he murmured in her ears, 'Look outside.'

The submarine was slowly slipping beneath the waves.

Margaret smiled up at Harry and then kissed him.

CHAPTER TWENTY-NINE

W HEN IT was all over, Carol-Ann would not touch Eddie.

She sat in the dining room, sipping hot milky coffee prepared by Davy the steward. She was pale and shaky, but she kept saying she was all right. However, she flinched every time Eddie put his hand on her.

He sat close, looking at her, but she would not meet his eyes. They spoke in low voices about what had happened. She told him obsessively, again and again, how the men had burst into the house and dragged her out into their car. 'I was standing there bottling plums!' she kept saying, as if that was the most outrageous aspect of the whole episode.

'It's all over now,' he would say each time, and she would nod her head vigorously, but he could tell she did not believe it.

At last she looked at him and said, 'When will you have to fly next?'

Then he understood. She was frightened about how she would feel the next time he left her alone. He felt relieved: he could reassure her about that, easily. 'I won't be flying any more,' he told her. 'I'm resigning

634

right away. They'd have to fire me otherwise: they can't employ an engineer who's deliberately brought a plane down the way I did.'

Captain Baker overheard part of the conversation, and interrupted him. 'Eddie, there's something I have to say to you. I understand what you did. You were put in an impossible position and you handled it the best you could. More than that: I don't know another man that would have handled it so well. You were brave and you were smart, and I'm proud to fly with you.'

'Thank you, sir,' Eddie said, and there was a lump in his throat. 'I can't tell you how good that makes me feel.' Out of the corner of his eye he spotted Percy Oxenford, sitting alone, looking shocked: 'Sir, I think we all should thank young Percy: he saved the day!'

Percy heard him and looked up.

'Good point,' said the Captain. He patted Eddie on the shoulder and went over to shake the boy's hand. 'You're a brave man, Percy.'

Percy brightened instantly. 'Thank you!' he said.

The Captain sat down to chat with him, and Carol-Ann said to Eddie, 'If you're not flying, what will we do?'

'I'll start that business we've been talking about.'

He could see the hope in her face, but she did not really believe it yet. 'Can we?'

'I've got enough money saved to buy the airfield, and I'll borrow what I need to get started.'

She was visibly cheering by the second. 'Could we run it together?' she said. 'Maybe I could keep the books and answer the phone while you do repairs and refuelling?'

He smiled and nodded. 'Sure, at least until the baby comes.'

'Just like a Mom and Pop store.'

He reached out and took her hand, and this time she did not flinch, but squeezed his hand in return. 'Mom and Pop,' he said, and at last she smiled.

Nancy was hugging Mervyn when Diana tapped him on the shoulder.

Nancy had been lost in joy and relief, overwhelmed by the pleasure of being alive and with the man she loved. Now she wondered if Diana would cast a cloud over this moment. Diana had left Mervyn indecisively, and she had shown signs of regretting it, off and on, ever since. He had just proved that he still cared for her by bargaining with the gangsters to save her. Was she about to beg him to take her back?

Mervyn turned and gave his wife a guarded look. 'Well, Diana?'

Her face was wet with tears, but she had a determined expression. 'Will you shake hands?' she said.

Nancy was not sure what this meant, and Mervyn's wary manner told her that he, too, was uncertain. However, he offered his hand, saying, 'Of course.'

Diana held his hand in both of hers. New tears came, and Nancy felt sure she was about to say, 'Let's try again,' but instead she said, 'Good luck, Mervyn. I wish you happiness.'

Mervyn looked solemn. 'Thank you, Di. I wish you the same.'

Then Nancy understood: they were forgiving one another for the hurt that had been done. They were still going to split up, but they would part friends.

On impulse, Nancy said to Diana, 'Will you shake hands with me?'

The other woman hesitated only for a fraction of a second. 'Yes,' she said. They shook hands. 'I wish you well,' Diana said.

'And I you.'

Diana turned round without saying any more and went aft along the aisle to her compartment.

Mervyn said, 'But what about us? What are we going to do?'

Nancy realized she had not yet had time to tell him of her plan. 'I'm going to be Nat Ridgeway's European manager.'

Mervyn was surprised. 'When did he offer you the job?'

'He hasn't – but he will,' she said, and she laughed happily.

She heard the sound of an engine. It was not one of the Clipper's mighty engines, but a smaller one. She looked out of the window, wondering if the Navy had arrived.

To her surprise, she saw that the gangsters' motor launch had been untied from the Clipper and from the little seaplane and was pulling rapidly away.

But who was driving it?

*

Margaret opened the throttle wide and steered the launch away from the Clipper.

The wind blew her hair off her face, and she gave a whoop of sheer exhilaration. 'Free!' she yelled. 'I'm free!'

She and Harry had been standing in the aisle of the Clipper, wondering what to do next, when Eddie the engineer brought the skipper of the launch down the stairs and put him in No. 1 compartment with Luther; and both of them had been struck by the identical thought.

The passengers and crew were too busy congratulating one another to take much notice of Margaret and Harry as they slipped into the bow compartment and boarded the launch. The engine was idling. Harry had untied the ropes while Margaret figured out the controls, which were just like Father's boat in Nice, and they were away in seconds.

She did not think they would be chased. The naval cutter summoned by the engineer was in hot pursuit of a German submarine, and could not be expected to take an interest in a man who had stolen a pair of cufflinks in London. When the police arrived they would be investigating murder, kidnapping and piracy: it would be a long time before they worried about Harry.

Harry rummaged in a locker and found some maps. After studying them for a while he said, 'There are lots of charts of the waters around a bay called Black's Harbour, which is right on the border between the

USA and Canada. I think we must be near there. We should head for the Canadian side.'

A little later he said, 'There's a big place about seventy-five miles north of here called St John. It has a railway station. Are we heading north?'

She looked at the compass. 'More or less, yes.'

'I don't know anything about navigating, but if we keep in sight of the coast I don't see how we can go wrong. We should get there around nightfall.'

She smiled at him.

He put the charts down and stood beside her at the wheel, staring at her hard.

'What?' she said. 'What is it?'

He shook his head as if in disbelief. 'You're so beautiful,' he said. 'And you like me!'

She laughed. 'Anyone would like you, if they knew you.'

He put his arm around her waist. 'This is a hell of a thing, sailing along in the sunshine with a girl like you. My old ma always said I was lucky, and she was right, wasn't she?'

'What will we do when we get to St John?' she said.

'We'll beach the launch, walk into town, get a room for the night and take the first train out in the morning.'

'I don't know what we're going to do for money,' she said with a little frown of worry.

'Yes, that is a problem. I've only got a few pounds, and we'll have to pay for hotels, rail tickets, new clothes . . .'

'I wish I'd brought my overnight case, like you.'

He looked mischievous. 'That's not my case,' he said. 'It's Mr Luther's.'

She was mystified. 'Why did you bring Mr Luther's case?'

'Because it's got a hundred thousand dollars in it,' he said, and he started to laugh.

AFTERWORD

T HE GOLDEN age of the flying boats was very short.

Only twelve Boeing B-314's were built, six of the first model and six more of a slightly modified version called the B-314A. Nine were handed over to the US military early in the war. One of these, the *Dixie Clipper*, carried President Roosevelt to the Casablanca Conference in January 1943. Another, the *Yankee Clipper*, crashed at Lisbon in February 1943 with twenty-nine casualties, the only crash in the history of the aircraft.

The three planes Pan American did not give to the US military were sold to the British, and were also used to carry VIPs across the Atlantic: Churchill flew on two, the *Bristol* and the *Berwick*.

The point of flying boats was that they did not need expensive long concrete runways. During the war, however, long runways were built in many parts of the world to accommodate heavy bombers, and the advantage of the flying boats disappeared.

After the war the B-314 was uneconomic, and one by one the planes were scrapped or scuttled.

There are now none left anywhere in the world.

ACKNOWLEDGEMENTS

I THANK the many people and organizations who helped me research this book, especially:

In New York: Pan American Airlines, most particularly their librarian Liwa Chiu;

In London: Lord Willis;

In Manchester: Chris Makepeace;

In Southampton: Ray Facey of Associated British Ports and Ian Sinclair of RAF Hythe;

In Foynes: Margaret O'Shaughnessy of the Flying Boat Museum;

In Botwood: Tip Evans, the Botwood Heritage Museum, and the hospitable people of Botwood;

In Shediac: Ned Belliveau and his family, and Charles Allain and the Moncton Museum;

Former Pan American crew and other employees who flew on the Clipper: Madeline Cuniff, Bob Fordyce, Lew Lindsey, Jim McLeod, States Mead, Roger Wolin and Stan Zedalis;

For finding most of the above: Dan Starer and Pam Mendez.

A DANGEROUS
FORTUNE

ACKNOWLEDGEMENTS

For generous help in the writing of this book I thank the following friends, relations and colleagues: Carole Baron, Joanna Bourke, Ben Braber, George Brennan, Jackie Farber, Barbara Follett, Emanuele Follett, Katya Follett, Michael Haskoll, Pam Mendez, M. J. Orbell, Richard Overy, Dan Starer, Kim Turner, Ann Ward, Jane Wood and Al Zuckerman.

THE FAMILY TREE OF THE
Pilasters

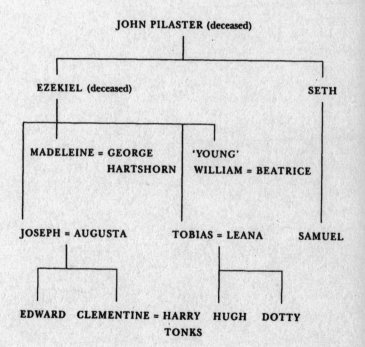

PROLOGUE

1866

[I]

O N THE DAY of the tragedy, the boys of Windfield
  School had been confined to their rooms.

It was a hot Saturday in May, and they would normally
have spent the afternoon on the south field, some playing
cricket and others watching from the shady fringes of
Bishop's Wood. But a crime had been committed. Six gold
sovereigns had been stolen from the desk of Dr Offerton,
the Latin master, and the whole school was under
suspicion. All the boys were to be kept in until the thief was
caught.

Micky Miranda sat at a table scarred with the initials of
generations of bored schoolboys. In his hand was a
government publication called *Equipment of Infantry*. The
engravings of swords, muskets and rifles usually fascinated
him, but he was too hot to concentrate. On the other side
of the table his room-mate, Edward Pilaster, looked up
from a Latin exercise book. He was copying out Micky's
translation of a page from Plutarch, and now he pointed an
inky finger and said: 'I can't read this word.'

Micky looked. 'Decapitated,' he said. 'It's the same word
in Latin, *decapitare*.' Micky found Latin easy, perhaps
because many of the words were similar in Spanish, which
was his native language.

Edward's pen scratched on. Micky got up restlessly and
went to the open window. There was no breeze. He looked
wistfully across the stable yard to the woods. There was a
shady swimming-hole in a disused quarry at the north end
of Bishop's Wood. The water was cold and deep. . . .

'Let's go swimming,' he said suddenly.

'We can't,' Edward said.

'We could go out through the synagogue.' The

3

'synagogue' was the room next door, which was shared by three Jewish boys. Windfield School taught divinity with a light touch and was tolerant of religious differences, which was why it appealed to Jewish parents, to Edward's Methodist family, and to Micky's Catholic father. But, despite the school's official attitude, Jewish boys came in for a certain amount of persecution. Micky went on: 'We can go through their window and drop on to the wash-house roof, climb down the blind side of the stable and sneak into the woods.'

Edward looked scared. 'It's the Striper if you're caught.'

The Striper was the ash cane wielded by the headmaster, Dr Poleson. The punishment for breaking detention was twelve agonizing strokes. Micky had been flogged once by Dr Poleson, for gambling, and he still shuddered when he thought of it. But the chance of getting caught was remote, and the idea of undressing and slipping naked into the pool was so immediate that he could almost feel the cold water on his sweaty skin.

He looked at his room-mate. Edward was not well liked at school: he was too lazy to be a good student, too clumsy to do well in games and too selfish to make many friends. Micky was the only friend he had, and he hated Micky to spend time with other boys. 'I'll see if Pilkington wants to go,' Micky said, and he went to the door.

'No, don't do that,' said Edward anxiously.

'I don't see why I shouldn't,' said Micky. 'You're too scared.'

'I'm not scared,' Edward said implausibly. 'I've got to finish my Latin.'

'Then finish it while I go swimming with Pilkington.'

Edward looked stubborn for a moment, then caved in. 'All right, I'll go,' he said reluctantly.

Micky opened the door. There was a low rumble of noise

4

from the rest of the house, but no masters to be seen in the corridor. He darted into the next room. Edward followed.

'Hello, Hebrews,' Micky said.

Two of the boys were playing cards at the table. They glanced up at him then continued their game without speaking. The third, Fatty Greenbourne, was eating a cake. His mother sent him food all the time. 'Hello, you two,' he said amiably. 'Want some cake?'

'By God, Greenbourne, you eat like a pig,' Micky said.

Fatty shrugged and continued to tuck in to his cake. He suffered a good deal of mockery, being fat as well as Jewish, but none of it seemed to touch him. His father was said to be the richest man in the world, and perhaps that made him impervious to name-calling, Micky thought.

Micky went to the window, opened it and looked around. The stable yard was deserted. Fatty said: 'What are you fellows doing?'

'Going swimming,' said Micky.

'You'll be flogged.'

Edward said plaintively: 'I know.'

Micky sat on the windowsill, rolled over on to his stomach, wriggled backwards and then dropped the few inches on to the sloping roof of the wash-house. He thought he heard a slate crack, but the roof held his weight. He glanced up and saw Edward looking anxiously out. 'Come on!' Micky said. He scrambled down the roof and used a convenient drainpipe to ease himself to the ground. A minute later Edward landed beside him.

Micky peeked around the corner of the wash-house wall. There was no one in sight. Without further hesitation he darted across the stable yard and into the woods. He ran through the trees until he judged he was out of sight of the school buildings, then he stopped to rest. Edward came up beside him. 'We did it!' Micky said. 'Nobody spotted us.'

'We'll probably be caught going back in,' Edward said morosely.

Micky smiled at him. Edward was very English-looking, with straight fair hair and blue eyes and a big nose like a broad-bladed knife. He was a tall boy with wide shoulders, strong but uncoordinated. He had no sense of style, and wore his clothes awkwardly. He and Micky were the same age, sixteen, but in other ways they were very different: Micky had curly dark hair and dark eyes, and he was meticulous about his appearance, hating to be untidy or dirty. 'Trust me, Pilaster,' Micky said. 'Don't I always take care of you?'

Edward grinned, mollified. 'All right, let's go.'

They followed a barely discernible path through the wood. It was a little cooler under the leaves of the beech and elm trees, and Micky began to feel better. 'What will you do this summer?' he asked Edward.

'We usually go to Scotland in August.'

'Do your people have a shooting-box there?' Micky had picked up the jargon of the English upper classes, and he knew that 'shooting-box' was the correct term even if the house in question was a fifty-room castle.

'They rent a place,' Edward replied. 'But we don't shoot over it. My father's not a sportsman, you know.'

Micky heard a defensive note in Edward's voice and pondered its significance. He knew that the English aristocracy liked to shoot birds in August and hunt foxes all winter. He also knew that aristocrats did not send their sons to this school. The fathers of Windfield boys were businessmen and engineers rather than earls and bishops, and such men did not have time to waste hunting and shooting. The Pilasters were bankers, and when Edward said 'My father's not a sportsman' he was acknowledging that his family was not in the very highest rank of society.

It amused Micky that Englishmen respected the idle more than people who worked. In his own country, respect was given neither to aimless nobles nor to hard-working businessmen. Micky's people respected nothing but power. If a man had the power to control others – to feed or starve them, imprison or free them, kill them or let them live – what more did he need?

'What about you?' Edward said. 'How will you spend the summer?'

Micky had wanted him to ask that. 'Here,' he said. 'At school.'

'You're not staying at school all through the vacation again?'

'I have to. I can't go home. It takes six weeks one way – I'd have to start back before I got there.'.

'By Jove, that's hard.'

In fact Micky had no wish to go back. He loathed his home, and had done since his mother died. There were only men there now: his father, his older brother Paulo, some uncles and cousins, and four hundred cowboys. Papa was a hero to the men and a stranger to Micky: cold, unapproachable, impatient. But Micky's brother was the real problem. Paulo was stupid but strong. He hated Micky for being smarter, and he liked to humiliate his little brother. He never missed a chance to prove to everyone that Micky could not rope steers or break horses or shoot a snake through the head. His favourite trick was to scare Micky's horse so it would bolt, and Micky would have to shut his eyes tight and cling on, scared to death, while the horse charged madly across the pampas until it exhausted itself. No, Micky did not want to go home for the vacation. But he did not want to remain at school, either. What he really wanted was to be invited to spend the summer with the Pilaster family.

Edward did not immediately suggest this, however, and Micky let the subject drop. He felt sure it would come up again.

They clambered over a decaying picket fence and walked up a low hill. As they breasted the rise they came upon the swimming-hole. The chiselled sides of the quarry were steep, but agile boys could find a way to scramble down. At the bottom was a deep pool of murky green water that contained toads, frogs and the occasional water-snake.

To Micky's surprise, there were also three boys in it.

He narrowed his eyes against the sunlight glinting off the surface and peered at the naked figures. All three were in the lower fourth at Windfield.

The mop of carrot-coloured hair belonged to Antonio Silva, who despite his colouring was a compatriot of Micky's. Tonio's father did not have as much land as Micky's, but the Silvas lived in the capital and had influential friends. Like Micky, Tonio could not go home in the vacations, but he was lucky enough to have friends at the Cordovan Ministry in London, so he did not have to stay at the school all summer.

The second boy was Hugh Pilaster, a cousin of Edward's. There was no resemblance between the cousins: Hugh had black hair and small, neat features, and he usually wore an impish grin. Edward resented Hugh for being a good scholar and making Edward look like the dunce of the family.

The other was Peter Middleton, a rather timid boy who attached himself to the more confident Hugh. All three had white, hairless thirteen-year-old bodies with thin arms and legs.

Then Micky saw a fourth boy. He was swimming on his own at the far end of the pool. He was older than the other three and did not seem to be with them. Micky could not see his face well enough to identify him.

Edward was grinning evilly. He had seen an opportunity to make mischief. He put his finger to his lips in a hushing gesture then started down the side of the quarry. Micky followed.

They reached the ledge where the small boys had left their clothes. Tonio and Hugh were diving underneath, investigating something, while Peter swam quietly up and down on his own. Peter was the first to spot the newcomers. 'Oh, no,' he said.

'Well, well,' said Edward. 'You boys are breaking bounds, aren't you?'

Hugh Pilaster noticed his cousin then, and shouted back: 'So are you!'

'You'd better go back, before you're caught,' Edward said. He picked up a pair of trousers from the ground. 'But don't get your clothes wet, or everyone will know where you've been.' Then he threw the trousers into the middle of the pool and cackled with laughter.

'You cad!' Peter yelled as he made a grab for the floating trousers.

Micky smiled, amused.

Edward picked up a boot and threw it in.

The small boys began to panic. Edward picked up another pair of trousers and threw them in. It was hilarious to see the three victims yelling and diving for their clothes, and Micky started to laugh.

As Edward continued to throw boots and clothes into the water, Hugh Pilaster scrambled out. Micky expected him to make his escape, but unexpectedly he ran straight at Edward. Before Edward could turn around, Hugh gave him a mighty shove. Although Edward was much bigger, he was caught off balance. He staggered on the ledge then toppled over and fell into the pool with a terrific splash.

It was done in a twinkling, and Hugh snatched up an armful of clothes and went up the quarry side like a monkey. Peter and Tonio shrieked with mocking laughter.

Micky chased Hugh a short way but realized he could not hope to catch the smaller, nimbler boy. Turning back, he looked to see whether Edward was all right. He need not have worried. Edward had surfaced. He got hold of Peter Middleton and started ducking the boy's head again and again, punishing him for that mocking laugh.

Tonio swam away and reached the edge of the pool, clutching a bundle of sodden clothing. He turned to look back. 'Leave him alone, you big ape!' he yelled at Edward. Tonio had always been reckless and now Micky wondered what he would do next. Tonio went further along the side, then turned again with a stone in his hand. Micky yelled a warning to Edward, but it was too late. Tonio threw the stone with surprising accuracy and hit Edward on the head. A bright splash of blood appeared on his brow.

Edward gave a roar of pain and, leaving Peter, struck out across the pool after Tonio.

[II]

HUGH RACED naked through the wood towards the school, clutching what remained of his clothes, trying to ignore the pain of his bare feet on the rough ground. Coming to a place where the path was crossed by another, he dodged to the left, ran on a little way, then dived into the bushes and hid.

He waited, trying to calm his hoarse breathing and listen. His cousin Edward and Edward's crony, Micky

Miranda, were the worst beasts in the entire school: slackers, bad sports and bullies. The only thing to do was to keep out of their way. But he felt sure Edward would come after him. Edward had always hated Hugh.

Their fathers had quarrelled, too. Hugh's father, Toby, had taken his capital out of the family business and started his own enterprise, trading in dyes for the textile industry. Even at thirteen Hugh knew that the worst crime in the Pilaster family was to take your capital out of the bank. Edward's father, Joseph, had never forgiven his brother Toby.

Hugh wondered what had happened to his friends. There had been four of them in the pool before Micky and Edward turned up: Tonio, Peter and Hugh had been splashing about on one side of the pool, and an older boy, Albert Cammel, had been swimming alone at the far end.

Tonio was normally brave to the point of recklessness, but he was terrified of Micky Miranda. They came from the same place, a South American country called Cordova, and Tonio said that Micky's family were powerful and cruel. Hugh did not really understand what that meant, but the effect was striking: Tonio might cheek the other fifth-formers but he was always polite, even subservient, to Micky.

Peter would be scared out of his wits: he was frightened of his own shadow. Hugh hoped he had got away from the bullies.

Albert Cammel, nicknamed Hump, had not been with Hugh and friends, and he had left his clothes in a different place, so he had probably escaped.

Hugh too had escaped, but he was not yet out of trouble. He had lost his underclothes, socks and boots. He would have to sneak into school in his soaking wet shirt and trousers and hope he would not be seen by a master or one of the senior boys. He groaned aloud at the thought. Why do things like this always happen to me? he asked himself miserably.

He had been in and out of trouble ever since he came to Windfield eighteen months ago. He had no trouble studying: he worked hard and came top of his class in every test. But the petty rules irritated him beyond reason. Ordered to go to bed every night at a quarter to ten, he always had some compelling reason for staying up until a quarter past. He found forbidden places tantalizing, and was irresistibly drawn to explore the rectory garden, the headmaster's orchard, the coal-hole and the beer cellar. He ran when he should have walked, read when he was supposed to go to sleep, and talked during prayers. And he always ended up like this, guilty and scared, wondering why he let himself in for so much grief.

The wood was silent for several minutes while he reflected gloomily on his destiny, wondering whether he would end up an outcast from society, or even a criminal, thrown in jail or transported to Australia in chains or hanged.

At last he decided that Edward was not coming after him. He stood up and pulled on his wet trousers and shirt. Then he heard someone crying.

Cautiously, he peeped out – and saw Tonio's shock of carrot-coloured hair. His friend was walking slowly along the path, naked, wet, carrying his clothes and sobbing.

'What happened?' Hugh asked. 'Where's Peter?'

Tonio suddenly became fierce. 'I'll never tell, never!' he said. 'They'll kill me.'

'All right, don't tell me,' Hugh said. As always, Tonio was terrified of Micky: whatever had happened, Tonio would keep quiet about it. 'You'd better get dressed,' Hugh said practically.

Tonio looked blankly at the bundle of sodden garments in his arms. He seemed too shocked to sort them out. Hugh took them from him. He had boots and trousers and one sock, but no shirt. Hugh helped him put on what he had, then they walked towards the school.

Tonio stopped crying, though he still looked badly shaken. Hugh hoped those bullies hadn't done something really nasty to Peter. But he had to think of saving his own skin now. 'If we can get into the dormitory, we can put on fresh clothes and our spare boots,' he said, planning ahead. 'Then as soon as the detention is lifted we can walk into town and buy new clothes on credit at Baxted's.'

Tonio nodded. 'All right,' he said dully.

As they wound their way through the trees, Hugh wondered again why Tonio was so disturbed. After all, bullying was nothing new at Windfield. What had happened back there at the pool after Hugh had escaped? But Tonio said nothing more about it all the way back.

The school was a collection of six buildings that had once been the hub of a large farm, and their dormitory was in the old dairy near the chapel. To get there they had to go over a wall and cross the fives court. They climbed the wall and peeped over. The courtyard was deserted, as Hugh had expected, but all the same he hesitated. The thought of the Striper whipping his behind made him cringe. But there was no alternative. He had to get back into school and put on dry clothes.

'All clear,' he hissed. 'Off we go!'

They jumped over the wall together and sprinted across the court to the cool shade of the stone-built chapel. So far, so good. Then they crept around the east end, staying close to the wall. Next there was a short dash across the drive and into their building. Hugh paused. There was no one in sight. 'Now!' he said.

The two boys ran across the road. Then, as they reached the door, disaster struck. A familiar, authoritative voice rang out: 'Pilaster Minor! Is that you?' And Hugh knew that the game was up.

His heart sank. He stopped and turned. Dr Offerton had chosen that very moment to come out of the chapel, and now stood in the shadow of the porch, a tall, dyspeptic figure in a college gown and mortar-board hat. Hugh stifled a groan. Dr Offerton, whose money had been stolen, was the least likely of all the masters to show mercy. It would be the Striper. The muscles of his bottom clenched involuntarily.

'Come here, Pilaster,' Dr Offerton said.

Hugh shuffled over to him, with Tonio following behind. Why do I take such risks? Hugh thought in despair.

'Headmaster's study, right away,' said Dr Offerton.

'Yes, sir,' Hugh said miserably. It was getting worse and worse. When the head saw how he was dressed he would probably be sacked from the school. And how would he explain it to his mother?

'Off you go!' the master said impatiently.

The two boys turned away, but Dr Offerton said: 'Not you, Silva.'

Hugh and Tonio exchanged a quick mystified look. Why should Hugh be punished and not Tonio? But they could not question orders, and Tonio escaped into the dormitory while Hugh made for the head's house.

He could feel the Striper already. He knew he would cry, and that was even worse than the pain, for at the age of thirteen he felt he was too old to cry.

The head's house was on the far side of the school compound, and Hugh walked very slowly, but he got there all too soon, and the maid opened the door a second after he rang.

He met Dr Poleson in the hall. The headmaster was a bald man with a bulldog's face, but for some reason he did not look as thunderously angry as he should have. Instead of demanding to know why Hugh was out of his room *and* dripping wet, he simply opened the study door and said quietly: 'In here, young Pilaster.' No doubt he was saving his rage for the flogging. Hugh went in with his heart pounding.

He was astonished to see his mother sitting there.

Worse yet, she was weeping.

'I only went swimming!' Hugh blurted out.

The door closed behind him and he realized the head had not followed him in.

Then he began to understand that this had nothing to do with his breaking detention and going swimming, and losing his clothing, and being found half-naked.

He had a dreadful feeling it was much worse than that.

'Mother, what is it?' he said. 'Why have you come?'

'Oh, Hugh,' she sobbed, 'your father's dead.'

[III]

SATURDAY WAS the best day of the week for Maisie Robinson. On Saturday Papa got paid. Tonight there would be meat for supper, and new bread.

She sat on the front doorstep with her brother Danny, waiting for Papa to come home from work. Danny was thirteen, two years older than Maisie, and she thought he was wonderful, even though he was not always kind to her.

The house was one of a row of damp, airless dwellings in the dockland neighbourhood of a small town on the northeast coast of England. It belonged to Mrs MacNeil, a widow. She lived in the front room downstairs. The

Robinsons lived in the back room and another family lived upstairs. When it was time for Papa to arrive home, Mrs MacNeil would be out on the doorstep, waiting to collect the rent.

Maisie was hungry. Yesterday she had begged some broken bones from the butcher and Papa had bought a turnip and made a stew, and that was the last meal she had had. But today was Saturday!

She tried not to think about supper, for it made the pain in her stomach worse. To take her mind off food she said to Danny: 'Papa swore this morning.'

'What did he say?'

'He said Mrs MacNeil is a *paskudniak*.'

Danny giggled. The word meant shitbag. Both children spoke English fluently after a year in the new country, but they remembered their Yiddish.

Their name was not really Robinson, it was Rabinowicz. Mrs MacNeil had hated them ever since she discovered they were Jews. She had never met a Jew before and when she rented them the room she thought they were French. There were no other Jews in this town. The Robinsons had never intended to come here: they had paid for passage to a place called Manchester, where there were lots of Jews, and the ship's captain had told them this was Manchester, but he had cheated them. When they discovered they were in the wrong place, Papa said they would save up enough money to move to Manchester; but then Mama had fallen ill. She was still ill, and they were still here.

Papa worked on the waterfront, in a high warehouse with the words 'Tobias Pilaster and Co' in big letters over the gate. Maisie often wondered who Co was. Papa worked as a clerk, keeping records of the barrels of dyes that came in and out of the building. He was a careful man, a taker of notes and a maker of lists. Mama was the reverse. She had

16

always been the daring one. It was Mama who wanted to come to England. Mama loved to make parties, go on trips, meet new people, dress up and play games. That was why Papa loved her so much, Maisie thought: because she was something he could never be.

She was not spirited any more. She lay all day on the old mattress, drifting in and out of sleep, her pale face shiny with sweat, her breath hot and odorous. The doctor had said she needed building up, with plenty of fresh eggs and cream, and beef every day; and then Papa had paid him with the money for that night's dinner. But now Maisie felt guilty every time she ate, knowing that she was taking food that might save her mother's life.

Maisie and Danny had learned to steal. On market day they would go into the centre of town and pilfer potatoes and apples from the stalls in the square. The traders were sharp-eyed but every now and again they would be distracted by something – an argument over change, a dog fight, a drunk – and the children would grab what they could. When their luck was in, they would meet a rich kid their own age; then they would set on him and rob him. Such children often had an orange or a bag of sweets in their pockets as well as a few pennies. Maisie was afraid of being caught because she knew Mama would be so ashamed, but she was hungry too.

She looked up and saw some men coming along the street in a knot. She wondered who they were. It was still a little too early for the dock workers to be coming home. They were talking angrily, waving their arms and shaking their fists. As they came closer she recognized Mr Ross, who lived upstairs and worked with Papa at Pilasters. Why was he not at work? Had they been sacked? He looked angry enough for that. He was red in the face and swearing, talking about stupid gits, lousy bleeders and lying bastards.

When the group drew level with the house Mr Ross left them abruptly and stomped inside, and Maisie and Danny had to dive out of the way to avoid his hobnailed boots.

When Maisie looked up again she saw Papa. A thin man with a black beard and soft brown eyes, he was following the others at a distance, walking with his head bowed; and he looked so dejected and hopeless that Maisie wanted to cry. 'Papa, what's happened?' she said. 'Why are you home early?'

'Come inside,' he said, his voice so low that Maisie could only just hear.

The two children followed him into the back of the house. He knelt by the mattress and kissed Mama's lips. She woke up and smiled at him. He did not smile back. 'The firm's bust,' he said, speaking Yiddish. 'Toby Pilaster went bankrupt.'

Maisie was not sure what that meant but Papa's tone of voice made it sound like a disaster. She shot a look at Danny: he shrugged. He did not understand it either.

'But why?' Mama said.

'There's been a financial crash,' Papa said. 'A big bank in London failed yesterday.'

Mama frowned, struggling to concentrate. 'But this isn't London,' she said. 'What's London to us?'

'The details I don't know.'

'So you've got no work?'

'No work, and no pay.'

'But today they've paid you.'

Papa bowed his head. 'No, they didn't pay us.'

Maisie looked at Danny again. This they understood. No money meant no food for any of them. Danny looked scared. Maisie wanted to cry.

'They must pay you,' Mama whispered. 'You worked all week, they have to pay you.'

18

'They've no money,' Papa said. 'That's what bankrupt means, it means you owe people money and can't pay them.'

'But Mr Pilaster is a good man, you always said.'

'Toby Pilaster's dead. He hanged himself, last night, in his office in London. He had a son Danny's age.'

'But how are we to feed our children?'

'I don't know,' Papa said, and to Maisie's horror he began to cry. 'I'm sorry, Sarah,' he said as the tears rolled into his beard. 'I've brought you to this awful place where there are no Jews and no one to help us. I can't pay the doctor, I can't buy medicines, I can't feed our children. I've failed you. I'm sorry, I'm sorry.' He leaned forward and buried his wet face in Mama's breast. She stroked his hair with a shaky hand.

Maisie was appalled. Papa never cried. It seemed to mean the end of any hope. Perhaps they would all die now.

Danny stood up, looked at Maisie, and jerked his head toward the door. She got up and together they tiptoed out of the room. Maisie sat on the front step and began to cry. 'What are we going to do?' she said.

'We'll have to run away,' Danny said.

Danny's words gave her a cold feeling in her chest. 'We can't,' she said.

'We must. There's no food. If we stay we'll die.'

Maisie didn't care if she died, but a different thought occurred to her: Mama would surely starve herself to feed the children. If they stayed, she would die. They had to leave to save her. 'You're right,' Maisie said to Danny. 'If we go, perhaps Papa will be able to find enough food for Mama. We've got to go, for her sake.' Hearing herself say the words, she was awestruck by what was happening to her family. It was worse even than the day they had left Viskis, with the village houses still burning behind them, and got on a cold train with all their belongings in two sailcloth bags; for then she had known that Papa would always look after her, no matter what else happened; and now she had to take care of herself.

'Where will we go?' she said in a whisper.

'I'm going to America.'

'America! How?'

'There's a ship in the harbour that's bound for Boston on the morning tide – I'll shin up a rope tonight and hide on deck in one of the boats.'

'You'll stow away,' Maisie said, with fear and admiration in her voice.

'That's right.'

Looking at her brother, she saw for the first time that there was the shadow of a moustache beginning to show on his upper lip. He was becoming a man, and one day he would have a full black beard like Papa's. 'How long does it take to get to America?' she asked him.

He hesitated, then looked foolish and said: 'I don't know.'

She realized that she was not included in his plans, and she felt miserable and scared. 'We're not going together, then,' she said sadly.

He looked guilty, but he did not contradict her. 'I'll tell you what you should do,' he said. 'Go to Newcastle. You can walk there in about four days. It's a huge city, bigger than Gdansk – no one will notice you there. Cut your hair, steal a pair of trousers and pretend to be a boy. Go to a big stables and help with the horses – you've always been good with horses. If they like you, you'll get tips, and after a while they might give you a proper job.'

Maisie could not imagine being totally alone. 'I'd rather go with you,' she said.

'You can't. It's going to be hard enough anyway, to hide

myself on the ship, and steal food and so on. I couldn't look after you too.'

'You wouldn't have to look after me. I'd be as quiet as a mouse.'

'I'd feel worried about you.'

'Won't you worry about leaving me all on my own?'

'We've got to take care of ourselves!' he said angrily.

She saw that his mind was made up. She had never been able to talk him round when his mind was made up. With dread in her heart she said: 'When should we go? In the morning?'

He shook his head. 'Now. I'll need to get aboard the ship as soon as it's dark.'

'Do you really mean it?'

'Yes.' As if to prove it, he stood up.

She stood up too. 'Should we take anything?'

'What?'

She shrugged. She had no spare clothes, no souvenirs, no possessions of any kind. There was no food or money to take. 'I want to kiss Mama goodbye,' she said.

'Don't,' said Danny harshly. 'If you do, you'll stay.'

It was true. If she saw Mama now she would break down and tell everything. She swallowed hard. 'All right,' she said, fighting back the tears. 'I'm ready.'

They walked away side by side.

When they got to the end of the street she wanted to turn around and take a last look at the house; but she was afraid that if she did she would weaken; so she walked on, and never looked back.

[IV]

From *The Times*:

CHARACTER OF THE ENGLISH SCHOOLBOY – The Deputy-Coroner for Ashton, Mr H. S. Wasbrough, held an inquest yesterday at the Station Hotel, Windfield, on the body of Peter James St John Middleton, aged 13, a schoolboy. The boy had been swimming in a pool at a disused quarry near Windfield School when two older boys had seen him apparently in difficulties, the court was told. One of the older boys, Miguel Miranda, a native of Cordova, gave evidence that his companion, Edward Pilaster, aged 15, stripped off his outer clothing and dived in to try to save the younger boy, but to no avail. The headmaster of Windfield, Dr Herbert Poleson, testified that the quarry was out of bounds to pupils, but he was aware that the rule was not always obeyed. The jury returned a verdict of accidental death by drowning. The Deputy-Coroner then called attention to the bravery of Edward Pilaster in trying to save the life of his friend, and said the character of the English schoolboy, as formed by such institutions as Windfield, was a thing of which we might justifiably feel proud.

[V]

MICKY MIRANDA was captivated by Edward's mother.

Augusta Pilaster was a tall, statuesque woman in her thirties. She had black hair and black eyebrows and a haughty, high-cheekboned face with a straight, sharp nose and a strong chin. She was not exactly beautiful, and certainly not pretty, but somehow that proud face was deeply fascinating. She wore a black coat and a black hat to the inquest, and that made her even more dramatic. And yet what was so bewitching was the unmistakable feeling she gave Micky that the formal clothes covered a voluptuous body, and the arrogant, imperious manner concealed a passionate nature. He could hardly take his eyes off her.

Beside her sat her husband Joseph, Edward's father, an ugly, sour-faced man of about forty. He had the same big blade of a nose as Edward, and the same fair colouring, but his blond hair was receding, and he had bushy Dundreary side-whiskers sprouting from his cheeks as if to compensate for his baldness. Micky wondered what had made such a splendid woman marry him. He was very rich – perhaps that was it.

They were returning to the school in a carriage hired from the Station Hotel: Mr and Mrs Pilaster, Edward and Micky, and the headmaster, Dr Poleson. Micky was amused to see that the headmaster was also bowled over by Augusta Pilaster. Old Pole asked if the inquest had tired her, inquired if she was comfortable in the carriage, ordered the coachman to go slower, and leaped out at the end of the journey to have the thrill of holding her hand as she stepped down. His bulldog face had never looked so animated.

The inquest had gone well. Micky put on his most open and honest expression to tell the story he and Edward had made up, but inside he had been scared. The British could be very sanctimonious about telling the truth, and if he was found out he would be in deep trouble. But the court was so enchanted by the story of schoolboy heroism that no one questioned it. Edward was nervous, and stammered his evidence, but the coroner excused him, suggesting that he was distraught over his failure to save Peter's life, and insisting he should not blame himself.

None of the other boys was asked to the inquest. Hugh had been taken away from the school on the day of the drowning because of the death of his father. Tonio was not asked to give evidence because nobody knew he had witnessed the death: Micky had scared him into silence. The other witness, the unknown boy at the far end of the pool, had not come forward.

Peter Middleton's parents were too grief-stricken to attend. They sent their lawyer, a sleepy-eyed old man whose only object was to get the whole thing over with a minimum of fuss. Peter's older brother David was there, and became quite agitated when the lawyer declined to ask Micky or Edward any questions, but to Micky's relief the old man waved aside his whispered protests. Micky was thankful for his laziness: Edward might have crumbled under sceptical questioning.

In the head's dusty drawing-room Mrs Pilaster embraced Edward and kissed the wound on his forehead where Tonio's stone had hit him. 'My poor dear child,' she said. Micky and Edward had not told anyone that Tonio had thrown a stone at Edward, for then they would have to explain why he did it. Instead they had said that Edward banged his head when he dived in to rescue Peter.

As they drank their tea, Micky saw a new side to Edward. His mother, sitting beside him on the sofa, touched him constantly and called him Teddy. Instead of being embarrassed, as most boys would, he seemed to like it, and kept giving her a winning little smile that Micky had never seen before. She's stupid about him, Micky thought, and he loves it.

After a few minutes of small talk Mrs Pilaster stood up abruptly, startling the men, who scrambled to their feet.

'I'm sure you want to smoke, Dr Poleson,' she said. Without waiting for a reply she went on: 'Mr Pilaster will take a turn around the garden with you and have a cigar. Teddy, dear, go with your father. I should like to have a few quiet minutes in the chapel. Perhaps Micky would show me the way.'

'By all means, by all means, by all means,' the head stuttered, falling over himself in his eagerness to assent to this series of commands. 'Off you go, Miranda.'

Micky was impressed. How effortlessly she made them all do her bidding! He held the door open for her and followed her out.

In the hall he said politely: 'Would you like a parasol, Mrs Pilaster? The sun is quite strong.'

'No, thank you.'

They went outside. There were a lot of boys hanging around outside the head's house. Micky realized that word had got around about Pilaster's stunning mother, and they had all come to catch a glimpse of her. Feeling pleased to be her escort, he led her through a series of courtyards and quadrangles to the school chapel. 'Shall I wait outside for you?' he offered.

'Come inside. I want to talk to you.'

He began to feel nervous. His pleasure in escorting a striking mature woman around the school started to fade, and he wondered why she wanted to interview him alone.

The chapel was empty. She took a back pew and invited him to sit beside her. Looking straight into his eyes, she said: 'Now tell me the truth.'

Augusta saw the flash of surprise and fear in the boy's expression and knew that she was right.

However, he recovered in an instant. 'I've already told you the truth,' he said.

She shook her head. 'You have not.'

He smiled.

The smile took her by surprise. She had caught him out; she knew he was on the defensive; yet he could smile at her. Few men could resist the force of her will, but it seemed he was exceptional, despite his youth. 'How old are you?' she said.

'Sixteen.'

She studied him. He was outrageously good-looking, with his curly dark-brown hair and smooth skin, although there was already a hint of decadence in the heavy-lidded eyes and full lips. He reminded her somewhat of the Earl of Strang, with his poise and good looks. . . . She pushed that thought aside with a guilty pang. 'Peter Middleton was not in difficulties when you arrived at the pool,' she said. 'He was swimming around quite happily.'

'What makes you say this?' he said coolly.

He was scared, she sensed, but he maintained his composure. He was really quite remarkably mature. She found herself unwillingly showing more of her hand. 'You're forgetting that Hugh Pilaster was there,' she said. 'He is my nephew. His father took his own life last week, as you probably heard, and that is why he isn't here. But he has spoken to his mother, who is my sister-in-law.'

'What did he say?'

Augusta frowned. 'He said that Edward threw Peter's clothes into the water,' she said reluctantly. She did not really understand why Teddy would do such a thing.

'And then?'

Augusta smiled. This boy was taking control of the conversation. She was supposed to be questioning him, but instead he was interrogating her. 'Just tell me what really happened,' she said.

He nodded. 'Very well.'

When he said that, Augusta was relieved, but worried as well. She wanted to know the truth, but she feared what it might be. Poor Teddy – he had almost died, as a baby, because there had been something wrong with Augusta's breast-milk, and he nearly wasted away before the doctors discovered the nature of the problem and proposed a wet-nurse. Ever since then he had been vulnerable, needing her special protection. Had she had her way he would not have gone to boarding school, but his father had been intransigent about that. . . . She returned her attention to Micky.

'Edward didn't mean any harm,' Micky began. 'He was just ragging. He threw the other boys' clothes into the water as a joke.'

Augusta nodded. That sounded normal to her: boys teasing one another. Poor Teddy must have suffered that sort of thing himself.

'Then Hugh pushed Edward in.'

'That little Hugh has always been a troublemaker,' Augusta said. 'He's just like his wretched father was.' And like his father he would probably come to a bad end, she thought to herself.

'The other boys all laughed, and Edward pushed Peter's head under, to teach him a lesson. Hugh ran off. Then Tonio threw a stone at Edward.'

Augusta was horrified. 'But he might have been knocked unconscious, and drowned!'

'However, he wasn't, and he went chasing after Tonio. I was watching them: no one was looking at Peter Middleton. Tonio got away from Edward eventually. That was when we noticed that Peter had gone quiet. We don't really know what happened to him: perhaps Edward's ducking exhausted him, so that he was too tired or too breathless to get out of the pool. Anyway, he was floating face down. We got him out of the water right away, but he was dead.'

It was hardly Edward's fault, Augusta thought. Boys were always rough with one another. All the same she was deeply grateful that this story had not come out at the inquest. Micky had covered up for Edward, thank heavens. 'What about the other boys?' she said. 'They must know what happened.'

'It was lucky that Hugh left the school that very day.'

'And the other one – did you call him Tony?'

'Antonio Silva. Tonio for short. Don't worry about him. He's from my country. He'll do as I tell him.'

'How can you be sure?'

'He knows that if he gets me into trouble, his family will suffer back home.'

There was something chilling in the boy's voice as he said this, and Augusta shivered.

'May I fetch you a shawl?' Micky said attentively.

Augusta shook her head. 'No other boys saw what happened?'

Micky frowned. 'There was another boy swimming in the pool when we got there.'

'Who?'

He shook his head. 'I couldn't see his face, and I didn't know it was going to be important.'

'Did he see what happened?'

'I don't know. I'm not sure at what point he left.'

'But he had gone by the time you got the body out of the water?'

'Yes.'

'I wish we knew who it was,' Augusta said anxiously.

'He may not even have been a schoolboy,' Micky pointed out. 'He could be from the town. Anyway, for whatever reason, he hasn't come forward as a witness, so I suppose he's no danger to us.'

No danger to us. It struck Augusta that she was involved with Micky in something dishonest, possibly illegal. She did not like the situation. She had got into it without realizing, and now she was trapped. She looked hard at him and said: 'What do you want?'

She caught him off guard for the first time. Looking bewildered, he said: 'What do you mean?'

'You covered up for my son. You committed perjury today.' He was unbalanced by her directness, she saw. That pleased her: she was in control again. 'I don't believe you took such a risk out of the goodness of your heart. I think you want something in return. Why don't you just tell me what it is?'

She saw his gaze drop momentarily to her bosom, and for a wild moment she thought he was going to make an indecent suggestion. Then he said: 'I want to spend the summer with you.'

She had not expected that. 'Why?'

'My home is six weeks' journey away. I have to stay at school during the holidays. I hate it – it's lonely and boring. I'd like to be invited to spend the summer with Edward.'

Suddenly he was a schoolboy again. She had thought he would ask for money, or perhaps a job at Pilasters Bank. But this seemed such a small, almost childish request. However, it clearly was not small to him. After all, she thought, he is only sixteen.

'You shall stay with us for the summer, and welcome,' she said. The thought did not displease her. He was a rather formidable young man in some ways, but his manners were perfect and he was good-looking: it would be no hardship to have him as a guest. And he might be a good influence on Edward. If Teddy had a fault it was that he was rather aimless. Micky was just the opposite. Perhaps some of his strength of will would rub off on her Teddy.

Micky smiled, showing white teeth. 'Thank you,' he said. He seemed sincerely delighted.

She felt an urge to be alone for a while and mull over what she had heard. 'Leave me now,' she said. 'I can find my way back to the headmaster's house.'

He got up from the pew where they were sitting. 'I'm very grateful,' he said, and offered his hand.

She took it. 'I'm grateful to you, for protecting Teddy.'

He bent down, as if he were going to kiss her hand; and then, to her astonishment, he kissed her lips. It was so quick that she had no time to turn away. She searched for words of protest as he straightened up, but she could not think what to say. A moment later he was gone.

It was outrageous! He should not have kissed her at all, let alone on the lips. Who did he think he was? Her first thought was to rescind the summer invitation. But that would never do.

Why not? she asked herself. Why could she not cancel an invitation extended to a mere schoolboy? He had acted presumptuously, so he should not come to stay.

But the thought of going back on her promise made her uncomfortable. It was not just that Micky had saved Teddy from disgrace, she realized. It was worse than that. She had entered into a criminal conspiracy with him. It made her unpleasantly vulnerable to him.

She sat in the cool chapel for a long time, staring at the bare walls and wondering, with a distinct feeling of apprehension, how that handsome, knowing boy would use his power.

PART ONE

1873

CHAPTER ONE

May

[I]

WHEN MICKY MIRANDA was twenty-three his father
came to London to buy rifles.

Señor Carlos Raul Xavier Miranda, known always as
Papa, was a short man with massive shoulders. His tanned
face was carved in lines of aggression and brutality. In
leather chaps and a broad-brimmed hat, seated on a
chestnut stallion, he could make a graceful, commanding
figure; but here in Hyde Park, wearing a frock-coat and a
top hat, he felt foolish, and that made him dangerously
bad-tempered.

They were not alike. Micky was tall and slim, with
regular features, and he got his way by smiling rather than
frowning. He was deeply attached to the refinements of
London life: beautiful clothes, polite manners, linen sheets
and indoor plumbing. His great fear was that Papa would
want to take him back to Cordova. He could not bear to
return to days in the saddle and nights sleeping on the hard
ground. Even worse was the prospect of being under the
thumb of his older brother Paulo, who was a replica of
Papa. Perhaps Micky would go home one day, but it would

33

be as an important man in his own right, not as the younger son of Papa Miranda. Meanwhile he had to persuade his father that he was more useful here in London than he would be at home in Cordova.

They were walking along South Carriage Drive on a sunny Saturday afternoon. The park was thronged with well-dressed Londoners on foot, on horseback or in open carriages, enjoying the warm weather. But Papa was not enjoying himself. 'I must have those rifles!' he muttered to himself in Spanish. He said it twice.

Micky spoke in the same language. 'You could buy them back home,' he said tentatively.

'Two thousand of them?' Papa said. 'Perhaps I could. But it would be such a big purchase that everyone would know about it.'

So he wanted to keep it secret. Micky had no idea what Papa was up to. Paying for two thousand guns, and the ammunition to go with them, would probably take all the family's reserves of cash. Why did Papa suddenly need so much ordnance? There had been no war in Cordova since the now-legendary March of the Cowboys, when Papa had led his men across the Andes to liberate Santamaria Province from its Spanish overlords. Who were the guns for? If you added up Papa's cowboys, relatives, placemen and hangers-on it would come to fewer than a thousand men. Papa had to be planning to recruit more. Whom would they be fighting? Papa had not volunteered the information and Micky was afraid to ask.

Instead he said: 'Anyway, you probably couldn't get such high-quality weapons at home.'

'That's true,' said Papa. 'The Westley-Richards is the finest rifle I've ever seen.'

Micky had been able to help Papa with his choice of rifles. Micky had always been fascinated by weapons of all kinds, and he kept up with the latest technical developments. Papa needed short-barrelled rifles that would not be too cumbersome for men on horseback. Micky had taken Papa to a factory in Birmingham and shown him the Westley-Richards carbine with the breech-loading action, nicknamed the Monkeytail because of its curly lever.

'And they make them so fast,' Micky said.

'I expected to wait six months for the guns to be manufactured. But they can do it in a few days!'

'It's the American machinery they use.' In the old days, when guns had been made by blacksmiths who fitted the parts together by trial and error, it would indeed have taken six months to make two thousand rifles; but modern machinery was so precise that the parts of any gun would fit any other gun of the same pattern, and a well-equipped factory could turn out hundreds of identical rifles a day, like pins.

'And the machine that makes two hundred thousand cartridges a day!' Papa said, and he shook his head in wonderment. Then his mood switched again and he said grimly: 'But how can they ask for the money before the rifles are delivered?'

Papa knew nothing about international trade, and he had assumed the manufacturer would deliver the rifles in Cordova and accept payment there. On the contrary, the payment was required before the weapons left the Birmingham factory.

But Papa was reluctant to ship silver coins across the Atlantic Ocean in barrels. Worse still, he could not hand over the entire family fortune before the arms were safely delivered.

'We'll solve this problem, Papa,' Micky said soothingly. 'That's what merchant banks are for.'

'Go over it again,' Papa said. 'I want to make sure I understand this.'

Micky was pleased to be able to explain something to Papa. 'The bank will pay the manufacturer in Birmingham. It will arrange for the guns to be shipped to Cordova, and insure them on the voyage. When they arrive, the bank will accept payment from you at their office in Cordova.'

'But then they have to ship the silver to England.'

'Not necessarily. They may use it to pay for a cargo of salt beef coming from Cordova to London.'

'How do they make a living?'

'They take a cut of everything. They will pay the rifle manufacturer a discounted price, take a commission on the shipping and insurance, and charge you extra for the guns.'

Papa nodded. He was trying not to show it, but he was impressed, and that made Micky happy.

They left the park and walked along Kensington Gore to the home of Joseph and Augusta Pilaster.

In the seven years since Peter Middleton drowned, Micky had spent every vacation with the Pilasters. After school he had toured Europe with Edward for a year, and he had roomed with Edward during the three years they had spent at Oxford University, drinking and gambling and raising Cain, making only the barest pretence of being students.

Micky had never again kissed Augusta. He would have liked to. He wanted to do more than just kiss her. And he sensed that she might let him. Underneath that veneer of frozen arrogance there was the hot heart of a passionate and sensual woman, he was sure. But he had held back out of prudence. He had achieved something priceless by being accepted almost as a son in one of the richest families in England, and it would be insane to jeopardize that cherished position by seducing Joseph's wife. All the same he could not help daydreaming about it.

Edward's parents had recently moved into a new house. Kensington Gore, which not so long ago had been a country road leading from Mayfair through the fields to the village of Kensington, was now lined, along its south side, by splendid mansions. On the north side of the street were Hyde Park and the gardens of Kensington Palace. It was the perfect location for the home of a rich commercial family.

Micky was not so sure about the style of architecture.

It was certainly striking. It was of red brick and white stone, with big leaded windows on the ground and first floors. Above the first floor was a huge gable, its triangular shape enclosing three rows of windows – six, then four, then two at the apex: bedrooms, presumably, for innumerable relatives, guests and servants. The sides of the gable were stepped, and on the steps were perched stone animals – lions and dragons and monkeys. At the very top was a ship in full sail. Perhaps it represented the slave ship which, according to family legend, was the foundation of the Pilasters' wealth.

'I'm sure there's not another house like this in London,' Micky said as he and his father stood outside staring at it.

Papa replied in Spanish. 'No doubt that is what the lady intended.'

Micky nodded. Papa had not met Augusta, but he had her measure already.

The house also had a big basement. A bridge crossed the basement area and led to the entrance porch. The door was open, and they went in.

Augusta was having a drum, an afternoon tea-party, to show off her house. The oak-panelled hall was jammed with people and servants. Micky and his father handed their hats to a footman then pushed through the crowd to the vast drawing-room at the back of the house. The french windows were open, and the party spilled out on to a flagged terrace and a long garden.

Micky had deliberately chosen to introduce his father at a crowded occasion, for Papa's manners were not always up to London standards, and it was better that the Pilasters should get to know him gradually. Even by Cordovan standards he paid little attention to social niceties, and escorting him around London was like having a lion on a leash. He insisted on carrying his pistol beneath his coat at all times.

Papa did not need Micky to point Augusta out to him.

She stood in the centre of the room, draped in a royal blue silk dress with a low square neckline that revealed the swell of her breasts. As Papa shook her hand she gazed at him with her hypnotic dark eyes and said in a low, velvet voice: 'Sênor Miranda – what a pleasure to meet you at last.'

Papa was immediately entranced. He bowed low over her hand. 'I can never repay your kindness to Miguel,' he said in halting English.

Micky studied her as she cast her spell over his father. She had changed very little since the day he had kissed her in the chapel at Windfield School. The extra line or two around her eyes only made them more fascinating; the touch of silver in her hair enhanced the blackness of the rest; and if she was a little heavier than she had been it made her body more voluptuous.

'Micky has often told me of your splendid ranch,' she was saying to Papa.

Papa lowered his voice. 'You must come and visit us one day.'

God forbid, Micky thought. Augusta in Cordova would be as out of place as a flamingo in a coal mine.

'Perhaps I shall,' Augusta said. 'How far is it?'

'With the new fast ships, only a month.'

He still had hold of her hand, Micky noticed. And his voice had gone furry. He had fallen for her already. Micky felt a stab of jealousy. If anyone was going to flirt with Augusta it should be Micky, not Papa.

'I hear Cordova is a beautiful country,' Augusta said.

Micky prayed Papa would not do anything embarrassing. However, he could be charming when it suited him, and he was now playing the role of romantic South American grandee for Augusta's benefit. 'I can promise you that we would welcome you like the queen you are,' he said in a low voice; and now it was obvious that he was making up to her.

But Augusta was a match for him. 'What an extraordinarily tempting prospect,' she said with a shameless insincerity that went right over Papa's head. Withdrawing her hand from his without missing a beat, she looked over his shoulder and cried: 'Why, Captain Tillotson, how kind of you to come!' And she turned away to greet the latest arrival.

Papa was bereft. It took him a moment to regain his composure. Then he said abruptly: 'Take me to the head of the bank.'

'Certainly,' Micky said nervously. He looked around for Old Seth. The entire Pilaster clan was here, including maiden aunts, nephews and nieces, in-laws and second cousins. He recognized a couple of Members of Parliament and a sprinkling of lesser nobility. Most of the other guests were business connections, Micky judged – and rivals, too, he thought as he saw the thin, upright figure of Ben Greenbourne, head of Greenbournes Bank, said to be the richest man in the world. Ben was the father of Solomon, the boy Micky had always known as Fatty Greenbourne. They had lost touch since school: Fatty had not studied at a university or done a European tour, but had gone straight into his father's business.

The aristocracy generally thought it vulgar to talk about money, but this group had no such inhibitions, and Micky kept hearing the word 'crash'. In the newspapers it was sometimes spelt 'Krach' because it had started in Austria. Share prices were down and the Bank Rate was up, according to Edward, who had recently started work at the family bank. Some people were alarmed, but the Pilasters felt confident that London would not be pulled down with Vienna.

Micky took Papa out through the french windows on to the paved terrace, where wooden benches were placed in the shade of striped awnings. There they found Old Seth, sitting with a rug over his knees despite the warm spring weather. He was weak from some unspecified illness, and he looked as frail as an eggshell, but he had the Pilaster nose, a big curved blade that made him formidable still.

Another guest was gushing over the old man, saying: 'What a shame you aren't well enough to go to the royal levee, Mr Pilaster!'

Micky could have told the woman this was the wrong thing to say to a Pilaster.

'On the contrary, I'm glad of the excuse,' Seth harrumphed. 'I don't see why I should bow the knee to people who have never earned a penny in their lives.'

'But the Prince of Wales – such an honour!'

Seth was in no mood to be argued with – indeed he rarely was – and he now said: 'Young lady, the name of Pilaster is an accepted guarantee of honest dealing in corners of the globe where they've never heard of the Prince of Wales.'

'But Mr Pilaster, you almost sound as if you disapprove of the royal family!' the woman persisted, with a strained attempt at a playful tone.

Seth had not been playful for seventy years. 'I disapprove of idleness,' he said. 'The Bible says, "If any would not work, neither should he eat." St Paul wrote that, in Second Thessalonians, chapter three, verse ten, and he conspicuously omitted to say that royalty were an exception to the rule.'

The woman retired in confusion. Suppressing a grin, Micky said: 'Mr Pilaster, may I present my father, Señor Carlos Miranda, who is over from Cordova for a visit.'

Seth shook Papa's hand. 'Cordova, eh? My bank has an office in your capital city, Palma.'

'I go to the capital very little,' Papa said. 'I have a ranch in Santamaria Province.'

'So you're in the beef business.'

'Yes.'

'Look into refrigeration.'

Papa was baffled. Micky explained: 'Someone has invented a machine for keeping meat cold. If they can find a way to install it in ships, we will be able to send fresh meat all over the world without salting it.'

Papa frowned. 'This could be bad for us. I have a big salting plant.'

'Knock it down,' said Seth. 'Go in for refrigeration.'

Papa did not like people telling him what to do, and Micky felt a little anxious. Out of the corner of his eye he spotted Edward. 'Papa, I want to introduce you to my best friend,' he said. He managed to ease his father away from Seth. 'Allow me to present Edward Pilaster.'

41

Papa examined Edward with a cold, clear-eyed gaze. Edward was not good-looking – he took after his father, not his mother – but he looked like a healthy farm boy, muscular and fair-skinned. Late nights and quantities of wine had not taken their toll – not yet, anyway. Papa shook his hand and said: 'You two have been friends for many years.'

'Soul mates,' Edward said.

Papa frowned, not understanding.

Micky said: 'May we talk business for a moment?'

They stepped off the terrace and on to the newly-laid lawn. The borders were freshly planted, all raw earth and tiny shrubs. 'Papa has been making some large purchases here, and he needs to arrange shipping and finance,' Micky went on. 'It could be the first small piece of business you bring into your family bank.'

Edward looked keen. 'I'll be glad to handle that for you,' he said to Papa. 'Would you like to come into the bank tomorrow morning, so that we can make all the necessary arrangements?'

'I will,' said Papa.

Micky said: 'Tell me something. What if the ship sinks? Who loses – us, or the bank?'

'Neither,' Edward said smugly. 'The cargo will be insured at Lloyd's. We would simply collect the insurance money and ship a new consignment to you. You don't pay until you get your goods. What is the cargo, by the way?'

'Rifles.'

Edward's face fell. 'Oh. Then we can't help you.'

Micky was mystified. 'Why?'

'Because of Old Seth. He's a Methodist, you know. Well, the whole family is, but he's rather more devout than most. Anyway, he won't finance arms sales, and as he's Senior Partner, that's bank policy.'

'The devil it is,' Micky cursed. He shot a fearful look at his father. Fortunately, Papa had not understood the conversation. Micky had a sinking feeling in his stomach. Surely his scheme could not founder on something as stupid as Seth's religion? 'The damned old hypocrite is practically dead, why should he interfere?'

'He is about to retire,' Edward pointed out. 'But I think Uncle Samuel will take over, and he's the same, you know.'

Worse and worse. Samuel was Seth's bachelor son, fifty-three years old and in perfect health. 'We'll just have to go to another merchant bank,' Micky said.

Edward said: 'That should be straightforward, provided you can give a couple of sound business references.'

'References? Why?'

'Well, a bank always takes the risk that the buyer will renege on the deal, leaving them with a cargo of unwanted merchandise on the far side of the globe. They just need some assurance that they're dealing with a respectable businessman.'

What Edward did not realize was that the concept of a respectable businessman did not yet exist in South America. Papa was a *caudillo*, a provincial landowner with a hundred thousand acres of pampas and a workforce of cowboys that doubled as his private army. He wielded power in a way the British had not known since the Middle Ages. It was like asking William the Conqueror for references.

Micky pretended to be unperturbed. 'No doubt we can provide something,' he said. In fact he was stumped. But if he was going to stay in London he had to bring this deal off.

They turned and strolled back towards the crowded terrace, Micky hiding his anxiety. Papa did not yet understand that they had encountered a serious difficulty, but Micky would have to explain it later – and then there would be trouble. Papa had no patience with failure, and his anger was terrifying.

Augusta appeared on the terrace and spoke to Edward. 'Find Hastead for me, Teddy darling,' she said. Hastead was her obsequious Welsh butler. 'There's no cordial left and the wretched man has disappeared.' Edward went off. She favoured Papa with a warm, intimate smile. 'Are you enjoying our little gathering, Señor Miranda?'

'Very well, thank you,' said Papa.

'You must have some tea, or a glass of cordial.'

Papa would have preferred tequila, Micky knew, but alcoholic drink was not served at Methodist tea-parties.

Augusta looked at Micky. Always quick to sense other people's moods, she said: 'I can see that you're not enjoying the party. What's the matter?'

He did not hesitate to confide in her. 'I was hoping Papa could help Edward by bringing new business to the bank, but it involves guns and ammunition, and Edward has just explained that Uncle Seth won't finance weapons.'

'Seth won't be Senior Partner much longer,' Augusta said.

'Apparently Samuel feels the same as his father.'

'Does he?' Augusta said, and her tone was arch. 'And who says that Samuel is to be the next Senior Partner?'

[II]

HUGH PILASTER was wearing a new sky-blue ascot-style cravat, slightly puffed at the neckline and held in place with a pin. He really should have been wearing a new coat, but he earned only £68 a year, so he had to brighten up his old clothes with a new tie. The ascot was the latest fashion, and sky-blue was a daring colour choice; but when he spied his reflection in the huge mirror over the mantelpiece in Aunt Augusta's drawing-room he saw that the blue tie and black suit looked rather fetching with his blue eyes and black hair, and he hoped the ascot gave him an attractively rakish air. Perhaps Florence Stalworthy would think so, anyway. He had started to take an interest in clothes since he met her.

It was a bit embarrassing, living with Augusta and being so poor; but there was a tradition at Pilasters Bank that men were paid what they were worth, regardless of whether they were family members. Another tradition was that everyone started at the bottom. Hugh had been a star pupil at school, and would have been head boy if he had not got into trouble so much; but his education counted for little at the bank, and he was doing the work of an apprentice clerk – and was paid accordingly. His aunt and uncle never offered to help him out financially, so they had to put up with his looking a little shabby.

He did not much care what they thought about his appearance, of course. It was Florence Stalworthy he was worried about. She was a pale, pretty girl, the daughter of the Earl of Stalworthy; but the most important thing about her was that she was interested in Hugh Pilaster. The truth was that Hugh could be fascinated by any girl who would talk to him. This bothered him, because it surely meant that his feelings were shallow; but he could not help it. If a girl touched him accidentally it was enough to make his mouth go dry. He was tormented by curiosity about what their legs looked like under all those layers of skirt and petticoat. There were times when his desire hurt like a wound. He was twenty years old, he had felt like this since he was fifteen, and in those five years he had never kissed anyone except his mother.

A party such as this drum of Augusta's was exquisite torture. Because it was a party, everyone went out of their way to be pleasant, find things to talk about, and show an interest in one another. The girls looked lovely and smiled and sometimes, discreetly, flirted. So many people were crowded into the house that inevitably some of the girls would brush up against Hugh, bump into him as they turned around, touch his arm, or even press their breasts against his back as they squeezed by. He would have a week of restless nights afterwards.

Many of the people here were his relations, inevitably. His father, Tobias, and Edward's father, Joseph, had been brothers. But Hugh's father had withdrawn his capital from the family business, started his own enterprise, gone bankrupt, and killed himself. That was why Hugh had left the expensive Windfield boarding school and become a day-boy at the Folkestone Academy for the Sons of Gentlemen; it was why he started work at nineteen instead of doing a European tour and wasting a few years at a university; it was why he lived with his aunt; and it was why he did not have new clothes to wear to the party. He was a relation, but a poor one; an embarrassment to a family whose pride, confidence and social standing were based on its wealth.

It would never have occurred to any of them to solve the problem by giving him money. Poverty was the punishment for doing business badly, and if you started to ease the pain for failures, why, there would be no incentive to do well. 'You might as well put feather-beds in prison cells,' they would say whenever someone suggested helping life's losers.

His father had been the victim of a financial crisis, but that made no difference. He had failed on 11 May 1866, a date known to bankers as Black Friday. On that day a bill-broker called Overend and Gurney Ltd had gone bankrupt for five million pounds, and many firms were dragged down, including the London Joint Stock Bank and Sir Samuel Peto's building company, as well as Tobias Pilaster and Co. But there were no excuses in business, according to the Pilaster philosophy. Just at present there was a financial crisis, and no doubt one or two firms would fail before it was over; but the Pilasters were vigorously protecting themselves, shedding their weaker clients, tightening credit, and ruthlessly turning down all but the most unquestionably secure new business. Self-preservation was the highest duty of the banker, they believed.

Well, I'm a Pilaster, too, Hugh thought. I may not have the Pilaster nose, but I understand about self-preservation. There was a rage that boiled in his heart sometimes when he brooded about what had happened to his father, and it made him all the more determined to become the richest and most respected of the whole damn crew. His cheap day school had taught him useful arithmetic and science while his better-off cousin Edward was struggling with Latin and Greek; and not going to university had given him an early start in the business. He was never tempted to follow a different way of life, become a painter or a Member of Parliament or a clergyman. Finance was in his blood. He could give the current Bank Rate quicker than he could say whether it was raining. He was determined he would never be as smug and hypocritical as his older relatives, but all the same he was going to be a banker.

However, he did not think about it much. Most of the time he thought about girls.

He stepped out of the drawing-room on to the terrace and saw Augusta bearing down on him with a girl in tow.

'Dear Hugh,' she said, 'here's your friend Miss Bodwin.'

Hugh groaned inwardly. Rachel Bodwin was a tall, intellectual girl of radical opinions. She was not pretty –

she had dull brown hair and light eyes set rather close together – but she was lively and interesting, full of subversive ideas, and Hugh had liked her a lot when he first came to London to work at the bank. But Augusta had decided he should marry Rachel, and that had ruined the relationship. Before that they had argued fiercely and freely about divorce, religion, poverty and votes for women. Since Augusta had begun her campaign to bring them together, they just stood and exchanged awkward chit-chat.

'How lovely you look, Miss Bodwin,' he said automatically.

'You're very kind,' she replied in a bored tone.

Augusta was turning away when she caught sight of Hugh's tie. 'Heavens!' she exclaimed. 'What is that? You look like an innkeeper!'

Hugh blushed crimson. If he could have thought of a sharp rejoinder he would have risked it, but nothing came to mind, and all he could do was mutter: 'It's just a new tie. It's called an ascot.'

'You shall give it to the boot-boy tomorrow,' she said, and she turned away.

Resentment flared in Hugh's breast against the fate that forced him to live with his overbearing aunt. 'Women ought not to comment on a man's clothes,' he said moodily. 'It's not ladylike.'

Rachel said: 'I think women should comment on anything that interests them, so I shall say that I like your tie, and that it matches your eyes.'

Hugh smiled at her, feeling better. She was very nice, after all. However, it was not her niceness that caused Augusta to want him to marry her. Rachel was the daughter of a lawyer specializing in commercial contracts. Her family had no money other than her father's professional income, and on the social ladder they were several rungs below the Pilasters; indeed they would not be at this party at all except that Mr Bodwin had done useful work for the bank. Rachel was a girl in a low station in life, and by marrying her Hugh would confirm his status as a lesser breed of Pilaster; and that was what Augusta wanted.

He was not completely averse to the thought of proposing to Rachel. Augusta had hinted that she would give him a generous wedding present if he married her choice. But it was not the wedding present that tempted him, it was the thought that every night he would be able to get into bed with a woman, and lift her nightdress up, past her ankles and her knees, past her thighs—

'Don't look at me that way,' Rachel said shrewdly. 'I only said I liked your tie.'

Hugh blushed again. Surely she could not guess what had been in his mind? His thoughts about girls were so grossly physical that he felt ashamed of himself much of the time. 'Sorry,' he mumbled.

'What a lot of Pilasters there are,' she said brightly, looking around. 'How do you cope with them all?'

Hugh looked around too, and saw Florence Stalworthy come in. She was extraordinarily pretty, with her fair curls falling over her delicate shoulders, a pink dress trimmed with lace and silk ribbons, and ostrich feathers in her hat. She met Hugh's eye and smiled at him across the room.

'I can see I've lost your attention,' Rachel said with characteristic bluntness.

'I'm most awfully sorry,' Hugh said.

Rachel touched his arm. 'Hugh, dear, listen to me for a moment. I like you. You're one of the few people in London society who aren't unspeakably dull. But I don't love you and I will never marry you, no matter how often your aunt throws us together.'

Hugh was startled. 'I say—' he began.

49

But she had not finished. 'And I know you feel much the same about me, so please don't pretend to be heartbroken.'

After a stunned moment, Hugh grinned. This directness was what he liked about her. But he supposed she was right: liking was not loving. He was not sure what love was, but she seemed to know. 'Does this mean we can go back to quarrelling about women's suffrage?' he said cheerfully.

'Yes, but not today. I'm going to talk to your old school friend, Señor Miranda.'

Hugh frowned. 'Micky couldn't spell "suffrage" let alone tell you what it means.'

'All the same, half the debutantes in London are swooning over him.'

'I can't imagine why.'

'He's a male Florence Stalworthy,' Rachel said, and with that she left him.

Hugh frowned, thinking about that. Micky knew Hugh was a poor relation and he treated him accordingly, so it was difficult for Hugh to be objective about him. He was very personable, and always beautifully dressed. He reminded Hugh of a cat, sleek and sensual with glossy fur. It was not quite the thing to be so carefully groomed, and men said he was not very manly, but women did not seem to care about that.

Hugh followed Rachel with his eyes as she crossed the room to where Micky stood with his father, talking to Edward's sister Clementine, Aunt Madeleine, and young Aunt Beatrice. Now Micky turned to Rachel, giving her his full attention as he shook her hand and said something that made her laugh. He was always talking to three or four women, Hugh realized.

All the same Hugh disliked the suggestion that Florence was somehow like Micky. She was attractive and popular,

as he was, but Micky was something of a cad, Hugh
thought.

He made his way to Florence's side, feeling thrilled but
nervous. 'Lady Florence, how are you?'

She smiled dazzlingly. 'What an extraordinary house!'

'Do you like it?'

'I'm not sure.'

'That's what most people say.'

She laughed as if he had made a witty remark, and he
felt inordinately pleased.

He went on: 'It's very modern, you know. There are five
bathrooms! And a huge boiler in the basement warms the
whole place with hot-water pipes.'

'Perhaps the stone ship on top of the gable is a little too
much.'

Hugh lowered his voice. 'I think so too. It reminds me of
the cow's head outside a butcher's shop.'

She giggled again. Hugh was pleased that he could make
her laugh. He decided it would be nice to get her away
from the crowd. 'Come and see the garden,' he said.

'How lovely.'

It was not lovely, having only just been planted, but that
did not matter in the least. He led her out of the drawing-
room on to the terrace but there he was waylaid by
Augusta, who shot him a look of reproof and said: 'Lady
Florence, how kind of you to come. Edward will show you
the garden.' She grabbed Edward, who was standing
nearby, and ushered the two of them away before Hugh
could say a word. He clenched his teeth in frustration and
vowed he would not let her get away with this. 'Hugh,
dear, I know you want to talk to Rachel,' she said. She took
Hugh's arm and moved him back inside, and there was
nothing he could do to resist her, short of snatching his arm

51

away and making a scene. Rachel was standing with Micky Miranda and his father. 'Micky, I want your father to meet my brother-in-law, Mr Samuel Pilaster.' She detached Micky and his father and took them off, leaving Hugh with Rachel again.

Rachel was laughing. 'You can't argue with her.'

'It would be like arguing with a dashed railway train,' Hugh fumed. Through the window he could see the bustle of Florence's dress as it swayed down the garden beside Edward.

Rachel followed his eyes and said: 'Go after her.'

He grinned. 'Thanks.'

He hurried down the garden. As he caught up, a wicked idea occurred to him. Why should he not play his aunt's game and detach Edward from Florence? Augusta would be spitting mad when she found out – but it would be worth it for the sake of a few minutes alone in the garden with Florence. To hell with it, he thought. 'Oh, Edward,' he said. 'Your mother asked me to send you to her. She's in the hall.'

Edward did not question this: he was used to sudden changes of mind by his mother. He said: 'Please excuse me, Lady Florence.' He left them and went into the house.

Florence said: 'Did she really send for him?'

'No.'

'You're so bad!' she said, but she was smiling.

He looked into her eyes, basking in the sunshine of her approval. There would be hell to pay later, but he would suffer much worse for the sake of a smile like that. 'Come and see the orchard,' he said.

[III]

AUGUSTA WAS amused by Papa Miranda. Such a squat peasant of a man! He was so different from his lithe, elegant son. Augusta was very fond of Micky Miranda. She always felt more of a woman when she was with him, even though he was so young. He had a way of looking at her as if she were the most desirable thing he had ever seen. There were times when she wished he would do more than just look. It was a foolish wish, of course, but all the same she felt it now and again.

She had been alarmed by their conversation about Seth. Micky assumed that when Old Seth died or retired, his son Samuel would take over as Senior Partner of Pilasters Bank. Micky would not have made that assumption on his own: he must have picked it up from the family. Augusta did not want Samuel to take over. She wanted the job for her husband Joseph, who was Seth's nephew.

She glanced through the drawing-room window and saw the four partners in Pilasters Bank together on the terrace. Three were Pilasters: Seth, Samuel and Joseph – the early nineteenth-century Methodists had favoured Biblical names. Old Seth looked like the invalid he was, sitting with a blanket over his knees, outliving his usefulness. Beside him was his son. Samuel was not as distinguished-looking as his father. He had the same beak-like nose, but below it was a rather soft mouth with bad teeth. Tradition would favour him to succeed because he was the eldest of the partners after Seth. Augusta's husband Joseph was speaking, making a point to his uncle and his cousin with short jabbing movements of his hand, a characteristically impatient gesture. He, too, had the Pilaster nose, but the rest of his features were rather irregular and he was losing his hair. The fourth partner was standing back, listening with his arms folded. He was Major George Hartshorn, husband of Joseph's sister Madeleine. A former army officer, he had a prominent scar on his forehead from a wound received twenty years ago in the Crimean War. He was no hero, however: his horse had been frightened by a steam-traction engine and he had fallen and banged his head on the wheel of a kitchen wagon. He had retired from the army and joined the bank when he married Madeleine. An amiable man who followed where others led, he was not clever enough to run the bank, and anyway they had never had a Senior Partner whose name was not Pilaster. The only serious candidates were Samuel and Joseph.

Technically, the decision was made by a vote of the partners. By tradition, the family generally reached a consensus. In reality, Augusta was determined to have her way. But it would not be easy.

The Senior Partner of Pilasters Bank was one of the most important people in the world. His decision to grant a loan could save a monarch; his refusal could start a revolution. Along with a handful of others — J. P. Morgan, the Rothschilds, Ben Greenbourne — he held the prosperity of nations in his hands. He was flattered by heads of state, consulted by prime ministers, and courted by diplomats; and his wife was fawned upon by them all.

Joseph wanted the job, but he had no subtlety. Augusta was terrified that he would let the opportunity slip through his fingers. Left to himself he might say bluntly that he would like to be considered, then simply allow the family to decide. It might not occur to him that there were other things he should do to make sure he won the contest. For instance, he would never do anything to discredit his rival.

Augusta would have to find ways to do that for him.

She had no trouble identifying Samuel's weakness. At

the age of fifty-three he was a bachelor, and lived with a young man who was blithely referred to as his 'secretary'. Until now the family had paid no attention to Samuel's domestic arrangements, but Augusta was wondering if she could change all that.

Samuel had to be handled carefully. He was a fussy, finicky man, the kind who would change his entire outfit of clothes because a drop of wine had fallen on the knee of his trousers; but he was not weak, and could not be intimidated. A frontal assault was not the way to attack him.

She would have no regrets about injuring him. She had never liked him. He sometimes acted as if he found her amusing, and he had a way of refusing to take her at face value that she found deeply annoying.

As she moved among her guests, she put out of her mind the irritating reluctance of her nephew Hugh to pay court to a perfectly suitable young girl. That branch of the family had always been troublesome and she was not going to let it distract her from the more important problem that Micky had alerted her to, the threat of Samuel.

She spotted her sister-in-law, Madeleine Hartshorn, in the hall. Poor Madeleine, you could tell she was Joseph's sister, for she had the Pilaster nose. On some of the men it looked distinguished, but no woman could look anything but plain with a great beak like that.

Madeleine and Augusta had once been rivals. Years ago, when Augusta first married Joseph, Madeleine had resented the way the family began to centre around Augusta – even though Madeleine never had the magnetism or the energy to do what Augusta did, arranging weddings and funerals, matchmaking, patching up quarrels, and organizing support for the sick, the pregnant and the bereaved. Madeleine's attitude had come close to

55

causing a rift within the family. Then she had delivered a weapon into Augusta's hands. One afternoon Augusta had stepped into an exclusive Bond Street silverware shop just in time to see Madeleine slipping into the back of the store. Augusta had lingered for a while, pretending to hesitate over a toast rack, until she saw a handsome young man follow the same route. She had heard that the rooms above such stores were sometimes used for romantic rendezvous, and she was now almost certain that Madeleine was having a love affair. A five pound note had persuaded the proprietress of the shop, a Mrs Baxter, to divulge the name of the young man, Viscount Tremain.

Augusta had been genuinely shocked, but the first thought that had occurred to her was that what Madeleine could do with Viscount Tremain, Augusta could do with Micky Miranda. But that was out of the question, of course. Besides, if Madeleine could be found out, the same could happen to Augusta.

It could have ruined Madeleine socially. A man who had a love affair was considered wicked but romantic; a woman who did the same was a whore. If her secret got out she would be shunned by society and her family would be ashamed of her. Augusta's first thought was to use the secret to control Madeleine, holding over her head the threat of exposure. But that would make Madeleine forever hostile. It was foolish to multiply enemies unnecessarily. There had to be a way she could disarm Madeleine and at the same time make an ally of her. After much thought she had evolved a strategy. Instead of intimidating Madeleine with the information, she pretended to be on her side. 'A word to the wise, dear Madeleine,' she had whispered. 'Mrs Baxter cannot be trusted. Tell your viscount to find a more discreet rendezvous.' Madeleine had begged her to keep the secret and had been pathetically grateful when

Augusta willingly promised eternal silence. Since then there had been no rivalry between them.

Now Augusta took Madeleine's arm, saying: 'Come and see my room – I think you'll like it.'

On the first floor of the house were her bedroom and dressing-room, Joseph's bedroom and dressing-room, and a study. She led Madeleine into her bedroom, closed the door, and waited for her reaction.

She had furnished the room in the latest Japanese style, with fretwork chairs, peacock-feather wallpaper and a display of porcelain over the mantelpiece. There was an immense wardrobe painted with Japanese motifs, and the window-seat in the bay was partly concealed by dragonfly curtains.

'Augusta, how daring!' said Madeleine.

'Thank you.' Augusta was almost completely happy with the effect. 'There was a better curtain material I wanted but Liberty's had sold out of it. Come and see Joseph's room.'

She took Madeleine through the communicating door. Joseph's bedroom was furnished in a more moderate version of the same style, with dark leather-paper on the walls and brocade curtains. Augusta was especially proud of a lacquered display cabinet that held his collection of jewelled snuff-boxes.

'Joseph is so eccentric,' said Madeleine, looking at the snuff-boxes.

Augusta smiled. Her husband was not in the least eccentric, generally speaking, but it was odd for a hard-headed Methodist businessman to collect something so frivolous and exquisite, and the whole family found it amusing. 'He says they're an investment,' she said. A diamond necklace for her would have been an equally good investment, but he never bought her such things, for

Methodists considered jewellery to be a needless extravagance.

'A man should have a hobby,' Madeleine said. 'It keeps him out of trouble.'

Out of whorehouses was what she meant. The implied reference to men's peccadilloes reminded Augusta of her purpose. Softly, softly, she said to herself. 'Madeleine, dear, what *are* we going to do about cousin Samuel and his "secretary"?'

Madeleine looked puzzled. 'Ought we to do something?'

'If Samuel is to become Senior Partner, we must.'

'Why?'

'My dear, the Senior Partner of Pilasters has to meet ambassadors, heads of state, even royalty – he must be quite, *quite* irreproachable in his private life.'

Comprehension dawned, and Madeleine flushed. 'Surely you're not suggesting that Samuel is in some way . . . depraved?'

That was exactly what Augusta was suggesting, but she did not want to say it outright, for fear of provoking Madeleine to defend her cousin. 'I trust that I shall never know,' she said evasively. 'The important thing is what people think.'

Madeleine was unconvinced. 'Do you really suppose people think . . . that?'

Augusta forced herself to have patience with Madeleine's delicacy. 'My dear, we are both married women, and we know what men are like. They have animal appetites. The world assumes that a single man of fifty-three living with a pretty boy is vicious, and heaven knows, in most cases the world is probably right.'

Madeleine frowned, looking worried. Before she could say anything else there was a knock at the door and Edward came in. 'What is it, mother?' he asked.

Augusta was annoyed by the interruption and she had no idea what the boy was talking about. 'What do you mean?'

'You sent for me.'

'I most certainly did not. I told you to show Lady Florence around the garden.'

Edward looked hurt. 'Hugh said you wanted to see me!'

Augusta understood. 'Did he? And I suppose he is showing Lady Florence the garden now?'

Edward saw what she was getting at. 'I do believe he is,' he said, looking wounded. 'Don't be cross with me, Mother, please.'

Augusta melted instantly. 'Don't worry, Teddy dear,' she said. 'Hugh is such a sly boy.' But if he thought he could outwit his Aunt Augusta he was also foolish.

This distraction had irritated her, but on reflection she thought she had said enough to Madeleine about Cousin Samuel. At this stage all she wanted was to plant the seed of doubt: anything more might be too heavy-handed. She decided to leave well enough alone. She ushered her sister-in-law and her son out of the room, saying: 'Now I must return to my guests.'

They went downstairs. The party was going well, to judge by the cacophony of talk, laughter, and a hundred silver teaspoons clinking in bone china saucers. Augusta briefly checked the dining-room where the servants were dispensing lobster salad, fruit cake and iced drinks. She moved through the hall, speaking a word or two to each guest who caught her eye, but looking for a particular one – Florence's mother, Lady Stalworthy.

She was worried by the possibility that Hugh might marry Florence. Hugh was already doing far too well at the bank. He had the quick commercial brain of a barrow-boy and the engaging manners of a card-sharp. Even Joseph spoke approvingly of him, oblivious of the threat to their own son. Marriage to the daughter of an earl would give Hugh social status to add to his native talents, and then he would be a dangerous rival to Edward. Dear Teddy did not have Hugh's superficial charm or his head for figures, so he needed all the help Augusta could give him.

She found Lady Stalworthy standing in the bay window of the drawing-room. She was a pretty middle-aged woman in a pink dress and a little straw hat with silk flowers all over it. Augusta wondered anxiously how she would feel about Hugh and Florence. Hugh was no great catch, but from Lady Stalworthy's point of view he was not a disaster. Florence was the youngest of three daughters, and the other two had married well, so Lady Stalworthy might be indulgent. Augusta had to prevent that. But how?

She stood at Lady Stalworthy's side and saw that she was watching Hugh and Florence in the garden. Hugh was explaining something, and Florence's eyes sparkled with pleasure as she looked at him and listened. 'The careless happiness of youth,' said Augusta.

'Hugh seems a nice boy,' Lady Stalworthy said.

Augusta looked hard at her for a moment. Lady Stalworthy had a dreamy smile on her face. She had once been as pretty as her daughter, Augusta guessed. Now she was remembering her own girlhood. She needed to be brought down to earth with a thump, Augusta decided. 'How quickly they pass, those carefree days.'

'But so idyllic while they last.'

It was time for the poison. 'Hugh's father died, as you know,' Augusta said. 'And his mother lives very quietly at Folkestone, so Joseph and I feel an obligation to take a parental interest.' She paused. 'It is hardly necessary for me to say that an alliance with your family would be a remarkable triumph for Hugh.'

'How kind of you to say that,' said Lady Stalworthy, as if she had been paid a pretty compliment. 'The Pilasters themselves are a family of distinction.'

'Thank you. If Hugh works hard he will one day earn a comfortable living.'

Lady Stalworthy looked a little taken aback. 'His father left nothing at all, then?'

'No.' Augusta needed to let her know that Hugh would get no money from his uncles when he married. She said: 'He will have to work his way up in the bank, living on his salary.'

'Ah, yes,' said Lady Stalworthy, and her face showed a hint of disappointment. 'Florence has a small independence, happily.'

Augusta's heart sank. So Florence had money of her own. That was bad news. Augusta wondered how much it was. The Stalworthys were not as rich as the Pilasters – few people were – but they were comfortable, Augusta believed. At any rate, Hugh's poverty was not enough to turn Lady Stalworthy against him. Augusta would have to use stronger measures. 'Dear Florence would be such a help to Hugh . . . a stabilizing influence, I feel sure.'

'Yes,' said Lady Stalworthy vaguely, and then she frowned. 'Stabilizing?'

Augusta hesitated. This kind of thing was dangerous, but the risk had to be taken. 'I never listen to gossip, and I'm sure you don't either,' she said. 'Tobias *was* quite unfortunate, of that there is no doubt, but Hugh shows *hardly* any sign of having inherited the weakness.'

'Good,' said Lady Stalworthy, but her face showed deep anxiety.

'All the same, Joseph and I would be very happy to see him married to such a sensible girl as Florence. One feels she would be firm with him, if . . .' Augusta trailed off.

'I . . .' Lady Stalworthy swallowed. 'I don't seem to recall just what his father's weakness was.'

'Well, it wasn't true, really.'

'Strictly between you and me, of course.'

'Perhaps I shouldn't have raised it.'

'But I must know everything, for my daughter's sake. I'm sure you understand.'

'Gambling,' Augusta said in a lowered voice. She did not want to be overheard: there were people here who would know she was lying. 'It was what led him to take his own life. The shame, you know.' Pray heaven the Stalworthys don't bother to check the truth of this, she thought fervently.

'I thought his business failed.'

'That, too.'

'How tragic.'

'Admittedly, Joseph has had to pay Hugh's debts once or twice, but he has spoken very firmly to the boy, and we feel sure it will not happen again.'

'That's reassuring,' said Lady Stalworthy, but her face told a different story.

Augusta felt she had probably said enough. The pretence that she was in favour of the match was wearing dangerously thin. She glanced out of the window again. Florence was laughing at something Hugh was saying, throwing her head back and showing her teeth in a way that was rather . . . unseemly. He was practically eating her up with his eyes. Everyone at the party could see they were attracted to one another. 'I judge it won't be long before matters come to a head,' Augusta said.

'Perhaps they have talked enough for one day,' Lady Stalworthy said with a troubled look. 'I had better intervene. Do excuse me.'

'Of course.'

Lady Stalworthy headed rapidly for the garden.

Augusta felt relieved. She had carried off another delicate conversation. Lady Stalworthy was suspicious of Hugh now, and once a mother began to feel uneasy about a suitor she rarely came to favour him in the end.

She looked around and spotted Beatrice Pilaster, another sister-in-law. Joseph had had two brothers: one was Tobias, Hugh's father, and the other was William, always called Young William because he was born twenty-three years after Joseph. William was now twenty-five and not yet a partner in the bank. Beatrice was his wife. She was like a large puppy, happy and clumsy and eager to be everyone's friend. Augusta decided to speak to her about Samuel and his secretary. She went over to her and said: 'Beatrice, dear, would you like to see my bedroom?'

[IV]

MICKY AND HIS father left the party and set out to walk back to their lodgings in Camberwell. Their route lay entirely through parks – first Hyde Park, then Green Park, and St James's Park – until they reached the river. They stopped in the middle of Westminster Bridge to rest for a spell and look at the view.

On the north shore of the river was the greatest city in the world. Upstream were the Houses of Parliament, built in a modern imitation of the neighbouring thirteenth-century Westminster Abbey. Downstream they could see the gardens of Whitehall, the Duke of Buccleuch's palace, and the vast brick edifice of the new Charing Cross Railway Station.

The docks were out of sight, and no big ships came this far up, but the river was busy with small boats and barges and pleasure-cruisers, a pretty sight in the evening sun.

The southern shore might have been in a different country. It was the site of the Lambeth potteries, and there, in mud fields dotted with ramshackle workshops, crowds of grey-faced men and ragged women were still at work boiling bones, sorting rubbish, firing kilns and pouring paste into moulds to make the drain-pipes and chimney-pots needed by the fast-expanding city. The smell was strong even here on the bridge, a quarter of a mile away. The squat hovels in which the workers lived were crowded around the walls of Lambeth Palace, the London home of the Archbishop of Canterbury, like the filth left by high tide on the muddy foreshore. Despite the nearness of the archbishop's palace the neighbourhood was known as the Devil's Acre, presumably because the fires and the smoke, the shuffling workers and the awful smell made people think of Hell.

Micky's lodgings were in Camberwell, a respectable suburb beyond the potteries; but he and his father hesitated on the bridge, reluctant to plunge into the Devil's Acre. Micky was still cursing the scrupulous Methodist conscience of Old Seth Pilaster for frustrating his plans. 'We will solve this problem about shipping the rifles, Papa,' he said. 'Don't worry about it.'

Papa shrugged. 'Who is standing in our way?' he asked.

It was a simple question, but it had a deep meaning in the Miranda family. When they had an intractable problem, they asked: *Who is standing in our way?* It really meant: *Who do we have to kill to get this done?* It brought back to Micky all the barbarism of life in Santamaria Province, all the grisly legends he preferred to forget: the story about how Papa had punished his mistress for being unfaithful to

64

him by putting a rifle up her and pulling the trigger; the time a Jewish family opened a store next to his in the provincial capital, so he set fire to it and burned the man and his wife and children alive; the one about the dwarf who had dressed up to look like Papa during the carnival, and made everyone laugh by strutting up and down in a perfect imitation of Papa's walk – until Papa calmly went up to the dwarf, drew a pistol, and blew his head off.

Even in Cordova this was not normal, but there Papa's reckless brutality had made him a man to be feared. Here in England it would get him thrown in jail. 'I don't anticipate the need for drastic action,' Micky said, trying to cover his nervousness with an air of unconcern.

'For now, there is no hurry,' Papa said. 'Winter is beginning at home. There will be no fighting until the summer.' He gave Micky a hard look. 'But I *must* have the rifles by the end of October.'

That look made Micky feel weak at the knees. He leaned against the stone parapet of the bridge to steady himself. 'I'll see to it, Papa, don't worry,' he said anxiously.

Papa nodded as if there could be no doubt about it. They were silent for a minute. Out of the blue, Papa said: 'I want you to stay in London.'

Micky felt his shoulders slump with relief. It was what he had been hoping for. He must have done something right, then. 'I think it might be a good idea, Papa,' he said, trying to hide his eagerness.

Then Papa dropped his bombshell. 'But your allowance will stop.'

'What?'

'The family can't keep you. You must support yourself.'

Micky was appalled. Papa's meanness was as legendary as his violence, but still this was unexpected. The Mirandas were rich. Papa had thousands of head of cattle, monopolized all horse-dealing over a huge territory, rented land to small farmers and owned most of the stores in Santamaria Province.

It was true that their money did not buy much in England. Back home a Cordovan silver dollar would get you a slap-up meal, a bottle of rum and a whore for the night; here it would hardly stretch to a cheap meal and a glass of weak beer. That had come as a blow to Micky when he went to Windfield School. He had managed to supplement his allowance by playing cards, but he had found it hard to make ends meet until he befriended Edward. Even now Edward paid for all the expensive entertainments they shared: the opera, visits to racecourses, hunting and whores. Still, Micky needed a basic income to pay his rent, tailor's bills, subscriptions to the gentlemen's clubs that were an essential element of London life, and tips to servants. How did Papa expect him to find that? Take a job? The idea was appalling. No member of the Miranda family worked for wages.

He was about to ask how he was expected to live on no money when Papa abruptly changed the subject and said: 'I will now tell you what the rifles are for. We are going to take over the desert.'

Micky did not understand. The Miranda property covered a big area of Santamaria Province. Bordering their land was a smaller property owned by the Delabarca family. To the north of both was land so arid that neither Papa nor his neighbour had ever bothered to claim it. 'What do we want the desert for?' Micky said.

'Beneath the dust there is a mineral called nitrate. It's used as a fertilizer, much better than dung. It can be shipped all over the world and sold for high prices. The reason I want you to stay in London is to take charge of selling it.'

66

'How do we know this stuff is there?'

'Delabarca has started mining it. It has made his family rich.'

Micky felt excited. This could transform the family's future. Not instantly, of course; not soon enough to solve the problem of how he would live with no allowance. But in the long term. . . .

'We have to act fast,' Papa said. 'Wealth is power, and the Delabarca family will soon be stronger than we are. Before that happens, we have to destroy them.'

CHAPTER TWO

June

[I]

Whitehaven House
Kensington Gore
London, S.W.
June 2nd, 1873

My dear Florence,
Where are you? I hoped to see you at Mrs Bridewell's ball,
then at Richmond, then at the Muncasters' on Saturday . . .
but you weren't at any of them! Write me a line and say
you're still alive.

 Affectionately yours,
 Hugh Pilaster.

23, Park Lane
London, W.
June 3rd, 1873

To Hugh Pilaster, Esq.
Sir:
You will oblige me by not communicating with my daughter
under any circumstances whatsoever henceforth.

 Stalworthy.

Whitehaven House
Kensington Gore
London, S.W.
June 6th, 1873

Dearest Florence,

At last I have found a confidential messenger to smuggle a
note to you. Why have you been hidden away from me? Have
I offended your parents? Or – which heaven forbid – you?
Your cousin Jane will bring your reply to me. Write it quickly!

With fond regards,

Hugh.

Stalworthy Manor
Stalworthy
Buckinghamshire
June 7th, 1873

Dear Hugh,

I am forbidden to see you because you are a gambler like
your father. I am truly sorry but I must believe that my
parents know what is best for me.

Sorrowfully,

Florence.

Whitehaven House
Kensington Gore
London, S.W.
June 8th, 1873

Dear Mother,

A young lady has just rejected me because my father was a
gambler. Is it true? Please answer right away. I must know!

Your loving son,

Hugh.

2, Wellington Villas
Folkestone
Kent
June 9th, 1873

My dear son,

I never knew your father to gamble. I cannot imagine who would say such a wicked thing about him. He lost his money in a business collapse, as you have always been told. There was no other cause.

I hope you are well and happy, my dear, and that your beloved will accept you. I continue much the same. Your sister Dorothy sends her best love, as does,

Your Mother.

Whitehaven House
Kensington Gore
London, S.W.
June 10th, 1873

Dear Florence,

I believe someone may have told you a wrong thing about my father. His business failed, it is true. It was no fault of his own: a large firm called Overend and Gurney went bankrupt for five million pounds, and many of their creditors were destroyed. He took his own life the same day. But he never gambled; and nor do I.

If you explain this to the noble earl your father, I believe all will be well.

Fondly yours,
Hugh.

Stalworthy Manor
Stalworthy
Buckinghamshire
June 11th, 1873

Hugh,

Writing falsehoods to me will do no good. I now know for sure that my parents' advice to me is right, and I must forget you.
  Florence.

Whitehaven House
Kensington Gore
London, S.W.
June 12th, 1873

Dear Florence,

You must believe me! It is possible that I have not been told the truth about my father – although I cannot in all sincerity doubt my mother's word – but in my own case I *know* the truth! When I was fourteen years old I put a shilling on the Derby and lost it, and since then I have never seen the point of gambling. When I see you I will swear an oath.
  In hope –
  Hugh.

FOLJAMBE & MERRIWEATHER, SOLICITORS
GRAYS'S INN
LONDON, W.C.
June 13th, 1873

To Hugh Pilaster, Esq.
Sir:
We are instructed by our client, the Earl of Stalworthy, to require you to desist from communication with his daughter.

Please be informed that the noble earl will take any and all necessary steps, including a High Court injunction, to enforce his will in this matter, unless you refrain immediately.

For Messrs. Foljambe & Merriweather,

Albert C. Merriweather.

Hugh –

She showed your last letter to my aunt, her mother. They have taken her to Paris until the end of the London Season, and then they go to Yorkshire. It is no good – she no longer cares for you. Sorry –

Jane.

[II]

THE ARGYLL ROOMS were the most popular place of entertainment in London, but Hugh had never been there. It would never have occurred to him to visit such a place: although not actually a brothel, it had a low reputation. However, a few days after Florence Stalworthy finally rejected him, Edward casually invited Hugh to join him and Micky for an evening's debauchery, and he accepted.

Hugh did not spend much time with his cousin. Edward had always been spoilt rotten, a bully and a slacker who got others to do his work. Hugh had long ago been cast in the role of black sheep of the family, following in his father's footsteps. They had little in common. But despite that Hugh decided to try the pleasures of dissipation. Low dives and loose women were a way of life for thousands of upper-class Englishmen. Perhaps they knew best: perhaps this, rather than true love, was the way to happiness.

In fact he was not sure whether he had truly been in love with Florence. He was angry that her parents had turned her against him, even more so because the reason was a wicked falsehood about his father. But he found, somewhat to his shame, that he was not heartbroken. He thought about Florence often, but nevertheless he continued to sleep well, eat heartily, and concentrate on his work without difficulty. Did that mean he had never loved her? The girl he liked best in the whole world, apart from his six-year-old sister Dotty, was Rachel Bodwin, and he had certainly toyed with the idea of marrying her. Was that love? He did not know. Perhaps he was too young to understand love. Or perhaps it simply had not happened to him yet.

The Argyll Rooms were next door to a church in Great Windmill Street, just off Piccadilly Circus. Edward paid a shilling admission for each of them and they went inside. The three of them wore evening dress: black tail-coats with silk lapels, black trousers with silk braid, low-cut white waistcoats, white shirts and white bow-ties. Edward's suit was new and expensive; Micky's rather cheaper, but fashionably cut; and Hugh's was inherited from his father.

The ballroom was an extravagantly gas-lit arena, with huge gilt mirrors intensifying the brilliant light. The dance floor was crowded with couples, and behind an elaborate gold trellis-work screen a half-concealed orchestra was playing a vigorous polka. Some of the men wore evening dress, a sign that they were upper-class people going slumming; but most wore respectable black daytime suits, identifying them as clerks and small businessmen.

Above the ballroom was a shadowed gallery. Edward

pointed to it and said to Hugh: 'If you make friends with a dollymop, you can pay another shilling and take her up there: plush seats, dim light, and blind waiters.'

Hugh felt dazzled, not just by the lights but by the possibilities. All around him were girls who had come here for the sole purpose of flirting! Some were with boyfriends but others had come alone, intending to dance with total strangers. And they were all dressed up to the nines, in evening gowns with bustles, many of them cut very low at the neckline, and the most amazing hats. But he noticed that on the dance floor they all modestly wore their cloaks. And Micky and Edward had assured him that they were not prostitutes but ordinary girls, shop assistants and parlourmaids and dressmakers.

'How do you meet them?' Hugh asked. 'Surely you don't just accost them like streetwalkers?'

Edward answered him by pointing to a tall, distinguished-looking man in white-tie-and-tails, who wore some kind of badge and appeared to be supervising the dancing. 'That's the master of ceremonies. He'll effect an introduction, if you tip him.'

The atmosphere was a curious but exciting mixture of respectability and licence, Hugh found.

The polka ended and some of the dancers returned to their tables. Edward pointed and cried: 'Well I'm damned, there's Fatty Greenbourne!'

Hugh followed his finger and saw their old schoolmate, bigger than ever, bulging out of his white waistcoat. On his arm was a stunningly beautiful girl. Fatty and the girl sat down at a table, and Micky said quietly: 'Why don't we join them for a while?'

Hugh was keen for a closer look at the girl, and he assented readily. The three young men threaded their way through the tables. 'Good evening, Fatty!' Edward said cheerfully.

'Hello, you lot,' he replied. 'People call me Solly nowadays,' he added amiably.

Hugh had seen Solly now and again in the City, London's financial district. For some years Solly had been working at the head office of his family's bank, which was just around the corner from Pilasters. Unlike Hugh, Edward had only been working in the City for a few weeks, which was why he had not previously run into Solly.

'We thought we'd join you,' Edward said casually, and looked an inquiry at the girl.

Solly turned to his companion. 'Miss Robinson, may I present some old school friends: Edward Pilaster, Hugh Pilaster, and Micky Miranda.'

Miss Robinson's reaction was startling. She went pale beneath her rouge and said: 'Pilaster? Not the same family as Tobias Pilaster?'

'My father was Tobias Pilaster,' said Hugh. 'How do you know the name?'

She recovered her composure quickly. 'My father used to work for Tobias Pilaster and Co. As a child, I used to wonder who Co was.' They laughed, and the moment of tension passed. She added: 'Would you lads like to sit down?'

There was a bottle of champagne on the table. Solly poured some for Miss Robinson and called for more glasses. 'Well, this is a real reunion of old Windfield chums,' he said. 'Guess who else is here: Tonio Silva.'

'Where?' said Micky quickly. He seemed displeased to hear that Tonio was around, and Hugh wondered why. At school Tonio had always been frightened of Micky, he remembered.

75

'He's on the dance floor,' Solly said. 'He's with Miss Robinson's friend, Miss April Tilsley.'

Miss Robinson said: 'You could call me Maisie. I'm not a *formal* girl.' And she threw a lascivious wink at Solly.

A waiter brought a plate of lobster and set it in front of Solly. He tucked a napkin into his shirt collar and started to eat.

'I thought you Jewboys weren't supposed to eat shellfish,' Micky said with lazy insolence.

Solly was as impervious as ever to such remarks. 'I'm only kosher at home,' he said.

Maisie Robinson gave Micky a hostile glare. 'We Jewgirls eat what we like,' she said, and took a morsel from Solly's plate.

Hugh was surprised that she was Jewish: he always thought of Jews as having dark colouring. He studied her. She was quite short, but added about a foot to her height by piling her tawny hair into a high chignon and topping it with a huge hat decorated with artificial leaves and fruit. Underneath the hat was a small, impudent face with a wicked twinkle in the green eyes. The cut of her chestnut-coloured gown revealed an astonishing acreage of freckled bosom. Freckles were not generally thought to be attractive, but Hugh could hardly take his eyes off them. After a while Maisie felt his stare and returned it. He turned away with an apologetic smile.

He took his mind off her bosom by looking around the group and noting how his old schoolmates had changed in the last seven years. Solly Greenbourne had matured. Although he was still fat, and had the same easygoing grin, he had acquired an air of authority in his middle twenties. Perhaps it came from being so rich – but Edward was rich and he had no such aura. Solly was already respected in the City; and while it was easy to earn respect when you were the heir to Greenbournes Bank, all the same a foolish young man in that position could rapidly become a laughing-stock.

Edward had grown older but unlike Solly he had not matured. For him, as for a child, play was everything. He was not stupid, but he found it difficult to concentrate on his work at the bank because he would rather be elsewhere, dancing and drinking and gambling.

Micky had become a handsome devil, with dark eyes and black eyebrows and curly hair grown a little too long. His evening dress was correct but rather dashing: his jacket had a velvet collar and cuffs, and his shirt was frilled. He had already attracted admiring glances and inviting looks from several girls seated at nearby tables, Hugh had noticed. But Maisie Robinson had taken a dislike to him, and Hugh guessed that was not just because of the remark about Jewboys. There was something sinister about Micky. He was unnervingly quiet, watchful and self-contained. He was not frank, he rarely showed hesitation, uncertainty, or vulnerability, and he never revealed anything of his soul – if he had one. Hugh did not trust him.

The next dance ended and Tonio Silva came to the table with Miss April Tilsley. Hugh had run into Tonio several times since school, but even if he had not seen him for years he would have recognized him instantly by the shock of carrot-coloured hair. They had been best friends until that awful day in 1866 when Hugh's mother had come to tell him that his father was dead and take him away from the school. They had been the bad boys of the lower fourth, always getting into scrapes, but they had enjoyed life, despite the floggings.

Hugh had often wondered, over the years, what had really happened that day at the swimming-hole. He had never believed the newspaper story about Edward trying to

77

rescue Peter Middleton: Edward would not have the courage. But Tonio still would not speak of it, and the only other witness, Albert 'Hump' Cammel, had gone to live in the Cape Colony.

Hugh studied Tonio's face as he shook hands with Micky. Tonio still seemed somewhat in awe of Micky. 'How are you, Miranda?' he said in a normal voice, but his expression showed a mixture of fear and admiration. It was the attitude a man might have towards a champion prizefighter famous for his quick temper.

Tonio's companion April was a little older than her friend Maisie, Hugh judged, and there was a pinched, sharp look about her that made her less attractive; but Tonio was having a great time with her, touching her arm and whispering in her ear and making her laugh.

Hugh turned back to Maisie. She was talkative and vivacious, with a lilting voice that had a trace of the accent of north-east England, where Tobias Pilaster's warehouses had been. Her expression was endlessly fascinating as she smiled, frowned, pouted, wrinkled her turned-up nose and rolled her eyes. She had fair eyelashes, he noticed, and there was a sprinkling of freckles on her nose. She was an unconventional beauty but no one would deny she was the prettiest woman in the room.

Hugh was obsessed by the thought that, since she was here at the Argyll Rooms, she was presumably willing to kiss, cuddle and perhaps even Go All The Way tonight with one of the men around the table. Hugh daydreamed about a sexual encounter with almost every girl he met – he was ashamed of how much and how often he thought about it – but normally it could only happen after courtship, engagement and marriage. Whereas Maisie might do it tonight!

She caught his eye again, and he had that embarrassing

feeling that Rachel Bodwin sometimes gave him, that she knew what he was thinking. He searched around desperately for something to say, and finally blurted out: 'Have you always lived in London, Miss Robinson?'

'Only for three days,' she said.

It might be mundane, he thought, but at least they were talking. 'So recently!' he said. 'Where were you before?'

'Travelling,' she said, and turned away to speak to Solly.

'Ah,' Hugh said. That seemed to put an end to the conversation, and he felt disappointed. Maisie acted almost as if she had a grudge against him.

But April took pity on him and explained. 'Maisie's been with a circus for three years.'

'Heavens! Doing what?'

Maisie turned around again. 'Bareback horse-riding,' she said. 'Standing on the horses, jumping from one to another, all those tricks.'

April added: 'In tights, of course.'

The thought of Maisie in tights was unbearably tantalizing. Hugh crossed his legs and said: 'How did you get into that line of work?'

She hesitated, then seemed to make up her mind about something. She turned around in her chair to face Hugh directly, and a dangerous glint came into her eyes. 'It was like this,' she said. 'My father worked for Tobias Pilaster and Co. Your father cheated my father out of a week's wages. At that time my mother was sick. Without that money, either I would starve or she would die. So I ran away from home. I was eleven years old at the time.'

Hugh felt his face flush. 'I don't believe my father cheated anyone,' he said. 'And if you were eleven you can't possibly have understood what happened.'

'I understood hunger and cold!'

'Perhaps your father was at fault,' Hugh persisted though

he knew it was unwise. 'He shouldn't have had children if he couldn't afford to feed them.'

'He could feed them!' Maisie blazed. 'He worked like a slave – and then you stole his money!'

'My father went bankrupt, but he never stole.'

'It's the same thing when you're the loser!'

'It's not the same, and you're foolish and insolent to pretend that it is.'

The others obviously felt he had gone too far, and several people began to speak at the same time. Tonio said: 'Let's not quarrel about something that happened so long ago.'

Hugh knew he should stop but he was still angry. 'Ever since I was thirteen years old I've had to listen to the Pilaster family running my father down but I'm not going to take it from a circus performer.'

Maisie stood up, her eyes flashing like cut emeralds. For a moment Hugh thought she was going to slap him. Then she said: 'Dance with me, Solly. Perhaps your rude friend will have gone when the music stops.'

[III]

Hugh's quarrel with Maisie broke up the party. Solly and Maisie went off on their own, and the others decided to go ratting. Ratting was against the law, but there were half a dozen regular pits within five minutes of Piccadilly Circus, and Micky Miranda knew them all.

It was dark when they emerged from the Argyll into the district of London known as Babylon. Here, out of sight of the palaces of Mayfair, but conveniently close to the gentlemen's clubs of St James's, was a warren of narrow streets dedicated to gambling, blood sports, opium smoking, pornography, and – most of all – prostitution. It was a hot, sweaty night, and the air was heavy with the smells of cooking, beer and drains. Micky and his friends moved slowly down the middle of the crowded street. Within the first minute an old man in a battered top hat offered to sell him a book of lewd verses, a young man with rouge on his cheeks winked at him, a well-dressed woman of his own age opened her jacket quickly and gave him a glimpse of two beautiful bare breasts, and a ragged older woman offered him sex with an angel-faced girl about ten years old. The buildings, mostly pubs, dance-halls, brothels and cheap lodging-houses, had grimy walls and small, filthy windows through which could occasionally be glimpsed a gaslit revel. Passing along the street were white-waistcoated swells such as Micky, bowler-hatted clerks and shopkeepers, goggle-eyed farmers, soldiers in unbuttoned uniforms, sailors with their pockets temporarily full of money, and a surprising number of respectable-looking middle-class couples walking arm-in-arm.

Micky was enjoying himself. It was the first time for several weeks that he had managed to get away from Papa for an evening. They were waiting for Seth Pilaster to die so that they could close the deal for the rifles, but the old man was clinging to life like a limpet on a rock. Going to music-halls and brothels was no fun with your father; and besides, Papa treated him more like a servant, sometimes even telling him to wait outside while he went with a whore. Tonight was a blessed relief.

He was glad to have run into Solly Greenbourne again. The Greenbournes were even richer than the Pilasters, and Solly might one day be useful.

He was not glad to have seen Tonio Silva. Tonio knew too much about the death of Peter Middleton seven years ago. In those days Tonio had been terrified of Micky. He was still wary, and he still looked up to Micky, but that was not the same as being frightened. Micky was worried about him but at the moment he did not know what he could do about it.

He turned off Windmill Street into a narrow alley. The eyes of cats blinked at him from piles of refuse. Checking that the others were in tow, he entered a dingy pub, walked through the bar and out of the back door, crossed a yard where a prostitute was kneeling in front of a client in the moonlight, and opened the door of a ramshackle wooden building like a stable.

A dirty-faced man in a long greasy coat demanded fourpence as the price of admission. Edward paid and they went in.

The place was brightly lit and full of tobacco smoke, and there was a foul smell of blood and excrement. Forty or fifty men and a few women stood around a circular pit. The men were of all classes, some in the heavy wool suits and spotted neckerchiefs of well-off workers, others in frock-coats or evening dress; but the women were all more or less disreputable types like April. Several of the men had dogs with them, carried in their arms or tied to chair-legs.

Micky pointed out a bearded man in a tweed cap who held a muzzled dog on a heavy chain. Some of the spectators were examining the dog closely. It was a squat, muscular animal with a big head and a powerful jaw, and it looked angry and restless. 'He'll be on next,' Micky said.

Edward went off to buy drinks from a woman with a tray. Micky turned to Tonio and addressed him in Spanish. It was bad form to do this in front of Hugh and April, who could not understand; but Hugh was a nobody and April was even less, so it hardly mattered. 'What are you doing these days?' he asked.

'I'm an attaché to the Cordovan Minister in London,' Tonio replied.

'Really?' Micky was intrigued. Most South American countries saw no point in having an ambassador in London, but Cordova had had an envoy for ten years. No doubt Tonio had got the post of attaché because his family, the Silvas, were well connected in the Cordovan capital, Palma. By contrast Micky's Papa was a provincial baron and had no such strings to pull. 'What do you have to do?'

'I answer letters from British firms that want to do business in Cordova. They ask about the climate, the currency, internal transport, hotels, all kinds of things.'

'Do you work all day?'

'Not often.' Tonio lowered his voice. 'Don't tell a soul, but I have to write only two or three letters most days.'

'Do they pay you?' Many diplomats were men of independent means who worked for nothing.

'No. But I have a room at the Minister's residence, and all my meals; plus an allowance for clothing. They also pay my subscriptions to clubs.'

Micky was fascinated. It was just the kind of job that would have suited him, and he felt envious. Free board and lodging, and the basic expenses of a young man-about-town paid, in return for an hour's work every morning. Micky wondered if there might be some way Tonio could be eased out of the post.

Edward came back with five tots of brandy in small glasses and handed them around. Micky swallowed his at once. It was cheap and fiery.

Suddenly the dog growled and started to run around in frantic circles, pulling on its chain, the hair on its neck standing up. Micky looked around to see two men coming in carrying a cage of huge rats. The rats were even more frenzied than the dog, running over and under one another and squeaking with terror. All the dogs in the room started to bark, and for a while there was a terrific cacophony as the owners yelled at the animals to shut up.

The entrance was locked and barred from the inside, and the man in the greasy coat started to take bets. Hugh Pilaster said: 'By Jove, I never saw such big rats. Where do they get them?'

Edward answered him. 'They're specially bred for this,' he said, and turned away to speak to one of the handlers. 'How many this contest?'

'Six dozen,' the man replied.

Edward explained: 'That means they will put seventy-two rats into the pit.'

Tonio said: 'How does the betting work?'

'You can bet on the dog or the rats; and if you think the rats will win, you can bet on how many will be left when the dog dies.'

The dirty man was calling out odds and taking money in exchange for scraps of paper on which he scribbled numbers with a thick pencil.

Edward put a sovereign on the dog, and Micky bet a shilling on six rats surviving, for which he got odds of five to one. Hugh declined to bet, like the dull stick he was.

The pit was about four feet deep, and it was surrounded by a wood fence another four feet high. Crude candelabra set at intervals around the fence threw strong light into the hole. The dog was unmuzzled and let into the pit through a wooden gate that was shut tight behind him. He stood stiff-legged, hackles raised, staring up, waiting for the rats. The rat handlers picked up the cage. There was a quiet moment of anticipation.

Suddenly Tonio said: 'Ten guineas on the dog.'

Micky was surprised. Tonio had talked about his job and its perquisites as if he had to be quite careful how he spent money. Was that a sham? Or was he making bets he could not afford?

The bookmaker hesitated. It was a big bet for him, too. Nevertheless, after a moment he scribbled a slip, handed it over, and pocketed Tonio's money.

The handlers swung the cage back, then forward, as if they were going to throw the whole thing into the pit; then, at the last minute, a hinged flap at one end opened, and the rats were hurled out of the cage and through the air, squealing with terror. April screamed with shock, and Micky laughed.

The dog went to work with lethal concentration. As the rats rained down on him his jaws snapped rhythmically. He would pick one up, break its back with one hard shake of his huge head, and drop it for another.

The smell of blood became nauseating. All the dogs in the room barked madly, and the spectators added to the noise, the women shrieking to see the carnage and the men shouting encouragement to the dog or to the rats. Micky laughed and laughed.

It took a moment for the rats to realize they were trapped in the pit. Some ran around the edge, looking for a way out; others jumped up, trying without success to get a grip on the sheer sides; others formed themselves into a heap. For a few seconds the dog had it all his own way, and killed a dozen or more.

Then the rats turned, all at once, as if they had heard a signal. They began to fly at the dog, biting his legs, his haunches and his short tail. Some got on his back and bit his neck and ears, and one sank its sharp little teeth into his lower lip and clung on, swinging from his lethal jaws, until he howled with rage and slammed it against the ground, and at last it released his bleeding flesh.

The dog kept turning around in dizzying circles and caught rat after rat, killing them all; but there were always more behind him. Half the rats were dead when he began to tire. The people who had bet on thirty-six, and got long odds, now tore up their slips; but those who had bet on lower numbers cheered louder.

The dog was bleeding from twenty or thirty bites, and the ground became slippery with his blood and the moist corpses of the dead rats. Still he swung his great head; still he cracked their brittle spines in his terrible mouth; but he moved a little less quickly, and his feet were not so sure on the slimy earth. Now, Micky thought, it starts to get interesting.

Sensing the dog's fatigue, the rats became bolder. When he had one in his jaws, another would spring for his throat. They ran between his legs and under his belly and leaped at the soft parts of his hide. One particularly big creature dug its teeth into his hind leg and refused to let go. He turned to snap at it but another rat distracted him by leaping on his snout. Then the leg seemed to give way – the rat must have severed a tendon, Micky thought – and suddenly the dog was limping.

He was much slower to turn, now. As if they knew that, the dozen or so remaining rats all attacked his rear end. Wearily he snapped them up in his jaws; wearily he broke their backs; wearily he dropped them on the bloody ground. But his underside was raw flesh, and he could not hold out much longer. Micky thought he might have bet wisely, and there would be six rats left when the dog died.

Then the dog gained a sudden access of energy. Spinning around on three legs, he killed another four rats in as many seconds. But it was his last gasp. He dropped a rat and then his legs buckled under him. Once more he turned his head to snap at the creatures, but this time he caught none, and his head drooped.

The rats began to feed.

Micky counted: there were six left.

He looked at his companions. Hugh looked ill. Edward said to him: 'A bit strong for your stomach, eh?'

'The dog and the rats are simply behaving as nature intended,' Hugh said. 'It's the humans who disgust me.'

Edward grunted and went to buy more drinks.

April's eyes were sparkling as she looked up at Tonio, a man – she thought – who could afford to lose ten guineas in a bet. Micky looked more closely at Tonio and saw in his face a hint of panic. I don't believe he *can* afford to lose ten guineas, Micky thought.

Micky collected his winnings from the bookmaker: five shillings. He had made a profit on the evening already. But he had a feeling that what he had learned about Tonio could in the end be worth a great deal more.

[IV]

IT WAS MICKY who had most disgusted Hugh. Throughout the contest, Micky had been laughing hysterically. At first Hugh could not think why that laughter sounded so chillingly familiar. Then he remembered Micky laughing just the same way when Edward threw Peter Middleton's clothes into the swimming-hole. It was an unpleasant reminder of a grim memory.

Edward came back with the drinks and said: 'Let's go to Nellie's.'

They swallowed their tots of brandy and went out. In

the street, Tonio and April took their leave and slipped into a building that looked like a cheap hotel. Hugh presumed they were going to take a room for an hour, or perhaps for the night. He wondered whether to go on with Edward and Micky. He was not having a very good time, yet he was curious to know what went on at Nellie's. He had decided to try debauchery, so he probably ought to see the evening out, not quit half-way, he thought in the end.

Nellie's was in Prince's Street, off Leicester Square. There were two uniformed commissionaires at the door. As the three young men arrived, the commissionaires were turning away a middle-aged man in a bowler hat. 'Evening dress only,' said one of the commissionaires over the man's protests.

They seemed to know Edward and Micky, for one touched his hat and the other opened the door. They went down a long passage to another door. They were inspected through a peephole, and then the door opened.

It was a bit like walking into a large drawing-room in a big London house. Fires blazed in two large grates, there were sofas, chairs and small tables everywhere, and the room was full of men and women in evening dress.

However, it only took another moment to see that this was no ordinary drawing-room. Most of the men had their hats on. About half of them were smoking – something that was not permitted in polite drawing-rooms – and some had their coats off and their ties undone. Most of the women were fully dressed but a few seemed to be in their underwear. Some of them were sitting on men's laps, others were kissing men, and one or two were permitting themselves to be fondled intimately.

For the first time in his life Hugh was in a brothel.

It was noisy, with men shouting jokes, women laughing, and a fiddler somewhere playing a waltz. Hugh followed

Micky and Edward as they walked the length of the room. The walls were hung with pictures of naked women and copulating couples, and Hugh began to feel aroused. At the far end, under a huge oil painting of a complex outdoor orgy, sat the fattest person Hugh had ever seen: a vast-bosomed, heavily painted woman in a silk gown like a purple tent. She was sitting on a chair like a throne, surrounded by girls. Behind her was a broad, red-carpeted staircase that presumably led up to bedrooms.

Edward and Micky approached the throne and bowed, and Hugh followed suit.

Edward said: 'Nell, my pet, allow me to present my cousin, Mr Hugh Pilaster.'

'Welcome, boys,' said Nell. 'Come and entertain these beautiful girls.'

'In a while, Nell. Is there a game tonight?'

'There's always a game at Nellie's,' she said, and waved towards a door at one side of the room.

Edward bowed again and said: 'We'll be back.'

'Don't fail me, boys!'

They moved off. 'She acts like royalty!' Hugh murmured.

Edward laughed. 'This is the top stew in London. Some of the people who bow to her tonight will be bowing to the Queen in the morning.'

They went into the next room, where twelve or fifteen men were sitting around two baccarat tables. Each table had a white line chalked about a foot from its edge, and the players pushed coloured counters across the line to place bets. Most of them had drinks beside them, and the air was full of cigar smoke.

There were a few empty chairs at one of the tables, and Edward and Micky immediately sat down. A waiter brought them some counters, and they each signed a receipt. Hugh said quietly to Edward: 'What are the stakes?'

'A pound minimum.'

It occurred to Hugh that if he played and won he could afford one of the women in the next room. He did not actually have as much as a pound in his pockets, but obviously Edward's credit was good here. . . . Then he remembered Tonio losing ten guineas at the ratting. 'I shan't play,' he said.

Micky said languidly: 'We never imagined you would.'

Hugh felt awkward. He wondered whether to ask a waiter to bring him a drink, then he reflected that it would probably cost him a week's wages. The banker dealt cards from a shoe and Micky and Edward placed bets. Hugh decided to slip away.

He returned to the main drawing-room. Looking more closely at the furniture, he could see that it was quite tawdry: there were stains on the velvet upholstery and burn marks on the polished wood, and the carpets were worn and ripped. Beside him a drunk man was on his knees, singing to a whore, while two of his friends laughed uproariously. On the next couch a couple were kissing with their mouths open. Hugh had heard that people did this but he had never seen it. He watched, mesmerized, as the man unbuttoned the front of the woman's dress and started to caress her breasts. They were white and flabby, with big dark-red nipples. The whole scene aroused and revolted Hugh at the same time. Despite his distaste, his prick grew hard. The man on the couch bent his head to the woman's bosom and began to kiss her breasts. Hugh could not believe what he was seeing. The woman looked over the top of the man's head, caught Hugh's eye, and winked.

A voice in Hugh's ear said: 'You could do that to me, if you like.'

He spun round, feeling as guilty as if he had been caught doing something shameful. Beside him was a dark-haired girl of about his own age, heavily rouged. He could not help glancing down at her bosom. He looked away again quickly, feeling embarrassed.

'Don't be shy,' she said. 'Look as long as you want. They're for you to enjoy.' To his horror he felt her hand on his groin. She found his stiff prick and squeezed it. 'My goodness, you are excited,' she said. Hugh was suffering exquisite anguish. He felt about to explode. The girl tilted her head up and kissed his lips, rubbing his prick at the same time.

It was too much. Unable to control himself, Hugh ejaculated into his underwear.

The girl felt it. For a moment she just looked surprised, then she burst out laughing. 'My God, you are a green one!' she said loudly. Hugh felt humiliated. The girl looked around and said to the nearest whore: 'I only touched him, and he creamed himself!' Several people laughed.

Hugh turned away and headed for the exit. The laughter seemed to follow him the length of the room. He had to restrain himself from running. At last he reached the door. A moment later he was out in the street.

The night had cooled a little, and he took a deep breath and paused to calm himself. If this was dissipation, he did not like it. The dollymop Maisie had been rude about his father; the ratting had been revolting; the whores had laughed at him. The whole lot of them could go to the devil.

A commissionaire gave him a sympathetic look. 'Decided to have an early night, sir?'

'What a good idea,' said Hugh, and he walked away.

Micky was losing money. He could cheat at baccarat if he had the bank, but tonight the bank would not come to him.

He was secretly relieved when Edward said: 'Let's get a couple of girls.'

'You go,' he said, feigning indifference. 'I'll play on.'

A gleam of panic showed in Edward's eyes. 'It's getting late.'

'I'm trying to win back my losses,' Micky said stubbornly.

Edward lowered his voice. 'I'll pay for your chips.'

Micky pretended to hesitate, then give in. 'Oh, all right.'

Edward smiled.

He settled up and they went into the main room. Almost immediately, a blonde girl with large breasts came up to Edward. He put his arm around her bare shoulders, and she pressed her bosom against his chest.

Micky scanned the girls. A slightly older woman with a nicely debauched look caught his eye. He smiled at her and she came over. She put her hand on his shirt front, dug her nails into his chest, stood on tiptoe and gently bit his lower lip.

He saw Edward watching him, flushed with excitement. Micky began to feel eager. He looked at his own woman. 'What's your name?' he said.

'Alice.'

'Let's go upstairs, Alice,' he said.

They all went up the stairs together. On the landing was a marble statue of a centaur with a huge erect penis, which Alice rubbed as they went by. Next to it a couple were performing the sexual act standing up, oblivious of a drunk man sitting on the floor watching them.

The women headed for separate rooms, but Edward steered them into the same room. 'All together tonight, boys?' said Alice.

'We're saving money,' Micky said, and Edward laughed.

'At school together, were you?' she said knowingly, as

she closed the door behind them. 'Used to frig each other off?'

'Shut up,' Micky said, embracing her.

While Micky kissed Alice, Edward came up behind her, put his arms around her, and cupped her breasts. She looked faintly surprised but made no objection. Micky felt Edward's hands moving between his body and the woman's, and he knew that Edward was rubbing himself against her rump.

After a moment the other girl said: 'What shall I do? I feel a bit left out.'

'Get your drawers off,' Edward told her. 'You're next.'

CHAPTER THREE

July

[I]

As a little boy, Hugh had thought Pilasters Bank was owned by the walkers. These personages were in fact lowly messengers, but they were all rather portly, and wore immaculate morning dress with silver watch-chains across their ample waistcoats, and they moved about the bank with such ponderous dignity that to a child they appeared the most important people there.

Hugh had been brought here at the age of ten by his grandfather, Old Seth's brother. The marble-walled banking hall on the ground floor had seemed like a church: huge, gracious, silent, a place where incomprehensible rites were performed by an elite priesthood in the service of a divinity called Money. Grandfather had shown him all around: the carpeted hush of the first floor, occupied by the partners and their correspondence clerks, where little Hugh had been given a glass of sherry and a plate of biscuits in the Partners' Room; the senior clerks at their tables on the second floor, bespectacled and anxious, surrounded by bundles of papers tied with ribbon like gifts; and the juniors on the top floor, sitting at their high desks in lines like

Hugh's toy soldiers, scratching entries in ledgers with inky fingers. But best of all, for Hugh, had been the basement, where contracts even older than Grandfather were kept in vaults, thousands of postage stamps waited to be licked, and there was a whole room full of ink stored in enormous glass jars. It had amazed him to reflect on the process. The ink came into the bank, it was spread over the papers by the clerks, and then the papers were returned to the basement to be stored for ever; and somehow this made money.

The mystery had gone out of it now. He knew that the massive leather-bound ledgers were not arcane texts but simple lists of financial transactions, laboriously compiled and scrupulously updated; and his own fingers had become cramped and ink-stained by days of writing in them. A Bill of Exchange was no longer a magic spell but merely a promise to pay money at a future date, written on a piece of paper and guaranteed by a bank. Discounting, which as a child he had thought must mean counting backwards from a hundred down to one, turned out to be the practice of buying Bills of Exchange at a little less than their face value, keeping them until their due date then cashing them at a small profit.

Hugh was a general assistant to Jonas Mulberry, the Principal Clerk. A bald man of about forty, Mulberry was good-hearted but a little sour. He would always take time to explain things to Hugh, but he was very quick to find fault if Hugh was in the least hasty or careless. Hugh had been working under him for the past year, and yesterday he had made a serious mistake. He had lost a Bill of Lading for a consignment of Bradford cloth destined for New York. The Bradford manufacturer had been downstairs in the banking hall asking for his money, but Mulberry had needed to check the Bill before authorizing payment, and

Hugh could not find the document. They had been obliged to ask the man to come back in the morning.

In the end Hugh had found the bill, but he had spent most of the night worrying about it, and this morning he had devised a new system of dealing with papers for Mulberry.

On the table in front of him he had two cheap wooden trays, two oblong cards, a quill pen and an inkwell. He wrote slowly and neatly on one card:

For the attention of the Principal Clerk

On the second card he wrote:

Having been dealt with by the Principal Clerk

He carefully blotted his writing then fixed one card to each tray with thumbtacks. He put the trays on Jonas Mulberry's table and stood back to survey his work. At that moment Mr Mulberry came in. 'Good morning, Mr Hugh,' he said. All family members were addressed this way at the bank because otherwise there would be confusion among all the different Mr Pilasters.

'Good morning, Mr Mulberry.'

'And what the dickens is this?' Mulberry said tetchily, looking at the trays.

'Well,' Hugh began. 'I found that Bill of Lading.'

'Where was it?'

'Mixed up with some letters you had signed.'

Mulberry narrowed his eyes. 'Are you trying to say it was my fault?'

'No,' Hugh said quickly. 'It's my responsibility to keep your papers in order. That's why I've instituted the tray system – to separate papers you've already dealt with from papers you haven't yet looked at.'

Mulberry grunted non-committally. He hung his bowler

hat on the hook behind the door and sat down at the table. Finally he said: 'We'll try it – it might be quite effective. But next time, have the courtesy to consult me before implementing your ingenious ideas. This is my room, after all, and I am the Principal Clerk.'

'Certainly,' Hugh said. 'I'm sorry.' He knew he should have asked Mulberry's permission, but he had been so keen on his new idea that he had not had the patience to wait.

'The Russian Loan issue closed yesterday,' Mulberry went on. 'I want you to go down to the post room and organize the counting of the applications.'

'Right.' The bank was raising a loan of two million pounds for the government of Russia. It had issued £100 bonds which paid £5 interest per year; but they were selling the bonds for £93, so the true interest rate was over five and three-eighths. Most of the bonds had been bought by other banks in London and Paris, but some had been offered to the general public, and now the applications would have to be counted.

'Let's hope we have more applications than we can fulfil,' Mulberry said.

'Why?'

'That way the unlucky applicants will try to buy the bonds tomorrow on the open market, and that will drive the price up perhaps to £95 – and all our customers will feel they've bought a bargain.'

Hugh nodded. 'And what if we have too few applications?'

'Then the bank, as underwriter, has to buy the surplus – at £93. And tomorrow the price may go down to £92 or £91, and we will have made a loss.'

'I see.'

'Off you go.'

Hugh left Mulberry's office, which was on the second

floor, and ran down the stairs. He was happy that Mulberry had accepted his tray idea and relieved that he was not in worse trouble over the lost Bill of Lading. As he reached the first floor, where the Partners' Room was, he saw Samuel Pilaster, looking dapper in a silver-grey frock-coat and a navy-blue satin tie. 'Good morning, Uncle Samuel,' Hugh said.

'Morning, Hugh. What are you up to?' He showed more interest in Hugh than the other partners did.

'Going to count the applications for the Russian loan.'

Samuel smiled, showing his crooked teeth. 'I don't know how you can be so cheerful with a day of that in front of you!'

Hugh continued down the stairs. Within the family people were beginning to talk in hushed tones about Uncle Samuel and his secretary. Hugh did not find it shocking that Samuel was what people called effeminate. Women and vicars might pretend that sex between men was perverted, but it went on all the time at schools such as Windfield and it never did anyone any harm.

He reached the ground floor and entered the grand banking hall. It was only half-past nine, and the dozens of clerks who worked at Pilasters were still streaming through the grand front door, smelling of bacon breakfasts and underground railway trains. Hugh nodded to Miss Greengrass, the only female clerk. A year ago, when she had been hired, debate had raged through the bank as to whether a woman could possibly do the work. In the event she had settled the matter by proving herself supremely competent. There would be more female clerks in the future, Hugh guessed.

He took the back stairs to the basement and made his way to the post room. Two messengers were sorting mail, and applications for the Russian Loan already filled one big sack. Hugh decided he would get two junior clerks to add up the applications, and he would check their arithmetic.

The work took most of the day. It was a few minutes before four o'clock when he doublechecked the last bundle and added the last column of figures. The issue was undersubscribed: a little more than one hundred thousand pounds of bonds remained unsold. It was not a big shortfall, as a proportion of a two-million-pound issue, but there was a big psychological difference between oversubscribed and undersubscribed, and the partners would be disappointed.

He wrote the tally on a clean sheet of paper and went in search of Mulberry. The banking hall was quiet now. A few customers stood at the long polished counter. Behind the counter, clerks lifted the big ledgers on and off the shelves. Pilasters did not have many private accounts. It was a merchant bank, lending money to traders to finance their ventures. As Old Seth would say, the Pilasters weren't interested in counting the greasy pennies of a grocer's takings or the grubby banknotes of a tailor – there was not enough profit in it. But all the family kept accounts at the bank, and the facility was extended to a small number of very rich clients. Hugh spotted one of them now: Sir John Cammel. Hugh had known his son at Windfield. A thin man with a bald head, Sir John earned vast incomes from coal mines and docks on his lands in Yorkshire. Now he was pacing the marble floor looking impatient and bad-tempered. Hugh said: 'Good afternoon, Sir John, I hope you're being attended to?'

'No, I'm not, lad. Doesn't anyone do any work in this place?'

Hugh glanced around rapidly. None of the partners or

senior clerks was in sight. He decided to use his initiative. 'Will you come upstairs to the Partners' Room, sir? I know they will be keen to see you.'

'All right.'

Hugh led him upstairs. The partners all worked together in the same room – so that they could keep an eye on one another, according to tradition. The room was furnished like the reading-room in a gentlemen's club, with leather sofas, bookcases and a central table with newspapers. In framed portraits on the walls, ancestral Pilasters looked down their beak-like noses at their descendants.

The room was empty. 'One of them will be back in a moment, I'm sure,' Hugh said. 'May I offer you a glass of madeira?' He went to the sideboard and poured a generous measure while Sir John settled himself in a leather armchair. 'I'm Hugh Pilaster, by the way.'

'Oh, yes?' Sir John was somewhat mollified to find he was talking to a Pilaster, rather than an ordinary office boy. 'Did you go to Windfield?'

'Yes, sir. I was there with your son, Albert. We called him Hump.'

'All Cammels are called Hump.'

'I haven't seen him since . . . since then.'

'He went to the Cape Colony, and liked it there so much that he never came back. He raises horses now.'

Albert Cammel had been at the swimming-hole on that fateful day in 1866. Hugh had never heard his version of how Peter Middleton drowned. 'I'd like to write to him,' Hugh said.

'I dare say he'll be glad of a letter from an old school-friend. I'll give you his address.' Sir John moved to the table, dipped a quill in the inkwell and scribbled on a sheet of paper. 'There you are.'

'Thank you.' Sir John was mollified now, Hugh noted with satisfaction. 'Is there anything else I can do for you while you're waiting?'

'Well, perhaps you can deal with this.' He took a cheque out of his pocket. Hugh examined it. It was for a hundred and ten thousand pounds, the largest personal cheque Hugh had ever handled. 'I've just sold a coal mine to my neighbour,' Sir John explained.

'I can certainly deposit it for you.'

'What interest will I get?'

'Four per cent, at present.'

'That'll do, I suppose.'

Hugh hesitated. It occurred to him that if Sir John could be persuaded to buy Russian bonds, the loan issue could be transformed from being slightly undersubscribed to slightly oversubscribed. Should he mention it? He had already overstepped his authority by bringing a guest into the Partners' Room. He decided to take a chance. 'You could get five and three-eighths by buying Russian bonds.'

Sir John narrowed his eyes. 'Could I now?'

'Yes. The subscription closed yesterday, but for you. . . .'

'Are they safe?'

'As safe as the Russian government.'

'I'll think about it.'

Hugh's enthusiasm had been aroused now and he wanted to close the sale. 'The rate may not be the same tomorrow, as you know. When the bonds come on the open market the price may go up or down.' Then he decided he was sounding too eager, so he backed off. 'I'll place this cheque to your account immediately, and if you wish you could talk to one of my uncles about the bonds.'

'All right, young Pilaster – off you go.'

Hugh went out and met Uncle Samuel in the hall. 'Sir

John Cammel is in there, Uncle,' he said. 'I found him in the banking hall looking bad-tempered, so I've given him a glass of madeira – I hope I did the right thing.'

'I'm sure you did,' said Samuel. 'I'll take care of him.'

'He brought in this cheque for a hundred and ten thousand. I mentioned the Russian Loan – it's undersubscribed by a hundred thousand.'

Samuel raised his eyebrows. 'That was precocious of you.'

'I only said he might talk to one of the partners about it if he wanted a higher rate of interest.'

'All right. It's not a bad idea.'

Hugh returned to the banking hall, pulled out Sir John's ledger and entered the deposit, then took the cheque to the clearing clerk. Then he went up to the second floor to Mulberry's office. He handed over the tally of Russian bonds, mentioned the possibility that Sir John Cammel might buy the balance, and sat down at his own table.

A walker came in with tea and bread-and-butter on a tray. This light refreshment was served to all clerks who stayed at the office after four-thirty. When work was light most people left at four. Bank staff were the elite among clerks, much envied by merchants' and shippers' clerks, who often worked until late and sometimes right through the night.

A little later Samuel came in and handed some papers to Mulberry. 'Sir John bought the bonds,' he said to Hugh. 'Good work – that was an opportunity well taken.'

'Thank you.'

Samuel spotted the labelled trays on Mulberry's desk. 'What's this?' he said in a tone of amusement. 'For the attention of the Principal Clerk . . . Having been dealt with by the Principal Clerk.'

Mulberry answered him. 'The purpose is to keep

incoming and outgoing papers separate. It avoids confusion.'

'What a good scheme. I think I might do the same.'

'As a matter of fact, Mr Samuel, it was young Mr Hugh's idea.'

Samuel turned an amused look on Hugh. 'I say, you are keen, dear boy.'

Hugh was sometimes told he was too cocky, so now he pretended to be humble. 'I know I've got an awful lot to learn, still.'

'Now, now, no false modesty. Tell me something. If you were to be released from Mr Mulberry's service, what job would you like to do next?'

Hugh did not have to think about his answer. The most coveted job was that of correspondence clerk. Most clerks saw only a part of a transaction – the part they recorded – but the correspondence clerk, drafting letters to clients, saw the whole deal. It was the best position in which to learn, and the best from which to win promotion. And Uncle Samuel's correspondence clerk, Bill Rose, was due to retire.

Without hesitation Hugh said: 'I'd like to be your correspondence clerk.'

'Would you, now? After only a year in the bank?'

'By the time Mr Rose goes it will be eighteen months.'

'So it will.' Samuel still seemed amused, but he had not said no. 'We'll see, we'll see,' he said, and he went out.

Mulberry said to Hugh: 'Did you advise Sir John Cammel to buy the surplus Russian bonds?'

'I just mentioned it,' said Hugh.

'Well, well,' said Mulberry. 'Well, well.' And he sat staring at Hugh speculatively for several minutes thereafter.

[II]

I T WAS A SUNNY Sunday afternoon, and all London was out for a stroll in best Sunday-go-to-meeting clothes. Piccadilly was free from traffic, for only an invalid would drive on the Sabbath. Maisie Robinson and April Tilsley were strolling down the wide avenue, looking at the palaces of the rich and trying to pick up men.

They lived in Soho, sharing a single room in a slum house in Carnaby Street, near the St James's Workhouse. They would get up around midday, dress carefully, and go out on the streets. By evening they had generally found a couple of men to pay for their dinner: if not, they went hungry. They had almost no money but they needed little. When the rent was due April would ask a boyfriend for a 'loan'. Maisie always wore the same clothes and washed her underwear every night. One of these days someone would buy her a new gown. Sooner or later, she hoped, one of the men who bought her dinner would either marry her or set her up as his mistress.

April was still excited about the South American she had met, Tonio Silva. 'Just think, he can afford to lose ten guineas on a bet!' she said. 'And I've always liked red hair.'

'I didn't like the other South American, the dark one,' Maisie said.

'Micky? He was gorgeous.'

'Yes, but there was something sly about him, I thought.'

April pointed to a huge mansion. 'That's Solly's father's house.'

It was set back from the road, with a semicircular drive in front. It was like a Greek temple, with a row of pillars across the front that reached all the way up to the roof.

Brass gleamed on the big front door and there were red velvet curtains at the windows.

April said: 'Just think, you could be living there one day.'

Maisie shook her head. 'Not me.'

'It's been done before,' April said. 'You just have to be more randy than upper-class girls, and that's not difficult. Once you're married, you can learn to imitate the accent and all that in no time. You speak nice already, except when you get cross. And Solly's a nice boy.'

'A nice fat boy,' Maisie said with a grimace.

'But so rich! People say his father keeps a symphony orchestra at his country house just in case he wants to hear some music after dinner!'

Maisie sighed. She did not want to think about Solly. 'Where did the rest of you go, after I shouted at that boy Hugh?'

'Ratting. Then me and Tonio went to Batt's Hotel.'

'Did you do it with him?'

'Of course! Why do you think we went to Batt's?'

'To play whist?'

They giggled.

April looked suspicious. 'You did it with Solly, though, didn't you?'

'I made him happy,' Maisie said.

'What does that mean?'

Maisie made a gesture with her hand, and they both giggled again.

April said: 'You only frigged him off? Why?'

Maisie shrugged.

'Well, perhaps you're right,' April said. 'Sometimes it's best not to let them have it all first time. If you lead them on a bit it can make them more keen.'

Maisie changed the subject. 'It brought back bad memories, meeting people called Pilaster,' she said.

April nodded. 'Bosses, I hate their fucking guts,' she said with sudden venom. April's language was even more earthy than what Maisie had been used to in the circus. 'I'll never work for one. That's why I do this. I set my own price and get paid in advance.'

'My brother and me left home the day Tobias Pilaster went bankrupt,' Maisie said. She smiled ruefully. 'You could say it's because of the Pilasters that I'm here today.'

'What did you do after you left? Did you join the circus straight away?'

'No.' Maisie felt a tug at her heart as she remembered how frightened and lonely she had been. 'My brother stowed away on a ship going to Boston. I've not seen him or heard from him since. I slept at a rubbish tip for a week. Thank God the weather was mild – it was May. It only rained one night: I covered myself with rags and had fleas for years afterwards. . . . I remember the funeral.'

'Whose?'

'Tobias Pilaster's. The procession went through the streets. He'd been a big man in the town. I remember a little lad, not much older than me, wearing a black coat and a top hat, holding his mam's hand. It must have been Hugh.'

'Fancy that,' said April.

'After that I walked to Newcastle. I dressed as a lad and worked at a stables, helping out. They let me sleep in the straw at night, alongside the horses. I stayed there three years.'

'Why did you leave?'

'I grew these,' Maisie said, and jiggled her breasts. A middle-aged man walking by saw her, and his eyes nearly popped out. 'When the head stablehand realized I was a lass he tried to rape me. I smacked him across the face with a riding-crop, and that was the end of the job.'

'I hope you cut him,' April said.

'I certainly cooled his ardour.'

'You should have whacked his thing.'

'He might have liked it.'

'Where did you go when you left the stable?'

'That's when I joined the circus. I started as a stablehand and eventually became one of the riders.' She sighed nostalgically. 'I liked the circus. The people are warm.'

'Too warm, I gather.'

Maisie nodded. 'I never really got on with the ringmaster, and when he told me to gam him it was time to leave. I decided that if I'm going to suck cocks for a living I want a better wage. And here I am.' She always picked up speech mannerisms and she had adopted April's unrestrained vocabulary.

April gave her a shrewd look. 'Just how many cocks have you sucked since then?'

'None, to tell the truth.' Maisie felt embarrassed. 'I can't lie to you, April – I'm not sure I'm cut out for this trade.'

'You're perfect for it!' April protested. 'You've got that twinkle in your eye that men can't resist. Listen. Persist with Solly Greenbourne. Give him a bit more each time. Let him feel your pussy one day, let him see you naked the next. . . . In about three weeks he'll be panting for it. One night when you've got his trousers down and his tool in your mouth, say: "If you bought me a little house in Chelsea, we could do this any time you wanted to." I swear to you, Maisie, if Solly says no to that, I'll become a nun.'

Maisie knew she was right, but her soul revolted against it. She was not sure why. It was partly because she was not attracted to Solly. Paradoxically, another reason was that he was so nice. She could not bring herself to manipulate him heartlessly. But worst of all, she felt she would be giving up all hope of real love – a real marriage with a man she really burned for. On the other hand, she had to live somehow, and she was determined not to live like her parents, waiting all week for a pittance on payday and forever at risk of unemployment because of some financial crisis hundreds of miles away.

April said: 'What about one of the others? You could have had your pick of them.'

'I liked Hugh, but I offended him.'

'He's got no money, anyway.'

'Edward's a pig, Micky frightens me, and Tonio is yours.'

'Solly's your man, then.'

'I don't know.'

'I do. If you let him slip through your fingers, you'll spend the rest of your life walking down Piccadilly and thinking "I could be living in that house now."'

'Yes, I probably will.'

'And if not Solly, who? You could end up with a nasty little middle-aged grocer who keeps you short of money and expects you to launder your own sheets.'

Maisie brooded on that prospect as they came to the western end of Piccadilly and turned north into Mayfair. She probably could make Solly marry her if she put her mind to it. And she would be able to play the part of a grand lady without too much difficulty. Speech was half the battle and she had always been a good mimic. But the thought of trapping kind Solly into a loveless marriage sickened her.

Cutting through a mews, they passed a big livery stable. Maisie felt nostalgic for the circus, and stopped to pet a tall chestnut stallion. The horse immediately nuzzled her hand. A man's voice said: 'Redboy don't generally allow strangers to touch him.'

Maisie turned around to see a middle-aged man in a black morning coat with a yellow waistcoat. His formal clothes clashed with his weatherbeaten face and uneducated speech, and she guessed he was a former stablehand who had started his own business and done well. She smiled and said: 'He doesn't mind me, do you, Redboy?'

'I don't suppose you could ride him, now, could you?'

'Ride him? Yes, I could ride him, without a saddle, and stand upright on his back, too. Is he yours?'

The man made a small bow and said: 'George Sammles, at your service, ladies; proprietor, as it says there.' He pointed to where his name was painted over the door.

Maisie said: 'I shouldn't boast, Mr Sammles, but I've spent the last four years in a circus, so I can probably ride anything you have in your stables.'

'Is that a fact?' he said thoughtfully. 'Well, well.'

April put in: 'What's on your mind, Mr Sammles?'

He hesitated. 'This may seem a mite sudden, but I was asking myself whether this lady might be interested in a business proposition.'

Maisie wondered what was coming next. Until this moment she had thought the conversation was no more than idle banter. 'Go on.'

April said suggestively: 'We're always interested in business propositions.' But Maisie had a feeling Sammles was not after what April had in mind.

'You see, Redboy's for sale,' the man began. 'But you don't sell horses by keeping them indoors. Whereas, if you was to ride him around the park for an hour or so, a lady such as yourself, looking, if I may be so bold, as pretty as a pitcher, you'd attract a deal of attention, and chances are that sooner or later someone would ask you how much you wanted for the horse.'

Was there money in this, Maisie wondered? Did it offer her a way of paying the rent without selling her body or her soul? But she did not ask the question that was on her mind. Instead she said: 'And then I'd tell the person: "Away and see Mr Sammles in the Curzon Mews, for the nag's his." Is that what you mean?'

'Exackly so, except that, rather than call Redboy a nag, you might term him "this magnificent creature", or "this fine specimen of horseflesh", or such.'

'Maybe,' said Maisie, thinking to herself that she would use her own words, not Sammles's. 'Now then, to business.' She could no longer pretend to be casual about the money. 'How much would you pay?'

'What do you think it's worth?'

Maisie picked a ridiculous sum. 'A pound a day.'

'Too much,' he said promptly. 'I'll give you half that.'

She could hardly believe her luck. Ten shillings a day was an enormous wage: girls of her age who worked as housemaids were lucky to get a shilling a day. Her heart beat faster. 'Done,' she said quickly, afraid he might change his mind. 'When do I start?'

'Come tomorrow at half-past ten.'

'I'll be here.'

They shook hands and the girls moved off. Sammles called after her: 'Mind you wear the dress you've got on today – it's fetching.'

'Have no fear,' Maisie said. It was the only one she had. But she did not tell Sammles that.

[III]

TRAFFIC IN THE PARK
TO THE EDITOR OF THE TIMES

Sir, – There has been noted in Hyde Park, in recent days, at about half past eleven o'clock each morning, a jamb of carriages, so large, that there has been no getting forward for up to an hour. Numerous explanations have been suggested; as, that too many Country residents come up to Town for the Season; or, that the prosperity of London is now such that even tradesmen's wives keep carriages and drive in the Park; but the real truth has nowhere been mentioned. The fault lies with a lady, whose name is unknown, but whom men term 'The Lioness', doubtless on account of the tawny colour of her hair; a charming creature, beautifully dressed, who rides, with ease and spirit, horses that would daunt many males; and drives, with equal facility, a carriage, drawn by perfectly matched pairs. The fame of her beauty and equestrian daring is such that all London migrates to the Park at the hour when she is expected; and, once there, finds it cannot move. Could not you, sir, whose business it is to know everything and everyone, and who possibly, therefore, may know the true identity of The Lioness, prevail upon her to desist, so that the Park may return to its normal state of quiet decorum and ease of passage?

I am, Sir, your obedient servant,

AN OBSERVER

The letter had to be a joke, Hugh thought as he put down the newspaper. The Lioness was real enough – he had heard the clerks at the bank talking about her – but she was not the cause of carriage congestion. All the same he was intrigued. He gazed through the leaded windows of Whitehaven House to the park. Today was a holiday. The sun was shining and there were already lots of people walking, riding and driving carriages. Hugh thought he might just go to the park in the hope of seeing what the fuss was all about.

Aunt Augusta was also planning to go into the park. Her barouche was drawn up in front of the house. The coachman was wearing his wig and the liveried footman was ready to ride behind. She drove in the park at this time most mornings, as did all upper-class women and idle men. They said they did it for fresh air and exercise, but more importantly it was a place to see and be seen. The real cause of congestion was people stopping their carriages to gossip, and blocking the road.

Hugh heard his aunt's voice. He got up from the breakfast table and went into the hall. As usual, Aunt Augusta was beautifully dressed. Today she wore a purple day gown with a tight jacket bodice and yards of ruffles below. The hat was a mistake, though: it was a miniature straw boater, no more than three inches across, perched on top of her coiffure at the front. It was the latest fashion, and on pretty girls it was sweet; but Augusta was anything but sweet, and on her it was ludicrous. She did not often make such errors, but when she did it was usually because she was following fashion too faithfully.

She was talking to Uncle Joseph. He had the harassed air he often wore when Augusta was talking to him. He stood in front of her, half-turning away, stroking his bushy side-whiskers impatiently. Hugh wondered whether there was any affection between them. There must have been at one time, he supposed, for they had conceived Edward and Clementine. They rarely showed fondness, but every now and again, Hugh reflected, Augusta would do something thoughtful for Joseph. Yes, he thought they probably still loved each other.

Augusta carried on speaking as if Hugh were not there, which was her usual way. 'The whole family is worried,' she was saying insistently, as if Uncle Joseph had suggested the opposite. 'There could be a scandal.'

'But the situation – whatever it may be – has been going on for years, and no one has ever thought it scandalous.'

'Because Samuel is not the Senior Partner. An ordinary person can do many things without attracting notice. But the Senior Partner of Pilasters Bank is a public figure.'

'Well, the matter may not be urgent. Uncle Seth is still alive and shows every sign of hanging on indefinitely.'

'I know,' Augusta said, and there was a telling note of frustration in her voice. 'I sometimes wish. . . .' She stopped before revealing herself too much. 'Sooner or later he will hand over the reins. It could happen tomorrow. Cousin Samuel cannot pretend there is nothing to worry about.'

'Perhaps,' said Joseph. 'But if he does so pretend, I'm not sure what can be done.'

'Seth may have to be told about the problem.'

Hugh wondered how much Old Seth knew about his son's life. In his heart he probably knew the truth, but perhaps he never admitted it, even to himself.

Joseph looked uneasy. 'Heaven forbid.'

'It would certainly be unfortunate,' Augusta said with brisk hypocrisy. 'But you must make Samuel understand that unless he gives way his father will have to be brought in, and if that happens Seth must have all the facts.'

Hugh could not help admiring her cunning and ruthlessness. She was sending Samuel a message: Give up your secretary or we'll force your father to confront the reality that his son is more or less married to a man.

In truth she did not care a straw about Samuel and his secretary. She just wanted to make it impossible for him to become Senior Partner – so that the mantle would fall on her husband. It was pretty low, and Hugh wondered whether Joseph fully understood what Augusta was doing.

Now Joseph said uneasily: 'I should like to resolve matters without such drastic action.'

Augusta lowered her voice to an intimate murmur. When she did this, Hugh always thought, she was transparently insincere, like a dragon trying to purr. 'I'm quite sure you'll find a way to do just that,' she said. She smiled beseechingly. 'Will you drive with me today? I should so like your company.'

He shook his head. 'I must go to the bank.'

'What a shame, to be shut up in a dusty office on a beautiful day like this.'

'There has been a panic in Bologna.'

Hugh was intrigued. Since the Vienna 'Krach' there had been several bank failures and company liquidations in different parts of Europe, but this was the first 'panic'. London had escaped damage, so far. In June the Bank Rate, the thermometer of the financial world, had risen to seven per cent – not quite fever level – and it had already dropped back to six per cent. However, there might be some excitement today.

Augusta said: 'I trust the panic won't affect us.'

'So long as we take care, no,' said Joseph.

'But it's a holiday today – there will be no one at the bank to make your tea!'

'I dare say I shall survive half a day without tea.'

'I'll send Sara to you in an hour. She's made a cherry cake, your favourite – she shall bring you some, and make your tea.'

Hugh saw an opportunity. 'Shall I come with you, Uncle? You may want a clerk.'

Joseph shook his head. 'I shan't need you.'

Augusta said: 'You may want him to run errands, my dear.'

Hugh said with a grin: 'Or he may want to ask my advice.'

Joseph did not appreciate the joke. 'I shall just read the

telegraph messages and decide what is to be done when the markets open again tomorrow morning.'

Foolishly, Hugh persisted. 'I should like to come, all the same – just out of interest.'

It was always a mistake to badger Joseph. 'I tell you I don't need you,' he said irritably. 'Drive in the park with your aunt, she needs an escort.' He put his hat on his head and went out.

Augusta said: 'You have a talent for needlessly annoying people, Hugh. Get your hat, I'm ready to go.'

Hugh did not really want to drive with Augusta, but his uncle had commanded him to do so, and he was curious to see The Lioness, so he did not argue.

Augusta's daughter Clementine appeared, dressed to go out. Hugh had played with his cousin when they were children, and she had always been a tell-tale. At the age of seven she had asked Hugh to show her his doodle, and then told her mother what he had done, and Hugh had been thrashed. Now twenty years old, Clementine looked like her mother, but where Augusta was overbearing, Clementine was sly.

They all went out. The footman handed them up into the carriage. It was a new vehicle, painted bright blue and drawn by a superb pair of grey geldings – an equipage fit for the wife of a great banker. Augusta and Clementine sat facing forward, and Hugh settled himself opposite them. The top was down because of the brilliant sunshine, but the ladies opened their parasols. The coachman flicked his whip and they set off.

A few moments later they were on the South Carriage Drive. It was as crowded as the writer of the letter to *The Times* had claimed. There were hundreds of horses ridden by top-hatted men and sidesaddle women; dozens of carriages of every type – open and closed, two-wheel and four-wheel; plus children on ponies, couples on foot, nurses with baby carriages and people with dogs. The carriages gleamed with new paint, the horses were brushed and combed, the men wore full morning dress and the women sported all the bright colours that the new chemical dyes could produce. Everyone moved slowly, the better to scrutinize horses and carriages, dresses and hats. Augusta talked to her daughter, and the conversation required no contribution from Hugh other than the occasional indication of agreement.

'There's Lady St Ann in a Dolly Varden hat!' Clementine exclaimed.

'They went out of fashion a year ago,' said Augusta.

'Well, well,' said Hugh.

Another carriage pulled alongside, and Hugh saw his Aunt Madeleine Hartshorn. If she had whiskers she'd look just like her brother Joseph, he thought. She was Augusta's closest crony. Together they controlled the social life of the family. Augusta was the driving force, but Madeleine was her faithful acolyte.

Both carriages stopped, and the ladies exchanged greetings. They were obstructing the road, and two or three carriages pulled up behind them. Augusta said: 'Take a turn with us, Madeleine, I want to talk to you.' Madeleine's footman helped her down from her own carriage and into Augusta's and they drove off again.

'They're threatening to tell Old Seth about Samuel's secretary,' Augusta said.

'Oh, no!' said Madeleine. 'They mustn't!'

'I've spoken to Joseph, but they won't be stopped,' Augusta went on. Her tone of sincere concern took Hugh's breath away. How did she manage it? Perhaps she convinced herself that the truth was whatever it suited her to say at any moment.

'I shall speak to George,' said Madeleine. 'The shock could kill dear Uncle Seth.'

Hugh toyed with the idea of reporting this conversation to his Uncle Joseph. Surely, he thought, Joseph would be appalled to know how he and the other partners were being manipulated by their wives? But they would not believe Hugh. He was a nobody – and that was why Augusta did not care what she said in front of him.

Their carriage slowed almost to a halt. There was a knot of horses and vehicles up ahead. Augusta said irritably: 'What's the cause of this?'

'It must be The Lioness,' Clementine said excitedly.

Hugh scanned the crowd eagerly but could not see what was causing the holdup. There were several carriages of different kinds, nine or ten horses and some pedestrians.

Augusta said: 'What's this about a lioness?'

'Oh, Mother, she's notorious!'

As Augusta's carriage drew nearer, a smart little victoria emerged from the ruck, pulled by a pair of high-stepping ponies and driven by a woman.

'It *is* The Lioness!' Clementine squealed.

Hugh looked at the woman driving the victoria and was astonished to recognize her.

It was Maisie Robinson.

She cracked a whip and the ponies picked up speed. She was wearing a brown merino costume with flounces of silk, and a mushroom-coloured tie with a bow at her throat. On her head was a perky little top hat with a curly brim.

Hugh felt angry with her all over again for what she had said about his father. She knew nothing about finance and she had no right to accuse people of dishonesty in that casual way. But all the same he could not help thinking that she looked absolutely ravishing. There was something

117

irresistibly charming about the set of that small, neat body in the driving seat, the tilt of the hat, even the way she held the whip and shook the reins.

So The Lioness was Maisie Robinson! But how come she had horses and carriages? Had she come into money? What was she up to?

While Hugh was still marvelling, there was an accident.

A nervous thoroughbred trotted past Augusta's carriage and was startled by a small, noisy terrier. It reared up and the rider fell off into the road – right in front of Maisie's victoria.

Quickly she changed direction, showing impressive control of her vehicle, and pulled across the road. Her evasive action took her right in front of Augusta's horses, causing the coachman to haul on his reins and let out an oath.

She brought her carriage to an abrupt stop alongside. Everyone looked at the thrown rider. He appeared unhurt. He got to his feet unaided, dusted himself down, and walked off, cursing, to catch his horse.

Maisie recognized Hugh. 'Hugh Pilaster, I do declare!' she cried.

Hugh blushed. 'Good morning,' he said, and had no idea what to do next.

He realized immediately that he had made a serious error of etiquette. He ought not to have acknowledged Maisie while he was with his aunts, for he could not possibly introduce such a person to them. He should have snubbed her.

However, Maisie made no attempt to address the ladies. 'How do you like these ponies?' she said. She seemed to have forgotten their quarrel.

Hugh was completely thrown by this beautiful, surprising woman, her skilful driving and her careless manners. 'They're very fine,' he said without looking at them.

'They're for sale.'

Aunt Augusta said icily: 'Hugh, kindly tell this *person* to let us pass!'

Maisie looked at Augusta for the first time. 'Shut your gob, you old bitch,' she said casually.

Clementine gasped and Aunt Madeleine gave a small scream of horror. Hugh's mouth dropped open. Maisie's gorgeous clothes and expensive equipage had made it easy to forget that she was an urchin from the slums. Her words were so splendidly vulgar that for a moment Augusta was too stunned to reply. Nobody ever dared to speak to her this way.

Maisie did not give her time to recover. Turning back to Hugh she said: 'Tell your cousin Edward he should buy my ponies!' Then she cracked her whip and drove away.

Augusta erupted. 'How dare you expose me to such a person!' she boiled. 'How dare you take off your hat to her!'

Hugh was staring after Maisie, watching her neat back and jaunty hat recede along the drive.

Aunt Madeleine joined in. 'How can you possibly know her, Hugh?' she said. 'No well-bred young man would be acquainted with that type! And it seems you have even introduced her to Edward!'

It was Edward who had introduced Maisie to Hugh, but Hugh was not going to try to shift the blame. They would not have believed him anyway. 'I don't actually know her very well,' he said.

Clementine was intrigued. 'Where on earth did you meet her?'

'A place called the Argyll Rooms.'

Augusta frowned at Clementine and said: 'I don't wish to know such things. Hugh, tell Baxter to drive home.'

Hugh said: 'I'm going to walk for a while.' He opened the door of the carriage.

'You're going after that woman!' Augusta said. 'I forbid it!'

'Drive on, Baxter,' said Hugh as he stepped down. The coachman shook the reins, the wheels turned, and Hugh politely doffed his hat as his angry aunts were driven away.

He had not heard the last of this. There would be more trouble later. Uncle Joseph would be told, and soon all the partners would know that Hugh consorted with low women.

But it was a holiday, the sun was shining, and the park was full of people enjoying themselves, and Hugh could not get worried about his aunt's rage today.

He felt light-hearted as he strode along the path. He headed in the direction opposite to that Maisie had taken. People drove around in circles, so he might run into her again.

He was keen to talk to her more. He wanted to set her straight about his father. Oddly enough he no longer felt angry with her about what she had said. She was simply mistaken, he thought, and she would understand if it was explained to her. Anyway, just talking to her was exciting.

He reached Hyde Park Corner and turned north along Park Lane. He doffed his hat to numerous relations and acquaintances: Young William and Beatrice in a brougham, Uncle Samuel on a chestnut mare, Mr Mulberry with his wife and children. Maisie might have stopped on the far side, or she might have left by now. He began to feel that he would not see her again.

But he did.

She was just leaving, crossing Park Lane. It was undoubtedly her, with that mushroom-coloured silk tie at her throat. She did not see him.

On impulse he followed her across the road, into Mayfair, and down a mews, running to keep up with her. She pulled the victoria up to a stable and jumped down. A groom came out and began to help her with the horses.

Hugh came up beside her, breathing hard. He wondered why he had done this. 'Hello, Miss Robinson,' he said.

'Hello again!'

'I followed you,' he said superfluously.

She gave him a frank look. 'Why?'

Without thinking he blurted out: 'I was wondering if you would go out with me one night.'

She put her head on one side and frowned slightly, considering his proposal. Her expression was friendly, as if she liked the idea, and he thought she would accept. But it seemed some practical consideration was at war with her inclinations. She looked away from him, and a little frown appeared on her brow; then she appeared to make up her mind. 'You can't afford me,' she said decisively; and she turned her back on him and walked into the stable.

[IV]

Cammel Farm
Cape Colony
South Africa
14th July, 1873

Dear Hugh,

Jolly nice to hear from you! One is rather isolated out here, and you can't imagine the pleasure we get out of a long, newsy letter from home. Mrs Cammel, who used to be the Hon. Amelia Clapham until she married me, was especially amused by your account of The Lioness. . . .

It's a bit late to say this, I know, but I was dreadfully

shocked by the death of your father. Schoolboys don't write condolence notes. And your own tragedy was somewhat eclipsed by the drowning of Peter Middleton on the very same day. But believe me, many of us thought of you and talked about you after you were so abruptly taken away from school. . . .

I'm glad you asked me about Peter. I have felt guilty ever since that day. I didn't actually see the poor chap die, but I saw enough to guess the rest.

Your Cousin Edward was, as you so colourfully put it, more rotten than a dead cat. You managed to get most of your clothes out of the water and scarper, but Peter and Tonio weren't so quick.

I was over the other side, and I don't think Edward and Micky even noticed me. Or perhaps they didn't recognize me. At any rate they never spoke to me about the incident.

Anyway, after you had gone Edward proceeded to torment Peter even more, pushing his head under the water and splashing his face while the poor boy struggled to retrieve his clothes.

I could see it was getting out of hand but I was a complete coward, I'm afraid. I should have gone to Peter's aid but I was not much bigger myself, certainly no match for Edward and Micky Miranda, and I didn't want my clothes soaked as well. Do you remember the punishment for breaking bounds? It was twelve strokes of the Striper, and I don't mind admitting I was more frightened of that than anything else. Anyway, I grabbed my clothes and sneaked away without attracting any attention.

I looked back once, from the lip of the quarry. I don't know what had happened in the meantime, but Tonio was scrambling up the side, naked and clutching a bundle of wet clothes, and Edward was swimming across the pool after him, leaving Peter gasping and spluttering in the middle.

I thought Peter would be all right, but obviously I was wrong. He must have been at the end of his tether. While Edward was chasing Tonio, and Micky was watching, Peter drowned without anyone noticing.

I didn't know that until later, of course. I got back to school and slipped into my dorm. When the masters started asking questions, I swore I had been there all afternoon. As the ghastly story began to emerge I never had the guts to admit that I had seen what happened.

Not a tale to be proud of, Hugh. But telling the truth at last has made me feel a bit better, at any rate. . . .

Hugh put down Albert Cammel's letter and stared out of his bedroom window. The letter explained both more and less than Cammel imagined.

It explained how Micky Miranda had insinuated himself into the Pilaster family to such an extent that he spent every vacation with Edward and had all his expenses paid by Edward's parents. No doubt Micky had told Augusta that Edward had virtually killed Peter. But in court Micky said Edward had tried to rescue the drowning boy. And in telling that lie Micky had saved the Pilasters from public disgrace. Augusta would have been powerfully grateful – and perhaps, also, fearful that Micky might one day turn against them and reveal the truth. It gave Hugh a cold, rather scared feeling in the pit of his stomach. Albert Cammel, all unknowing, had revealed that Augusta's relationship with Micky was deep, dark and corrupt.

But another puzzle remained. For Hugh knew something about Peter Middleton that almost no one else was aware of. Peter had been something of a weakling, and all the boys treated him as a weed. Embarrassed about his weakness, he had embarked on a training programme – and his main exercise was swimming. He stroked across that pool hour after hour, trying to build his physique. It had not worked: a thirteen-year-old boy could not become broad-shouldered and deep-chested except by growing into a man, and that was a process that could not be hurried.

The only effect of all his efforts was to make him like a fish in the water. He could dive to the bottom, hold his breath for several minutes, float on his back, and keep his eyes open under water. It would have taken more than Edward Pilaster to drown him.

So why had he died?

Albert Cammel had told the truth, as far as he knew it, Hugh was sure. But there had to be more. Something else had happened on that hot afternoon in Bishop's Wood. A poor swimmer might have been killed accidentally, drowned because Edward's rough-housing was too much for him to take. But casual horseplay could not have killed Peter. And if his death was not accidental, it was deliberate.

And that was murder.

Hugh shuddered.

There had been only three people there: Edward, Micky and Peter. Peter must have been murdered by Edward or Micky.

Or both.

[V]

Augusta was already dissatisfied with her Japanese decor. The drawing-room was full of oriental screens, angular furniture on spindly legs, and Japanese fans and vases in black lacquered cabinets. It was all very expensive, but cheap copies were already appearing in the Oxford Street stores, and the look was no longer exclusive to the very best houses. Unfortunately, Joseph would not permit redecoration so soon, and Augusta would have to live with increasingly common furniture for several years.

The drawing-room was where Augusta held court at tea-time every weekday. The women usually came first: her sisters-in-law, Madeleine and Beatrice, and her daughter Clementine. The partners would arrive from the bank at about five: Joseph, Old Seth, Madeleine's husband George Hartshorn, and occasionally Samuel. If business was quiet the boys would come too: Edward, Hugh and Young William. The only non-member of the family who was a regular tea-time guest was Micky Miranda, but occasionally there would be a visiting Methodist clergyman, perhaps a missionary seeking funds to convert the heathens in the South Seas, Malaya, or the newly opened-up Japan.

Augusta worked hard to keep people coming. All the Pilasters liked sweet things, and she provided delicious buns and cakes as well as the very best tea from Assam and Ceylon. Big events such as family holidays and weddings would be planned during these sessions, so anyone who stopped coming would soon lose touch with what was going on.

Despite all that, every now and again one of them would go through a phase of wanting to be independent. The most recent example had been Young William's wife Beatrice a year or so ago, after Augusta had been rather insistent about a dress fabric Beatrice had chosen that did not suit her. When this happened Augusta would leave them for a while, then win them back with some extravagantly generous gesture. In Beatrice's case Augusta had thrown an expensive birthday party for Beatrice's old mother, who was borderline senile and only barely presentable in public. Beatrice had been so grateful that she had forgotten all about the dress fabric – just as Augusta had intended.

Here at these tea-time gatherings Augusta found out what was going on in the family and at the bank. Right now she was anxious about Old Seth. She was carefully working the family around to the idea that Samuel could not be the next Senior Partner, but Seth showed no inclination to retire, despite his failing health. She found it maddening to have her careful plans held up by the stubborn tenacity of an old man.

It was the end of July, and London was becoming quieter. The aristocracy moved out of town at this time of year, on their way to yachts at Cowes or shooting-boxes in Scotland. They would stay in the country, slaughtering birds, hunting foxes and stalking deer, until after Christmas. Between February and Easter they would start to drift back, and by May the London Season would be in full swing.

The Pilaster family did not follow this routine. Although richer by far than most of the aristocracy, they were business people, and had no thought of spending half the year idly persecuting dumb animals in the countryside. However, the partners could generally be persuaded to holiday for most of the month of August, provided there was no undue excitement in the banking world.

This year the holiday had been in doubt all summer, as a distant storm had rumbled threateningly across the financial capitals of Europe; but the worst seemed to be over, the Bank Rate was down to three per cent, and Augusta had rented a small castle in Scotland. She and Madeleine planned to leave in a week or so, and the men would follow a day or two later.

A few minutes before four o'clock, as she was standing in the drawing-room feeling discontented with her furniture and Old Seth's obstinacy, Samuel walked in.

All the Pilasters were ugly, but Samuel was the worst,

Augusta thought. He had the big nose, but he also had a weak, womanish mouth and irregular teeth. He was a fussy man, immaculately dressed, fastidious about his food, a lover of cats and a hater of dogs.

But what made Augusta dislike him was that of all the men in the family he was the most difficult to persuade. She could charm Old Seth, who was susceptible to an attractive woman even at his advanced age; she could generally get around Joseph by wearing down his patience; George Hartshorn was under Madeleine's thumb and so could be manipulated indirectly; and the others were young enough to be intimidated, although Hugh sometimes gave her trouble.

Nothing worked on Samuel – least of all her feminine charms. He had an infuriating way of laughing at her when she thought she was being subtle and clever. He gave the impression that she was not to be taken seriously – and that offended her mortally. She was much more wounded by Samuel's quiet mockery than she was at being called an old bitch by a trollop in the park.

Today, however, Samuel did not wear that amused, sceptical smile. He looked angry, so angry that for a moment Augusta was alarmed. He had obviously come early in order to find her alone. It struck her that for two months she had been conspiring to ruin him, and that people had been murdered for less than that. He did not shake her hand, but stood in front of her, wearing a pearl-grey morning-coat and a deep wine-red tie, smelling faintly of cologne. Augusta held up her hands in a defensive gesture.

Samuel gave a humourless laugh and moved away. 'I'm not going to strike you, Augusta,' he said. 'Though heaven knows you deserve a whipping.'

Of course he would not touch her. He was a gentle soul

who refused to finance the export of rifles. Augusta's confidence came back in a rush, and she said disdainfully: 'How dare you criticize me!'

'Criticize?' he said, and the rage flashed again in his eyes. 'I don't stoop to criticize you.' He paused, then spoke again in a voice of controlled anger. 'I despise you.'

Augusta could not be intimidated a second time. 'Have you come here to tell me that you are willing to give up your vicious ways?' she said in a ringing voice.

'My vicious ways,' he repeated. 'You're willing to destroy my father's happiness and make my own life miserable, all for the sake of your ambition, and yet you can talk about *my* vicious ways! I believe you're so steeped in evil that you've forgotten what it is.'

He was so convinced and passionate that Augusta wondered if perhaps it really was wicked of her to threaten him. Then she realized he was trying to weaken her resolve by playing on her sympathy. 'I'm only concerned for the bank,' she said coldly.

'Is that your excuse? Is that what you'll tell the Almighty, on the Day of Judgement, when he asks you why you blackmailed me?'

'I'm doing my duty.' Now that she felt in control again she began to wonder why he had come here. Was it to concede defeat – or to defy her? If he gave in she could rest assured that soon she would be the wife of the Senior Partner. But the alternative made her want to bite her nails. If he defied her there was a long, difficult struggle ahead, with no certainty of the outcome.

Samuel went to the window and looked out at the garden. 'I remember you as a pretty little girl,' he said meditatively. Augusta grunted impatiently. 'You used to come to church in a white dress with white ribbons in your hair,' he went on. 'The ribbons didn't fool anyone. You were a tyrant even then. Everyone used to walk in the park after the service, and the other children were scared of you, but they played with you because you organized the games. You even terrorized your parents. If you didn't get what you wanted you could throw a tantrum so noisy that people would stop their carriages to see what was going on. Your father, God rest his soul, had the haunted look of a man who cannot understand how he had brought such a monster into the world.'

What he was saying was close to the truth and it made her uncomfortable. 'That all happened years ago,' she said, looking away.

He went on as if she had not spoken. 'It's not for myself that I'm worried. I'd like to be Senior Partner, but I can live without it. I'd be a good one – not as dynamic as my father, perhaps; more of a teamworker. But Joseph isn't up to the job. He's bad-tempered and impulsive, and he makes poor decisions; and you make it worse, by inflaming his ambition and clouding his vision. He's all right in a group, where others can guide him and restrain him. But he can't be the leader, his judgement isn't good enough. He'll harm the bank, in the long run. Don't you care about that?'

For a moment Augusta wondered if he was right. Was she in danger of killing the goose that laid the golden eggs? But there was so much money in the bank that they could never spend it all even if none of them ever did another day's work. Anyway, it was ridiculous to say that Joseph would be bad for the bank. There was nothing very difficult about what the partners did: they went into the bank, read the financial pages of the newspaper, loaned people money and collected the interest. Joseph could do that as well as any of them. 'You men always pretend that banking is

complex and mysterious,' she said. 'But you don't fool me.'
She realized that she was being defensive. 'I'll justify myself
to God, not to you,' she said.

'Would you really go to my father, as you have
threatened?' Samuel said. 'You know it could kill him.'

She hesitated only for an instant. 'There is no
alternative,' she said firmly.

He stared at her for a long time. 'You devil, I believe
you,' he said.

Augusta held her breath. Would he give in? She felt that
victory was almost in her grasp, and in her imagination she
heard someone say respectfully: *Allow me to present Mrs
Joseph Pilaster – the wife of the Senior Partner of Pilasters
Bank. . . .*

He hesitated, then spoke with obvious distaste. 'Very
well. I shall tell the others that I don't wish to become
Senior Partner when my father retires.'

Augusta repressed a smile of triumph. She had won. She
turned away to conceal her elation.

'Enjoy your victory,' Samuel said bitterly. 'But
remember, Augusta, that we all have secrets – even you.
One day someone will use your secrets against you this
way, and you'll remember what you did to me.'

Augusta was mystified. What was he referring to? For no
reason at all the thought of Micky Miranda came into her
mind, but she pushed it aside. 'I have no secrets to be
ashamed of,' she said.

'Don't you?'

'No!' she said, but his confidence worried her.

He gave her a peculiar look. 'A young lawyer called
David Middleton came to see me yesterday.'

For a moment she did not understand. 'Should I know
him?' The name was disturbingly familiar.

'You met him once, seven years ago, at an inquest.'

Suddenly Augusta felt cold. Middleton: that had been the name of the boy who drowned.

Samuel said: 'David Middleton believes that his brother Peter was killed – by Edward.'

Augusta wanted desperately to sit down, but she refused to give Samuel the satisfaction of seeing her rattled. 'Why on earth is he trying to make trouble now, after seven years?'

'He told me he was never satisfied with the inquest, but he remained silent for fear of causing his parents even more distress. However, his mother died soon after Peter, and his father died this year.'

'Why did he approach you – not me?'

'He belongs to my club. Anyway, he has re-read the inquest records and he says that there were several eyewitnesses who were never called to give evidence.'

There certainly were, Augusta thought anxiously. There was mischievous Hugh Pilaster; a South American boy called Tony or something; and a third person who had never been identified. If David Middleton got hold of one of them the whole story might come out.

Samuel was looking thoughtful. 'From your point of view it was a pity the coroner made those remarks about Edward's heroism. That made people suspicious. They would have believed that Edward stood on the edge dithering while a boy drowned. But everyone who's ever met him knows he wouldn't cross the street to help someone, let alone dive into a pool to rescue a drowning boy.'

This sort of talk was complete rubbish, and insulting too. 'How dare you,' Augusta said, but she could not muster her usual tone of authority.

Samuel ignored her. 'The schoolboys never believed it. David had been to the same school not many years earlier

131

and he knew many of the older boys. Talking to them increased his suspicions.'

'The whole idea is absurd.'

'Middleton is a quarrelsome individual, like all lawyers,' Samuel said, heedless of her protests. 'He's not going to let this rest.'

'He doesn't frighten me in the least.'

'That's good, because I'm sure you'll be receiving a visit from him soon.' He went to the door. 'I won't stay for tea. Good afternoon, Augusta.'

Augusta sat down heavily on a sofa. She had not foreseen this – how could she? Her triumph over Samuel was blighted. That old business had come up again, seven years later, when it ought to have been completely forgotten! She was dreadfully frightened for Edward. She could not bear anything bad to happen to him. She held her head to stop it throbbing. What could she do?

Hastead, her butler, came in, followed by two parlourmaids with trays of tea and cakes. 'With your permission, madam?' he said in his Welsh accent. Hastead's eyes seemed to look in different directions and people were never quite sure which one to concentrate on. At first this was disconcerting, but Augusta was used to him. She nodded. 'Thank you, madam,' he said, and they began to set out the china. Augusta could sometimes be soothed by Hastead's obsequious manner and the sight of servants doing her bidding; but today it did not work. She got up and went to the open french doors. The sunny garden did nothing for her either. How was she going to stop David Middleton?

She was still agonizing over the problem when Micky Miranda arrived.

She was glad to see him. He looked as fetching as always, in his black morning coat and striped trousers, a spotless white collar around his neck, a black satin tie knotted at his throat. He saw that she was distressed and he was instantly sympathetic. He came across the room with the grace and speed of a jungle cat, and his voice was like a caress: 'Mrs Pilaster, what on earth has upset you?'

She was grateful that he was the first to come. She grabbed him by the arms. 'Something frightful has happened.'

His hands rested on her waist, as if they were dancing, and she felt a shiver of pleasure as his fingers pressed her hips. 'Don't be distressed,' he said soothingly. 'Tell me about it.'

She began to feel calmer. At moments like these she was very fond of Micky. It reminded her of how she had felt about the young Earl of Strang, when she was a girl. Micky reminded her powerfully of Strang: his easy grace, his attentiveness, his beautiful clothes, and most of all the way he moved, the suppleness of his limbs and the oiled machinery of his body. Strang had been fair and English, where Micky was dark and Latin, but they both had that ability to make her feel so feminine. She wanted to draw his body to hers and rest her cheek on his shoulder. . . .

She saw the maids staring at her, and realized that it was mildly indecent for Micky to stand there with both hands on her hips. She detached herself from him, took his arm and led him through the french windows into the garden, where they would be out of earshot of the servants. The air was warm and balmy. They sat close together on a wooden bench in the shade, and Augusta turned sideways to look at him. She longed to hold his hand but that would have been improper.

He said: 'I saw Samuel leaving — has he got something to do with this?'

Augusta spoke quietly, and Micky leaned close to hear

her, so close she could have kissed him almost without moving. 'He came to tell me he will not seek the position of Senior Partner.'

'Good news!'

'Yes. It means that the post will certainly go to my husband.'

'And Papa can have his rifles.'

'As soon as Seth retires.'

'It's maddening the way Old Seth hangs on!' Micky exclaimed. 'Papa keeps asking me when it will happen.'

Augusta knew why Micky was so worried: he was afraid his father would send him back to Cordova. 'I can't imagine Seth will last much longer,' she said to comfort him.

He looked into her eyes. 'But that's not what has upset you.'

'No. It's that wretched boy who drowned at your school – Peter Middleton. Samuel told me that his brother, the lawyer, has started asking questions.'

Micky's fine face darkened. 'After all these years?'

'Apparently he kept quiet for his parents' sake, but now they're dead.'

Micky frowned. 'How much of a problem is this?'

'You may know better than I.' Augusta hesitated. There was a question she had to ask, but she was afraid of the answer. She screwed up her nerve. 'Micky . . . do you think it was Edward's fault the boy died?'

'Well. . . .'

'Say yes or no!' she commanded.

Micky paused, then at last said: 'Yes.'

Augusta closed her eyes. Darling Teddy, she thought, why did you do it?

Micky sat quietly: 'Peter was a poor swimmer. Edward didn't drown him, but he did exhaust him. Peter was alive when Edward left him to chase after Tonio. But I believe he was too weak to swim to the side, and he drowned while no one was watching.'

'Teddy didn't want to kill him.'

'Of course not.'

'It was just schoolboy horseplay.'

'Edward meant no real harm.'

'So it's not murder.'

'I'm afraid it is,' Micky said gravely, and Augusta's heart missed a beat. 'If a thief throws a man to the ground, intending only to rob him, but the man suffers a heart attack and dies, the thief is guilty of murder, even though he did not intend to kill.'

'How do you know this?'

'I checked with a lawyer, years ago.'

'Why?'

'I wanted to know Edward's position.'

Augusta buried her face in her hands. It was worse than she had imagined.

Micky prised her hands away from her face and kissed each hand in turn. The gesture was so tender that it made her want to cry. He continued to hold her hands as he said: 'No sensible person would persecute Edward over something that happened when he was a child.'

'But is David Middleton a sensible person?' Augusta cried.

'Perhaps not. He appears to have nursed his obsession through the years. God forbid that his persistence should lead him to the truth.'

Augusta shuddered as she imagined the consequences. There would be a scandal; the gutter press would say SHAMEFUL SECRET OF BANKING HEIR; the police would be brought in; poor dear Teddy might have to go on trial; and if he should be found guilty—

'Micky, it's too awful to contemplate!' she whispered.

135

'Then we must do something.'

Augusta squeezed his hands, then released them and took stock. She had faced the magnitude of the problem. She had seen the shadow of the gallows fall on her only son. It was time to stop agonizing and take action. Thank God Edward had a true friend in Micky. 'We must make sure David Middleton's inquiries lead nowhere. How many people know the truth?'

'Six,' Micky said immediately. 'Edward, you and me make three, but we aren't going to tell him anything. Then there is Hugh.'

'He wasn't there when the boy died.'

'No, but he saw enough to know that the story we told the coroner was false. And the fact that we lied makes us look guilty.'

'Hugh is a problem, then. The others?'

'Tonio Silva saw it all.'

'He never said anything at the time.'

'He was too frightened of me then. But I'm not sure he is now.'

'And the sixth?'

'We never found out who that was. I didn't see his face at the time, and he has never come forward. I'm afraid there's nothing we can do about him. However, if nobody knows who he is I don't suppose he's any danger to us.'

Augusta felt a fresh tremor of fear: she was not sure about that. There was always a danger the unknown witness might reveal himself. But Micky was right to say there was nothing they could do. 'Two people we can deal with, then: Hugh and Tonio.'

There was a thoughtful silence.

Hugh could no longer be regarded as a minor nuisance, Augusta reflected. His pushy ways were gaining him credit at the bank, and Teddy looked plodding by comparison.

Augusta had managed to sabotage the romance between Hugh and Lady Florence Stalworthy. But now Hugh was threatening Teddy in a much more dangerous way. Something had to be done about him. But what? He was a Pilaster, albeit a bad one. She racked her brains and came up with nothing.

Micky said thoughtfully: 'Tonio has a weakness.'

'Ah, yes?'

'He's a bad gambler. Bets more than he can afford, and loses.'

'Perhaps you could arrange a game?'

'Perhaps.'

The thought crossed Augusta's mind that Micky might know how to cheat at cards. However, she could not possibly ask him: the suggestion would be mortally insulting to any gentleman.

Micky said: 'It might be expensive. Would you stake me?'

'How much would you need?'

'A hundred pounds, I fear.'

Augusta did not hesitate: Teddy's life was at stake. 'Very well,' she said. She heard voices in the house: other tea-time guests were beginning to arrive. She stood up. 'I'm not sure how to deal with Hugh,' she went on worriedly. 'I'll have to think about it. We must go inside.'

Her sister-in-law Madeleine was there, and began talking as soon as they stepped through the door. 'That dressmaker will drive me to drink, two hours to pin a hem, I can't wait for a cup of tea, oh, and you've got more of that heavenly almond cake, but my goodness, isn't the weather hot?'

Augusta gave Micky's hand a conspiratorial squeeze and sat down to pour the tea.

CHAPTER FOUR

August

[I]

London was hot and sticky, and the population longed for fresh air and open fields. On the first day of August everyone went to the races at Goodwood.

They travelled by special trains from Victoria Station in south London. The divisions of British society were carefully mirrored in the transport arrangements – high society in the upholstered luxury of the first-class coaches, shopkeepers and schoolteachers crowded but comfortable in second class, factory workers and domestic servants crammed together on hard wooden benches in third. When they got off the train the aristocracy took carriages, the middle class boarded horse-buses, and the workers walked. The picnics of the rich had been sent by earlier trains: scores of hampers, carried on the shoulders of strapping young footmen, packed with china and linen, cooked chickens and cucumbers, champagne and hothouse peaches. For the less wealthy there were stalls selling sausages, shellfish and beer. The poor brought bread and cheese wrapped in handkerchiefs.

Maisie Robinson and April Tilsley went with Solly

Greenbourne and Tonio Silva. Their position in the social hierarchy was dubious. Solly and Tonio clearly belonged in first class, but Maisie and April should have gone third. Solly compromised by buying second-class tickets, and they took the horse-bus from the station across the Downs to the racecourse.

However, Solly was too fond of his food to settle for a lunch bought off a stall, and he had sent four servants ahead with a vast picnic of cold salmon and white wine packed in ice. They spread a snow-white tablecloth on the ground and sat around it on the springy turf. Maisie fed Solly titbits. She was growing more and more fond of him. He was kind to everyone, full of fun, and interesting to talk to. Gluttony was his only real vice. She still had not let him have his way with her, but it seemed that the more she refused him, the more devoted to her he became.

The racing began after lunch. There was a bookmaker nearby, standing on a box and shouting odds. He wore a loud check suit, a flowing silk tie, a huge spray of flowers in his buttonhole, and a white hat. He carried a leather satchel full of money slung over his shoulder and stood under a banner which read: 'Wm. Tucker, the King's Head, Chichester'.

Tonio and Solly bet on every race. Maisie got bored: one horserace was the same as another if you didn't gamble. April would not leave Tonio's side, but Maisie decided to look around.

The horses were not the only attraction. The Downs around the racecourse were crowded with tents, stalls and carts. There were gambling booths, freak shows, and dark-skinned gypsies in bright headscarves telling fortunes. People were selling gin, cider, meat pies, oranges and bibles. Barrel organs and bands competed with one another, and through the crowds wandered conjurors and jugglers and acrobats, all asking for pennies. There were dancing dogs, dwarfs and giants and men on stilts. The boisterous carnival atmosphere reminded Maisie powerfully of the circus, and she suffered a nostalgic twinge of regret for the life she had left behind. The entertainers were here to take money from the public any way they could and it warmed her heart to see them succeed.

She knew she should be taking more from Solly. It was crazy to be walking out with one of the richest men in the world and living in one room in Soho. By now she ought to be wearing diamonds and furs and have her eye on a little suburban house in St John's Wood or Clapham. Her job riding Sammles's horses would not last much longer: the London season was coming to an end and the people who could afford to buy horses were leaving for the country. But she would not let Solly give her anything but flowers. It drove April mad.

Maisie passed a big marquee. Outside were two girls dressed as bookmakers and a man in a black suit shouting: 'The only racing certainty at Goodwood today, is the coming Day of Judgement! Stake your faith on Jesus, and the payout is eternal life.' The interior of the tent looked cool and shady, and on impulse she went in. Most of the people sitting on the benches looked as if they were already converted. Maisie sat near the exit and picked up a hymn book.

She could understand why people joined chapels and went preaching at race meetings. It made them feel they belonged to something. The feeling of belonging was the real temptation Solly offered her: not so much the diamonds and furs, but the prospect of being Solly Greenbourne's mistress, with somewhere to live and a regular income and a position in the scheme of things. It was not a respectable position, nor permanent – the arrangement would end the moment Solly got bored with her – but it was a lot more than she had now.

The congregation stood up to sing a hymn. It was all about being washed in the blood of the lamb, and it made Maisie feel ill. She went out.

She passed a puppet show as it was reaching its climax, with the irascible Mr Punch being knocked from one side of the little stage to the other by his club-wielding wife. Maisie studied the crowd with a knowledgeable eye. There was not much money in a Punch-and-Judy show if it was operated honestly: most of the audience would slip away without paying anything and the rest would give halfpennies. But there were other ways to fleece the customers. After a few moments she spotted a boy at the back robbing a man in a top hat. Everyone but Maisie was watching the show, and no one else saw the small grubby hand sliding into the man's waistcoat pocket.

Maisie had no intention of doing anything about it. Wealthy and careless young men deserved to lose their pocket watches, and bold thieves earned their loot, in her opinion. But when she looked more closely at the victim she recognized the black hair and blue eyes of Hugh Pilaster. She recalled April telling her that Hugh had no money. He could not afford to lose his watch. She decided on impulse to save him from his own carelessness.

She made her way quickly around to the back of the crowd. The pickpocket was a ragged sandy-haired boy of about eleven years, just the age Maisie had been when she ran away from home. He was delicately drawing Hugh's watch-chain out of his waistcoat. There was a burst of uproarious laughter from the audience watching the show, and at that moment the pickpocket edged away with the watch in his hand.

Maisie grabbed him by the wrist.

He gave a small cry of fear and tried to wriggle free, but she was too strong for him. 'Give it to me and I'll say nothing,' she hissed.

He hesitated for a moment. Maisie saw fear and greed at war on his dirty face. Then a kind of weary resignation took over, and he dropped the watch on the ground.

'Away and steal someone else's watch,' she said. She released his hand and he was gone in a twinkling.

She picked up the watch. It was a gold hunter. She opened the front and checked the time: ten past three. On the back of the watch was inscribed:

> *Tobias Pilaster*
> *from your loving wife*
> *Lydia*
> *23rd May 1851*

The watch had been a gift from Hugh's mother to his father. Maisie was glad she had rescued it. She closed the face and tapped Hugh on the shoulder.

He turned around, annoyed at being distracted from the entertainment; then his bright blue eyes widened in surprise. 'Miss Robinson!'

'What's the time?' she said.

He reached automatically for his watch and found his pocket empty. 'That's funny. . . .' He looked around as if he might have dropped it. 'I do hope I haven't—'

She held it up.

'By Jove!' he said. 'How on earth did you find it?'

'I saw you being robbed, and rescued it.'

'Where's the thief?'

'I let him go. He was only a wee lad.'

'But. . . .' He was nonplussed.

'I'd have let him take the watch, only I know you can't afford to buy another.'

'You don't really mean that.'

'I do. I used to steal, when I was a child, any time I could get away with it.'

'How dreadful.'

Maisie found herself once again becoming annoyed by him. To her way of thinking there was something sanctimonious in his attitude. She said: 'I remember your father's funeral. It was a cold day, and raining. Your father died owing my father money – yet you had a coat that day, and I had none. Was that honest?'

'I don't know,' he said with sudden anger. 'I was thirteen years old when my father went bankrupt – does that mean I have to turn a blind eye to villainy all my life?'

Maisie was taken aback. It was not often that men snapped at her, and this was the second time Hugh had done it. But she did not want to quarrel with him again. She touched his arm. 'I'm sorry,' she said. 'I didn't mean to criticize your father. I just wanted you to understand why a child might steal.'

He softened immediately. 'And I haven't thanked you for saving my watch. It was my mother's wedding gift to my father, so it's more precious than its price.'

'And the child will find another fool to rob.'

He laughed. 'I've never met anyone like you!' he said. 'Would you like to have a glass of beer? I'm so hot.'

It was just what she felt like. 'Yes, please.'

A few yards off there was a heavy four-wheeled cart loaded with huge barrels. Hugh bought two pottery tankards of warm, malty ale. Maisie took a long draught: she had been thirsty. It tasted better than Solly's French wine. Fixed to the cart was a sign chalked in rough capital letters saying WALK OFF WITH A POT AND IT WILL BE BROKE OVER YOUR HED.

A meditative look came over Hugh's usually lively face,

and after a while he said: 'Do you realize we were both victims of the same catastrophe?'

She did not. 'What do you mean?'

'There was a financial crisis in 1866. When that happens, perfectly honest companies fail . . . like when one horse in a team falls and drags the others down with it. My father's business collapsed because people owed him money and didn't pay; and he was so distraught that he took his own life, and left my mother a widow and me fatherless at the age of thirteen. Your father couldn't feed you because people owed him money and couldn't pay, and you ran away at the age of eleven.'

Maisie saw the logic of what he was saying, but her heart would not let her agree: she had hated Tobias Pilaster for too long. 'It's not the same,' she protested. 'Working men have no control over these things – they just do what they're told. Bosses have the power. It's their fault if things go wrong.'

Hugh looked thoughtful. 'I don't know, perhaps you're right. Bosses certainly take the lion's share of the rewards. But I'm sure of one thing, at least: bosses or workers, their children aren't to blame.'

Maisie smiled. 'It's hard to believe we've found something to agree about.'

They finished their drinks, returned the pots and walked a few yards to a merry-go-round with wooden horses. 'Do you want a ride?' said Hugh.

Maisie smiled. 'No.'

'Are you here on your own?'

'No, I'm with . . . friends.' For some reason she did not want him to know she had been brought here by Solly. 'And you? Are you with your awful aunt?'

He grimaced. 'No. Methodists don't approve of race meetings – she'd be horrified if she knew I was here.'

'Is she fond of you?'

'Not in the least.'

'Then why does she let you live with her?'

'She likes to keep people in sight, so she can control them.'

'Does she control you?'

'She tries.' He grinned. 'Sometimes I escape.'

'It must be hard, living with her.'

'I can't afford to live on my own. I have to be patient and work hard at the bank. Eventually I'll get promoted and then I'll be independent.' He grinned again. 'And then I'll tell her to shut her gob like you did.'

'I hope you didn't get into trouble.'

'I did, but it was worth it to see the expression on her face. That was when I started to like you.'

'Is that why you asked me to dine with you?'

'Yes. Why did you refuse?'

'Because April told me you haven't a penny to your name.'

'I've enough for a couple of chops and a plum pudding.'

'How could a girl resist that?' she said mockingly.

He laughed. 'Come out with me tonight. We'll go to Cremorne Gardens and dance.'

She was tempted, but she thought of Solly and felt guilty. 'No, thank you.'

'Why not?'

She asked herself the same question. She was not in love with Solly and she was taking no money from him: why was she saving herself for him? I'm eighteen years old, she thought, and if I can't go out dancing with a boy I like, what's the point in living? 'All right, then.'

'You'll come?'

'Aye.'

He grinned. She had made him happy. 'Shall I fetch you?'

She did not want him to see the Soho slum where she shared a room with April. 'No, let's meet somewhere.'

'All right – we'll go to Westminster Pier and take the steamer to Chelsea.'

'Yes!' She felt more excited than she had for months. 'What time?'

'Eight o'clock?'

She made a rapid calculation. Solly and Tonio would want to stay until the last race. Then they had to get the train back to London. She would say goodbye to Solly at Victoria Station and walk to Westminster. She thought she could make it. 'But if I'm late, you'll wait?'

'All night, if necessary.'

Thinking of Solly made her feel guilty. 'I'd better get back to my friends now.'

'I'll walk with you,' he said eagerly.

She did not want that. 'Best you don't.'

'As you wish.'

She put out her hand and they shook. It seemed oddly formal. 'Until tonight,' she said.

'I'll be there.'

She turned and walked away, feeling that he was watching her. Now why did I do that? she thought. Do I want to go out with him? Do I really like him? The first time we met we had a quarrel that broke up the party, and today he was ready to squabble again if I hadn't smoothed it over. We really don't get on. We'll never be able to dance together. Perhaps I won't go.

But he's got lovely blue eyes.

She made up her mind not to think about it any more. She had agreed to meet him and she would. She might enjoy it or she might not, but fretting beforehand would not help.

She would have to invent a reason for leaving Solly. He was expecting to take her out to dinner. However, he never questioned her – he would accept any excuse, no matter how implausible. All the same she would try and think of something convincing, for it made her feel bad to abuse his easygoing nature.

She found the others where she had left them. They had spent the whole afternoon between the rail and the bookmaker in the check suit. April and Tonio were looking bright-eyed and triumphant. As soon as April saw Maisie she said: 'We've won a hundred and ten pounds – isn't it wonderful?'

Maisie was happy for April. It was such a lot of money to get for nothing. As she was congratulating them, Micky Miranda appeared, strolling along with his thumbs in the pockets of his dove-grey waistcoat. She was not surprised to see him: everyone went to Goodwood.

Although Micky was startlingly good-looking, Maisie disliked him. He reminded her of the circus ringmaster, who had thought all women should be thrilled to be propositioned by him, and was highly affronted when one turned him down. Micky had Edward Pilaster in tow, as always. Maisie was curious about their relationship. They were so different: Micky slim, immaculate, confident; Edward big, clumsy, hoggish. Why were they so inseparable? But most people were enchanted by Micky. Tonio regarded him with a kind of nervous veneration, like a puppy with a cruel master.

Behind them were an older man and a young woman. Micky introduced the man as his father. Maisie studied him with interest. He did not resemble Micky at all. He was a short man with bowed legs, very broad shoulders and a weatherbeaten face. Unlike his son he did not look comfortable in a stiff collar and a top hat. The woman was clinging to him like a lover but she had to be younger than him by thirty years. Micky introduced her as Miss Cox.

They all talked about their winnings. Both Edward and Tonio had made a lot on a horse called Prince Charlie. Solly had won money then lost it again, and seemed to enjoy both equally. Micky did not say how he had fared, and Maisie guessed he had not bet as much as the others: he seemed too careful a person, too calculating, to be a heavy gambler.

However, with his next breath he surprised her. He said to Solly: 'We're going to have a heavyweight game tonight, Greenbourne – a pound minimum. Will you join in?'

She was struck by the thought that Micky's languid posture was covering up considerable tension. He was a deep one.

Solly would go along with anything. 'I'll join in,' he said.

Micky turned to Tonio. 'Would you care to join us?' His take-it-or-leave-it tone sounded false to Maisie.

'Count on me,' Tonio said excitedly. 'I'll be there!'

April looked troubled and said: 'Tonio, not tonight – you promised me.' Maisie suspected that Tonio could not afford to play when the minimum stake was a pound.

'What did I promise?' he said with a wink at his friends.

She whispered something in his ear, and all the men laughed.

Micky said: 'It's the last big game of the season, Silva. You'll be sorry if you miss it.'

That surprised Maisie. At the Argyll Rooms she had got the impression that Micky disliked Tonio. Why was he now trying to talk him into joining the card game?

Tonio said: 'I'm lucky today – look how much I've won on the horses! I shall play cards tonight.'

Micky glanced at Edward, and Maisie caught a look of

relief in their eyes. Edward said: 'Shall we all dine together at the club?'

Solly looked at Maisie, and she realized she had been provided with a ready-made excuse for not spending the evening with him. 'Dine with the boys, Solly,' she said. 'I don't mind.'

'Are you sure?'

'Yes. I've had a lovely day. You spend the evening at your club.'

'That's settled, then,' said Micky.

He and his father, Miss Cox and Edward took their leave.

Tonio and April went to place a bet on the next race. Solly offered Maisie his arm and said: 'Shall we walk for a while?'

They strolled along the white-painted rail that bounded the track. The sun was warm and the country air smelled good. After a while Solly said: 'Do you like me, Maisie?'

She stopped, stood on tiptoe, and kissed his cheek. 'I like you a lot.'

He looked into her eyes, and she was mystified to see tears behind his spectacles. 'Solly, dear, what is it?' she said.

'I like you, too,' he said. 'More than anyone I've ever met.'

'Thank you.' She was touched. It was unusual for Solly to show any emotion stronger than mild enthusiasm.

Then he said: 'Will you marry me?'

She was flabbergasted. This was the last thing in the world she had expected. Men of Solly's class did not propose to girls like her. They seduced them, gave them money, kept them as mistresses, and had children by them, but they did not marry them. She was too astounded to speak.

Solly went on: 'I'd give you anything you want. Please say yes.'

Marriage to Solly! Maisie realized she would be unbelievably rich for ever and ever. A soft bed every night, a blazing fire in every room of the house, and as much butter as she could eat. She would get up when she pleased, not when she had to. She would never be cold again, never hungry, never shabbily dressed, never weary.

The word *Yes* trembled on the tip of her tongue.

She thought of April's tiny room in Soho, with its nest of mice in the wall; she thought of how the privy stank on warm days; she thought of the nights they went without dinner; she thought of how her feet ached after a day of walking the streets.

She looked at Solly. How hard could it be, to marry this man?

He said: 'I love you so much, I'm just desperate for you.'

He really did love her, she could tell.

And that was the trouble.

She did not love him.

He deserved better. He deserved a wife who really loved him, not a hard-hearted guttersnipe on the make. If she married him she would be cheating him. And he was too good for that.

She felt close to tears. She said: 'You're the kindest, most gentle man I've ever met—'

'Don't say no, please?' he interrupted. 'If you can't say yes, say nothing. Think about it, at least for a day, perhaps longer.'

Maisie sighed. She knew she should turn him down, and it would have been easier to do so right away. But he was begging her. 'I'll think about it,' she said.

He beamed. 'Thank you.'

She shook her head ruefully. 'Whatever happens, Solly, I believe I'll never be proposed to by a better man.'

[II]

HUGH AND MAISIE took the penny ride on the pleasure-steamer from Westminster Pier to Chelsea. It was a warm, light evening, and the muddy river was busy with cockle-boats, barges and ferries. They steamed upstream, under the new railway bridge for Victoria Station, passing Christopher Wren's Chelsea Hospital on the north shore and, on the south, the flowers of Battersea Fields, London's traditional duelling ground. Battersea Bridge was a ramshackle wooden structure that looked ready to fall down. At its south end were chemical factories, but on the opposite side pretty cottages clustered around Chelsea Old Church, and naked children splashed in the shallows.

Less than a mile beyond the bridge they disembarked and walked up the wharf to the magnificent gilded gateway of Cremorne Gardens. The Gardens consisted of twelve acres of groves and grottoes, flower-beds and lawns, ferneries and copses between the river and the King's Road. It was dusk when they arrived, and there were Chinese lanterns in the trees and gaslight along the winding paths. The place was packed: many of the younger people who had been at the races had decided to finish the day here. Everyone was dressed up to the nines, and they sauntered carefree through the gardens, laughing and flirting, the girls in pairs, the young men in larger groups, the couples arm-in-arm.

The weather had been fine all day, sunny and warm, but now it was becoming a hot, thundery night that threatened a storm. Hugh felt at once elated and nervous. He was thrilled to have Maisie on his arm, but he had the insecure sense that he did not know the rules of the game he was playing. What did she expect? Would she let him kiss her? Would she let him do anything he wanted? He longed to touch her body, but he did not know where to begin. Would she expect him to go all the way? He wanted to, but he had never done it before and he was afraid of making a fool of himself. The other clerks at Pilasters talked a lot about dollymops, and what they would and would not do, but Hugh suspected that much of what they said was boasting. Anyway, Maisie could not be treated as a dollymop. She was more complex than that.

He was also a little worried that he might be seen by someone he knew. His family would disapprove powerfully of what he was doing. Cremorne Gardens was not only a lower-class place, it was thought by Methodists to encourage immorality. If he were found out, Augusta would be sure to use it against him. It was one thing for Edward to take loose women to disreputable places: he was the son and heir. It was different for Hugh, penniless and poorly educated and expected to be a failure like his father: they would say that licentious pleasure gardens were his natural habitat, and he belonged with clerks and artisans and girls like Maisie.

Hugh was at a critical stage in his career. He was on the point of getting promoted to correspondence clerk – at a salary of £150 a year, more than double what he was getting now – and that could be jeopardized by a report of dissolute behaviour.

He looked anxiously at the other men walking along the winding paths between the flower-beds, fearful of recognizing someone. There was a sprinkling of upper-class men, some with girls on their arms; but they all carefully avoided Hugh's eye, and he realized they too were apprehensive about being seen. He decided that if he saw people he knew they would be as keen as he to keep it quiet; and he felt reassured.

He was proud of Maisie. She was wearing a blue-green gown with a low neckline and a bustle behind, and a sailor hat poised jauntily on her piled-up hair. She attracted a lot of admiring glances.

They passed a ballet theatre, an oriental circus, an American bowling green and several shooting galleries, then went into a restaurant to dine. This was a new experience for Hugh. Although restaurants were becoming more common, they were mostly used by the middle classes: upper-class people still did not like the idea of eating in public. Young men such as Edward and Micky ate out quite often, but they thought of themselves as slumming, and they only did it when they were either looking for or had already found dollymops to keep them company.

All through dinner Hugh tried not to think about Maisie's breasts. The tops of them showed lusciously above the neckline of her gown, and they were very pale, with freckles. He had seen bare breasts, just once – at Nellie's weeks ago. But he had never touched one. Were they firm, like muscles, or limp? When a woman took off her corset, did her breasts move as she walked, or remain rigid? If you touched them, would they yield to pressure, or were they hard, like kneecaps? Would she let him touch them? He sometimes even thought about kissing them, the way the man in the brothel had kissed the whore's breasts, but this was a secret desire that he felt ashamed of. In fact he was vaguely ashamed of all these feelings. It seemed brutish to sit with a woman and think all the time of her naked body, as if he cared nothing for her, but just wanted to use her.

However, he could not help it, especially with Maisie, who was so alluring.

While they were eating there was a firework display in another part of the gardens. The bangs and flashes upset the lions and tigers in the menagerie, and they roared their disapproval. Hugh recalled that Maisie had worked in a circus, and he asked her what it was like.

'You get to know people very well when you live so close together,' she said thoughtfully. 'It's good in some ways, bad in others. People help each other all the time. There are love affairs, lots of quarrels, sometimes fights – there were two murders in the three years I was with the circus.'

'Good heavens.'

'And the money is unreliable.'

'Why?'

'When people need to economize, entertainment is the first thing they cut out.'

'I'd never thought of that. I must remember not to invest the bank's money in any form of entertainment business.'

She smiled. 'Do you think about finance all the time?'

No, Hugh thought, I think about your breasts all the time. He said: 'You have to understand that I'm the son of the black sheep of the family. I know more about banking than the other young Pilaster men, but I have to work doubly hard to prove my worth.'

'Why is it so important to prove yourself?'

Good question, Hugh thought. He considered. After a minute he said: 'I've always been that way, I suppose. At school I just had to be top of the class. And my father's failure made it worse: everyone thinks I'm going to go the same way, and I have to show them they're wrong.'

'In a way I feel the same, you know. I'm never going to live as my mam did, always on the edge of destitution. I'm going to have money, I don't care what I have to do.'

As gently as he could, Hugh said: 'Is that why you go around with Solly?'

She frowned, and for a moment he thought she was going to be angry, but that passed and she smiled ironically. 'I suppose that's a fair question. If you want to know the truth, I'm not proud of my connection with Solly. I misled him with certain . . . expectations.'

Hugh was surprised. Did that mean she had not gone all the way with Solly? 'He seems to like you.'

'And I like him. But comradeship isn't what he wants, and it never was, and I always knew that.'

'I see what you mean.' Hugh decided she had not gone all the way with Solly, and that meant she might not be willing to do it with him. He felt both disappointed and relieved: disappointed because he was so hungry for her, relieved because he was so nervous about it.

'You seem pleased about something,' said Maisie.

'I suppose I'm glad to hear that you and Solly are only comrades.'

She looked a little sad, and he wondered if he had said the wrong thing.

He paid for their dinner. It was quite expensive but he had brought the money he had been saving for his next suit of clothes, nineteen shillings, so he had plenty of cash. When they left the restaurant the people in the gardens seemed more boisterous than they had earlier, no doubt because they had consumed a good deal of beer and gin in the interim.

They came upon a dance floor. Dancing was something Hugh felt confident about: it was the only subject that had been well taught at the Folkestone Academy for the Sons of Gentlemen.

He led Maisie on to the floor and took her in his arms for the first time. His fingertips tingled as he rested his right

155

hand in the small of her back, just above her bustle. He could feel the warmth of her body through her clothing. With his left hand he held hers, and she gave it a squeeze: the sensation thrilled him.

At the end of the first dance he smiled at her, feeling pleased, and to his surprise she reached up and touched his mouth with a fingertip. 'I like it when you grin,' she said. 'You look boyish.'

'Boyish' was not exactly the impression he was trying to give, but at this point anything that pleased her was all right with him.

They danced again. They were good partners: although Maisie was short, Hugh was only a little taller, and they were both light on their feet. He had danced with dozens of girls, if not hundreds, but he had never enjoyed it this much. He felt as if he was only now discovering the delightful sensation of holding a woman close, moving and swaying with the music, and executing complicated steps in unison.

'Are you tired?' he asked her at the end of the dance.

'Certainly not!'

They danced again.

At society balls it was bad manners to dance with the same girl more than twice. You had to lead her off the floor and offer to fetch her some champagne or sorbet. Hugh had always chafed at such regulations, and now he felt joyfully liberated to be an anonymous reveller at this public dance.

They stayed on the floor until midnight, when the music stopped.

All the couples left the dance floor and moved on to the garden paths. Hugh noticed that many of the men kept their arms around their partners, even though they were no longer dancing; so, with some trepidation, he did the same. Maisie did not seem to mind.

The festivities were becoming unruly. Beside the paths there were occasional small cabins, like boxes at the opera, where people could sit and dine and watch the crowds walk by. Some of the cabins had been rented by groups of undergraduates who were now drunk. A man walking in front of Hugh had his top hat playfully knocked off his head, and Hugh himself had to duck to avoid a flying loaf of bread. He held Maisie closer to him, protectively, and to his delight she wound her arm around his waist and gave him a squeeze.

There were numerous shadowy groves and bowers off the main footpath, and Hugh could dimly perceive couples on the wooden seats, although he could not be sure whether they were embracing or just sitting together. He was surprised when the couple walking in front of them stopped and kissed passionately in the middle of the path. He led Maisie around them, feeling awkward. But after a while he got over his embarrassment and began to feel excited. A few minutes later they passed another embracing couple. Hugh caught Maisie's eye, and she smiled at him in a way that he felt sure was meant to be encouraging. But somehow he could not summon up the nerve to just go ahead and kiss her.

The gardens were becoming more rowdy. They had to detour around a scuffle involving six or seven young men, all shouting drunkenly, punching and knocking one another down. Hugh began to notice a number of unaccompanied women, and wondered if they were prostitutes. The atmosphere was turning threatening and he felt the need to protect Maisie.

Then a group of thirty or forty young men came charging along, tipping people's hats off, pushing women aside and throwing men to the ground. There was no escaping them: they spread out across the lawns either side of the path.

Hugh acted quickly. He stood in front of Maisie with his back to the onslaught, then took off his hat and put both arms around her, holding her tight. The mob swept by. A heavy shoulder hit Hugh in the back, and he staggered, still holding Maisie; but he managed to remain upright. On one side of him a girl was knocked over, and on the other a man was punched in the face. Then the hooligans were gone.

Hugh relaxed his grip and looked down at Maisie. She looked back at him expectantly. Hesitantly, he leaned down and kissed her lips. They were deliciously soft and mobile. He closed his eyes. He had waited years for this: it was his first kiss. And it was as delightful as he had dreamed. He breathed in the scent of her. Her lips moved delicately against his. He wanted never to stop.

She broke the kiss. She looked hard at him, then hugged him tight, pulling his body against hers. 'You could spoil all my plans,' she said quietly.

He was not sure what she meant.

He looked to one side. There was a bower with an empty seat. Screwing up his courage, he said: 'Shall we sit down?'

'All right.'

They made their way into the darkness and sat on the wooden seat. Hugh kissed her again.

This time he felt a little less tentative. He put his arm around her shoulders and pulled her to him, and with his other hand he tilted her chin; and he kissed her more passionately than before, pressing his lips to hers hard. She responded enthusiastically, arching her back so that he could feel her bosom crushed against his chest. It surprised him that she should be so keen, though he knew of no reason why girls should not like kissing as much as men did. Her eagerness made it doubly exciting.

He stroked her cheek and her neck, and his hand fell to

her shoulder. He wanted to touch her breasts, but he was afraid she would be offended, so he hesitated. She put her lips to his ear, and in a whisper that was also a kiss, she said: 'You can touch them.'

It startled him that she had been able to read his mind, but the invitation excited him almost beyond endurance – not just because she was willing, but that she should actually speak of it. *You can touch them.* His fingertips traced a line from her shoulder, across her collarbone, down to her bosom, and he touched the swell of her breast above the neckline of her gown. Her skin was soft and warm. He was not sure what he should do next. Should he try to put his hand inside?

Maisie answered his unspoken question by taking his hand and pressing it to her dress below the neckline. 'Squeeze them, but gently,' she whispered.

He did so. They were not like muscles or kneecaps, he found, but more yielding, except for the hard nipples. His hand went from one to the other, stroking and squeezing alternately. Maisie's breath was hot against his neck. He felt as if he could do this all night, but he paused to kiss her lips again. This time she kissed him briefly then pulled away, kissed then pulled away, again and again, and that was even more thrilling. There were lots of ways to kiss, he realized.

Suddenly she froze. 'Listen,' she said.

Hugh had been vaguely aware that the gardens were getting very noisy, and now he realized he was hearing shouting and crashing. Looking towards the footpath he saw that everyone was running in different directions. 'There must be a fight,' he said.

Then he heard a police whistle.

'Damn,' he said. 'Now there'll be trouble.'

'We'd better leave,' Maisie said.

'Let's find our way to the King's Road entrance and see if we can pick up a hansom cab.'

'All right.'

He hesitated, reluctant to leave. 'One more kiss.'

'Yes.'

He kissed her and she hugged him hard.

'Hugh,' she said, 'I'm glad I met you.'

He thought it was the nicest thing anyone had ever said to him.

They regained the footpath and headed north, hurrying. A moment later two young men came hurtling along, one chasing the other; and the first crashed into Hugh, sending him flying. When he scrambled to his feet they had gone.

Maisie was concerned. 'Are you all right?'

He brushed himself off and picked up his hat. 'No damage,' he said. 'But I don't want it to happen to you. Let's cut across the lawns – it might be safer.'

As they stepped off the path, the gaslights went out.

They pressed forward in the dark. Now there was a continuous clamour of men shouting and women screaming, punctuated by police whistles. It suddenly occurred to Hugh that he might be arrested. Then everyone would find out what he had been up to. Augusta would say he was too dissolute to be given a responsible post at the bank. He groaned. Then he recalled how it had felt to touch Maisie's breasts, and he decided he did not care what Augusta said.

They kept away from paths and open spaces, and picked their way through trees and shrubbery. The ground rose slightly from the river bank, so Hugh knew they were headed the right way as long as they were going uphill.

In the distance he saw lanterns twinkling, and steered towards the lights. They began to meet up with other couples going in the same direction. Hugh hoped there would be less chance of trouble with the police if they were in a group of obviously respectable and sober people.

As they approached the gate a troop of thirty or forty policemen entered. Fighting to get into the park against the flow of the crowd, the police started indiscriminately clubbing men and women. The crowd turned and began to run in the opposite direction.

Hugh thought fast. 'Let me carry you,' he said to Maisie. She looked puzzled but said: 'All right.'

He stooped and picked her up, with one arm under her knees and the other around her shoulders. 'Pretend you've fainted,' he said, and she closed her eyes and went limp. He walked forward, against the press of the crowd, shouting: 'Make way, there! Make way!' in his most authoritative voice. Seeing an apparently sick woman, even the fleeing people tried to get out of the way. He came up against the advancing policemen, who were as panicky as the public. 'Stand aside, constable! Let the lady through!' he shouted at one of them. The man looked hostile and for a moment he thought his bluff would be called. Then a sergeant shouted: 'Let the gentleman pass!' He advanced through the line of police and suddenly found himself in the clear.

Maisie opened her eyes and he smiled at her. He liked holding her this way and he was in no hurry to lay down his burden. 'Are you all right?'

She nodded. She seemed tearful. 'Put me down.'

He put her down gently and hugged her. 'I say, don't cry,' he said. 'It's all over now.'

She shook her head. 'It's not the riot,' she said. 'I've seen fights before. But this is the first time anyone ever took care of me. All my life I've had to look after myself. It's a new experience.'

He did not know what to say. All the girls he had ever

met assumed that men would take care of them automatically. Being with Maisie was a constant revelation.

Hugh looked about for a cab. There were none to be seen. 'I'm afraid we may have to walk.'

'When I was eleven years old I walked for four days to get to Newcastle,' she said. 'I think I can make it from Chelsea to Soho.'

[III]

MICKY MIRANDA had begun to cheat at cards while he was at Windfield School, to supplement the inadequate allowance he received from home. The methods he had invented for himself had been crude, but good enough to fool schoolboys. Then, on the long transatlantic voyage home which he had taken between school and university, he had tried to fleece a fellow-passenger who turned out to be a professional card-sharp. The older man had been amused, and had taken Micky under his wing, teaching him all the basic principles of the craft.

Cheating was most dangerous when the stakes were high. If people were playing for pennies it never occurred to them that someone would cheat. Suspicion mounted with the size of the bets.

If he were caught tonight it would not just mean the failure of his scheme to ruin Tonio. Cheating at cards was the worst crime a gentleman could commit in England. He would be asked to resign from his clubs, his friends would be 'not at home' any time he called at their houses, and no one would speak to him in the street. The rare stories he had heard about Englishmen cheating always ended with the culprit leaving the country to make a fresh start in some untamed territory such as Malaya or Hudson Bay. Micky's fate would be to go back to Cordova, endure the taunts of his elder brother, and spend the rest of his life raising cattle. The thought made him feel ill.

But the rewards tonight were as dramatic as the risks.

He was not doing this just to please Augusta. That was important enough: she was his passport into the society of London's wealthy and powerful people. But he also wanted Tonio's job.

Papa had said Micky would have to earn his keep in London – there would be no more money from home. Tonio's job was ideal. It would enable Micky to live like a gentleman while doing hardly any work. And it would also be a step on the ladder to a higher position. One day Micky might become the Minister. And then he would be able to hold his head high in any company. Even his brother would not be able to sneer at that.

Micky, Edward, Solly and Tonio dined early at the Cowes, the club they all favoured. By ten o'clock they were in the card room. They were joined at the baccarat table by two other club gamblers who had heard of the high stakes: Captain Carter and Viscount Montagne. Montagne was a fool, but Carter was a hard-headed type, and Micky would have to be wary of him.

There was a white line drawn around the table ten or twelve inches from the edge. Each of the players had a pile of gold sovereigns in front of him, outside the white square. Once money crossed the line into the square it was staked.

Micky had spent the day pretending to drink. At lunch he had wet his lips with champagne and surreptitiously poured it out on the grass. On the train back to London he had accepted the offer of Edward's flask several times, but had always blocked the neck with his tongue while appearing to toss off a swig. At dinner he had poured himself a small glass of claret then added to it twice without ever drinking any. Now he quietly ordered ginger beer, which looked like brandy-and-soda. He had to be stone-cold sober to perform the delicate sleight-of-hand operations that would enable him to ruin Tonio Silva.

He licked his lips nervously, caught himself, and tried to relax.

Of all games the card-sharp's favourite was baccarat. It might have been invented, Micky thought, to enable the smart to steal from the rich.

In the first place, it was a game purely of chance, with no skill or strategy. The player received two cards and added up their values: a three and a four would make seven, a two and a six would make eight. If the total came to more than nine, only the last digit counted; so fifteen was five, twenty was zero, and the highest possible score was nine.

A player with a low score could draw a third card, which would be dealt face up, so everyone could see it.

The banker dealt just three hands: one to his left, one to his right, and one to himself. Players bet on either the left or the right hand. The banker paid out to any hand higher than his own.

The second great advantage of baccarat, from the cheat's point of view, was that it was played with a pack of at least three decks of cards. This meant the cheat could use a fourth deck and confidently deal a card out of his sleeve without worrying whether another player already had the same card in his hand.

While the others were still making themselves comfortable and lighting their cigars he asked a waiter for three new decks of cards. When the man came back he naturally handed the cards to Micky.

In order to control the game Micky had to deal, so his

first challenge was to make sure he was banker. This involved two tricks: neutralizing the cut, and second-card-dealing. They were both relatively simple, but he was stiff with tension, and that could make a man bungle the easiest manoeuvres.

He broke the seals. The cards were always packed the same way, with the jokers on top and the ace of spades at the bottom. Micky took out the jokers and shuffled, enjoying the clean slippery feel of the new cards. It was the simplest of operations to move an ace from the bottom to the top of the pack; but then he had to let one of the other players cut the cards without moving the ace from top.

He passed the pack to Solly, sitting on his right. As he put it down he contracted his hand a fraction, so that the top card – the ace of spades – stayed in his palm, concealed by the breadth of his hand. Solly cut. Keeping his hand palm-downward all the time to conceal the ace, Micky picked up the pack, replacing the hidden card on top as he did so. He had successfully neutralized the cut.

'High card gets the bank?' he said, forcing himself to sound indifferent as to whether they said yes or no.

There was a murmur of assent.

Holding the pack firmly, he slid the top card back a fraction of an inch and began to deal fast, keeping the top card back and always dealing the second until he came to himself, when at last he dealt the ace. They all turned over their cards. Micky's was the only ace, so he was banker.

He managed a casual smile. 'I think I'm going to be lucky tonight,' he said.

No one commented.

He relaxed a little.

Concealing his relief, he dealt the first hand.

Tonio was playing on his left, with Edward and Viscount

Montagne. On his right were Solly and Captain Carter. Micky did not want to win: that was not his purpose tonight. He just wanted Tonio to lose.

He played fair for a while, losing a little of Augusta's money. The others relaxed and ordered another round of drinks. When the time was right, Micky lit a cigar.

In the inside pocket of his dress coat, next to his cigar case, was another deck of cards – bought at the stationer's in St James's Street where the club's playing-cards came from so that they would match.

He had arranged the extra deck in winning pairs, all giving a total of nine, the highest score: four and five, nine and ten, nine and jack, and so on. The surplus cards, all tens and court cards, he had left at home.

Returning his cigar-case to his pocket, he palmed the extra deck; then, picking up the pack from the table with his other hand, he slid the new cards to the bottom of the old pack. While the others mixed their brandy-and-water he shuffled, carefully bringing to the top of the pack, in order, one card from the bottom, two cards at random, another from the bottom, and another two at random. Then, dealing first to his left, then to his right, then to himself, he gave himself the winning pair.

Next time around he gave Solly's side a winning hand. For a while he continued the same way, making Tonio lose and Solly win. The money he won from Tonio's side was thus paid out to Solly's side, and no suspicion attached to Micky, for the pile of sovereigns in front of him remained about the same.

Tonio had started by putting on the table most of the money he had won at the races – about a hundred pounds. When it was down to about fifty, he stood up and said: 'This side is unlucky – I'm going to sit by Solly.' He moved to the other side of the table.

That won't help you, Micky thought. It was no more difficult to make the left side win and the right side lose from now on. But it made him nervous to hear Tonio talk about bad luck. He wanted Tonio to go on thinking he was lucky today, even while he was losing money.

Occasionally Tonio would vary his style by betting five or ten sovereigns on a hand instead of two or three. When this happened, Micky dealt him a winning hand. Tonio would rake in his winnings and say gleefully: 'I'm lucky today, I'm sure of it!' even though his pile of coins was steadily getting smaller.

Micky was feeling more relaxed now. He studied his victim's mental state while he smoothly manipulated the cards. It was not enough that Tonio should be cleaned out. Micky wanted him to play with money he didn't have, to gamble on borrowed money and be unable to repay his debts. Only then would he be thoroughly disgraced.

Micky waited with trepidation while Tonio lost more and more. Tonio was awestruck by Micky and would generally do whatever Micky suggested, but he was not a complete fool and there was still a chance he might have the sense to draw back from the brink of ruin.

When Tonio's money was almost gone Micky made his next move. He took out his cigar case again. 'These are from home, Tonio,' he said. 'Try one.' To his relief, Tonio accepted. The cigars were long and would take a good half-hour to smoke. Tonio would not want to leave before finishing his cigar.

When they had lit up Micky moved in for the kill.

A couple of hands later Tonio was broke. 'Well, that's everything I won at Goodwood this afternoon,' he said despondently.

'We ought to give you a chance to win it back,' Micky said. 'Pilaster will lend you a hundred pounds, I'm sure.'

Edward looked a little startled, but it would have seemed ungenerous to refuse when he had such a big pile of winnings in front of him, and he said: 'By all means.'

Solly intervened. 'Perhaps you should retire, Silva, and be grateful that you've had a great day's gambling at no cost.'

Micky silently cursed Solly for being a good-natured nuisance. If Tonio did the sensible thing now the whole scheme was ruined.

Tonio hesitated.

Micky held his breath.

But it was not in Tonio's nature to gamble prudently, and as Micky had calculated, he could not resist the temptation to carry on. 'All right,' he said. 'I might as well play on until I finish my cigar.'

Micky let out a discreet sigh of relief.

Tonio beckoned to a waiter and ordered pen, paper and ink. Edward counted out a hundred sovereigns and Tonio scribbled an IOU. Micky knew that if Tonio lost all that he could never repay the debt.

The game went on. Micky found himself sweating a little as he held the delicate balance, ensuring that Tonio lost steadily, with the occasional big win to keep him optimistic. But this time when he was down to fifty pounds he said: 'I only win when I gamble high. I'm putting the lot on this next hand.'

It was a big bet even for the Cowes Club. If Tonio lost he was finished. One or two club members saw the size of the stake and stood near the table to watch the play.

Micky dealt the cards.

He looked at Edward, on the left, who shook his head to indicate that he did not want another card.

On the right, Solly did the same.

Micky turned over his own cards. He had given himself an eight and an ace, making nine.

Edward turned over the hand on the left. Micky did not know what the cards were: he knew in advance what he himself was going to get, but he dealt the others at random. Edward had a five and a two, making seven. He and Captain Carter had lost their money.

Solly turned over his hand, the cards on which Tonio had staked his future.

He had a nine and a ten. That made nineteen, which counted as nine. This equalled the bank's score, so there was no winner or loser, and Tonio got to keep his fifty pounds.

Micky cursed under his breath.

He wanted Tonio to leave those fifty sovereigns on the table now. He gathered up the cards quickly. With a mocking note into his voice he said: 'Going to reduce your stake, Silva?'

'Certainly not,' said Tonio. 'Deal the cards.'

Micky thanked his stars and dealt, giving himself another winning hand.

This time Edward tapped his cards, indicating that he wanted a third. Micky dealt him a four of clubs and turned to Solly. Solly passed.

Micky turned over his cards and showed a five and a four. Edward had a four showing, and turned over a worthless king and another four, making eight. His side had lost.

Solly turned up a two and a four, making six. The right side had also lost to the banker.

And Tonio was ruined.

He turned pale and looked ill, and muttered something that Micky recognized as a Spanish curse.

Micky suppressed a smile of triumph and raked in his winnings – then he saw something that took his breath away and stopped his heart with dread.

There were four fours of clubs on the table.

They were supposed to be playing with three decks of cards. Anyone who noticed the four identical fours would immediately know that extra cards had somehow been added to the pack.

It was a hazard of this particular method of cheating, and the chances of its happening were roughly one in a hundred thousand.

If the anomaly were seen, it would be Micky, not Tonio, who was ruined.

So far no one had spotted it. Suits had no significance in this game, so the irregularity was not glaring. Micky picked up the cards swiftly, his heart beating hard. He was just thanking his stars that he had got away with it when Edward said: 'Hang on – there were four fours of clubs on the table.'

Micky cursed him for a blundering elephant. Edward was just thinking aloud. Of course he had no idea of Micky's scheme.

'Couldn't be,' said Viscount Montagne. 'We're playing with three decks of cards, so there are only three fours of clubs.'

'Exactly,' said Edward.

Micky puffed on his cigar. 'You're drunk, Pilaster. One of them was a four of spades.'

'Oh, sorry.'

Viscount Montagne said: 'At this time of night, who can tell the difference between spades and clubs?'

Once again Micky thought he had got away with it – and once again his elation was premature.

Tonio said belligerently: 'Let's look at the cards.'

Micky's heart seemed to stop. The cards from the last hand were placed on a pile which was shuffled and reused when the pack ran out. If the discards were turned over, the four identical fours would be seen, and Micky would be finished.

Desperately he said: 'I hope you're not questioning my word.'

This was a dramatic challenge to make in a gentlemen's club: it was not very many years since such words would have led to a duel. People at the neighbouring tables began to watch what was happening. Everyone looked at Tonio for his response.

Micky was thinking fast. If he could produce the four of spades from the top of the discard pile he would have proved his point – and with luck no one would look at the rest of the discards.

But first he had to find a four of spades. There were three. Some might be in the discard pile on the table, but the odds were that at least one was in the pack they had been playing with, which was in his hand.

It was his only chance.

While all eyes were on Tonio, he turned the pack so that the cards faced him. With infinitesimal movements of his thumb he exposed a corner of each card in turn. He kept his eyes firmly fixed on Tonio, but held the cards within his vision so that he could still read the letters and symbols in the corners.

Tonio said stubbornly: 'Let's look at the discards.'

The others turned to Micky. Steeling his nerve, he carried on fiddling with the pack, praying for a four of spades. In the midst of such drama no one remarked on what he was doing. The cards in contention were in the pile on the table, so it would seem to make no difference what he did with those in his hand. They would have to

171

look quite hard to see that behind his hands he was sorting through the pack, but even if they did so they would not immediately realize he was up to no good.

But he could not stand on his dignity indefinitely. Sooner or later one of them would lose patience, abandon courtesy, and pick up the discards. To gain a few precious moments he said: 'If you can't lose like a man, perhaps you oughtn't to play.' He felt a slight sweat break out on his forehead. He wondered whether he had missed a four of spades in his haste.

Solly said mildly: 'It can't hurt to look, can it?'

Damn Solly, always so sickeningly reasonable, Micky thought desperately.

Then at last he found a four of spades.

He palmed it.

'Oh, very well,' he said with a feigned nonchalance that was the polar opposite of what he was feeling.

Everyone became very still and quiet.

Micky put down the pack he had been furtively sorting through, keeping the four of spades in his palm. He reached out and picked up the discard pile, dropping the four on top. He placed the pile in front of Solly and said: 'There will be a four of spades in there, I guarantee.'

Solly turned over the top card, and they all saw that it was the four of spades.

A hum of conversation broke out around the room as they all relaxed.

Micky was still terrified that someone might turn over more cards and see that there were four fours of clubs underneath.

Viscount Montagne said: 'I think that settles it, and speaking for myself, Miranda, I can only apologize if any doubt has been cast upon your word.'

'Good of you to say so,' Micky said.

They all looked at Tonio. He stood up, his face working. 'Damn the lot of you, then,' he said, and he walked out.

Micky swept up all the cards on the table. Now no one would ever know the truth.

His palms were wet with perspiration. He wiped them surreptitiously on his trousers. 'I'm sorry about my compatriot's behaviour,' he said. 'If there's one thing I hate, it's a fellow who can't play cards like a gentleman.'

[IV]

I N THE EARLY hours of the morning Maisie and Hugh walked north through the raw new suburbs of Fulham and South Kensington. The night became hotter and the stars disappeared. They held hands, even though their palms were sweaty in the heat. Maisie felt bewildered but happy.

Something odd had happened tonight. She did not understand it but she liked it. In the past, when men had kissed her and touched her breasts, she had felt it was part of a transaction, something she gave in return for whatever she needed from them. Tonight had been different. She had *wanted* him to touch her – and he had been too polite to do anything without being asked!

It had started while they were dancing. Until then she had not been aware that this was going to be radically different from any previous evening spent with an upper-class young man. Hugh was more charming than most, and he looked good in his white waistcoat and silk tie, but still he was just a nice boy. Then, on the dance floor, she had begun to think how nice it would be to kiss him. The feeling had got stronger as they walked around the gardens after the dancing and saw all the other courting couples. His hesitation had been engaging. Other men saw dinner and conversation as a tedious preliminary to the important business of the evening, and could hardly wait to get her in a dark place and start groping, but Hugh had been shy.

In other respects he was the opposite of shy. In the riot he had been completely fearless. After he was knocked to the ground his only concern had been to make sure the same thing did not happen to her. There was a lot more to Hugh than the average young man-about-town.

When finally she had made him understand that she wanted to be kissed, it had been delicious, quite unlike any kiss she had had before. Yet he was not skilful or experienced. Quite the reverse: he was naive and uncertain. So why had she enjoyed it so much? And why had she suddenly longed to feel his hands on her breasts?

She was not tormented by these questions, just intrigued. She was contented, walking through London in the darkness with Hugh. Now and again she felt a few drops of rain, but the threatened cloudburst did not materialize. She began to think it would be nice to be kissed again soon.

They reached Kensington Gore and turned right, along the south side of the park, heading for the city centre where she lived. Hugh stopped opposite a huge house whose front was illuminated by two gaslights. He put his arm around her shoulders. 'That's my Aunt Augusta's house,' he said. 'That's where I live.'

She put her arm around his waist and stared at the house, wondering what it was like to live in such a vast mansion. She found it hard to imagine what you would do with all the rooms. After all, if you had somewhere to sleep and somewhere to cook, and perhaps the luxury of another room in which to entertain guests, what else did you need? There was no point in having two kitchens or two sitting rooms: you could only be in one at a time. It reminded her that she and Hugh lived on separate islands in society, divided by an ocean of money and privilege. The thought troubled her. 'I was born in a one-room hut,' she said.

'In the north-east?'

'No, in Russia.'

'Really? "Maisie Robinson" doesn't sound like a Russian name.'

'I was born Miriam Rabinowicz. We all changed our names when we came here.'

'Miriam,' he said softly. 'I like it.' He drew her to him and kissed her. Her anxiety evaporated and she gave herself up to the sensation. He was less hesitant now: he knew what he liked. She drank his kisses thirstily, like a glass of cold water on a hot day. She hoped he would touch her breasts again.

He did not disappoint her. A moment later she felt his hand close gently over her left breast. Almost immediately her nipple grew taut, and his fingertips touched it through the silk of her dress. She felt embarrassed that her desire should be so obvious, but it only inflamed him more.

After a while she wanted to feel his body. She reached inside his dress coat and ran her hands up and down his back, feeling the hot skin through the thin cotton of his shirt. She was behaving like a man, she thought. She wondered if he minded. But she was enjoying it too much to stop.

Then it started to rain.

It happened not gradually but all at once. There was a flash of lightning, a clap of thunder right afterwards, and an instant downpour. By the time they broke the kiss their faces were wet.

Hugh seized her hand and pulled. 'Let's take shelter in the house!' he said.

They ran across the road. Hugh led her down the steps,

past a sign saying 'Tradesmen's Entrance', to the basement area. By the time they reached the doorway she was soaked to the skin. Hugh unlocked the door. Putting a finger to his lips to indicate silence, he ushered her inside.

She hesitated for a fraction of a second, wondering whether she should ask exactly what he had in mind; but the thought slipped away and she stepped through the door.

They tiptoed through a kitchen the size of a small church to a narrow staircase. Hugh put his mouth to her ear and said: 'There'll be clean towels upstairs. We'll take the back staircase.'

She followed him up three long flights, then they passed through another door and emerged on a landing. He glanced through an open doorway into a bedroom where a nightlight burned. In a normal voice he said: 'Edward's still out. There's no one else on this floor. Aunt and Uncle's rooms are on the floor below us and the servants' above. Come.'

He led her into his bedroom and turned up the gaslight. 'I'll fetch towels,' he said, and went out again.

She took off her hat and looked around the room. It was surprisingly small, and furnished simply, with a single bed, a dresser, a plain wardrobe, and a small desk. She had expected something much more luxurious – but Hugh was a poor relation, and his room reflected that.

She looked with interest at his things. He had a pair of silver-backed hair brushes engraved with the initials *T.P.* – another heirloom from his father. He was reading a book called *The Handbook of Good Commercial Practice*. On the desk was a framed photograph of a woman and a girl about six years old. She slid open the drawer of his bedside table. There was a bible and another book underneath it. She moved the bible aside and read the title of the concealed book: it was called *The Duchess of Sodom*. She realized she was prying. Feeling guilty, she closed the drawer quickly.

Hugh came back with a pile of towels. Maisie took one. It was warm from an airing cupboard, and she buried her wet face in it gratefully. This is what it's like to be rich, she thought; great piles of warm towels whenever you need them. She dried her bare arms and her bosom. 'Who's the picture of?' she asked him.

'My mother and my sister. My sister was born after my father died.'

'What's her name?'

'Dorothy. I call her Dotty. I'm very fond of her.'

'Where do they live?'

'In Folkestone, by the sea.'

Maisie wondered if she would ever meet them.

Hugh drew up the chair from the desk and made her sit down. He knelt in front of her, took off her shoes, and dried her wet feet with a fresh towel. She closed her eyes: the sensation of the warm, soft towel on the soles of her feet was exquisite.

Her dress was wet through, and she shivered. Hugh removed his coat and boots. Maisie knew she could not get dry without taking off her dress. Underneath she was quite decent. She was not wearing knickers – only rich women did – but she had on a full-length petticoat and a chemise. Impulsively she stood up, turned her back to Hugh and said: 'Will you undo me?'

She could feel his hands shaking as his fingers fumbled with the hooks-and-eyes that fastened her dress. She was nervous too, but she could not back out now. When he had done she thanked him and stepped out of the dress.

She turned to face him.

His expression was a touching mixture of embarrassment and desire. He stood like Ali Baba staring at the thieves' treasure. She had thought vaguely that she would simply dry herself with a towel and put her dress back on later, when it had dried, but now she realized it was not going to be like that. And she was glad.

She put her hands on his cheeks, pulled his head down and kissed him. This time she opened her mouth, expecting him to do the same, but he did not. He had never kissed that way, she realized. She teased his lips with the tip of her tongue. She sensed that he was shocked but excited too, and after a moment he opened his mouth a fraction and responded shyly with his tongue. He began to breathe harder.

After a while he broke the kiss, reached for the top of her chemise and tried to undo the button. He fumbled for a moment then grasped the garment with both hands and tore it open, sending buttons flying. His hands closed over her bare breasts and he shut his eyes and groaned. She felt as if she were melting inside. She wanted more of this, now and always.

'Maisie,' he said.

She looked at him.

'I want to. . . .'

She smiled. 'So do I.'

When the words were out she wondered where they came from. She had spoken without thinking. But she had no doubts. She wanted him more than she had ever wanted anything.

He stroked her hair. 'I've never done it before,' he said.

'Nor have I.'

He stared at her. 'But I thought—' He stopped.

She felt a spasm of anger, then controlled herself. It was her own fault if he had thought she was promiscuous. 'Let's lie down,' she said.

He sighed happily, then said: 'Are you sure?'

'Am I sure?' she repeated. She could hardly believe he had said that. She had never known a man who would ask that question. They never thought about how she felt. She took his hand in hers and kissed the palm. 'If I wasn't sure before, I am now.'

She lay down on the narrow bed. The mattress was hard but the sheet was cool. He lay beside her and said: 'What now?'

They were approaching the limits of her experience, but she knew the next step. 'Feel me,' she said. He touched her tentatively through her clothing. Suddenly she was impatient. She pulled up her petticoat – she had nothing on underneath – and pressed his hand to her mound.

He stroked her, kissing her face, his breath hot and fast. She knew she should be afraid of getting pregnant, but she could not focus on the danger. She was out of control: the pleasure was too intense for her to think. This was as far as she had ever gone with a man, but all the same she knew exactly what she wanted next. She put her lips to his ear and murmured: 'Push your finger in.'

He did so. 'It's all wet,' he said wonderingly.

'That's to help you.'

His fingers explored her delicately. 'It seems so small.'

'You'll have to be gentle,' she said, although a part of her wanted to be taken furiously.

'Shall we do it now?'

She was suddenly impatient. 'Yes, please, quickly.'

She sensed him fumbling with his trousers, then he lay between her legs. She was frightened – she had heard stories about how much it hurt the first time – but she was also consumed by longing for him.

She felt him ease into her. After a moment he encountered resistance. He pushed gently, and it hurt. 'Stop!' she said.

He looked at her worriedly. 'I'm sorry—'

'It will be all right. Kiss me.'

He lowered his face to hers and kissed her lips, gently at first and then passionately. She put her hands on his waist, lifted her hips off the bed a little, then pulled him to her. There was a pain, sharp enough to make her cry out, then something gave way inside her and she felt a tremendous release of tension. She broke the kiss and looked at him.

'Are you all right?' he said.

She nodded. 'Did I make a noise?'

'Yes, but I don't think anyone heard.'

'Don't stop,' she said.

He hesitated a moment longer. 'Maisie,' he murmured, 'is this a dream?'

'If it is, let's not wake up yet.' She moved against him, guiding him with her hands on his hips. He followed her lead. It reminded her of how they had danced together just a few hours earlier. She gave herself up to the sensation. He began to pant.

Distantly, above the noise of his breathing and hers, she heard a door open.

She was so absorbed in her feelings and Hugh's body that the sound failed to alarm her.

Suddenly a harsh voice shattered the mood like a stone through a window. 'Well, well, Hugh – what's all this?'

Maisie froze.

Hugh gave a despairing groan, and she felt his seed spurt warm inside her.

She wanted to cry.

The sneering voice came again. 'What do you think this house is, a brothel?'

Maisie whispered: 'Hugh – get off me.'

He withdrew from her and rolled off the bed. She saw his cousin Edward standing in the doorway, smoking a cigar and staring at them intently. Hugh quickly covered her with a big towel. She sat upright and pulled it up to her neck.

Edward grinned nastily. 'Well, if you've finished I might give her a go.'

Hugh wrapped a towel around his waist. Controlling his anger with a visible effort, he said: 'You're drunk, Edward – go to your room before you say something completely unforgivable.'

Edward ignored him and approached the bed. 'Why, it's Solly Greenbourne's dollymop! But I won't tell him – so long as you're nice to me.'

Maisie saw that he was in earnest, and she shuddered with loathing. She knew that some men were inflamed by a woman who had just been with another man – April had told her the slang term for a woman in that state, a buttered bun – and she knew intuitively that Edward was such a man.

Hugh was enraged. 'Get out of here, you damn fool,' he said.

'Be a sport,' Edward persisted. 'After all, she's only a damned whore.' With that he reached down and snatched away Maisie's towel.

She jumped off the bed the other side, covering herself with her arms; but there was no need. Hugh took two strides across the little room and hit Edward a mighty punch on the nose. Blood spurted and Edward let out a roar of agony.

Edward was rendered harmless instantly, but Hugh was still angry, and he hit him again.

Edward screamed in fear and pain and blundered to the door. Hugh went after him, throwing punches at the back of his head. Edward began to yell: 'Leave me alone, stop it, please!' He fell through the doorway.

Maisie followed them out. Edward was stretched out on the floor and Hugh was sitting on top of him, still hitting him. She cried: 'Hugh, stop, you'll kill him!' She tried to grab Hugh's arms, but he was in a fury and it was hard to restrain him.

A moment later she glimpsed a movement out of the corner of her eye. She looked up and saw Hugh's Aunt Augusta standing at the top of the stairs in a black silk peignoir, staring at her. In the flickering gaslight she looked like a voluptuous ghost.

There was a strange look in Augusta's eyes. At first Maisie could not read her expression; then, after a moment, she understood, and she was frightened.

It was a look of triumph.

[V]

As SOON AS Augusta saw the naked girl she sensed that this was her chance to get rid of Hugh once and for all.

She recognized her immediately. This was the trollop who had insulted Augusta in the park, the one they called The Lioness. The thought had crossed her mind even then that this little minx might one day get Hugh into serious trouble: there was something arrogant and uncompromising in the set of her head and the light in her eyes. Even now, when she ought to be mortified by shame, she stood there, stark naked, and stared back at Augusta coolly. She had a magnificent body, small but shapely, with plump white breasts and a riot of sand-coloured hair at her groin. Her look was so haughty that she almost made Augusta feel like the intruder. But she would be the downfall of Hugh.

The outlines of a plan were forming in Augusta's mind when suddenly she saw Edward lying on the floor with blood all over his face.

All her old fears rose up in force, and she was taken back twenty-three years, to when he nearly died as a baby. Blind panic swamped her. 'Teddy!' she screamed. 'What's happened to Teddy!' She fell to her knees beside him. 'Speak to me, speak to me!' she yelled. She was possessed by an unbearable dread, just as she had been when her baby kept getting thinner and thinner every day and the doctors could not understand why.

Edward sat up and groaned.

'Say something!' she pleaded.

'Don't call me Teddy,' he said.

Her terror eased a fraction. He was conscious and could speak. But his voice was thick and his nose looked out of shape. 'What happened?' she said.

'I caught Hugh with his whore, and he just went mad!' Edward said.

Forcing down her rage and fear, she reached out gently and touched Edward's nose. He gave a loud yelp, but permitted her to press delicately. There was nothing broken, she thought; it was just swelling up.

She heard her husband's voice say: 'What the deuce is going on?'

She stood up. 'Hugh has attacked Edward,' she said.

'Is the boy all right?'

'I think so.'

Joseph turned to Hugh. 'Damnation, sir, what do you mean by it?'

'The silly fool asked for it,' Hugh said defiantly.

That's right, Hugh, make it worse, Augusta thought. Whatever you do, don't apologize. I want your uncle to stay angry with you.

However, Joseph's attention was torn between the boys and the woman, and his eyes kept switching to her naked body. Augusta felt a stab of jealousy.

That made her calmer. There was nothing much wrong with Edward. She began to think rapidly. How could she best exploit this situation? Hugh was totally vulnerable now: she could do anything to him. She thought immediately of her conversation with Micky Miranda. Hugh had to be silenced, for he knew too much about the death of Peter Middleton. Now was the moment to strike.

First she had to separate him from the girl.

Some servants had appeared in their nightclothes and were hovering in the doorway that led to the back stairs, looking aghast but fascinated by the scene on the landing. Augusta saw her butler, Hastead, in a yellow silk dressing-gown that Joseph had discarded some years ago, and Williams, a footman in a striped nightshirt. 'Hastead and Williams, help Mr Edward to his bed, will you?' The two men bustled forward and got Teddy to his feet.

Next Augusta spoke to her housekeeper. 'Mrs Merton, cover this girl with a sheet, or something, and take her to my room and get her dressed.' Mrs Merton took off her own dressing-gown and draped it around the girl's shoulders. She pulled it closed over her nakedness but made no move to leave.

Augusta said: 'Hugh, run to Dr Humbold's house in Church Street: he'd better have a look at poor Edward's nose.'

'I'm not leaving Maisie,' Hugh said.

Augusta said sharply: 'Since you've done the damage, it's the least you can do to fetch a doctor!'

Maisie said: 'I'll be all right, Hugh. Fetch the doctor. I'll be here when you get back.'

Still Hugh stood his ground.

Mrs Merton said: 'This way, please,' and indicated the back stairs.

Maisie said: 'Oh, I think we'll use the main staircase.' Then, walking like a queen, she crossed the landing and went down the stairs. Mrs Merton followed.

Augusta said: 'Hugh?'

He was still reluctant to go, she could see, but on the other hand he could think of no good reason to refuse. After a moment he said: 'I'll put my boots on.'

Augusta concealed her relief. She had separated them. Now, if her luck held, she would be able to seal Hugh's fate. She turned to her husband. 'Come. Let's go to your room and discuss this.'

They went down the stairs and entered his bedroom. As soon as the door was closed Joseph took her in his arms and kissed her. She realized he wanted to make love.

That was unusual. They made love once or twice a week, but she was always the initiator: she would go to his room and get into his bed. She saw it as part of her wifely duty to keep him satisfied, but she liked to be in control, so she discouraged him from coming to her room. When they were first married he had been harder to restrain. He had insisted on taking her whenever he wanted, and for a while she had been obliged to let him have his way; but eventually he had come round to her way of thinking. Then, for a while, he had bothered her with unseemly suggestions, such as that they should make love with the light on, that she should lie on top of him, and even that she should do unspeakable things to him with her mouth. But she had firmly resisted and he had long ago ceased to express such ideas.

Now, however, he was breaking the pattern. She knew why. He had been inflamed by the sight of Maisie's naked body, those firm young breasts and that bush of sandy hair.

The thought left a bad taste in her mouth, and she pushed him away.

He looked resentful. She wanted him angry with Hugh, not with her, so she touched his arm in a conciliatory gesture. 'Later,' she said. 'I'll come to you later.'

He accepted that. 'There's bad blood in Hugh,' he said. 'He gets it from my brother.'

'He can't continue to live here after this,' Augusta said in a tone that did not invite discussion.

Joseph was not disposed to argue that point. 'Indeed not.'

'You must discharge him from the bank,' she went on.

Joseph looked mulish. 'I beg you not to make announcements about what should happen at the bank.'

'Joseph, he has just insulted you by bringing into the house an unfortunate woman,' she said, using the euphemism for prostitute.

Joseph went and sat at his writing table. 'I know what he's done. I merely ask that you keep what happens in the house separate from what happens at the bank.'

She decided to retreat for a moment. 'Very well. I'm sure you know best.'

It always deflated him when she gave in unexpectedly. 'I suppose I had better discharge him,' he said after a moment. 'I imagine he will go back to his mother in Folkestone.'

Augusta was not sure about that. She had not yet worked out her strategy: she was thinking on her feet. 'What would he do for work?'

'I don't know.'

Augusta realized she had made a mistake. Hugh would be even more dangerous if he were unemployed, resentful and knocking around with nothing to do. David Middleton had not yet approached him – possibly Middleton had not yet learned that Hugh had been at the swimming-hole on the fateful day – but sooner or later he would. She became flustered, wishing she had thought more before insisting Hugh should be dismissed. She felt exasperated with herself.

Could she make Joseph change his mind back again?

She had to try. 'Perhaps we're being harsh,' she said.

He raised his eyebrows, surprised at this sudden display of mercy.

Augusta went on: 'Well, you keep saying that he has a great deal of potential as a banker. Perhaps it's unwise to throw that away.'

Joseph became annoyed. 'Augusta, do make up your mind what you want!'

She sat down on a low chair near his desk. She let her nightdress ride up and stretched out her legs. She still had good legs. He looked at them and his expression softened.

While he was distracted she racked her brains. Suddenly she was inspired. 'Send him abroad,' she said.

'Eh?'

The more she thought of the idea, the better she liked it. He would be out of reach of David Middleton, but still within her sphere of influence. 'The Far East, or South America,' she went on, warming to her theme. 'Some place where his bad behaviour will not reflect directly on my house.'

Joseph forgot his irritation with her. 'It's not a bad idea,' he said reflectively. 'There's an opening in the United States. The old boy who runs our Boston office needs an assistant.'

America would be perfect, Augusta thought. She was pleased with her own brilliance.

But at the moment Joseph was only toying with the idea. She wanted him to commit himself to it. 'Let Hugh go as soon as possible,' she said. 'I don't want him in the house another day.'

'He can book his passage in the morning,' Joseph said. 'After that there is no reason for him to stay in London. He can go down to Folkestone to say goodbye to his mother, and stay there until his ship sails.'

And he won't see David Middleton for years, Augusta thought with satisfaction. 'Splendid. It's settled, then.' Were there any other snags? She remembered Maisie. Did Hugh care for her? It seemed unlikely, but anything was possible. He might refuse to be parted from her. It was a loose end, and it worried Augusta. Hugh could not possibly take a trollop to Boston with him, but on the other hand he might refuse to leave London without her. Augusta wondered if she could nip the romance in the bud, just as a precaution.

She stood up and moved to the door that communicated with her bedroom. Joseph looked disappointed. 'I must get rid of that girl,' she said.

'Anything I can do?'

The question surprised her. It was not like him to make generalized offers of help. He wanted another look at the whore, she thought sourly. She shook her head. 'I'll come back. Get into bed.'

'Very well,' he said reluctantly.

She went into her own room and closed the door firmly behind her.

Maisie was clothed again and pinning her hat to her hair. Mrs Merton was folding up a rather flashy blue-green gown and cramming it into a cheap bag. 'I've loaned her a dress of mine, as hers is soaked, mum,' said the housekeeper.

That answered a little question that had been nagging Augusta. She had thought it was unlike Hugh to do something as blatantly stupid as to bring home a whore. Now she saw how it had come about. They had been caught in the sudden storm, and Hugh had brought the woman inside to get dry, then one thing had led to another.

'What is your name?' she said to the girl.

'Maisie Robinson. I know yours.'

Augusta found that she loathed Maisie Robinson. She was not sure why: the girl was hardly worthy of such strong feelings. It had something to do with the way she had looked when naked: so proud, so voluptuous, so independent. 'I suppose you want money,' Augusta said disdainfully.

'You hypocritical cow,' Maisie said. 'You didn't marry that rich, ugly husband of yours for love.'

It was the truth, and the words took Augusta's breath away. She had underestimated this young woman. She had made a bad beginning, and now she had to dig herself out of the hole. From now on she must handle Maisie carefully. This was a providential opportunity, and she must not waste it.

She swallowed hard and forced herself to sound neutral. 'Will you sit down for a moment?' She indicated a chair.

Maisie looked surprised, but after a moment's hesitation she took a seat.

Augusta sat opposite her.

The girl had to be made to give Hugh up. She had been scornful when Augusta had hinted at a bribe, and Augusta was reluctant to repeat the offer: she sensed that money would not work with this girl. But she was clearly not the type to be bullied either.

Augusta would have to make her believe that separation would be the best thing for both Maisie and Hugh. It would work best if Maisie thought that giving Hugh up was her own idea. And that might be best achieved by

Augusta arguing the opposite. Now, there was a good notion. . . .

Augusta said: 'If you want to marry him, I can't stop you.' The girl looked surprised, and Augusta congratulated herself on having caught her off guard.

'What makes you think I want to marry him?' Maisie said.

Augusta almost laughed. She wanted to say: *The fact that you're a scheming little gold-digger*, but instead she said: 'What girl wouldn't want to marry him? He's personable and good-looking and he comes from a great family. He has no money, but his prospects are excellent.'

Maisie narrowed her eyes and said: 'It almost sounds as if you want me to marry him.'

Augusta intended to give exactly that impression, but she had to tread delicately. Maisie was suspicious and seemed too bright to be easily hoodwinked. 'Let's not be fanciful, Maisie,' she said. 'Forgive me for saying so, but no woman of my class would wish a man of her family to marry quite so far below him.'

Maisie showed no resentment. 'She might if she hated him enough.'

Feeling encouraged, Augusta continued to lead her on. 'But I don't hate Hugh,' she said. 'Whatever gave you that idea?'

'He did. He told me you treat him as a poor relation and make sure everyone else does the same.'

'How ungrateful people can be. But why would I wish to ruin his career?'

'Because he shows up that ass of a son of yours, Edward.'

A wave of anger engulfed Augusta. Once again Maisie had come uncomfortably close to the truth. It was true that Edward lacked Hugh's low cunning, but Edward was a fine, sweet young man and Hugh was ill-bred. 'I think you had better not mention the name of my son,' Augusta said in a low voice.

Maisie grinned. 'I seem to have touched a sore place.' She immediately became grave again. 'So that's your game. Well, I won't play it.'

'What do you mean?' said Augusta.

Suddenly there were tears in Maisie's eyes. 'I like Hugh too much to ruin him.'

Augusta was surprised and pleased by the strength of Maisie's passion. This was working out perfectly, despite the bad beginning. 'What are you going to do?' Augusta asked.

Maisie struggled not to cry. 'I shan't see him any more. You may yet destroy him, but you won't have my help.'

'He might come after you.'

'I shall disappear. He doesn't know where I live. I'll stay away from the places where he might look for me.'

A good plan, Augusta thought; you'll only need to keep it up for a short while, then he will go abroad and be away for years, perhaps for ever. But she said nothing. She had led Maisie to the obvious conclusion and now the girl needed no further help.

Maisie wiped her face on her sleeve. 'I'd better go now, before he comes back with the doctor.' She stood up. 'Thank you for lending me your dress, Mrs Merton.'

The housekeeper opened the door for her. 'I'll show you out.'

'We'll take the back stairs this time, please,' Maisie said. 'I don't want—' She stopped, swallowed hard, and said in a near-whisper: 'I don't want to see Hugh again.'

Then she went out.

Mrs Merton followed and closed the door.

Augusta let out a long breath. She had done it. She had stunted Hugh's career, neutralized Maisie Robinson, and averted the danger from David Middleton, all in one night. Maisie had been a formidable opponent, but in the end she had proved too emotional.

Augusta savoured her triumph for a few moments then went up to Edward's room.

He was sitting up in bed, sipping brandy from a goblet. His nose was bruised and there was dried blood around it, and he looked somewhat sorry for himself. 'My poor boy,' Augusta said. She went to his nightstand and damped a corner of a towel, then sat on the edge of the bed and wiped the blood from his upper lip. He winced. 'Sorry!' she said.

He gave her a smile. 'That's all right, Mother,' he said. 'Do carry on. It's very soothing.'

While she was washing him Dr Humbold came in, closely followed by Hugh. 'Have you been fighting, young man?' the doctor said cheerily.

Augusta took exception to that suggestion. 'He certainly has not,' she said crossly. 'He has been attacked.'

Humbold was crushed. 'Quite so, quite so,' he muttered.

Hugh said: 'Where's Maisie?'

Augusta did not want to talk about Maisie in front of the doctor. She stood up and took Hugh outside. 'She left.'

'Did you send her away?' he demanded.

Augusta was inclined to tell him not to speak to her in that tone of voice, but she decided there was nothing to be gained by angering him: her victory over him was already total, though he did not know it. She said in a conciliatory tone: 'If I had thrown her out, do you not think she would have been waiting in the street to tell you so? No, she left of her own accord, and she said she would write to you tomorrow.'

'But she said she would still be here when I got back with the doctor.'

'Then she changed her mind. Have you never known a girl of her age to do that?'

Hugh looked bewildered, but he did not know what to say next.

Augusta added: 'No doubt she wished to extricate herself as quickly as possible from the embarrassing position in which you had put her.'

That seemed to make sense to him. 'I suppose you made her feel so uncomfortable that she couldn't bear to remain in the house.'

'That will do,' she said severely. 'I don't wish to hear your opinions. Your Uncle Joseph will see you first thing in the morning, before you leave for the bank. Now goodnight.'

For a moment he seemed as if he would argue. However, there was really nothing for him to say. 'Very well,' he muttered at last. He turned into his room.

Augusta went back into Edward's room. The doctor was closing his bag. 'No real damage,' he said. 'His nose will feel tender for a few days, and he may have a black eye tomorrow; but he's young, and he'll soon heal.'

'Thank you, doctor. Hastead will see you out.'

'Good night.'

Augusta bent over the bed and kissed Edward. 'Good night, dear Teddy. Go to sleep, now.'

'Very well, Mother dear. Good night.'

She had one more task to perform.

She went down the stairs and entered Joseph's room. She was hoping he would have gone to sleep waiting for her, but he was sitting up in bed, reading the *Pall Mall Gazette*. He put it aside immediately and lifted the covers to let her in.

He embraced her immediately. She realized it was quite

light in the room: dawn had broken without her noticing it. She closed her eyes.

He entered her quickly. She put her arms around him and responded to his movements. She thought of herself when she was sixteen, lying on a river bank in a raspberry-pink dress and a straw hat, being kissed by the young Earl of Strang; only in her mind he did not stop at kissing her, but lifted her skirts and made love to her in the hot sunshine, with the river lapping at their feet. . . .

When it was over she lay beside Joseph for a while, reflecting on her victory.

'Extraordinary night,' he murmured sleepily.

'Yes,' she said. 'That awful girl.'

'Mmm,' he grunted. 'Very striking-looking . . . arrogant and wilful . . . thinks she's as good as anyone . . . lovely figure . . . just like you at that age.'

Augusta was mortally offended. 'Joseph!' she said. 'How could you say such an awful thing?'

He made no reply, and she saw that he was asleep.

Enraged, she threw back the covers, got out of bed and stamped out of the room.

She did not go back to sleep that night.

[VI]

MICKY MIRANDA's lodgings in suburban Camberwell consisted of two rooms in a terraced house belonging to a widow with a grown-up son. None of his high-class friends had ever visited him there, not even Edward Pilaster. Micky played the role of a young man-about-town on a very tight budget, and elegant accommodation was one of the things he could manage without.

At nine o'clock each morning the landlady brought coffee

and hot rolls for him and Papa. Over breakfast, Micky explained how he had caused Tonio Silva to lose a hundred pounds he did not have. He did not expect his father to sing his praises, but he did hope for a grudging acknowledgement of his ingenuity. However, Papa was not impressed. He blew on his coffee and slurped it noisily. 'So, has he gone back to Cordova?'

'Not yet, but he will.'

'You hope. So much trouble, and still you only *hope* he will go.'

Micky felt wounded. 'I'll seal his fate today,' he protested.

'When I was your age . . .'

'You would have slit his throat, I know. But this is London, not Santamaria Province, and if I go around cutting people's throats they'll hang me.'

'There are times when you have no choice.'

'But there are other times when it's better to tread softly, Papa. Think of Samuel Pilaster, and his milk-and-water objections to dealing in guns. I got him out of the way without bloodshed, didn't I?' In fact Augusta had done it, but Micky had not told Papa that.

'I don't know,' Papa said stubbornly. 'When do I get the rifles?'

It was a sore point. Old Seth was still alive, still Senior Partner of Pilasters Bank. It was August. In September the winter snow would start to melt on the mountains of Santamaria. Papa wanted to go home – with his weapons. As soon as Joseph became Senior Partner, Edward would put the deal through and the guns would be shipped. But Old Seth clung on with infuriating stubbornness to his post and his life.

'You'll get them soon, Papa,' said Micky. 'Seth can't last much longer.'

'Good,' said Papa, with the smug expression of one who has won an argument.

Micky buttered a roll. It had always been like this. He could never please his father no matter how he tried.

He turned his mind to the day ahead. Tonio now owed money he could never pay. The next step was to turn a problem into a crisis. He wanted Edward and Tonio to quarrel publicly. If he could arrange that, Tonio's disgrace would become general knowledge and he would be obliged to resign from his job and go home to Cordova. That would put him comfortably out of the reach of David Middleton.

Micky wanted to do all this without making an enemy of Tonio. For he had another purpose: he wanted Tonio's job. Tonio could make matters difficult, if he felt so inclined, by maligning Micky to the Minister. Micky wanted to persuade him to smooth the path.

The whole situation was complicated by the history of his relationship with Tonio. At school Tonio had hated and feared Micky; more recently Tonio had been admiring of him. Now Micky needed to become Tonio's best friend – at the same time as he ruined his life.

While Micky was brooding over the tricky day ahead of him, there was a knock at the door to the room and the landlady announced a visitor. A moment later Tonio came in.

Micky had been planning to call on him after breakfast. This would save him the trouble.

'Sit down, have some coffee,' he said cheerfully. 'Bad luck last night! Still, winning and losing, that's what cards are all about.'

Tonio bowed to Papa and sat down. He looked as if he had not slept. 'I lost more than I can afford,' he said.

Papa grunted impatiently. He had no patience with

people feeling sorry for themselves, and anyway he despised the Silva family as lily-livered city dwellers who lived by patronage and corruption.

Micky pretended sympathy and said solemnly: 'I'm sorry to hear that.'

'You know what it means. In this country, a man who doesn't pay his gambling debts isn't a gentleman. And a man who isn't a gentleman can't be a diplomat. I might have to resign and go home.'

Exactly, thought Micky; but he said in a sorrowful voice: 'I do see the problem.'

Tonio went on: 'You know what fellows are like about these things – if you don't pay up the next day you're already under suspicion. But it would take me years to pay back a hundred pounds. That's why I've come to you.'

'I don't understand,' said Micky, though he understood perfectly.

'Will you give me the money?' Tonio pleaded. 'You're Cordovan, not like these English; you don't condemn a man for one mistake. And I would pay you back, eventually.'

'If I had the money I'd give it to you,' said Micky. 'I wish I were that well off.'

Tonio looked at Papa, who stared at him coldly and said simply: 'No.'

Tonio hung his head. 'I'm such a fool about gambling,' he said in a hollow voice. 'I don't know what I'm going to do. If I go home in disgrace I won't be able to face my family.'

Micky said thoughtfully: 'Perhaps there is something else I can do to help.'

Tonio brightened. 'Oh, please, anything!'

'Edward and I are good friends, as you know. I could

speak to him on your behalf, explain the circumstances, and ask him to be lenient – as a personal favour to me.'

'Would you?' Tonio's face was suffused with hope.

'I'll ask him to wait for his money, and not to tell anyone. I don't say he'll agree to it, mind you. The Pilasters have money by the bucketful but they're a hard-headed bunch. I'll try, anyway.'

Tonio clasped Micky's hand. 'I don't know how to thank you,' he said fervently. 'I'll never forget this.'

'Don't raise your hopes too high—'

'I can't help it. I've been in despair, and you've given me a reason to go on.' Tonio looked shamefaced and added: 'I thought of killing myself this morning. I walked across London Bridge and I was going to throw myself into the river.'

There was a soft grunt from Papa, who clearly thought that would have been the best thing all round.

Micky said hastily: 'Thank God you changed your mind. Now, I'd better go along to Pilasters Bank and talk to Edward.'

'When will I see you?'

'Will you be at the club at lunch time?'

'Of course, if you want me to.'

'Meet me there, then.'

'Right.' Tonio stood up. 'I'll leave you to finish your breakfast. And—'

'Don't thank me,' Micky said, holding up his hand in a silencing gesture. 'It's unlucky. Wait and hope.'

'Yes. All right.' Tonio bowed again to Papa. 'Goodbye, Señor Miranda.' He went out.

'Stupid boy,' Papa muttered.

'A complete fool,' Micky agreed.

Micky went into the next room and dressed in his morning clothes: a white shirt with a stiff upright collar and starched cuffs, buff-coloured trousers, a black satin stock which he took the trouble to tie perfectly, and a black double-breasted frock-coat. His shoes gleamed with wax and his hair shone with macassar oil. He always dressed elegantly but conservatively: he would never wear one of the fashionable new turndown collars, or carry a monocle like a dandy. The English were ever ready to believe that a foreigner was a cad, and he took care to give them no excuse.

Leaving Papa to his own devices for the day, he went out and walked across the bridge into the financial district, which was called the City, because it covered the square mile of the original Roman city of London. Traffic was at a complete standstill around St Paul's Cathedral as carriages, horse-buses, brewers' drays, hansom cabs and costermongers' barrows competed for space with a huge flock of sheep being driven to Smithfield meat market.

Pilasters Bank was a big new building with a long classical frontage and an imposing entrance flanked by massive fluted pillars. It was a few minutes past noon when Micky went through the double doors into the banking hall. Although Edward rarely got to work before ten, he could generally be persuaded to leave for lunch any time after twelve.

Micky approached one of the walkers and said: 'Be good enough to tell Mr Edward Pilaster that Mr Miranda has called.'

'Very good, sir.'

Here more than anywhere Micky envied the Pilasters. Their wealth and power was proclaimed by every detail: the polished marble floor, the rich panelling, the hushed voices, the scratch of pens in ledgers, and perhaps most of all by the overfed, overdressed messengers. All this space and all these people were basically employed in counting the Pilaster family's money. No one here raised cattle, mined nitrate or built railroads: the work was done by others far away. The Pilasters just watched the money multiply. To Micky it seemed the best possible way to live now that slavery had been abolished.

There was also something false about the atmosphere here. It was solemn and dignified, like a church, or the court of a president, or a museum. They were moneylenders, but they acted as if charging interest was a noble calling, like the priesthood.

After a few minutes Edward appeared – with a bruised nose and a black eye. Micky raised his eyebrows. 'My dear fellow, what happened to you?'

'I had a fight with Hugh.'

'What about?'

'I told him off for bringing a whore into the house and he lost his temper.'

It occurred to Micky that this might have given Augusta the opportunity she had been seeking to get rid of Hugh. 'What happened to Hugh?'

'You won't see him again for a long time. He's been sent to Boston.'

Well done, Augusta, thought Micky. It would be neat if both Hugh and Tonio could be dealt with on the same day. He said: 'You look as if you might benefit from a bottle of champagne and some lunch.'

'Splendid idea.'

They left the bank and headed west. There was no point in getting into a hansom here because the streets were blocked by the sheep and the cabs were all stuck in the traffic. They passed the meat market which was the destination of the sheep. The stench from the slaughterhouses was unbearably disgusting. The sheep were thrown from the street through a trapdoor down into the underground abattoir. The fall was sufficient to break their legs, which rendered them motionless until the slaughterer was ready to cut their throats. 'It's enough to put you off mutton for life,' Edward said as they covered their faces with handkerchiefs. Micky thought it would take a lot more than that to put Edward off his lunch.

Once out of the City they hailed a hansom and directed it to Pall Mall. As soon as they were on their way, Micky began his prepared speech. He started by saying: 'I hate a chap who spreads reports about another chap's bad behaviour.'

'Yes,' Edward said vaguely.

'But when it affects a chap's friends, a chap is more or less obliged to say something.'

'Mmm.' Edward clearly had no idea what Micky was talking about.

'And I'd hate you to think I kept quiet about it just because he was a countryman of mine.'

There was a moment's silence, then Edward said: 'I'm not quite sure I follow you.'

'I'm talking about Tonio Silva.'

'Ah, yes. I suppose he can't afford to pay what he owes me.'

'Utter nonsense. I know his family. They're almost as rich as yours.' Micky was not afraid to tell this outrageous lie: people in London had no idea how wealthy South American families might be.

Edward was surprised. 'Good Lord. I thought the opposite.'

'Not at all. He can afford it easily. That makes it worse.'

'What? Makes what worse?'

Micky gave a heavy sigh. 'I'm afraid he has no intention of paying you. And he's been going around boasting about it, saying you aren't man enough to make him pay.'

Edward reddened. 'Has he, by the devil! Not man enough! We'll see about that.'

'I warned him not to underestimate you. I told him I was afraid you might not stand to be made a fool of. But he chose to ignore my advice.'

'The scoundrel. Well, if he won't listen to wise counsel he may have to find out the truth the hard way.'

'It's a shame,' said Micky.

Edward fumed in silence.

Micky fretted impatiently while the hansom crawled along the Strand. Tonio should be at the club by now. Edward was in just the right mood to quarrel. Everything was working out just right.

At last the cab pulled up outside the club. Micky waited while Edward paid the driver. They went inside. In the cloakroom, in a knot of people hanging up their hats, they met Tonio.

Micky tensed. He had put everything in place: now he could only cross his fingers and hope that the drama he had envisioned would play itself out as planned.

Tonio caught Edward's eye, looked awkward, and said: 'By Jove . . . Good morning, you two.'

Micky looked at Edward. His face turned pink and his eyes bulged, and he said: 'See here, Silva.'

Tonio stared at him fearfully. 'What is it, Pilaster?'

Edward said loudly: 'About that hundred pounds.'

The room went suddenly quiet. Several people looked around and two men on their way out stopped in the doorway and turned to see. It was bad behaviour to talk about money, and a gentleman would do so only in extreme circumstances. Everyone knew that Edward Pilaster had more money than he knew what to do with, so it was obvious he had some other motive for publicly mentioning Tonio's debt. Bystanders sensed a scandal.

Tonio went white. 'Yes?'

Edward said brutally: 'You can let me have it today, if it would suit your convenience.'

A challenge had been issued. Plenty of people knew the debt was real, so there was no point in arguing about it. As a gentleman, Tonio had only one option. He had to say: *By all means. If it's important, you shall have your money right away. Let's go upstairs, and I'll write you a cheque – or shall we step around the corner to my bank?* If he did not do that, everyone would know he could not pay, and he would be ostracized.

Micky watched with horrid fascination. At first a look of panic came over Tonio's face, and for a moment Micky wondered whether he would do something crazy. Then fear gave way to anger, and he opened his mouth to protest, but no words came out. Instead he spread his hands in a pleading gesture; but he quickly abandoned that, too. Finally his face crumpled like the face of a child about to cry. At that point he turned and ran. The two men in the doorway dodged out of his way, and he dashed through the lobby and out into the street without his hat.

Micky was elated: it had all gone perfectly.

The men in the cloakroom all coughed and fidgeted to disguise their embarrassment. An older member muttered: 'That was a bit hard, Pilaster.'

Micky said quickly: 'He deserved it.'

'No doubt, no doubt,' said the older man.

Edward said: 'I need a drink.'

Micky said: 'Order a brandy for me, would you? I'd better go after Silva and make sure he doesn't throw himself under the wheels of a horse-bus.' He dashed out.

This was the most subtle part of his plan: he now had to convince the man he had ruined that he was his best friend.

Tonio was hurrying along in the direction of St James's, not looking where he was going, bumping into people.

Micky ran and caught up with him. 'I say, Silva, I'm dreadfully sorry,' he said.

Tonio stopped. There were tears on his cheeks. 'I'm finished,' he said. 'It's all over.'

'Pilaster turned me down flat,' Micky said. 'I did my best. . . .'

'I know. Thank you.'

'Don't thank me. I failed.'

'But you tried. I wish there was something I could do to show my appreciation.'

Micky hesitated, thinking: *Do I dare to ask him for his job, right now?* He decided to be bold. 'As a matter of fact there is – but we should talk about it another time.'

'No, tell me now.'

'I'd feel bad. Let's leave it until another day.'

'I don't know how many more days I'll be here. What is it?'

'Well . . .' Micky feigned embarrassment. 'I suppose the Cordovan Minister will eventually be looking for someone to replace you.'

'He'll need someone right away.' Comprehension showed on Tonio's tear-stained face. 'Of course – you should have the job! You'd be perfect!'

'If you could put in a word . . .'

'I'll do more than that. I'll tell him what a help you've been, and how you tried to get me out of the mess I got myself into. I'm sure he'll want to appoint you.'

'I wish I weren't benefiting from your troubles,' Micky said. 'I feel I'm behaving like a rat.'

'Not at all.' Tonio took Micky's hand in both his. 'You're a true friend.'

CHAPTER FIVE

September

[I]

Hugh's six-year-old sister Dorothy was folding his shirts and packing them into his trunk. He knew that as soon as she went to bed he would have to take them all out and do them again, because her folding was hopelessly untidy; but he pretended she was very good at it, and encouraged her.

'Tell me about America again,' she said.

'America is so far away that in the morning the sun takes four hours to get there.'

'Do they stay in bed all morning?'

'Yes – then they get up at lunch time and have breakfast!' She giggled. 'They're lazy.'

'Not really. You see, it doesn't get dark until midnight, so they have to work all evening.'

'And they go to bed late! I like going to bed late. I'd like America. Why can't we go with you?'

'I wish you could, Dotty.' Hugh felt rather wistful: he would not see his baby sister again for years. She would be changed when he returned. She would understand time zones.

September rain drummed on the windows, and down in the bay the wind lashed the waves, but here there was a coal fire and a soft hearth-rug. Hugh packed a handful of books: *Modern Business Methods*, *The Successful Commercial Clerk*, *The Wealth of Nations*, *Robinson Crusoe*. The older clerks at Pilasters Bank were contemptuous of what they called 'book-learning', and were fond of saying that experience was the best teacher, but they were wrong: Hugh had been able to understand the workings of the different departments much more quickly because he had studied the theory beforehand.

He was going to America at a time of crisis. In the early 1870s several of the banks had made large loans on the security of speculative railway stocks, and when railway construction ran into trouble in the middle of 1873 the banks started to look shaky. A few days ago Jay Cooke & Co., the agents of the American government, had gone bust, dragging the First National Bank of Washington down with them; and the news had reached London the same day via the transatlantic telegraph cable. Now five New York banks had suspended business, including the Union Trust Company – a major bank – and the old-established Mechanics' Banking Association. The Stock Exchange had closed its doors. Businesses would fail, thousands of people would be thrown out of work, trade would suffer, and Pilasters' American operation would get smaller and more cautious – so that it would be harder for Hugh to make his mark.

So far the crisis had had little impact in London. The Bank Rate had gone up a point, to four per cent, and a small London bank with close American links had failed, but there was no panic. All the same, Old Seth insisted there was trouble ahead. He was quite weak, now. He had moved into Augusta's house and spent most days in bed.

But he stubbornly refused to resign until he had steered Pilasters through the storm.

Hugh began to fold his clothes. The bank had paid for two new suits: he had a suspicion his mother had persuaded his grandfather to authorize that. Old Seth was as tight-fisted as the rest of the Pilasters but he had a soft spot for Hugh's mother; in fact it was the small allowance Seth gave her that she had been living on all these years.

Mother had also insisted Hugh be allowed a few weeks off before leaving, to give him more time to get ready and say his goodbyes. She had not seen much of him since he had gone to work at the bank – he could not afford the train fare to Folkestone very often – and she wanted to have some time with him before he left the country. They had spent most of August here, at the seaside, while Augusta and her family had been on holiday in Scotland. Now the holidays were over and it was time to leave, and Hugh was saying goodbye to his mother.

While he was thinking of her she came into the room. She was in her eighth year of widowhood but she still wore black. She did not seem to want to marry again, although she easily could have – she was still beautiful, with serene blue eyes and thick blonde hair.

He knew she was sad that she would not see him for years. But she had not spoken of her sadness: rather, she shared his excitement and trepidation at the challenge of a new country.

'It's almost bedtime, Dorothy,' she said. 'Go and put on your nightdress.' As soon as Dotty was out of the room, Mother began to refold Hugh's shirts.

He wanted to talk to her about Maisie, but he felt shy. Augusta had written to her, he knew. She might also have heard from other family members, or even seen them on one of her rare shopping trips to London. The story she had heard might be a long way from the truth. After a moment he said: 'Mother . . .'

'What is it, dear?'

'Aunt Augusta doesn't always say quite what is true.'

'No need to be so polite,' she said with a bitter smile. 'Augusta has been telling lies about your father for years.'

Hugh was startled by her frankness. 'Do you think it was she who told Florence Stalworthy's parents that he was a gambler?'

'I'm quite sure of it, unfortunately.'

'Why is she this way?'

Mother put down the shirt she was folding and thought for a minute. 'Augusta was a very beautiful girl,' she said. 'Her family worshipped at Kensington Methodist Hall, which is how we knew them. She was an only child, wilful and spoilt. Her parents were nothing special: her father was a shop assistant who had started his own business and ended up with three little grocery stores in the west London suburbs. But Augusta was clearly destined for higher things.'

She went to the rainy window and looked out, seeing not the stormy English Channel but the past. 'When she was seventeen the Earl of Strang fell for her. He was a lovely boy – comely, kind, high-born, and rich. Naturally his parents were horrified at the prospect that he should marry a grocer's daughter. However, she was very beautiful, and even then, though she was young, she had a dignified air that could carry her through most social situations.'

'Did they become engaged?' Hugh asked.

'Not formally. But everyone assumed it was a foregone conclusion. Then there was a dreadful scandal. Her father was accused of systematically giving short weight in his shops. An employee he had sacked reported him to the Board of Trade. It was said that he had even cheated the church, which bought tea from him for the Tuesday evening Bible study groups and so on. There was a chance he would go to jail. He denied everything vehemently, and in the end nothing came of it. But Strang dropped Augusta.'

'She must have been heartbroken.'

'No,' Mother said. 'Not heartbroken. She was wild with rage. All her life she had been able to have her own way. Now she wanted Strang more than she had ever wanted anything – and she couldn't have him.'

'And she married Uncle Joseph on the rebound, as they say.'

'I'd say she married him in a fit of temper. He was older than she by seven years, which is a lot when you're seventeen; and he wasn't much better looking then than he is now; but he was very rich, even richer than Strang. To give her credit, she has done all she can to be a good wife to him. But he will never be Strang, and she is still angry about that.'

'What happened to Strang?'

'He married a French countess and died in a hunting accident.'

'I almost feel sorry for Augusta.'

'No matter what she has, she always wants more: more money, a more important job for her husband, a higher social position for herself. The reason she is so ambitious – for herself, for Joseph and for Edward – is that she still yearns for what Strang could have given her: the title, the ancestral home, the life of endless leisure, wealth without work. But that isn't what Strang offered her, in truth. He offered her love. That's what she's really lost. And nothing will ever make up for it.'

Hugh had never had such an intimate conversation with his mother. He felt encouraged to open his heart to her. 'Mother,' he began. 'About Maisie . . .'

She looked puzzled. 'Maisie?'

'The girl . . . all the trouble is about. Maisie Robinson.'

Her face cleared. 'Augusta never told anyone her name.'

He hesitated, then blurted out: 'She's not an "unfortunate" woman.'

Mother was embarrassed: men never mentioned such things as prostitution to their mothers. 'I see,' she said, looking away.

Hugh ploughed on. 'She is lower-class, that much is right. And Jewish.' He looked at her face and saw that she was startled, but not horrified. 'She's nothing worse than that. In fact . . .' He hesitated.

Mother looked at him. 'Go on.'

'In fact, she was a maiden.'

Mother blushed.

'I'm sorry to speak of such things, Mother,' he said. 'But if I don't you'll only know Aunt Augusta's version of the story.'

Mother swallowed. 'Were you fond of her, Hugh?'

'Rather.' He felt tears come to his eyes. 'I don't understand why she disappeared. I've no idea where she went. I never knew her address. I've inquired at the livery stables she worked for, and at the Argyll Rooms where I met her. Solly Greenbourne was fond of her too, and he's as baffled as I am. Tonio Silva knew her friend April, but Tonio has gone back to South America and I can't find April.'

'How mysterious.'

'I'm sure Aunt Augusta arranged this somehow.'

'I have no doubt of it. I can't imagine how, but she is appallingly devious. However, you must look to the future now, Hugh. Boston will be such an opportunity for you. You must work hard and conscientiously.'

'She really is an extraordinary girl, Mother.'

Mother did not believe him, he could tell. She said: 'But you'll forget her.'

'I wonder if I ever shall.'

Mother kissed his forehead. 'You will. I promise.'

[II]

THERE WAS only one picture on the wall in the attic room Maisie shared with April. It was a garish circus poster showing Maisie, in spangled tights, standing on the back of a galloping horse. Underneath, in red letters, were the words THE AMAZING MAISIE. The picture was not very true to life, for the circus had not actually had any white horses, and Maisie's legs had never been that long. All the same she cherished the poster. It was her only souvenir of those days.

Otherwise the room contained only a narrow bed, a wash-stand, one chair and a three-legged stool. The girls' clothes hung from nails banged into the wall. The dirt on the window served instead of curtains. They tried to keep the place clean but it was impossible. Soot fell down the chimney, mice came up through the cracks in the floorboards, and dirt and insects crept in through the gaps between the window-frame and the surrounding brickwork. Today it was raining, and water dripped from the windowsill and from a crack in the ceiling.

Maisie was getting dressed. It was Rosh Hashanah, when the Book of Life was open, and at this time of year she always wondered what was being written for her. She never actually prayed, but she did hope, in a solemn kind of way, that something good was going on her page of the Book.

April had gone to make tea in the communal kitchen,

but now she came back, bursting into the room with a newspaper in her hand. 'It's you, Maisie, it's you!' she said.

'What?'

'In the *Lloyd's Weekly News*. Listen to this "Miss Maisie Robinson, formerly Miriam Rabinowicz. If Miss Robinson will contact Messrs Goldman and Jay, Solicitors, at Gray's Inn, she will learn something to her advantage." It must be you!'

Maisie's heart beat faster, but she made her expression stern and her voice cold. 'It's Hugh,' she said. 'I'll not go.'

April looked disappointed. 'You might have inherited money from a long-lost relation.'

'I might be the Queen of Mongolia, but I'll not walk all the way to Gray's Inn on the off-chance.' She was managing to sound flippant, but her heart ached. She thought about Hugh every day and every night, and she was miserable. She hardly knew him, but it was impossible to forget him.

Nevertheless she was determined to try. She knew he had been searching for her. He had been at the Argyll Rooms every night, he had badgered Sammles the stable-owner, and he had inquired for her at half the cheap lodging-houses in London. Then the inquiries had ceased, and Maisie assumed he had given up. Now it seemed he had merely changed his tactics, and was trying to reach her with newspaper advertisements. It was very hard to continue to avoid him when he was searching so persistently for her and she wanted so badly to see him again. But she had made her decision. She loved him too much to ruin him.

She put her arms into her corset. 'Help me with my stays,' she said to April.

April began pulling the laces. 'I've never had my name in the paper,' she said enviously. 'You have twice, now, if you count "The Lioness" as a name.'

'And how much good has it done me? By God, I'm getting fat.'

April tied the laces and helped her into her gown. They were going out tonight. April had a new lover, a middle-aged magazine editor with a wife and six children in Clapham. This evening he and a friend were taking April and Maisie to a music-hall.

Between now and then they would walk along Bond Street and stare into the windows of fashionable shops. They would not buy anything. In order to hide from Hugh, Maisie had been obliged to give up working for Sammles – much to Sammles's regret, for she had sold five horses and a pony-and-trap – and the money she had saved was rapidly running out. But they had to go out, regardless of the weather: it was too depressing to stay in the room.

Maisie's gown was tight across her breasts and she winced as April did it up. April gave her a curious look and said: 'Are your nipples sore?'

'Yes, they are – I wonder why?'

'Maisie,' said April in a worried tone, 'when did you last have the curse?'

'I never keep count.' Maisie thought for a moment, and a chill descended on her. 'Oh, dear God,' she said.

'When?'

'I think it was before we went to the races at Goodwood. Do you think I'm pregnant?'

'Your waist is bigger and your nipples hurt and you haven't had the curse for two months – yes, you're pregnant,' April said in an exasperated voice. 'I can't believe you've been so stupid. Who was it?'

'Hugh, of course. But we only did it once. How can you get pregnant from one fuck?'

'You *always* get pregnant from one fuck.'

'Oh, my God.' Maisie felt as if she had been hit by a

train. Shocked, bewildered and frightened, she sat down on the bed and began to cry. 'What am I going to do?' she said helplessly.

'We could go to that lawyer's office, for a start.'

Suddenly everything was different.

At first Maisie was scared and angry. Then she realized that she was now obliged to get in touch with Hugh, for the sake of the child inside her. And when she admitted this to herself she felt more glad than frightened. She was longing to see him again. She had convinced herself that it would be wrong to. But the baby made everything different. Now it was her duty to contact Hugh, and the prospect made her weak with relief.

All the same she was nervous as she and April climbed the steep staircase to the lawyer's rooms at Gray's Inn. The advertisement might not have been placed by Hugh. It would hardly be surprising if he had given up the search for her. She had been as discouraging as a girl could, and no man would carry the torch for ever. The advertisement might be something to do with her parents, if they were still alive. Perhaps things had begun to go well for them at last, and they had the money to search for her. She was not sure how she felt about that. There had been many times when she had longed to see Mama and Papa again, but she was afraid they would be ashamed of her way of life.

They reached the top of the stairs and entered the outer office. The lawyer's clerk was a young man wearing a mustard-coloured waistcoat and a condescending smile. The girls were wet and bedraggled, but all the same he was disposed to flirt. 'Ladies!' he said. 'How could two such goddesses have need of the services of Messrs Goldman and Jay? What could I possibly do for you?'

April rose to the occasion. 'You could take off that waistcoat, it's hurting my eyes,' she said.

Maisie had no patience with gallantry today. 'My name is Maisie Robinson,' she said.

'Aha! The advertisement. By a happy chance, the gentleman in question is with Mr Jay at this very minute.'

Maisie felt faint with trepidation. 'Tell me something,' she said hesitantly. 'The gentleman in question . . . Is he by any chance Mr Hugh Pilaster?' She looked pleadingly at the clerk.

He failed to notice her look and replied in his ebullient tone: 'Good Lord, no!'

Maisie's hopes collapsed again. She sat down on a hard wooden bench by the door, fighting back tears. 'Not him,' she said.

'No,' said the clerk. 'As a matter of fact, I know Hugh Pilaster – we were at school together in Folkestone. He's gone to America.'

Maisie rocked back as if she had been punched. 'America?' she whispered.

'Boston, Massachusetts. Took a ship a couple of weeks ago. You know him, then?'

Maisie ignored the question. Her heart felt like a stone, heavy and cold. Gone to America. And she had his child inside her. She was too horrified to cry.

April said aggressively: 'Who is it, then?'

The clerk began to realize he was out of his depth. He lost his superior air and said nervously: 'I'd better let him tell you himself. Excuse me for a moment.' He disappeared through an inner door.

Maisie stared blankly at the boxes of papers stacked against the wall, reading the titles marked on the sides: *Blenkinsop Estate, Regina versus Wiltshire Flour Millers, Great Southern Railway, Mrs Stanley Evans (deceased)*. Everything that happened in this office was a tragedy for someone, she reflected: death, bankruptcy, divorce, prosecution.

When the door opened again, a different man came out, a man of striking appearance. Not much older than Maisie, he had the face of a Biblical prophet, with dark eyes staring out from under black eyebrows, a big nose with flaring nostrils, and a bushy beard. He looked familiar, and after a moment she realized that he reminded her a little of her father, although Papa had never looked so fierce.

'Maisie?' he said. 'Maisie Robinson?'

His clothes were a little odd, as if they had been bought in a foreign country, and his accent was American. 'Yes, I'm Maisie Robinson,' she said. 'Who the devil are you?'

'Don't you recognize me?'

Suddenly she remembered a wire-thin boy, ragged and barefoot, with the first shadow of a moustache on his lip and a do-or-die look in his eye. 'Oh, my God!' she yelped. 'Danny!' For a moment she forgot her troubles as she ran to his arms. 'Danny, is it really you?'

He hugged her so hard it hurt. 'Sure it's me,' he said.

'Who?' April was saying. 'Who is he?'

'My brother!' Maisie said. 'The one that ran away to America! He came back!'

Danny broke their embrace to stare at her. 'How did you get to be beautiful?' he said. 'You used to be a skinny little runt!'

She touched his beard. 'I might have known you without all this fur round your gob.'

There was a discreet cough from behind Danny, and Maisie looked up to see an elderly man standing in the doorway looking faintly disdainful. 'Apparently we have been successful,' he said.

Danny said: 'Mr Jay, may I present my sister, Miss Robinson.'

'Your servant, Miss Robinson. If I may make a suggestion . . . ?'

'Why not?' said Danny.

'There is a coffee house in Theobalds Road, just a few steps away. You must have a lot to talk about.'

He obviously wanted them out of his office, but Danny did not seem to care what Mr Jay wanted. Whatever else might have happened he had not learned to be deferential. 'What do you say, girls? Would you like to talk here, or shall we go and drink coffee?'

'Let's go,' Maisie said.

Mr Jay added: 'And perhaps you might come back to settle your account a little later, Mr Robinson?'

'I won't forget. Come on, girls.'

They left the office and went down the stairs. Maisie was bursting with questions, but controlled her curiosity with an effort while they found the coffee-house and settled themselves at a table. At last she said: 'What have you been doing for the last seven years?'

'Building railways,' he said. 'It so happened that I arrived at a good time. The civil war had just ended and the railway boom was beginning. They were so desperate for workers that they were shipping them over from Europe. Even a skinny fourteen-year-old could get a job. I worked on the first-ever steel bridge, over the Mississippi at St Louis; then I got a job building the Union Pacific Railroad in Utah. I was a ganger by the time I was nineteen – it's young men's work. And I joined the trade union and led a strike.'

'Why did you come back?'

'There's been a stock market crash. The railroads have

run out of money, and the banks that were financing them have gone bust. There are thousands of men, hundreds of thousands, looking for work. I decided to come home and make a new start.'

'What will you do – build railroads here?'

He shook his head. 'I've got a new idea. You see, it's happened to me twice, that my life has been wrecked by a financial crash. The men who own banks are the stupidest people in the world. They never learn, so they make the same mistakes again and again. And it's the working men who suffer. Nobody ever helps them – nobody ever will. They have to help each other.'

April said: 'People never help each other. It's every one for himself in this world. You've got to be selfish.'

April often said that, Maisie recalled, even though in practice she was a generous person and would do anything for a friend.

Danny said: 'I'm going to start a kind of club for working men. They'll pay sixpence a week, and if they're thrown out of work through no fault of their own the club will pay them a pound a week while they look for a new job.'

Maisie stared at her brother in admiration. The plan was formidably ambitious – but she had thought the same when at the age of fourteen he had said: *There's a ship in the harbour that's bound for Boston on the morning tide – I'll shin up a rope tonight and hide on deck in one of the boats*. He had done what he said then and he probably would now. He said he had led a strike. He seemed to have grown into the kind of person other men would follow.

'But what about Papa and Mama?' he said. 'Have you been in touch with them?'

Maisie shook her head and then, surprising herself, she began to cry. Suddenly she felt the pain of losing her family, a pain she had refused to acknowledge all these years.

Danny put a hand on her shoulder. 'I'll go back up north and see if I can trace them.'

'I hope you find them,' Maisie said. 'I miss them so much.' She caught the eye of April, who was staring at her in astonishment. 'I'm so afraid they'll be ashamed of me.'

'And why should they?' he said.

'I'm pregnant.'

His face reddened. 'And not married?'

'No.'

'Going to get married?'

'No.'

Danny was angry. 'Who is the swine?'

Maisie raised her voice. 'Spare me the outraged brother act, will you?'

'I'd like to break his neck—'

'Shut up, Danny!' Maisie said angrily. 'You left me alone seven years ago and you've no business to come back and act as if you own me.' He looked abashed, and she went on in a quieter voice: 'It doesn't matter. He would have married me, I expect, but I didn't want him to, so forget about him. Anyway, he's gone to America.'

Danny calmed down. 'If I wasn't your brother I'd marry you myself. You're pretty enough! Anyway, you can have what little money I've got left.'

'I don't want it.' She realized she was sounding ungracious, but she could not help it. 'There's no need for you to take care of me, Danny. Use your money for your working men's club. I'll look after myself. I managed when I was eleven years old, so I suppose I can now.'

[III]

MICKY MIRANDA and Papa were in a small eating-house in Soho, lunching off oyster stew – the cheapest dish on the menu – and strong beer. The restaurant was a few minutes from the Cordovan Ministry in Portland Place, where Micky now sat at a writing-table every morning for an hour or two, dealing with the Minister's mail. He was finished for the day and had met Papa for lunch. They sat opposite one another on hard wooden high-backed benches. There was sawdust on the floor and years of grease on the low ceiling. Micky hated eating in such places, but all the same he did it often, to save money. He ate at the Cowes Club only when Edward was paying. Besides, taking Papa to the club was a strain: Micky was constantly afraid the old man would start a fight, or pull a gun, or spit on the rug.

Papa wiped his bowl with a chunk of bread and pushed it aside. 'I must explain something to you,' he said.

Micky put down his spoon.

Papa said: 'I need rifles to fight the Delabarca family. When I have destroyed them I will take over their nitrate mines. The mines will make our family rich.'

Micky nodded silently. He had heard all this before but he would not dare to say so.

'The nitrate mines are only the beginning, the first step,' Papa went on. 'When we have more money, we will buy more rifles. Different family members will become important people in the province.'

Micky's ears pricked up. This was a new line.

'Your cousin Jorge will be a colonel in the army. Your brother Paulo will become chief of police in Santamaria Province.'

220

So that he can be a professional bully instead of an amateur, Micky thought.

Papa said: 'Then I will become governor of the province.'

Governor! Micky had not realized that Papa's aspirations were so high.

But he had not finished. 'When we control the province, we will look to the nation. We will become fervent supporters of President Garcia. You will be his envoy in London. Your brother will become his Minister of Justice, perhaps. Your uncles will be generals. Your half-brother Dominic, the priest, will become Archbishop of Palma.'

Micky was astonished: he never knew he had a half-brother. But he said nothing, for he did not want to interrupt.

'And then,' Papa said, 'when the time is right, we will move the Garcia family aside and we will step in.'

'You mean we will take over the government?' Micky said, wide-eyed. He was bowled over by Papa's audacity and confidence.

'Yes. In twenty years' time, my son, either I will be president of Cordova . . . or you will.'

Micky tried to take it in. Cordova had a constitution which provided for democratic elections, but none had ever been held. President Garcia had taken power in a coup ten years ago; previously he had been commander-in-chief of the armed forces under President Lopez, who had led the rebellion against the Spanish rule in which Papa and his cowboys had fought.

Papa surprised Micky by the subtlety of his strategy: to become a fervent supporter of the current ruler and then betray him. But what was Micky's role? He should become the Cordovan Minister in London. He had already taken the first step by elbowing Tonio Silva aside and getting his job. He would have to find a way to do the same to the Minister.

And then what? If his father were president, Micky might be Foreign Minister, and travel the world as the representative of his country. But Papa had said Micky himself might be president – not Paulo, not Uncle Rico, but Micky. Was it really possible?

Why not? Micky was clever, ruthless and well-connected: what more did he need? The prospect of ruling a whole country was intoxicating. Everyone would bow to him; the most beautiful women in the land would be his to take, whether they wished it or not; he would be as rich as the Pilasters.

'President,' he said dreamily. 'I like it.'

Papa reached out casually and slapped his face.

The old man had a powerful arm and a horny hand, and the slap rocked Micky. He cried out, shocked and hurt, and leaped to his feet. He tasted blood in his mouth. The place went quiet and everyone looked.

'Sit down,' Papa said.

Slowly and reluctantly, Micky obeyed.

Papa reached across the table with both hands and grabbed him by the lapels. In a voice full of scorn he said: 'This entire plan has been put at risk because you have completely failed in the simple, small task allotted to you!'

Micky was terrified of him in this mood. 'Papa, you'll get your rifles!' he said.

'In one more month it will be spring in Cordova. We have to take the Delabarca mines this season – next year will be too late. I have booked passage on a freighter bound for Panama. The captain has been bribed to put me and the weapons ashore on the Atlantic coast of Santamaria.' Papa stood up, dragging Micky upright, tearing his shirt by the force of his grip. His face was suffused with anger.

'The ship sails in five days' time,' he said in a voice that filled Micky with fear. 'Now get out of here and buy me those guns!'

Augusta Pilaster's servile butler, Hastead, took Micky's wet coat and hung it near the fire that blazed in the hall. Micky did not thank him. They disliked one another. Hastead was jealous of anyone Augusta favoured, and Micky despised the man for fawning. Besides, Micky never knew which way Hastead's eyes were looking, and that unnerved him.

Micky went into the drawing-room and found Augusta alone. She looked pleased to see him. She held his hand in both of hers and said: 'You're so cold.'

'I walked across the park.'

'Foolish boy, you should have taken a hansom.' Micky could not afford hansom cabs, but Augusta did not know that. She pressed his hand to her bosom and smiled. It was like a sexual invitation, but she acted as if she were innocently warming his cold fingers.

She did this kind of thing a lot when they were alone together, and normally Micky enjoyed it. She would hold his hand and touch his thigh, and he would touch her arm or her shoulder, and look into her eyes, and they would talk in low voices, like lovers, without ever acknowledging that they were flirting. He found it exciting, and so did she. But today he was too desperately worried to dally with her. 'How is Old Seth?' he asked, hoping to hear of a sudden relapse.

She sensed his mood and let go of his hand without protest, although she looked disappointed. 'Come close to the fire,' she said. She sat on a sofa and patted the seat beside her. 'Seth is much better.'

Micky's heart sank.

She went on: 'He may be with us for years yet.' She could not keep the irritation out of her voice. She was impatient for her husband to take over. 'You know he is living here now. You shall visit him when you have had some tea.'

'He must retire soon, surely?' said Micky.

'There is no sign of it, regrettably. Just this morning he forbade another issue of Russian railway stock.' She patted his knee. 'Be patient. Your Papa shall have his rifles eventually.'

'He can't wait much longer,' Micky said worriedly. 'He has to leave next week.'

'So that's why you're looking so tense,' she said. 'Poor boy. I wish I could do something to help.'

'You don't know my father,' Micky said, and he could not keep the note of despair out of his voice. 'He pretends to be civilized when he sees you, but in reality he's a barbarian. God knows what he'll do to me if I let him down.'

There were voices in the hall. 'There's something I must tell you before the others come in,' Augusta said hastily. 'I finally met Mr David Middleton.'

Micky nodded. 'What did he say?'

'He was polite, but frank. Said he did not believe that the entire truth about his brother's death had been told, and asked if I could put him in touch with either Hugh Pilaster or Antonio Silva. I told him they were both abroad, and he was wasting his time.'

'I wish we could solve the problem of Old Seth as neatly as we solved that one,' Micky said as the door opened.

Edward came in, then his sister Clementine. Clementine looked like Augusta but did not have the same force of personality, and although she was younger she had none of her mother's sexual allure. Augusta poured tea. Micky talked to Edward in a desultory way about their plans for the evening. There were no parties or balls in September: the aristocracy stayed away from London until after Christmas, and only the politicians and their wives were in town. But there was no shortage of middle-class entertainment, and Edward had tickets for a play. Micky pretended to be looking forward to it, but his mind was on Papa.

Hastead brought in hot buttered muffins. Edward ate several but Micky had no appetite. More family members arrived: Joseph's brother Young William; Joseph's ugly sister Madeleine; and Madeleine's husband, Major Hartshorn, with the scar on his forehead. They all talked of the financial crisis, but Micky could tell they were not afraid: Old Seth had seen it coming and had made sure that Pilasters Bank was not exposed. High-risk securities had lost value – Egyptian, Peruvian and Turkish bonds had crashed – but English government securities and English railway shares had suffered only modest falls.

One by one they all went up to visit Seth; one by one they came down and said how marvellous he was. Micky waited until last. He finally went up at half-past five.

Seth was in what used to be Hugh's room. A nurse sat outside with the door ajar in case he should call her. Micky went in and closed the door.

Seth was sitting up in bed reading *The Economist*. Micky said: 'Good afternoon, Mr Pilaster. How are you feeling?'

The old man put his journal aside with obvious reluctance. 'I'm feeling well, I thank you. How is your father?'

'Impatient to be home.' Micky stared at the frail old man on the white sheets. The skin of his face was translucent, and the curved knife of the Pilaster nose seemed sharper than ever, but there was lively intelligence in the eyes. He looked as if he could live and run the bank for another decade.

Micky seemed to hear his father's voice in his ear, saying: *Who is standing in our way?*

The old man was weak and helpless, and there was only Micky in the room and the nurse outside.

Micky realized he had to kill Seth.

His father's voice said: *Do it now.*

He could suffocate the old man with a pillow and leave no evidence. Everyone would think he had died a natural death.

Micky's heart filled with loathing and he felt ill.

'What's the matter?' Seth said. 'You look sicker than I.'

'Are you quite comfortable, sir?' Micky said. 'Let me adjust your pillows.'

'Please don't trouble, they're all right,' said Seth, but Micky reached behind him and pulled out a big feather pillow.

Micky looked at the old man and hesitated.

Fear flashed in Seth's eyes and he opened his mouth to call out.

Before he could make a sound Micky smothered his face with the pillow and pushed his head back down.

Unfortunately, Seth's arms were outside the bedclothes, and now his hands grasped Micky's forearms with surprising strength. Micky stared in horror at the aged talons clamped to his coat sleeves, but he held on with all his might. Seth clawed desperately at Micky's arms but the younger man was stronger.

When that failed Seth began to kick his legs and squirm. He could not escape from Micky's grasp, but Hugh's old bed squeaked, and Micky was terrified that the nurse might hear and come in to investigate. The only way he could think of to keep the old man still was to lie on top of him. Still holding the pillow over Seth's face, Micky got on the bed and lay on the writhing body. It was grotesquely reminiscent of sex with an unwilling woman, Micky thought crazily, and he suppressed the hysterical laughter that bubbled to his lips. Seth continued to struggle but his movements were restrained by Micky's weight and the bed ceased to squeak. Micky held on grimly.

At last all movement ceased. Micky remained in place as long as he dared, to make sure; then he cautiously removed the pillow and stared at the white, still face. The eyes were closed but the features were still. The old man looked dead. Micky realized he should check for a heartbeat. Slowly and fearfully, he lowered his head to Seth's chest.

Suddenly the old man's eyes opened wide and he took a huge, dragging breath.

Micky almost cried aloud with horror. A moment later he regained his wits and shoved the pillow over Seth's face again. He felt himself shaking weakly with fear and disgust as he held it down; but there was no more resistance.

He knew he should keep it there for several minutes, to be sure the old man really was dead this time; but he was worried about the nurse. She might notice the silence. He had to speak, for a pretence of normality. But he could not think what to say to a dead man. Say anything, he told himself, it doesn't matter so long as she hears the murmur of conversation. 'I'm pretty well,' he mumbled desperately. 'Pretty well, pretty well. And how are you? Well, well. I'm glad to hear you're feeling better. Splendid, Mr Pilaster. I'm very glad to see you looking so well, so splendid, so much better, oh, dear God, I can't keep this up, very well, splendid, splendid . . .'

He could stand it no longer. He took his weight off the pillow. Grimacing with distaste, he put his hand on Seth's chest where he imagined the heart would be. There were sparse white hairs on the old man's pale skin. The body was warm beneath the nightshirt, but there was no heartbeat. *Are you really dead this time?* he thought. And then he seemed to hear Papa's voice, angry and impatient, saying: *Yes, you fool, he's dead, now get out of there!* Leaving the pillow over the face, he rolled off the corpse and stood up.

A wave of nausea engulfed him. He felt weak and faint, and he grabbed the bedpost to steady himself. I killed him, he thought. I killed him.

There was a voice on the landing.

Micky looked at the body on the bed. The pillow was still over Seth's face. He snatched it up. Seth's dead eyes were open and staring.

The door opened.

Augusta walked in.

She stood in the doorway, looking at the rumpled bed, the still face of Seth with its staring eyes, and the pillow in Micky's hands. The blood drained from her cheeks.

Micky stared at her, silent and helpless, waiting for her to speak.

She stood there, looking from Seth to Micky and back again, for a long moment.

Then, slowly and quietly, she closed the door.

She took the pillow from Micky. She lifted Seth's lifeless head and replaced the pillow, then she straightened the sheets. She picked up *The Economist* from the floor, placed it on his chest, and folded his hands over it, so that he looked as if he had fallen asleep reading it.

Then she closed his eyes.

She came to Micky. 'You're shaking,' she said. She took his face in her hands and kissed his mouth.

For a moment he was too stunned to react. Then he went from terror to desire in a flash. He put his arms around her

228

and embraced her, feeling her bosom against his chest. She opened her mouth and their tongues met. Micky grasped her breasts in both hands and squeezed them hard. She gasped. His erection came immediately. Augusta began to grind her pelvis against his, rubbing herself on his stiff penis. They were both breathing hard. Augusta took his hand, put it in her mouth, and bit down, to stop herself crying out. Her eyes closed tight and she shuddered. He realized she was coming, and he was so inflamed that he, too, reached a climax.

It had taken only a few moments. Afterwards they clung together, panting, for a little longer. Micky was too bewildered to think.

When Augusta had caught her breath she broke the embrace. 'I'm going to my room,' she said quietly. 'You should leave the house immediately.'

'Augusta—'

'Call me Mrs Pilaster!'

'All right—'

'This never happened,' she said in a fierce whisper. 'Do you understand me? *None of it ever happened!*'

'All right,' he said again.

She smoothed the front of her dress and patted her hair. He watched helplessly, immobilized by the force of her will. She turned and went to the door. Automatically he opened it for her. He followed her out.

The nurse looked an inquiry at them. Augusta put her finger to her lips in a hushing gesture. 'He's just dropped off to sleep,' she said quietly.

Micky was amazed and appalled by her coolness.

'Best thing for him,' said the nurse. 'I'll leave him in peace for an hour or so.'

Augusta nodded agreement. 'I should, if I were you. Believe me, he's quite comfortable now.'

PART TWO

1879

CHAPTER ONE

January

[I]

HUGH RETURNED to London after six years.

In that period the Pilasters had doubled their wealth – and Hugh was partly responsible.

He had done extraordinarily well in Boston, better than he could have dreamed. Transatlantic trade was booming as the United States recovered from the civil war, and Hugh had made sure Pilasters Bank was financing a healthy chunk of that business.

Then he had guided the partners into a series of lucrative issues of North American stocks and bonds. After the war, government and business needed cash, and Pilasters Bank raised the money.

Finally he had developed an expertise in the chaotic market for railway stocks, learning to tell which railroads would make fortunes and which would never get past the first mountain range. Uncle Joseph had been wary at first, remembering the New York crash of 1873; but Hugh had inherited the anxious conservatism of the Pilasters, and he had recommended only the good-quality shares, scrupulously avoiding anything that smacked of flashy speculation; and his judgement had proved sound. Now Pilasters was the world leader in the business of raising capital for the industrial development of North America. Hugh was being paid a thousand pounds a year, and he knew he was worth more.

When he docked at Liverpool he was met off the ship by the chief clerk of Pilaster's local branch, a man with whom he had exchanged telegrams at least once a week ever since he went to Boston. They had never met, and when they identified each other the clerk said: 'Goodness me, I didn't know you were so young, sir!' This pleased Hugh as he had found a silver hair in his otherwise jet-black head that very morning. He was twenty-six.

He went by train to Folkestone, not pausing in London. The partners of Pilasters Bank might have felt he should call on them before going to see his mother but he thought otherwise: he had given them the last six years of his life and he owed his mother at least a day.

He found her more serenely beautiful than ever but still wearing black in memory of his father. His sister Dotty, now twelve, hardly remembered him and was shy until he sat her on his knee and reminded her how badly she had folded his shirts.

He begged his mother to move to a bigger house: he could easily afford to pay the rent. She refused, and told him to save his money and build up his capital. However, he persuaded her to take on another servant to help Mrs Builth, her ageing housekeeper.

Next day he took the London, Chatham and Dover Railway and arrived in London at Holborn Viaduct Station. A vast new hotel had been built at the station by people who thought Holborn was going to become a busy stopover for Englishmen on their way to Nice or St Petersburg. Hugh would not have put money into it:

he guessed the station would be used mostly by City workers who lived in the expanding suburbs of south-east London.

It was a bright spring morning. He walked to Pilasters Bank. He had forgotten the smoky taste of London's air, much worse than Boston or New York. He paused for a moment outside the bank, looking at its grandiose facade.

He had told the partners that he wanted to come home on furlough, to see his mother and sister and the old country. But he had another reason for returning to London.

He was about to drop a bombshell.

He had arrived with a proposal to merge Pilasters' North American operation with the New York bank of Madler and Bell, forming a new partnership that would be called Madler, Bell and Pilaster. It would make a lot of money for the bank; it would crown his achievements in the United States; and it would allow him to return to London and graduate from scout to decision-maker. It would mean the end of his period of exile.

He straightened his tie nervously and went in.

The banking hall, that years ago had so impressed him with its marble floors and ponderous walkers, now seemed merely staid. As he started up the stairs he met Jonas Mulberry, his former supervisor. Mulberry was startled and pleased to see him. 'Mr Hugh!' he said, shaking hands vigorously. 'Are you back permanently?'

'I hope so. How is Mrs Mulberry?'

'Very well, thank you.'

'Give her my regards. And the three little ones?'

'Five, now. All in fine health, God be thanked.'

It occurred to Hugh that the Principal Clerk might know the answer to a question on Hugh's mind. 'Mulberry, were you here when Mr Joseph was made a partner?'

'I was a new junior. That was twenty-five years ago come June.'

'So Mr Joseph would have been . . .'

'Twenty-nine.'

'Thank you.'

Hugh went on up to the Partners' Room, knocked on the door and went in. The four partners were there: Uncle Joseph, sitting at the Senior Partner's desk, looking older and balder and more like Old Seth; Aunt Madeleine's husband Major Hartshorn, his nose turning red to match the scar on his forehead, reading *The Times* beside the fire; Uncle Samuel, beautifully dressed as ever in a charcoal-grey double-breasted cutaway jacket with a pearl-grey waistcoat, frowning over a contract; and the newest partner, Young William, now thirty-one, sitting at his desk and writing in a notebook.

Samuel was the first to greet Hugh. 'My dear boy!' he said, getting up and shaking hands. 'How well you look!'

Hugh shook hands with all of them and accepted a glass of sherry. He looked around at the portraits of previous Senior Partners on the walls. 'Six years ago in this room I sold Lord Liversedge a hundred thousand pounds' worth of Russian government bonds,' he remembered.

'So you did,' said Samuel.

'Pilasters' commission on that sale, at five per cent, still amounts to more than I've been paid in the entire eight years I've worked for the bank,' he said with a smile.

Joseph said tetchily: 'I hope you're not asking for a rise in salary. You're already the highest-paid employee in the entire firm.'

'Except the partners,' said Hugh.

'Naturally,' Joseph snapped.

Hugh perceived that he had got off to a bad start. Too eager, as always, he told himself. Slow down. 'I'm not asking for a rise,' he said. 'However, I do have a proposition to put to the partners.'

Samuel said: 'You'd better sit down and tell us about it.'

Hugh put his drink down untasted and gathered his thoughts. He desperately wanted them to agree to his proposition. It was both the culmination and the proof of his triumph over adversity. It would bring more business to the bank at one stroke than most partners could attract in a year. And if they agreed they would be more or less obliged to make him a partner.

'Boston is no longer the financial centre of the United States,' he began. 'New York's the place now. We really ought to move our office. But there's a snag. A good deal of the business I've done in the last six years has been undertaken jointly with the New York house of Madler and Bell. Sidney Madler rather took me under his wing when I was green. If we moved to New York we'd be in competition with them.'

'Nothing wrong with competition, where appropriate,' Major Hartshorn asserted. He rarely had anything of value to contribute to a discussion, but rather than stay silent he would state the obvious in a dogmatic way.

'Perhaps. But I've got a better idea. Why not merge our North American operation with Madler and Bell?'

'Merge?' said Hartshorn. 'What do you mean?'

'Set up a joint venture. Call it Madler, Bell and Pilaster. It would have an office in New York and one in Boston.'

'How would it work?'

'The new house would deal with all the import–export financing currently done by both separate houses, and the profits would be shared. Pilasters would have the chance to participate in all new issues of bonds and stocks marketed by Madler and Bell. I would handle that business from London.'

'I don't like it,' said Joseph. 'It's just handing over our business to someone else's control.'

'But you haven't heard the best part,' Hugh said. 'All of Madler and Bell's European business, currently distributed among several agents in London, would be handed over to Pilasters.'

Joseph grunted in surprise. 'That must amount to . . .'

'More than fifty thousand pounds a year in commissions.'

Hartshorn said: 'Good Lord!'

They were all startled. They had never set up a joint venture before and they did not expect such an innovative proposition from someone who was not even a partner. But the prospect of fifty thousand a year in commission was irresistible.

Samuel said: 'You've obviously talked this over with them.'

'Yes. Madler is very keen, and so is his partner, John James Bell.'

Young William said: 'And you would supervise the joint venture from London.'

Hugh saw that William regarded him as a rival who was much less dangerous three thousand miles away. 'Why not?' he said. 'After all, London is where the money is raised.'

'And what would your status be?'

It was a question Hugh would have preferred not to answer so soon. William had shrewdly raised it to embarrass him. Now he had to bite the bullet. 'I think Mr Madler and Mr Bell would expect to deal with a partner.'

'You're too young to be a partner,' Joseph said immediately.

'I'm twenty-six, Uncle,' Hugh said. 'You were made a partner when you were twenty-nine.'

'Three years is a long time.'

'And fifty thousand pounds is a lot of money.' Hugh realized he was sounding cocky – a fault he was prone to – and he backed off quickly. He knew that if he pushed them into a corner they would turn him down just out of conservatism. 'But there is much to be weighed up. I know you'll want to talk it over. Perhaps I should leave you?' Samuel nodded discreetly and Hugh went to the door.

Samuel said: 'Whether this works out or not, Hugh, you're to be congratulated on a jolly enterprising proposition – I'm sure we all agree on that.'

He looked inquiringly at his partners and they all nodded assent. Uncle Joseph murmured: 'Quite so, quite so.'

Hugh did not know whether to be frustrated, because they had not agreed to his plan, or pleased that they had not turned it down flat. He had a dispiriting sense of anticlimax. But there was no more he could do. 'Thank you,' he said, and he went out.

At four o'clock that afternoon he stood outside Augusta's enormous, elaborate house in Kensington Gore.

Six years of London soot had darkened the red brick and smudged the white stone, but it still had the statues of birds and beasts on the stepped gable, with the ship in full sail at the apex of the roof. And they say Americans are ostentatious! thought Hugh.

He knew from his mother's letters that Joseph and Augusta had spent some of their ever-growing wealth on two other homes, a castle in Scotland and a country mansion in Buckinghamshire. Augusta had wanted to sell the Kensington house and buy a mansion in Mayfair, but Joseph had put his foot down: he liked it here.

The place had been relatively new when Hugh left, but still it was a house full of memories for him. Here he had suffered Augusta's persecution, courted Florence Stalworthy, punched Edward's nose, and made love to Maisie Robinson. The recollection of Maisie was the most poignant. It was not the humiliation and disgrace he recalled so much as the passion and the thrill. He had not seen or heard anything of Maisie since that night but he still thought about her every day of his life.

The family would remember the scandal as retailed by Augusta: how Tobias Pilaster's depraved son had brought a whore into the house and then, on being caught, had viciously attacked poor blameless Edward. So be it. They could think what they liked, but they had to acknowledge him as a Pilaster and a banker, and soon, with luck, they would have to make him a partner.

He wondered how much the family had changed in six years. His mother had kept him abreast of domestic events in monthly letters. His cousin Clementine was engaged to be married; Edward was not, despite Augusta's efforts; Young William and Beatrice had a baby girl. But Mother did not tell him the underlying changes. Did Uncle Samuel still live with his 'secretary'? Was Augusta as ruthless as ever, or had she mellowed with age? Had Edward sobered up and settled down? Had Micky Miranda finally married one of the flock of girls who fell in love with him every season?

It was time to face them all. He crossed the street and knocked on the door.

It was opened by Hastead, Augusta's oily butler. He did not appear to have changed: his eyes still looked in different directions. 'Good afternoon, Mr Hugh,' he said, but his Welsh voice was frosty, which indicated that Hugh was still out of favour in this house. Hastead's welcome could always be relied upon to reflect what Augusta was feeling.

He passed through the entrance lobby and into the hall.

There, like a reception committee, stood the three harridans of the Pilaster family: Augusta, her sister-in-law Madeleine, and her daughter Clementine. Augusta at forty-seven was as striking-looking as ever: she still had a classic face with dark eyebrows and a proud look, and if she was a little heavier than six years ago she had the height to carry it. Clementine was a slimmer edition of the same book, but she did not have the indomitable air of her mother and she missed being beautiful. Aunt Madeleine was every inch a Pilaster, from the curved nose down the thin, angular figure to the expensive lace trim around the hem of her ice-blue dress.

Hugh gritted his teeth and kissed them all.

Augusta said: 'Well, Hugh, I trust your foreign experiences have made you a wiser young man than you were?'

She was not going to let anyone forget that he had left under a cloud. Hugh replied: 'I trust we all grow wiser as we age, dear aunt,' and he had the satisfaction of seeing her face darken with anger.

'Indeed!' she said frostily.

Clementine said: 'Hugh, allow me to present my fiancé, Sir Harry Tonks.'

Hugh shook hands. Harry was too young to have a knighthood, so the 'sir' must mean he was a baronet, a kind of second-class aristocrat. Hugh did not envy him marriage to Clementine. She was not as bad as her mother, but she had always had a mean streak.

Harry asked Hugh: 'How was your crossing?'

'Very quick,' said Hugh. 'I came in one of the new screw steamers. It only took seven days.'

'By Jove! Marvellous, marvellous.'

'What part of England are you from, Sir Harry?' Hugh asked, probing into the man's background.

'I've a place in Dorsetshire. Most of my tenants grow hops.'

Landed gentry, Hugh concluded; if he has any sense he will sell his farms and put the money into Pilasters Bank. In fact Harry did not seem very bright, but he might be biddable. The Pilaster women liked to marry men who would do as they were told, and Harry was a younger version of Madeleine's husband George. As they grew older they became grumpy and resentful but they rarely rebelled.

'Come into the drawing-room,' Augusta commanded. 'Everyone's waiting to see you.'

He followed her in, but stopped short in the doorway. The familiar wide room, with its big fireplaces at either end and the french windows leading to the long garden, had been quite transformed. All the Japanese furniture and fabrics had gone, and the room had been redecorated in a profusion of bold, richly coloured patterns. Looking more closely, Hugh saw that they were all flowers: big yellow daisies in the carpet, red roses climbing a trellis in the wallpaper, poppies in the curtains, and pink chrysanthemums in the silk that draped chair-legs, mirrors, occasional tables and the piano. 'You've changed this room, Aunt,' he said superfluously.

Clementine said: 'It all comes from William Morris's new shop in Oxford Street – it's the latest thing.'

Augusta said: 'The carpet has to be changed, though. It's not the right colour.'

She was never satisfied, Hugh recalled.

Most of the Pilaster family were here. They were all curious about Hugh, he realized. He had gone away in disgrace and they may have thought they would never see him again – but they had underestimated him, and he had returned a conquering hero. Now they were all keen to take a second look.

The first person he shook hands with was his cousin Edward. He was twenty-nine but he looked older: he was already becoming stout and his face had the flushed look of a glutton. 'So, you're back,' he said. He tried a smile but it turned into a resentful sneer. Hugh could hardly blame him. The two cousins had always been compared to one another. Now Hugh's success drew attention to Edward's lack of achievement at the bank.

Micky Miranda stood next to Edward. Still handsome and immaculately dressed, Micky seemed even more sleek and self-assured. Hugh said: 'Hello, Miranda, are you still working for the Cordovan Minister?'

'I *am* the Cordovan Minister,' Micky replied.

Somehow Hugh was not surprised.

He was pleased to see his old friend Rachel Bodwin. 'Hello, Rachel, how are you?' he said. She had never been a pretty girl but she was turning into a handsome woman, he realized. She had angular features and eyes set too close together, but what had seemed plain six years ago was now oddly intriguing. 'What are you doing with yourself these days?'

'Campaigning to reform the law on women's property,' she said. Then she grinned and added: 'Much to the embarrassment of my parents, who would prefer me to campaign for a husband.'

She had always been alarmingly candid, Hugh recalled. He found her interesting on that account, but he could imagine that many eligible bachelors would be intimidated by her. Men liked women to be a little shy and not too clever.

As he exchanged small talk with her, he wondered whether Augusta still wanted to make a match between the two of them. It hardly mattered: the only man Rachel had ever shown any real interest in was Micky Miranda. Even now she was taking care to include Micky in the conversation with Hugh. He had never understood why girls found Micky irresistible, and Rachel surprised him more than most, for she was intelligent enough to realize that Micky was a rotter; yet it was almost as if he fascinated them more on that account.

He moved on and shook hands with Young William and his wife. Beatrice greeted Hugh warmly, and he concluded that she was not as much under Augusta's influence as the other Pilaster women.

Hastead interrupted them to give Hugh an envelope. 'This just arrived by messenger,' he said.

It contained a note in what looked to Hugh like a secretary's handwriting:

> 123, Piccadilly
> London, W.
> Tuesday

Mrs Solomon Greenbourne requests the pleasure of your company at dinner tonight.

Below, in a familiar scrawl, was written:

Welcome home! – Solly.

He was pleased. Solly was always amiable and easygoing. Why could the Pilasters not be as relaxed, he wondered? Were Methodists naturally more tense than Jews? But perhaps there were tensions he did not know about in the Greenbourne family.

Hastead said: 'The messenger is waiting for a reply, Mr Hugh.'

Hugh said: 'My compliments to Mrs Greenbourne, and I shall be delighted to join them for dinner.'

Hastead bowed and withdrew. Beatrice said: 'My

goodness, are you dining with the Solomon Greenbournes? How marvellous!'

Hugh was surprised. 'I don't expect it to be marvellous,' he said. 'I was at school with Solly and I've always liked him, but an invitation to dine with him was never a coveted privilege.'

'It is now,' said Beatrice.

'Solly married a fireball,' William explained. 'Mrs Greenbourne loves to entertain, and her parties are the best in London.'

'They're part of the Marlborough Set,' Beatrice said reverently. 'They're friends with the Prince of Wales.'

Clementine's fiancé Harry overheard this and said in a resentful tone: 'I don't know what English society is coming to, when the heir to the throne prefers Jews to Christians.'

'Really?' said Hugh. 'I must say I've never understood why people dislike Jews.'

'Can't stand 'em, myself,' Harry said.

'Well, you're marrying into a banking family, so you're going to meet an awful lot more of them in the future.'

Harry looked mildly offended.

William said: 'Augusta disapproves of the entire Marlborough Set, Jews and others. Apparently their morals aren't what they should be.'

Hugh said: 'And I bet they don't invite Augusta to their parties.'

Beatrice giggled at the thought and William said: 'Certainly not!'

'Well,' said Hugh, 'I can't wait to meet Mrs Greenbourne.'

*

Piccadilly was a street of palaces. At eight o'clock on a chilly January evening it was busy, the wide road hectic with carriages and cabs, the gaslit pavements thronged by men dressed like Hugh in white-tie-and-tails, women in velvet cloaks and fur collars, and painted prostitutes of both sexes.

Hugh walked along deep in thought. Augusta was as implacably hostile to him as ever. He had cherished a secret faint hope that she might have mellowed, but she had not. And she was still the matriarch, so to have her as an enemy was to be at odds with the family.

The situation at the bank was better. The business obliged the men to be more objective. Inevitably Augusta would try to block his advancement there, but he had more chance to defend himself on that territory. She knew how to manipulate people but she was hopelessly ignorant about banking.

On balance the day had not gone badly and now he looked forward to a relaxing evening with friends.

When Hugh left for America, Solly Greenbourne had been living with his father, Ben, in a vast house overlooking Green Park. Now Solly had a house of his own, just down the street from his father's place and not much smaller. Hugh passed through an imposing doorway into a vast hall lined with green marble, and stopped to stare at the extravagant sweep of a black-and-orange marble staircase. Mrs Greenbourne had something in common with Augusta Pilaster: neither woman believed in understatement.

A butler and two footmen were in the hall. The butler took Hugh's hat, only to hand it to a footman: then the second footman led him up the staircase. On the landing he glanced through an open door and saw the bare polished floor of a ballroom with a long sweep of curtained windows, then he was led into a drawing-room.

Hugh was no expert on decoration but he immediately recognized the gorgeous, extravagant style of Louis XVI. The ceiling was a riot of plaster moulding, the walls had inset panels of flock wallpaper, and all the tables and chairs were perched on thin gilded legs that looked as if they might snap. The colours were yellow, orange-red, gold and green. Hugh could easily imagine prim people saying it was vulgar, concealing their envy beneath a pretence of distaste. In fact it was sensual. It was a room in which impossibly wealthy people did anything they pleased.

Several other guests had arrived already and stood around drinking champagne and smoking cigarettes. This was new to Hugh: he had never seen people smoking in a drawing-room. Solly caught his eye and detached himself from a group of laughing people to come over. 'Pilaster, how nice of you to come! How are you, for goodness' sake?'

Hugh perceived that Solly had become a little more extrovert. He was still fat and bespectacled, and there was already a stain of some kind on his white waistcoat, but he was jollier than ever and, Hugh immediately sensed, happier too.

'I'm very well, thanks, Greenbourne,' Hugh said.

'I know it! I've been watching your progress. I wish our bank had someone like you in America. I hope the Pilasters are paying you a fortune – you deserve it.'

'And you've become a socialite, they say.'

'None of my doing. I got married, you know.' He turned and tapped the bare white shoulder of a short woman in an eggshell-green dress. She was facing the other way but her back was oddly familiar, and a strange feeling like déjà vu came over Hugh, making him feel unaccountably sad. Solly said to her: 'My dear, do you remember my old friend Hugh Pilaster?'

She paused a moment longer, finishing what she was

saying to her companions, and Hugh thought: Why do I feel breathless at the sight of her? Then she turned very slowly, like a door opening into the past, and Hugh's heart stopped as he saw her face.

'Of course I remember him,' she said. 'How are you, Mr Pilaster?'

Hugh stared, speechless, at the woman who had become Mrs Solomon Greenbourne.

It was Maisie.

[II]

AUGUSTA SAT at her dressing-table and put on the single row of pearls that she always wore at dinner parties. It was her most expensive piece of jewellery. Methodists did not believe in costly ornament, and her parsimonious husband Joseph used that as an excuse not to buy her jewellery. He would have liked to stop her redecorating the house so often, but she did it without asking him: if he had his way they might live no better than his clerks. He accepted the redecoration grumpily, insisting only that she leave his bedroom alone.

She took from her open jewellery box the ring Strang had given her thirty years ago. It was in the form of a gold serpent with a diamond head and ruby eyes. She put it on her finger and, as she had done a thousand times before, brushed the raised head against her lips, remembering.

Her mother had said: 'Send back his ring, and try to forget him.'

The seventeen-year-old Augusta had said: 'I have sent it back already, and I will forget him,' but it was a lie. She kept the ring concealed in the spine of her bible, and she had never forgotten Strang. If she could not have his love, she vowed, all the other things he could have given her would be hers somehow, one day.

She would never be the Countess of Strang, she had accepted that years ago. But she was determined to have a title. And since Joseph did not have one she would have to get him one.

She had brooded over the problem for years, studying the mechanisms by which men gained titles, and many sleepless nights of planning and longing had gone into her strategy. Now she was ready and the time was right.

She would begin her campaign tonight, over dinner. Among her guests were three people who would play a crucial part in having Joseph made an earl.

He might take the title Earl of Whitehaven, she thought. Whitehaven was the port where the Pilaster family had begun in business, four generations ago. Joseph's great-grandfather Amos Pilaster had made his fortune with a legendary gamble, putting all his money in a slave ship. But then he had gone into a less chancy business, buying serge cloth and printed calico from Lancashire textile mills and shipping it to the Americas. Their London home was already called Whitehaven House in acknowledgement of the birthplace of the business. Augusta would be Countess of Whitehaven if her plans worked out.

She imagined herself and Joseph entering a grand drawing-room as a butler announced: 'The Earl and Countess of Whitehaven,' and the thought made her smile. She saw Joseph making his maiden speech in the House of Lords, on a topic connected with high finance, and the other peers listening with respectful attention. Shopkeepers would call her 'Lady Whitehaven' in loud tones and people would look around to see who it was.

However, she wanted this for Edward as much as anything else, she told herself. One day he would inherit his father's title, and meanwhile he would be able to put 'The Hon. Edward Pilaster' on his visiting card.

She knew exactly what she had to do, but all the same she felt uneasy. Getting a peerage was not like buying a carpet – you could not go to the supplier and say: 'I want that one, how much is it?' Everything had to be done with hints. She would need to be very surefooted tonight. If she made a wrong move, her careful plans could go wrong very quickly. If she had misjudged her people she was doomed.

A parlourmaid knocked and said: 'Mr Hobbes has arrived, madam.'

She'll have to call me 'My lady' soon, Augusta thought.

She put Strang's ring away, got up from her dressing-table, and went through the communicating door into Joseph's room. He was dressed for dinner, sitting at the cabinet where he kept his collection of jewelled snuff-boxes, looking at one of them in the gaslight. Augusta wondered whether to mention Hugh to him now.

Hugh continued to be a nuisance. Six years ago she thought she had dealt with him once and for all, but he was once again threatening to overshadow Edward. There was talk of his becoming a partner: Augusta could not tolerate that. She was determined that Edward would be Senior Partner one day, and she could not let Hugh get ahead.

Was she right to worry so much? Perhaps it would be as well to let Hugh run the business. Edward could do something else, go into politics perhaps. But the bank was the heart of this family. People who left, like Hugh's father Tobias, always came to nothing in the end. The bank was where the money was made and the power exercised. Pilasters could bring down a monarch by refusing him a loan: few politicians had that ability. It was dreadful to think of Hugh being Senior Partner, entertaining ambassadors, drinking coffee with the Chancellor of the

Exchequer, and taking first place at family gatherings, lording it over Augusta and her side of the family.

But it would be difficult to get rid of Hugh this time. He was older and wiser and he had an established position in the bank. The wretched boy had worked hard and patiently for six years to rehabilitate his reputation. Could she undo all that?

However, this was not the moment to confront Joseph about Hugh. She wanted him in a good mood for the dinner party. 'Stay up here a few more minutes, if you like,' she said to him. 'Only Arnold Hobbes has arrived.'

'Very well, if you don't mind,' he said.

It would suit her to have Hobbes alone for a while.

Hobbes was the editor of a political journal called *The Forum*. It generally sided with the Conservatives, who stood for the aristocracy and the established Church, and against the Liberals, the party of businessmen and Methodists. The Pilasters were both businessmen and Methodists, but the Conservatives were in power.

She had met Hobbes only once or twice before, and she guessed he might have been surprised to receive her invitation. However, she had been confident he would accept. He would not get many invitations to homes as wealthy as Augusta's.

Hobbes was in a curious position. He was powerful, because his journal was widely read and respected; yet he was poor, for he did not make much money out of it. The combination was awkward for him – and perfectly suited to Augusta's purpose. He had the power to help her and he might be bought.

There was just one possible snag. She hoped he did not have high principles: that would destroy his usefulness. But if she had judged him aright he was corruptible.

She felt nervous and jittery. She stood outside the

drawing-room door for a moment, saying to herself: *Relax, Mrs Pilaster, you're good at this.* After a moment she felt calmer, and she went in.

He stood up eagerly to greet her. He was a nervous, quick-witted man, bird-like in his movements. His dress suit was at least ten years old, Augusta thought. She led him to the window-seat, to give their conversation a feeling of intimacy even though they were not old friends. 'Tell me what mischief you have been at today,' she said playfully. 'Trouncing Mr Gladstone? Undermining our India policy? Persecuting Catholics?'

He peered at her through smeared spectacles. 'I've been writing about the City of Glasgow Bank,' he said.

Augusta frowned. 'This is the bank that failed a little while ago.'

'Exactly. Many of the Scottish trade unions have been ruined, you know.'

'I seem to remember hearing talk of it,' she said. 'My husband said the City of Glasgow had been known for years to be unsound.'

'I don't understand this,' he said excitedly. 'People know a bank is no good, yet it is allowed to continue in business until it crashes, and thousands of people lose their life savings!'

Augusta did not understand it either. She knew next to nothing about business. But she now saw a chance to lead the conversation in the direction she wanted. 'Perhaps the worlds of commerce and government are too widely separated,' she said.

'It must be so. Better communication between businessmen and statesmen might prevent such catastrophes.'

'I wonder. . . .' Augusta hesitated as if considering an idea that had just struck her. 'I wonder whether someone

such as yourself would consider becoming a director of one
or two companies.'

He was surprised. 'Indeed, I might.'

'You see . . . some first-hand experience of participating
in the direction of a business enterprise might help you
when you comment, in your journal, on the world of
commerce.'

'I've no doubt it would.'

'The rewards are not great – a hundred or two a year, at
best.' She saw his eyes light up: that was a lot of money to
him. 'But the obligations are small.'

'A most interesting thought,' he said. He was working
hard to conceal his excitement, she could tell.

'My husband could arrange it, if you were interested. He
has constantly to recommend directors for the boards of
enterprises in which he has some interest. Do think it over
and tell me if you would like me to mention it.'

'Very well, I shall.'

So far, so good, Augusta thought. But showing him the
bait was the easy part. Now she had to get him on the
hook. She said thoughtfully: 'And the world of commerce
should reciprocate, of course. More businessmen should
serve their country in the House of Lords, I feel.'

His eyes narrowed slightly, and she guessed that his
quick mind was beginning to understand the bargain he
was being offered. 'No doubt,' he said non-committally.

Augusta developed her theme. 'Both Houses of
Parliament would benefit from the knowledge and wisdom
of senior businessmen, especially when debating the
nation's finances. Yet there is a curious prejudice against a
businessman being elevated to the peerage.'

'There is, and it is quite irrational,' Hobbes admitted.
'Our merchants, manufacturers and bankers are
responsible for the nation's prosperity, much more so than

landowners and clergymen; yet it is the latter who are ennobled for their services to the nation, while the men who really make and do things are overlooked.'

'You should write an article about the question. It is the kind of cause for which your journal has campaigned in the past – the modernization of our ancient institutions.' She gave him her warmest smile. Her cards were on the table now. He could hardly fail to see that this campaign was the price he had to pay for the company directorships she was offering. Would he stiffen, look offended, and beg to differ? Would he walk out in a huff? Would he smile and turn her down gracefully? If he did any of those things she would have to start all over again with someone else.

There was a long pause, then he said: 'Perhaps you're right.'

Augusta relaxed.

'Perhaps we should take this up,' he went on. 'Closer links between commerce and government.'

'Peerages for businessmen,' Augusta said.

'And company directorships for journalists,' he added.

Augusta sensed that they had gone as far as they could in the direction of frankness, and it was time to pull back. If it were admitted that she was bribing him he might be humiliated and refuse. She was well satisfied with what she had achieved, and she was about to change the subject when more guests arrived and she was saved the trouble.

The rest of the party arrived in a bunch, and Joseph appeared at the same time. A few moments later Hastead came in and said: 'Dinner is served, sir,' and Augusta longed to hear him say *My lord* instead of *Sir*.

They walked from the drawing-room through the hall to the dining-room. The rather short procession bothered Augusta. In aristocratic houses there was often a long and very elegant walk to the dining-room, and it was a high point of the dinner-party ritual. The Pilasters traditionally scorned to copy upper-class manners, but Augusta felt differently. To her this house seemed irredeemably suburban. But she had failed to persuade Joseph to move.

Tonight she had arranged for Edward to walk in to dinner with Emily Maple, a shy, pretty girl of nineteen who was with her father, a Methodist minister, and her mother. They were plainly overwhelmed by the house and the company, and hardly fitted in, but Augusta was getting desperate in her search for a suitable bride for Edward. The boy was now twenty-nine years old and he had never shown a spark of interest in any eligible girl, to his mother's frustration. He could hardly fail to find Emily attractive: she had big blue eyes and a sweet smile. The parents would be thrilled by such a match. As for the girl, she would have to do as she was told. But Edward might need to be pushed. The trouble was, he saw no reason to marry. He enjoyed his life with his male friends, going to his club and so on, and settling down to married life had little appeal. For a while she had blithely assumed this was just a normal phase in a young man's life, but it had gone on too long, and lately she had begun to worry whether he would ever come out of it. She would have to put pressure on him.

On her left at the table Augusta placed Michael Fortescue, a personable young man with political aspirations. He was said to be close to the Prime Minister, Benjamin Disraeli, who had been ennobled and was now Lord Beaconsfield. Fortescue was the second of the three people Augusta needed to help her get Joseph a peerage. He was not as clever as Hobbes but he was more sophisticated and self-assured. Augusta had been able to overawe Hobbes, but she would have to seduce Fortescue.

Mr Maple said grace and Hastead poured wine. Neither Joseph nor Augusta would drink wine, but they offered it to their guests. As the consommé was served Augusta smiled warmly at Fortescue and said in a low, intimate voice: 'When are we going to see you in Parliament?'

'I wish I knew,' he said.

'Everyone speaks of you as a brilliant young man, as you must know.'

He was pleased but embarrassed by her flattery. 'I'm not sure I do know.'

'And you're so good-looking, too – that never hurts.'

He looked rather startled. He had not expected her to flirt – but he was not averse to it.

'You shouldn't wait for a General Election,' she went on. 'Why don't you stand in a by-election? It should be easy enough to arrange – people say you have the ear of the Prime Minister.'

'You're very kind – but by-elections are expensive, Mrs Pilaster.'

It was the response she had been hoping for, but she did not let him know that. 'Are they?' she said.

'And I am not a wealthy man.'

'I didn't know that,' she lied. 'You should find a sponsor, then.'

'A banker, perhaps?' he said in a tone that was half playful, half wistful.

'It's not impossible. Mr Pilaster is keen to take a more active part in the government of the nation.' He would be, if a peerage were offered. 'And he doesn't see why commercial men should feel obliged to be Liberals. Between you and me, he often finds himself more in agreement with the younger Conservatives.'

Her confidential tone encouraged him to be frank – as she intended – and now he said directly: 'In what way would Mr Pilaster like to serve the nation – other than by sponsoring a by-election candidate?'

This was a challenge. Should she answer his question, or continue to be indirect? Augusta decided to match his frankness. 'Perhaps in the House of Lords. Do you think it is possible?' She was enjoying this – and so was he.

'Possible? Certainly. Whether it is likely, is another question. Shall I inquire?'

This was more straightforward than Augusta had anticipated. 'Could you do so discreetly?'

He hesitated. 'I believe I could.'

'It would be most kind,' she said with satisfaction. She had turned him into a co-conspirator.

'I shall let you know what I find out.'

'And if a suitable by-election should be called . . .'

'You're very good.'

She touched his arm. He was a very attractive young man, she thought. She enjoyed plotting with him. 'I believe we understand one another perfectly,' she murmured. She noticed that he had unusually big hands. She held his arm a moment longer, looking into his eyes; then she turned away.

She was feeling good. She had dealt with two of the three key people and she had not yet slipped. Throughout the next course she talked to Lord Morte, who was sitting on her right. With him she made polite, pointless conversation: it was his wife she wanted to influence and for that she had to wait until after dinner.

The men stayed in the dining-room to smoke and Augusta took the ladies upstairs to her bedroom. There she got Lady Morte alone for a few minutes. Fifteen years older than Augusta, Harriet Morte was a lady-in-waiting to Queen Victoria. She had iron-grey hair and a superior manner. Like Arnold Hobbes and Michael Fortescue, she had influence; and Augusta hoped that, like them, she would be corruptible. Hobbes and Fortescue were vulnerable because they were poor. Lord and Lady Morte were not so much poor as improvident: they had plenty of money, but they spent more than they had. Lady Morte's gowns were splendid and her jewellery was magnificent, and Lord Morte believed, against the evidence of forty years, that he had a good eye for a racehorse.

Augusta was more nervous about Lady Morte than she had been about the men. Women were more difficult. They would not take anything at face value and they knew when they were being manipulated. Thirty years as a courtier would have refined Lady Morte's sensibility to the point where nothing could slip by her.

Augusta began by saying: 'Mr Pilaster and I are such admirers of the dear Queen.'

Lady Morte nodded, as if to say *Of course*. However, there was no *of course* about it: Queen Victoria was disliked by much of the nation for being withdrawn, staid, remote and inflexible.

Augusta went on: 'If there were ever anything we could do to help you with your noble duties, we would be thrilled.'

'How very kind.' Lady Morte looked a little puzzled. She hesitated, then decided to ask. 'But what could you possibly do?'

'What do bankers do? They lend.' Augusta lowered her voice. 'Court life must be cripplingly expensive, I imagine.'

Lady Morte stiffened. There was a taboo on talking about money in her class and Augusta was breaking it flagrantly.

But Augusta ploughed on. 'If you were to open an account with Pilasters, there would never be any problems in that area. . . .'

Lady Morte was offended, but on the other hand she was being offered the remarkable privilege of unlimited credit at one of the largest banks in the world. Her instincts told her to snub Augusta, but greed held her back: Augusta could read the conflict in her face.

Augusta did not give her time to think about it. 'Please forgive my being so frightfully candid,' Augusta went on. 'It comes only from a wish to be of service.' Lady Morte would not believe that, but she would assume Augusta simply wanted to curry favour with royalty. She would not look for a more specific motive, and Augusta would give her no more clues tonight.

Lady Morte hesitated a moment longer, then said: 'You're very kind.'

Mrs Maple, the mother of Emily, returned from the bathroom, and Lady Morte took her turn. She went out with an expression of mild embarrassment frozen to her face. Augusta knew that she and Lord Morte would agree, in the carriage going home, that commercial people were impossibly vulgar and ill-mannered; but one day soon he would lose a thousand guineas on a horse, and on the same day her dressmaker would demand payment of a six-month-old bill for three hundred pounds, and the two of them would remember Augusta's offer, and they would decide that vulgar commercial people did after all have their uses.

Augusta had cleared the third hurdle. If she had assessed the woman correctly, Lady Morte would be hopelessly in debt to Pilasters Bank within six months. Then she would find out what Augusta wanted from her.

The ladies reconvened in the drawing-room on the ground floor and took coffee. Lady Morte was still distant, but stopped short of being rude. The men joined them a few minutes later. Joseph took Mr Maple upstairs to show him his collection of snuff-boxes. Augusta was pleased: Joseph only did that when he liked someone. Emily played the piano. Mrs Maple asked her to sing, but she said she had a cold, and stuck to her refusal with remarkable obstinacy despite her mother's pleas, making Augusta think anxiously that she might not be as submissive as she looked.

Augusta had done her work for the night: she wanted them all to go home now so that she could run over the evening in her mind and assess how much she had achieved. She did not actually like any of them except for Michael Fortescue. However, she forced herself to be polite and make conversation for another hour. Hobbes was hooked, she thought; Fortescue had made a bargain and would keep it; Lady Morte had been shown the slippery slope that led to perdition and it was only a matter of time before she started down it. Augusta was relieved and satisfied.

When at last they departed, Edward was ready to go to his club, but Augusta stopped him. 'Sit down and listen for a moment,' she said. 'I want to talk to you and your father.' Joseph, who was heading for bed, sat down again. She addressed him. 'When are you going to make Edward a partner in the bank?'

Joseph immediately looked cross. 'When he is older.'

'But I hear that Hugh may be made a partner, and he is three years younger than Edward.' Although Augusta had no idea how money was made she always knew what was happening at the bank in terms of the personal advancement or otherwise of family members. Men did not normally talk business in front of ladies, but Augusta got it all out of them at her tea-time gatherings.

'Seniority is only one of the ways in which a man may qualify as a partner,' Joseph said irritably. 'Another is the ability to bring in business, which Hugh has to a degree I have never seen in so young a man. Other qualifications would be a large capital investment in the bank, high social position, or political influence. I am afraid that as yet Edward has none of these.'

'But he is your son.'

'A bank is a business, not a dinner party,' Joseph said, getting angrier. He hated her to challenge him. 'Position is not merely a question of rank or precedence. Ability to make money is the test.'

Augusta suffered a moment of doubt. Ought she to push for Edward's advancement if he was not really able? But that was nonsense. He was perfectly all right. He might not be able to add up a column of figures as fast as Hugh, but breeding would tell in the end. She said: 'Edward could have a large capital investment in the bank, if you so wished. You can settle money on him any time you please.'

Joseph's face took on the stubborn look that Augusta knew well, the look he wore when he refused to move house or forbade her to redecorate his bedroom. 'Not before the boy marries!' he said, and with that he left the room.

Edward said: 'You've made him angry.'

'It's only for your sake, Teddy darling.'

'But you've made matters worse!'

'No, I haven't.' Augusta sighed. 'Sometimes your generous outlook prevents you from seeing what is going on. Your Papa may believe that he has taken a firm stand, but if you think about what he said you'll realize that he has promised to settle a large sum on you *and* make you a partner as soon as you get married.'

'Goodness, I suppose he has,' Edward said in surprise. 'I didn't look at it that way.'

'That's your trouble, dear. You're not sly, like Hugh.'

'Hugh was very lucky in America.'

'Of course he was. You would like to get married, wouldn't you?'

He sat beside her and took her hand. 'Why should I, when I have you to take care of me?'

'But who will you have when I'm gone? Did you like that little Emily Maple? I thought she was charming.'

'She told me that hunting is cruel to the fox,' Edward said in a tone of disdain.

'Your father will settle at least a hundred thousand on you – perhaps more, perhaps a quarter of a million.'

Edward was not impressed. 'I have everything I want, and I like living with you,' he said.

'And I like having you near me. But I want to see you happily married, with a lovely wife and your own fortune and a partnership at the bank. Say you'll think about it.'

'I'll think about it.' He kissed her cheek. 'And now I really must go, Mama. I promised to meet some fellows half an hour ago.'

'Go on, then.'

He got up and went to the door. 'Good night, Mama.'

'Good night,' she said. 'Think about Emily!'

[III]

KINGSBRIDGE MANOR was one of the largest houses in England. Maisie had stayed there three or four times and she still had not seen half of it. The house had twenty principal bedrooms, not counting the rooms of the fifty or so servants. It was heated by coal fires and lit by candles, and it had only one bathroom, but what it lacked in modern conveniences it made up in old-fashioned luxury: four-poster beds curtained with heavy silk, delicious old wines from the vast underground cellars, horses and guns and books and games without end.

The young Duke of Kingsbridge had once owned a

hundred thousand acres of best Wiltshire farmland, but on Solly's advice he had sold half of it and bought a big chunk of South Kensington with the proceeds. Consequently the agricultural depression that had impoverished many great families had left 'Kingo' untouched, and he was still able to entertain his friends in the grand style.

The Prince of Wales had been with them for the first week. Solly and Kingo and the prince shared a taste for boisterous fun, and Maisie had helped to provide it. She had substituted soapsuds for whipped cream on Kingo's dessert; she had unbuttoned Solly's braces while he dozed in the library, so that his trousers fell down when he stood up; and she had glued together the pages of *The Times* so that it could not be opened. By hazard the prince himself had been the first to pick up the newspaper, and as he fumbled with the pages there had been a moment of suspense when everyone wondered how he would take it – for though the heir to the throne loved practical jokes, he was never the victim – but then he began to chuckle as he realized what had happened, and the others all laughed uproariously, from relief as much as amusement.

The prince had left, and Hugh Pilaster had arrived; and then the trouble had started.

It was Solly's idea to get Hugh invited here. Solly liked Hugh. Maisie could not think of a plausible reason to object. It had been Solly who asked Hugh to dinner in London, too.

He had recovered his composure quickly enough, that evening, and had proved himself a perfectly eligible dinner guest. Perhaps his manners were not quite as refined as they might have been if he had spent the last six years in London drawing-rooms instead of Boston warehouses, but his natural charm made up for any shortcomings. In the two days he had been at Kingsbridge he had entertained them all with tales of life in America, a place none of them had visited.

It was ironic that Maisie should find Hugh's manners a little rough. Six years ago it had been the other way around. But she was a quick learner. She had acquired the accent of the upper classes with no trouble. The grammar had taken her a little longer. Hardest of all had been the little subtleties of behaviour, the grace-notes of social superiority: the way they walked through a door, spoke to a pet dog, changed the subject of a conversation, ignored a drunk. But she had studied hard, and now it all came naturally to her.

Hugh had recovered from the shock of their meeting, but Maisie had not. She would never forget his expression when he first saw her. She had been prepared, but for Hugh it had been a complete surprise. Because of his surprise he had shown his feelings quite nakedly, and Maisie had been dismayed to see the hurt in his eyes. She had wounded him deeply, six years ago, and he had not got over it.

The look on his face had haunted her ever since. She had been upset when she learned he was coming here. She did not want to see him. She did not want the past brought back. She was married to Solly, who was a good husband, and she could not bear the thought of hurting him. And there was Bertie, her reason for living.

Their child was named Hubert, but they called him Bertie, which was also the name of the Prince of Wales. Bertie Greenbourne would be five years old on 1 May, but that was a secret: his birthday was celebrated in September, to hide the fact that he had been born only six months after the wedding. Solly's family knew the truth, but no one else did: Bertie had been born in Switzerland, during the twelve-month European tour that had been their honeymoon. Since then Maisie had been happy.

Solly's parents had not welcomed Maisie. They were

stiff-necked snobbish German Jews who had been living in England for generations, and they looked down on Yiddish-speaking Russian Jews just off the boat. The fact that she was carrying another man's child confirmed their prejudice and gave them an excuse for rejecting her. However, Solly's sister Kate, who was about Maisie's age and had a six-year-old daughter, was nice to Maisie when her parents were not around.

Solly loved her, and he loved Bertie too, although he did not know whose child he was; and that was enough for Maisie – until Hugh came back.

She got up early, as always, and went along to the nursery wing of the great house. Bertie was having breakfast in the nursery dining-room with Kingo's children Anne and Alfred, supervised by three nursery maids. She kissed Bertie's sticky face and said: 'What are you having?'

'Porridge with honey.' He spoke with the drawling accent of the upper classes, the accent Maisie had been at pains to learn, and from which she still occasionally slipped.

'Is it nice?'

'The honey's nice.'

'I think I'll have some,' said Maisie, sitting down. It would be more digestible than the kippers and devilled kidneys the adults had for breakfast.

Bertie did not take after Hugh. As a baby he had resembled Solly, for all babies looked like Solly; and now he was getting more and more like Maisie's father, with dark hair and brown eyes. Maisie could see something of Hugh in him now and again, especially when he gave a mischievous grin; but there was no obvious resemblance, fortunately.

A nursery maid brought Maisie a dish of porridge with honey and she tasted it.

'Do you like it, Mama?' said Bertie.

Anne said: 'Don't speak with your mouth full, Bertie.'
Anne Kingsbridge was a superior seven-year-old and she
lorded it over Bertie and her five-year-old brother Freddy.

'It's delicious,' said Maisie

Another maid said: 'Would you like some buttered toast,
children?' and they all said yes in a chorus.

Maisie had at first felt it was unnatural for a child to
grow up surrounded by servants, and she feared that Bertie
would be over-protected; but she had learned that rich
children played in the dirt and climbed walls and got into
fights just as much as the poor, and the main difference
was that the people who cleaned up after them got paid.

She would have liked to have more children, Solly's
children, but something had gone wrong inside her when
Bertie was born and the Swiss doctors had said she would
not conceive again. They had been proved right, for she
had been sleeping with Solly for five years without once
missing the monthly curse. Bertie was the only child she
would ever have. She was bitterly sorry for Solly, who
would never have children of his own; although he said he
already had more happiness than any man deserved.

Kingo's wife the duchess, known to her friends as Liz,
joined the nursery breakfast party soon after Maisie. As
they were washing their children's hands and faces, Liz
said: 'You know, my mother would never have done this.
She only saw us when we were scrubbed clean and dressed
up. So unnatural.' Maisie smiled. Liz thought herself very
down-to-earth because she washed her own children's faces.

They stayed in the nursery until ten o'clock, when the
governess arrived and set the children to work drawing and
painting. Maisie and Liz returned to their rooms. Today
was a quiet day, with no hunting. Some of the men were
going fishing and others would stroll in the woods with a
dog or two, shooting rabbits. The ladies, and the men who

liked ladies better than dogs, would walk around the park before lunch.

Solly had eaten breakfast and was getting ready to go out. He was dressed in a brown tweed lounge suit with a short jacket. Maisie kissed him and helped him put on his ankle-boots: if she had not been there he would have called his valet, for he could not bend down far enough to tie the laces himself. She put on a fur coat and hat and Solly donned a heavy plaid Inverness coat with a cape and matching bowler hat, then they went down to the draughty hall to meet the others.

It was a bright, frosty morning, delightful if you had a fur coat, torture if you lived in a draughty slum and had to walk barefoot. Maisie liked to remember the privations of her childhood: it intensified the pleasure she took in being married to one of the richest men in the world.

She walked with Kingo on one side of her and Solly on the other. Hugh was behind with Liz. Although Maisie could not see him she could feel his presence, hear him chatting with Liz and making her giggle, and imagine the twinkle in his blue eyes. After about half a mile they came to the main gate. As they were turning to stroll through the orchard Maisie saw a familiar tall, black-bearded figure approaching from the village. For a moment she imagined it was her Papa; then she recognized her brother Danny.

Danny had returned to their home town six years ago to find that their parents no longer lived in the old house, and had left no other address. Disappointed, he travelled further north, to Glasgow, and founded the Working Men's Welfare Association, which not only insured working men against unemployment but also campaigned for safety rules in factories, the right to join trade unions, and financial regulation of corporations. His name started appearing in the newspapers – Dan Robinson, not Danny, for he was too formidable to be a Danny now. Papa read about him and came to his office, and there was a joyful reunion.

It turned out that Papa and Mama had at last met other Jews soon after Maisie and Danny ran away. They borrowed the money to move to Manchester, where Papa found another job, and they never sank so low again. Mama survived her illness and was now quite healthy.

Maisie was married to Solly by the time the family was reunited. Solly would cheerfully have given Papa a house and an income for life, but Papa did not want to retire, and instead asked Solly to lend him the money to open a shop. Now Mama and Papa sold caviar and other delicacies to the wealthy citizens of Manchester. When Maisie went to visit she took off her diamonds, put on a pinafore and served behind the counter, confident that none of the Marlborough Set were likely to go to Manchester and if they did they would not do their own shopping.

Seeing Danny here at Kingsbridge, Maisie immediately feared something had happened to their parents, and she ran to him, her heart in her mouth, saying: 'Danny! What's wrong? Is it Mama?'

'Papa and Mama are just fine, so are all the rest,' he said in his American accent.

'Thank God. How did you know I was here?'

'You wrote to me.'

'Oh, yes.'

Danny looked like a Turkish warrior with his curly beard and flashing eyes, but he was dressed like a clerk, in a well-worn black suit and a bowler hat, and he appeared to have walked a long way, for he had muddy boots and a weary expression. Kingo looked at him askance, but Solly rose to the occasion with his usual social grace. He shook Danny's hand and said: 'How are you, Robinson? This is my friend the Duke of Kingsbridge. Kingo, allow me to present my brother-in-law, Dan Robinson, general secretary of the Working Men's Welfare Association.'

Many men would have been dumbstruck to be introduced to a duke, but not Danny. 'How do you do, Duke?' he said with easy courtesy.

Kingo shook hands warily. Maisie guessed he was thinking that being polite to the lower classes was all very well up to a point, but it should not be taken too far.

Then Solly said: 'And this is our friend Hugh Pilaster.'

Maisie tensed. In her anxiety about Mama and Papa she had forgotten that Hugh was behind her. Danny knew secrets about Hugh, secrets Maisie had never told her husband. He knew that Hugh was the father of Bertie. Danny had once wanted to break Hugh's neck. They had never met, but Danny had not forgotten. What would he do?

However, he was six years older now. He gave Hugh a cold look, but shook hands civilly.

Hugh, who did not know he was a father and had no inkling of these undertones, spoke to Danny in a friendly way. 'Are you the brother who ran away from home and went to Boston?'

'I sure am.'

Solly said: 'Fancy Hugh knowing that!'

Solly had no idea how much Hugh and Maisie knew about one another: he did not know that they had spent a night together telling one another their life stories.

Maisie felt bewildered by the conversation: it was skating over the surface of too many secrets, and the ice was thin. She hastened to get back on to firm ground. 'Danny, why are you here?'

His weary face took on an expression of bitterness. 'I'm

no longer the secretary of the Working Men's Welfare Association,' he said. 'I'm ruined, for the third time in my life, by incompetent bankers.'

'Danny, please!' Maisie protested. He knew perfectly well that both Solly and Hugh were bankers.

But Hugh said: 'Don't worry! We hate incompetent bankers too. They're a menace to everyone. But what exactly has happened, Mr Robinson?'

'I spent five years building up the Welfare Association,' Danny said. 'It was a mighty big success. We paid out hundreds of pounds every week in benefits and took in thousands in subscriptions. But what were we to do with the surplus?'

Solly said: 'I assume you put it aside against the possibility of a bad year.'

'And where do you think we put it?'

'In a bank, I trust.'

'In the City of Glasgow Bank, to be exact.'

'Oh, dear,' said Solly.

Maisie said: 'I don't understand.'

Solly explained: 'The City of Glasgow Bank went bust.'

'Oh, no!' Maisie cried. It made her want to weep.

Danny nodded. 'All those shillings paid in by hard-working men – lost by fools in top hats. And you wonder why they talk about revolution.' He sighed. 'I've been trying to rescue the Association since it happened, but the task was hopeless, and I've given up.'

Kingo said abruptly: 'Mr Robinson, I am sorry for you and your members. Will you take some refreshment? You must have walked seven miles if you came from the railway station.'

'I will, and thank you.'

Maisie said: 'I'll take Danny indoors, and leave you to finish your walk.' She felt her brother was wounded, and she wanted to get him alone and do what she could to ease his pain.

The others obviously felt the tragedy too. Kingo said: 'Will you stop for the night, Mr Robinson?'

Maisie winced. Kingo was being too generous. It was easy enough to be civil to Danny for a few minutes out here in the park, but if he stayed overnight Kingo and his lotus-eating friends would soon get fed up with Danny's coarse clothes and working-class concerns, then they would snub him and he would be hurt.

But Danny said: 'I have to be back in London tonight. I just came to spend a few hours with my sister.'

Kingo said: 'In that case allow me to have you driven to the station in my carriage, whenever you're ready.'

'That's real kind of you.'

Maisie took her brother's arm. 'Come with me and I'll get you some lunch.'

After Danny left for London, Maisie joined Solly for an afternoon nap.

Solly lay on the bed in a red silk bathrobe and watched her undress. 'I can't rescue Dan's Welfare Association,' he said. 'Even if it made financial sense to me – which it doesn't – I couldn't persuade the other partners.'

Maisie felt a sudden surge of affection for him. She had not asked him to help Danny. 'You're such a good man,' she said. She opened his bathrobe and kissed his vast belly. 'You've already done so much for my family, you never have to apologize. Besides, Danny won't take anything from you, you know that; he's too proud.'

'But what will he do?'

She stepped out of her petticoats and rolled down her stockings. 'Tomorrow he's meeting with the Amalgamated

Society of Engineers. He wants to be a Member of Parliament and he hopes they will sponsor him.'

'And I suppose he'll campaign for stricter government regulation of banks.'

'Would you be against that?'

'We never like the government to tell us what to do. True, there are too many crashes; but there might be even more if the politicians ran the banks.' He rolled on his side and propped his head up on his elbow to get a better view of her taking off her underwear. 'I wish I weren't leaving you tonight.'

Maisie wished the same. A part of her was excited at the prospect of being with Hugh when Solly was away, but that made her feel more guilty still. 'I don't mind,' she said.

'I feel so ashamed of my family.'

'You shouldn't.' It was Passover, and Solly was going to celebrate the ritual of seder with his parents. Maisie was not invited. She understood Ben Greenbourne's dislike of her, and half felt she deserved the way he treated her, but Solly was deeply upset by it. Indeed, he would have quarrelled with his father if Maisie had let him, but she did not want that on her conscience too, and she insisted he continue to see his parents in a normal way.

'Are you sure you don't mind?' he said anxiously.

'I'm sure. Listen, if I felt strongly about it I could go to Glasgow and spend Passover with my own parents.' She became thoughtful. 'The fact is that I've never felt part of all that Jewish stuff, not since we left Russia. When we came to England there were no Jews in the town. The people I lived with in the circus had no religion at all, mostly. Even when I married a Jew, your family made me feel unwelcome. I'm fated to be an outsider, and to tell you the truth I don't mind. God never did anything for me.'

She smiled. 'Mama says God gave you to me, but that's rubbish: I got you all by myself.'

He was reassured. 'I'll miss you tonight.'

She sat on the edge of the bed and leaned over him so that he could nuzzle her breasts. 'I'll miss you too.'

'Mmm.'

After a while they lay side by side, head to tail, and he caressed her between her legs while she kissed and licked and then sucked his penis. He loved to do this in the afternoon, and he cried out softly as he came in her mouth.

She changed her position and nestled in the crook of his arm.

'What does it taste like?' he said sleepily.

She smacked her lips. 'Caviar.' He giggled and closed his eyes.

She began to stroke herself. Soon he was snoring. When she came he did not stir.

'The men who ran the City of Glasgow Bank should go to jail,' Maisie said shortly before dinner.

'That's a bit hard,' Hugh responded.

The remark struck her as smug. 'Hard?' she said irritably. 'Not as hard as what happened to the working men whose money was lost!'

'Still, no one is perfect, not even those working men,' Hugh persisted. 'If a carpenter makes a mistake, and a house falls down, should he go to jail?'

'It's not the same!'

'And why not?'

'Because the carpenter is paid thirty shillings a week and obliged to follow a foreman's orders, whereas a banker gets thousands, and justifies it by saying he carries a weight of responsibility.'

'All true. But the banker is human, and has a wife and children to support.'

'You might say the same of murderers, yet we hang them regardless of the fate of their orphaned children.'

'But if a man kills another accidentally, for example by shooting at a rabbit and hitting a man behind a bush, we don't even send him to jail. So why should we jail bankers who lose other people's money?'

'To make other bankers more careful!'

'And by the same logic we might hang the man who shot at the rabbit, to make other shooters more careful.'

'Hugh, you're just being perverse.'

'No, I'm not. Why treat careless bankers more harshly than careless rabbit-shooters?'

'The difference is that careless shots do not throw thousands of working people into destitution every few years, whereas careless bankers do.'

At this point Kingo interjected languidly: 'The directors of the City of Glasgow Bank probably *will* go to jail, I hear; and the manager too.'

Hugh said: 'So I believe.'

Maisie felt like screaming with frustration. 'Then why have you been contradicting me?'

He grinned. 'To see whether you could justify your attitude.'

Maisie remembered that Hugh had always had the power to do this to her, and she bit her tongue. Her spitfire personality was part of her appeal to the Marlborough Set, one of the reasons they accepted her despite her background; but they would get bored if she let her tantrums go on too long. Her mood changed in a flash. 'Sir, you have insulted me!' she cried theatrically. 'I challenge you to a duel!'

'What weapons do ladies duel with?' Hugh laughed.

'Crochet hooks at dawn!'

They all laughed at that, then a servant came in and announced dinner.

They were always eighteen or twenty around the long table. Maisie never ceased to love the crisp linen and fine china, the hundreds of candles reflected in the shining glassware, the immaculate black-and-white evening dress of the men and the gorgeous colours and priceless jewellery of the women. There was champagne every night, but it went straight to Maisie's waist, so she allowed herself only a sip or two.

She found herself seated next to Hugh. The duchess normally put her next to Kingo, for Kingo liked pretty women and the duchess was tolerant; but tonight she had apparently decided to vary the formula. No one said grace, for in this set religion was kept for Sundays only. The soup was served and Maisie chatted brightly to the men on either side of her. However, her mind was on her brother. Poor Danny! So clever, so dedicated, such a great leader – and so unlucky. She wondered if he would succeed in his new ambition of becoming a Member of Parliament. She hoped so. Papa would be so proud.

Today, unusually, her background had intruded visibly into her new life. It was surprising how little difference it made. Like her, Danny did not appear to belong to any particular class of society. He represented working men; his dress was middle-class; yet he had the same confident, slightly arrogant manners as Kingo and his friends. They could not easily tell whether he was an upper-class boy who chose martyrdom among the workers or a working-class boy who had risen in life.

Something similar was true of Maisie. Anyone with the least instinct for class differences could tell she was not a born lady. However, she played the part so well, and she was so pretty and charming, that they could not quite bring themselves to believe the persistent rumour that Solly had picked her up in a dance parlour. If there had been any question of her acceptance by London society, it had been answered when the Prince of Wales, son of Queen Victoria and future king, had confessed himself 'captivated' by her and sent her a gold cigarette box with a diamond clasp.

As the meal progressed she felt the presence of Hugh by her side more and more. She made an effort to keep the conversation light, and took care to talk at least as much to the man on her other side; but the past seemed to stand at her shoulder, waiting to be acknowledged, like a weary, patient supplicant.

She and Hugh had met three or four times since his return to London, and now they had spent forty-eight hours in the same house, but they had never spoken of what had happened six years ago. All Hugh knew was that she had disappeared without trace, only to surface as Mrs Solomon Greenbourne. Sooner or later she was going to have to give him some explanation. She was afraid that talking about it would bring back all the old feelings, in him as well as her. But it had to be done, and perhaps this was a good time, when Solly was away.

A moment came when several people around them were talking noisily. Maisie decided she should speak now. She turned to Hugh, and suddenly she was overcome with emotion. She began speaking three or four times and could not go on. Finally she managed to get a few words out. 'I would have ruined your career, you know.' Then she had to make such an effort not to cry that she could say no more.

He understood right away what she was talking about. 'Who told you that you would have ruined my career?'

If he had been sympathetic she might have broken down, but luckily he was aggressive, and that enabled her to reply: 'Your Aunt Augusta.'

'I suspected she was involved somehow.'

'But she was right.'

'I don't believe that,' he said, getting angry very quickly. 'You didn't ruin Solly's career.'

'Calm down. Solly wasn't already the black sheep of the family. Even so it was difficult enough. His family hate me still.'

'Even though you're Jewish?'

'Yes. Jews can be as snobbish as anyone else.' He would never know the real reason – that Bertie was not Solly's child.

'Why didn't you simply tell me what you were doing, and why?'

'I couldn't.' Remembering those awful days, she felt choked up again and had to take a deep breath to calm herself. 'I found it very hard to cut myself off like that, it broke my heart. I couldn't have done it at all if I'd had to justify myself to you as well.'

Still he would not let her off the hook. 'You could have sent me a note.'

Maisie's voice dropped almost to a whisper. 'I couldn't bring myself to write it.'

At last he seemed to relent. He took a gulp of his wine and averted his eyes from her. 'It was awful, not understanding, not knowing if you were even alive.' He was speaking harshly, but now she could see the remembered pain in his eyes.

'I'm sorry,' she said feebly. 'I'm so sorry I hurt you. I didn't want to. I wanted to save you from unhappiness. I did it for love.' As soon as she heard herself say the word *love* she regretted it.

277

He picked up on it. 'Do you love Solly now?' he said abruptly.

'Yes.'

'The two of you seem very settled.'

'The way we live . . . it isn't difficult to be contented.'

He had not finished being angry with her. 'You've got what you always wanted.'

That was a bit hard, but she felt that perhaps she deserved it, so she just nodded.

'What happened to April?'

Maisie hesitated. This was going a bit too far. 'You class me with April, then, do you?' she said, feeling hurt.

Somehow that deflated his anger. He smiled ruefully and said: 'No, you were never like April, I know that. All the same I'd like to know what became of her. Do you still see her?'

'Yes – discreetly.' April was a neutral topic: talking about her would get them off this dangerously emotional ground. Maisie decided to satisfy his curiosity. 'Do you know a place called Nellie's?'

He lowered his voice. 'It's a brothel.'

She could not restrain herself from asking: 'Did you ever go there?'

He looked embarrassed. 'Yes, once. It was a fiasco.'

That did not surprise her: she remembered how naive and inexperienced the twenty-year-old Hugh had been. 'Well, April now owns the place.'

'Goodness! How did that happen?'

'First she became the mistress of a famous novelist and lived in the prettiest little cottage in Clapham. He tired of her at about the time Nell was thinking about retirement. So April sold the cottage and bought Nell out.'

'Fancy that,' said Hugh. 'I'll never forget Nell. She was the fattest woman I've ever seen.'

The table had suddenly gone quiet, and his last sentence was heard by several people nearby. There was general laughter, and someone said: 'Who was this fat lady?' Hugh just grinned and made no reply.

After that they stayed off dangerous topics, but Maisie felt subdued and somewhat fragile, as if she had suffered a fall and bruised herself.

When dinner was over and the men had smoked their cigars, Kingo announced that he wanted to dance. The drawing-room carpet was rolled up and a footman who could play polkas on the piano was summoned and set to work.

Maisie danced with everyone except Hugh, then it was obvious she was avoiding him, so she danced with him; and it was as if six years had rolled back and they were in Cremorne Gardens again. He hardly led her: they seemed instinctively to do the same thing. Maisie could not suppress the disloyal thought that Solly was a clumsy dancer.

After Hugh she took another partner; but then the other men stopped asking her. As ten o'clock turned to eleven and the brandy appeared, convention was abandoned: white ties were loosened, some of the women kicked off their shoes, and Maisie danced every dance with Hugh. She knew she ought to feel guilty, but she had never been much good at guilt: she was enjoying herself and she was not going to stop.

When the piano-playing footman was exhausted, the duchess demanded a breath of air, and maids were sent scurrying for coats so they could all take a turn around the garden. Out in the darkness, Maisie took Hugh's arm. 'The whole world knows what I've been doing for the last six years, but what about you?'

'I like America,' he said. 'There's no class system. There

are rich and poor, but no aristocracy, no nonsense about rank and protocol. What you've done, in marrying Solly and becoming a friend of the highest in the land, is pretty unusual here, and even now I bet you never actually tell the truth about your origins—'

'They have their suspicions, I think – but you're right, I don't own up.'

'In America you'd boast about your humble beginnings the way Kingo boasts about his ancestors fighting at the battle of Agincourt.'

She was interested in Hugh, not America. 'You haven't married.'

'No.'

'In Boston . . . was there a girl you liked?'

'I tried, Maisie,' he said.

Suddenly she wished she had not asked him about this, for she had a premonition that his answer would destroy her happiness; but it was too late, the question had been raised and he was already speaking.

'There were pretty girls in Boston, and pleasant girls, and intelligent girls, and girls who would make wonderful wives and mothers. I paid attention to some of them, and they seemed to like me. But when it came to the point where I had to make a proposal or back off I realized, each time, that what I felt was not enough. It was not what I felt for you. It wasn't love.'

Now he had said it. 'Stop,' Maisie whispered.

'Two or three mothers got rather cross with me, then my reputation spread around, and the girls became wary. They were nice enough to me, but they knew there was something wrong with me, I wasn't serious, not the marrying kind. Hugh Pilaster, the English banker and breaker of hearts. And if a girl did seem to fall for me, despite my record, I would discourage her. I don't like to break people's hearts. I know too well what it feels like.'

Her face was wet with tears, she realized, and she was glad of the tactful dark. 'I'm sorry,' she said, but she whispered so softly that she could hardly hear her own voice.

'Anyway, I know what's wrong with me now. I guess I always knew, but the last two days have removed any doubts.'

They had fallen behind the others, and now he stopped and faced her.

She said: 'Don't say it, Hugh, please.'

'I still love you. That's all.'

It was out, and everything was ruined.

'I think you love me too,' he went on mercilessly. 'Don't you?'

She looked up at him. She could see, reflected in his eyes, the lights of the house across the lawn, but his face was in shadow. He inclined his head and kissed her lips, and she did not turn away. 'Salt tears,' he said after a minute. 'You do love me. I knew it.' He took a folded handkerchief from his pocket and touched her face gently, mopping the teardrops from her cheeks.

She had to put a stop to this. 'We must catch up with the others,' she said. 'People will talk.' She turned and began to walk, so that he had to either release her arm or go with her. He went with her.

'I'm surprised that you worry about people talking,' he said. 'Your set is famous for not minding anything of that sort.'

She was not really concerned about the others. It was herself she was worried about. She made him walk faster until they rejoined the rest of the party, then she let go of his arm and talked to the duchess.

She was obscurely bothered by Hugh's saying that the Marlborough Set was famous for its tolerance. It was true, but she wished he hadn't used the phrase *anything of that sort*; she was not sure why.

When they re-entered the house the tall clock in the hall was striking midnight. Maisie suddenly felt drained by the tensions of the day. 'I'm going to bed,' she announced.

She saw the duchess look reflexively at Hugh, then back at her, and suppress a little smile; and she realized that they all thought Hugh would sleep with her tonight.

The ladies went upstairs together, leaving the men to play billiards and drink a nightcap. As the women kissed her goodnight Maisie saw the same look in the eyes of each one, a gleam of excitement tinged with envy.

She went into her bedroom and closed the door. A coal fire burned merrily in the grate, and there were candles on the mantelpiece and the dressing-table. On the bedside table, as usual, there was a plate of sandwiches and a bottle of sherry in case she got peckish in the night: she never touched them, but the well-trained staff of Kingsbridge Manor put a tray beside every bed without fail.

She began to take off her clothes. They might all be wrong: perhaps Hugh would not come to her tonight. The thought stabbed her like a pain, and she realized she was longing for him to come through the door so that she could take him in her arms and kiss him, really kiss him, not guiltily as she had in the garden, but hungrily and shamelessly. The feeling brought back an overwhelming memory of the night of the Goodwood Races six years ago, the narrow bed in his aunt's house, and the expression on his face when she took off her dress.

She looked at her body in the long mirror. Hugh would notice how it had changed. Six years ago she had had tiny turned-in pink nipples like dimples, but now, after nursing

Bertie, they were enlarged and strawberry-coloured, and stuck out. As a girl she had not needed to wear a corset — she had been naturally wasp-shaped — but her waist had never quite returned to normal after pregnancy.

She heard the men coming up the stairs, heavy-footed and laughing at some joke. Hugh had been right: not one of them would be shocked by a little adultery at a country-house party. Did they not feel disloyal to their friend Solly, she thought derisively? And then it hit her like a slap in the face that she was the one who ought to feel disloyal.

She had put Solly out of her mind all evening, but now he came back to her in spirit: harmless, amiable Solly; kind, generous Solly; the man who loved her to distraction, the man who cared for Bertie, knowing he was another man's child. Within hours of his leaving the house Maisie was about to let another man come into her bed. What kind of woman am I? she thought.

On impulse she went to the door and locked it.

She realized now why she had disliked Hugh's saying: *Your set is famous for not minding anything of that sort.* It made her feeling for Hugh seem commonplace, just another one of the many flirtations, romances and infidelities that gave society ladies something to gossip about. Solly deserved better than to be betrayed by a commonplace affair.

But I want Hugh, she thought.

The idea of forgoing this night with him made her want to weep. She thought of his boyish grin and his bony chest, his blue eyes and smooth white skin; and she remembered the expression on his face when he looked at her body, the expression of wonder and happiness, desire and delight; and it seemed so hard to give that up.

There was a soft tap at the door.

She stood naked in the middle of the room, paralysed and dumb.

The handle turned and the door was pushed; but of course it would not open.

She heard her name spoken in a low voice.

She went to the door and put her hand to the key.

'Maisie!' he called softly. 'It's me, Hugh.'

She longed for him so much that the sound of his voice made her moist inside. She put her finger in her mouth and bit herself hard, but the pain did not mask the desire.

He tapped on the door again. 'Maisie! Let me in?'

She leaned her back against the wall, and the tears streamed down her face, dripping off her chin on to her breasts.

'At least let us talk!'

She knew that if she opened the door there would be no talking – she would take him in her arms and they would fall to the floor in a frenzy of desire.

'Say *something*. Are you there? I know you're there.'

She stood still, crying silently.

'Please?' he said. 'Please?'

After a while he went away.

Maisie slept badly and woke early, but as the new day dawned her spirits lifted a little. Before the other guests were up she went along to the nursery wing as usual. Outside the door of the nursery dining-room she stopped suddenly. She was not the first guest to rise, after all. She could hear a man's voice inside. She paused and listened. It was Hugh.

He was saying: 'And just at that moment, the giant woke up.'

There was a childish squeal of delighted terror that Maisie recognized as coming from Bertie.

Hugh went on: 'Jack went down the beanstalk as fast as his legs could carry him – but the giant came after him!'

Kingo's daughter Anne said in the superior voice of a knowing seven-year-old: 'Bertie's hiding behind his chair because he's scared. I'm not scared.'

Maisie wanted to hide like Bertie, and she turned and began to walk back to her room, but she stopped again. She had to face Hugh some time today, and here in the nursery might be the easiest place. She composed herself and went in.

Hugh had the three children enraptured. Bertie hardly saw his mother come in. Hugh looked up at Maisie with hurt in his eyes. 'Don't stop,' Maisie said, and she sat down by Bertie and hugged him.

Hugh returned his attention to the children. 'And what do you think Jack did next?'

'I know,' said Anne. 'He got an axe.'

'That's right.'

Maisie sat there hugging Bertie, while Bertie stared big-eyed at the man who was his real father. If I can stand this, I can do anything, Maisie thought.

Hugh said: 'And while the giant was still half-way up the beanstalk, Jack chopped it down! And the giant fell all the way to the earth . . . and died. And Jack and his mother lived happily ever after.'

Bertie said: 'Tell it again.'

[IV]

THE CORDOVAN Ministry was busy. Tomorrow was Cordovan Independence Day and there would be a big afternoon reception for Members of Parliament, Foreign

Office officials, diplomats and journalists. This morning, to add to his worries, Micky Miranda had received a stiff note from the British Foreign Secretary about two English tourists who had been murdered while exploring the Andes. But when Edward Pilaster called, Micky Miranda dropped everything, for what he had to say to Edward was much more important than either the reception or the note. He needed half a million pounds, and he was hoping to get the money from Edward.

Micky had been the Cordovan Minister for a year. Getting the job had required all his cunning, but it had also cost his family a fortune in bribes back home. He had promised Papa that all that money would come back to the family, and now he had to make good his promise. He would rather die than let his father down.

He brought Edward into the Minister's chamber, a grand first-floor room dominated by a full-size Cordovan flag. He went to the big table and spread out a map of Cordova, weighing down the corners with his cigar case, the sherry decanter, a glass, and Edward's grey top hat. He hesitated. It was the first time he had ever asked someone for half a million pounds.

'Here is Santamaria Province, in the north of the country,' he began.

'I do know the geography of Cordova,' Edward said peevishly.

'Of course you do,' said Micky in a soothing voice. It was true. Pilasters Bank did a healthy volume of business with Cordova, financing its exports of nitrate, salt beef and silver and its imports of mining equipment, guns and luxury goods. Edward handled all that business, thanks to Micky, who as attaché and then Minister had made life difficult for anyone who did not want to use Pilasters Bank to finance their trade with his country. In consequence Edward was now seen as the leading London expert on Cordova. 'Of course you do,' Micky repeated. 'And you know that all the nitrate mined by my father has to be transported by mule train from Santamaria to Palma. But what you may not realize is that it is perfectly possible to build a railroad along that route.'

'How can you be sure? A railroad is a complicated thing.'

Micky took a bound volume from his desk. 'Because my father commissioned a survey by a Scottish engineer, Gordon Halfpenny. All the details are in here – including the costs. Take a look.'

'How much?' Edward said.

'Five hundred thousand pounds.'

Edward riffled through the pages of the report. 'What about politics?'

Micky glanced up at the big portrait of President Garcia in the uniform of Commander-in-Chief. Every time Micky looked at the picture he vowed that one day his own portrait would occupy that spot on the wall. 'The president favours the idea. He believes it will strengthen his military grip on the countryside.' Garcia trusted Papa. Ever since Papa had become Governor of Santamaria Province – with the help of two thousand Westley-Richards short-barrelled rifles made in Birmingham – the Miranda family had been the president's fervent supporters and close allies. Garcia did not suspect Papa's motive for wanting a railway to the capital: it would enable the Miranda family to attack the capital within two days instead of two weeks.

'How will it be paid for?' said Edward.

'We'll raise the money on the London market,' Micky said airily. 'In fact I thought Pilasters Bank might like to have the business.' He tried to breathe slowly and normally.

This was the climax of his long and painstaking cultivation of the Pilaster family: this was to be his reward for years of preparation.

But Edward shook his head and said: 'I don't think so.'

Micky was astonished and dismayed. At worst he had thought Edward would agree to think about it. 'But you raise money for railroads all the time – I thought you'd be pleased to have the opportunity!'

'Cordova isn't the same as Canada or Russia,' Edward said. 'Investors don't like your political set-up, with every provincial *caudillo* having his own personal army. It's medieval.'

Micky had not thought of that. 'You floated Papa's silver mine.' That had happened three years ago, and had brought Papa a useful hundred thousand pounds.

'Exactly! It turned out to be the only silver mine in South America that struggles to make a profit.'

In truth the mine was very rich, but Papa was skimming the profits off the top and leaving nothing for the shareholders. If only he had left a little margin for the sake of respectability! But Papa never listened to such counsel.

Micky fought down a panicky feeling, but his emotions must have shown on his face, for Edward said worriedly: 'I say, old boy, is it terribly important? You look upset.'

'To tell you the truth, it would mean quite a lot to my family,' Micky admitted. He felt that Edward must be able to raise this money if he really wanted to; it could not be impossible. 'Surely, if a bank with the prestige of Pilasters were to back the project, people would conclude that Cordova must be a good place to invest.'

'There's something in that,' Edward said. 'If one of the partners put the idea up, and really wanted to push it through, it could probably be done. But I'm not a partner.'

Micky realized he had underestimated the difficulty of

raising half a million pounds. But he was not beaten. He would find a way. 'I'll have to think again,' he said with forced cheerfulness.

Edward drained his sherry glass and stood up. 'Shall we go to lunch?'

That night Micky and the Pilasters went to see *HMS Pinafore* at the Opera Comique. Micky got there a few minutes early. While he was waiting in the foyer he ran into the Bodwin family, who were Pilaster hangers-on: Albert Bodwin was a lawyer who did a lot of work for the bank, and Augusta had once tried quite hard to get the daughter, Rachel Bodwin, to marry Hugh.

Micky's mind was on the problem of raising the money for the railroad, but he flirted with Rachel Bodwin automatically, as he did with all girls and many married women. 'And how is the movement for female emancipation, Miss Bodwin?'

Her mother blushed and said: 'I wish you wouldn't speak of it, Señor Miranda.'

'Then I shan't, Mrs Bodwin, for your wishes are to me as Acts of Parliament, legally binding.' He turned back to Rachel. She was not exactly pretty – her eyes were a little too close together – but she had a good figure: long legs, a narrow waist and a deep bust. In a sudden flash of fantasy he imagined her with her hands tied to the head of a bed and her naked legs spread, and he enjoyed the picture. Glancing up from her bosom he caught her eye. Most girls would have blushed and turned away, but she gave him a look of remarkable frankness and smiled, and it was he who felt embarrassed. Looking for something to talk about he said: 'Did you know that our old friend Hugh Pilaster has returned from the colonies?'

'Yes, I saw him at Whitehaven House. You were there.'

'Ah yes, I forgot.'

'I always liked Hugh.'

But you didn't want to marry him, Micky thought. Rachel had now been on offer in the marriage market for many years, and she was beginning to look like stale goods, he thought unkindly. Yet his instincts told him she was a deeply sexual person. Her problem was undoubtedly that she was too formidable. She frightened men off. But she must be getting desperate. Approaching thirty and still single, she would surely be wondering if she were doomed to the life of a spinster. Some women might contemplate that with equanimity, but not Rachel, Micky felt.

She was attracted to him, but then so was almost everyone, old and young, male and female. Micky liked it when rich and influential people fell for him, for it gave him power; but Rachel was nobody and her interest in him was valueless.

The Pilasters arrived and Micky turned his attention to Augusta. She was wearing a striking evening gown in deep raspberry pink. 'You look . . . delicious, Mrs Pilaster,' he said in a low voice, and she smiled with pleasure. The two families chatted for a few minutes, then it was time to take their seats.

The Bodwins were in the stalls but the Pilasters had a box. As they separated, Rachel gave Micky a warm smile and said quietly: 'Perhaps we will see you later, Señor Miranda.' Her father overheard and looked disapproving as he took her arm and hurried her away, but Mrs Bodwin smiled at Micky as they left. Mr Bodwin doesn't want his daughter to fall for a foreigner, Micky thought, but Mrs Bodwin is not so choosy any more.

He worried over his railroad loan throughout the first act. It had not occurred to him that Cordova's primitive political setup, which had allowed the Miranda family to fight their way to wealth and power, might be seen by investors as risky. That probably meant he could not get the railroad project financed by any other bank. The only way to raise the money would be to use his inside influence with Pilasters. And the only people he might be able to influence were Edward and Augusta.

During the first interval he found himself alone in the box with Augusta for a few moments, and he tackled her immediately, knowing that she appreciated the direct approach. 'When will Edward be made a partner in the bank?'

'That's a sore point,' she said sourly. 'Why do you ask?'

He told her briefly about the railroad, leaving out Papa's long-term aim of attacking the capital. 'I can't get the money from another bank – none of them know anything about Cordova, because I've kept them all away for Edward's sake.' It was not the real reason but Augusta would not know that: she did not understand the business. 'But it would be a success if Edward could push it through.'

Augusta nodded. 'My husband has promised to make Edward a partner as soon as he marries,' she said.

Micky was surprised. Edward marry! The idea was startling – and yet why should it be?

Augusta went on: 'We have even agreed on a bride: Emily Maple, the daughter of Deacon Maple.'

'What's she like?'

'Pretty, young – she's only nineteen – and sensible. Her parents approve of the match.'

She sounded about right for Edward, Micky thought: he liked pretty girls but he needed one he could dominate. 'So what obstacle is there?'

Augusta frowned. 'I simply don't know. But somehow Edward never quite gets around to asking her.'

This did not surprise Micky. He could not imagine Edward marrying, no matter how suitable the girl. What did he have to gain from marriage? He had no desire for children. But now there was an incentive: the partnership. Even if Edward did not care about that, Micky did. 'What can we do to encourage him?' he said.

Augusta gave Micky a sharp look and said: 'I have a funny feeling that he might go ahead if you were married.'

Micky looked away. That was perceptive of her. She had no idea what went on in the private rooms of Nellie's brothel – but she had a mother's intuition. He, too, felt that if he married first, Edward might be more willing. 'Me, marry?' he said with a little laugh. Naturally he would marry, sooner or later – everyone did – but he saw no reason to do so yet.

However, if it was the price of financing the railroad . . .

It was not just the railroad, he reflected. One successful loan would lead to another. Countries such as Russia and Canada raised fresh loans every year on the London market – for railroads, harbours, water supply companies, and general government finance. There was no reason why Cordova should not do the same. Micky would take a commission, official or unofficial, on every penny raised; but more importantly, the money would be channelled to his family's interests back home, making them ever richer and more powerful.

And the alternative was unthinkable. If he let his father down over this he would never be forgiven. To avert his father's wrath he would marry three times over.

He looked back at Augusta. They never spoke of what had happened in Old Seth's bedroom back in the September of 1873, but she could not possibly have forgotten it. It had been sex without intercourse, infidelity without adultery, something and nothing. They had both been fully clothed, it had lasted only seconds, yet it had been more passionate and moving and searingly unforgettable than anything Micky had ever done with the whores at Nellie's brothel, and he felt sure it had been a momentous passage for Augusta too. How did she really feel about the prospect of Micky getting married? Half the women in London would be jealous, but it was so hard to know what Augusta felt in her heart. He decided to ask her directly. He looked into her eyes and said: 'Do you want me to marry?'

She hesitated. He saw regret in her face for a moment. Then her expression hardened and she said firmly: 'Yes.'

He stared at her. She held his look. He saw that she meant what she said, and he was oddly disappointed.

Augusta said: 'It must be settled soon. Emily Maple and her parents won't be kept in suspense indefinitely.'

In other words I'd better get married quickly, Micky thought.

I will, then. So be it.

Joseph and Edward returned to the box and the conversation turned to other matters.

Throughout the next act Micky thought about Edward. They had been friends now for fifteen years. Edward was weak and insecure, eager to please but without initiative or drive. His life's project was to get people to encourage and support him, and Micky had been supplying that need ever since he started doing Edward's Latin prep at school. Now Edward needed to be pushed into the marriage that was necessary for his career – and for Micky's.

During the second interval Micky said to Augusta: 'Edward needs someone to help him at the bank – a clever clerk who will be loyal to him and look after his interests.'

Augusta thought for a moment. 'That's a very good notion indeed,' she said. 'Someone you and I know and trust.'

'Exactly.'

Augusta said: 'Do you have someone in mind?'

'I have a cousin working for me at the Ministry. His name is Simon Oliver. It was Olivera but he anglicized it. He's a smart boy and completely trustworthy.'

'Bring him to tea,' Augusta said. 'If I like the looks of him I'll speak to Joseph.'

'Very well.'

The last act began. He and Augusta often thought alike, Micky mused. It was Augusta he should be married to: together they could conquer the world. He pushed that fantastic notion out of his head. Who was he going to marry? She should not be an heiress, for he had nothing to offer such a girl. There were several heiresses he could easily captivate, but winning their hearts was only the start: there would be a prolonged battle with the parents and no guarantee of the right result. No, he needed a girl of modest background, one who liked him already and would accept him with alacrity. His eye roamed idly around the stalls of the theatre – and lit on Rachel Bodwin.

She fitted the bill perfectly, he realized. She was already half in love with him. She was getting desperate for a husband. Her father did not like Micky much but her mother did, and the mother and daughter together would soon overcome the father's opposition.

But most importantly, she aroused him.

She would be a virgin, innocent and apprehensive. He would do things to her that would bewilder and disgust her. She might resist, which would make it even better. In the end a wife had to give in to her husband's sexual demands, regardless of how bizarre or distasteful they might be, for she had no one to complain to. Once again he pictured her tied to the bed, only this time she was writhing, either in pain or desire or both. . . .

The show came to an end. As they left the theatre Micky looked out for the Bodwins. They met on the pavement, as the Pilasters were waiting for their carriage and Albert Bodwin was hailing a hansom. Micky gave Mrs Bodwin a winning smile and said: 'May I do myself the honour of calling on you tomorrow afternoon?'

She was obviously startled. 'The honour would be all mine, Señor Miranda.'

'You're too kind.' He shook hands with Rachel, looked her in the eye, and said: 'Until tomorrow, then.'

'I look forward to it,' she said.

Augusta's carriage arrived and Micky opened the door. 'What do you think of her?' he murmured.

'Her eyes are too close together,' Augusta said as she climbed in. She settled in her seat then spoke to him through the open door. 'Other than that, she looks like me.' She slammed the door and the carriage drove off.

An hour later Micky and Edward were eating supper in a private room at Nellie's. Apart from the table, the room contained a sofa, a wardrobe, a wash-stand and a big bed. April Tilsley had redecorated the whole place, and this room had fashionable William Morris fabrics, and a set of framed drawings of people performing sexual acts with a variety of fruits and vegetables. But it was in the nature of the business that people got drunk and misbehaved, and already the wallpaper was torn, the curtains stained and the carpet ripped. However, low candlelight hid the tawdriness of the room as well as taking years off the ages of the women.

The men were being waited on by two of their favourite girls, Muriel and Lily, who were wearing red silk shoes and huge, elaborate hats but were otherwise naked. From outside the room came the sounds of raucous singing and some kind of heated quarrel, but in here it was peaceful, with the crackling of the coal fire and the murmured words of the two girls as they served supper. The atmosphere relaxed Micky, and he began to feel less anxious about the railroad loan. He had a plan, at least. He could only try it out. He looked across the table at Edward. Theirs had been a fruitful friendship, he mused. There were times when he felt almost fond of Edward. Edward's dependency was tiresome, but it was what gave Micky power over him. He had helped Edward, Edward had helped him, and together they had enjoyed all the vices of the most sophisticated city in the world.

When they finished eating Micky poured another glass of wine and said: 'I'm going to marry Rachel Bodwin.'

Muriel and Lily giggled.

Edward stared at him for a long moment then said: 'I don't believe it.'

Micky shrugged. 'Believe what you wish. It's true, all the same.'

'Do you really mean it?'

'Yes.'

'You swine.'

Micky stared at his friend in surprise. 'What? Why shouldn't I marry?'

Edward stood up and leaned over the table aggressively. 'You're a damned swine, Miranda, and that's all there is to say.'

Micky had not anticipated such a reaction. 'What the devil has got into you?' he said. 'Aren't you going to marry Emily Maple?'

'Who told you that?'

'Your mother.'

'Well, I'm not marrying anyone.'

'Why not? You're twenty-nine years old. So am I. It's time for a man to equip himself with the semblance of a respectable household.'

'To the devil with a respectable household!' Edward roared, and he overturned the table. Micky sprang back as crockery smashed and wine spilled. The two naked women cringed away fearfully.

'Calm down!' Micky cried.

'After all these years!' Edward raged. 'After all I've done for you!'

Micky was baffled by Edward's fury. He realized he had to calm the man down. A scene like this could prejudice him against marriage, and that was the opposite of what Micky wanted. 'It's not a disaster,' he said in a reasonable tone. 'It's not going to make any difference to us.'

'It's bound to!'

'No, it's not. We'll still come here.'

Edward looked suspicious. In a quieter voice he said: 'Will we?'

'Yes. And we'll still go to the club. That's what clubs are for. Men go to clubs to get away from their wives.'

'I suppose they do.'

The door opened and April swept in. 'What's the noise about?' she said. 'Edward, have you been breaking my china?'

'I'm sorry, April. I'll pay for it.'

Micky said to April: 'We were just explaining to Edward that he can still come here after he's married.'

'Good God, I should hope so,' April said. 'If no married men came here I'd have to close the place.' She turned toward the doorway and called out: 'Sidney! Fetch a broom.'

Edward was calming down rapidly, to Micky's relief. Micky said: 'When we're first married, we should probably spend a few evenings at home, and give the occasional dinner party. But after a while we'll go right back to normal.'

Edward frowned. 'Don't wives mind that?'

Micky shrugged. 'Who cares whether they mind? What can a wife do?'

'If she's discontented I suppose she can bother her husband.'

Micky realized that Edward was taking his mother as a typical wife. Fortunately few women were as strong-willed or as clever as Augusta. 'The trick is not to be too good to them,' Micky said, speaking from observation of married cronies at the Cowes Club. 'If you're good to a wife she'll want you to stay with her. Treat her roughly and she'll be only too glad to see you go off to your club in the evening and leave her in peace.'

Muriel put her arms around Edward's neck. 'It'll be just the same when you're married, Edward, I promise,' she said. 'I'll suck your cock while you watch Micky fuck Lily, just the way you like.'

'Will you?' he said with a foolish grin.

"Course I will.'

'So nothing will change, really,' he said, looking at Micky.

'Oh, yes,' said Micky. 'One thing will change. You'll be a partner in the bank.'

CHAPTER TWO

April

[I]

THE MUSIC-HALL was as hot as a Turkish bath. The air smelled of beer, shellfish and unwashed people. On stage a young woman dressed in elaborate rags stood in front of a painted backdrop of a pub. She was holding a doll, to represent a new-born baby, and singing about how she had been seduced and abandoned. The audience, sitting on benches at long trestle-tables, linked arms and joined in the chorus:

And all it took was a little drop of gin!

Hugh sang at the top of his voice. He was feeling good. He had eaten a pint of winkles and drunk several glasses of warm, malty beer, and he was pressed up against Nora Dempster, a pleasant person to be squashed by. She had a soft, plump body and a beguiling smile, and she had probably saved his life.

After his visit to Kingsbridge Manor he had fallen into the pit of a black depression. Seeing Maisie had raised old ghosts, and since she rejected him again the ghosts had haunted him without respite.

299

He had been able to live through the daytime, for at work there were challenges and problems to take his mind off his grief: he was busy organizing the joint enterprise with Madler and Bell, which the Pilasters partners had finally approved. And he was soon to become a partner himself, something he had dreamed of. But in the evenings he had no enthusiasm for anything. He was invited to a great many parties, balls and dinners, for he was a member of the Marlborough Set by virtue of his friendship with Solly, and he often went, but if Maisie was not there he was bored, and if she was he was miserable. So most evenings he sat in his rooms thinking about her, or walked the streets hoping against all likelihood to bump into her.

It was on the street that he had met Nora. He had gone to Peter Robinson's in Oxford Street – a shop that had once been a linen draper's but was now called a 'department store' – to get a birthday present for his sister Dotty: he planned to take the train to Folkestone immediately afterwards. But he was so miserable that he did not know how he was going to face his family, and a kind of paralysis of choice made him incapable of selecting a gift. He came out empty-handed as it was getting dark, and Nora literally bumped into him. She had stumbled and he had caught her in his arms.

He would never forget how it had felt to hold her. Even though she was wrapped up, her body was soft and yielding, and she smelled warm and scented. For a moment the cold, dark London street vanished and he was in a closed world of sudden delight. Then she dropped her purchase, a pottery vase, and it smashed on the pavement. She gave a cry of dismay and looked as if she might burst into tears. Hugh naturally insisted on buying a replacement.

She was a year or two younger than he, twenty-four or twenty-five. She had a pretty round face with sandy blonde curls poking out from a bonnet, and her clothes were cheap but pleasing: a pink wool dress embroidered with flowers and worn over a bustle, and a tight-fitting French-navy velvet jacket trimmed with rabbit fur. She spoke with a broad Cockney drawl.

While they were buying the replacement vase he told her, by way of conversation, that he could not decide what to give his sister for her birthday. Nora suggested a colourful umbrella, and then she insisted on helping him choose it.

Finally he took her home in a hansom. She told him she lived with her father, a travelling salesman of patent medicines. Her mother was dead. The neighbourhood where she lived was rather less respectable than he had guessed, poor working-class rather than middle-class.

He assumed he would never see her again, and all day Sunday at Folkestone he brooded about Maisie as always. On Monday at the bank he got a note from Nora, thanking him for his kindness: her handwriting was small, neat and girlish, he noticed before screwing the note up into a ball and dropping it into the waste-paper basket.

Next day he stepped out of the bank at midday, on his way to a coffee house for a plate of lamb cutlets, and saw her walking along the street towards him. At first he did not recognize her, but simply thought what a nice face she had; then she smiled at him and he remembered. He doffed his hat and she stopped to talk. She worked as an assistant to a corset maker, she told him with a blush, and she was on her way back to the shop after visiting a client. A sudden impulse made him ask her to go dancing with him that night.

She said she would like to go but she did not have a respectable hat, so he took her to a milliner's shop, and bought her one, and that settled the matter.

Much of their romance was conducted while shopping. She had never owned much and she took unashamed delight in Hugh's affluence. For his part he enjoyed buying her gloves, shoes, a coat, bracelets, and anything else she wanted. His sister Dotty, with all the wisdom of her twelve years, had announced that Nora only liked him for his money. He had laughed and said: 'But who would love me for my looks?'

Maisie did not disappear from his mind – indeed, he still thought of her every day – but the memories no longer plunged him into despair. He had something to look forward to now, his next rendezvous with Nora. In a few weeks she gave him back his *joie de vivre*.

On one of their shopping expeditions they met Maisie in a furrier's store in Bond Street. Feeling rather bashful, Hugh introduced the two women. Nora was bowled over to meet Mrs Solomon Greenbourne. Maisie invited them to tea at the Piccadilly house. That evening Hugh saw Maisie again at a ball, and to his surprise Maisie was quite ungracious about Nora. 'I'm sorry, but I don't like her,' Maisie had said. 'She strikes me as a hard-hearted grasping woman and I don't believe she loves you one bit. For God's sake don't marry her.'

Hugh had been hurt and offended. Maisie was just jealous, he decided. Anyway, he was not thinking of marriage.

When the music-hall show came to an end they went outside into a fog, thick and swirling and tasting of soot. They wrapped scarves around their necks and over their mouths and set off for Nora's home in Camden Town.

It was like being underwater. All sound was muffled, and

people and things loomed out of the fog suddenly, without warning: a whore soliciting beneath a gaslight, a drunk staggering out of a pub, a policeman on patrol, a crossing sweeper, a lamplit carriage creeping along the road, a damp dog in the gutter and a glint-eyed cat down an alley. Hugh and Nora held hands and stopped every now and again in the thickest darkness to pull down their scarves and kiss. Nora's lips were soft and responsive, and she let him slip his hand inside her coat and caress her breasts. The fog made everything hushed and secret and romantic.

He usually left her at the corner of her street but tonight, because of the fog, he walked her to the door. He wanted to kiss her again there, but he was afraid her father might open the door and see them. However, Nora surprised him by saying: 'Would you like to come in?'

He had never been inside her house. 'What will your Papa think?' he said.

'He's gone to Huddersfield,' she said, and she opened the door.

Hugh's heart beat faster as he stepped inside. He did not know what was going to happen next but it was sure to be exciting. He helped Nora out of her cloak, and his eyes rested longingly on the curves beneath her sky-blue gown.

The house was tiny, smaller even than the house in Folkestone that Hugh's mother had moved to after his father's death. The staircase took up most of the narrow hall. There were two doors off the hall, leading presumably to a front parlour and a back kitchen. Upstairs there must be two bedrooms. There would be a tin bath in the kitchen and a privy in the back yard.

Hugh hung his hat and coat on a stand. A dog was barking in the kitchen, and Nora opened the door to release a small black Scottish terrier with a blue ribbon around its neck. It greeted her enthusiastically then circled Hugh warily. 'Blackie protects me when Pa's away,' Nora said, and Hugh registered the double meaning.

He followed Nora into the parlour. The furniture was old and worn, but Nora had brightened the room with things they had bought together: gay cushions, a colourful rug and a painting of Balmoral Castle. She lit a candle and drew the curtains.

Hugh stood in the middle of the room, not knowing what to do with himself, until she put him out of his misery by saying: 'See if you can get the fire going.' There were a few embers in the hearth, and Hugh put on kindling and blew the fire back to life with a small bellows.

When he was done he turned around to see her sitting on the sofa with her hat off and her hair let down. She patted the cushion beside her and he sat down obediently. Blackie glared jealously at him, and he wondered how soon he could get the dog out of the room.

They held hands and looked into the fire. Hugh felt at peace. He could not imagine wanting to do anything else for the rest of his life. After a while he kissed her again. Tentatively he touched her breast. It was firm, and filled his hand. He squeezed it gently, and she sighed heavily. Hugh had not felt this good for years, but he wanted more. He kissed her harder, still touching her breasts.

By degrees she leaned back until Hugh was half lying on her. They both began to breathe hard. He was sure she must be able to feel his prick pressing against her plump thigh. In the back of his mind the voice of conscience told him he was taking advantage of a young girl in her father's absence, but it was a faint voice and could not prevail against the desire that welled up inside him like a volcano.

He longed to touch her most intimate places. He put his hand between her legs. She stiffened immediately, and the dog barked, sensing the tension. Hugh pulled away a little and said: 'Let's put the dog outside.'

Nora looked troubled. 'Perhaps we should stop.'

Hugh could not bear the thought of stopping. However, the word *perhaps* encouraged him. 'I can't stop now,' he said. 'Put the dog out.'

'But . . . we're not even engaged, or anything.'

'We could get engaged,' he said without thinking.

She went slightly pale. 'Do you mean it?'

He asked himself the same question. From the start he had thought of this as a dalliance, not a serious courtship; yet only a few moments ago he had been thinking how much he would like to spend the rest of his life holding hands with Nora in front of a fire. Did he really want to marry her? He realized that he did, in fact there was nothing he would like better. There would be a fuss, of course. The family would say he was marrying beneath him. They could go to the devil. He was twenty-six years old, he earned a thousand pounds a year, and he was about to be made a partner in one of the most prestigious banks in the world: he could marry who the hell he liked. His mother would be troubled but supportive: she would worry, but she would be glad to see her son happy. And the rest of them could say what they pleased. They had never done anything for him.

He looked at Nora, pink and pretty and lovable, lying back on the old sofa with her hair around her bare shoulders. He wanted her badly, now, quickly. He had been alone too long. Maisie was thoroughly settled with Solly: she would never be his. It was time he had some-one warm and soft to share his bed and his life. Why not Nora?

He snapped his fingers at the dog. 'Come here, Blackie.' It approached him warily. He stroked its head then grabbed the ribbon around its neck. 'Come and guard the hall,' he said, and he put the dog outside and closed the door. It barked twice and subsided into silence.

He sat beside Nora and took her hand. She looked wary. He said: 'Nora, will you marry me?'

She flushed red. 'Yes, I will.'

He kissed her. She opened her mouth and kissed him back passionately. He touched her knee. She took his hand and guided it beneath the skirts of her dress, up between her legs to the fork of her thighs. Through the flannelette of her underwear he could feel the rough hair and soft flesh of her mound. Her lips tracked across his cheek to his ear, and she whispered: 'Hugh, darling, make me yours, tonight, now.'

'I will,' he said hoarsely. 'I will.'

[II]

THE DUCHESS of Tenbigh's costume ball was the first great event of the 1879 London season. Everyone was talking about it weeks in advance. Fortunes were spent on fancy dress, and people would go to any length to get an invitation.

Augusta and Joseph Pilaster were not invited. That was hardly surprising: they did not belong in the very highest echelon of London society. But Augusta wanted to go, and she made up her mind she would be there.

As soon as she heard about the ball she mentioned it to Harriet Morte, who responded by looking embarrassed and saying nothing. As a lady-in-waiting to the Queen, Lady Morte had great social power; and on top of that she was a distant cousin of the Duchess of Tenbigh. But she did not offer to get Augusta invited.

Augusta checked Lord Morte's account with Pilasters Bank and found that he had an overdraft of a thousand pounds. The next day he got a note asking him when he hoped to regularize the account.

Augusta called on Lady Morte the same day. She apologized, saying that the note had been an error and the clerk who sent it had been sacked. Then she mentioned the ball again.

Lady Morte's normally impassive face was momentarily animated by a glare of pure hatred as she understood the bargain that was being offered. Augusta was unmoved. She had no wish to be liked by Lady Morte, she just wanted to use her. And Lady Morte was confronted with a simple choice: exert her influence to get Augusta invited to the ball, or find a thousand pounds to pay off her overdraft. She took the easier option, and the invitation cards arrived the following day.

Augusta was annoyed that Lady Morte had not helped her willingly. It was hurtful that Lady Morte had to be coerced. Feeling spiteful, Augusta made her get Edward an invitation too.

Augusta was going as Queen Elizabeth and Joseph as the Earl of Leicester. On the night of the ball they had dinner at home and changed afterwards. When she was dressed Augusta went into Joseph's room to help him with his costume and talk to him about his nephew Hugh.

She was incensed that Hugh was to be made a partner in the bank at the same time as Edward. Worse still, everyone knew that Edward had been made a partner only because he had married and been given a £250,000 investment in the bank, whereas Hugh was being made a partner because

307

he had brought off a spectacularly profitable deal with Madler and Bell of New York. People were already talking of Hugh as a potential Senior Partner. The thought made Augusta grind her teeth.

Their promotion was to take place at the end of April, when the annual partnership agreement was formally renewed. But earlier in the month, to Augusta's delight, Hugh made the unbelievably foolish mistake of marrying a plump little working-class girl from Camden Town.

The Maisie episode six years ago had shown that he had a weakness for girls from the gutter, but Augusta had never dared to hope that he would marry one. He had done the deed quietly, in Folkestone, with just his mother and sister and the bride's father in attendance, then he had presented the family with a *fait accompli*.

As Augusta adjusted Joseph's Elizabethan ruff she said: 'I presume you'll have to think again about Hugh's being made a partner, now that he's married a housemaid.'

'She's not a housemaid, she's a corsetière. Or was. Now she's Mrs Pilaster.'

'All the same, a partner in Pilasters can hardly have a shop-girl as a wife.'

'I must say I think he can marry whom he likes.'

Augusta had been afraid he would take this line. 'You wouldn't say that if she were ugly, bony and sour,' she said acidly. 'It's only because she's pretty and flirtatious that you're so tolerant.'

'I just don't see the problem.'

'A partner has to meet cabinet ministers, diplomats, leaders of great businesses. She won't know how to act. She could embarrass him at any moment.'

'She can learn.' Joseph hesitated, then added: 'I sometimes think you forget your own background, my dear.'

Augusta drew herself up to her full height. 'My father

had three shops!' she said vehemently. 'How dare you compare me to that little trollop!'

He backed down instantly. 'All right, I'm sorry.'

Augusta was outraged. 'Furthermore, I never worked in my father's shops,' she said. 'I was brought up to be a lady.'

'I've apologized, let's say no more about it. It's time to go.'

Augusta clamped her mouth shut but inside she was seething.

Edward and Emily were waiting for them in the hall, dressed as Henry II and Eleanor of Aquitaine. Edward was having trouble with his gold braid cross-garters, and he said: 'You go on, Mother, and send the carriage back for us.'

But Emily quickly put in: 'Oh, no, I want to go now. Fix your garters on the way.'

Emily had big blue eyes and the pretty face of a little girl, and she was very fetching in the embroidered twelfth-century gown and cloak, with a long wimple on her head. However, Augusta had discovered that she was not as timid as she looked. During the preparations for the wedding it had become clear that Emily had a will of her own. She had been happy to let Augusta take over the wedding breakfast, but she had insisted, rather stubbornly, on having her own way about her wedding dress and her bridesmaids.

As they got into their carriage and drove off, Augusta recalled vaguely that the marriage of Henry II and Eleanor had been stormy. She hoped Emily would not give Edward too much trouble. Since the wedding Edward had been bad-tempered, and Augusta suspected there was something wrong. She had tried to find out by questioning Edward delicately, but he would not say a word.

However, the important thing was that he was married and a partner in the bank. He was settled. Everything else could be worked out.

The ball began at half-past ten and the Pilasters arrived on time. Lights blazed from every window of Tenbigh House. There was already a crowd of onlookers outside, and in Park Lane a line of carriages waited to enter the courtyard. The crowd applauded each costume as the guests descended from their vehicles and mounted the steps to the door. Looking ahead as she waited, Augusta saw Anthony and Cleopatra, several Roundheads and Cavaliers, two Greek goddesses and three Napoleons enter the house.

At last her carriage reached the door and they got out. Once inside the house there was another queue, from the hall up the curving staircase to the landing where the Duke and Duchess of Tenbigh, dressed as Solomon and Sheba, were greeting their guests. The hall was a mass of flowers and a band played to entertain them while they waited.

The Pilasters were followed in by Micky Miranda — invited because of his diplomatic status — and his new wife Rachel. Micky looked more dashing than ever in the red silk of a Cardinal Wolsey outfit, and for a moment the sight of him made Augusta's heart flutter. She looked critically at his wife, who had chosen to come as a slave girl, rather surprisingly. Augusta had encouraged Micky to marry but she could not suppress a stab of resentment towards the rather plain girl who had won his hand. Rachel returned Augusta's stare coolly, and took Micky's arm possessively after he kissed Augusta's hand.

As they slowly mounted the stairs Micky said to Rachel: 'The Spanish Envoy is here – be sure to be nice to him.'

'You be nice to him,' Rachel said crisply. 'I think he's a slug.'

Micky frowned but said no more. With her extreme views and forceful manner, Rachel would have made a good wife for a campaigning journalist or a Radical Member of Parliament. Micky deserved someone less eccentric and more beautiful, Augusta felt.

Up ahead of them Augusta spotted another pair of newlyweds, Hugh and Nora. Hugh was a member of the Marlborough Set, because of his friendship with the Greenbournes, and to Augusta's chagrin he was invited to everything. He was dressed as an Indian rajah and Nora seemed to have come as a snake-charmer, in a sequined gown cut away to reveal harem trousers. Artificial snakes were wound around her arms and legs, and one laid its papier-mâché head on her ample bosom. Augusta shuddered. 'Hugh's wife really is impossibly vulgar,' she murmured to Joseph.

He was inclined to be lenient. 'It is a costume ball, after all.'

'Not one of the other women here has been so tasteless as to show her legs.'

'I don't see any difference between loose trousers and a dress.'

He was probably enjoying the sight of Nora's legs, Augusta thought with distaste. It was so easy for such a woman to befuddle men's judgement. 'I just don't think she's fit to be the wife of a partner in Pilasters Bank.'

'Nora won't have to make any financial decisions.'

Augusta could have screamed with frustration. Evidently it was not enough that Nora was a working-class girl. She would have to do something unforgivable before Joseph and his partners would turn against Hugh.

Now there was a thought.

Augusta's anger died down as quickly as it had flared. Perhaps, she thought, there was a way she could get Nora into trouble. She looked up the stairs again and studied her prey.

Nora and Hugh were talking to the Hungarian attaché, Count de Tokoly, a man of doubtful morals who was appropriately dressed as Henry VIII. Nora was just the kind of girl the count would be charmed by, Augusta thought biliously. Respectable ladies would cross the room to avoid speaking to him, but all the same he had to be invited everywhere because he was a senior diplomat. There was no sign of disapproval on Hugh's face as he watched his wife bat her eyelashes at the old roué. Indeed Hugh's expression showed nothing but adoration. He was still too much in love to find fault. That would not last. 'Nora is talking to de Tokoly,' Augusta murmured to Joseph. 'She had better take care of her reputation.'

'Now don't you be rude to him,' Joseph replied brusquely. 'We're hoping to raise two million pounds for his government.'

Augusta did not care a straw for de Tokoly. She continued to brood about Nora. The girl was most vulnerable right now, when everything was unfamiliar and she had not had time to learn upper-class manners. If she could be brought to disgrace herself somehow tonight, preferably in front of the Prince of Wales . . .

Just as she was thinking about the prince, a great cheer went up outside the house, indicating that the royal party had arrived.

A moment later the prince and Princess Alexandra came in, dressed as King Arthur and Queen Guinevere, followed by their entourage got up as knights in armour and medieval ladies. The band stopped abruptly in the middle of a Strauss waltz and struck up the national anthem. All the guests in the hall bowed and curtsied, and the queue on the staircase dipped like a wave as the royal party came up. The prince was getting fatter every year, Augusta thought as she curtsied to him. She was not sure whether there was any grey in his beard yet, but he was rapidly going bald on top. She always felt sorry for the pretty princess, who had a great deal to put up with from her spendthrift, philandering husband.

At the top of the stairs, the duke and duchess welcomed their royal guests and ushered them into the ballroom. The guests on the staircase surged forward to follow them.

Inside the long ballroom, masses of flowers from the hothouse at the Tenbighs' country home were banked up all around the walls, and the light from a thousand candles glittered back from the tall mirrors between the windows. The footmen handing round champagne were dressed as Elizabethan courtiers in doublet and hose. The prince and princess were ushered to a dais at the end of the room. It had been arranged that some of the more spectacular costumes should pass in front of the royal party in procession, and as soon as the royals were seated the first group came in from the salon. A crush formed near the dais, and Augusta found herself shoulder-to-shoulder with Count de Tokoly.

'What a delightful girl your nephew's wife is, Mrs Pilaster,' he said.

Augusta gave him a frosty smile. 'How generous you are to say so, Count.'

He raised an eyebrow. 'Do I detect a note of dissent? No doubt you would have preferred young Hugh to choose a bride from his own class.'

'You know the answer to that without my telling you.'

'But her charm is irresistible.'

'Doubtless.'

'I shall ask her to dance later on. Do you think she will accept?'

Augusta could not resist an acid retort. 'I am sure of it. She is not fastidious.' She turned away. No doubt it was too much to hope for that Nora would cause some kind of incident with the count –

She was suddenly inspired.

The count was the critical factor. If she put him together with Nora the combination could be explosive.

Her mind was racing. Tonight was a perfect opportunity. She had to do it now.

Feeling a little breathless with excitement, Augusta looked around, spotted Micky, and went over to him. 'There's something I want you to do for me, now, quickly,' she said.

Micky gave her a knowing look. 'Anything,' he murmured.

She ignored the innuendo. 'Do you know Count de Tokoly?'

'Indeed. All we diplomats know one another.'

'Tell him that Nora is no better than she ought to be.'

Micky's mouth curled in a half-smile. 'Just that?'

'You may elaborate if you wish.'

'Should I hint that I know this from, let us say, personal experience?'

This conversation was transgressing the boundaries of propriety, but Micky's idea was a good one and she nodded. 'Even better.'

'You know what he will do?' Micky said.

'I trust he will make an indecent suggestion to her.'

'If that's what you want . . .'

'Yes.'

Micky nodded. 'I am your slave, in this as in all things.'

Augusta waved the compliment aside impatiently: she was too tense to listen to facetious gallantry. She looked for Nora and saw her staring around in wonderment at the lavish decor and the extravagant costumes: the girl had never seen anything like this in her life. She was quite off-guard. Without further reflection Augusta made her way through the crowd to Nora's side.

She spoke into her ear. 'A word of advice.'

'Much obliged for it, I'm sure,' Nora said.

Hugh had presumably given Nora a malevolent account of Augusta's character, but to the girl's credit she showed no sign of hostility. She appeared not to have made up her mind about Augusta, and was neither warm nor cold to her.

Augusta said: 'I noticed you talking to Count de Tokoly.'

'A dirty old man,' Nora said immediately.

Augusta winced at her vulgarity but pressed on. 'Be careful of him, if you value your reputation.'

'Be careful?' Nora said. 'What do you mean, exactly?'

'Be polite, of course – but whatever happens, don't let him take any liberties. The least encouragement is enough for him and if he is not set straight immediately he can be very embarrassing.'

Nora nodded, understanding. 'Don't worry, I know how to deal with his type.'

Hugh was standing nearby talking to the Duke of Norwich. Now he noticed Augusta, looked suspicious, and came to his wife's side. However, Augusta had already said all she needed to say, and she turned away to watch the procession. She had done her work: the seeds were planted. Now she had to wait anxiously and hope for the best.

Passing in front of the prince were some of the Marlborough Set, including the Duke and Duchess of Kingsbridge and Solly and Maisie Greenbourne. They were dressed as Eastern potentates, shahs and pashas and sultanas, and instead of bowing and curtsying they knelt and salaamed, which drew a laugh from the portly prince and a round of applause from the crowd. Augusta loathed Maisie Greenbourne, but she hardly noticed. Her mind was rapidly turning over possibilities. There were a hundred ways her plot could go wrong: de Tokoly could be captivated by a different pretty face, Nora might deal with him graciously, Hugh might stay too close for de Tokoly to do anything offensive. But with a little luck the drama she had plotted would be played out – and then there would be ructions.

The procession was coming to an end when, to Augusta's dismay, she saw the face of David Middleton pushing through the crowd towards her.

She had last seen him six years ago, when he had questioned her about his brother Peter's death at Windfield School, and she had told him that the two witnesses, Hugh Pilaster and Antonio Silva, had gone abroad. But now Hugh was back and here was Middleton. How had a mere lawyer got invited to such a grand occasion? She recalled vaguely that he was a distant relation of the Duke of Tenbigh. She could hardly have foreseen this. It was a potential disaster. I can't think of everything! she said to herself frenziedly.

To her horror Middleton walked straight up to Hugh.

Augusta edged closer through the crush. She heard Middleton say: 'Hello, Pilaster, I heard you were back in England. Do you remember me? I'm Peter Middleton's brother.'

Augusta turned her back so that he would not notice her and strained to hear over the hum of conversation around her.

'I do remember – you were at the inquest,' Hugh said. 'Allow me to present my wife.'

'How do you do, Mrs Pilaster,' Middleton said

316

perfunctorily, and returned his attention to Hugh. 'I was never happy with that inquest, you know.'

Augusta went cold. Middleton had to be obsessed to bluntly bring up such an inappropriate subject in the middle of a costume ball. This was insupportable. Would poor Teddy never be free of that old suspicion?

She could not hear Hugh's reply but his tone was guardedly neutral.

Middleton's voice was louder and she picked up what he said next. 'You must know that the whole school disbelieved Edward's story about trying to rescue my brother from drowning.'

Augusta was taut with fear of what Hugh might say, but he continued to be circumspect, and said something about its having taken place a long time ago.

Suddenly Micky was at Augusta's side. His face was a mask of relaxed urbanity but she could see the tension in the set of his shoulders. 'Is that the Middleton fellow?' he murmured in her ear.

She nodded.

'I thought I recognized him.'

'Hush, listen,' she said.

Middleton had become slightly aggressive. 'I think you know the truth about what happened,' he said in a challenging voice.

'Do you, indeed?' Hugh grew audible as his tone became less friendly.

'Forgive me for being so blunt, Pilaster. He was my brother. For years I've wondered what happened. Don't you think I've a right to know?'

There was a pause. Augusta knew that such an appeal to the rights and wrongs of the case was just the kind of thing to move the sanctimonious Hugh. She wanted to intervene, to shut them up or change the subject or break up the group, but that would be tantamount to a confession that she had something to hide; so she stood helpless and terrified, rooted to the spot, straining her ears to hear over the murmur of the crowd.

At last Hugh replied. 'I didn't see Peter die, Middleton. I can't tell you what happened. I don't know for certain, and it would be wrong to speculate.'

'You have your suspicions, then? You can guess how it happened?'

'There's no room for guesswork in a case such as this. It would be irresponsible. You want the truth, you say. I'm all for that. If I knew the truth I'd consider myself duty bound to tell it. But I don't.'

'I think you're protecting your cousin.'

Hugh was offended. 'Damn it, Middleton, that's too strong. You're entitled to be upset, but don't cast doubt on my honesty.'

'Well, somebody's lying,' Middleton said rudely, and with that he went away.

Augusta breathed again. Relief made her weak at the knees and she surreptitiously leaned on Micky for support. Hugh's precious principles had worked in her favour. He suspected that Edward had contributed to the death of Peter, but because it was only a suspicion he would not say it. And now Middleton had put Hugh's back up. It was the mark of a gentleman never to tell a lie, and for young men such as Hugh the suggestion that they might not be speaking the truth was a serious insult. Middleton and Hugh were not likely to talk further.

The crisis had blown up suddenly, like a summer storm, scaring her badly; but it had vanished just as fast, leaving her feeling battered but safe.

The procession ended. The band struck up a quadrille.

The prince led the duchess on to the floor, and the duke took the princess, to make the first foursome. Other groups rapidly followed suit. The dancing was rather sedate, probably because so many people were wearing heavy costumes and cumbersome head-dresses.

Augusta said to Micky: 'Perhaps Mr Middleton is no longer a danger to us.'

'Not if Hugh continues to keep his mouth shut.'

'And so long as your friend Silva stays in Cordova.'

'His family has less and less influence as the years go by. I don't expect to see him in Europe again.'

'Good.' Augusta's mind reverted to her plot. 'Did you speak to de Tokoly?'

'I did.'

'Good.'

'I just hope you know what you're doing.'

She gave him a reproving look.

'How foolish of me,' he said. 'You always know what you're doing.'

The second dance was a waltz, and Micky asked her for the pleasure. When Augusta was a girl the waltz had been considered indecent, because the partners were so close together, the man's arm going all the way around the woman's waist in an embrace. But nowadays even royalty waltzed.

As soon as Micky took her in his arms she felt changed. It was like being seventeen again, and dancing with Strang. When Strang danced he was thinking about his partner, not his feet, and Micky had the same talent. He made Augusta feel young and beautiful and carefree. She was aware of the smoothness of his hands, the masculine smell of tobacco and macassar oil, and the heat of his body as it pressed against hers. She felt a pang of envy towards Rachel, who shared his bed. Momentarily she recalled the scene in Old Seth's bedroom six years ago, but it seemed unreal, like a dream she had once had, and she could never quite believe it had actually happened.

Some women in her position would have had a clandestine love affair, but although Augusta sometimes daydreamed of secret meetings with Micky, in reality she could not face the skulking in back streets, the hole-in-corner meetings, the furtive embraces, the evasions and excuses. And besides, such affairs were often found out. She was more likely to leave Joseph and run away with Micky. He might be willing. At any rate she could make him willing if she put her mind to it. But whenever she toyed with that dream she thought of all the things she would have to give up: her three houses, her carriage, her dress allowance, her social position, the entrée to balls such as this. Strang could have given her all that, but Micky could offer only his seductive self, and it was not enough.

'Look over there,' Micky said.

She followed the direction of his nod and saw Nora dancing with Count de Tokoly. She tensed. 'Let's get closer to them,' she said.

It was not easy, for the royal group was in that corner, and everyone was trying to be near them; but Micky skilfully steered her through the crush until they were close.

The waltz ground on, endlessly repeating the same banal tune. So far Nora and the count looked like any other dancing couple. He made occasional remarks in a low voice, she nodded and smiled. Perhaps he was holding her a little too closely, but not enough to cause remark. As the orchestra played on, Augusta wondered whether she had misjudged her two victims. The worry made her tense and she danced badly.

The waltz began to wind up to its climax. Augusta continued to watch Nora and the count. Suddenly there was a change. Nora's face took on a look of frozen consternation: the count must have said something she did not like. Augusta's hopes rose. But whatever he had said clearly was not sufficiently offensive for Nora to make a scene, and they danced on.

Augusta was ready to give up hope, and the waltz was in its last few bars, when the explosion came.

Augusta was the only person to see how it started. The count put his lips close to Nora's ear and spoke. She coloured up, then stopped dancing abruptly and pushed him away; but nobody except Augusta noticed this because the dance was just ending. However, the count pushed his luck and spoke again, his face creasing with a characteristic lascivious grin. At that second the music stopped, and in the momentary silence that followed, Nora slapped him.

The smack sounded throughout the ballroom like a gunshot. It was not a polite ladylike slap, designed for drawing-room use, but the kind of blow that would deter a drunken groper in a saloon-bar. The count staggered back – and bumped into the Prince of Wales.

There was a collective gasp from the people around. The prince stumbled and was caught by the Duke of Tenbigh. In the horrified silence, Nora's cockney accent rang out loud and clear: 'Don't you ever come near me again, you filthy old reprobate!'

For another second they formed a still tableau: the outraged woman, the humiliated count and the startled prince. Augusta was possessed by jubilation. It had worked – it had worked better than she could have imagined!

Then Hugh appeared at Nora's side and took her arm; the count drew himself up to his full height and stalked out; and an anxious group clustered protectively around the prince, hiding him from view. Conversation broke out around the room like a roll of thunder.

Augusta looked triumphantly at Micky.

'Brilliant,' he murmured with real admiration. 'You're brilliant, Augusta.' He squeezed her arm and led her off the dance floor.

Her husband was waiting for her. 'That wretched girl!' he expostulated. 'To cause a scene like that under the nose of the prince – she's brought disgrace on the whole family, and doubtless lost us a major contract too!'

It was just the reaction Augusta had hoped for. 'Now perhaps you'll believe that Hugh can't be made a partner,' she said triumphantly.

Joseph gave her an appraising stare. For one dreadful moment she feared she had overplayed her hand, and he had guessed that she had orchestrated the whole incident. But if the thought had crossed his mind he must have dismissed it, for he said: 'You're right, my dear. You've been right all along.'

Hugh was steering Nora to the door. 'We're leaving, of course,' he said neutrally as they passed.

'We'll all have to leave now,' Augusta said. However, she did not want them to go immediately. If no more was said tonight, there was a danger that tomorrow when people cooled off they might say the incident was not as bad as it had seemed. To guard against that, Augusta wanted more of a row now: hot tempers, angry words, accusations that could not easily be forgotten. She put a detaining hand on Nora's arm. 'I tried to warn you about Count de Tokoly,' she said accusingly.

Hugh said: 'When such a man insults a lady on the dance floor, there isn't much she can do other than cause a scene.'

'Don't be ridiculous,' Augusta snapped. 'Any well-bred young girl would have known exactly what to do. She should have said she felt unwell and sent for her carriage.'

Hugh knew this was true and he did not try to deny it. Once again Augusta worried that everyone might calm down and the incident would fizzle out. But Joseph was still angry, and he said to Hugh: 'Heaven knows how much damage you've done to the family and the bank tonight.'

Hugh coloured. 'What precisely do you mean?' he said stiffly.

By challenging Joseph to back up the accusation Hugh was making things worse for himself, Augusta thought with satisfaction. He was too young to know that he should shut up and go home at this point.

Joseph grew more angry. 'We've certainly lost the Hungarian account, and we'll never again be invited to a royal event.'

'I know that perfectly well,' Hugh said. 'I meant to ask why you said the damage has been done by *me*.'

'Because you brought into the family a woman who doesn't know how to behave!'

Better and better, Augusta thought with malicious glee.

Hugh was bright red now but he spoke with controlled fury. 'Let me get this straight. A Pilaster wife must be willing to suffer insult and humiliation at dances rather than do anything to jeopardize a business deal, is that your philosophy?'

Joseph was mightily offended. 'You insolent young pup,' he raged. 'What I'm saying is that by marrying beneath yourself you have disqualified yourself from ever becoming a partner in the bank!'

He said it! Augusta thought jubilantly. He said it!

Hugh was jolted into silence. Unlike Augusta he had not thought ahead, had not worked out the implications of the row. Now the significance of what had happened was sinking in, and she watched his expression change from rage, through anxiety and comprehension, to despair.

She fought to conceal a victorious smile. She had what she wanted: she had won. Later Joseph might regret his pronouncement but it was most unlikely he would withdraw it – he was too proud.

'So that's it,' Hugh said at last, and he was looking at Augusta rather than Joseph. To her surprise she saw that he was close to tears. 'Very well, Augusta. You win. I don't know how it was done but I've no doubt you provoked this incident somehow.' He turned to Joseph. 'But you ought to reflect on it, Uncle Joseph. You should think about who genuinely cares about the bank. . . .' He looked again at Augusta and finished: 'And who are its real enemies.'

[III]

THE NEWS OF Hugh's fall spread around the City in hours. By the following afternoon, people who had clamoured to see him with money-making schemes for railways, steel mills, shipyards and suburban housing were cancelling their appointments. In the bank, clerks who had venerated him now regarded him as just another manager. He found he could go into a coffee-house in the streets around the Bank of England without immediately attracting a cluster of people eager to know his views on the Grand Trunk Railroad, the price of Louisiana Bonds and the American national debt.

Within the Partners' Room there was a row. Uncle Samuel had been indignant when Joseph announced that Hugh could not be made a partner. However, Young William had sided with his brother Joseph, and Major Hartshorn did the same, so Samuel was outvoted.

It was Jonas Mulberry, the bald, lugubrious Principal

Clerk, who told Hugh what had happened between the partners. 'I must say I regret the decision, Mr Hugh,' he said with evident sincerity. 'When you worked under me as a youngster you never tried to blame your mistakes on me – unlike certain other family members I have dealt with in the past.'

'I wouldn't have dared, Mr Mulberry,' said Hugh with a smile.

Nora cried for a week. Hugh refused to blame her for what had happened. No one had forced him to marry her: he had to take responsibility for his own decisions. If his family had any decency they would stand by him in such a crisis, but he had never been able to count on them for that kind of support.

When Nora got over her upset she became rather unsympathetic, revealing a hard-hearted side that surprised Hugh. She could not understand the significance of the partnership to him. He realized, with a sense of disappointment, that she was not very good at imagining other people's feelings. He thought it must be because she had grown up poor and motherless, and had been forced to put her own interests first all her life. Although he was a little shaken by her attitude, he forgot about it every night when they climbed into the big soft bed together in their nightwear and made love.

Hugh's resentment grew inside him like an ulcer, but he now had a wife, a big new house and six servants to support, so he had to stay on at the bank. He was given his own room, on the floor above the Partners' Room, and he put a big map of North America on the wall. Every Monday morning he wrote a summary of the previous week's North American business and cabled it to Sidney Madler in New York. On the second Monday after the Duchess of

Tenbigh's ball, in the telegraph office on the ground floor, he met a stranger, a dark haired man of about twenty-one. Hugh smiled and said: 'Hello, who are you?'

'Simon Oliver,' the man said in an accent that sounded vaguely Spanish.

'You must be new here,' Hugh said, and stuck out his hand. 'I'm Hugh Pilaster.'

'How do you do,' Oliver said. He seemed rather sulky.

'I work on North American loans,' Hugh said. 'What about you?'

'I'm clerk to Mr Edward.'

Hugh made a connection. 'Are you from South America?'

'Yes, Cordova.'

That made sense. As Edward's specialty was South America in general and Cordova in particular, it could be useful to have a native of that country to work with him, especially as Edward did not speak Spanish. 'I was at school with the Cordovan Minister, Micky Miranda,' Hugh said. 'You must know him.'

'He is my cousin.'

'Ah.' There was no family resemblance, but Oliver was immaculately groomed, his well-tailored clothes pressed and brushed, his hair oiled and combed, his shoes shiny: no doubt he modelled himself on his successful older cousin. 'Well, I hope you enjoy working with us.'

'Thank you.'

Hugh was thoughtful as he returned to his own office on the next floor up. Edward needed all the help he could get, but Hugh was a little bothered at having a cousin of Micky's in such a potentially influential position at the bank.

His unease was vindicated a few days later.

Once again it was Jonas Mulberry who told him what was going on in the Partners' Room. Mulberry came into

Hugh's room with a schedule of payments the bank had to make in London on behalf of the US government, but his real reason was to talk. His spaniel face was longer than ever as he said: 'I don't like it, Mr Hugh. South American bonds have never been good.'

'We're not launching a South American bond, are we?'

Mulberry nodded. 'Mr Edward proposed it and the partners have agreed.'

'What's it for?'

'A new railroad from the capital city, Palma, to Santamaria Province.'

'Where the provincial governor is Papa Miranda . . .'

'The father of Mr Edward's friend, Señor Miranda.'

'And the uncle of Edward's clerk, Simon Oliver.'

Mulberry shook his head disapprovingly. 'I was a clerk here when the Venezuelan government defaulted on its bonds fifteen years ago. My father, God rest his soul, could remember the Argentine default of 1828. And look at Mexican bonds – they pay individuals now and again. Whoever heard of bonds that paid out now and again?'

Hugh nodded. 'Anyway, investors who like railroads can get five and six per cent on their money in the United States – why go to Cordova?'

'Exactly.'

Hugh scratched his head. 'Well, I'll try to find out what they're thinking about.'

Mulberry flourished a bundle of papers. 'Mr Samuel asked for a summary of liabilities on Far East acceptances. You could take the figures to him.'

Hugh grinned. 'You think of everything.' He took the papers and went down to the Partners' Room.

Only Samuel and Joseph were there. Joseph was dictating letters to a shorthand-writer and Samuel was poring over a map of China. Hugh put the report on

Samuel's table and said: 'Mulberry asked me to give you this.'

'Thank you.' Samuel looked up and smiled. 'Something else on your mind?'

'Yes. I'm wondering why we're backing the Santamaria Railroad.'

Hugh heard Joseph pause in his dictation, then resume.

Samuel said: 'It's not the most attractive investment we've ever launched, I grant you, but with the backing of the Pilaster name it should go off all right.'

'You could say that of just about any issue that is proposed to us,' Hugh objected. 'The reason we have such a high reputation is that we never do offer the investors a bond that is only "all right".'

'Your Uncle Joseph feels that South America may be ready for a revival.'

Hearing his name, Joseph joined in. 'This is a toe dipped into the water to feel the temperature.'

'It's risky, then.'

'If my great-grandfather had never taken a risk he would not have put all his money into one slave ship and there would be no such thing as Pilasters Bank today.'

Hugh said: 'But since then, Pilasters has always left it to smaller, more speculative houses to dip their toes into unknown waters.'

Uncle Joseph did not like to be argued with and he replied in an irritated tone: 'One exception will not harm us.'

'But the willingness to make exceptions may harm us deeply.'

'That's not for you to judge.'

Hugh frowned. His instinct had been right: the investment did not make commercial sense, and Joseph could not justify it. So why had they done it? As soon as he put the question to himself that way he realized what the answer was. 'You've done this because it's Edward, haven't you? You want to encourage him, and this is the first deal he has come up with since you made him a partner, so you're letting him do it, even though it's a poor prospect.'

'It's not your place to question my motives!'

'It's not your place to risk other people's money as a favour to your son. Small investors in Brighton and Harrogate will put up the money for this railroad, and they will lose everything if it fails.'

'You're not a partner, so your opinion on these matters is not sought.'

Hugh hated people to shift their ground during a discussion and he responded waspishly. 'I'm a Pilaster, though, and when you damage the good name of the bank you injure me.'

Samuel cut in: 'I think you've probably said enough, Hugh—'

Hugh knew he should shut up but he could not restrain himself. 'I'm afraid I haven't said enough.' He heard himself shouting and tried to lower his voice. 'You're dissipating the bank's reputation by doing this. Our good name is our greatest asset. To use it up in this way is like spending your capital.'

Uncle Joseph was now beyond civility. 'Don't you dare stand here in my bank and lecture me on the principles of investment, you insolent young whippersnapper. Get out of this room.'

Hugh stared at his uncle for a long moment. He was furious and depressed. Foolish, weak Edward was a partner, and leading the bank into bad business deals with the help of his injudicious father, and there was nothing

anyone could do about it. Boiling with frustration, Hugh
turned and left the room, slamming the door.

Ten minutes later he went to ask Solly Greenbourne for a
job.

He was not certain Greenbournes would take him on. He
was an asset that any bank would covet, because of his
contacts in the United States and Canada, but bankers felt
it was not quite gentlemanly to pirate top managers from
their rivals. In addition, the Greenbournes might fear that
Hugh would tell secrets to his family at the dinner table,
and the fact that he was not Jewish could only increase that
fear.

However, Pilasters had become a dead end street for
him. He had to get out.

It had rained earlier but by mid-morning the sun was
out, and steam rose from the horse manure that carpeted
the streets of London. The architecture of the City was a
mixture of grand classical buildings and tumbledown old
houses: the Pilaster building was the grand type,
Greenbournes the other. You would not have guessed that
Greenbournes Bank was bigger and more important than
Pilasters from the appearance of the head office. The
business had started, three generations ago, lending to fur
importers out of two rooms of an old house in Thames
Street. Whenever more space was needed they simply took
over another house in the row, and now the bank occupied
four adjacent buildings and three others nearby. But more
business was done in these ramshackle houses than in the
ostentatious splendour of the Pilaster building.

Inside there was none of the devotional hush of Pilasters'
banking hall. Hugh had to fight his way through a crowd

of people in the lobby, like petitioners waiting to see a medieval king, every one of them convinced that if only he could get a word with Ben Greenbourne, present his case or pitch his proposal, he could make a fortune. The zig-zag corridors and narrow staircases of the interior were obstructed by tin boxes of old files, cartons of stationery and demijohns of ink, and every spare cubbyhole had been made into an office for a clerk. Hugh found Solly in a large room with an uneven floor and a wonky window looking out over the river. Solly's bulk was half-hidden behind a desk piled with papers. 'I live in a palace and work in a hovel,' Solly said ruefully. 'I keep trying to persuade Father to commission a purpose-built office like yours, but he says there's no profit in property.'

Hugh sat on a lumpy sofa and accepted a large glass of expensive sherry. He was uncomfortable, because in the back of his mind he was thinking about Maisie. He had seduced her before she became Solly's wife and he would have done it again afterwards if she had let him. But all that was over now, he told himself. Maisie had locked the door at Kingsbridge Manor, and he had married Nora. He did not intend to be an unfaithful husband.

Still he felt awkward.

'I came to see you here because I want to talk business,' he said.

Solly made an open-handed gesture. 'You have the floor.'

'My area of expertise is North America, as you know.'

'Don't I just! You've got it so well wrapped up that we can't get a look in.'

'Exactly. And you're missing out on a good deal of profitable business as a result.'

'No need to rub it in. Father asks me constantly why I'm not more like you.'

331

'What you need is someone with North American experience to come in, set up a New York office for you, and go after the business.'

'That and a fairy godmother.'

'I'm serious, Greenbourne. I'm your man.'

'You!'

'I want to work for you.'

Solly was staggered. He peered over his glasses as if checking that it really was Hugh who had said that. After a moment he said: 'It's because of that incident at the Duchess of Tenbigh's ball, I suppose.'

'They've said they won't make me a partner because of my wife.' Solly would sympathize, Hugh thought, because he too had married a lower-class girl.

'I'm sorry to hear that,' Solly said.

Hugh said: 'But I'm not asking for kindness. I know what I'm worth and you'll have to pay my price if you want me. I'm earning a thousand a year now and I expect it to go up every year as long as I continue to make more and more money for the bank.'

'That's no problem.' Solly thought for a moment. 'This could be a great coup for me, you know. I'm grateful for the offer. You're a good friend and a formidable businessman.' Hugh, thinking of Maisie again, felt a guilty pang at the words 'good friend'. Solly continued: 'There's nothing I'd like better than to have you working alongside me.'

'I detect an unspoken "but",' Hugh said with trepidation in his heart.

Solly shook his owlish head. 'No buts, as far as I'm concerned. Of course I can't hire you the way I'd hire a ledger clerk. I'll have to clear it with my father. But you know how it is in the world of banking: profit is an argument that outweighs all others. I don't see Father turning down the prospect of a chunk of the North American market.'

Hugh did not want to seem too eager, but he could not help saying: 'When will you speak to him?'

'Why not now?' Solly said. He stood up. 'I shan't be a minute. Have another glass of sherry.' He went out.

Hugh sipped his sherry but he found it hard to swallow, he was so tense. He had never applied for a job before. It was unnerving to realize that his future depended on the whim of old Ben Greenbourne. For the first time he understood the feelings of the scrubbed young men in starched collars whom he had occasionally interviewed for jobs as clerks. Restlessly he got up and went to the window. On the far side of the river a barge was unloading bales of tobacco into a warehouse: if it was Virginia tobacco, he had probably financed the transaction.

He had a doomy feeling, a bit like the sensation he had had when he boarded ship for Boston six years ago: a sense that nothing would ever be the same again.

Solly came back in with his father. Ben Greenbourne had the upright carriage and bullet-shaped head of a Prussian general. Hugh stood up to shake hands and looked anxiously at his face. It was solemn. Did that mean no?

Ben said: 'Solly tells me your family has decided not to offer you a partnership.' His speech was coldly precise, the accent clipped. He was so different from his son, Hugh thought.

'To be exact, they offered it then withdrew the offer,' Hugh said.

Ben nodded. He was a man who appreciated exactness. 'It's not for me to criticize their judgement. However, if your North American expertise is for sale, as it were, then I'm certainly a buyer.'

Hugh's heart leaped. That sounded like a job offer. 'Thank you!' he said.

'But I shouldn't wish to take you on under false pretences, so there's something I must make clear. It is not at all likely that you will ever become a partner here.'

Hugh had not actually thought that far ahead, but all the same it was a blow. 'I see,' he said.

'I say this now so that you will never think it a reflection on your work. Many Christians are valued colleagues and dear friends, but the partners have always been Jews, and it will ever be so.'

'I appreciate your frankness,' Hugh said. He was thinking: By God, you're a cold-hearted old man.

'Do you still want the job?'

'Yes, I do.'

Ben Greenbourne shook his hand again. 'Then I look forward to working with you,' he said, and he left the room.

Solly smiled broadly. 'Welcome to the firm!'

Hugh sat down. 'Thank you,' he said. His relief and pleasure were somewhat blighted by the thought that he would never be a partner, but he made an effort to put a good face on it. He would make a good salary, and live comfortably; it was just that he would never be a millionaire – to make that sort of money you had to be a partner.

'When can you start?' Solly said eagerly.

Hugh had not thought of that. 'I probably should give ninety days' notice.'

'Make it less if you can.'

'Of course. Solly, this is great. I can't tell you how pleased I am.'

'Me, too.'

Hugh could not think what to say next, so he stood up to go, but Solly said: 'Can I make another suggestion?'

'By all means.' He sat down again.

'It's about Nora. I hope you won't take offence.'

Hugh hesitated. They were old friends, but he really did not want to talk to Solly about his wife. His own feelings were too ambivalent. He was embarrassed about the scene she had made, yet he also felt she had been justified. He felt defensive about her accent, her manners and her low-class background, but he was also proud of her for being so pretty and charming.

However, he could hardly be touchy with the man who had just rescued his career, so he said: 'Go ahead.'

'As you know, I too married a girl who was . . . not used to high society.'

Hugh nodded. He knew it perfectly well, but he did not know how Maisie and Solly had coped with the situation, for he had been abroad when they married. They must have handled it well, for Maisie had become one of London's leading society hostesses, and if anyone remembered her humble origin they never spoke of it. This was unusual, but not unique: Hugh had heard of two or three celebrated working-class beauties who had been accepted by high society in the past.

Solly went on: 'Maisie knows what Nora's going through. She could help her a lot: tell her what to do and say, what mistakes to avoid, where to get gowns and hats, how to manage the butler and the housekeeper, all that. Maisie's always been fond of you, Hugh, so I feel sure she'd be glad to help. And there's no reason Nora shouldn't pull off the trick Maisie did and end up as a pillar of society.'

Hugh found himself moved almost to tears. This gesture of support from an old friend touched his heart. 'I'll suggest it,' he said, speaking rather curtly to hide his feelings. He stood up to go.

'I hope I haven't overstepped the mark,' Solly said anxiously as they shook hands.

Hugh went to the door. 'On the contrary. Damn it, Greenbourne, you're a better friend than I deserve.'

When Hugh got back to Pilasters Bank there was a note waiting for him. It read:

> *10.30 a.m.*
> *My dear Pilaster:*
>   *I must see you right away. You will find me in Plage's Coffee House around the corner. I will wait for you. Your old friend –*
>   *Antonio Silva*

So Tonio was back! His career had been ruined when he lost more than he could pay in a card game with Edward and Micky. He had left the country in disgrace at about the same time as Hugh. What had happened to him since? Full of curiosity, Hugh went straight to the coffee house.

He found an older, shabbier, more subdued Tonio, sitting in a corner reading *The Times*. He still had a shock of carrot-coloured hair, but otherwise there was nothing left of the mischievous schoolboy or the profligate young man. Although he was only Hugh's age, twenty-six, there were already tiny lines of worry around his eyes.

'I made a big success of Boston,' Hugh said in answer to Tonio's first question. 'I came back in January. But now I'm having trouble with my damned family all over again. How about you?'

'There have been a lot of changes in my country. My family is not as influential as it once was. We still control Milpita, the provincial city we come from, but in the capital others have come between us and President Garcia.'

'Who?'

'The Miranda faction.'

'Micky's family?'

336

'Absolutely. They took over the nitrate mines in the north of the country and that has made them rich. They also monopolize trade with Europe, because of their connection with your family's bank.'

Hugh was surprised. 'I knew Edward was doing a lot of business with Cordova, but I didn't realize it was all going through Micky. Still, I don't suppose it matters.'

'But it does,' said Tonio. He took a sheaf of papers from inside his coat. 'Take a minute to read this. It's an article I've written for *The Times*.'

Hugh took the manuscript and began to read. It was a description of conditions at a nitrate mine owned by the Mirandas. Because the trade was financed by Pilasters Bank, Tonio held the bank responsible for the ill-treatment of the miners. At first Hugh was unmoved: long hours, poor wages and child labour were features of mines all over the world. But as he read on he realized this was worse. At the Miranda mines, the overseers were armed with whips and guns, and they used them freely to enforce discipline. Labourers – including women and children – were flogged for being too slow, and if they tried to leave before they had worked out their contracts they could be shot. Tonio had eyewitness accounts of such 'executions'.

Hugh was horrified. 'But this is murder!' he said.

'Exactly.'

'Doesn't your president know about it?'

'He knows. But the Mirandas are his favourites now.'

'And your own family . . .'

'Once upon a time we could have put a stop to it. Now it takes all our efforts to retain control of our own province.'

Hugh was mortified to think his own family and their bank were financing such a brutal industry, but for a moment he tried to put aside his feelings and think coolly about consequences. The article Tonio had written was just the kind of material *The Times* liked to publish. There would be speeches in Parliament and letters in the weekly journals. The social conscience of businessmen, many of whom were Methodists, would make them hesitate before getting involved with Pilasters. It would all be extremely bad for the bank.

Do I care? thought Hugh. The bank had treated him badly and he was about to leave it. But despite that he could not ignore this problem. He was still an employee, he would draw his salary at the end of the month, and he owed Pilasters his loyalty at least until then. He had to do something.

What did Tonio want? The fact that he was showing Hugh the article before publishing it suggested that he wanted to make a deal. 'What's your objective?' Hugh asked him. 'Do you want us to stop financing the nitrate trade?'

Tonio shook his head. 'If Pilasters pulled out, someone else would take over – another bank with a thicker hide. No, we must be more subtle.'

'You've got something specific in mind.'

'The Mirandas are planning a railway.'

'Ah, yes. The Santamaria Railroad.'

'That railway will make Papa Miranda the wealthiest and most powerful man in the country, excepting only the president. And Papa Miranda is a brute. I want the railway stopped.'

'And that's why you're going to publish this article.'

'Several articles. And I'll hold meetings, make speeches, lobby members of Parliament, and try to get an appointment with the Foreign Secretary: anything to undermine the financing of this railway.'

It might work, too, Hugh thought. Investors would shy away from anything controversial. It struck him that Tonio had changed a lot, from the young tearaway who couldn't stop gambling into the sober adult who campaigned against ill-treatment of miners. 'So why have you come to me?'

'We could shortcut the process. If the bank decides not to underwrite the railway bonds, I won't publish the article. That way, you avoid a great deal of unpleasant publicity and I get what I want too.' Tonio gave an embarrassed smile. 'I hope you don't think of this as blackmail. It is a bit crude, I know, but nowhere near as crude as flogging children in a nitrate mine.'

Hugh shook his head. 'Not crude at all. I admire your crusading spirit. The consequences for the bank don't affect me directly – I'm about to resign.'

'Really!' Tonio was astonished. 'Why?'

'It's a long story. I'll tell you another time. However, the upshot is that all I can do is tell the partners that you've approached me with this proposition. They can decide how they feel about it and what they want to do. I'm quite sure they won't ask my opinion.' He was still holding Tonio's manuscript. 'May I keep this?'

'Yes. I have a copy.'

The sheets of paper bore the letterhead of the Hotel Russe, Berwick Street, Soho. Hugh had never heard of it: it was not one of London's fancy establishments. 'I'll let you know what the partners say.'

'Thank you.' Tonio changed the subject. 'I'm sorry our conversation has been all business. Let's get together and talk about the old days.'

'You must meet my wife.'

'I'd love to.'

'I'll be in touch.' Hugh left the coffee-house and walked back to the bank. When he looked at the big clock in the banking hall he was surprised it was not yet one o'clock: so much had happened this morning. He went straight to the

Partners' Room, where he found Samuel, Joseph and Edward. He handed Tonio's article to Samuel, who read it and passed it on to Edward.

Edward became apoplectic with rage and was unable to finish it. He went red in the face, pointed his finger at Hugh and said: 'You've cooked this up with your old school friend! You're trying to undermine our entire South American business! You're just jealous of me because you weren't made a partner!'

Hugh understood why he was so hysterical. The South American trade was Edward's only significant contribution to business. If that went he was useless. Hugh sighed. 'You were Bonehead Ned at school, and you still are,' he said. 'The question is whether the bank wants to be responsible for increasing the power and influence of Papa Miranda, a man who apparently thinks nothing of flogging women and murdering children.'

'I don't believe that!' Edward said. 'The Silva family are enemies of the Mirandas. This is just malicious propaganda.'

'I'm sure that's what your friend Micky will say. But is it true?'

Uncle Joseph looked suspiciously at Hugh. 'You came in here just a few hours ago and tried to talk me out of this issue. I have to wonder whether this whole thing isn't some scheme to undermine Edward's first major piece of business as a partner.'

Hugh stood up. 'If you're going to cast doubt on my good faith I'll leave right away.'

Uncle Samuel stepped in. 'Sit down, Hugh,' he said. 'We don't have to find out whether this tale is true or not. We're bankers, not judges. The fact that the Santamaria Railroad is going to be controversial makes the bond issue riskier, and that means we have to reconsider.'

Uncle Joseph said aggressively: 'I'm not willing to be bullied. Let this South American popinjay publish his article and go to the devil.'

'That's one way to handle it,' Samuel mused, treating Joseph's belligerence more seriously than it deserved. 'We can wait and see what effect the article has on the price of existing South American stocks: there aren't many, but it's enough to serve as a gauge. If they crash, we'll cancel the Santamaria Railroad. If not, we go ahead.'

Joseph, somewhat mollified, said: 'I don't mind submitting to the decision of the market.'

'There is one other option we might consider,' Samuel went on. 'We could get another bank to come in with us on the issue of bonds, and float it jointly. That way, any hostile publicity would be enfeebled by having a divided target.'

That made a lot of sense, Hugh thought. It was not what he would have done: he would prefer to cancel the bond issue. But the strategy worked out by Samuel would minimize the risk, and that was what banking was all about. Samuel was a much better banker than Joseph.

'All right,' Joseph said with his usual impulsiveness. 'Edward, see if you can find us a partner.'

'Who should I approach?' Edward said anxiously. Hugh realized he had no idea how to go about something like this.

Samuel answered him. 'It's a big issue. On reflection, not many banks would want such a big exposure to South America. You should go to Greenbournes: they might be the only people big enough to take the risk. You know Solly Greenbourne, don't you?'

'Yes. I'll see him.'

Hugh wondered whether he should advise Solly to turn Edward down, and immediately thought better of it: he was being hired as an expert on North America, and it

341

would seem presumptuous if he started out by passing judgement on a completely different area. He decided to have one more try at persuading Uncle Joseph to cancel the issue completely. 'Why don't we just wash our hands of the Santamaria Railroad?' he said. 'It's low-grade business. The risk has always been high, and now we're threatened with bad publicity on top. Do we need this?'

Edward said petulantly: 'The partners have made their decision and it's not for you to question them.'

Hugh gave up. 'You're quite right,' he said. 'I'm not a partner, and soon I won't be an employee either.'

Uncle Joseph frowned at him. 'What does that mean?'

'I'm resigning from the bank.'

Joseph was jolted. 'You can't do that!'

'I certainly can. I'm a mere employee, and you've treated me as such. So, like an employee, I'm leaving you for a better job elsewhere.'

'Where?'

'As a matter of fact I shall be working at Greenbournes.'

Uncle Joseph's eyes looked as if they would pop out. 'But you're the one who knows all the North Americans!'

'I imagine that's why Ben Greenbourne was so keen to hire me,' Hugh said. He could not help being pleased that Uncle Joseph was so irate.

'But you'll take business away from us!'

'You should have thought of that when you decided to go back on your offer of a partnership.'

'How much are they paying you?'

Hugh stood up to leave. 'That's not for you to ask,' he said firmly.

Edward shrieked: 'How dare you speak to my father that way!'

Joseph's indignation burst like a bubble, and to Hugh's

surprise he suddenly calmed down. 'Oh, shut up, Edward,' he said mildly. 'A certain amount of low cunning is part of what goes to make a good banker. There are times when I wish you were more like Hugh. He may be the black sheep of the family but at least he's got some spunk.' He turned back to Hugh. 'Go on, clear off,' he said without malice. 'I hope you'll come a cropper, but I'm not betting on it.'

'No doubt that's the nearest to good wishes that I'm likely to get from your branch of the family,' Hugh said. 'Good day to you.'

[IV]

'AND HOW IS dear Rachel?' Augusta asked Micky as she poured tea.

'She's fine,' Micky said. 'She may come along later.'

In fact he did not quite understand his wife. She had been a virgin when they married, but she acted like a whore. She submitted to him at any time, anywhere, and always with enthusiasm. One of the first things he had tried was tying her to the bedhead, to re-create the vision he had enjoyed when he first became attracted to her; and somewhat to his disappointment she had complied willingly. So far nothing he was able to do had succeeded in making her resist him. He had even taken her in the drawing-room, where there was a constant risk that the servants would see; and she had seemed to enjoy it more than ever.

On the other hand, she was the opposite of submissive in every other area of life. She argued with him about the house, the servants, money, politics and religion. When he got fed up with contradicting her he tried ignoring her, then insulting her, but nothing made any difference. She suffered from the delusion that she had as much right to her point of view as a man.

'I hope she's a help to you in your work,' Augusta said.

Micky nodded. 'She's a good hostess at Ministry functions,' he said. 'Attentive and gracious.'

'I thought she did very well at the party you gave for Ambassador Portillo,' Augusta said. Portillo was the Portuguese envoy and Augusta and Joseph had attended the dinner.

'She has a stupid plan to open a maternity hospital for women without husbands,' Micky said, allowing his irritation to show.

Augusta shook her head in disapproval. 'It's impossible for a woman in her position in society. Besides, there are already one or two such hospitals.'

'She says they're all religious institutions that tell women how wicked they are. Her place will help without preaching.'

'Worse and worse,' Augusta said. 'Think what the press would say!'

'Exactly. I've been very firm with her about it.'

'She's a lucky girl,' Augusta said, and favoured Micky with an intimate smile.

He realized that she was flirting and he was failing to respond. The truth was that he was too involved with Rachel. He certainly did not love her, but he was deeply engrossed by his relationship with her and she absorbed all his sexual energy. To compensate for his distraction he held Augusta's hand for a moment as she passed him a cup of tea. 'You're flattering me,' he said softly.

'No doubt I am. But something is worrying you, I can tell.'

'Dear Mrs Pilaster, as perceptive as always. Why do I ever imagine I can hide anything from you?' He released her hand and took his tea. 'Yes, I'm a little tense about the Santamaria Railroad.'

'I thought the partners had agreed to that.'

'They have, but these things take so long to organize.'

'The financial world moves slowly.'

'I understand that, but my family doesn't. Papa sends me cables twice a week. I curse the day the telegraph reached Santamaria.'

Edward came in bursting with news. 'Antonio Silva's back!' he said before he had closed the door behind him.

Augusta paled. 'How do you know?'

'Hugh saw him.'

'That's a blow,' she said, and Micky was surprised to see that her hand was shaking as she put down her cup and saucer.

'And David Middleton is still asking questions,' said Micky, recalling Middleton's conversation with Hugh at the Duchess of Tenbigh's ball. Micky was pretending to be worried, but in truth he was not altogether displeased. He liked to have Edward and Augusta reminded, from time to time, of the guilty secret they all shared.

'It's not just that,' Edward said. 'He's trying to sabotage the Santamaria Railroad bond issue.'

Micky frowned. Tonio's family had opposed the railway scheme back home in Cordova, but they had been overruled by President Garcia. What could Tonio possibly do here in London?

The same question occurred to Augusta. 'How can he do anything?'

Edward handed his mother a sheaf of papers. 'Read that.'

345

Micky said: 'What is it?'

'An article Tonio plans to publish in *The Times* about your family's nitrate mines.'

Augusta skimmed the pages rapidly. 'He claims that life as a nitrate miner is unpleasant and dangerous,' she said derisively. 'Who ever supposed it was a garden party?'

Edward said: 'He also reports that women are flogged and children shot for disobedience.'

She said: 'But what has this to do with your bond issue?'

'The railway is to carry nitrate to the capital. Investors don't like anything controversial. Many of them will already be wary of a South American bond. Something like this could scare them off completely.'

Micky was shaken. This sounded like very bad news. He asked Edward: 'What does your father say about all this?'

'We're trying to get another bank to come in with us on the deal, but basically we're going to let Tonio publish and see what happens. If the publicity causes a crash in South American stocks we'll have to abandon the Santamaria Railroad.'

Damn Tonio to hell. He was clever – and Papa was a fool, to run his mines like slave camps and then expect to raise money in the civilized world.

But what was to be done? Micky racked his brains. Tonio had to be silenced, but he would not be persuaded or bribed. A chill descended over Micky's heart as he realized he would have to use cruder, riskier methods.

He pretended to be calm. 'May I see the article, please?'

Augusta handed it to him.

The first thing he noticed was the hotel address at the top of the paper. Putting on an air of insouciance that he did not feel, he said: 'Why, this is no problem at all.'

Edward protested: 'But you haven't read it yet!'

'I don't need to. I've seen the address.'

'So what?'

'Now that we know where to find him, we can deal with him,' Micky said. 'Leave it to me.'

CHAPTER THREE

May

[I]

SOLLY LOVED to watch Maisie getting dressed.

Each evening she would put on her dressing-jacket and summon her maids to pin her hair up and thread it with flowers or feathers or beads; then she would dismiss the servants and wait for her husband.

Tonight they were going out, which they did most evenings. The only time they stayed in, during the London season, was when they were giving a party. Between Easter and the end of July they never dined alone.

He came in at half-past six, in his dress trousers and white waistcoat, carrying a large glass of champagne. Maisie's hair was decorated with yellow silk flowers tonight. She slipped out of her bedroom gown and stood naked in front of the mirror. She did a pirouette for Solly's benefit then began to dress.

First she put on a linen chemise with a neckline embroidered with flowers. It had silk tapes at the shoulders to tie it to her dress so that it would not be seen. Next she drew on fine white woollen stockings and fastened them just above her knees with elastic garters. She stepped into

348

a pair of knee-length loose cotton lawn drawers with pretty braiding at the hems and a drawstring waist, then put on yellow silk evening slippers.

Solly picked up her corset from its frame and helped her into it, then drew the laces tight at the back. Most women were helped to dress by one or two maids, for it was impossible for a woman to manage the elaborate corset and gown alone. However, Solly had learned to perform these services himself rather than go without the pleasure of watching.

Crinolines and bustles were no longer in fashion, but Maisie put on a cotton petticoat with a flounced train and a ruffled hem to support the train of her gown. The petticoat was fastened at the back with a bow, and Solly tied it.

At last she was ready for the gown. It was of yellow-and-white striped silk taffeta. The bodice was loosely draped, which flattered her large bosom, and caught at the shoulder with a bow. The rest of the garment was similarly swagged and caught at the waist, knee and hem. It took a maid all day to iron it.

She sat on the floor and Solly lifted the dress over her so that she was sitting inside it like a tent. Then she stood up carefully, putting her hands through the armholes and her head through the neck. Together she and Solly arranged the folds of the drapery until they looked right.

She opened her jewellery box and took out a diamond-and-emerald necklace and matching earrings that Solly had given her on their first wedding anniversary. As she was putting them on he said: 'We're going to be seeing a lot more of our old friend Hugh Pilaster from now on.'

Maisie muffled a sigh. Solly's trusting nature could be tiresome. The normal suspicious-minded husband would have divined the attraction between Maisie and Hugh, and would be bad-tempered every time the other man's name was mentioned, but Solly was too innocent. He had no idea he was putting temptation in her way. 'Why, what's happened?' she said neutrally.

'He's coming to work at the bank.'

That was not so bad. Maisie had half feared Solly had invited Hugh to live with them. 'Why is he leaving Pilasters? I thought he was doing so well.'

'They refused him a partnership.'

'Oh, no!' She knew Hugh better than anyone did, and she understood how badly he had suffered because of his father's bankruptcy and suicide. She could guess how broken he was by the refusal of a partnership. 'The Pilasters are a mean-spirited family,' she said with feeling.

'It's because of his wife.'

Maisie nodded. 'I'm not surprised.' She had witnessed the incident at the Duchess of Tenbigh's ball. Knowing the Pilasters as she did, she could not help wondering if Augusta had somehow stage-managed the whole incident in order to discredit Hugh.

'You have to feel sorry for Nora.'

'Mmm.' Maisie had met Nora, some weeks before the wedding, and had taken an instant dislike to her. Indeed, she had wounded Hugh by telling him Nora was a heartless gold-digger and he should not marry her.

'Anyway, I suggested to Hugh that you might help her.'

'What?' Maisie said sharply. She looked away from her mirror. 'Help her?'

'Rehabilitate her. You know what it's like to be looked down on because of your background. You overcame all that prejudice.'

'And now I'm supposed to work the same transformation on every other guttersnipe who marries into society?' Maisie snapped.

'I've obviously done something wrong,' Solly said worriedly. 'I thought you'd be glad to help, you've always been so fond of Hugh.'

Maisie went to her cupboard for her gloves. 'I wish you'd consulted me first, before volunteering me for this job.' She opened the cupboard. On the back of the door, framed in wood, hung the old poster she had saved from the circus, showing her in tights, standing on the back of a white horse, over the legend 'The Amazing Maisie'. The picture jerked her out of her tantrum and she suddenly felt ashamed of herself. She ran to Solly and threw her arms around him. 'Oh, Solly, how can I be so ungrateful?'

'There, there,' he murmured, stroking her bare shoulders.

'You've been so kind and generous to me and my family, of course I'll do this for you, if you wish.'

'I'd hate to force you into something—'

'No, no, you're not forcing me. Why shouldn't I help her get what I got?' She looked at her husband's chubby face, creased now with lines of anxiety. She stroked his cheek. 'Stop worrying. I was being horribly selfish for a minute but it's over. Go and put your jacket on. I'm ready.' She stood on tiptoe and kissed his lips, then turned away and put on her gloves.

She knew what had really made her cross. The irony of the situation was bitter. She was being asked to train Nora for the role of Mrs Hugh Pilaster – the position Maisie herself had longed to occupy. In her innermost heart she still wanted to be Hugh's wife, and she hated Nora for winning what she had lost. All in all it was a shameful attitude and Maisie resolved to drop it. She should be glad Hugh had married. He had been very unhappy, and it was at least partly her fault. Now she could stop worrying about him. She felt a sense of loss, if not grief, but she should keep those feelings locked away in a room no one ever entered. She would throw herself energetically into the task of bringing Nora Pilaster back into the good graces of London's high society.

Solly came back with his jacket on and they went along to the nursery. Bertie was in his nightshirt, playing with a wooden model of a railway train. He loved to see Maisie in her gowns and would be very disappointed if for some reason she went out in the evening without showing him what she was wearing. He told her what had happened in the park that afternoon – he had befriended a large dog – and Solly got down on the floor and played trains for a while. Then it was Bertie's bedtime, and Maisie and Solly went downstairs and got into their carriage.

They were going to a dinner party, then on to a ball afterwards. Both would take place within half a mile of their house in Piccadilly, but Maisie could not walk the streets in such an elaborate gown: the hem and train, and her silk shoes, would be filthy by the time she arrived. All the same she still smiled to think that the girl who had once walked for four days to get to Newcastle could not now go half a mile without her carriage.

She was able to begin her campaign for Nora that very night. When they reached their destination and entered the drawing-room of the Marquis of Hatchford, the first person she saw was Count de Tokoly. She knew him quite well and he always flirted with her, so she felt free to be direct. 'I want you to forgive Nora Pilaster for slapping you,' she said.

'Forgive?' he said. 'I'm flattered! To think that at my age I can still make a young woman slap my face – it's a great compliment.'

That wasn't how you felt at the time, Maisie thought.

However, she was glad he had decided to make light of the whole incident.

He went on: 'Now, if she had refused to take me seriously – that would have been an insult.'

It was exactly what Nora ought to have done, Maisie reflected. 'Tell me something,' she said. 'Did Augusta Pilaster encourage you to flirt with her daughter-in-law?'

'Grisly suggestion!' he replied. 'Mrs Joseph Pilaster as a pander! She did nothing of the kind.'

'Did anyone encourage you?'

He looked at Maisie through narrowed eyes. 'You're clever, Mrs Greenbourne; I've always respected you for that. Cleverer than Nora Pilaster. She'll never be what you are.'

'But you haven't answered my question.'

'I'll tell you the truth, as I admire you so much. The Cordovan Minister, Señor Miranda, told me that Nora was . . . what shall we say . . . susceptible.'

So that was it. 'And Micky Miranda was put up to it by Augusta, I'm sure of it. Those two are as thick as thieves.'

De Tokoly was miffed. 'I do hope I haven't been used as a pawn.'

'That's the danger of being so predictable,' Maisie said waspishly.

Next day she took Nora to her dressmaker.

As Nora tried on styles and fabrics Maisie found out a little more about the incident at the Duchess of Tenbigh's ball. 'Did Augusta say anything to you beforehand about the count?' she asked.

'She warned me not to let him take any liberties,' Nora replied.

'So you were ready for him, so to speak.'

'Yes.'

'And if Augusta had said nothing, would you have behaved the same way?'

Nora looked thoughtful. 'I probably wouldn't have slapped him – I wouldn't have had the nerve. But Augusta made me think it was important to take a stand.'

Maisie nodded. 'There you are. She wanted this to happen. She also got someone to tell the count you were easy.'

Nora was amazed. 'Are you sure?'

'He told me. She's a devious bitch and she has no scruples at all.' Maisie realized she was speaking in her Newcastle accent, something that rarely happened nowadays. She reverted to normal. 'Never underestimate Augusta's capacity for treachery.'

'She doesn't scare me,' Nora said defiantly. 'I haven't got too many scruples myself.'

Maisie believed her – and felt sorry for Hugh.

A polonaise was the perfect dress style for Nora, she thought as the dressmaker pinned a gown around Nora's generous figure. The fussy details suited her pretty looks: the pleated frills, the front opening decorated with bows, and the tie-back skirt with flounces all looked sweet on her. Perhaps she was a little too voluptuous, but a long corset would restrain her tendency to wobble.

'Looking pretty is half the battle,' she said as Nora admired herself in the mirror. 'As far as the men are concerned it's really all that matters. But you have to do more to get accepted by the women.'

Nora said: 'I've always got on better with men than women.'

Maisie was not surprised: Nora was that type.

Nora went on: 'You must be the same. That's why we've got where we are.'

Are we the same? wondered Maisie.

'Not that I put myself on the same level as you,' Nora added. 'Every ambitious girl in London envies you.'

Maisie winced at the thought that she was looked up to as a hero by fortune-hunting women, but she said nothing because she probably deserved it. Nora had married for money, and she was quite happy to admit it to Maisie because she assumed that Maisie had done the same. And she was right.

Nora said: 'I'm not complaining, but I did pick the black sheep of the family, the one with no capital. You married one of the richest men in the world.'

How surprised you would be, Maisie thought, if you knew how willingly I'd swap.

She put the thought out of her mind. All right, she and Nora were two of a kind. She would help Nora win the acceptance of the snobs and shrews who ruled society.

'Never talk about how much anything costs,' she began, remembering her own early mistakes. 'Always remain calm and unruffled, no matter what happens. If your coachman has a heart attack, your carriage crashes, your hat blows off and your drawers fall down, just say: "Goodness me, such excitement", and get in a hansom. Remember that the country is better than the town, idleness is superior to work, old is preferable to new and rank is more important than money. Know a little about everything, but never be an expert. Practise talking without moving your mouth – it will improve your accent. Tell people that your great-grandfather farmed in Yorkshire: Yorkshire is too big for anyone to check, and agriculture is an honourable way to become poor.'

Nora struck a pose, looked vague, and said languidly: 'Goodness me, *such* a lot to remember, how shall I *ever* manage?'

'Perfect,' said Maisie. 'You'll do very well indeed.'

[II]

Mᴵᶜᴷʏ Mᴵᴿᴬᴺᴰᴬ stood in a doorway in Berwick Street, wearing a light overcoat to keep out the chill of a spring evening. He was smoking a cigar and watching the street. There was a gas lamp nearby but he stood in the shadow so that his face could not easily be seen by passers-by. He felt anxious, dissatisfied with himself, soiled. He disliked violence. It was Papa's way, Paulo's way. For Micky it always seemed such an admission of failure.

Berwick Street was a narrow, filthy passage of cheap pubs and lodging-houses. Dogs rummaged in the gutters and small children played in the gaslight. Micky had been there since nightfall and he had not seen a single policeman. Now it was almost midnight.

The Hotel Russe was across the street. It had seen better days, but still it was a cut above its surroundings. There was a light over the door and inside Micky could see a lobby with a reception counter. However, there did not appear to be anyone at the counter.

Two other men loitered on the far pavement, one on either side of the hotel entrance. All three of them were waiting for Antonio Silva.

Micky had pretended to be calm in front of Edward and Augusta but in fact he was desperately worried about Tonio's article appearing in *The Times*. He had put so much effort into getting Pilasters to launch the Santamaria

Railroad. He had even got married to that bitch Rachel for the sake of the damned bonds. His entire career depended on its success. If he let his family down over this, his father would be not only raging but vengeful. Papa had the power to get Micky fired as Minister. With no money and no position he could hardly stay in London: he would have to return home and face humiliation and disgrace. Either way, the life he had enjoyed for so many years would be over.

Rachel had demanded to know where he was planning to spend this evening. He had laughed at her. 'Never try to question me,' he had said.

She had surprised him by saying: 'Then I shall go out for the evening, too.'

'Where?'

'Never try to question me.'

Micky had locked her in the bedroom.

When he got home she would be incandescent with wrath, but that had happened before. On previous occasions when she had raged at him he had thrown her on the bed and torn off her clothes, and she had always submitted to him eagerly. She would do it yet again tonight, he felt sure.

He wished he could feel as sure of Tonio.

He was not even certain the man was still living at this hotel, but he could not go in and ask without arousing suspicion.

He had moved as quickly as possible, but still it had taken forty-eight hours to locate and hire two ruthless toughs, reconnoitre the location and set up the ambush. In that time Tonio might have moved. Then Micky would be in trouble.

A careful man would move hotels every few days. But a careful man would not use notepaper that bore an address. Tonio was not the cautious type. On the contrary, he had always been reckless. In all probability he was still at this hotel, Micky thought.

He was right.

A few minutes after midnight, Tonio appeared.

Micky thought he recognized the walk as the figure turned into the far end of Berwick Street, coming from the direction of Leicester Square. He tensed, but resisted the temptation to move right away. Restraining himself with an effort, he waited until the man passed a gaslamp, when the face became clearly visible for a moment. Then there was no doubt: it was Tonio. Micky could even see the carroty colour of the side-whiskers. He felt relief and heightened anxiety at the same time: relief that he had Tonio in his sights, anxiety about the crude, dangerous attack he was about to make.

Then he saw the policemen.

It was the worst possible luck. There were two of them, coming down Berwick Street from the opposite direction, helmeted and caped, their truncheons hanging from their belts, shining their bull's-eye lanterns into dark corners. Micky stood stock still. There was nothing he could do. They saw Micky, noted his top hat and his cigar, and nodded deferentially: it was none of their business what an upper-class man might be doing loitering in a doorway – they were after criminals, not gentlemen. They passed Tonio fifteen or twenty yards from the hotel door. Micky fidgeted in frustration. Another few moments and Tonio would be safe inside his hotel.

Then the two policemen turned a corner and were gone from sight.

Micky gestured to his two accomplices.

They moved fast.

Before Tonio reached the door of his hotel, the two men

seized him and bundled him into the alley alongside the building. He shouted once, but after that his cries were muffled.

Throwing away the remains of his cigar, Micky crossed the road and entered the alley. They had stuffed a scarf into Tonio's mouth, to prevent his making a noise, and they were beating him with iron bars. His hat had fallen off, and his head and face were already covered with blood. His body was protected by a coat, but they slashed at his knees and shins and his unprotected hands.

The sight made Micky feel ill. 'Stop it, you fools!' he hissed at them. 'Can't you see he's had enough?' Micky did not want them to kill Tonio. As things stood, the incident looked like a routine robbery, accompanied by a savage beating. A murder would create a great deal more fuss – and the policemen had seen Micky's face, however briefly.

With apparent reluctance the two thugs stopped hitting Tonio, who slumped to the ground and lay still.

'Empty his pockets!' Micky whispered.

Tonio did not move as they took from him a watch and chain, a pocketbook, some coins, a silk handkerchief and a key.

'Give me the key,' Micky said. 'The rest is yours.'

The older of the two men, Barker – humorously known as Dog – said: 'Give us the money.'

He gave them each ten pounds in gold sovereigns.

Dog gave him the key. Tied to it with a small piece of thread was a slip of card with the number eleven scrawled on it. It was all Micky needed.

He turned to leave the alley – and saw that they were being watched. A man stood in the street staring at them. Micky's heart raced.

Dog saw him a moment later. He grunted an oath and

raised his iron bar as if to strike the man down. Suddenly Micky realized something and grabbed Dog's arm. 'No,' he said. 'That won't be necessary. Look at him.'

The watching man had a slack mouth and an empty look in his eyes: he was an idiot.

Dog lowered his weapon. 'He'll do us no harm,' he said. 'He's two sticks short of a bundle.'

Micky pushed past him into the street. Looking back, he saw Dog and his companion taking off Tonio's boots.

Micky walked away, hoping he would never see them again.

He turned into the Hotel Russe. To his relief the desk in the little lobby was still unoccupied. He went up the stairs.

The hotel consisted of three houses knocked together, and it took Micky a while to find his way around, but two or three minutes later he let himself into Room No.11.

It was a cramped, grimy room stuffed with furniture that had once been pretentious but was now merely shabby. Micky put his hat and cane on a chair and began to search quickly and methodically. In the writing-desk he found a copy of the article for *The Times*, which he took. However, it was not worth much. Tonio either had copies or could rewrite it from memory. But in order to get the article published he would have to produce some kind of evidence, and it was the evidence that Micky was looking for.

In the chest of drawers he found a novel called *The Duchess of Sodom* which he was tempted to steal, but he decided it was an unnecessary risk. He tipped Tonio's shirts and underwear out of the drawers on to the floor. There was nothing hidden there.

He had not really expected to find it in an obvious place.

He looked behind and underneath the chest, the bed and the wardrobe. He climbed on the table so that he could look on top of the wardrobe: there was nothing there but thick dust.

He pulled the sheets off the bed, probed the pillows for something hard, and examined the mattress. He finally found what he wanted underneath the mattress.

Inside a large envelope was a wad of papers tied together with lawyers' ribbons.

Before he could examine the documents he heard footsteps in the hall.

He dropped the bundle and stood behind the door.

The footsteps went past and faded.

He untied the ribbons and scanned the documents. They were in Spanish, and bore the stamp of a lawyer in Palma, the capital of Cordova. They were the sworn affidavits of witnesses who had seen floggings and executions at Micky's family's nitrate mines.

Micky lifted the sheaf of papers to his lips and kissed them. They were the answer to his prayers.

He stuffed them into the bosom of his coat. Before destroying them he had to make a note of the names and addresses of the witnesses. The lawyers would have copies of the affidavits, but the copies were no use without the witnesses. And now that Micky knew who the witnesses were, their days were numbered. He would send their addresses to Papa, and Papa would silence them.

Was there anything else? He looked around the room. It was a mess. There was nothing more for him here. He had what he needed. Without proof, Tonio's article was worthless.

He left the room and went down the stairs.

To his surprise there was a clerk at the desk in the lobby. The man looked up and said challengingly: 'May I ask your business?'

Micky made an instant decision. If he ignored the clerk, the man would probably just think he was rude. To stop and give an account of himself would allow the clerk to study his face. He said nothing and went out. The clerk did not follow.

As he passed the alley he heard a feeble cry for help. Tonio was crawling toward the street, leaving a trail of blood. The sight made Micky want to throw up. Disgusted, he grimaced, looked away and walked on.

[III]

IN THE AFTERNOONS, wealthy ladies and idle gentlemen called on one another. It was a tiresome practice and four days of the week Maisie told her servants to say she was not at home. On Fridays she received people, and there might be twenty or thirty during the course of an afternoon. It was always more or less the same crowd: the Marlborough Set, the Jewish set, women with 'advanced' ideas such as Rachel Bodwin, and a few wives of Solly's more important business acquaintances.

Emily Pilaster was in the last category. Her husband Edward was involved in a deal with Solly about a railway in Cordova, and Maisie assumed it was on the strength of that that Emily called. But she stayed all afternoon and at half-past five, when everyone else had gone, she was still there.

A pretty girl with big blue eyes, she was only about twenty years old and anyone could tell she was miserable, so Maisie was not surprised when she said: 'Please can I talk to you about something personal?'

'Of course, what is it?'

'I do hope you won't be offended but there's no one I can discuss it with.'

This sounded like a sexual problem. It would not be the first time that a well-bred girl had come to Maisie for advice on a subject she would not discuss with her mother. Perhaps they had heard rumours about her racy past, or perhaps they just found her approachable. 'It's hard to offend me,' Maisie said. 'What do you want to discuss?'

'My husband hates me,' she said, and she burst into tears.

Maisie felt sorry for her. She had known Edward in the old Argyll Rooms days and he had been a pig then. No doubt he had got worse since. She could sympathize with anyone unfortunate enough to have married him.

'You see,' Emily said between sobs, 'his parents wanted him to marry, but he didn't want to, so they offered him a huge settlement, and a partnership in the bank, and that persuaded him. And I agreed because my parents wanted me to and he seemed as good as anyone and I wanted to have babies. But he never liked me and now that he's got his money and his partnership he can't stand the sight of me.'

Maisie sighed. 'This may sound hard, but you're in the same position as thousands of women.'

Emily wiped her eyes with a handkerchief and made an effort to stop crying. 'I know, and I don't want you to think I'm feeling sorry for myself. I realize I've got to make the best of it. And I know I could cope with the situation if only I could have a baby. That's all I ever really wanted.'

Children were the consolation of most unhappy wives, Maisie reflected. 'Is there any reason why you shouldn't have babies?'

Emily was shifting restlessly on the couch, almost writhing with embarrassment, but her childlike face was set in lines of determination. 'I've been married for two months and *nothing's happened*.'

'Early days yet—'

'No, I don't mean I expected to be pregnant by now.'

Maisie knew it was difficult for such girls to be specific, so she led her with questions. 'Does he come to your bed?'

'He did at first, but not any more.'

'When he did, what went wrong?'

'The trouble is, I'm not sure what's supposed to happen.'

Maisie sighed. How could mothers allow their daughters to walk up the aisle in such ignorance? She recalled that Emily's father was a Methodist minister. That did not help. 'What's supposed to happen is this,' she began. 'Your husband kisses and touches you, his doodle gets long and stiff, and he puts it into your cunny. Most girls like it.'

Emily blushed scarlet. 'He did the kissing and touched, but nothing else.'

'Did his doodle get stiff?'

'It was dark.'

'Didn't you feel it?'

'He made me rub it once.'

'And what was it like? Rigid, like a candle, or limp, like an earthworm? Or in between, like a sausage before it's cooked?'

'Limp.'

'And when you rubbed it, did it stiffen?'

'No. It made him very angry and he slapped me and said I was no good. *Is* it my fault, Mrs Greenbourne?'

'No, it's not your fault, though men generally blame women. It's a common problem and it's called impotence.'

'What causes it?'

'Lots of different things.'

'Does it mean I can't have a baby?'

'Not until you can make his doodle stiff.'

Emily looked as if she might cry. 'I do so want a baby. I'm so lonely and unhappy but if I had a baby I could put up with everything else.'

Maisie wondered what Edward's problem was. He certainly had not been impotent in the old days. Was there anything she could do to help Emily? She could probably find out whether Edward was impotent all the time or just with his wife. April Tilsley would know. Edward had still been a regular customer at Nellie's brothel last time Maisie spoke to April – although that had been years ago: it was difficult for a society lady to remain close friends with London's leading madam. 'I know someone close to Edward,' she said cautiously. 'She might be able to shed some light on the problem.'

Emily swallowed. 'Do you mean that he has a mistress? Please tell me – I must face the facts.'

She was a determined girl, Maisie thought. She may be ignorant and naive but she's going to get what she wants. 'This woman isn't his mistress. But if he has one she might know.'

Emily nodded. 'I'd like to meet your friend.'

'I don't know that you personally should—'

'I want to. He's my husband, and if there's something bad to be told I want to hear it.' Her face took on that set, stubborn look again, and she said: 'I'll do anything, you must believe me – anything. My whole life is going to be a wasteland unless I save myself.'

Maisie decided to test her resolve. 'My friend's name is April. She owns a brothel near Leicester Square. It's two minutes from here. Are you prepared to go there with me now?'

'What's a brothel?' said Emily.

*

The hansom pulled up outside Nellie's. Maisie peeked out, scanning the street. She did not want to be seen going into a brothel by anyone she knew. However, this was the hour when most people of her class were dressing for dinner, and there were only a few poor people on the street. She and Emily got out of the cab. She had paid the driver in advance. The door to the brothel was not locked. They went inside.

Daylight was not kind to Nellie's. At night it might have a certain seedy glamour, Maisie thought, but at the moment it looked threadbare and grubby. The velvet upholstery was faded, the tables were scarred with cigar burns and glass rings, the silk wallpaper was peeling and the erotic paintings just looked vulgar. An old woman with a pipe in her mouth was sweeping the floor. She did not appear surprised to see two society ladies in expensive dresses. When Maisie asked for April, the old woman jerked a thumb at the staircase.

They found April in an upstairs kitchen, drinking tea at the table with several other women, all in dressing-gowns or housecoats; obviously it was some hours before business would begin. At first April did not recognize Maisie and they stared at one another for a long moment. Maisie found her old friend little changed: still thin, hard-faced and sharp-eyed; a little weary-looking, perhaps, from too many late nights and too much cheap champagne; but with the confident, assertive air of a successful businesswoman. 'What can we do for you?' she said.

'Don't you know me, April?' said Maisie; and at once April shrieked with delight and jumped up and threw her arms around her.

When they had embraced and kissed, April turned to the other women in the kitchen and said: 'Girls, this is the woman who did what we all dream of. Formerly Miriam

Rabinowicz, later Maisie Robinson, she is now Mrs Solomon Greenbourne!'

The women all cheered as if Maisie were some kind of hero. She felt bashful: she had not anticipated that April would give such a frank account of her story – especially in front of Emily Pilaster – but it was too late now.

'Let's have a gin to celebrate,' April said. They sat down and one of the women produced a bottle and some glasses and poured them drinks. Maisie had never enjoyed gin, and now that she was accustomed to the best champagne she liked it even less, but she knocked it back to be companionable. She saw Emily sip hers and grimace. Their glasses were immediately recharged.

'Well, what brings you here?' April said.

'A marital problem,' Maisie said. 'My friend here has an impotent husband.'

'Bring him here, my love,' April said to Emily. 'We'll sort him out.'

'He's already a customer, I suspect,' Maisie said.

'What's his name?'

'Edward Pilaster.'

April was startled. 'My God.' She stared hard at Emily. 'So you're Emily. You poor cow.'

'You know my name,' Emily said. She looked mortified. 'That means he speaks to you about me.' She drank some more gin.

One of the other women said: 'Edward's not impotent.'

Emily blushed.

'I'm sorry,' the woman said. 'Only he usually asks for me.' She was a tall girl with dark hair and a deep bosom. Maisie thought she did not look very impressive in her grubby robe, smoking a cigarette like a man: but perhaps she was attractive when she was dressed up.

Emily recovered her composure. 'It's so strange,' she

said. 'He's my husband, but you know more about him than I do. And I don't even know your name.'

'Lily.'

There was a moment of awkward silence. Maisie sipped her drink: the second gin tasted better than the first. This was a very bizarre scene, she realized: the kitchen, the women in *déshabillé*, the cigarettes and gin, and Emily, who an hour ago had not been sure what sexual intercourse consisted of, discussing her husband's impotence with his favourite whore.

'Well,' April said briskly, 'now you know the answer to the question. Why is Edward impotent with his wife? Because Micky's not around. He can never get hard if he's alone with a woman.'

'Micky?' said Emily incredulously. 'Micky Miranda? The Cordovan Minister?'

April nodded. 'They do everything together, especially here. Once or twice Edward has come in on his own but it never works.'

Emily was looking bewildered. Maisie asked the obvious question: 'What, exactly, do they do?'

It was Lily who answered. 'Nothing very complicated. Over the years they've tried several variations. At the moment what they like is, the two of them go to bed with one girl, usually me or Muriel.'

Maisie said: 'But Edward really does it, properly, does he? I mean, he gets hard, and everything?'

Lily nodded. 'No question of that.'

'Do you think that's the only way he could ever manage it?'

Lily frowned. 'I don't think it matters much exactly what happens, how many girls and so on. If Micky is there, it works, and if he's not, it doesn't.

Maisie said: 'Almost as if Micky is the one Edward really loves.'

Emily said faintly: 'I feel as if I'm in a dream, or something.' She took a long swallow of gin. 'Can all this be true? Do these things really go on?'

April said: 'If you but knew. Edward and Micky are tame by comparison with some of our customers.'

Even Maisie was startled. The thought of Edward and Micky in bed together with a woman was so odd it made her want to laugh out loud, and she had to make an effort to suppress the chuckle that bubbled up in her throat.

She recalled the night Edward had discovered her and Hugh making love. Edward had been uncontrollably aroused, she remembered; and she had felt intuitively that what inflamed him was the idea of fucking her immediately after Hugh. 'A buttered bun!' she said.

Some of the women giggled.

'That's right,' April laughed.

Emily smiled and looked puzzled. 'I don't understand.'

April said: 'Some men like a buttered bun.' The whores laughed louder. 'It means a woman who's just been fucked by another man.'

Emily started to giggle, and in a moment they were all laughing hysterically. It was a combination of the gin, the weird situation, and the talk of men's peculiar sexual preferences, Maisie thought. Her use of the vulgar phrase had released the tension. Every time the laughter eased one of them would say: 'A buttered bun!' and they would all collapse into giggles again.

At last they were too exhausted to laugh any more. When they quietened down, Maisie said: 'But where does this leave Emily? She wants to have a baby. She can hardly invite Micky to bed with her and her husband.'

Emily looked miserable.

April caught her eye and held it. 'How determined are you, Emily?' she said.

'I'll do anything,' said Emily. 'Really, anything in the world.'

'If you mean that,' said April slowly, 'there is something we could try.'

[IV]

JOSEPH PILASTER finished off a large plate of grilled lamb's kidneys and scrambled eggs, and began to butter a slice of toast. Augusta often wondered whether the customary bad temper of middle-aged men had to do with the amount of meat they ate. The thought of kidneys for breakfast made her feel quite ill.

'Sidney Madler has come to London,' he said. 'I have to see him this morning.'

For a moment Augusta was not sure who he was talking about. 'Madler?'

'From New York. He's angry about Hugh not being a partner.'

'What is it to do with him?' Augusta said. 'The insolence!' She spoke superciliously but she was bothered.

'I know what he'll say,' Joseph said. 'When we formed our joint enterprise with Madler and Bell there was an implicit understanding that the London end of the operation would be run by Hugh. Now Hugh has resigned, as you know.'

'But you did not wish Hugh to resign.'

'No, but I could keep him by offering him a partnership.'

There was some risk of Joseph weakening, Augusta could see. The thought scared her. She had to stiffen his nerve. 'I trust you won't allow outsiders to decide who shall and who shall not be a partner in Pilasters Bank.'

'Indeed I won't.'

A thought occurred to Augusta. 'Can Mr Madler terminate the joint enterprise?'

'He could, though he hasn't threatened to, so far.'

'Is it worth a lot of money?'

'It was. But when Hugh goes to work at Greenbournes he's likely to take most of the business with him.'

'So it really makes very little difference what Mr Madler thinks.'

'Perhaps not. But I'll have to tell him something. He's come all the way from New York just to make a fuss about this.'

'Tell him Hugh has married an impossible wife. He can hardly fail to understand that.'

'Of course.' Joseph stood up. 'Goodbye, dear.'

Augusta stood up and kissed her husband on the lips. 'Don't be bullied, Joseph,' she said.

His shoulders straightened and his mouth set in a stubborn line. 'I shan't.'

When he had gone she sat at the table sipping coffee for a while, wondering how serious this threat was. She had tried to bolster Joseph's resistance but there was a limit to how much she could do. She would have to keep a very close eye on that situation.

She was surprised to hear that Hugh's departure would cost the bank a lot of money. It had not occurred to her that in promoting Edward and undermining Hugh she was also losing money. For a moment she wondered whether she might be endangering the bank that was the foundation of all her hopes and schemes. But that was ridiculous. Pilasters Bank was hugely wealthy: nothing she could do would threaten it.

While she was finishing her breakfast Hastead sidled in to tell her that Mr Fortescue had called. She immediately put Sidney Madler out of her mind. This was much more important. Her heart beat faster.

Michael Fortescue was her tame politician. Having won the Deaconridge by-election with financial help from Joseph, he was now a Member of Parliament, and indebted to Augusta. She had made it very clear how he could repay that debt: by helping her to get a peerage for Joseph. The by-election had cost five thousand pounds, enough to buy the finest house in London, but that was a cheap price to pay for a title. The afternoon was the time for calls, so morning visitors generally had urgent business. She felt sure Fortescue would not have called so early unless he had news of the peerage, and her heart beat faster. 'Put Mr Fortescue in the lookout,' she told the butler. 'I shall be with him directly.' She sat still for a few moments, trying to make herself calm.

Her campaign had gone according to plan so far. Arnold Hobbes had published a series of articles in his journal *The Forum* calling for peerages for commercial men. Lady Morte had talked to the Queen about it, and had sung Joseph's praises; and she said Her Majesty had seemed impressed. And Fortescue had told Prime Minister Disraeli that there was a groundswell of public opinion in favour of the idea. Now perhaps the whole effort was about to bear fruit.

The tension was almost too much for Augusta, and she felt a little breathless as she hurried up the stairs, her head full of the phrases she hoped soon to hear: *Lady Whitehaven . . . the Earl and Countess of Whitehaven . . . very good, m'lady . . . as your ladyship pleases . . .*

The lookout was a curious room. It was over the front lobby, and was reached by a door half-way up the stairs. It had a bay window over the street, but that was not what gave the room its name. What was unusual about it was an interior window that looked down into the main hall. People in the hall did not suspect they were observed, and over the years Augusta had seen some strange sights from that vantage point. The room was informal, small and cosy, with a low ceiling and a fireplace. Augusta received visitors there in the morning.

Fortescue was a tall, good-looking young man with unusually big hands. He looked a little tense. Augusta sat close to him on the window-seat and gave him a warm, reassuring smile.

'I've just been with the Prime Minister,' he said.

Augusta could hardly speak. 'Did you talk about peerages?'

'We did indeed. I've managed to convince him that it is time the banking industry was represented in the House of Lords, and he's now minded to grant a peerage to a City man.'

'Wonderful!' said Augusta. But Fortescue had an uncomfortable expression, not at all like the bringer of glad tidings. 'So why do you look so glum?' she said uneasily.

'There's also bad news,' Fortescue said, and suddenly he looked a little frightened.

'What?'

'I'm afraid he wants to give the peerage to Ben Greenbourne.'

'No!' Augusta felt as if she had been punched. 'How can that be?'

Fortescue became defensive. 'I suppose he can give peerages to whomever he pleases. He is the Prime Minister.'

'But I didn't go to all this trouble for the benefit of Ben Greenbourne!'

'I agree it's ironic,' Fortescue said languidly. 'But I did my best.'

'Don't be so smug,' she snapped. 'Not if you want my help in future elections.'

Rebellion flashed in his eyes, and for a moment she thought she had lost him, thought he was going to say that he had repaid the debt and now he no longer needed her; but then he dropped his gaze and said: 'I assure you I'm devastated by this news—'

'Be quiet, let me think,' she said, and she began to pace up and down the little room. 'We must find a way to change the Prime Minister's mind. . . . We must make it into a scandal. What are Ben Greenbourne's weaknesses? His son is married to a guttersnipe, but that's not really enough. . . .' It occurred to her that if Greenbourne got a title it would be inherited by his son Solly, which would mean that Maisie would eventually be a countess. The thought was sickening. 'What are Greenbourne's politics?'

'None known.'

She looked at the young man and saw that he was sulking. She had spoken too harshly to him, she realized. She sat down beside him and took one of his big hands in both her own. 'Your political instincts are remarkable, in fact that's what first made me notice you. Tell me what your guess would be.'

Fortescue melted immediately, as men generally did when she took the trouble to be nice to them. 'If pressed he would probably be Liberal. Most businessmen are Liberal, and so are most Jews. But as he has never expressed any opinion publicly, it will be hard to make him out to be an enemy of the Conservative government—'

'He's a Jew,' Augusta said. 'That's the key.'

Fortescue looked dubious. 'The Prime Minister himself

is a Jew by birth, and he has now been made Lord Beaconsfield.'

'I know, but he's a practising Christian. Besides . . .'

Fortescue raised an inquiring eyebrow.

'I have instincts too,' Augusta said. 'Mine tell me that Ben Greenbourne's Jewishness is the key to it all.'

'If there is anything I can do . . .'

'You've been wonderful. There's nothing for the moment. But when the Prime Minister begins to have doubts about Ben Greenbourne, just remind him that there is a safe alternative in Joseph Pilaster.'

'Rely on me, Mrs Pilaster.'

Lady Morte lived in a house in Curzon Street which her husband could not afford. The door was opened by a liveried footman in a powdered wig. Augusta was shown into a morning-room crowded with costly knick-knacks from Bond Street shops: gold candelabra, silver picture-frames, porcelain ornaments, crystal vases, and an exquisite antique jewelled inkstand that must have cost as much as a young racehorse. Augusta despised Harriet Morte for her weakness in spending money she did not have; but at the same time she was reassured by these signs that the woman was as extravagant as ever.

She paced up and down the room as she waited. A feeling of panic grew over her every time she faced the prospect that Ben Greenbourne would get the honour instead of Joseph. She did not think she could mount a campaign like this a second time. And it made her squirm to think that the result of all her efforts might be that the title of countess would eventually go to that little sewer rat Maisie Greenbourne. . . .

Lady Morte came in, saying distantly: 'What a lovely surprise to see you at this time of day!' It was a reproof to Augusta for calling before lunch. Lady Morte's iron-grey hair looked hastily combed, and Augusta guessed she had not been fully dressed.

But you had to receive me, didn't you? thought Augusta. You were afraid I might be calling about your bank account, so you had no choice.

However, she spoke in a subservient tone that would flatter the woman. 'I've come to ask your advice over something urgent.'

'Anything I can do . . .'

'The Prime Minister has agreed to give a peerage to a banker.'

'Splendid! I mentioned it to Her Majesty, as you know. Doubtless that had its effect.'

'Unfortunately he wants to give it to Ben Greenbourne.'

'Oh, dear. That is unfortunate.'

Augusta could tell that Harriet Morte was secretly pleased by this news. She hated Augusta. 'It's more than unfortunate,' Augusta said. 'I've expended a good deal of effort over this and now it seems the benefits will go to my husband's greatest rival!'

'I do see that.'

'I wish we could prevent it happening.'

'I'm not sure what we can do.'

Augusta pretended to be thinking aloud. 'Peerages have to be approved by the Queen, don't they?'

'Yes, indeed. Technically it is she who grants them.'

'Then she could do something, if you asked her.'

Lady Morte gave a little laugh. 'My dear Mrs Pilaster, you overestimate my power.' Augusta held her tongue and ignored the condescending tone. Lady Morte went on: 'Her Majesty is not likely to take my advice over that of the

Prime Minister. Besides, what would be my grounds of objection?'

'Greenbourne is a Jew.'

Lady Morte nodded. 'There was a time when that would have finished it. I remember when Gladstone wanted to make Lionel Rothschild a peer: the Queen refused point-blank. But that was ten years ago. Since then we have had Disraeli.'

'But Disraeli is a Christian. Greenbourne is a practising Jew.'

'I wonder if that would make a difference,' Lady Morte mused. 'It might, you know. And she's constantly criticizing the Prince of Wales for having so many Jews among his friends.'

'Then if you were to mention to her that the Prime Minister is proposing to ennoble one of them . . .'

'I can bring it up in conversation. I'm not sure it will be enough to effect your purpose.'

Augusta thought hard. 'Is there anything we can do to make the whole question a matter of more concern to Her Majesty?'

'If there were to be some public protest – questions in Parliament, perhaps, or articles in the press . . .'

'The press,' Augusta said. She thought of Arnold Hobbes. 'Yes!' she said. 'I think that could be arranged.'

Hobbes was splendidly discombobulated by Augusta's presence in his cramped, inky office. He could not make up his mind whether to tidy up, attend to her or get rid of her. Consequently he did all three in a hysterical muddle: he moved sheets of paper and bundles of proofs from the floor to the table and back again; he fetched her a chair, a glass of sherry and a plate of biscuits; and at the same time he proposed that they go elsewhere to talk. She let him run wild for a minute or two then said: 'Mr Hobbes, please sit down and listen to me.'

'Of course, of course,' he said, and he subsided into a chair and peered at her through his grimy spectacles.

She told him in a few crisp sentences about Ben Greenbourne's peerage.

'Most regrettable, most regrettable,' he blabbered nervously. 'However, I don't think *The Forum* could be accused of lack of enthusiasm in promoting the cause which you so kindly suggested to me.'

And in exchange for which you got two lucrative directorships of companies controlled by my husband, Augusta thought. 'I know it's not your fault,' she said irritably. 'The point is, what can you do about it?'

'My journal is in a difficult position,' he said worriedly. 'Having campaigned so vociferously for a banker to get a peerage, it's hard for us to turn around and protest when it actually happens.'

'But you never intended for a Jew to be so honoured.'

'True, true, although so many bankers are Jews.'

'Couldn't you write that there are enough Christian bankers for the Prime Minister to choose from?'

He remained reluctant. 'We might . . .'

'Then do so!'

'Excuse me, Mrs Pilaster, but it's not quite enough.'

'I don't understand you,' she said impatiently.

'A professional consideration, but I need what we journalists call a slant. For instance, we could accuse Disraeli – or Lord Beaconsfield, as he now is – of partiality to members of his own race. Now that would be a slant. However, he is in general a man so upright that that particular charge might not stick.'

Augusta hated dithering, but she reined in her

impatience because she could see there was a genuine problem here. She thought for a moment and was struck by an idea. 'When Disraeli took his seat in the House of Lords, was the ceremony normal?'

'In every way, I believe.'

'He took the oath of loyalty on a Christian bible?'

'Indeed.'

'Old and New Testament?'

'I begin to see your drift, Mrs Pilaster. Would Ben Greenbourne swear on a Christian bible? From what I know of him, I doubt it.'

Augusta shook her head dubiously. 'He might, though, if nothing were said about it. He's not a man to look for a confrontation. But he's very stiff-necked when challenged. If there were to be a noisy public demand for him to swear the same way as everyone else he might well rebel. He wouldn't let people say he had been pushed into anything.'

'A noisy public demand,' Hobbes mused. 'Yes . . .'

'Could you create that?'

Hobbes warmed to the idea. 'I see it already,' he said excitedly. 'BLASPHEMY IN THE HOUSE OF LORDS. Now that, Mrs Pilaster, is what we call a slant. You're quite brilliant. You ought to be a journalist yourself!'

'How flattering,' she said. The sarcasm was lost on him.

Hobbes suddenly looked pensive. 'Mr Greenbourne is a very powerful man.'

'So is Mr Pilaster.'

'Of course, of course.'

'Then I may rely on you?'

Hobbes rapidly weighed the risks and decided to back the Pilaster cause. 'Leave everything to me.'

Augusta nodded. She was beginning to feel better. Lady Morte would turn the Queen against Greenbourne, Hobbes would make an issue of it in the press, and Fortescue was standing by to whisper into the ear of the Prime Minister the name of a blameless alternative: Joseph. Once again the prospects looked good.

She stood up to go, but Hobbes had more to say. 'If I might venture a question on another topic?'

'By all means.'

'I've been offered a printing-press rather cheaply. At present, you know, we use outside printers. If we had our own press it would reduce our costs, and we could perhaps make a little extra by printing other publications as a service.'

'Obviously,' Augusta said impatiently.

'I was wondering whether Pilasters Bank might be persuaded into a commercial loan.'

It was the price of his continuing support. 'How much?'

'A hundred and sixty pounds.'

It was a peppercorn. And if he campaigned against peerages for Jews with as much energy and bile as he had brought to his campaign in favour of peerages for bankers, it would be well worth it.

He said: 'A bargain, I assure—'

'I'll speak to Mr Pilaster.' He would assent, but she did not want to let Hobbes have it too easily. He would value it more highly if it was granted reluctantly.

'Thank you. Always a pleasure to meet with you, Mrs Pilaster.'

'Doubtless,' she said, and she went out.

CHAPTER FOUR

June

[I]

THE CORDOVAN MINISTRY was quiet. The offices on the ground floor were empty, the three clerks having gone home hours ago. Micky and Rachel had given a dinner-party in the first-floor dining-room for a small group – Sir Peter Mountjoy, an under-secretary at the Foreign Office, and his wife; the Danish Minister; and the Chevalier Michele from the Italian embassy – but the guests had left and the domestic staff had cleared away. Micky was about to go out.

The novelty of being married was beginning to wear off. He had tried and failed to shock or disgust his sexually inexperienced wife. Her unfailing enthusiasm for whatever perversion he proposed was beginning to unnerve him. She had decided that whatever he wanted was all right with her, and when she made a decision like that there was no moving her. He had never met a woman who could be so implacably logical.

She would do anything he asked in bed, but she believed that outside the bedroom a woman should not be a slave to her husband, and she was equally rigid about both rules.

Consequently they were always fighting about domestic issues. Sometimes Micky could turn one situation into the other. In the middle of a row about servants or money he would say: 'Lift up your dress and lie on the floor,' and the quarrel would end in a passionate embrace. But that no longer worked every time: sometimes she would recommence the argument as soon as he rolled off her.

Lately he and Edward had been spending more and more evenings in their old haunts. Tonight was Mask Night at Nellie's brothel. This was one of April's innovations: all the women would be wearing masks. April claimed that sexually frustrated high-society ladies came in and mingled with the regular girls on Mask Nights. Certainly some of the women were not regulars, but Micky suspected that the strangers were in fact middle-class women in desperate financial straits, rather than bored aristocrats in search of degenerate thrills. Whatever the truth of the matter, Mask Night never failed to be interesting.

Micky combed his hair and filled his cigar-case, then he went downstairs. To his surprise, Rachel was standing in the hall, barring the way to the door. Her arms were folded and she wore a determined expression. He braced himself for a fight.

'It's eleven o'clock in the evening,' she said. 'Where are you going?'

'To the devil,' he replied. 'Get out of my way.' He picked up his hat and cane.

'Are you going to a brothel called Nellie's?'

He was startled enough to be silenced for a moment.

'I see you are,' she said.

'Who have you been talking to?' he said.

She hesitated, then said: 'Emily Pilaster. She told me that you and Edward go there regularly.'

'You shouldn't listen to women's gossip.'

Her face was white. He realized she was scared. That was unusual. Perhaps this fight would be different.

'You must stop going there,' she said.

'I've told you, don't try to give orders to your master.'

'It's not an order. It's an ultimatum.'

'Don't be silly. Get out of my way.'

'Unless you promise not to go there any more, I shall leave you. I'll go away from this house tonight and never come back.'

She meant it, he saw. That was why she looked scared. She even had her outdoor shoes on ready. 'You're not leaving,' he said. 'I shall lock you in your room.'

'You'll find that difficult. I've collected all the room keys and thrown them away. There isn't a single room in this house that can be locked.'

That was clever of her. It seemed that this was going to be one of their more interesting contests. He grinned at her and said: 'Take off your knickers.'

'That won't work tonight, Micky,' she said. 'I used to think it meant you loved me. Now I've realized sex is just your way of controlling people. I doubt whether you even enjoy it.'

He reached out and grasped her breast. It was warm and heavy in his hand, despite the layers of clothing. He caressed it, watching her face, but her expression did not change. He realized she was not going to give in to passion tonight. He squeezed hard, hurting her, then let go. 'What's got into you?' he said with genuine curiosity.

'Men catch infectious diseases at places such as Nellie's.'

'The girls there are very clean—'

'Please, Micky – don't pretend to be stupid.'

She was right. There was no such thing as a clean prostitute. In fact he had been very lucky: he had only caught one mild case of the pox during many years of visiting brothels. 'All right,' he conceded. 'I might catch an infectious disease.'

'And give it to me.'

He shrugged. 'It's one of the hazards of being a wife. I might give you the measles, too, if I catch it.'

'But syphilis can be hereditary.'

'What are you driving at?'

'I might give it to our children, if we have any. And that is what I am not willing to do. I will not bring a child into the world with such a dreadful disease.' She was breathing in short gasps, a sign of severe tension. She means it, he thought. She finished: 'So I'm going to leave you, unless you agree to cease all contact with prostitutes.'

There was no point in further discussion. 'We'll see whether you can leave with a broken nose,' he said, and he raised his cane to strike her.

She was ready for him. She dodged the blow and ran to the door. To Micky's surprise it was ajar – she must have opened it earlier, in anticipation of violence, he thought – and she slipped outside in a flash.

Micky went after her. Another surprise awaited him outside: there was a carriage at the kerb. Rachel jumped into it. Micky was amazed at how meticulously she had planned everything. He was about to leap into the carriage after her when his way was blocked by a large figure in a top hat. It was her father, Mr Bodwin, the lawyer.

'I take it you refuse to mend your ways,' he said.

'Are you abducting my wife?' Micky replied. He was angry at having been outmanoeuvred.

'She's leaving of her own free will.' Bodwin's voice was a little shaky, but he stood his ground. 'She will return to you whenever you agree to give up your vicious habits. Subject of course to a satisfactory medical examination.'

For a moment Micky was tempted to strike him – but

only for a moment. Violence was not Micky's style. Anyway, the lawyer would undoubtedly charge him with assault, and such a scandal could blight a diplomatic career. Rachel was not worth that.

It was a stand-off, he realized. What am I fighting for? he asked himself. 'You can keep her,' he said. 'I've finished with her.' He went back into the house and slammed the door.

He heard the carriage drive away. To his surprise he found himself regretting Rachel's departure. He had married her purely for convenience, of course – it had been a way of persuading Edward to marry – and in some respects life would be simpler without her. But in a curious way he had enjoyed the daily clash of wits. He had never had that with a woman. However, it was often tiresome too, and he told himself that on balance he would be better off alone.

When he had caught his breath, he put on his hat and went out. It was a mild summer night with a clear sky and bright stars. London's air always tasted better in summer, when people did not need to burn coal to warm their houses.

As he walked down Regent Street he turned his mind to business. Since he had had Tonio Silva beaten up a month ago he had heard no more of his article about the nitrate mines. Tonio was probably still recovering from his wounds. Micky had sent Papa a coded telegram with the names and addresses of the witnesses who had signed Tonio's affidavits, and they were probably dead by now. Hugh had been made to look foolish for having started an unnecessary scare, and Edward was delighted.

Meanwhile, Edward had got Solly Greenbourne to agree in principle to float the Santamaria Railroad bonds jointly with Pilasters. It had not been easy: Solly was as suspicious

385

of South America as most investors were. Edward had been obliged to offer a higher commission and take a share in a speculative scheme of Solly's before the deal could be closed. Edward had also played on the fact that they were old school friends, and Micky suspected it was Solly's soft-heartedness that had tipped the balance in the end.

Now they were drawing up contracts. It was a painfully slow business. What made life difficult for Micky was that Papa could not understand why these things could not be done in a few hours. He was demanding the money right away.

However, when Micky thought of the obstacles he had overcome he was quite pleased with himself. After Edward turned him down flat the task had seemed impossible. But with Augusta's help he had manoeuvred Edward into marriage and a partnership in the bank. Then he had dealt with opposition from Hugh Pilaster and Tonio Silva. Now the fruits of all his efforts were about to fall into his hands. Back home the Santamaria Railroad would always be Micky's railroad. Half a million pounds was a vast sum, greater than the military budget of the entire country. This one achievement would count for more than everything his brother Paulo had ever done.

A few minutes later he stepped into Nellie's. The party was in full swing: every table was occupied, the air was thick was cigar smoke, and ribald banter and raucous laughter could be heard over the sound of a small orchestra playing loud dance tunes. All the women wore masks. Some were simple dominoes but most were more elaborate, and a few were entire headdresses covering everything but the eyes and mouth.

Micky pushed his way through the crowd, nodding at acquaintances and kissing some of the girls. Edward was in the card-room, but he got up as soon as Micky walked in.

'April's got a virgin for us,' he said thickly. It was late, and he had drunk a lot.

Virginity had never been Micky's particular obsession, but there was always something stimulating about a girl who was frightened, and he was titillated. 'How old?'

'Seventeen.'

Which probably meant twenty-three, Micky thought, knowing how April estimated the ages of her girls. Still he was intrigued. 'Have you seen her?'

'Yes. She's masked, of course.'

'Of course.' Micky wondered what her story was. She might be a provincial girl who had run away from home and found herself destitute in London; she might have been abducted from a farm; she might just be a housemaid fed up with slaving sixteen hours a day for six shillings a week.

A woman in a little black domino touched his arm. The mask was no more than a token, and he recognized April. 'A genuine virgin,' April said.

No doubt she was charging Edward a small fortune for the privilege of taking the girl's maidenhead. 'Have you put your own hand up her, to feel her hymen?' Micky said sceptically.

April shook her head. 'I don't need to. I know when a girl is telling the truth.'

'If I don't feel it pop you won't get paid,' he said, even though they both knew Edward would be paying.

'Agreed.'

'What's her story?'

'She's an orphan, brought up by an uncle. He was eager to get her off his hands as soon as possible, and arranged for her to marry an older man. When she refused he put her out on the street. I rescued her from a life of drudgery.'

'You're an angel,' Micky said sarcastically. He did not believe a word of it. Even though he could not read April's expression behind the mask he had the strongest feeling that she was up to something. He gave her a sceptical look. 'Tell me the truth,' he said.

'I have,' April said. 'If you don't want her, there are six other men here who'll pay just as much as you.'

Edward said impatiently: 'We want her. Stop arguing, Micky. Let's have a look at her.'

'Room three,' April said. 'She's waiting for you.'

Micky and Edward made their way up the stairs, which were littered with embracing couples, and went into Room No. 3.

The girl stood in the corner. She wore a simple muslin gown, and her entire head was covered with a hood, leaving only slits for the eyes and an opening for the mouth. Once again Micky was seized by suspicion. They could see nothing of her face and head: she might be hideously ugly, perhaps deformed. Was this some kind of prank?

He realized, as he stared at her, that she was trembling with fear, and he put his doubts aside as he felt a stirring of desire in his loins. To frighten her more he crossed the room quickly, pulled the neckline of her gown aside, and plunged his hand into her bosom. She flinched, and there was terror in her bright blue eyes, but she stood her ground. She had small, firm breasts.

Her fear made him want to be brutal. Normally he and Edward would toy with a woman for a while, but he decided to take this one suddenly. 'Kneel on the bed,' he told her.

She did as he said. He got behind her and pulled up her skirt. She gave a little cry of fright. She was wearing nothing underneath.

It was easier to penetrate her than he had expected: April must have given her some cream to lubricate herself. He felt the obstruction of her maidenhead. He grabbed her hips and pulled her roughly to him as he thrust deep inside her, and the membrane broke. She began to sob, and that excited him so much that he reached his climax immediately.

He withdrew to make way for Edward. There was blood on his prick. He felt dissatisfied, now that it was over, and he wished he had stayed at home and gone to bed with Rachel. Then he remembered that she had left him and he felt worse.

Edward turned the girl over on her back. She almost rolled off the bed, and he grabbed her ankles and pulled her back into the middle. As he did so her hood came partly off.

Edward said: 'Good God!'

'What's the matter?' Micky said without much interest.

Edward was kneeling between the girl's thighs with his prick in his hand, staring at her half-revealed face. Micky realized that the girl must be someone they knew. He watched, fascinated, as she tried to tug the hood down again. Edward prevented her, and pulled it right off.

Then Micky saw the big blue eyes and child-like face of Edward's wife, Emily.

'I never heard of such a thing!' he said, and he started to laugh.

Edward gave a roar of rage. 'You filthy cow!' he yelled. 'You did this to shame me!'

'No, Edward, no!' she cried. 'To help you – to help us!'

'Now they all know!' he shouted, and he punched her face.

She screamed and struggled, and he hit her again.

Micky laughed all the more. It was the funniest thing he had ever seen: a man going into a whorehouse and meeting his own wife!

April came rushing in, in response to the screams.

'Leave her alone!' she yelled, and she tried to pull Edward off.

He pushed her aside. 'I'll chastize my own wife if I please!' he roared.

'You great big fool, she only wants to have a baby!'

'She'll have my fist instead!'

They struggled for a moment. Edward punched his wife again, then April punched him on the ear. He gave a cry of pain and surprise, making Micky collapse with hysterical laughter.

At last April managed to haul Edward off his wife.

Emily got off the bed. Astonishingly, she did not immediately rush out. Instead she spoke to her husband. 'Please don't give up, Edward. I'll do anything you want, anything!'

He lunged at her again. April clung to his legs and tripped him up. He fell to his knees. April said: 'Get out, Emily, before he kills you!'

Emily rushed out, weeping.

Edward was still raging. 'I'll never come to this poxy whorehouse again!' he yelled, wagging his finger at April.

Micky fell on the sofa, holding his sides, laughing fit to bust.

[II]

MAISIE GREENBOURNE'S Midsummer Ball was one of the fixtures of the London season. She always had the best band, the most delicious food, outrageously extravagant decorations, and endless champagne. But the main reason everyone wanted to go was that the Prince of Wales always came.

This year Maisie decided to use the occasion to launch the new Nora Pilaster.

It was a high-risk strategy, for if it went wrong both Nora and Maisie would be humiliated. But if it went well no one would ever dare to snub Nora again.

Maisie gave a small dinner for twenty-four people earlier in the evening, before the ball. The prince could not come to the dinner. Hugh and Nora were there, and Nora looked quite bewitching in a gauzy sky-blue gown covered with little satin bows. The off-the-shoulder style made the most of her pink skin and voluptuous figure.

The other guests were surprised to see her at the table, but assumed Maisie knew what she was doing. She hoped they were right. She understood how the prince's mind worked, and she was fairly sure she could predict his reactions; but now and again he defied expectations and turned on his friends, particularly if he felt he was being used. If that happened Maisie would end up like Nora, cold-shouldered by London society. When she thought about it she was amazed that she had allowed herself to take that risk merely for the sake of Nora. But it was not for Nora, it was for Hugh.

Hugh was working out his notice at Pilasters Bank. It was now two months since he had resigned. Solly was impatient for Hugh to start at Greenbournes, but the Pilasters partners had insisted he stay the full three months. No doubt they wanted to postpone as long as possible the moment when Hugh went to work for their rivals.

After dinner Maisie talked briefly to Nora as the ladies used the bathroom. 'Stay as close to me as you can,' she said. 'When the moment comes for me to present you to the prince, I won't be able to go looking for you: you'll have to be right there.'

'I'll stick to you like a Scotchman to a five-pound note,' Nora said in her cockney accent, then she changed to an upper-class drawl and said: 'Never fear! I shan't run off!'

The guests began to arrive at ten-thirty. Maisie did not normally invite Augusta Pilaster, but she had this year, wanting Augusta to see Nora's triumph, if triumph it should be. She had half-expected Augusta to decline, but she was among the first to arrive. Maisie had also invited Hugh's New York mentor, Sidney Madler, a charming man of about sixty with a white beard. He turned up in a distinctly American version of evening dress, with a short jacket and a black tie.

Maisie and Solly stood shaking hands for an hour, then the prince arrived. They escorted him into the ballroom and presented Solly's father. Ben Greenbourne bowed stiffly from the waist, as straight-backed as a Prussian guardsman. Then Maisie danced with the prince.

'I've a splendid titbit of gossip for you, sir,' she said as they waltzed. 'Although I hope it won't make you cross.'

He held her closer and spoke in her ear. 'How intriguing, Mrs Greenbourne – do go on.'

'It's about the incident at the Duchess of Tenbigh's ball.'

She felt him go stiff. 'Ah, yes. Faintly embarrassing, I do confess.' He lowered his voice. 'When that girl called de Tokoly a filthy old reprobate I thought for a minute she was talking to me!'

Maisie laughed gaily, as if the idea were absurd, although she knew that quite a lot of people had made the same assumption.

'But do go on,' said the prince. 'Was there more to it than met the eye?'

'It seems so. De Tokoly had been told, quite falsely, that the young woman was, how shall I put it, open to invitation.'

'Open to invitation!' He chuckled fruitily. 'I must remember that one.'

'And she, for her part, had been warned to slap him instantly if he tried to take liberties.'

'So there was almost certain to be a scene. Cunning. Who was behind it all?'

Maisie hesitated momentarily. She had never before used her friendship with the prince to do someone down. But Augusta was wicked enough to deserve it. 'Do you know who I mean by Augusta Pilaster?'

'Indeed. Matriarch of the *other* banking family.'

'It was she. The girl, Nora, is married to Augusta's nephew, Hugh. Augusta did it to spite Hugh, whom she hates.'

'What a snake she must be! But she ought not to cause such scenes when I am present. I rather feel like punishing her.'

This was the moment Maisie had been leading up to. 'All you would have to do is notice Nora, to show that she is forgiven,' she said; and she held her breath for his reply.

'And ignore Augusta, perhaps. Yes, I think I might do that.'

The dance ended. Maisie said: 'Shall I present Nora to you? She's here tonight.'

He looked at her shrewdly. 'Did you plan all this, you little minx?'

She had been afraid of this. He was not stupid and he could guess that she had been scheming. It would be better not to deny it. She looked bashful and did her best to blush. 'You have found me out. How foolish of me to think I might pull the wool over *your* eagle eyes.' She changed her expression and favoured him with a direct, candid gaze. 'What shall I do for a penance?'

A lascivious smile passed over his face. 'Don't tempt me. Come, I forgive you.'

Maisie breathed easier: she had got away with it. Now it was up to Nora to charm him.

'Where is this Nora?' he said.

She was hovering close by, as instructed. Maisie caught her eye and she approached instantly. Maisie said: 'Your Royal Highness, may I present Mrs Hugh Pilaster?'

Nora curtsied and batted her eyelashes.

The prince eyed her bare shoulders and plump, rosy bosom. 'Charming,' he said enthusiastically. 'Quite charming.'

Hugh watched in astonishment and delight as Nora chatted happily with the Prince of Wales.

Yesterday she had been a social outcast, living proof that you can't make a silk purse out of a sow's ear. She had lost the bank a big contract and run Hugh's career into a brick wall. Now she was the envy of every woman in the room: her clothes were perfect, her manners were charming and she was flirting with the heir to the throne. And the transformation had been brought about by Maisie.

Hugh glanced at his Aunt Augusta, standing near him, with Uncle Joseph by her side. She was staring at Nora and the prince. Augusta was trying to look unconcerned, but Hugh could see she was horrified. How it must gall her, Hugh thought, to know that Maisie, the working-class girl she derided six years ago, is now so much more influential than she is.

With perfect timing, Sidney Madler came over. Looking incredulous, he said to Joseph: 'Is *that* the woman you say is hopelessly unsuitable to be a banker's wife?'

Before Joseph could reply, Augusta spoke. In a

deceptively mild voice she said: 'She did lose the bank a major contract.'

Hugh said: 'As a matter of fact, she didn't. That loan is going through.'

Augusta turned on Joseph. 'Count de Tokoly didn't interfere?'

'He seems to have got over his fit of pique rather quickly,' Joseph said.

Augusta had to pretend to be pleased. 'How fortunate,' she said, but her insincerity was transparent.

Madler said: 'Financial need generally outweighs social prejudice in the end.'

'Yes,' said Joseph. 'So it does. I think I may have been too hasty in denying Hugh a partnership.'

Augusta interrupted in a voice of deadly sweetness. 'Joseph, what are you saying?'

'This is business, my dear – men's talk,' he said firmly. 'You need not concern yourself with it.' He turned to Hugh. 'We certainly don't want you working for Greenbournes.'

Hugh did not know what to say. He knew that Sidney Madler had made a fuss, and that Uncle Samuel had backed him – but it was almost unknown for Uncle Joseph to admit a mistake. And yet, he thought with mounting excitement, why else was Joseph raising the subject? 'You know why I'm going to Greenbournes, Uncle,' he said.

'They'll never make you a partner, you know,' Joseph said. 'You have to be Jewish for that.'

'I'm well aware of it.'

'Given that, wouldn't you rather work for the family?'

Hugh felt let down: after all, Joseph was only trying to talk him into staying on as an employee. 'No, I wouldn't rather work for the family,' he said indignantly. He saw that his uncle was taken aback by his strength of feeling. He went on: 'To be quite honest, I'd prefer to work for the

395

Greenbournes, where I would be free from family intrigues' – he darted a defiant glance at Augusta – 'and where my responsibility and rewards would depend on nothing but my ability as a banker.'

Augusta said in a scandalized tone: 'You prefer Jews to your own family?'

'Keep out of this,' Joseph told her brusquely. 'You know why I'm saying all this, Hugh. Mr Madler feels that we have let him down, and all the partners are worried about your taking our North American business with you when you go.'

Hugh tried to steady his nerves. It was time to drive a hard bargain. 'I wouldn't come back if you doubled my salary,' he said, burning his boats. 'There's only one thing you can offer me that would make me change my mind, and that's a partnership.'

Joseph sighed. 'You're the very devil to negotiate with.'

Madler put in: 'As every good banker should be.'

'Very well,' Joseph said at last. 'I'm offering you a partnership.'

Hugh felt weak. They've backed down, he thought. They've given in. I've won. He could hardly believe it had really happened.

He glanced at Augusta. Her face was a rigid mask of self-control, but she said nothing: she knew she had lost.

'In that case . . .' he said, and he hesitated, savouring the moment. He took a deep breath. 'In that case, I accept.'

Augusta finally lost her composure. She turned red and her eyes seemed to bulge. 'You're going to regret this for the rest of your lives!' she spat. Then she stalked off.

She cut a swathe through the crowd in the ballroom as she headed for the door. People stared at her and looked nervous. She realized her rage was showing on her face, and she wished she could hide her feelings, but she was too distraught. All the people she loathed and despised had triumphed. The guttersnipe Maisie, the underbred Hugh and the appalling Nora had thwarted her and got what they wanted. Her stomach was twisted in knots of frustration and she felt nauseated.

At last she reached the door and passed out on to the first-floor landing, where the crowd was thinner. She buttonholed a passing footman. 'Call Mrs Pilaster's carriage instantly!' she commanded. He went off at a run. At least she could still intimidate footmen.

She left the party without speaking to anyone else. Her husband could go home in a hansom. She fumed all the way to Kensington.

When she got to the house her butler, Hastead, was waiting in the hall. 'Mr Hobbes is in the drawing-room, ma'am,' he said sleepily. 'I told him you might not be back until dawn, but he insisted on waiting.'

'What the dickens does he want?'

'He didn't say.'

Augusta was in no mood to see the editor of *The Forum*. What was he doing here in the early hours of the morning? She was tempted to ignore him and go straight to her room, but then she thought of the peerage and decided she had better talk to him.

She went into the drawing-room. Hobbes was asleep by the dying fire. 'Good morning!' Augusta said loudly.

He started and sprang to his feet, peering at her through his smeared spectacles. 'Mrs Pilaster! Good – ah, yes, morning.'

'What brings you here so late?'

'I thought you would like to be the first to see this,' he said, and he handed her a journal.

It was the new number of *The Forum*, still warm and smelling of the printing-press. She opened it to the title page and read the headline over the leading article:

CAN A JEW BE A LORD?

Her spirits lifted. Tonight's fiasco was only one defeat, she reminded herself. There were other battles to be fought. She read the first few lines:

We trust there is no truth in the rumours, currently circulating at Westminster and in the London clubs, that the Prime Minister is contemplating the grant of a peerage to a prominent banker of the Jewish race and faith.

We have never favoured persecution of heathen religions. However, tolerance can go too far. To give the highest accolade to one who openly rejects Christian salvation would be perilously close to blasphemy.

Of course, the Prime Minister himself is a Jew by race. But he has been converted, and took his oath of allegiance to Her Majesty on the Christian bible. No constitutional question was therefore raised by his ennoblement. But we have to ask whether the unbaptized banker of whom rumour speaks would be prepared so far to compromise his faith as to swear on the combined Old and New Testaments. If he were to insist on the Old Testament alone, how could the bishops in the House of Lords stand by without protest?

We have no doubt that the man himself is a loyal citizen and an honest man of business. . . .

There was much more of the same. Augusta was pleased. She looked up from the page. 'Well done,' she said. 'That should cause a stir.'

'I hope so.' With a quick, bird-like gesture, Hobbes reached inside his jacket and pulled out a sheet of paper. 'I have taken the liberty of contracting to buy the printing-press I mentioned to you. The bill of sale—'

'Go to the bank in the morning,' Augusta snapped, ignoring the proffered paper. Somehow she could never bring herself to be civil to Hobbes for long, even when he had served her well. Something about his manner irritated her. She made an effort to be more pleasant. In a softer voice she said: 'My husband will give you a cheque.'

Hobbes bowed. 'In that case I will take my leave.' He went out.

Augusta breathed a sigh of satisfaction. This would show them all. Maisie Greenbourne thought she was the leader of London society. Well, she could dance with the Prince of Wales all night long, but she couldn't fight the power of the press. It would take the Greenbournes a long time to recover from this onslaught. And meanwhile Joseph would have his peerage.

Feeling better, she sat down to read the article again.

[III]

O N T H E M O R N I N G after the ball Hugh woke up feeling jubilant. His wife had been accepted into high society and he was going to be made a partner in Pilasters Bank. The partnership gave him the chance to make not just thousands of pounds but, over the years, hundreds of thousands. One day he would be rich.

Solly would be disappointed that Hugh would not be working for him after all. But Solly was nothing if not easygoing: he would understand.

He put on his robe. From his bedside drawer he took a gift-wrapped jeweller's box and slipped it into his pocket. Then he went into his wife's bedroom.

Nora's room was large but it always felt cramped. The windows, the mirrors and the bed were all draped with patterned silk; the floor was covered with rugs two and three deep; the chairs were piled with embroidered cushions; and every shelf and tabletop was crowded with framed pictures, china dolls, miniature porcelain boxes and other knick-knacks. The predominant colours were her favourite pink and blue, but just about every other colour was represented somewhere, in the wallpapers, bedclothes, curtains or upholstery.

Nora was sitting up in bed, surrounded by lace pillows, sipping tea. Hugh perched on the edge of the bed and said: 'You were wonderful last night.'

'I showed them all,' she said, looking pleased with herself. 'I danced with the Prince of Wales.'

'He couldn't stop looking at your bosom,' Hugh said. He reached over and caressed her breasts through the silk of her high-buttoned nightdress.

She pushed his hand aside irritably. 'Hugh! Not now.'

He felt hurt. 'Why not now?'

'It's the second time this week.'

'When we were first married we used to do it constantly.'

'Exactly – when we were first married. A girl doesn't expect to have to do it every day for ever.'

Hugh frowned. He would have been perfectly happy to do it every day for ever – wasn't that what marriage was all about? But he did not know what was normal. Perhaps he was over-active. 'How often do you think we should do it, then?' he said uncertainly.

She looked pleased to have been asked, as if she had been waiting for an opportunity to clear this up. 'Not more than once a week,' she said firmly.

'Really?' His feeling of exultation went away and he suddenly felt very cast down. A week seemed an awfully long time. He stroked her thigh through the sheets. 'Perhaps a little more than that.'

'No!' she said, moving her leg.

Hugh was upset. Once upon a time she had seemed enthusiastic about lovemaking. It had been something they enjoyed together. How had it become a chore she performed for his benefit? Had she never really liked it, but just pretended? There was something dreadfully depressing about that idea.

He no longer felt like giving her his gift, but he had bought it and he did not want to take it back to the shop. 'Well, anyway, I got you this, to commemorate your triumph at Maisie Greenbourne's ball,' he said rather dolefully, and he gave her the box.

Her manner changed instantly. 'Oh, Hugh, you know how I love presents!' she said. She tore off the ribbon and opened the box. It contained a pendant in the shape of a spray of flowers, made of rubies and sapphires on gold stems. The pendant hung from a fine gold chain. 'It's beautiful,' she said.

'Put it on, then.'

She put it over her head.

The pendant did not show to best advantage against the front of her nightdress. 'It will look better with a low-cut evening gown,' Hugh said.

Nora gave him a coquettish look and began to unbutton her nightdress. Hugh watched hungrily as she exposed more and more of her chest. The brooch hung in the swelling of her cleavage like a drop of rain on a rosebud. She smiled at Hugh and carried on undoing buttons, then she pulled the nightdress open, showing him her bare breasts. 'Do you want to kiss them?' she said.

Now he did not know what to think. Was she toying with him or did she want to make love? He leaned over and kissed her breasts with the jewel nestling between them. He took her nipple into his mouth and sucked it gently.

'Come to bed,' she said.

'I thought you said . . .'

'Well . . . a girl has to show she's grateful, doesn't she?' She drew back the covers.

Hugh felt sick. It was the jewellery that had changed her mind. All the same he could not resist the invitation. He shrugged out of his dressing-gown, hating himself for being so weak, and climbed in beside her.

When he came, he felt like crying.

With Hugh's morning mail there was a letter from Tonio Silva.

Tonio had vanished shortly after Hugh met him in Plage's Coffee House. No article had appeared in *The Times*. Hugh had looked rather foolish, having made such a fuss about the danger to the bank. Edward had taken every opportunity to remind the partners of Hugh's false alarm. However, the incident had been eclipsed by the drama of Hugh's threatened move to Greenbournes.

Hugh had written to the Hotel Russe but got no reply. He had been worried about his friend, but there was no more he could do.

He opened the letter anxiously. It came from a hospital, asking Hugh to visit. The letter finished: 'Whatever you do, *tell no one where I am.*'

What had happened? Tonio had been in perfect health two months ago. And why was he in a public hospital? Hugh was dismayed. Only the poor went to hospitals, which were grim, insanitary places: anyone who could afford it had doctors and nurses come to the house, even for operations.

Mystified and concerned, Hugh went straight to the hospital. He found Tonio in a dark, bare ward of thirty close-packed beds. His ginger hair had been shaved and his face and head were scarred. 'Dear God!' Hugh said. 'Have you been run over?'

'Beaten up,' said Tonio.

'What happened?'

'I was attacked in the street outside the Hotel Russe a couple of months ago.'

'You were robbed, I suppose.'

'Yes.'

'You're a mess!'

'It's not quite as bad as it looks. I had a broken finger and a cracked ankle, but otherwise it was only cuts and bruises – although rather a lot of them. However, I'm almost better now.'

'You should have contacted me before. We must get you out of here. I'll send my doctor to you, and arrange a nurse—'

'No, thanks, old boy. I appreciate your generosity. But money isn't the only reason I stayed here. It's also safer. Other than you, only one person knows where I am: a trusted colleague who brings me beefsteak pies and brandy and messages from Cordova. I hope you didn't tell anyone you were coming.'

'Not even my wife,' Hugh said.

'Good.'

Tonio's old recklessness seemed to have vanished, Hugh thought; in fact he was going to the other extreme. 'But you can't stay in hospital for the rest of your life to hide from street ruffians.'

'The people who attacked me were not just thieves, Pilaster.'

Hugh took off his hat and sat on the edge of the bed. He

tried to ignore the intermittent groaning of the man in the next bed. 'Tell me what happened,' he said.

'It wasn't a routine theft. My key was taken and the thieves used it to get into my room. Nothing of value was stolen but all the papers pertaining to my article for *The Times* were taken, including the affidavits signed by the witnesses.'

Hugh was horrified. It chilled his heart to think that the immaculately respectable transactions taking place in the hushed halls of Pilasters should have any link with violent crime in the streets and the battered face in front of him. 'It almost sounds as if the bank is under suspicion.'

'Not the bank,' Tonio said. 'Pilasters is a powerful institution, but I don't believe it could organize murders in Cordova.'

'Murders?' This was getting worse and worse. 'Who has been murdered?'

'All the witnesses whose names and addresses were on the affidavits that were stolen from my hotel room.'

'I can hardly believe it.'

'I'm lucky to be alive myself. They would have killed me, I think, were it not that murders are investigated more thoroughly here in London than they are back at home, and they were afraid of the fuss.'

Hugh was still dazed and disgusted by the revelation that people had been murdered because of a bond issue by Pilasters Bank. 'But who is behind all this?'

'Micky Miranda.'

Hugh shook his head incredulously. 'I'm not fond of Micky, as you know, but I can't believe he would do this.'

'The Santamaria Railroad is vital to him. It will make his family the second most powerful in the land.'

'I realize that, and I don't doubt that Micky would bend a lot of rules to achieve his aims. But he's not a killer.'

'Yes, he is,' Tonio said.

'Come on.'

'I know it for sure. I haven't always acted as if I knew – in fact I've been a damn fool about Miranda. But that's because he has a devilish charm. For a while he made me think he was my friend. The truth is that he's evil through and through and I've known it since school.'

'How could you?'

Tonio shifted in the bed. 'I know what really happened thirteen years ago, the afternoon Peter Middleton drowned in the swimming-hole at Bishop's Wood.'

Hugh was electrified. He had been wondering about this for years. Peter Middleton had been a strong swimmer: it was most unlikely that he had died by accident. Hugh had long been convinced that there had been some kind of foul play. Perhaps at last he was going to learn the truth. 'Go on, man,' he said. 'I can't wait to hear this.'

Tonio hesitated. 'Could you give me a little wine?' he said. There was a bottle of madeira on the floor beside the bed. Hugh poured some into a glass. While Tonio sipped it, Hugh recalled the heat of that day, the stillness of the air in Bishop's Wood, the scarred rock walls of the swimming-hole, and the cold, cold water.

'The coroner was told that Peter was in difficulty in the pool. He was never told that Edward was ducking him repeatedly.'

'I knew that much,' Hugh interrupted. 'I had a letter from "Hump" Cammel in the Cape Colony. He was watching from the far side of the pool. But he didn't stay to see the end.'

'That's right. You escaped and Hump ran away. That left me, Peter, Edward and Micky.'

'What happened after I left?' Hugh said impatiently.

'I got out and threw a stone at Edward. It was a lucky

shot: it hit him square in the middle of the forehead, and drew blood. It caused him to leave off tormenting Peter and come after me. I scrambled up the side of the quarry, trying to get away from him.'

'Edward was never light on his feet, even then,' Hugh observed.

'That's right. I got well ahead of him then, half-way up I looked back. Micky was continuing to bully Peter. Peter had swum to the side and was trying to get out of the water, but Micky kept pushing his head under. I only glanced at them for a moment, but I could see very clearly what was going on. Then I continued to climb.'

He took another sip of the wine. 'When I got to the rim of the quarry I looked back again. Edward was still coming after me but he was a long way behind and I had time to catch my breath.' Tonio paused, and an expression of revulsion crossed his bruised face. 'By this time Micky was in the water with Peter. What I saw – perfectly clearly, and I can see it in my memory now as if it were yesterday – was Micky holding Peter under the water. Peter was thrashing about, but Micky had Peter's head under his arm and Peter couldn't break the hold. Micky was drowning him. There is absolutely no doubt about it. It was straightforward murder.'

'Dear God,' Hugh breathed.

Tonio nodded. 'It makes me feel ill to think of it even now. I stared at them for I don't know how long. Edward almost caught me. Peter had stopped thrashing about, and was just struggling feebly, when Edward reached the rim of the quarry and I had to run away.'

'So that's how Peter died.' Hugh was stunned and horrified.

'Edward followed me through the woods a little way, but he was puffed out and I shook him off. Then I found you.'

Hugh remembered the thirteen-year-old Tonio wandering through Bishop's Wood, naked, wet, carrying his clothes and sobbing. The memory brought back the shock and pain he had suffered later that same day, when he learned that his father was dead. 'But why did you never tell anyone what you had seen?'

'I was afraid of Micky – afraid he'd do to me what he did to Peter. I'm still afraid of Micky – look at me now! You should be afraid of him too.'

'I am, don't worry.' Hugh was thoughtful. 'You know, I don't believe Edward and Augusta know the truth about this.'

'What makes you say so?'

'They had no reason to cover up for Micky.'

Tonio looked dubious. 'Edward might have, out of friendship.'

'Perhaps – although I doubt he could have kept the secret more than a day or two. Anyway, Augusta knew that the story they had told, about Edward trying to rescue Peter, was a lie.'

'How did she know that?'

'My mother told her, and I told my mother. Which means that Augusta was involved in covering up the truth. Now, I can believe that Augusta would tell any amount of lies for the sake of her son – but not for Micky. In those days she didn't even know him.'

'So what do you think happened?'

Hugh frowned. 'Imagine this. Edward gives up chasing you and goes back to the swimming-hole. He finds Micky dragging Peter's body out of the water. As Edward arrives, Micky says: "You fool, you've killed him!" Remember, Edward hasn't seen Micky holding Peter's head under. Micky pretends that Peter was so exhausted by Edward's ducking that he could swim no longer and he just drowned.

"What am I going to do?" says Edward. Micky says: "Don't worry. We'll say it was an accident. In fact, we'll say you jumped in and tried to rescue him." Micky thereby covers up his own crime and earns the undying gratitude of both Edward and Augusta. Does that make sense?'

Tonio nodded. 'By God, I think you're right.'

'We must go to the police,' Hugh said angrily.

'To what purpose?'

'You're witness to a murder. The fact that it happened thirteen years ago makes no difference. Micky must be brought to book.'

'You're forgetting something. Micky has diplomatic immunity.'

Hugh had not thought of that. As the Cordovan Minister, Micky could not be put on trial in Britain. 'He could still be disgraced and sent home.'

Tonio shook his head. 'I'm the only witness. Micky and Edward will both tell a different story. And it's well known that Micky's family and mine are sworn enemies back home. If it had happened yesterday we'd have trouble convincing anyone.' Tonio paused. 'But you might want to tell Edward that he's not a murderer.'

'I don't think he'd believe me. He'd suspect me of trying to stir up trouble between him and Micky. There is one person I must tell, though.'

'Who?'

'David Middleton.'

'Why?'

'I think he's entitled to know how his brother died,' Hugh said. 'He questioned me about it at the Duchess of Tenbigh's ball. He was rather rude, in fact. But I said that if I knew the truth I would be honour bound to tell him. I'll go and see him today.'

'Do you think he'll go to the police?'

408

'I assume he'll see that it would be pointless, as you and I have realized.'

Suddenly he felt oppressed by the drab hospital ward and the grim talk of past murder. 'I'd better go to work.' He stood up. 'I'm going to be made a partner in the bank.'

'Congratulations! I'm sure you deserve it.' Tonio suddenly looked hopeful. 'Will you be able to stop the Santamaria Railroad?'

Hugh shook his head. 'I'm sorry, Tonio. Much as I dislike the project, I can't do anything about it now. Edward has made a deal with Greenbournes Bank to float the bonds jointly. The partners of both banks have approved the issue and contracts are being drawn up. I'm afraid we've lost that battle.'

'Damn.' Tonio was crestfallen.

'Your family will have to find other ways to oppose the Mirandas.'

'I fear they may be unstoppable.'

'I'm sorry,' Hugh repeated. A new thought struck him and he frowned in puzzlement. 'You know, you've solved a mystery for me. I couldn't understand how Peter drowned when he was such a good swimmer. But your answer is an even greater mystery.'

'I'm not sure I follow you.'

'Think about it. Peter was innocently swimming; Edward ducked him, just out of general nastiness; we all ran away; Edward gave chase – and then Micky cold-bloodedly killed Peter. *It has nothing to do with what went before.* Why did it happen? What had Peter done?'

'I see what you mean. Yes, it's puzzled me for years.'

'Micky Miranda murdered Peter Middleton . . . but why?'

CHAPTER FIVE

July

[I]

AUGUSTA WAS like a hen that had laid an egg on the day Joseph's peerage was announced. Micky went to the house at tea-time as usual and found the drawing-room crowded with people congratulating her on becoming the Countess of Whitehaven. Her butler Hastead was wearing a smug smile and saying 'my lady' and 'your ladyship' at every opportunity.

She was amazing, Micky thought as he watched them buzzing around her like the bees in the sunny garden outside the open windows. She had planned her campaign like a general. At one point there had been a rumour that Ben Greenbourne was to get the peerage, but that had been killed by an eruption of anti-Jewish sentiment in the press. Augusta was not admitting, even to Micky, that she had been behind the press coverage, but he was sure of it. In some ways she reminded him of his father: Papa had the same remorseless determination. But Augusta was cleverer. Micky's admiration for her grew as the years went by.

The only person who had ever defeated her ingenuity

was Hugh Pilaster. It was astonishing how difficult he was to crush. Like a persistent garden weed, he could be stamped on time and time again and he would always grow back straighter and stronger than ever.

Happily, Hugh had been unable to stop the Santamaria Railroad. Micky and Edward had proved too strong for Hugh and Tonio. 'By the way,' Micky said to Edward over the teacups, 'when are you going to sign the contract with Greenbournes?'

'Tomorrow.'

'Good!' Micky would be relieved when the deal was finally sewn up. It had dragged on for half a year, and Papa was now sending angry cables every week asking irascibly if he would ever get the money.

That evening Edward and Micky dined at the Cowes Club. Throughout the meal Edward was interrupted every few minutes by people congratulating him. One day he would inherit the title, of course. Micky was pleased. His association with Edward and the Pilasters had been a key factor in everything he had achieved, and greater prestige for the Pilasters would mean more power for Micky.

After dinner they moved to the smoking-room. They were among the earliest diners and for a while they had the room to themselves. 'I have come to the conclusion that Englishmen are terrified of their wives,' said Micky as they lit their cigars. 'It is the only possible explanation for the phenomenon of the London club.'

'What the devil are you talking about?' said Edward.

'Look around you,' Micky said. 'This place is exactly like your home, or mine. Expensive furniture, servants everywhere, boring food and unlimited drink. We can eat all our meals here, get our mail, read the newspapers, take a nap, and if we get too drunk to fall into a cab we can even get a bed for the night. The only difference between an Englishman's club and his home is that there are no women in his club.'

'Don't you have clubs in Cordova, then?'

'Certainly not. No one would join. If a Cordovan man wants to get drunk, play cards, hear political gossip, talk about his whores, smoke and belch and fart in comfort he does it in his own home; and if his wife is foolish enough to object he slaps her until she sees reason. But an English gentleman is so frightened of his wife that he has to leave the house to enjoy himself. That's why there are clubs.'

'You don't seem to be frightened of Rachel. You've got rid of her, haven't you?'

'Sent her back to her mother,' Micky said airily. It had not happened quite that way but he was not going to tell Edward the truth.

'People must notice that she doesn't appear at Ministry functions any more. Don't they comment?'

'I tell them she's in poor health.'

'But everyone knows she's trying to start a hospital for unmarried women to have babies. It's a public scandal.'

'It doesn't matter. People sympathize with me for having a difficult wife.'

'Will you divorce her?'

'No. That would be a real scandal. A diplomat can't be divorced. I'm stuck with her as long as I'm the Cordovan Minister, I'm afraid. Thank God she didn't get pregnant before she left.' It was a miracle she hadn't, he thought. Perhaps she was infertile. He waved at a waiter and ordered brandy. 'Speaking of wives,' he said tentatively, 'what about Emily?'

Edward looked embarrassed. 'I see as little of her as you see of Rachel,' he said. 'You know I bought a country

house in Leicestershire a while ago – she spends all her time there.'

'So, we're both bachelors again.'

Edward grinned. 'We were never anything else, really, were we?'

Micky glanced across the empty room and saw the bulky form of Solly Greenbourne in the doorway. For some reason the sight of him made Micky feel nervous – which was odd, because Solly was the most harmless man in London. 'Here comes another friend to congratulate you,' Micky said to Edward as Solly approached.

When Solly was closer Micky realized he was not wearing his usual amiable smile. In fact he looked positively angry. That was rare. Micky felt intuitively that there was some problem with the Santamaria Railroad deal. He told himself that he was worrying like an old woman. But Solly was never angry. . . .

Anxiety made Micky fatuously amicable. 'Hello, Solly, old boy – how's the genius of the Square Mile?'

Solly was not interested in Micky, however. Without even acknowledging the greeting, he rudely turned his vast back on Micky and faced Edward. 'Pilaster, you're a damned cad,' he said.

Micky was astonished and horrified. Solly and Edward were on the point of signing the deal. This was very grave – Solly never quarrelled with people. What on earth had brought it about?

Edward was equally mystified. 'What the devil are you talking about, Greenbourne?'

Solly reddened and he could hardly speak. 'I've discovered that you and that witch you call Mother are behind those filthy articles in *The Forum*.'

'Oh, no!' Micky said to himself in dismay. This was a

413

catastrophe. He had suspected Augusta's involvement, although he had no evidence – but how on earth had Solly found out?

The same question occurred to Edward. 'Who's been filling your fat head with such rot?'

'One of your mother's cronies is a lady-in-waiting to the Queen,' Solly replied. Micky guessed he was speaking of Harriet Morte: Augusta seemed to have some kind of hold over her. Solly went on: 'She let the cat out of the bag – she told the Prince of Wales. I've just been with him.'

Solly must be practically insane with anger to speak so indiscreetly about a private conversation with royalty, Micky thought. It was a case of a gentle soul being pushed too far. He could not see how a quarrel such as this could possibly be patched up – certainly not in time for the signing of the contract tomorrow.

He tried desperately to cool the temperature. 'Solly, old man, you can't be sure this story is true—'

Solly rounded on him. His eyes were bulging and he was perspiring. 'Can't I? When I read in today's newspaper that Joseph Pilaster has got the peerage that was expected to go to Ben Greenbourne?'

'All the same—'

'Can you imagine what this means to my father?'

Micky began to understand how the armour of Solly's amiability had been breached. It was not for himself that he was angry, but for his father. Ben Greenbourne's grandfather had arrived in London with a bale of Russian furs, a five-pound note and a hole in his boot. For Ben to take a seat in the House of Lords would be the ultimate badge of acceptance into English society. No doubt Joseph too would like to crown his career with a peerage – his family had also risen by their own efforts – but it would be much more of an achievement for a Jew. Greenbourne's peerage would have been a triumph not just for himself and his family but for the entire Jewish community in Britain.

Edward said: 'I can't help it if you're a Jew.'

Micky butted in quickly. 'You two shouldn't let your parents come between you. After all, you're partners in a major business enterprise—'

'Don't be a damned fool, Miranda,' Solly said with a savagery that made Micky flinch. 'You can forget about the Santamaria Railroad, or any other joint venture with Greenbournes Bank. After our partners hear this story, they'll never do business with the Pilasters again.'

Micky tasted bile in his throat as he watched Solly leave the room. It was easy to forget how very powerful these bankers were – especially the unprepossessing Solly. Yet in a moment of fury he could wipe out all Micky's hopes with one simple sentence.

'Damned insolence,' Edward said feebly. 'Typical Jew.'

Micky almost told him to shut up. Edward would survive the collapse of this deal but Micky might not. Papa would be disappointed and angry and would look for someone to punish, and Micky would bear the brunt of his rage.

Was there really no hope? He tried to stop feeling destroyed and start thinking. Was there anything he could do to prevent Solly cancelling the deal? If there were, it would have to be done quickly, for once Solly told the other Greenbournes what he had learned, they would all turn against the deal.

Could Solly be talked round?

Micky had to try.

He stood up abruptly.

'Where are you going?' Edward said.

Micky decided not to tell Edward what he had in mind. 'To the card-room,' he replied. 'Don't you want to play?'

'Yes, of course.' Edward heaved himself out of his chair and they walked out of the room.

At the foot of the stairs Micky turned aside toward the toilets, saying: 'You go on up – I'll catch you.'

Edward went upstairs. Micky stepped into the cloakroom, grabbed his hat and cane, and dashed out through the front door.

He looked up and down Pall Mall, terrified that Solly might already be out of sight. It was dusk, and the gaslights were being lit. Micky could not see Solly anywhere. Then, a hundred yards away, he spotted him, a big figure in evening dress and a top hat heading toward St James's at a brisk waddle.

Micky went after him.

He would explain to Solly how important the railroad was to him and to Cordova. He would say that Solly was punishing millions of impoverished peasants on account of something Augusta had done. Solly was soft-hearted: if only he would calm down he might yet be talked around.

He had said he had just been with the Prince of Wales. That meant he might not yet have had time to tell anyone else the secret he had learned from the prince – that Augusta had arranged the anti-Jewish propaganda in the press. No one had overheard the row in the club: the smoking-room had been empty but for the three of them. In all probability Ben Greenbourne did not yet know who had cheated him out of his peerage.

Of course the truth might come out eventually. The Prince might tell someone else. But the contract was to be signed tomorrow. If the secret could be kept until then, all would be well. After that, the Greenbournes and the

Pilasters could quarrel until kingdom come: Papa would have his railroad.

Pall Mall was crowded with prostitutes strolling along the pavements, men going in and out of the clubs, lamplighters going about their work, and carriages and hansom cabs bowling along the road. Micky had trouble catching up. Panic bubbled up inside him. Then Solly turned up a side street, heading towards his house in Piccadilly.

Micky followed. The side street was less busy. Micky broke into a run. 'Greenbourne!' he called. 'Wait!'

Solly stopped and turned, breathing hard. He recognized Micky and turned away again.

Micky grabbed his arm. 'I must talk to you!'

Solly was so breathless he could hardly speak. 'Take your damned hands off me,' he panted. He broke away from Micky and walked on.

Micky went after him and grabbed him again. Solly tried to pull his arm away but this time Micky held on. 'Listen to me!'

'I told you to leave me alone!' Solly said fiercely.

'Just a minute, damn it!' Micky was getting angry now.

But Solly would not listen. He struggled furiously, jerked himself violently out of Micky's grasp, and turned away.

Two steps later he came to a cross-street and was forced to stop at the kerb as a carriage went by fast. Micky took the opportunity to speak to him again. 'Solly, calm down!' he said. 'I only want to reason with you!'

'Go to the devil!' Solly shouted.

The road cleared. To stop him moving away again Micky grabbed Solly's lapels. Solly struggled to free himself but Micky held on. 'Listen to me!' he yelled.

'Let me go!' Solly got one hand free and punched Micky on the nose.

The blow stung and Micky tasted blood. He lost his temper. 'Damn you!' he cried. He let go of Solly's coat and punched him back, hitting him on the cheek.

Solly turned and stepped into the street. At that moment they both saw a carriage coming towards them, being driven very fast. Solly jumped back to avoid being hit.

Micky saw a chance.

If Solly was dead, Micky's troubles would be over.

There was no time to reckon the odds, no room for hesitation and forethought.

Micky gave Solly a mighty shove, pushing him into the road in front of the horses.

The coachman yelled and hauled on the reins. Solly stumbled, saw the horses almost on top of him, fell to the ground and screamed.

For a frozen moment Micky saw the charging horses, the heavy carriage wheels, the terrified coachman and the huge helpless form of Solly, flat on his back in the road.

Then the horses charged over Solly. Micky saw the fat body twist and writhe as the ironclad hooves pounded it. Then the front nearside wheel of the carriage struck Solly's head a mighty blow, and he slumped unconscious. A split-second later the rear wheel ran over his face and crushed his skull like an eggshell.

Micky turned away. He thought he was going to throw up but he managed to control the urge. Then he began to shake. He felt weak and faint, and he had to lean on the wall.

He forced himself to look at the motionless body in the road. Solly's head was smashed, his face unrecognizable, blood and something else smeared over the road beside him. He was dead.

And Micky was saved.

Now Ben Greenbourne need never know what Augusta

had done to him: the deal could go ahead; the railroad would be built; and Micky would be a hero in Cordova.

He felt a warm trickle on his lip. His nose was bleeding. He pulled out a handkerchief and dabbed at it.

He stared a moment longer at Solly. You only lost your temper once in your life, and it killed you, he thought.

He looked up and down the street in the gaslight. There was no one around. Only the coachman had seen what happened.

The carriage juddered to a halt thirty yards down the road. The coachman leaped down and a woman looked out of the window. Micky turned and walked quickly away, heading back towards Pall Mall.

A few seconds later he heard the coachman call after him: 'Hey! You!'

He walked faster and turned the corner into Pall Mall without looking back. A moment later he was lost in the crowd.

By God, I did it, he thought. Now that he could no longer see the mangled body, the sense of disgust was passing, and he began to feel triumphant. Quick thinking and bold action had enabled him to overcome yet another obstacle.

He hurried up the steps of the club. With luck nobody would have noticed his absence, he hoped; but as he passed through the front door he had the bad fortune to bump into Hugh Pilaster going out.

Hugh nodded to him and said: 'Evening, Miranda.'

'Evening, Pilaster,' said Micky; and he went in, cursing Hugh under his breath.

He went to the cloakroom. His nose was red from Solly's punch but otherwise he just appeared a little rumpled. He straightened his clothing and brushed his hair. As he did so he thought about Hugh Pilaster. If Hugh had not been right there on the doorstep at the wrong moment, nobody would have known Micky had even left the club – he had been gone for only a few minutes. But did it really matter? No one was going to suspect Micky of killing Solly, and if they did, the fact that he had left his club for a few minutes would not prove anything. Still, he no longer had a watertight alibi, and that worried him.

He washed his hands thoroughly and hurried up the stairs to the card-room.

Edward was already playing baccarat and there was an empty seat at the table. Micky sat down. No one commented on the length of time he had been away.

He was dealt a hand. 'You look a bit seasick,' said Edward.

'Yes,' he said calmly. 'I think the fish soup may not have been perfectly fresh tonight.'

Edward waved at a waiter. 'Bring this man a glass of brandy.'

Micky looked at his cards. He had a nine and a ten, the perfect hand. He bet a sovereign.

He just could not lose today.

[II]

HUGH WENT to see Maisie two days after Solly died. He found her alone, sitting quiet and still on a sofa, neatly dressed in a black gown, looking small and insignificant in the splendour of the drawing-room at the palatial Piccadilly house. Her face was lined with grief and she looked as if she had not slept. His heart ached for her.

She threw herself into his arms and said: 'Oh, Hugh, he was the best of us!'

When she said that, Hugh himself could not keep the

tears back. Until this moment he had been too stunned to cry. It was a dreadful fate to die as Solly had, and he deserved it less than any man Hugh could name. 'There was no malice in him,' he said. 'He seemed incapable of it. I knew him for fifteen years and I can't remember a single time when he was unkind to someone.'

'Why do such things happen?' Maisie said miserably.

Hugh hesitated. Just a few days ago he had learned, from Tonio Silva, that Micky Miranda had killed Peter Middleton all those years ago. Because of that, Hugh could not help wondering whether Micky had had something to do with the death of Solly. The police were looking for a well-dressed man who had been arguing with Solly just before he was run over. Hugh had seen Micky entering the Cowes Club at around the time Solly died, so he had certainly been in the neighbourhood.

But there was no motive: quite the reverse. Solly had been on the point of closing the Santamaria Railroad deal that was so close to Micky's heart. Why would he kill his benefactor? Hugh decided to say nothing to Maisie about his unfounded suspicions. 'It seems to have been a tragic accident,' he said.

'The coachman thinks Solly was pushed. Why would the witness run away if he wasn't guilty?'

'He may have been attempting to rob Solly. That's what the newspapers are saying, anyway.' The papers were full of the story. It was a sensational case: the grisly death of a prominent banker, one of the richest men in the world.

'Do thieves wear evening dress?'

'It was almost dark. The coachman may have been mistaken about the man's clothing.'

Maisie detached herself from Hugh and sat down again: 'And if you had only waited a little longer you could have married me instead of Nora,' she said.

Hugh was startled by her frankness. The same thought had come to him within seconds of hearing the news – but he was ashamed of it. It was typical of Maisie to come right out and say what they were both thinking. He was not sure how to respond, so he made a foolish joke. 'If a Pilaster married a Greenbourne, it would be not so much a wedding as a merger.'

She shook her head. 'I'm not a Greenbourne. Solly's family never really accepted me.'

'You must have inherited a big chunk of the bank, though.'

'I've inherited nothing, Hugh.'

'But that's impossible!'

'It's true. Solly had no money of his own. His father gave him a huge monthly allowance, but he never settled any capital on him, because of me. Even this house is rented. I own my clothes, furniture and jewellery, so I'll never starve. But I'm not the heir to the bank – and nor is little Bertie.'

Hugh was astonished – and angry that anyone should be so mean to Maisie. 'The old man won't even provide for your son?'

'Not a penny. I saw my father-in-law this morning.'

It was a shabby way to treat her, and Hugh as her friend felt personally affronted. 'It's disgraceful,' he said.

'Not really,' Maisie said. 'I gave Solly five years of happiness, and in return I had five years of the high life. I can go back to normal. I'll sell my jewellery, invest the money and live quietly on the income.'

It was hard to take in. 'Will you go and live with your parents?'

'In Manchester. No, I don't think I can go quite that far back. I'll stay in London. Rachel Bodwin is opening a hospital for unmarried mothers: I might work with her.'

'There's a lot of fuss about Rachel's hospital. People think it's scandalous.'

'Then it should suit me very well!'

Hugh was still hurt and worried by Ben Greenbourne's ill-treatment of his daughter-in-law. He decided he would have a word with Greenbourne and try to change the man's mind. He would not mention it to Maisie beforehand, though. He did not want to raise her hopes and then disappoint them. 'Don't make any sudden decisions, will you?' he counselled.

'Such as?'

'Don't move out of the house, for example. Greenbourne might try to confiscate your furniture.'

'I won't.'

'And you need a lawyer of your own, to represent your interests.'

She shook her head. 'I no longer belong to the class of people who call in a lawyer the way they summon a footman. I have to count the cost. I shan't see a lawyer unless I feel sure I'm being cheated. And I don't think that will happen. Ben Greenbourne isn't dishonest. He's just hard: as hard as iron, and as cold. It's amazing that he fathered someone as warm-hearted as Solly.'

'You're very philosophical,' Hugh said. He admired her courage.

Maisie shrugged. 'I've had an amazing life, Hugh. I was destitute at eleven and fabulously wealthy at nineteen.' She touched a ring on her finger. 'This diamond is probably worth more money than my mother has ever seen. I gave the best parties in London; I met everyone who was anyone; I danced with the Prince of Wales. I've no regrets. Except that you married Nora.'

'I'm very fond of her,' he said unconvincingly.

'You were angry because I wouldn't have an affair with you,' Maisie said brutally. 'You were desperate for sexual release. And you picked Nora because she reminded you of me. But she's not me, and now you're unhappy.'

Hugh winced as if he had been struck. All this was painfully near the truth. 'You never liked her,' he said.

'And you may say I'm jealous, and you may be right, but I still say she never loved you and she married you for your money. I'll bet you've found that to be true since the wedding, haven't you?'

Hugh thought of how Nora refused to make love more than once a week, and how she changed her tune if he bought her gifts; and he felt miserable and looked away. 'She's always been deprived,' he said. 'It's not surprising that she became materialistic.'

'She was not as deprived as I was,' Maisie said scornfully. 'Even you were taken out of school for want of money, Hugh. It's no excuse for false values. The world is full of poor people who understand that love and friendship are more important than riches.'

Her scorn made Hugh defensive. 'She's not as bad as you make out.'

'All the same you're not happy.'

Feeling confused, Hugh fell back on what he knew to be right. 'Well, I've married her now, and I won't leave her,' he said. 'That's what the vows mean.'

Maisie smiled tearfully. 'I knew you would say that.'

Hugh had a sudden vision of Maisie naked, her round freckled breasts and the bush of red-gold hair at her groin, and he wished he could take back his high-principled words. Instead he stood up to go.

Maisie stood up too. 'Thank you for coming, dear Hugh,' she said.

He intended to shake her hand but instead he bent to

kiss her cheek; and then somehow he found himself kissing her lips. It was a soft, tender kiss that lingered for a long moment and almost destroyed Hugh's resolve; but then at last he tore himself away and left the room without another word.

Ben Greenbourne's house was another palace a few yards along Piccadilly. Hugh went straight there after seeing Maisie. He was glad to have something to do, some way of taking his mind off the turmoil in his heart. He asked for the old man. 'Say it's a matter of great urgency,' he told the butler. While he waited he noticed that the mirrors in the hall were covered, and he guessed this was part of the Jewish mourning ritual.

Maisie had thrown him off balance. When he saw her his heart had filled with love and longing. He knew he could never be truly happy without her. But Nora was his wife. She had brought warmth and affection into his life after Maisie rejected him, and that was why he had married her. What was the point of making promises in a wedding ceremony if you were going to change your mind later?

The butler showed Hugh into the library. Six or seven people were just going, leaving Ben Greenbourne alone. He had no shoes on and sat on a plain wooden stool. A table was piled with fruit and pastries for visitors.

Greenbourne was past sixty – Solly had been a late child – and he looked old and worn, but he showed no sign of tears. He stood up, straight-backed and formal as ever, and shook hands, then waved Hugh to another stool.

Greenbourne had an old letter in his hand. 'Listen to this,' he said, and he began to read. 'Dear Papa, We have a new Latin teacher, Reverend Green, and I am getting on

425

much better, ten out of ten every day last week. Waterford caught a rat in the broom cupboard and he is trying to train it to eat out of his hand. The food here is too little can you send me a cake? Your loving son, Solomon.' He folded the letter. 'He was fourteen when he wrote that.'

Hugh realized that Greenbourne was suffering despite his rigid self-control. 'I remember that rat,' he said. 'It bit Waterford's forefinger off.'

'How I wish I could turn back the years,' Greenbourne said, and Hugh saw that the old man's self-control was weakening.

'I must be one of Solly's oldest friends,' Hugh said.

'Indeed. He always admired you, although you were younger.'

'I can't think why. But he was always ready to think the best of people.'

'He was too soft.'

Hugh did not want the conversation to go that way. 'I've come here, not just as Solly's friend, but as Maisie's too.'

Greenbourne stiffened immediately. The sad look went from his face and he became the caricature of the upright Prussian again. Hugh wondered how anyone could so hate a woman as beautiful and full of fun as Maisie.

Hugh went on: 'I met her soon after Solly did. I fell in love with her myself, but Solly won her.'

'He was richer.'

'Mr Greenbourne, I hope you will allow me to be frank. Maisie was a penniless girl looking for a rich husband. But after she married Solly she kept her part of the bargain. She was a good wife to him.'

'And she has had her reward,' Greenbourne said. 'She has enjoyed the life of a lady for five years.'

'Funnily enough, that's what she said. But I don't think

it's good enough. What about little Bertie? Surely you don't want to leave your grandson destitute?'

'Grandson?' said Greenbourne. 'Hubert is no relation to me.'

Hugh had an odd premonition that something momentous was about to happen. It was like a nightmare in which a frightening but nameless horror was about to strike. 'I don't understand,' he said to Greenbourne. 'What do you mean?'

'That woman was already with child when she married my son.'

Hugh gasped.

'Solly knew it, and he knew the child was not his,' Greenbourne went on. 'He took her all the same – against my will, I need hardly add. People generally don't know this, of course: we went to great lengths to keep it secret, but there's no need to any longer, now that—' He broke off, swallowed hard, and continued. 'They went around the world after the wedding. The child was born in Switzerland; they gave out a false birth date; by the time they came home, having been away for almost two years, it was hard to tell that the baby was actually four months older than they said.'

Hugh felt as if his heart had stopped. There was a question he had to ask, but he was terrified of the answer. 'Who . . . who was the father?'

'She would never say,' Greenbourne said. 'Solly never knew.'

But Hugh did.

The child was his.

He stared at Ben Greenbourne, unable to speak.

He would talk to Maisie, and make her tell the truth, but he knew she would confirm his intuition. She had never been promiscuous, despite appearances. She had been a

427

virgin when he seduced her. He had made her pregnant, on that first night. Then Augusta had contrived to split them up, and Maisie had married Solly.

She had even called the baby Hubert, a name closely similar to Hugh.

'It is appalling, of course,' Greenbourne said, seeing his consternation and misunderstanding the reason for it.

I have a child, Hugh thought. A son. Hubert. Called Bertie. The thought wrenched at his heart.

'However, I'm sure you now see why I don't wish to have anything more to do with the woman or her child, now that my dear son has passed away.'

'Oh, don't worry,' Hugh said distractedly. 'I'll take care of them.'

'You?' Greenbourne said, mystified. 'Why should it be any concern of yours?'

'Oh . . . well, I'm all they've got, now, I suppose,' Hugh said.

'Don't get sucked in, young Pilaster,' Greenbourne said kindly. 'You've got a wife of your own to worry about.'

Hugh did not want to explain and he was too dazed to make up a story. He realized he had to get away. He stood up. 'I must go. My deepest condolences, Mr Greenbourne. Solly was the best man I ever knew.'

Greenbourne bowed his head. Hugh left him.

In the hall with the shrouded mirrors he took his hat from the footman and went out into the sunshine of Piccadilly. He walked west and entered Hyde Park, heading for his home in Kensington. He could have taken a hansom but he wanted time to think.

Everything was different now. Nora was his legal wife but Maisie was the mother of his son. Nora could look after herself – and so could Maisie, for that matter – but a child

428

needed a father. Suddenly the question of what he was to do with the rest of his life was open again.

No doubt a clergyman would say that nothing had changed and he should stay with Nora, the woman he had married in church; but clergymen did not know much. The strict Methodism of the Pilasters had passed Hugh by: he had never been able to believe that the answer to every modern moral dilemma could be found in the bible. Nora had seduced and married him for cold-hearted gain – Maisie was right about that – and all there was between them was a piece of paper. That was very little, weighed against a child – the child of a love so strong that it had persisted for many years and through many trials.

Am I just making excuses, he wondered? Is all this no more than specious justification for giving in to a desire I know to be wrong?

He felt torn in two.

He tried to consider the practicalities. He had no grounds for divorce, but he felt sure that Nora would be willing to divorce him, if she were offered enough money. However, the Pilasters would ask him to resign from the bank: the social stigma of divorce was too great to allow him to continue as a partner. He could get another job but no respectable people in London would entertain him and Maisie as a couple even after they married. They would almost certainly have to go abroad. But that prospect attracted him and he felt it would appeal to Maisie too. He could return to Boston or, better still, go to New York. He might never be a millionaire but what was that balanced against the joy of being with the woman he had always loved?

He found himself outside his own house. It was part of an elegant new red-brick terrace in Kensington, half a mile from his Aunt Augusta's much more extravagant place at

Kensington Gore. Nora would be in her overdecorated bedroom, dressing for lunch. What was to stop him walking in and announcing that he was leaving her?

That was what he wanted to do, he knew that now. But was it right?

It was the child that made the difference. It would be wrong to leave Nora for Maisie; but it was right to leave Nora for the sake of Bertie.

He wondered what Nora would say when he told her, and his imagination gave him the answer. He pictured her face set in lines of hard determination, and he heard the unpleasant edge to her voice, and he could guess the exact words she would use: 'It will cost you every penny you've got.'

Oddly enough, that decided him. If he had pictured her bursting into tears of sadness he would have been unable to go through with it, but he knew his first intuition was right.

He went into the house and ran up the stairs.

She was in front of the mirror, putting on the pendant he had given her. It was a bitter reminder that he had to buy her jewellery to persuade her to make love.

She spoke before he did. 'I've got some news,' she said.

'Never mind that now—'

But she would not be put off. She had an odd expression on her face: half-triumphant, half-sulky. 'You'll have to stay out of my bed for a while, anyway.'

He saw that he was not going to be allowed to speak until she had had her say. 'What on earth are you talking about?' he said impatiently.

'The inevitable has happened.'

Suddenly Hugh guessed. He felt as if he had been hit by a train. It was too late, he realized: he could never leave her now. He felt revulsion, and the pain of loss: loss of Maisie, loss of his son.

He looked into her eyes. There was defiance there, almost as if she had guessed what he had been planning. Perhaps she had.

He forced himself to smile. 'The inevitable?'

Then she said it. 'I'm going to have a baby.'

PART THREE

1890

CHAPTER ONE

September

[I]

JOSEPH PILASTER died in September 1890, having been Senior Partner of Pilasters Bank for seventeen years. During that period Britain had grown steadily richer, and so had the Pilasters. They were now almost as rich as the Greenbournes. Joseph's estate came to more than two million pounds, including his collection of sixty-five antique jewelled snuff-boxes – one for each year of his life – which was worth a hundred thousand pounds on its own, and which he left to his son Edward.

All the family kept all their capital invested in the business, which paid them an infallible five per cent interest when ordinary depositors were getting about one-and-a-half per cent on their money most of the time. The partners got even more. As well as five per cent on their invested capital they shared out the profits between them, according to complicated formulas. After a decade of such profit shares, Hugh was half-way to being a millionaire.

On the morning of the funeral Hugh inspected his face in his shaving mirror, looking for signs of mortality. He was thirty-seven years old. His hair was going grey, but the stubble he was scraping off his face was still black. Curly moustaches were fashionable and he wondered whether he should grow one to make himself look younger.

Uncle Joseph had been lucky, Hugh thought. During his tenure as Senior Partner the financial world had been stable. There had been only two minor crises: the failure of the City of Glasgow Bank in 1878 and the crash of the French bank Union Générale in 1882. In both cases the Bank of England had contained the crisis by raising interest rates briefly to six per cent, which was still a long way below panic level. In Hugh's opinion, Uncle Joseph had committed the bank much too heavily to investment in South America – but the crash which Hugh constantly feared had not come, and as far as Uncle Joseph was concerned it now never would. However, having risky investments was like owning a tumbledown house and renting it to tenants: the rent would keep coming in until the very end, but when the house finally fell down there would be no more rent and no more house either. Now that Joseph was gone Hugh wanted to put the bank on a sounder footing by selling or repairing some of those tumbledown South American investments.

When he had washed and shaved he put on his dressing-gown and went into Nora's room. She was expecting him: they always made love on Friday mornings. He had long ago accepted her once-a-week rule. She had become very plump, and her face was rounder than ever, but as a result she had very few lines, and she still looked pretty.

All the same, as he made love to her he closed his eyes and imagined he was with Maisie.

Sometimes he felt like giving up altogether. But these Friday morning sessions had so far given him three sons whom he loved to distraction: Tobias, named for Hugh's father; Samuel, for his uncle; and Solomon, for Solly

Greenbourne. Toby, the eldest, would start at Windfield School next year. Nora produced babies with little difficulty but once they were born she lost interest in them, and Hugh gave them a lot of attention to compensate for their mother's coldness.

Hugh's secret child, Maisie's son Bertie, now sixteen, had been at Windfield for years, and was a prizewinning scholar and star of the cricket team. Hugh paid his fees, visited the school on Speech Day, and generally acted like a godfather. Perhaps this led a few cynical people to suspect that he was Bertie's real father. But he had been Solly's friend, and everyone knew that Solly's father refused to support the boy, so most people assumed he was simply being generously faithful to the memory of Solly.

As he rolled off Nora she said: 'What time is the ceremony?'

'Eleven o'clock at Kensington Methodist Hall. And lunch afterwards at Whitehaven House.'

Hugh and Nora still lived in Kensington, but they had moved to a bigger house when the boys started coming. Hugh had left the choice to Nora, and she had picked a big house in the same ornate, vaguely Flemish style as Augusta's – a style that had become the height of fashion, or at any rate the height of suburban fashion, since Augusta built her place.

Augusta had never been satisfied with Whitehaven House. She wanted a Piccadilly palace like the Greenbournes'. But there was still a measure of Methodist puritanism in the Pilasters, and Joseph had insisted that Whitehaven House was enough luxury for anyone, no matter how rich. Now the house belonged to Edward. Perhaps Augusta would persuade him to sell it and buy her something grander.

When Hugh went down to breakfast his mother was

already there. She and his sister Dotty had come up from Folkestone yesterday. Hugh kissed his mother and sat down, and she said without preamble: 'Do you think he really loves her, Hugh?'

Hugh did not have to ask whom she was talking about. Dotty, now twenty-four, was engaged to Lord Ipswich, eldest son of the Duke of Norwich. Nick Ipswich was heir to a bankrupt dukedom, and Mama was afraid he only wanted Dotty for her money, or rather her brother's money.

Hugh looked fondly at his mother. She still wore black, twenty-four years after the death of his father. Her hair was now white, but in his eyes she was as beautiful as ever. 'He loves her, Mama,' he said.

As Dotty did not have a father, Nick had come to Hugh to ask formal permission to marry her. In such cases it was usual for the lawyers on both sides to draw up the marriage settlement before the engagement was confirmed, but Nick had insisted on doing things the other way around. 'I've told Miss Pilaster that I'm a poor man,' he had said to Hugh. 'She says she has known both affluence and poverty, and she thinks happiness comes from the people you are with, not the money you have.' It was all very idealistic, and Hugh would certainly give his sister a generous dowry; but he was happy to know that Nick genuinely loved her for richer or poorer.

Augusta was enraged that Dotty was marrying so well. When Nick's father died, Dotty would be a duchess, which was far superior to a countess.

Dotty came down a few minutes later. She had grown up in a way Hugh would never have expected. The shy, giggly little girl had become a sultry woman, fair-haired and sensual, strong-willed and quick-tempered. Hugh guessed that quite a lot of young men were intimidated by her, which was probably why she had reached the age of twenty-four without getting married. But Nick Ipswich had a quiet strength that did not need the prop of a compliant wife. Hugh thought they would have a passionate, quarrelsome marriage, quite the opposite of his own.

Nick called, by appointment, at ten, while they were still sitting round the breakfast table. Hugh had asked him to come. Nick sat next to Dotty and took a cup of coffee. He was an intelligent young man, twenty-two years old, just down from Oxford where, unlike most young aristocrats, he had actually sat examinations and got a degree. He had typically English good looks, fair hair and blue eyes and regular features, and Dotty looked at him as if she wanted to eat him with a spoon. Hugh envied their simple, lustful love.

At thirty-seven Hugh felt too young to be playing the role of head of the family, but he had asked for this meeting so he plunged right in. 'Dotty, your fiancé and I have had several long discussions about money.'

Mama got up to leave, but Hugh stopped her. 'Women are supposed to understand money nowadays, Mama – it's the modern way.' She smiled at him as if he were being a foolish boy, but she sat down again.

Hugh went on: 'As you all know, Nick had been planning a professional career, and thinking of reading for the bar, as the dukedom no longer provides a living.' As a banker Hugh understood exactly how Nick's father had lost everything. The duke had been a progressive landowner, and in the agricultural boom of the mid-century he had borrowed money to finance improvements: drainage schemes, the grubbing up of miles of hedges, and expensive steam-powered machinery for threshing, mowing and reaping. Then in the 1870s had come the great agricultural depression which was still going on now in 1890. The price of farmland had slumped and the duke's lands were worth less than the mortgages he had taken on them.

'However, if Nick could get rid of the mortgages that hang around his neck, and rationalize the dukedom, it could still generate a very considerable income. It just needs to be managed well, like any enterprise.'

Nick added: 'I'm going to sell quite a lot of outlying farms and miscellaneous property, and concentrate on making the most of what's left. And I'm going to build houses on the land we own at Sydenham in south London.'

Hugh said: 'We've worked out that the finances of the dukedom can be transformed, permanently, with about a hundred thousand pounds. So that is what I'm going to give you as a dowry.'

Dotty gasped, and Mama burst into tears. Nick, who had known the figure in advance, said: 'It is remarkably generous of you.' Dotty threw her arms around her fiancé and kissed him, then came around the table and kissed Hugh. Hugh felt a little awkward, but all the same he was glad to be able to make them so happy. And he was confident that Nick would use the money well and provide a secure home for Dotty.

Nora came down dressed for the funeral in purple and black bombazine. She had taken breakfast in her room, as always. 'Where are those boys?' she said irritably, looking at the clock. 'I told that wretched governess to have them ready—'

She was interrupted by the arrival of the governess and the children: eleven-year-old Toby; Sam, who was six; and Sol, four. They were all in black morning coats and black ties and carried miniature top hats. Hugh felt a glow of pride. 'My little soldiers,' he said. 'What was the Bank of England's discount rate last night, Toby?'

'Unchanged at two-and-a-half per cent, sir,' said Tobias, who had to look it up in *The Times* every morning.

Sam, the middle one, was bursting with news. 'Mama, I've got a pet,' he said excitedly.

The governess looked anxious. 'You didn't tell me. . . .'

Sam took a matchbox from his pocket, held it out to his mother, and opened it. 'Bill the spider!' he said proudly.

Nora screamed, knocked the box from his hand, and jumped away. 'Horrible boy!' she yelled.

Sam scrabbled on the floor for the box. 'Bill's gone!' he cried, and burst into tears.

Nora turned on the governess. 'How could you let him do such a thing!'

'I'm sorry, I didn't know—'

Hugh intervened. 'There's no harm done,' he said, trying to cool the temperature. He put an arm around Nora's shoulders. 'You were taken by surprise, that's all.' He ushered her out into the hall. 'Come on, everyone, it's time to leave.'

As they left the house he put a hand on Sam's shoulder. 'Now, Sam, I hope you've learned that you must always take care not to frighten ladies.'

'I lost my pet,' Sam said miserably.

'Spiders don't really like living in matchboxes anyway. Perhaps you should have a different kind of pet. What about a canary?'

He brightened immediately. 'Could I?'

'You'd have to make sure it was fed and watered regularly, or it would die.'

'I would, I would!'

'Then we'll look for one tomorrow.'

'Hooray!'

They drove to Kensington Methodist Hall in closed carriages. It was pouring with rain. The boys had never been to a funeral. Toby, who was a rather solemn child, said: 'Are we expected to cry?'

Nora said: 'Don't be so stupid.'

Hugh wished she would be more affectionate with the boys. She had been a baby when her own mother had died, and he guessed that was why she found it so difficult to mother her own children: she had never learned how. All the same she might try harder, he thought. He said to Toby: 'But you can cry if you feel like it. It's allowed at funerals.'

'I don't think I shall. I didn't love Uncle Joseph very much.'

Sam said: 'I loved Bill the spider.'

Sol, the youngest, said: 'I'm too big to cry.'

Kensington Methodist Hall expressed in stone the ambivalent feelings of prosperous Methodists, who believed in religious simplicity but secretly longed to display their wealth. Although it was called a hall, it was as ornate as any Anglican or Catholic church. There was no altar, but there was a magnificent organ. Pictures and statues were banned, but the architecture was baroque, the mouldings were extravagant and the decor was elaborate.

This morning the church was packed to the galleries, with people standing in the aisles and at the back. The employees of the bank had been given the day off to attend, and representatives had come from every important financial institution in the City. Hugh nodded to the Governor of the Bank of England, the First Lord of the Treasury, and Ben Greenbourne, more than seventy years old but still as straight-backed as a young guardsman.

The family were ushered to reserved seats in the front row. Hugh sat next to his Uncle Samuel, who was as immaculate as ever in a black frock coat, a wing collar and a fashionably knotted silk tie. Like Greenbourne, Samuel was in his seventies, and he too was alert and fit.

Samuel was the obvious choice as Senior Partner, now that Joseph was dead. He was the oldest and most experienced of the partners. However, Augusta and Samuel hated one another, and she would oppose him fiercely. She would probably back Joseph's brother, 'Young' William, now forty-two years old.

Among the other partners, two would not be considered because they did not bear the Pilaster name: Major Hartshorn and Sir Harry Tonks, husband of Joseph's daughter Clementine. The remaining partners were Hugh and Edward.

Hugh wanted to be Senior Partner – he wanted it with all his heart. Although he was the youngest of the partners, he was the ablest banker of them all. He knew he could make the bank bigger and stronger than it had ever been and at the same time reduce its exposure to the risky kind of loans Joseph had relied on. However, Augusta would oppose him even more bitterly than she would oppose Samuel. But he could not bear to wait until Augusta was old, or dead, before he took control. She was only fifty-eight: she could easily be around in another fifteen years, as vigorous and spiteful as ever.

The other partner was Edward. He was sitting next to Augusta in the front row. He was heavy and red-faced in middle age, and he had recently developed some kind of skin rash which was very unsightly. He was neither intelligent nor hard-working and in seventeen years he had managed to learn very little about banking. He arrived at work after ten and left for lunch around noon, and he quite often failed to return at all in the afternoon. He drank sherry for breakfast and was never quite sober all day, and he relied on his clerk, Simon Oliver, to keep him out of trouble. The idea of his being Senior Partner was unthinkable.

Edward's wife Emily was sitting next to him, which was a rare event. They led quite separate lives. He lived at Whitehaven House with his mother, and Emily spent all her time at their country house, only coming to London for ceremonial occasions such as funerals. Emily had once been very pretty, with big blue eyes and a child-like smile, but over the years her face had set in lines of disappointment. They had no children and it seemed to Hugh that they hated one another.

Next to Emily was Micky Miranda, fiendishly debonair in a grey coat with a black mink collar. Ever since finding out that Micky had murdered Peter Middleton, Hugh had been frightened of him. Edward and Micky were still as thick as thieves. Micky was involved in many of the South American investments the bank had backed over the last ten years.

The service was long and tedious, then the procession from the church to the cemetery, in the relentless September rain, took more than an hour, because of the hundreds of carriages following the hearse.

Hugh studied Augusta as her husband's coffin was lowered into the ground. She stood under a big umbrella held by Edward. Her hair was all silver, and she looked magnificent in a huge black hat. Surely now, when she had lost the companion of a lifetime, she would seem human and pitiable? But her proud face was carved in stern lines, like a marble sculpture of a Roman senator, and she showed no grief.

After the burial there was a lunch at Whitehaven House for the whole Pilaster extended family, including all the partners with their wives and children, plus close business associates and long-time hangers-on such as Micky Miranda. So that they could all eat together Augusta had put two dining tables end-to-end in the long drawing-room.

Hugh had not been inside the house for a year or two, and since his last visit it had been redecorated yet again, this time in the newly fashionable Arab style. Moorish arches had been inserted in the doorways, all the furniture featured carved fretwork, the upholstery was in colourful abstract Islamic designs, and here in the drawing-room were a Cairo screen and a Koran stand.

Augusta sat Edward in his father's chair. Hugh thought that was a bit tactless. Putting him at the head of the table cruelly emphasized how incapable he was of filling his father's shoes. Joseph had been an erratic leader but he had not been a fool.

However, Augusta had a purpose as always. Towards the end of the meal she said, with her customary abruptness: 'There must be a new Senior Partner as soon as possible, and obviously it will be Edward.'

Hugh was horrified. Augusta had always had a blind spot about her son, but all the same this was totally unexpected. He felt sure she could not possibly get her way, but it was unnerving that she should even make the suggestion.

There was a silence, and he realized that everyone was waiting for him to speak. He was regarded by the family as the opposition to Augusta.

He hesitated while he considered how best to handle it. He decided to try for a stand-off. 'I think the partners should discuss the question tomorrow,' he said.

Augusta was not going to let him off that easily. She said: 'I'll thank you not to tell me what I may and may not discuss in my own house, young Hugh.'

'If you insist.' He collected his thoughts rapidly. 'There's nothing obvious about the decision, although you, dear aunt, clearly don't understand the subtleties of the question, perhaps because you have never worked at the bank, or indeed worked at all—'

'How dare you—'

He raised his voice and overrode her. 'The oldest surviving partner is Uncle Samuel,' he said. He realized he was sounding too aggressive and he softened his voice again. 'I'm sure we would all agree that he would be a wise choice, mature and experienced and highly acceptable to the financial community.'

Uncle Samuel inclined his head in acknowledgement of the compliment but did not say anything.

Nobody contradicted Hugh – but nobody supported him either. He supposed they did not want to antagonize Augusta: the cowards preferred that he do it on their behalf, he thought cynically.

So be it. He went on: 'However, Uncle Samuel has declined the honour once before. If he should do so again, the eldest Pilaster would be Young William, who is also widely respected in the City.'

Augusta said impatiently: 'It is not the City that has to make the choice – it is the Pilaster family.'

'The Pilaster partners, to be exact,' Hugh corrected her. 'But just as the partners need the confidence of the rest of the family, so the bank needs to be trusted by the wider financial community. If we lose that trust we are finished.'

Augusta seemed to be getting angry. 'We have the right to choose whom we like!'

Hugh shook his head vigorously. Nothing annoyed him more than this kind of irresponsible talk. 'We have no rights, only duties,' he said emphatically. 'We're entrusted with millions of pounds of other people's money. We can't do what we like: we have to do what we must.'

Augusta tried another tack. 'Edward is the son and heir.'

'It's not a hereditary title!' Hugh said indignantly. 'It goes to the most able.'

It was Augusta's turn to be indignant. 'Edward is as good as anyone!'

Hugh looked around the table, dramatically holding the gaze of each man for a moment before moving on. 'Is there anyone here who will put his hand on his heart and say that Edward is the most able banker among us?'

No one spoke for a long minute.

Augusta said: 'Edward's South American bonds have made a fortune for the bank.'

Hugh nodded. 'It's true that we have sold many millions of pounds' worth of South American bonds in the last ten years, and Edward has handled all that business. But it's dangerous money. People bought the bonds because they trust Pilasters. If one of those governments should default on interest payments, the price of all South American bonds will go through the floor – and Pilasters will be blamed. Because of Edward's success in selling South American bonds our reputation, which is our most precious asset, is now in the hands of a set of brutish despots and generals who can't read.' Hugh found himself becoming emotional as he said this. He had helped to build up the reputation of the bank, by his own brains and hard work, and it made him angry that Augusta was willing to jeopardize it.

'You sell North American bonds,' Augusta said. 'There's always a risk. That's what banking is about.' She spoke triumphantly, as if she had caught him out.

'The United States of America has a modern democratic government, vast natural wealth and no enemies. Now that they've abolished slavery, there's no reason why the country shouldn't be stable for a hundred years. By contrast, South America is a collection of warring dictatorships that may not be the same for the next ten days. There is a risk in both cases, but in the north it's much smaller. Banking is about *calculating* risk.'

Augusta did not really understand business. 'You're just envious of Edward – you always were,' she said.

Hugh wondered why the other partners were so silent. As soon as he asked himself the question, he realized that Augusta must have spoken to them beforehand. But surely she could not have persuaded them to accept Edward as Senior Partner? He began to feel seriously worried.

'What has she said to you?' he said abruptly. He looked at each of them in turn. 'William? George? Harry? Come on, out with it. You've discussed this earlier and Augusta has nobbled you.'

They all looked a little foolish. Finally William said: 'Nobody has been nobbled, Hugh. But Augusta and Edward have made it clear that unless Edward becomes Senior Partner, they . . .' He seemed embarrassed.

'Out with it,' Hugh said.

'They will withdraw their capital from the business.'

'*What?*' Hugh was stunned. Withdrawing your capital was a cardinal sin in this family: his own father had done it and had never been forgiven. That Augusta should be willing even to threaten such a step was astonishing – and showed that she was deadly serious.

Between them, she and Edward controlled about forty per cent of the bank's capital, over two million pounds. If they withdrew the money at the end of the financial year, as they were legally entitled to do, the bank would be crippled.

It was startling that Augusta should make such a threat – and even worse that the partners were ready to give in to her. 'You're surrendering all authority to her!' he said. 'If you let her get away with it this time she'll do it again. Any time she wants something she can just threaten to withdraw her capital and you'll cave in. You might as well make *her* Senior Partner.'

Edward blustered: 'Don't you dare speak of my mother like that – mind your manners!'

'Manners be damned,' Hugh said rudely. He knew he was doing his cause no good by losing his temper, but he was too angry to stop. 'You're about to ruin a great bank. Augusta's blind, Edward is stupid and the rest of you are too cowardly to stop them.' He pushed back his chair and stood up, throwing his napkin down on the table like a challenge. 'Well, here's one person who won't be bullied.'

He stopped and took a breath, realizing he was about to say something that would change the course of the rest of his life. Around the table they all stared at him. He had no alternative, he realized. 'I resign,' he said.

As he turned from the table he caught Augusta's eye, and saw on her face a victorious smile.

Uncle Samuel came to see him that evening.

Samuel was an old man now, but no less vain than he had been twenty years ago. He still lived with Stephen Caine, his 'secretary'. Hugh was the only Pilaster who ever went to their home, which was a house in raffish Chelsea, decorated in the fashionable aesthetic style and full of cats. Once, when they were half-way down a bottle of port, Stephen had said he was the only Pilaster wife who was not a harridan.

When Samuel called, Hugh was in his library, where he generally retired after dinner. He had a book on his knee but he had not been reading it. Instead he had been staring into the fire, thinking about the future. He had plenty of money, enough to live comfortably for the rest of his life without working, but he would never be Senior Partner now.

Uncle Samuel looked weary and sad. 'I was at odds with my cousin Joseph for most of his life,' he said. 'I wish it had been otherwise.'

Hugh offered him a drink and he asked for port. Hugh called his butler and ordered a bottle decanted.

'How do you feel about it all?' Samuel asked. He was the only person in the world who asked Hugh how he felt.

'I was angry before, but now I'm just despondent,' Hugh replied. 'Edward is so hopelessly unsuited to be Senior Partner, but there's nothing to be done. How about you?'

'I feel as you do. I shall resign, too. I shan't withdraw my capital, at least not right away, but I shall go at the end of the year. I told them so after you made your dramatic exit. I don't know whether I should have spoken up earlier. It wouldn't have made any difference.'

'What else did they say?'

'Well, that's why I'm here, really, dear boy. I regret to say I'm a sort of messenger from the enemy. They asked me to persuade you not to resign.'

'Then they're damned fools.'

'That they certainly are. However, there is one thing you ought to think about. If you resign immediately, everyone in the City will know why. People will say that if Hugh Pilaster believes Edward can't run the bank he's probably right. It could cause a loss of confidence.'

'Well, if the bank has weak leadership people ought to lose confidence in it. Otherwise they'll lose their money.'

'But what if your resignation creates a financial crisis?'

Hugh had not thought of that. 'Is it possible?'

'I think so.'

'I wouldn't want to do that, needless to say.' A crisis

might bring down other, perfectly sound businesses, the way the collapse of Overend and Gurney had destroyed Hugh's father's firm in 1866.

'Perhaps you ought to stay until the end of the financial year, like me,' Samuel said. 'It's only a few months. By then Edward will have been in charge for a while and people will be used to it, and you can go with no fuss.'

The butler came back with the port. Hugh sipped it thoughtfully. He felt he had to agree to Samuel's proposal, much as he disliked the idea. He had given them all a lecture about their duty to their depositors and the wider financial community, and he had to heed his own words. If he were to allow the bank to suffer, just because of his own feelings, he would be no better than Augusta. Besides, the postponement would give him time to think about what to do with the rest of his life.

He sighed. 'All right,' he said at last. 'I'll stay until the end of the year.'

Samuel nodded. 'I thought you would,' he said. 'It's the right thing to do – and you always do the right thing, in the end.'

[II]

BEFORE MAISIE Greenbourne finally said goodbye to high society, eleven years ago, she had gone to all her friends – who were many and rich – and persuaded them to give money to Rachel Bodwin's Southwark Female Hospital. Consequently, the hospital's running costs were covered by the income from its investments.

The money was managed by Rachel's father, the only man involved in the running of the hospital. At first Maisie had wanted to handle the investments herself, but she had found that bankers and stockbrokers refused to take her seriously. They would ignore her instructions, ask for authority from her husband, and withhold information from her. She might have fought them, but in setting up the hospital she and Rachel had too many other fights on their hands, and they had let Mr Bodwin take over the finances.

Maisie was a widow, but Rachel was still married to Micky Miranda. Rachel never saw her husband but he would not divorce her. For ten years Rachel had been carrying on a discreet affair with Maisie's brother Dan Robinson, who was a Member of Parliament. The three of them lived together in Maisie's house in suburban Walworth.

The hospital was in working-class Southwark, in the heart of the city. They had taken a long lease on a row of four houses near Southwark Cathedral and had knocked internal doors through the walls on each level to make their hospital. Instead of rows of beds in cavernous wards they had small, comfortable rooms, each with only two or three beds.

Maisie's office was a cosy sanctuary near the main entrance. She had two comfortable chairs, flowers in a vase, a faded rug and bright curtains. On the wall was the framed poster of 'The Amazing Maisie' that was her only souvenir of the circus. The desk was unobtrusive, and the ledgers in which she kept her records were stowed in a cupboard.

The woman sitting opposite her was barefoot, ragged and nine months pregnant. In her eyes was the wary, desperate look of a starving cat that walks into a strange house hoping to be fed. Maisie said: 'What's your name, dear?'

'Rose Porter, mum.'

They always called her 'mum', as if she were a grand lady. She had long ago given up trying to make them call her Maisie. 'Would you like a cup of tea?'

'Yes, please, mum.'

Maisie poured tea into a plain china cup and added milk and sugar. 'You look tired.'

'I've walked all the way from Bath, mum.'

It was a hundred miles. 'It must have taken you a week!' said Maisie. 'You poor thing.'

Rose burst into tears.

This was normal, and Maisie was used to it. It was best to let them cry as long as they wanted to. She sat on the arm of Rose's chair, put her arm around her shoulders and hugged her.

'I know I've been wicked,' Rose sobbed.

'You aren't wicked,' Maisie said. 'We're all women here, and we understand. We don't talk of wickedness. That's for clergymen and politicians.'

After a while Rose calmed down and drank her tea. Maisie took the current ledger from the cupboard and sat at her writing-table. She kept notes on every woman admitted to the hospital. The records were often useful. If some self-righteous Conservative got up in Parliament and said that most unmarried mothers were prostitutes, or that they all wanted to abandon their babies, or some such rot, she would refute him with a careful, polite, factual letter, and repeat the refutation in the speeches she made up and down the country.

'Tell me what happened,' she said to Rose. 'How were you living, before you fell pregnant?'

'I was cook for a Mrs Freeman in Bath.'

'And how did you meet your young man?'

'He came up and spoke to me in the street. It was my afternoon off, and I had a new yellow parasol. I looked a treat, I know I did. That yellow parasol was the undoing of me.'

Maisie coaxed the story out of her. It was typical. The man was an upholsterer, respectable and prosperous working-class. He had courted her and they had talked of marriage. On warm evenings they had caressed one another, sitting in the park after dark, surrounded by other couples doing the same thing. Opportunities for sexual intercourse were few, but they had managed it four or five times, when her employer was away or his land-lady was drunk. Then he had lost his job. He moved to another town, looking for work; wrote to her once or twice; and vanished out of her life. Then she found she was pregnant.

'We'll try to get in touch with him,' Maisie said.

'I don't think he loves me any more.'

'We'll see.' It was surprising how often such men were willing to marry the girl, in the end. Even if they had run away on learning she was pregnant, they might regret their panic. In Rose's case the chances were high. The man had gone away because he had lost his job, not because he had fallen out of love with Rose; and he did not yet know he was going to be a father. Maisie always tried to get them to come to the hospital and see the mother and child. The sight of a helpless baby, their own flesh and blood, sometimes brought out the best in them.

Rose winced, and Maisie said: 'What's the matter?'

'My back hurts. It must be all the walking.'

Maisie smiled. 'It's not backache. Your baby's coming. Let's get you to a bed.'

She took Rose upstairs and handed her over to a nurse. 'It's going to be all right,' she said. 'You'll have a lovely bonny baby.'

She went into another room and stopped beside the bed

of a woman they called Miss Nobody, who refused to give any details about herself, not even her name. She was a dark-haired girl of about seventeen. Her accent was upper-class and her underwear was expensive, and Maisie was fairly sure she was Jewish. 'How do you feel, my dear?' Maisie asked her.

'I'm comfortable – and so grateful to you, Mrs Greenbourne.'

She was as different from Rose as could be – they might have come from opposite ends of the earth – but they were both in the same predicament, and they would both give birth in the same painful, messy way.

When Maisie got back to her room she resumed the letter she had been writing to the editor of *The Times*.

> *The Female Hospital*
> *Bridge Street*
> *Southwark*
> *London, S.E.*
> September 10th, 1890

To the Editor of 'The Times'
Dear Sir,

   I read with interest the letter from Dr Charles Wickam on the subject of women's physical inferiority to men.

She had not been sure how to go on, but the arrival of Rose Porter had given her inspiration.

   I have just admitted to this hospital a young woman in a certain condition who has walked here from Bath.

The editor would probably delete the words 'in a certain condition' as being vulgar, but Maisie was not going to do his censoring for him.

I note that Dr Wickham writes from the Cowes Club, and I cannot help but wonder how many members of the club could walk from Bath to London?

Of course as a woman I have never been inside the club, but I often see its members on the steps, hailing hansom cabs to take them distances of a mile or less, and I am bound to say that most of them look as if they would find it difficult to walk from Piccadilly Circus to Parliament Square.

They certainly could not work a twelve-hour shift in an East End sweatshop, as thousands of Englishwomen do every day—

She was interrupted again by a knock at the door. 'Come in,' she called.

The woman who entered was neither poor nor pregnant. She had big blue eyes and a girlish face, and she was richly dressed. She was Emily, the wife of Edward Pilaster.

Maisie got up and kissed her. Emily Pilaster was one of the hospital's supporters. The group included a surprising diversity of women – Maisie's old friend April Tilsley, now the owner of three London brothels, was a member. They gave cast-off clothes, old furniture, surplus food from their kitchens, and odd supplies such as paper and ink. They could sometimes find employment for the mothers after confinement. But most of all they gave moral support to Maisie and Rachel when they were vilified by the male establishment for not having compulsory prayers, hymn-singing and sermons on the wickedness of unmarried motherhood.

Maisie felt partly responsible for Emily's disastrous visit to April's brothel on Mask Night, when she had failed to seduce her own husband. Since then Emily and the loathsome Edward had led the discreetly separate lives of wealthy couples who hated one another.

This morning Emily was bright-eyed and excited. She sat down, then got up again and checked that the door was firmly shut. Then she said: 'I've fallen in love.'

Maisie was not sure this was unqualified good news, but she said: 'How wonderful! Who with?'

'Robert Charlesworth. He's a poet and he writes articles about Italian art. He lives in Florence most of the year but he's renting a cottage in our village, he likes England in September.'

It sounded to Maisie as if Robert Charlesworth had enough money to live well without doing any real work. 'He sounds madly romantic,' she said.

'Oh, he is, he's so soulful, you'd love him.'

'I'm sure I would,' Maisie said, although in fact she could not stand soulful poets with private incomes. However, she was happy for Emily, who had had more bad luck than she deserved. 'Have you become his mistress?'

Emily blushed. 'Oh, Maisie, you always ask the most embarrassing questions! Of course not!'

After what had happened on Mask Night, Maisie found it astonishing that Emily could be embarrassed about anything. However, experience had taught her that it was she, Maisie, who was peculiar in this respect. Most women were able to close their eyes to just about anything if they really wanted to. But Maisie had no patience with polite euphemisms and tactful phrases. If she wanted to know something she asked. 'Well,' she said brusquely, 'you can't be his wife, can you?'

The answer took her by surprise. 'That's why I came to see you,' Emily said. 'Do you know anything about getting a marriage annulled?'

'Goodness!' Maisie thought for a moment. 'On the grounds that the marriage has never been consummated, I presume?'

'Yes.'

Maisie nodded. 'I do know about it, yes.' It was no surprise that Emily had come to her for legal advice. There were no women lawyers, and a male lawyer would probably have gone straight to Edward and spilled the beans. Maisie was a campaigner for women's rights and she had studied the existing law on marriage and divorce. 'You would have to go to the Probate, Divorce and Admiralty Division of the High Court,' she said. 'And you would have to prove that Edward is impotent under all circumstances, not just with you.'

Emily's face fell. 'Oh, dear,' she said. 'We know that's not so.'

'Also, the fact that you're not a virgin would be a major problem.'

'Then it's hopeless,' Emily said miserably.

'The only way to do it would be to persuade Edward to co-operate. Do you think he would?'

Emily brightened. 'He might.'

'If he would sign an affidavit saying that he was impotent, and agree not to contest the annulment, your evidence won't be challenged.'

'Then I'll find a way to make him sign.' Emily's face took on a stubborn set and Maisie remembered how unexpectedly strong-willed the girl could be.

'Be discreet. It's against the law for a husband and wife to conspire in this way, and there's a man called the Queen's Proctor who acts as a kind of divorce policeman.'

'Will I be able to marry Robert afterwards?'

'Yes. Non-consummation is grounds for a full divorce under Church law. It will take about a year for the case to come to court, and then there's a waiting period of six months before the divorce becomes final, but in the end you will be allowed to remarry.'

'Oh, I hope Edward will do it.'

'How does he feel about you?'

'He hates me.'

'Do you think he'd like to get rid of you?'

'I don't think he cares, so long as I stay out of his way.'

'And if you didn't stay out of his way?'

'You mean if I were to make a nuisance of myself?'

'That's what I had in mind.'

'I suppose I could.'

Maisie was sure Emily could make an unbearable nuisance of herself once she put her mind to it.

'I'll need a lawyer to write the letter for Edward to sign,' Emily said.

'I'll ask Rachel's father, he's a lawyer.'

'Would you?'

'Certainly.' Maisie glanced at the clock. 'I can't see him today, it's the first day of term at Windfield School and I have to take Bertie. But I'll see him in the morning.'

Emily stood up. 'Maisie, you're the best friend a woman ever had.'

'I'll tell you what, this is going to stir up the Pilaster family. Augusta will have a fit.'

'Augusta doesn't scare me,' said Emily.

Maisie Greenbourne attracted a lot of attention at Windfield School. She always did. There were several reasons. She was known to be the widow of the fabulously wealthy Solly Greenbourne, although she had very little money herself. She was also notorious as an 'advanced' woman who believed in women's rights and, it was said, encouraged parlourmaids to have illegitimate babies. And then, when she brought Bertie to school, she was always accompanied by Hugh Pilaster, the handsome banker who

paid her son's fees: no doubt the more sophisticated among
the other parents suspected that Hugh was Bertie's real
father. But the main reason, she thought, was that at thirty-
four she was still pretty enough to turn men's heads.

Today she was wearing a tomato-red outfit, a dress with
a short jacket over it and a hat with a feather. She knew
she looked pretty and carefree. In fact these visits to the
school with Bertie and Hugh broke her heart.

It was seventeen years since she had spent a night with
Hugh, and she loved him as much as ever. Most of the time
she immersed herself in the troubles of the poor girls who
came to her hospital, and forgot her own grief; but two or
three times a year she had to see Hugh, and then the pain
came back.

He had known for eleven years that he was Bertie's real
father. Ben Greenbourne had given him a hint, and he had
confronted her with his suspicions. She told him the truth.
Since then he had done everything he could for Bertie short
of acknowledging him as his son. Bertie believed his father
was the late, lovable Solomon Greenbourne, and to tell him
the truth would just cause unnecessary pain.

His name was Hubert, and calling him Bertie had been
a sly compliment to the Prince of Wales, who was also a
Bertie. Maisie never saw the prince now. She was no longer
a society hostess and the wife of a millionaire: she was just
a widow living in a modest house in the south London
suburbs, and such women did not feature in the prince's
circle of friends.

She had chosen to call her son Hubert because the name
sounded like Hugh, but she had quickly become
embarrassed by the resemblance, and that was another
reason for calling the boy Bertie. She told her son that
Hugh was his dead father's best friend. Luckily there was

no obvious likeness between Bertie and Hugh. In fact Bertie was like Maisie's father, with soft dark hair and sad brown eyes. He was tall and strong, a good athlete and a hard-working student, and Maisie was so proud of him that she sometimes felt her heart would burst.

On these occasions Hugh was scrupulously polite to Maisie, playing the role of family friend, but she could tell that he felt the bitter-sweetness of the situation as painfully as she did.

Maisie knew, from Rachel's father, that Hugh was considered a prodigy in the City. When he talked about the bank his eyes sparkled and he was interesting and amusing. She could tell that his work was challenging and fulfilling. But if ever their conversation strayed into the domestic field he became sour and uncommunicative. He did not like to talk about his house, his social life, or – least of all – his wife. The only part of his family he told her about was his three sons, whom he loved to distraction. But there was a streak of regret even when he spoke of them, and Maisie had gathered that Nora was not a loving mother. Over the years she had watched him resign himself to a cold, sexually frustrating marriage.

Today he had on a silver-grey tweed suit that matched his silver-streaked hair, and a bright blue tie the colour of his eyes. He was heavier than he used to be but he still had a mischievous grin which appeared now and again. They made an attractive couple – but they were not a couple, and the fact that they looked and acted like one was what made her so sad. She took his arm as they walked into Windfield School, and she thought she would give her soul to be with him every day.

They helped Bertie unpack his trunk, then he made them tea in his study. Hugh had brought a cake which would probably feed the sixth form for a week. 'My boy Toby will be coming here next half,' Hugh said as they drank their tea. 'I wonder if you'd keep an eye on him for me?'

'I'll be glad to,' Bertie said. 'I'll make sure he doesn't go swimming in Bishop's Wood.' Maisie frowned at him, and he said: 'Sorry. Bad joke.'

'They still talk abou' that, do they?' Hugh said.

'Every year the head tells the story of how Peter Middleton drowned, to try and frighten chaps. But they still go swimming.'

After tea they said goodbye to Bertie, Maisie feeling tearful as always about leaving her little boy behind, even though he was now taller than she. They walked back into the town and took the train to London. They had a first-class compartment to themselves.

As they watched the scenery flash by, Hugh said: 'Edward is going to be Senior Partner at the bank.'

Maisie was startled. 'I didn't think he had the brains!'

'He hasn't. I shall resign at the end of the year.'

'Oh, Hugh!' Maisie knew how much he cared for that bank. All his hopes were tied up in it. 'What will you do?'

'I don't know. I'm staying on until the end of the financial year, so I've got time to think about it.'

'Won't the bank go to ruin under Edward?'

'I'm afraid it may.'

Maisie felt very sad for Hugh. He had had more bad luck than he deserved, while Edward had far too much good. 'Edward is Lord Whitehaven, too. Do you realize that if the title had gone to Ben Greenbourne, as it should have, Bertie would be in line to inherit it now?'

'Yes.'

'But Augusta put a stop to all that.'

'Augusta?' said Hugh with a puzzled frown.

'Yes. She was behind all that rubbish in the newspapers about "Can a Jew be a Peer?" Do you remember?'

'I do, but how can you be so sure that Augusta was behind it?'

'The Prince of Wales told us.'

'Well, well.' Hugh shook his head. 'Augusta never ceases to amaze me.'

'Anyway, poor Emily is Lady Whitehaven now.'

'At least she got something out of that wretched marriage.'

'I'm going to tell you a secret,' Maisie said. She lowered her voice even though there was no one within earshot. 'Emily is about to ask Edward for an annulment.'

'Good for her! On the grounds of non-consummation, I presume?'

'Yes. You don't seem surprised.'

'You can tell. They never touch. They're so awkward with one another, it's hard to believe they're man and wife.'

'She's been leading a false life all these years and she's decided to put an end to it.'

'She'll have trouble with my family,' Hugh said.

'With Augusta, you mean.' That had been Maisie's reaction too. 'Emily knows that. But she's got a streak of obstinacy that should serve her well.'

'Does she have a lover?'

'Yes. But she won't become his mistress. I can't think why she should be so scrupulous. Edward spends every night in a brothel.'

Hugh smiled at her, a sad, loving smile. 'You were scrupulous, once.'

Maisie knew he was talking about the night at Kingsbridge Manor when she had locked her bedroom door against him. 'I was married to a good man and you and I

463

were about to betray him. Emily's situation is quite different.'

Hugh nodded. 'All the same I think I understand how she feels. It's the lying that makes adultery shameful.'

Maisie disagreed. 'People should grab happiness where they can. You only have one life.'

'But when you grab happiness you may let go of something even more valuable – your integrity.'

'Too abstract for me,' Maisie said dismissively.

'No doubt it was for me, that night at Kingo's house, when I would have betrayed Solly's trust willingly, if you had let me. But it's become more concrete to me over the years. Now I think I value integrity more than anything else.'

'But what is it?'

'It means telling the truth, keeping promises, and taking responsibility for your mistakes. It's the same in business as it is in everyday life. It's a matter of being what you claim to be, doing what you say you'll do. And a banker of all people can't be a liar. After all, if his wife can't trust him, who can?'

Maisie realized she was getting angry with Hugh and she wondered why. She sat back in silence for a while, looking out of the window at the London suburbs in the dusk. Now that he was leaving the bank, what was there left in his life? He did not love his wife and his wife did not love their children. Why should he not find happiness in the arms of Maisie, the woman he had always loved?

At Paddington station he escorted her to the cab stand and helped her into a hansom. As they said goodbye she held his hands and said: 'Come home with me.'

He looked sad and shook his head.

'We love each other – we always have,' she pleaded. 'Come with me, and to hell with the consequences.'

'But life is consequences, isn't it?'

'Hugh! Please!'

He withdrew his hands and stepped back. 'Goodbye, dear Maisie.'

She stared at him helplessly. Years of suppressed yearning caught up with her. If she had been strong enough she would have seized him and dragged him into the cab by force. She felt maddened by frustration.

She would have stayed there for ever, but he nodded to the cabbie and said: 'Drive on.'

The man touched the horse with his whip, and the wheels turned.

A moment later Hugh was gone from her sight.

[III]

H UGH SLEPT badly that night. He kept waking up and running over his conversation with Maisie. He wished he had given in and gone home with her. He could be sleeping in her arms now, his head on her breasts, instead of tossing and turning alone.

But something else was bothering him too. He had a feeling she had said something momentous, something surprising and sinister, the significance of which had escaped him at the time. But it eluded him.

They had talked about the bank, and Edward becoming Senior Partner; Edward's title; Emily's plan to seek an annulment; the night at Kingsbridge Manor when they had almost made love; the conflicting values of integrity and happiness. . . . Where was the momentous revelation?

He tried running over the conversation backwards: *Come home with me . . . People should grab happiness where they can . . . Emily is about to ask Edward for an annulment . . . Emily is Lady*

Whitehaven now . . . Do you realize that if the title had gone to Ben Greenbourne, as it should have, Bertie would be in line to inherit it now?

No, he had missed something. Edward had got the title that should have gone to Ben Greenbourne – but Augusta had put a stop to all that. She had been behind all the nasty propaganda about whether a Jew could be a Lord. Hugh had not realized that, although looking back he thought he should have been able to guess. But the Prince of Wales had known, somehow, and he had told Maisie and Solly.

Hugh turned over restlessly. Why should that be such a momentous revelation? It was just another example of Augusta's ruthlessness. It had been kept quiet at the time. But Solly had known. . . .

Suddenly Hugh sat up in bed, staring into the darkness.

Solly had known.

If Solly knew that the Pilasters were responsible for a press campaign of racial hatred against his father, he would never again do business with Pilasters Bank. In particular, he would have cancelled the Santamaria Railroad issue. He would have told Edward that he was cancelling it. And Edward would have told Micky.

'Oh, my God,' Hugh said aloud.

He had always wondered whether Micky had something to do with the death of Solly. He knew Micky had been in the neighbourhood. But the motive had always puzzled him. As far as he knew, Solly had been about to consummate the deal and give Micky what he wanted; and if that was right Micky had every motive for keeping Solly alive. But if Solly had been about to cancel, Micky might have killed him to save the deal. Had Micky been the well-dressed man quarrelling with Solly a few seconds before he was run over? The coachman had always claimed Solly was pushed into his path. Had Micky shoved Solly under the wheels of that carriage? The thought was horrifying and disgusting.

Hugh got out of bed and turned up the gaslight. He would not go back to sleep tonight. He put on a dressing-gown and sat by the dying embers of the fire. Had Micky murdered *two* of his friends, Peter Middleton and Solly Greenbourne?

And if he had, what was Hugh going to do about it?

He was still agonizing over the question the next day when something happened that gave him the answer.

He spent the morning at his desk in the partners' room. He had once longed to sit here, in the quiet, luxurious centre of power, making decisions about millions of pounds, under the eyes of his ancestors' portraits; but now he was used to it. And soon he would be giving it up.

He was tying up loose ends, completing projects he had already begun but not starting new ones. His mind kept returning to Micky Miranda and poor Solly. It maddened him to think that a man as good as Solly had been done away with by a reptile and parasite such as Micky. What he really wanted to do was strangle Micky with his bare hands. But he could not kill Micky; in fact there was not even any point in reporting his beliefs to the police, for he had no proof.

His clerk, Jonas Mulberry, had been looking agitated all morning. Mulberry had come into the partners' room four or five times on different pretexts but had not said what was on his mind. Eventually Hugh divined that the man had something to say that he did not want the other partners to hear.

A few minutes before midday Hugh left the partners'

room and went along the corridor to the telephone room. They had had the phone installed two years ago, and they were already regretting the decision not to put it in the partners' room: each of them was called to the instrument several times a day.

On the way he met Mulberry in the corridor. He stopped him and said: 'Is there something on your mind?'

'Yes, Mr Hugh,' said Mulberry with evident relief. He lowered his voice. 'I happened to see some papers being drawn up by Simon Oliver, Mr Edward's clerk.'

'Come in here for a moment.' Hugh stepped into the telephone room and closed the door behind them. 'What was in the papers?'

'A proposal for a loan issue to Cordova – for two million pounds!'

'Oh, no!' said Hugh. 'This bank needs less exposure to South American debt – not more.'

'I knew you'd feel that way.'

'What is it for, specifically?'

'To build a new harbour in Santamaria Province.'

'Another scheme of Señor Miranda's.'

'Yes. I'm afraid that he and his cousin Simon Oliver have a great deal of influence over Mr Edward.'

'All right, Mulberry. Thank you very much for letting me know. I'll try to deal with it.'

Forgetting his phone call, Hugh returned to the partners' room. Would the other partners let Edward do this? They might. Hugh and Samuel no longer had much influence as they were leaving. Young William did not share Hugh's fear of a South American collapse. Major Hartshorn and Sir Harry would do as they were told. And Edward was Senior Partner now.

What was Hugh going to do about it? He had not left

yet, and he was still earning his share of the profits, so his responsibilities were not at an end.

The trouble was that Edward was not rational: as Mulberry had said, he was completely under the influence of Micky Miranda.

Was there any way Hugh could weaken that influence? He could tell Edward that Micky was a murderer. Edward would not believe him. But he began to feel that he had to try. He had nothing to lose. And he badly needed to do something about the dreadful revelation he had had in the night.

Edward had already left for lunch. On impulse, Hugh decided to follow him.

Guessing Edward's destination, he took a hansom to the Cowes Club. He spent the journey from the City to Pall Mall trying to think of words that would be plausible and inoffensive, to help convince Edward. But all the phrases he thought of sounded artificial, and when he arrived he decided to tell the unvarnished truth and hope for the best.

It was still early, and he found Edward alone in the smoking-room of the club, drinking a large glass of madeira. Edward's skin rash was getting worse, he noticed: where his collar chafed his neck it was red and raw.

Hugh sat down at the same table and ordered tea. When they were boys, Hugh had hated Edward passionately, for being a beast and a bully. But in recent years he had come to see his cousin as a victim. Edward was the way he was because of the influence of two wicked people, Augusta and Micky. Augusta had suffocated him and Micky had corrupted him. However, Edward had not softened towards Hugh, and he now made no bones about showing that he had no wish for Hugh's company. 'You didn't have to come this far for a cup of tea,' he said. 'What do you want?'

It was a bad start, but nothing could be done about that. Feeling pessimistic, Hugh began. 'I have something to say that will shock and horrify you.'

'Really?'

'You'll have trouble believing it, but all the same it's true. I think Micky Miranda is a murderer.'

'Oh, for God's sake,' Edward said angrily. 'Don't bother me with such nonsense.'

'Listen to me before you dismiss the idea out of hand,' Hugh said. 'I'm leaving the bank, you're Senior Partner, I have nothing left to fight for. But I discovered something yesterday. Solly Greenbourne knew that your mother was behind that press campaign to stop Ben Greenbourne getting a peerage.'

Edward gave an involuntary start, as if what Hugh had said chimed with something he already knew.

Hugh felt more hopeful. 'I'm on the right track, am I not?' he said. Guessing, he went on: 'Solly threatened to cancel the Santamaria Railroad deal, didn't he?'

Edward nodded.

Hugh sat forward, trying to contain his excitement.

Edward said: 'I was sitting at this very table, with Micky, when Solly came in, angry as the very devil. But—'

'And that night Solly died.'

'Yes – but Micky was with me all night. We played cards here then went on to Nellie's.'

'He must have left you, just for a few minutes.'

'No—'

'I saw him coming into the club about the time Solly died.'

'That must have been earlier.'

'He may have gone to the toilet, or something.'

'That hardly gives him enough time.' Edward's face settled into an expression of decided scepticism.

Hugh's hopes faded again. For a moment he had succeeded in creating a doubt in Edward's mind, but it had not lasted.

'You've lost your senses,' Edward went on. 'Micky's not a murderer. The notion is absurd.'

Hugh decided to tell him about Peter Middleton. It was an act of desperation, for if Edward refused to believe that Micky might have killed Solly eleven years ago, why would he believe that Micky had killed Peter twenty-four years ago? But Hugh had to try. 'Micky killed Peter Middleton, too,' he said, knowing that he was in danger of sounding wild.

'This is ridiculous!'

'You think you killed him, I know that. You ducked him repeatedly, then went chasing after Tonio; and you think that Peter was too exhausted to swim to the side, and drowned. But there's something you don't know.'

Despite his scepticism, Edward was intrigued. 'What?'

'Peter was a very strong swimmer.'

'He was a weed!'

'Yes – but he had been practising swimming, every day, all summer. He was a weed all right, but he could swim for miles. He swam to the side without difficulty – Tonio saw it.'

'What . . .' Edward swallowed. 'What else did Tonio see?'

'While you were climbing up the side of the quarry, Micky held Peter's head under the water until he drowned.'

To Hugh's surprise, Edward did not spurn the idea. Instead he said: 'Why have you waited so long to tell me this?'

'I didn't think you'd believe me. I'm only telling you now out of desperation, to try to dissuade you from this latest Cordovan investment.' He studied Edward's expression, and went on: 'But you do believe me, don't you?'

Edward nodded.

'Why?'

'Because I know why he did it.'

'Why?' said Hugh. He was inflamed by curiosity. He had wondered about this for years. 'Why did Micky kill Peter?'

Edward took a long swallow of his madeira, then he went silent. Hugh was afraid he would refuse to say any more. But eventually he spoke. 'In Cordova the Mirandas are a wealthy family, but their dollars don't buy much over here. When Micky came to Windfield he spent his entire year's allowance in a few weeks. But he had boasted of his family's riches, and he was much too proud to admit the truth. So, when he ran out of money . . . he stole.'

Hugh remembered the scandal that had rocked the school in June of 1866. 'The six gold sovereigns that were stolen from Dr Offerton,' he said wonderingly. 'Micky was the thief?'

'Yes.'

'Well, I'm damned.'

'And Peter knew.'

'How?'

'He saw Micky coming out of Offerton's study. When the theft was reported he guessed the truth. He said he would tell unless Micky owned up. We thought it was a piece of luck to catch him at the pool. When I ducked him I was trying to frighten him into silence. But I never thought. . . .'

'That Micky would kill him.'

'And all these years he's let me think it was my fault, and he was covering up for me,' Edward said. 'The swine.'

Hugh realized that, against the odds, he had succeeded in shaking Edward's faith in Micky. He was tempted to say: *Now that you know what he's like, forget about the Santamaria Harbour.* But he had to be careful not to overplay his hand. He decided he had said enough: Edward should be left to draw his own conclusions. Hugh stood up to go. 'I'm sorry to have given you such a blow,' he said.

Edward was deep in thought, rubbing his neck where the rash itched. 'Yes,' he said vaguely.

'I must go.'

Edward said nothing. He seemed to have forgotten Hugh's existence. He was staring into his glass. Hugh looked hard at him and realized, with a jolt, that he was crying.

He went out quietly and closed the door.

[IV]

AUGUSTA LIKED being a widow. For one thing, black suited her. With her dark eyes, silver hair and black eyebrows she was quite striking in mourning clothes.

Joseph had been dead for four weeks and it was remarkable how little she missed him. She found it a little odd that he was not there to complain if the beef was underdone or the library was dusty. She dined alone once or twice a week but she had always been able to enjoy her own company. She no longer had the status of wife of the Senior Partner, but she was the mother of the new Senior Partner. And she was the Dowager Countess of Whitehaven. She had everything Joseph had ever given her, without the nuisance of having Joseph himself.

And she might marry again. She was fifty-eight, and no longer capable of bearing children; but she still had the desires that she thought of as girlish feelings. In fact they had got worse since Joseph's death. When Micky Miranda touched her arm, or looked into her eyes, or let his hand rest on her hip as he ushered her into a room, she felt more strongly than ever that sensation of pleasure combined with weakness that made her head spin.

Looking at herself in the drawing-room mirror, she thought: We are so alike, Micky and I, even in our colouring. We would have had such pretty dark-eyed babies.

As she was thinking it, her blue-eyed, fair-haired baby came in. He was not looking well. He had gone from being stout to positively fat, and he had some kind of skin problem. He was often bad-tempered around tea-time, as the effects of the wine he drank at lunch wore off.

But she had something important to say to him and was in no mood to go easy on him. 'What's this I hear about Emily asking you for an annulment?' she said.

'She wants to marry someone else,' Edward said dully.

'She can't – she's married to you!'

'Not really,' Edward said.

What on earth was he talking about? Much as she loved him, he could be deeply irritating. 'Don't be silly,' she snapped. 'Of course she's married to you.'

'I only married her because you wanted me to. And she only agreed because her parents made her. We never loved one another, and . . .' He hesitated, then blurted: 'We never consummated the marriage.'

So that was what he was getting at. Augusta was astonished that he had the nerve to refer directly to the sexual act: such things were not said in front of women. However, she was not surprised to learn that the marriage was a sham: she had guessed it for years. All the same she was not going to let Emily get away with this. 'We can't have a scandal,' she said firmly.

'It wouldn't be a scandal—'

'Of course it would,' she barked, exasperated by his

474

short-sightedness. 'It would be the talk of London for a year, and it would be in all the cheap newspapers too.' Edward was Lord Whitehaven now, and a sexual sensation involving a peer was just the kind of thing featured in the weekly newspapers that servants bought.

Edward said miserably: 'But don't you think Emily has a right to her freedom?'

Augusta ignored that feeble appeal to justice. 'Can she force you?'

'She wants me to sign a document admitting that the marriage was never consummated. Then, apparently, it's straightforward.'

'And if you don't sign?'

'Then it's more difficult. These things are not easy to prove.'

'That settles it. We have nothing to worry about. Let's speak no more about this embarrassing topic.'

'But—'

'Tell her she can't have an annulment. I absolutely will not hear of it.'

'Very well, Mother.'

She was taken aback by his rapid capitulation. Although she generally got her way in the end, he normally put up more of a fight than this. He must have other problems on his mind. 'What's the matter, Teddy?' she said in a softer voice.

He sighed heavily. 'Hugh told me the devil of a thing,' he said.

'What?'

'He says Micky killed Solly Greenbourne.'

Augusta felt a shiver of horrid fascination. 'How? Solly was run over.'

'Hugh says Micky pushed him in front of that carriage.'

'Do you believe it?'

'Micky was with me that evening, but he might have slipped out for a few minutes. It's possible. Do you believe it, Mother?'

Augusta nodded. Micky was dangerous and bold: it was what made him so magnetic. She had no doubt he was capable of committing such a daring murder – and getting away with it.

'I find it hard to accept,' Edward said. 'I know Micky is wicked in some ways, but to think he would kill . . .'

'He would, though,' Augusta said.

'How can you be sure?'

Edward looked so pathetic that Augusta was tempted to share her own secret knowledge with him. Would it be wise? It could do no harm. And it might do some good. The shock of Hugh's revelation seemed to have made Edward more thoughtful than usual. Perhaps the truth was good for him. It might make him more serious. She decided to tell him. 'Micky killed your Uncle Seth,' she said.

'Good God!'

'He suffocated him with a pillow. I caught him red-handed.' Augusta felt a flush of heat in her loins as she remembered the scene that had followed.

Edward said: 'But why would Micky kill Uncle Seth?'

'He was in such a hurry to get those rifles shipped to Cordova, don't you remember?'

'I remember.' Edward was silent for a few moments. Augusta closed her eyes, reliving that long, wild embrace with Micky, in the room with the dead man.

Edward brought her out of her reverie. 'There's something else, and it's even worse. You remember that boy Peter Middleton?'

'Certainly.' Augusta would never forget him. His death had haunted the family ever since. 'What about him?'

'Hugh says Micky killed him.'

Now Augusta was shocked. 'What? No – I can't believe that.'

Edward nodded. 'Deliberately held his head under the water and drowned him.'

It was not the murder itself but the idea of Micky's betrayal that horrified her. 'Hugh must be lying.'

'He says Tonio Silva saw the whole thing.'

'But that would mean Micky has been wickedly deceiving us all these years!'

'I think it's true, Mother.'

Augusta realized, with a growing sense of dread, that Edward would not give credence to such a wild story without a reason. 'Why are you so willing to believe what Hugh says?'

'Because I know something Hugh didn't know, something that confirms the story. You see, Micky had stolen some money from one of the masters. Peter knew and was threatening to tell. Micky was desperate to find some way of shutting him up.'

'Micky was always short of money,' Augusta recalled. She shook her head in incredulity. 'And all these years we've thought . . .'

'That it was my fault Peter died.'

Augusta nodded.

Edward said: 'And Micky let us think it. I can't take it in, Mother. I believed I was a killer, and Micky knew I wasn't, but he said nothing. Isn't that a terrible betrayal of friendship?'

Augusta looked sympathetically at her son. 'Will you throw him over?'

'Inevitably.' Edward was grief-stricken. 'But he's my only friend, really.'

Augusta felt close to tears. They sat looking at each other, thinking about what they had done, and why.

Edward said: 'For nearly twenty-five years we've treated him as a member of the family. And he's a monster.'

A monster, Augusta thought. It was true.

And yet she loved him. Even if he had killed three people, she loved Micky Miranda. Despite the way he had deceived her, she knew that if he walked into the room at this moment she would long to take him in her arms.

She looked at her son. Reading his face, she realized he felt the same way. She had known it in her heart but now her mind acknowledged it.

Edward loved Micky too.

CHAPTER TWO

October

[I]

MICKY MIRANDA was worried. He sat in the lounge of the Cowes Club smoking a cigar, wondering what he had done to offend Edward. Edward was avoiding him. He stayed away from the club, he did not go to Nellie's, and he did not even appear in Augusta's drawing-room at tea-time. Micky had not seen him for a week.

He had asked Augusta what was wrong but she said she did not know. She was a little odd with him and he suspected that she knew but would not say.

This had not happened in twenty years. Every now and again Edward would take offence at something Micky did and go into a sulk, but it never lasted more than a day or two. This time it was serious – and that meant it could jeopardize the Santamaría Harbour money.

In the last decade, Pilasters Bank had issued Cordovan bonds about once a year. Some of the money had been capital for railways, waterworks and mines; some had been simple loans to the government. All of it had benefited the Miranda family directly or indirectly, and Papa Miranda

479

was now the most powerful man in Cordova after the president.

Micky had taken a commission on everything – although nobody at the bank knew this – and he was now personally very rich. More significantly, his ability to raise the money had made him one of the most important figures in Cordovan politics and the unquestioned heir to his father's power.

And Papa was about to start a revolution.

The plans were laid. The Miranda army would dash south by rail and lay siege to the capital. There would be a simultaneous attack on Milpita, the port on the Pacific coast that served the capital.

But revolutions cost money. Papa had instructed Micky to raise the biggest loan yet, two million pounds sterling, to buy weapons and supplies for a civil war. And Papa had promised a matchless reward. When Papa was president, Micky would be prime minister, with authority over everyone except Papa himself. And he would be designated Papa's successor, to become president when Papa died.

It was everything he had ever wanted.

He would return to his own country a conquering hero, the heir to the throne, the president's right-hand man, and lord over his cousins and uncles and – most gratifyingly – his older brother.

And now all of that had been put at risk by Edward.

Edward was essential to the plan. Micky had given Pilasters an unofficial monopoly of trade with Cordova, in order to boost Edward's prestige and power at the bank. It had worked: Edward was now Senior Partner, something he could never have achieved without help. But no one else in London's financial community had got a chance to develop any expertise in Cordovan trade. Consequently the other banks felt they did not know enough to invest there. And they were doubly suspicious of any project Micky brought to them because they assumed it had already been turned down by Pilasters. Micky had tried raising money for Cordova through other banks, but they had always turned him down.

Edward's sulk was therefore deeply disquieting. It was giving Micky sleepless nights. With Augusta unwilling or unable to shed any light on the problem, Micky had no one to ask: he himself was Edward's only close friend.

While he sat smoking and worrying, he spotted Hugh Pilaster. It was seven o'clock, and Hugh was in evening dress, having a drink alone, presumably on his way to meet people for dinner.

Micky did not like Hugh and he knew the feeling was mutual. However, Hugh might know what was going on. And Micky had nothing to lose by asking him. So he stood up and went over to Hugh's table. 'Evening, Pilaster,' he said.

'Evening, Miranda.'

'Have you seen your cousin Edward lately? He seems to have vanished.'

'He comes to the bank every day.'

'Ah.' Micky hesitated. When Hugh did not invite him to take a seat he said: 'May I join you?' and sat down without waiting for a reply. In a lower voice he said: 'Would you happen to know whether I've done anything to offend him?'

Hugh had looked thoughtful for a moment, then said: 'I can't think of any reason why I shouldn't tell you. Edward has discovered that you killed Peter Middleton, and you've been lying to him about it for twenty-four years.'

Micky almost jumped out of his chair. How the devil had that come out? He almost asked the question, then realized

481

he could not without admitting his guilt. Instead he feigned anger and stood up abruptly. 'I shall forget you ever said that,' he said, and he left the room.

It took him only a few moments to realize that he was in no more danger from the police than he had ever been. No one could prove what he had done and it had all happened so long ago that there would be no point in reopening the investigation. The real danger he faced was that Edward would refuse to raise the two million pounds Papa needed.

He had to win Edward's forgiveness. And to do that he had to see him.

That night he could do nothing for he was engaged to go to a diplomatic reception at the French Embassy and a supper party with some Conservative Members of Parliament. But the next day he went to Nellie's at lunchtime, woke April up, and persuaded her to send Edward a note, promising him 'something special' if he would come to the brothel that night.

Micky took April's best room and booked Edward's current favourite, Henrietta, a slim girl with short dark hair. He instructed her to dress in a man's evening clothes with a top hat, an outfit Edward found sexy.

By half-past nine in the evening he was waiting for Edward. The room had a huge four-poster bed, two sofas, a big ornate fireplace, the usual wash-stand, and a series of vividly obscene paintings set in a mortuary, showing the slavering attendant performing various sexual acts on the pale corpse of a beautiful young girl. Micky reclined on a velvet sofa, wearing nothing but a silk robe, sipping brandy, with Henrietta beside him.

She quickly got bored. 'Do you like these pictures?' she asked him.

He shrugged and did not answer. He did not want to talk to her. He had very little interest in women for their own sake. The sexual act itself was a humdrum mechanical process. What he liked about sex was the power it gave him. Women and men had always fallen in love with him and he never tired of using their infatuation to control, exploit and humiliate them. Even his youthful passion for Augusta Pilaster had been in part the desire to tame and ride a spirited wild mare.

From that point of view, Henrietta offered him nothing: it was no challenge to control her, she had nothing worth exploiting her for, and there was no satisfaction in humiliating someone as low down the scale as a prostitute. So he smoked his cigar and worried about whether Edward would come.

An hour went by, and then another. Micky began to lose hope. Was there some other way to reach Edward? It was very difficult to get to a man who really did not want to be seen. He could be 'not at home' at his house and unavailable at his place of work. Micky could hang around outside the bank to catch Edward leaving for lunch, but that was undignified, and anyway Edward could easily just ignore him. Sooner or later they would meet at some social occasion, but it might not happen for weeks, and Micky could not afford to wait that long.

Then, just before midnight, April put her head around the door and said: 'He's arrived.'

'At last,' Micky said with relief.

'He's having a drink but he says he doesn't want to play cards. He'll come in here in a few minutes, I'd guess.'

Micky's tension mounted. He was guilty of a betrayal about as bad as could be imagined. He had allowed Edward to suffer for a quarter of a century under the illusion that he had killed Peter Middleton when in fact Micky was

483

the guilty one all along. It was a lot to ask Edward to forgive.

But Micky had a plan.

He posed Henrietta on the sofa. He made her sit with the hat over her eyes and her legs crossed, smoking a cigarette. He turned the gaslights down low then went and sat on the bed, behind the door.

A few moments later Edward came in. In the dim light he did not notice Micky sitting on the bed. He stopped in the doorway, looking at Henrietta, and said: 'Hello – who are you?'

She looked up and said: 'Hello, Edward.'

'Oh, it's you,' he said. He shut the door and came inside. 'Well, what's the "something special" April has been talking about? I've seen you in a tail-coat before.'

'It's me,' Micky said, and stood up.

Edward frowned. 'I don't wish to see you,' he said, and turned toward the door.

Micky stood in his way. 'At least tell me why. We've been friends too long.'

'I've found out the truth about Peter Middleton.'

Micky nodded. 'Will you give me a chance to explain?'

'What is there to explain?'

'How I came to make such an awful mistake, and why I never had the courage to admit it.'

Edward looked mulish.

Micky said: 'Sit down, just for a minute, by Henrietta, and let me speak.'

Edward hesitated.

Micky said: 'Please?'

Edward sat on the sofa.

Micky went to the sideboard and poured him a brandy. Edward took it with a nod. Henrietta moved close to him on the sofa and took his arm. Edward sipped his drink, looked around, and said: 'I hate these paintings.'

'Me, too,' said Henrietta. 'They give me the shivers.'

'Shut up, Henrietta,' said Micky.

'Sorry I spoke, I'm sure,' she said indignantly.

Micky sat on the sofa opposite and addressed Edward. 'I was wrong, and I betrayed you,' he began. 'But I was fifteen years old, and we've been best friends for most of our lives. Are you really going to throw that away for a schoolboy peccadillo?'

'But you could have told me the truth at any time in the last twenty-five years!' Edward said indignantly.

Micky made his face sad. 'I could have, and I should have, but once a lie like that is told, it's hard to take it back. It would have ruined our friendship.'

'Not necessarily,' Edward said.

'Well, it has now . . . hasn't it?'

'Yes,' Edward said, but there was a tremor of uncertainty in his voice.

Micky realized the time had come to go all out.

He stood up and slipped off his robe.

He knew he looked good: his body was still lean, and his skin was smooth except for the curly hair at his chest and groin.

Henrietta immediately got up from the sofa and knelt in front of him. Micky watched Edward. Desire flickered in his eyes, but then he glowered obstinately and looked away.

In desperation Micky played his last card.

'Leave us, Henrietta,' he said.

She looked startled, but she got up and went out.

Edward stared at Micky. 'Why did you do that?' he said.

'What do we need her for?' Micky replied. He stepped

closer to the sofa, so that his groin was just inches from Edward's face. He put out a tentative hand, touched Edward's head, and gently stroked his hair. Edward did not move.

Micky said: 'We're better off without her . . . aren't we?'

Edward swallowed hard and said nothing.

'Aren't we?' Micky persisted.

At last Edward replied. 'Yes,' he whispered. 'Yes.'

The following week, Micky entered for the first time the hushed dignity of the partners' room at Pilasters Bank.

He had been bringing them business for seventeen years, but whenever he came to the bank he was shown to one of the other rooms, and a walker would fetch Edward from the partners' room. He suspected that an Englishman would have been admitted to the inner sanctum a lot faster. He loved London but he knew he would always be an outsider here.

Feeling nervous, he spread out the plan for Santamaria Harbour on the big table in the middle of the room. The drawing showed an entirely new port on the Atlantic coast of Cordova, with ship repair facilities and a rail link.

None of it would ever be built, of course. The two million pounds would go straight into the Miranda war chest. But the survey was genuine and the plans were professionally drawn, and if it had been an honest proposal it might even have made money.

Being a dishonest proposal it probably ranked as the most ambitious fraud in history.

While Micky explained it to them, talking of building materials, labour costs, customs duties and income projections, he struggled to maintain an appearance of calm. His entire career, the future of his family and the destiny of his country depended on the decision made in this room today.

The partners were also tense. All six were there: the two in-laws, Major Hartshorn and Sir Harry Tonks; Samuel, the old queen; Young William; and Edward and Hugh.

There would be a battle, but the odds were on Edward's side. He was Senior Partner. Major Hartshorn and Sir Harry always did what their Pilaster wives told them, and the wives got their orders from Augusta, so they would back Edward. Samuel would probably back Hugh. Young William was the only unpredictable one.

Edward was enthusiastic, as expected. He had forgiven Micky, they were the best of friends again, and this was his first major project as Senior Partner. He was pleased to have brought in such a big piece of business to launch his term of office.

Sir Harry spoke next. 'The proposal is carefully thought out, and we've been doing well with Cordovan bonds for a decade. It looks an attractive proposition to me.'

As anticipated, the opposition came from Hugh. It was Hugh who had told Edward the truth about Peter Middleton, and his motive had surely been to prevent this loan issue. 'I've been looking at what has happened to the last few South American issues we've handled,' he said, and he handed round copies of a table.

Micky studied the table while Hugh continued. 'The interest rate offered has gone up from six per cent three years ago to seven-and-a-half per cent last year. Despite that increase, the number of bonds remaining unsold has been higher each time.'

Micky knew enough about finance to understand what that meant: investors were finding South American bonds less and less attractive. Hugh's calm expression and relentless logic made Micky fume.

Hugh went on: 'Also, in each of the last three issues, the bank has been obliged to buy bonds in the open market to keep the price up artificially.' Which meant, Micky realized, that the figures in the table understated the problem.

'The consequence of our persistence in this saturated market is that we now hold almost a million pounds' worth of Cordovan bonds. Our bank is gravely over-exposed to that one sector.'

It was a powerful argument. Trying to stay cool, Micky reflected that if he were a partner he would now vote against the issue. But it would not be decided purely by the financial reasoning. There was more at stake here than money.

For a few seconds no one spoke. Edward looked angry, but he was restraining himself, knowing it would appear better if one of the other partners contradicted Hugh.

At last Sir Harry said: 'Point taken, Hugh, but I think you may be overstating the case a little.'

George Hartshorn concurred. 'We're all agreed that the plan itself is sound. The risk is small and the profits are considerable. I think we should accept.'

Micky had known in advance that those two would support Edward. He was waiting for Young William's verdict.

But it was Samuel who spoke next. 'I understand that you're all reluctant to veto the first major proposal brought in by a new Senior Partner,' he said. His tone suggested that they were not enemies divided into opposing camps, but reasonable men who could not help but agree, given a little goodwill. 'Perhaps you're not inclined to place much reliance on the views of two partners who have already announced their resignations. But I've been in the business twice as long as anyone else in this room, and Hugh is probably the most successful young banker in the world, and we both feel this project is more dangerous than it looks. Don't let personal considerations lead you to dismiss that advice out of hand.'

Samuel was eloquent, Micky thought, but his position had been known in advance. Everyone now looked at Young William.

At last he spoke. 'South American bonds have always seemed more risky,' he began. 'If we had allowed ourselves to be frightened of them we would have missed out on a great deal of profitable business during the last few years.' This sounded good, Micky thought. William went on: 'I don't think there's going to be a financial collapse. Cordova has gone from strength to strength under President Garcia. I believe we can anticipate increasing profits from our business there in future. We should be looking for more such business, not less.'

Micky let his breath out in a long, silent sigh of relief. He had won.

Edward said: 'Four partners in favour, then, and two against.'

'Just a minute,' said Hugh.

God forbid that Hugh should have something up his sleeve, Micky thought. He clenched his jaw. He wanted to cry out a protest but he had to suppress his feelings.

Edward looked crossly at Hugh. 'What is it? You're outvoted.'

'A vote has always been a last resort in this room,' Hugh said. 'When there is disagreement between the partners we try to reach a compromise that everyone can assent to.'

Micky could see that Edward was ready to squash this idea, but William said: 'What have you got in mind, Hugh?'

'Let me ask Edward something,' Hugh said. 'Are you confident that we can sell all or most of this issue?'

'Yes, if we price it right,' Edward said. It was clear from his expression that he did not know where this was heading. Micky had a dreadful premonition that he was about to be outmanoeuvred.

Hugh went on: 'Then why don't we sell the bonds on a commission basis, rather than underwriting the issue?'

Micky muffled a curse. That was not what he wanted. Normally, when the bank launched, say, a million pounds' worth of bonds, it agreed to buy any unsold bonds itself, thereby guaranteeing that the borrower would receive the full million. In return for that guarantee, the bank took a fat percentage. The alternative method was to offer the bonds for sale with no guarantee. The bank took no risk and received a much lower percentage, but if only ten thousand of the million bonds were sold, the borrower would get only ten thousand pounds. The risk remained with the borrower – and at this stage Micky did not want any risks.

William grunted. 'Hmm. That's a thought.'

Hugh had been cunning, Micky realized despondently. If he had continued to oppose the scheme outright, he would have been overruled. But he had suggested a way of reducing the risk. Bankers, being a conservative breed, loved to reduce their risks.

Sir Harry said: 'If we do sell them all, we still make about sixty thousand pounds, even at the reduced commission. And if we don't sell them all we shall have avoided a considerable loss.'

Say something, Edward! thought Micky. Edward was losing control of the meeting. But he seemed not to know how to get it back.

Samuel said: 'And we can record a unanimous decision of the partners – always a pleasant outcome.'

There was a general murmur of assent.

In desperation, Micky said: 'I can't promise that my principals will agree to that. In the past the bank has always underwritten Cordovan bonds. If you decide to change your policy . . .' He hesitated. 'I may have to go to another bank.' It was an empty threat, but would they know that?

William was offended. 'That's your privilege. Another bank may take a different view of the risks.'

Micky saw that his threat had only served to consolidate the opposition. Hastily he added: 'The leaders of my country value their relationship with Pilasters Bank and would not wish to jeopardize that.'

Edward said: 'And we reciprocate their feelings.'

'Thank you.' Micky realized there was no more to be said.

He began to roll up the map of the harbour. He had been defeated, but he was not ready to give up yet. That two million pounds was the key to the presidency of his country. He had to have it.

He would think of something.

Edward and Micky had arranged to have lunch together in the dining-room of the Cowes Club. It was planned as a celebration of their triumph, but now they had nothing to celebrate.

By the time Edward arrived, Micky had worked out what he had to do. His only chance now was to persuade Edward secretly to go against the decision of the partners, and underwrite the bonds without telling them. It was an outrageous, foolhardy and probably criminal act. But there was no alternative.

Micky was already sitting at the table when Edward came in. 'I'm very disappointed about what happened at the bank this morning,' Micky said right away.

'It was the fault of my damned cousin Hugh,' Edward said as he sat down. He waved at a waiter and said: 'Bring me a big glass of madeira.'

'The trouble is, if the issue isn't underwritten, there's no guarantee the harbour will be built.'

'I did my best,' Edward said plaintively. 'You saw that, you were there.'

Micky nodded. Unfortunately it was true. If Edward had been a brilliant manipulator of other people – like his mother – he might have defeated Hugh. But if Edward had been that sort of person he would not be Micky's pawn.

Pawn though he was, he might resist the proposal Micky had in mind. Micky cudgelled his brains for ways of persuading or coercing him.

They ordered their lunch. When the waiter had left Edward said: 'I've been thinking that I might get a place of my own. I've been living with my mother too long.'

Micky made an effort to be interested. 'You'd buy a house?'

'A small one. I don't want a palace, with dozens of parlourmaids running around putting coal on fires. A modest house that can be run by a good butler and a handful of servants.'

'But you've got everything you need at Whitehaven House.'

'Everything but privacy.'

Micky began to see what he was driving at. 'You don't want your mother to know everything you do. . . .'

'You might want to stay with me overnight, for example,' Edward said, giving Micky a very direct look.

Micky suddenly saw how he could exploit this idea. He feigned sadness and shook his head. 'By the time you get the house I shall probably have left London.'

Edward was devastated. 'What the devil do you mean?'

'If I don't raise the money for the new harbour, I'm sure to be recalled by the president.'

'You can't go back!' Edward said in a frightened voice.

'I certainly don't want to. But I may not have the choice.'

'The bonds will sell out, I'm sure,' Edward said.

'I hope so. If they don't . . .'

Edward hit the table with his fist, making the glasses shake. 'I wish Hugh had let me underwrite the issue!'

Micky said nervously: 'I suppose you have to abide by the decision of the partners.'

'Of course – what else?'

'Well . . .' He hesitated. He tried to sound casual. 'You couldn't just ignore what was said today, and simply have your staff draw up an underwriting deal, without telling anyone, could you?'

'I could, I suppose,' Edward said worriedly.

'After all, you are Senior Partner. That ought to mean something.'

'It damn well should.'

'Simon Oliver would do the paperwork discreetly. You can trust him.'

'Yes.'

Micky could hardly believe Edward was agreeing so readily. 'It might make the difference between my staying in London and my being recalled to Cordova.'

The waiter brought their wine and poured them each a glass.

Edward said: 'It would all come out, eventually.'

493

'By then it will be too late. And you can pass it off as a clerical error.' Micky knew this was implausible and he doubted if Edward would swallow it.

But Edward ignored it. 'If you stay . . .' He paused and dropped his eyes.

'Yes?'

'If you stay in London, will you spend nights at my new house, sometimes?'

That was the only thing Edward was interested in, Micky realized with a surge of triumph. He gave his most winning smile. 'Of course.'

Edward nodded. 'That's all I want. I'll speak to Simon this afternoon.'

Micky picked up his wine glass. 'To friendship,' he said.

Edward clinked glasses and smiled shyly. 'To friendship.'

[II]

WITHOUT WARNING, Edward's wife Emily moved into Whitehaven House.

Although everyone still thought of it as Augusta's house, Joseph had in fact bequeathed it to Edward. Consequently they could not throw Emily out: it would probably have been grounds for divorce, and that was just what Emily wanted.

In fact Emily was technically mistress of the house, and Augusta just a mother-in-law living there on sufferance. If Emily had openly confronted Augusta there would have been a mighty clash of wills. Augusta would have relished that, but Emily was too adroit to fight her openly. 'It is your home,' Emily would say sweetly. 'You must do whatever you wish.' The condescension was enough to make Augusta flinch.

Emily even had Augusta's title: as Edward's wife she was the Countess of Whitehaven now, and Augusta was the Dowager Countess.

Augusta continued to give orders to the servants as if she were still mistress of the house, and whenever she got the chance she would countermand Emily's instructions. Emily never complained. However, the servants became subversive. They liked Emily better than Augusta — because she was foolishly soft on them, Augusta thought — and they found ways to make Emily's life comfortable despite Augusta's efforts.

The most powerful weapon an employer had was the threat of dismissing a servant without a character reference. No one else would give the servant a job thereafter. But Emily had taken this weapon away from Augusta with an ease that was almost frightening. One day Emily ordered sole for lunch, Augusta changed it to salmon, sole was served, and Augusta dismissed the cook. But Emily gave the cook a glowing reference and she was hired by the Duke of Kingsbridge at a better wage. And for the first time ever, Augusta's servants were not terrified of her.

Emily's friends would call at Whitehaven House in the afternoon. Tea was a ritual presided over by the mistress of the house. Emily would smile sweetly and beg Augusta to take charge, but then Augusta would have to be polite to Emily's friends, which was almost as bad as letting Emily play the role of mistress.

Dinner was worse. Augusta sat at the head of the table, but everyone knew it was Emily's place, and one crass guest had even remarked how kind Emily was to defer to her mother-in-law that way.

Augusta had been outmanoeuvred, a new experience for her. Normally she held over people's heads the ultimate deterrent of expulsion from the circle of her favour. But

495

expulsion was what Emily wanted, and that made her impossible to frighten.

Augusta became all the more determined never to give in.

People began to invite Edward and Emily to social functions. Emily would go, whether Edward accompanied her or not. People began to notice. When Emily had hidden herself away in Leicestershire, her estrangement from her husband could be overlooked; but with both of them living in town it became embarrassing.

Once upon a time Augusta had been indifferent to the opinion of high society. It was a tradition among commercial people to regard the aristocracy as frivolous if not degenerate, and to ignore their opinions, or at least to pretend to. But Augusta had long ago left behind that simple middle-class pride. She was the Dowager Countess of Whitehaven and she craved the approval of London's elite. She could not allow her son churlishly to decline invitations from the very best people. So she forced him to go.

Tonight was a case in point. The Marquis of Hocastle was in London for a debate in the House of Lords, and the marchioness was giving a dinner party for such few of her friends as were not in the country hunting and shooting. Edward and Emily were going, and so was Augusta.

But when Augusta came downstairs in her black silk gown she found Micky Miranda in evening dress drinking whisky in the drawing-room. Her heart leaped at the sight of him, so dashing in his white waistcoat and high collar. He stood up and kissed her hand. She was glad she had chosen this gown, which had a low bodice that showed off her bosom.

Edward had dropped Micky, after finding out the truth about Peter Middleton, but it had only lasted a few days, and they were now closer friends than ever before. Augusta was glad. She could not be angry with Micky. She had always known he was dangerous: it made him even more desirable. She sometimes felt frightened of him, knowing that he had killed three people, but her fear was exciting. He was the most immoral person she had ever met, and she wished he would throw her to the floor and ravish her.

Micky was still married. He could probably divorce Rachel if he wanted to – there were persistent rumours about her and Maisie Robinson's brother Dan, the Radical Member of Parliament – but it could not be done while Micky was the Minister.

Augusta sat on the Egyptian sofa, intending that he should sit beside her, but to her disappointment he sat opposite. Feeling spurned, she said: 'What are you here for?'

'Edward and I are going to a prizefight.'

'No, you're not. He's dining with the Marquis of Hocastle.'

'Ah.' Micky hesitated. 'I wonder if I made a mistake . . . or he did.'

Augusta was quite sure Edward was responsible and she doubted whether it was a mistake. He loved to watch prizefighting and he was probably intending to slide out of the dinner engagement. She would soon put a stop to that. 'You'd better go on your own,' she said to Micky.

A rebellious look came into his eye, and for a moment she thought he was going to defy her. Was she losing her power over this young man, she wondered? But he stood up, albeit slowly, and said: 'I'll slope off, then, if you'll explain to Edward.'

'Of course.'

But it was too late. Before Micky reached the door Edward came in.

Augusta noticed that his skin rash was inflamed tonight. It covered his throat and the back of his neck and reached up to one ear. It troubled her, but he said the doctor insisted it was nothing to worry about.

Rubbing his hands in anticipation, he said: 'I'm looking forward to this.'

Augusta said in her most authoritative voice: 'Edward, you cannot go to the prizefight.'

He looked like a child who has been told that Christmas is cancelled. 'Why not?' he said plaintively.

For a moment Augusta felt sorry for him and almost backed down. Then she hardened her heart and said: 'You know perfectly well that we are engaged to dine with the Marquis of Hocastle.'

'That's not tonight, is it?'

'You know it is.'

'I shan't go.'

'You must!'

'But I dined out with Emily last night!'

'Then tonight will make two civilized dinners in a row.'

'Why the deuce are we invited anyway?'

'Don't swear in front of your mother! We're invited because they are friends of Emily's.'

'Emily can go to the—' He caught Augusta's look and stopped short. 'Tell them I've been taken ill,' he said.

'Don't be ridiculous.'

'I think I should be able to go where I like, Mother.'

'You cannot offend high-ranking people!'

'I want to see the fights!'

'You may not go!'

At that moment Emily came in. She could not help but notice the charged atmosphere in the room, and she said immediately: 'What's wrong?'

Edward said: 'Go and fetch me that blasted bit of paper you're always asking me to sign!'

'What are you talking about?' Augusta said. 'What bit of paper?'

'My agreement to the annulment,' he said.

Augusta was horrified – and she realized with sudden rage that none of this was accidental. Emily had planned it exactly this way. Her aim had been to irritate Edward so much that he would sign anything just to be rid of her. Augusta had even helped her, inadvertently, by insisting that Edward fulfil his social obligations. She felt a fool: she had allowed herself to be manipulated. And now Emily's plan was on the brink of succeeding.

Augusta said: 'Emily! Stay here!'

Emily smiled sweetly and went out.

Augusta turned on Edward. 'You are not to consent to an annulment!'

Edward said: 'I'm forty years old, Mother. I'm head of the family business and this is my own house. You ought not to tell me what to do.'

He had a sulky, stubborn look on his face, and the dreadful thought occurred to Augusta that he might actually defy her for the first time in his life.

She began to feel scared.

'Come and sit here, Teddy,' she said in a softer voice.

Reluctantly he sat beside her.

She reached out to stroke his cheek, but he flinched away.

'You can't take care of yourself,' she said. 'You've never been able to. That's why Micky and I have always looked after you, ever since you were at school.'

He looked even more obstinate. 'Perhaps it's time you stopped.'

A feeling of panic began to creep over Augusta. It was almost as if she was losing her grip.

Before she could say any more, Emily came back with a legal-looking document. She put it on the Moorish writing-table, where pens and ink were already laid out.

Augusta looked at her son's face. Could it be that he was more afraid of his wife than his mother? Augusta thought wildly about snatching the document away, throwing the pens on the fire and spilling the ink. She got a grip on herself. Better perhaps to give in and pretend it was of no great consequence. But the pretence would be useless: she had made a stand, and forbidden this annulment, and everyone would know she had been defeated.

She said to Edward: 'You'll have to resign from the bank if you sign that document.'

'I don't see why,' he replied. 'It's not like a divorce.'

Emily said: 'The Church has no objection to an annulment if the grounds are genuine.' It sounded like a quotation: she had obviously checked.

Edward sat at the table, selected a quill, and dipped its point into a silver inkwell.

Augusta fired her last shot. 'Edward!' she said in a voice quivering with rage. 'If you sign that I will never speak to you again!'

He hesitated, then put the pen to paper. Everyone was silent. His hand moved, and the scratch of the quill on the paper sounded like thunder.

Edward put down the pen.

'How could you treat your mother this way?' Augusta said, and the sob in her voice was genuine.

Emily sanded the signature and picked up the document.

Augusta moved between Emily and the door.

Both Edward and Micky looked on, bemused and motionless, as the two women faced each other.

Augusta said: 'Give me that paper.'

Emily stepped closer, hesitated in front of Augusta, and then, astonishingly, she slapped Augusta's face.

The blow stung. Augusta cried out with surprise and pain and staggered back.

Emily stepped past her quickly, opened the door, and left the room, still clutching the document.

Augusta sat down heavily in the nearest chair and began to cry.

She heard Edward and Micky leave the room.

She felt old, defeated and alone.

[III]

THE ISSUE OF two million pounds' worth of Santamaria Harbour bonds was a flop, much worse than Hugh had feared. By the deadline date Pilasters Bank had sold only four hundred thousand pounds' worth, and on the following day the price immediately fell. Hugh was deeply glad he had forced Edward to sell the bonds on commission rather than underwriting them.

On the following Monday morning his clerk Jonas Mulberry brought in the summary of the previous week's business that was handed to all the partners. Before the man had left the room Hugh noticed a discrepancy. 'Just a minute, Mulberry,' he said. 'This can't be right.' There was a huge fall in cash on deposit, well over a million pounds. 'There hasn't been a big withdrawal, has there?'

'Not that I know of, Mr Hugh,' said Mulberry.

Hugh looked around the room. All the partners were there except Edward, who had not yet arrived. 'Does anyone recall a big withdrawal last week?'

Nobody did.

Hugh stood up. 'Let's check,' he said to Mulberry.

They went up the stairs to the Senior Clerks' Room. The item they were looking for was too big to have been a cash withdrawal. It had to be an interbank transaction. Hugh recalled from his days as a clerk that there was a journal of such transactions updated daily. He sat at a table and said to Mulberry: 'Find me the interbank book, please.'

Mulberry pulled a big ledger from a shelf and set it in front of him. Another clerk piped up: 'Is there anything I can do to assist, Mr Hugh? I keep that ledger.' He had a worried look and Hugh realized he was afraid he might have made an error.

Hugh said: 'You're Clemmow, aren't you?'

'Yes, sir.'

'What big withdrawals were there last week – a million pounds or more?'

'Only one,' the clerk said immediately. 'The Santamaria Harbour Company withdrew one million, eight hundred thousand – the amount of the bond issue, less commission.'

Hugh shot to his feet. 'But they didn't have that much – they only raised four hundred thousand!'

Clemmow turned pale. 'The issue was two million pounds of bonds—'

'But it wasn't underwritten, it was a commission sale!'

'I checked their balance – it was a million eight.'

'Damnation!' Hugh shouted. All the clerks in the room stared at him. 'Show me the ledger!'

Another clerk on the other side of the room pulled down a huge book, brought it over to Hugh and opened it at a page marked: 'Santamaria Harbour Board'.

There were only three entries: a credit of two million pounds, a debit of two hundred thousand pounds' commission to the bank, and a transfer to another bank of the balance.

Hugh was livid. The money had gone. If it had simply been credited to the account in error, the mistake could have been rectified easily. But the money had been withdrawn from the bank the next day. That suggested a carefully planned fraud. 'By God, someone is going to jail for this,' he said wrathfully. 'Who wrote these entries?'

'I did, sir,' said the clerk who had brought him the book. He was shaking with fear.

'On what instructions?'

'The usual paperwork. It was all in order.'

'Where did it come from?'

'From Mr Oliver.'

Simon Oliver was a Cordovan by birth and the cousin of Micky Miranda. Hugh instantly suspected he was behind the fraud.

Hugh did not want to continue this inquiry in front of twenty clerks. He was already regretting that he had let them all know about the problem. But when he started he had not known he was going to uncover a massive embezzlement.

Oliver was Edward's clerk, and worked on the partners' floor alongside Mulberry. 'Find Mr Oliver right away and bring him to the partners' room,' Hugh said to Mulberry. He would continue the investigation there, with the other partners.

'Right away, Mr Hugh,' said Mulberry. 'All of you get back to your work, now,' he said to the rest of them. They returned to their desks and picked up their pens, but before Hugh was out of the room a buzz of excited conversation broke out.

Hugh returned to the partners' room. 'There's been a major fraud,' he said grimly. 'The Santamaria Harbour Company has been paid the full amount of the bond issue even though we only sold four hundred thousand.'

503

They were all horrified. 'How the devil did it happen?' said William.

'The amount was credited to their account and then immediately transferred to another bank.'

'Who's responsible?'

'I think it was done by Simon Oliver, Edward's clerk. I've sent for him, but my guess is the swine is already on a ship headed for Cordova.'

Sir Harry said: 'Can we get the money back?'

'I don't know. They may have moved it out of the country by now.'

'They can't build a harbour with stolen money!'

'Perhaps they don't want to build a harbour. The whole thing could have been a damned swindle.'

'Good God.'

Mulberry came in – and, to Hugh's surprise, he was accompanied by Simon Oliver. That suggested that Oliver had not stolen the money. He had a thick contract in his hand. He looked scared: no doubt Hugh's remark about someone going to jail had been repeated to him.

Without preamble Oliver said: 'The Santamaria issue was underwritten – the contract says so.' He held the document out to Hugh with a trembling hand.

Hugh said: 'The partners agreed that these bonds were to be sold on a commission basis.'

'Mr Edward told me to draw up an underwriting contract.'

'Can you prove it?'

'Yes!' He gave Hugh another sheet of paper. This was a contract brief, a short note of the terms of an agreement, given by a partner to the clerk who was to draw up the full contract. It was in Edward's handwriting and it quite clearly said that the loan was to be underwritten.

That settled it. Edward was responsible. There had been

no fraud, and there was no way the money could be got back. The whole transaction was perfectly legitimate. Hugh was dismayed and enraged.

'All right, Oliver, you can go,' he said.

Oliver stood his ground. 'I hope I may take it that no suspicion attaches to me, Mr Hugh.'

Hugh was not convinced that Oliver was totally innocent, but he was obliged to say: 'You are not to be blamed for anything you did under Mr Edward's orders.'

'Thank you, sir.' Oliver went out.

Hugh looked at his partners. 'Edward went against our collective decision,' he said bitterly. 'He changed the terms of the issue behind our backs. And it has cost us one million, four hundred thousand pounds.'

Samuel sat down heavily. 'How dreadful,' he said.

Sir Harry and Major Hartshorn just looked bewildered.

William said: 'Are we bankrupt?'

Hugh realized the question was addressed to him. Well, were they bankrupt? It was unthinkable. He reflected for a moment. 'Technically, no,' he said. 'Although our cash reserve has gone down by one million, four hundred thousand pounds, the bonds appear on the other side of our balance sheet, valued at nearly their purchase price. So our assets match our liabilities, and we're solvent.'

Samuel added: 'As long as the price doesn't collapse.'

'Indeed. If something happened to cause a fall in South American bonds we would be in deep trouble.' To think that the mighty Pilasters Bank was so weak made him feel sick with rage at Edward.

Sir Harry said: 'Can we keep this quiet?'

'I doubt it,' Hugh replied. 'I'm afraid I made no attempt to hide it up in the Senior Clerks' Room. It's gone around the building by now and it will be all over the City by the end of the lunch hour.'

505

Jonas Mulberry interjected a practical question. 'What about our liquidity, Mr Hugh? We'll need a large deposit before the end of the week to meet routine withdrawals. We can't sell the Harbour Bonds – it would depress the price.'

That was a thought. Hugh worried at the problem for a moment then said: 'I'll borrow a million from the Colonial Bank. Old Cunliffe will keep it quiet. That should tide us over.' He looked around at the others. 'That takes care of the immediate emergency. However, the bank is dangerously weak. In the medium term we have to correct the position just as fast as we can.'

William said: 'What about Edward?'

Hugh knew what Edward had to do: resign. But he wanted someone else to say it, so he remained silent.

Eventually Samuel said: 'Edward must resign from the bank. None of us could ever trust him again.'

William said: 'He may withdraw his capital.'

'He can't,' Hugh said. 'We haven't got the cash. That threat has lost its power.'

'Of course,' William said. 'I hadn't thought of that.'

Sir Harry said: 'Then who will be Senior Partner?'

There was a moment of silence. Samuel broke it by saying: 'Oh, for goodness' sake, can there be any question? Who uncovered Edward's deceit? Who took charge in the crisis? Who have you all looked to for guidance? During the last hour all the decisions have been made by one person. The rest of you have just asked questions and looked helpless. You *know* who the new Senior Partner must be.'

Hugh was taken by surprise. His mind had been on the problems facing the bank, and he had not given a thought to his own position. Now he saw that Samuel was right. The others had all been more or less inert. Ever since he noticed the discrepancy in the weekly summary he had been acting as if he were the Senior Partner. And he knew he was the only one capable of steering the bank through the crisis.

Slowly it dawned on him that he was about to achieve his life's ambition: he was going to be Senior Partner of Pilasters Bank. He looked at William, Harry and George. They all had a shamefaced air. They had brought about this disaster by allowing Edward to become Senior Partner. Now they knew Hugh had been right all along. They were wishing they had listened to him before, and they wanted to make up for their error. He could see in their faces that they wanted him to take over.

But they had to say it.

He looked at William, who was the most senior after Samuel. 'What do you think?'

He hesitated only for a second. 'I think you should be Senior Partner, Hugh,' he said.

'Major Hartshorn?'

'I agree.'

'Sir Harry?'

'Certainly – and I hope you'll accept.'

It was done. Hugh could hardly believe it.

He took a deep breath. 'Thank you for your confidence. I will accept. I hope I can bring us all through this calamity with our reputation and our fortunes intact.'

At that moment Edward came in.

There was a dismayed silence. They had been discussing him almost as if he were dead, and it was a shock to see him in the room.

At first he did not notice the atmosphere. 'This whole place is in turmoil,' he said. 'Juniors running around, senior clerks whispering in the corridors, hardly anyone doing any work – what the devil is going on?'

Nobody spoke.

Consternation spread over his face, then a look of guilt.

'What's wrong?' he said, but his expression told Hugh that he could guess. 'You'd better tell me why you're all staring at me,' he persisted. 'After all, I am the Senior Partner.'

'No, you're not,' said Hugh. 'I am.'

CHAPTER THREE

November

[I]

MISS DOROTHY PILASTER married Viscount
Nicholas Ipswich at Kensington Methodist Hall
on a cold, bright morning in November. The service was
simple though the sermon was long. Afterwards a lunch of
hot consommé, Dover sole, roast grouse and peach sherbet
was served to three hundred guests in a vast heated tent in
the garden of Hugh's house.

Hugh was very happy. His sister was radiantly beautiful
and her new husband was charming to everyone. But the
happiest person there was Hugh's mother. Smiling
beatifically, she sat beside the groom's father, the Duke of
Norwich. For the first time in twenty-four years she was
not wearing black: she had on a blue-grey cashmere outfit
that set off her thick silver hair and calm grey eyes. Her life
had been blighted by Hugh's father's suicide, and she had
suffered years of scrimping poverty, but now in her sixties
she had everything she wanted. Her beautiful daughter was
Viscountess Ipswich and would one day be the Duchess of
Norwich, and her son was rich and successful and the
Senior Partner of Pilasters Bank. 'I used to think I had

been unlucky,' she murmured to Hugh in between courses. 'I was wrong.' She put her hand on his arm in a gesture like a blessing. 'I'm very fortunate.' It made Hugh want to cry.

Because none of the women wanted to wear white (for fear of competing with the bride) or black (because it was for funerals) the women guests made a colourful splash. They seemed to have chosen hot colours to ward off the autumn chill: bright orange, deep yellow, raspberry red and fuchsia pink. The men were wearing black, white and grey, as always. Hugh had on a frock-coat with velvet lapels and cuffs: it was black, but as always he defied convention by wearing a bright blue silk tie, his only eccentricity. He was so responsible nowadays that he sometimes felt nostalgic for the time when he had been the black sheep of the family.

He took a sip of Château Margaux, his favourite red wine. It was a lavish wedding breakfast for a special couple, and Hugh was glad he could afford it. But he also felt a twinge of guilt about spending all that money when Pilasters Bank was so weak. They still had one million, four hundred thousand pounds' worth of Santamaria Harbour bonds, plus other Cordovan bonds valued at almost a million pounds: and they could not sell them without causing a drop in the price, which was the very thing Hugh feared. It was going to take him at least a year to strengthen the balance sheet. However, he had steered the bank through the immediate crisis, and they now had enough cash to meet normal withdrawals for the foreseeable future. Edward no longer came to the bank at all, although technically he would remain a partner until the end of the financial year. They were safe from everything except some unexpected catastrophe such as war, earthquake or plague.

On balance he felt he was entitled to give his only sister an expensive wedding.

And it was good for Pilasters Bank. Everyone in the financial community knew that the bank were down more than a million on Santamaria Harbour. This big party boosted confidence by assuring people that the Pilasters were still unimaginably rich. A cheapskate wedding would have aroused suspicion.

Dotty's dowry of a hundred thousand pounds had been made over to her husband, but it remained invested in the bank, earning five per cent. Nick could withdraw it, but he did not need it all at once. He would draw money gradually as he paid off his father's mortgages and reorganized the estate. Hugh was glad he did not want all the cash right away, for large withdrawals put a strain on the bank at present.

Everyone knew about Dotty's huge dowry. Hugh and Nick had not been able to keep it completely secret, and it was the kind of thing that got around very quickly. Now it was the talk of London. Hugh guessed it was being discussed this very moment at half the tables at least.

Looking around, he caught the eye of one guest who was not happy – indeed, she wore a miserable, cheated look, like a eunuch at an orgy: Aunt Augusta.

'London society has degenerated completely,' Augusta said to Colonel Mudeford.

'I fear you may be right, Lady Whitehaven,' he murmured politely.

'Breeding counts for nothing any more,' she went on. 'Jews are admitted everywhere.'

'Quite so.'

'I was the first Countess of Whitehaven, but the Pilasters were a distinguished family for a century before being honoured with a title; whereas today a man whose father was a navvy can get a peerage simply because he made a fortune selling sausages.'

'Indeed.' Colonel Mudeford turned to the woman on his other side and said: 'Mrs Telston, may I hand you some more redcurrant sauce?'

Augusta lost interest in him. She was seething at the spectacle she had been forced to attend. Hugh Pilaster, son of bankrupt Tobias, giving Château Margaux to three hundred guests; Lydia Pilaster, widow of Tobias, sitting next to the Duke of Norwich; Dorothy Pilaster, daughter of Tobias, married to Viscount Ipswich with the biggest dowry anyone had ever heard of. Whereas her son, dear Teddy, the offspring of the great Joseph Pilaster, had been summarily dismissed as Senior Partner and was soon to have his marriage annulled.

There were no rules any more! Anyone could enter society. As if to prove the point she caught sight of the greatest parvenu of them all: Mrs Solly Greenbourne, formerly Maisie Robinson. It was amazing that Hugh had the gall to invite her, a woman whose whole life had been scandal. First she had been practically a prostitute, then she had married the richest Jew in London, and now she ran a hospital where women who were no better than herself could give birth to their bastards. But there she was, sitting at the next table in a dress the colour of a new copper penny, chatting earnestly to the Governor of the Bank of England. She was probably talking about unmarried mothers. And he was listening!

*

'Put yourself in the position of an unmarried servant girl,' Maisie said to the governor. He looked startled, and she suppressed a grin. 'Think of the consequences if you become a mother: you will lose your job and your home, you will have no means of support, and your child will have no father. Would you then think to yourself: "Oh, but I can be delivered at Mrs Greenbourne's nice hospital in Southwark, so I may as well go ahead and do it?" Of course not. My hospital does nothing to encourage girls into immorality. I just save them from giving birth in the gutter.'

Maisie's brother Dan, sitting on her other side, joined in. 'It's rather like the Banking Bill I'm proposing in Parliament, which would oblige banks to take out insurance for the benefit of small depositors.'

'I know of it,' the governor said.

Dan went on: 'Some critics say it would encourage bankruptcy by making it less painful. But that's nonsense. No banker would want to fail, under any circumstances.'

'Indeed not.'

'When a banker is making a deal he does not think that he may make a widow in Bournemouth penniless by his rashness – he worries about his own wealth. Similarly, making illegitimate children suffer does nothing to discourage unscrupulous men from seducing servant girls.'

'I do see your point,' the governor said with a pained expression. 'A most . . . ah . . . original parallel.'

Maisie decided they had tormented him enough, and turned away, letting him concentrate on his grouse.

Dan said to her: 'Have you ever noticed how peerages always go to the wrong people? Look at Hugh and his cousin Edward. Hugh is honest, talented and hard-working, where Edward is foolish, lazy and worthless – yet

513

Edward is the Earl of Whitehaven and Hugh is just plain Mr Pilaster.'

Maisie was trying not to look at Hugh. Although she was glad to have been invited, she found it painful to see him in the bosom of his family. His wife, his sons, his mother and his sister made a closed circle which left her outside. She knew this marriage to Nora was unhappy: it was obvious from the way they spoke to one another, never touching, never smiling, never affectionate. But that was no consolation. They were a family and she would never be part of it.

She wished she had not come to the wedding.

A footman came to Hugh's side and said quietly: 'There's a telephone call for you from the bank, sir.'

'I can't speak now,' Hugh said.

A few minutes later his butler came out. 'Mr Mulberry from the bank is on the telephone, sir, asking for you.'

'I can't speak now!' Hugh said irritably.

'Very good, sir.' The butler turned away.

'No, wait a minute,' Hugh said. Mulberry knew Hugh would be in the middle of the wedding breakfast. He was an intelligent and responsible man. He would not insist on speaking to Hugh unless something was wrong.

Very wrong.

Hugh felt a chill of fear.

'I'd better speak to him,' he said. He stood up, saying: 'Please excuse me, Mother, Your Grace – something I have to attend to.'

He hurried out of the tent, across the lawn and into the house. The telephone was in his library. He picked up the instrument and said: 'Hugh Pilaster speaking.'

He heard the voice of his clerk. 'It's Mulberry, sir. I'm sorry to—'

'What's happened?'

'A telegram from New York. War has broken out in Cordova.'

'Oh, no!' It was catastrophic news for Hugh, his family and the bank. Nothing could be worse.

'Civil war, in fact,' Mulberry went on. 'A rebellion. The Miranda family has attacked the capital city, Palma.'

Hugh's heart was racing. 'Any indication of how strong they are?' If the rebellion could be crushed quickly there was still hope.

'President Garcia has fled.'

'The devil he has.' That meant it was serious. He cursed Micky and Edward bitterly. 'Anything else?'

'There's another cable from our Cordova office, but it's still being decoded.'

'Telephone to me again as soon as it's ready.'

'Very good, sir.'

Hugh cranked the machine, got the operator, and gave the name of the stockbroker used by the bank. He waited while the man was called to the telephone. 'Danby, this is Hugh Pilaster. What's happening to Cordovan bonds?'

'We're offering them at half par and getting no takers.'

Half price, Hugh thought. Pilasters was already bankrupt. Despair filled his heart. 'What will they fall to?'

'They'll go to zero, I should think. No one pays interest on government bonds in the middle of a civil war.'

Zero. Pilasters had just lost two-and-a-half million pounds. There was no hope now of gradually returning the balance sheet to strength. Clutching at straws, Hugh said: 'Suppose the rebels are wiped out in the next few hours – what then?'

515

'I shouldn't think anyone will buy the bonds even then,' said Danby. 'Investors will wait and see. At the very best it will take five or six weeks before confidence begins to return.'

'I see.' Hugh knew Danby was right. The broker was only confirming Hugh's own instincts.

'I say, Pilaster, your bank will be all right, won't it?' Danby said worriedly. 'You must have quite a lot of these bonds. It was noised about that you hardly sold any of the Santamaria Harbour issue.'

Hugh hesitated. He hated to tell lies. But the truth would destroy the bank. 'We've got more Cordovan bonds than I'd like, Danby. But we've got a lot of other assets as well.'

'Good.'

'I must get back to my guests.' Hugh had no intention of going back to his guests, but he wanted to give an impression of calm. 'I'm giving lunch to three hundred people – my sister got married this morning.'

'So I heard. Congratulations.'

'Goodbye.'

Before Hugh could ask for another number, Mulberry called again. 'Mr Cunliffe from the Colonial Bank is here, sir,' he said, and Hugh could hear the panic in his voice. 'He is asking for repayment of the loan.'

'Damn him,' Hugh said fervently. The Colonial had lent Pilasters a million pounds to tide them over the crisis, but the money was repayable on demand. Cunliffe had heard the news and seen the sudden slump in Cordovan bonds, and he knew Pilasters must be in trouble. Naturally he wanted to get his money out before the bank went bust.

And he was only the first. Others would be close behind. Tomorrow morning depositors would be queuing outside the doors, wanting cash. And Hugh would not be able to pay them.

'Have we got a million pounds, Mulberry?'

'No, sir.'

The weight of the world descended on to Hugh's shoulders, and he felt old. This was the end. It was the banker's nightmare: people came for their money, and the bank did not have it. And it was happening to Hugh.

'Tell Mr Cunliffe that you have been unable to get authorization to sign the cheque, because all the partners are at the wedding,' he said.

'Very good, Mr Hugh.'

'And then . . .'

'Yes, sir?'

Hugh paused. He knew he had no choice, but still he hesitated to say the dreadful words. He shut his eyes. Better get it over with.

'And then, Mulberry, you must close the doors of the bank.'

'Oh, Mr Hugh.'

'I'm sorry, Mulberry.'

There was an odd noise down the line, and Hugh realized that Mulberry was crying.

He put down the phone. Staring at the bookshelves of his library, he saw instead the grand facade of Pilasters Bank, and imagined the closing of the ornate iron doors. He saw passers-by stop and look. Before long a crowd would gather, pointing at the closed doors and chattering excitedly. The word would go around the City faster than a fire in an oil store: Pilasters has crashed.

Pilasters has crashed.

Hugh buried his face in his hands.

[11]

'WE ARE ALL absolutely penniless,' said Hugh.
     They did not understand, at first. He could tell
by their faces.

They gathered in the drawing-room of his house. It was
a cluttered room, having been decorated by Nora, who
loved to drape every stick of furniture with flowered fabrics
and crowd every surface with ornaments. The guests had
gone, at last – Hugh had not told anyone the bad news
until the party was over – but the family were still in their
wedding finery. Augusta sat with Edward, both of them
wearing scornful, disbelieving expressions. Uncle Samuel
sat next to Hugh. The other partners, Young William,
Major Hartshorn and Sir Harry, stood behind a sofa on
which sat their wives Beatrice, Madeleine and Clementine.
Nora, flushed from lunch and champagne, sat in her usual
chair beside the fire. The bride and groom, Nick and Dotty,
held hands, looking frightened.

Hugh felt most sorry for the newlyweds. 'Dotty's dowry
is gone, Nick. I'm afraid all our plans have come to
nothing.'

Aunt Madeleine said shrilly: 'You're the Senior Partner
– it must be your fault!'

She was being stupid and malicious. It was a predictable
reaction, yet all the same Hugh was wounded. It was so
unfair that she should blame him, after he had fought so
hard to prevent this.

However, William, her younger brother, corrected her
with surprising sharpness. 'Don't talk rot, Madeleine,' he
said. 'Edward deceived us all and burdened the bank with
huge amounts of Cordovan bonds which are now
worthless.' Hugh was grateful to him for being honest.

518

William went on: 'The blame lies with those of us who let Edward become Senior Partner.' He looked at Augusta.

Nora looked bewildered. 'We can't be *penniless*,' she said.

'But we are,' Hugh said patiently. 'All our money is in the bank and the bank has failed.' There was some excuse for his wife's not understanding: she had not been born into a banking family.

Augusta stood up and went to the fireplace. Hugh wondered whether she would try to defend her son, but she was not that foolish. 'Never mind whose fault it is,' she said. 'We must salvage what we can. There must be quite a lot of cash in the bank still, gold and banknotes. We must get it out and hide it somewhere safe before the creditors move in. Then—'

Hugh interrupted her. 'We'll do no such thing,' he said sharply. 'It's not our money.'

'Of course it's our money!' she cried.

'Be quiet and sit down, Augusta, or I'll have the footmen throw you out.'

She was sufficiently surprised to shut up, but she did not sit down.

Hugh said: 'There is cash at the bank, and as we have not officially been declared bankrupt, we can choose to pay some of our creditors. You'll all have to dismiss your servants; and if you send them to the side door of the bank with a note of how much they are owed I will pay them off. You should ask all tradesmen with whom you have accounts to give you a statement, and I will see that they are paid too – but only up to today's date: I will not pay any debts you incur from now on.'

'Who are you to tell me to dismiss my servants?' Augusta said indignantly.

Hugh was prepared to feel sympathy for their plight, even though they had brought it on themselves; but this deliberate obtuseness was very wearying, and he snapped at her: 'If you don't dismiss them they will leave anyway, because they won't get paid. Aunt Augusta, try to understand that *you haven't got any money.*'

'Ridiculous,' she muttered.

Nora spoke again. 'I can't dismiss our servants. It's not possible to live in a house like this with no servants.'

'That need not trouble you,' Hugh said. 'You won't be living in a house like this. I will have to sell it. We will all have to sell our houses, furniture, works of art, wine cellars and jewellery.'

'This is absurd!' Augusta cried.

'It's the law,' Hugh retorted. 'Each partner is personally liable for all the debts of the business.'

'I'm not a partner,' said Augusta.

'But Edward is. He resigned as Senior Partner but he remained a partner, on paper. And he owns your house – Joseph left it to him.'

Nora said: 'We have to live somewhere.'

'First thing tomorrow we must all look for small, cheap houses to rent. If you pick something modest our creditors will sanction it. If not you will have to choose again.'

Augusta said: 'I have absolutely no intention of moving house, and that's final. And I imagine the rest of the family feel the same.' She looked at her sister-in-law. 'Madeleine?'

'Quite right, Augusta,' said Madeleine. 'George and I will stay where we are. All this is nonsense. We can't possibly be destitute.'

Hugh despised them. Even now, when their arrogance and foolishness had ruined them, they still refused to listen to reason. In the end they would have to give up their illusions. But if they tried to cling to wealth that was no longer theirs, they would destroy the family's reputation as well as its fortune. He was determined to make them behave with scrupulous honesty, in poverty as in wealth. It was going to be an uphill struggle but he would not give in.

Augusta turned to her daughter. 'Clementine, I'm sure you and Harry will take the same view as Madeleine and George.'

Clementine said: 'No, Mother.'

Augusta gasped. Hugh was equally startled. It was not like his cousin Clementine to go against her mother. At least one family member had some common sense, he thought.

Clementine said: 'It was listening to you that got us all into this trouble. If we had made Hugh Senior Partner, instead of Edward, we would all still be as rich as Croesus.'

Hugh began to feel better. Some of the family understood what he had tried to do.

Clementine went on: 'You were wrong, Mother, and you've ruined us. I'm never going to heed your advice again. Hugh was right, and we had better let him do all he can to guide us through this dreadful disaster.'

William said: 'Quite right, Clementine. We should do whatever Hugh advises.'

The battle lines were drawn. On Hugh's side were William, Samuel, and Clementine, who ruled her husband Sir Harry. They would try to behave decently and honestly. Against him were Augusta, Edward, and Madeleine, who spoke for Major Hartshorn: they would try to snatch what they could and let the family's reputation go to hell.

Then Nora said defiantly: 'You'll have to carry me out of this house.'

There was a bitter taste in Hugh's mouth. His own wife was joining the enemy. 'You're the only person in the room who has gone against their husband or wife,' he said sadly. 'Don't you owe me any loyalty at all?'

She tossed her head. 'I didn't marry you to live in poverty.'

'All the same you *will* leave this house,' he said grimly. He looked at the other diehards: Augusta, Edward, Madeleine and Major Hartshorn. 'You will all have to give in, eventually,' he said. 'If you don't do it now, with dignity, you'll do it later, in disgrace, with bailiffs and policemen and newspaper reporters in attendance, vilified by the gutter press and slighted by your unpaid servants.'

'We shall see about that,' said Augusta.

When they had all gone Hugh sat staring into the fire, racking his brains for some way to pay the bank's creditors.

He was determined not to let Pilasters go into formal bankruptcy. The idea was almost too painful to contemplate. All his life he had lived under the shadow of his father's bankruptcy. His whole career had been an attempt to prove he was not tainted. In his heart of hearts he feared that if he suffered the same fate as his father, he too might be driven to take his own life.

Pilasters was finished as a bank. It had closed its doors on its depositors, and that was the end. But in the long term it ought to be able to repay its debts, especially if the partners were scrupulous about selling all their valuable possessions.

As the afternoon faded into twilight, the outlines of a plan began to form in his mind, and he allowed himself the faintest glimmer of hope.

At six p.m. he went to see Ben Greenbourne.

Greenbourne was seventy, but still fit, and he continued to run the business. He had a daughter, Kate, but Solly had been his only son; so when he retired he would have to hand over to his nephews, and he seemed reluctant to do that.

Hugh called at the mansion in Piccadilly. The house gave the impression not just of prosperity, but of limitless wealth. Every clock was a jewel, every stick of furniture a priceless antique; every panel was exquisitely carved, every carpet specially woven. Hugh was shown into the library, where gaslights blazed and a fire roared. In this room he had first realized that the boy called Bertie Greenbourne was his son.

Wondering if the books were just for show, he glanced at several while he was waiting. Some might have been chosen for their fine bindings, he thought, but others were well-thumbed, and several languages were represented. Greenbourne's learning was genuine.

The old man appeared fifteen minutes later, and apologized for keeping Hugh waiting. 'A domestic problem detained me,' he said with clipped Prussian courtesy. His family had never been Prussian; they had copied the manners of upper-class Germans, then retained them through a hundred years of living in England. He held himself as straight as ever, but Hugh thought he looked tired and worried. Greenbourne did not say what the domestic problem was and Hugh did not ask.

'You know that Cordovan bonds have crashed this afternoon,' Hugh said.

'Yes.'

'And you probably heard that my bank has closed its doors as a result.'

'Yes. I am very sorry.'

'It's twenty-four years since the last time an English bank failed.'

'That was Overend and Gurney. I remember it well.'

'So do I. My father went broke and hanged himself in his office in Leadenhall Street.'

Greenbourne was embarrassed. 'I am most terribly sorry, Pilaster. That dreadful fact had slipped my mind.'

'A lot of firms went down in that crisis. But much worse will happen tomorrow.' Hugh leaned forward on his stool and began his big pitch. 'In the last quarter of a century the business done in the City has increased tenfold. And because banking has become so sophisticated and complex, we are all more closely intertwined than ever. Some of the people whose money we have lost will be unable to pay their debts, so they will go bust too – and so on. Next week *dozens* of banks will fail, hundreds of businesses will be forced to close, and thousands upon thousands of people will suddenly find themselves destitute – unless we take action to prevent it.'

'Action?' said Greenbourne with more than a hint of irritation. 'What action can be taken? Your only remedy is to pay your debts; you cannot do so; therefore you are helpless.'

'Alone, yes, I'm helpless. But I am hoping that the banking community will do something.'

'Do you propose to ask other bankers to pay your debts? Why should they?' He was getting ready to be angry.

'You'll agree, surely, that it would be better for all of us if Pilasters' creditors could be paid in full.'

'Obviously.'

'Suppose a syndicate of bankers were formed to take over both the assets and the liabilities of Pilasters. The syndicate would guarantee to pay any creditor on demand. At the same time, it would begin to liquidate Pilasters' assets in an orderly fashion.'

Suddenly Greenbourne was interested, and his irritability vanished as he considered this novel proposal. 'I see. If the members of the syndicate were sufficiently respected and prestigious, their guarantee might be enough to reassure everyone, and creditors might not demand their cash immediately. With luck, the flow of money coming in from the sale of assets might cover the payments to creditors.'

'And a dreadful crisis would be averted.'

Greenbourne shook his head. 'But in the end, the members of the syndicate would lose money, for Pilasters' liabilities are greater than its assets.'

'Not necessarily.'

'How so?'

'We have more than two million pounds' worth of Cordovan bonds which are today valued at nothing. However, our other assets are substantial. A lot depends on how much we can raise by the sale of the partners' houses, and so on; but I estimate that even today the shortfall is only a million pounds.'

'So the syndicate must expect to lose a million.'

'Perhaps. But Cordovan bonds may not be worthless for ever. The rebels may be defeated. Or the new government may resume interest payments. At some point the price of Cordovan bonds will rise.'

'Possibly.'

'If the bonds came up to just half their previous level, the syndicate would break even. And if they did better than that, the syndicate would actually make a profit.'

Greenbourne shook his head. 'It might work, but for those Santamaria Harbour Bonds. That Cordovan Minister, Miranda, strikes me as an out-and-out thief; and his father is apparently the leader of the rebels. My guess is that the whole two million pounds has gone to pay for guns and ammunition. In which case investors will never see a penny.'

The old boy was as sharp as always, Hugh thought: he had exactly the same fear. 'I'm afraid you may be right. All the same there's a chance. And if you allow a financial panic you're sure to lose money in other ways.'

'It's an ingenious plan. You always were the cleverest of your family, young Pilaster.'

'But the plan depends on you.'

'Ah.'

'If you agree to head the syndicate, the City will follow your lead. If you refuse to be part of it, the syndicate will not have the prestige to reassure creditors.'

'I see that.' Greenbourne was not the man for false modesty.

'Will you do it?' Hugh held his breath.

The old man was silent for several seconds, thinking, then he said firmly: 'No, I won't.'

Hugh slumped in his chair. It was his last shot and it had failed. He felt a great weariness descend on him, as if his life were over and he were a tired old man.

Greenbourne said: 'All my life I have been cautious. Where other men see high profits, I see high risks, and I resist the temptation. Your Uncle Joseph was not like me. He would take the risk – and he pocketed the profits. His son Edward was worse. I say nothing about you: you have only just taken over. But the Pilasters must pay the price for their years of high profits. I didn't take those profits – why should I pay your debts? If I spend money to rescue you now, the foolish investor will be rewarded and the careful one will suffer. And if banking were run that way, why should anyone be cautious? We might as well all take risks, for there is no risk when failed banks can always be rescued. But there is always risk. Banking cannot be run your way. There will always be crashes. They are necessary to remind good and bad investors that risk is real.'

Hugh had wondered, before coming here, whether to tell the old man that Micky Miranda had murdered Solly. Now he considered it again, but he came to the same conclusion: it would shock and distress the old man but it would do nothing to persuade him to rescue Pilasters.

He was casting about for something to say, some last attempt to change Greenbourne's mind, when the butler came in and said: 'Pardon me, Mr Greenbourne, but you asked to be called the moment the detective arrived.'

Greenbourne stood up immediately, looking agitated, but his courtesy would not let him rush out without an explanation. 'I'm sorry, Pilaster, but I must leave you. My grand-daughter Rebecca has ... disappeared ... and we are all distraught.'

'I'm so sorry to hear that,' Hugh said. He knew Solly's sister Kate, and he had a vague memory of her daughter, a pretty dark-haired girl. 'I hope you find her safe and well.'

'We don't believe she has suffered violence – in fact we're quite sure she has only run off with a boy. But that's bad enough. Please excuse me.'

'By all means.'

The old man went out, leaving Hugh amid the ruins of his hopes.

[III]

MAISIE SOMETIMES wondered if there was something infectious about going into labour. It often happened, in a ward full of women nine months pregnant, that days would go by without incident, but as soon as one started labour the others would follow within hours.

It had been like that today. It had started at four o'clock in the morning and they had been delivering babies ever since. The midwives and nurses did most of the work, but when they were overstretched Maisie and Rachel had to leave their pens and ledgers and scurry around with towels and blankets.

By seven o'clock, however, it was all over, and they were enjoying a cup of tea in Maisie's office with Rachel's lover, Maisie's brother Dan, when Hugh Pilaster called. 'I bring very bad news, I'm afraid,' he said right away.

Maisie was pouring tea but his tone of voice shocked her and she stopped. Looking hard at his face she saw that he was grief-stricken, and she thought someone must have died. 'Hugh, what has happened?'

'I think you keep all the hospital's money in an account at my bank, don't you?'

If it was only money, Maisie thought, the news could not be that bad.

Rachel answered Hugh's question. 'Yes. My father handles the money, but he has kept his own private account with you ever since he became the bank's lawyer, and I suppose he found it convenient to do the same with the hospital's account.'

'And he invested your money in Cordovan bonds.'

'Did he?'

Maisie said: 'What's wrong, Hugh? For goodness' sake tell us!'

'The bank has failed.'

Maisie's eyes filled with tears, not for herself but for him. 'Oh, Hugh!' she cried. She knew how much he was hurting. For him this was almost like the death of a loved one, for he had invested all his hopes and dreams in the bank. She wished she could take some of the pain into herself, to ease his suffering.

Dan said: 'Good God. There will be a panic.'

'All your money has gone,' Hugh said. 'You'll probably have to close the hospital. I can't tell you how sorry I am.'

Rachel was white with shock. 'That's not possible!' she said. 'How can our money be gone?'

Dan answered her. 'The bank can't pay its debts,' he said bitterly. 'That's what bankruptcy means, it means you owe people money and you can't pay them.'

In a flash of recollection Maisie saw her father, a quarter of a century younger and looking much as Dan did today, saying exactly the same thing about bankruptcy. Dan had spent much of his life trying to protect ordinary people from the effects of these financial crises – but so far he had achieved nothing. 'Perhaps now they'll pass your Banking Bill,' she said to him.

Rachel said to Hugh: 'But what have you *done* with our money?'

Hugh sighed. 'Essentially this happened because of something Edward did while he was Senior Partner. It was a mistake, a huge mistake, and he lost a lot of money, more than a million pounds. I've been trying to hold everything together since then, but today my luck ran out.'

'I just didn't know this could happen!' said Rachel.

Hugh said: 'You should get some of your money back but not for a year or more.'

Dan put his arm around Rachel but she would not be consoled. 'And what is going to happen to all the wretched women who come here for help?'

Hugh looked so wounded that Maisie wanted to tell Rachel to shut up. 'I would gladly give you the money out of my own pocket,' he said. 'But I've lost everything too.'

'Surely something can be done?' she persisted.

'I did try. I've just come from Ben Greenbourne's house. I asked him to rescue the bank and pay the creditors, but he refused. He has troubles of his own, poor man: apparently his grand-daughter Rebecca has run off with her boyfriend. Anyway, without his support nothing can be done.'

Rachel stood up. 'I think I'd better go and see my father.'

'I must go to the House of Commons,' Dan said.

They went out.

Maisie's heart was full. She was dismayed at the prospect of closing the hospital, and rocked by the sudden destruction of all she had worked for; but most of all she ached for Hugh. She recalled, as if it were yesterday, the night seventeen years ago, after the Goodwood races, when Hugh had told her his life story; and she could hear now the agony in his voice when he told her that his father had gone bankrupt and taken his own life. He had said then that he was going to be the cleverest, most conservative and richest banker in the world one day – as if he believed that would ease the pain of his loss. And perhaps it would have. But instead he had suffered the same fate as his father.

Their eyes met across the room. Maisie read a silent appeal in his look. Slowly she got up and went to him. Standing beside his chair, she took his head in her hands and cradled it on her bosom, stroking his hair. Tentatively he put his arm around her waist, touching her gingerly at first, then hugging her to him hard. And then, at last, he began to cry.

When Hugh had gone Maisie made a tour of the wards. Now she saw everything with new eyes: the walls they had painted themselves, the beds they had bought in junk shops, the pretty curtains Rachel's mother had sewn. She remembered the superhuman efforts that had been required of her and Rachel to get the hospital opened: their battles with the medical establishment and the local council, the tireless charm they had used on the respectable householders and censorious clergy of the neighbourhood, the sheer dogged persistence that had enabled them to win through. She consoled herself with the thought that they had, after all, been victorious, and the hospital had been open for twelve years and had given comfort to hundreds of women. But she had wanted to make a permanent change. She had seen this as the first of dozens of Female Hospitals all over the country. In that she had failed.

She spoke to each of the women who had given birth today. The only one she was worried about was Miss Nobody. She was a slight figure and her baby had been very small. Maisie guessed she had been starving herself to help conceal her pregnancy from her family. Maisie was always astonished that girls managed to do this – she herself had ballooned when pregnant and could not have hidden it after five months – but she knew from experience it happened all the time.

She sat down on the edge of Miss Nobody's bed. The new mother was nursing her child, a girl. 'Isn't she beautiful?' she said.

Maisie nodded. 'She's got black hair, just like yours.'

'My mother has the same hair.'

Maisie reached out and stroked the tiny head. Like all babies, this one looked like Solly. In fact—

Maisie was jolted by a sudden revelation.

'Oh, my God, I know who you are,' she said.

The girl stared at her.

'You're Ben Greenbourne's grand-daughter Rebecca, aren't you? You kept your pregnancy secret as long as you could, then ran away to have the baby.'

The girl's eyes widened. 'How did you know? You haven't seen me since I was six years old!'

'But I knew your mother. I was married to her brother, after all. She was kind to me when her father wasn't around. And I remember you as a baby. You had black hair, just like your daughter.'

Rebecca was scared. 'Promise you won't tell them?'

'I promise I won't do anything without your consent. But I think you ought to send word to your family. Your grandfather is distraught.'

'He's the one I'm frightened of.'

Maisie nodded. 'I can understand why. He's a hard-hearted old curmudgeon, as I know from personal experience. But if you let me talk to him I think I can make him see sense.'

'Would you?' said Rebecca in a voice full of youthful optimism. 'Would you do that?'

'Of course,' Maisie said. 'But I won't tell him where you are unless he promises to be kind.'

Rebecca looked down. Her baby's eyes had closed and she had stopped sucking. 'She's asleep,' Rebecca said.

Maisie smiled. 'Have you chosen a name for her yet?'

'Oh, yes,' Rebecca said. 'I'm going to call her Maisie.'

Ben Greenbourne's face was wet with tears as he came out of the ward. 'I've left her with Kate for a while,' he said in a choked voice. He pulled a handkerchief from his pocket and dabbed ineffectually at his cheeks. Maisie had never seen her father-in-law lose his self-possession. He made a rather pathetic sight, but she felt it would do him a lot of good.

'Come to my room,' she said. 'I'll make you a cup of tea.'

'Thank you.'

She led him to her room and told him to sit down. He was the second man to weep in that chair this evening, she thought.

'All those young women,' the old man said. 'Are they all in the same position as Rebecca?'

'Not all,' Maisie said. 'Some are widows. Some have been abandoned by their husbands. Quite a lot have run away from men who beat them. A woman will suffer a lot of pain, and stay with a husband even if he injures her; but when she gets pregnant she worries that his blows will damage the child, and that's when she leaves. But most of our women are like Rebecca, girls who have simply made a stupid mistake.'

'I didn't think life had much more to teach me,' he said. 'Now I find I have been foolish and ignorant.'

Maisie handed him a cup of tea. 'Thank you,' he said. 'You're very kind. I was never kind to you.'

'We all make mistakes,' she said briskly.

'What a good thing you are here,' he said to her. 'Otherwise where would these poor girls go?'

'They would have their babies in ditches and alleyways,' Maisie said.

'To think that might have happened to Rebecca.'

'Unfortunately the hospital has to close,' Maisie said.

'Why is that?'

She looked him in the eye. 'All our money was in Pilasters Bank,' she said. 'Now we are penniless.'

'Is that so?' he said, and he looked very thoughtful.

Hugh undressed for bed but he felt far from sleep, so he sat up in his dressing-gown, staring into the fire, brooding. He went over and over the bank's situation in his mind, but he could think of no way to ameliorate it. Yet he could not stop thinking.

At midnight he heard a loud, determined knocking at the front door. He went downstairs in his nightclothes to answer it. There was a carriage at the kerb and a liveried footman on the doorstep. The man said: 'I beg pardon for knocking so late, sir, but the message is urgent.' He handed over an envelope and left.

As Hugh closed the door his butler came down the stairs. 'Is everything all right, sir?' he said worriedly.

'Just a message,' Hugh said. 'You can go back to bed.'

'Thank you, sir.'

Hugh opened the envelope and saw the neat, old-fashioned writing of a fussy elderly man. The words made his heart leap with joy.

> 12 Piccadilly
> London, S.W.
> November 23rd, 1890

Dear Pilaster,

On further reflection I have decided to consent to your proposal.

Yours, etc.

B. Greenbourne.

He looked up from the letter and grinned at the empty hall. 'Well, I'll be blowed,' he said delightedly. 'I wonder what made the old man change his mind?'

[IV]

AUGUSTA SAT IN the back room of the best jeweller's shop in Bond Street. Bright gaslights flared, making the jewellery glitter in the glass cases. The room was full of mirrors. An obsequious assistant padded across the room and placed in front of her a black velvet cloth bearing a diamond necklace.

The manager of the shop was standing beside Augusta. 'How much?' she asked him.

'Nine thousand pounds, Lady Whitehaven.' He breathed the price piously, like a prayer.

The necklace was simple and stark, just a plain row of identical large square-cut diamonds set in gold. It would look very striking against her black widow's gowns, she thought. But she was not buying it to wear.

'It's a wonderful piece, my lady; quite the loveliest thing we have in the shop.'

'Don't rush me, I'm thinking,' she replied.

This was her last desperate attempt to raise money. She had tried going openly to the bank and demanding a hundred pounds in gold sovereigns: the clerk, an insolent dog called Mulberry, had refused her. She had tried to have the house transferred from Edward's name into her own, but that had not worked either: the deeds were in the safe of old Bodwin, the bank's lawyer, and he had been got at by Hugh. Now she was going to try to buy diamonds on credit and sell them for cash.

Edward had at first been her ally, but now even he refused to help her. 'What Hugh is doing is for the best,' he had said stupidly. 'If word gets around that family members are trying to grab what they can, the syndicate could fall apart. They've been persuaded to put up money

535

to avert a financial crisis, not to keep the Pilaster family in luxury.' It was a long speech for Edward. A year ago it would have shaken Augusta to the core to have her son go against her, but since his rebellion over the annulment he was no longer the sweet, biddable boy she loved. Clementine had turned against her too, supporting Hugh's plans to turn them all into paupers. It made her shake with rage when she thought about it. But they would not get away with it.

She looked up at the shop manager. 'I'll take it,' she said decisively.

'A wise choice, I have no doubt, Lady Whitehaven,' he said.

'Send the bill to the bank.'

'Very good, my lady. We will deliver the necklace to Whitehaven House.'

'I'll take it with me,' Augusta said. 'I want to wear it tonight.'

The manager looked as if he were in pain. 'You put me in an impossible position, my lady.'

'What on earth are you talking about? Wrap it up!'

'I fear I cannot release the jewellery until payment has been received.'

'Don't be ridiculous. Do you know who I am?'

'Yes – but the newspapers say the bank has closed its doors.'

'This is an insult.'

'I am very, very sorry.'

Augusta stood up and picked up the necklace. 'I refuse to listen to this nonsense. I shall take it with me.'

Perspiring, the manager moved between her and the door. 'I beg you not to,' he said.

She moved towards him but he stood his ground. 'Get out of my way!' she blazed.

'I shall have to have the shop door locked and send for the police,' he said.

It dawned on Augusta that although the man was practically gibbering with terror he had not conceded one inch. He was afraid of her, but he was more frightened of losing nine thousand pounds' worth of diamonds. She realized she was defeated. Enraged, she threw the necklace on the floor. The man scooped it up with no attempt at dignity. Augusta opened the door herself, stalked through the shop, and went out to where her carriage waited.

She held her head high but she was mortified. The man had practically accused her of stealing. A small voice in the back of her mind said that stealing was exactly what she had been trying to do, but she stifled it. She rode home in a rage.

As she entered the house Hastead, the butler, tried to detain her, but she had no patience for domestic trivia at this moment, and she silenced him, saying: 'Bring me a glass of warm milk.' She had a pain in her stomach.

She went to her room. She sat at her dressing-table and opened her jewellery box. There was very little in it. What she had was worth only a few hundred pounds. She pulled out the bottom tray, took out a piece of folded silk and unwrapped it to reveal the serpent-shaped gold ring that Strang had given her. As always, she slipped it on her finger and brushed the jewelled head against her lips. She would never sell this. How different everything would have been if she had been allowed to marry Strang. For a moment she felt like crying.

Then she heard strange voices outside her bedroom door. A man . . . two men, perhaps . . . and a woman. They did not sound like servants and anyway her staff would not have the temerity to stand around conversing on the landing. She stepped outside.

The door to her late husband's room was open and the voices came from in there. When she went in Augusta saw a young man, obviously a clerk, and an older, well-dressed couple of her own class. She had never set eyes on any of them before. She said: 'In heaven's name who are you?'

The clerk said deferentially: 'Stoddart, from the agents, my lady. Mr and Mrs de Graaf are very interested in buying your beautiful house—'

'Get out!' she said.

The clerk's voice rose to a squeak. 'We have received instructions to put the house on the market—'

'Get out this minute! My house is not for sale!'

'But I personally spoke—'

Mr de Graaf touched Stoddart's arm and silenced him. 'An embarrassing mistake, quite obviously, Mr Stoddart,' he said mildly. He turned to his wife. 'Shall we leave, my dear?' The two of them walked out with a quiet dignity that made Augusta seethe, and Stoddart scurried after them, spilling apologies everywhere.

Hugh was responsible. Augusta did not have to make inquiries to establish that. The house was the property of the syndicate that had rescued the bank, he said, and they naturally wished to sell it. He had told Augusta to move out, but she had refused. His response was to send prospective buyers to view the place anyway.

She sat down in Joseph's chair. Her butler came in with her hot milk. She said: 'You are not to admit any more such people, Hastead – the house is not for sale.'

'Very good, my lady.' He set down her drink and hovered.

'Is there something else?' she asked him.

'M'lady, the butcher called personally today about his bill.'

'Tell him he will be paid at Lady Whitehaven's convenience, not his own.'

'Very good, m'lady. And both the footmen left today.'

'You mean they gave notice?'

'No, they just went.'

'Wretched people.'

'My lady, the rest of the staff are asking when they will get their wages.'

'Anything else?'

He looked bewildered. 'But what shall I tell them?'

'Tell them I did not answer your question.'

'Very good.' He hesitated, then said: 'I beg to give notice that I shall be leaving at the end of the week.'

'Why?'

'All the rest of the Pilasters have dismissed their staff. Mr Hugh told us we would be paid up to last Friday, but no more, regardless of how long we stay on.'

'Get out of my sight, you traitor.'

'Very good, my lady.'

Augusta told herself she would be glad to see the back of Hastead. She had always disliked his face: his eyes seemed to look in different directions. She was well rid of the lot of them, rats leaving the sinking ship.

She sipped her milk but the pain in her stomach did not ease.

She looked around the room. Joseph had never let her redecorate it, so it was still done out in the style she had chosen back in 1873, with leather-paper on the walls and heavy brocade curtains, and Joseph's collection of jewelled snuff-boxes in a lacquered display cabinet. The room seemed dead, as he was. She wished she could bring him back. None of this would have happened if he were still alive. She had a momentary vision of him standing by the bay window, holding one of his favourite snuff-boxes, turning it this way and that to see the play of light on the precious stones. She felt an unfamiliar choking sensation in her throat, and she shook her head to make the vision go away.

Soon Mr de Graaf or someone like him would move into this bedroom. No doubt he would tear down the curtains and the wallpaper and redecorate, probably in the currently fashionable arts-and-crafts style, with oak panelling and hard rustic chairs.

She would have to move out. She had accepted this, although she pretended otherwise. But she was not going to move to a cramped modern house in St John's Wood or Clapham, as Madeleine and Clementine had. She could not bear to live in reduced circumstances in London, where she could be seen by people she had once looked down upon.

She was going to leave the country.

She was not sure where to go. Calais was cheap but too close to London. Paris was elegant, but she felt too old to begin a new social life in a strange city. She had heard people talk of a place called Nice, on the Mediterranean coast of France, where a big house and servants could be had for next to nothing, and there was a quiet community of foreigners, many her own age, enjoying the mild winters and the sea air.

But she could not live on nothing a year. She had to have enough for rent and staff wages, and although she was prepared to live frugally she could not manage without a carriage. She had very little cash, no more than fifty pounds. Hence her desperate attempt to buy diamonds. Nine thousand pounds was not really enough, but it might have sufficed for a few years.

She knew she was jeopardizing Hugh's plans. Edward

had been right about that. The goodwill of the syndicate depended on the family being serious about paying off their debts. A family member running off to the Continent with her luggage full of jewellery was just the thing to upset a fragile coalition. In a way, that made the prospect more attractive: she would be happy to trip up the self-righteous Hugh.

But she had to have a stake. The rest would be easy: she would pack a single trunk, go to the steamship office to book passage, call a cab early in the morning, and slip away to the railway station without warning. But what could she use for money?

Looking around her husband's room she noticed a small notebook. She opened it, idly curious, and saw that someone – presumably Stoddart, the agent's clerk – had been making an inventory of the house contents. It angered her to see her possessions listed in a clerk's notebook and casually valued: *dining table £9; Egyptian screen 30s; portrait of a woman by Joshua Reynolds, £100.* There must be a few thousand pounds' worth of paintings in the house, but she could not pack those in a trunk. She turned the page and read *65 snuff boxes – refer to jewellery department.* She looked up. There in front of her, in the cabinet she had bought seventeen years ago, was the solution to her problem. Joseph's collection of jewelled snuff-boxes was worth thousands, perhaps as much as a hundred thousand pounds. She could pack it into her luggage easily: the boxes themselves were tiny, designed to fit into a man's waistcoat pocket. They could be sold one by one, as money was needed.

Her heart beat faster. This could be the answer to her prayers.

She reached out to open the cabinet. It was locked.

She suffered a moment of panic. She was not sure she

could break it open: the wood was stout, the panes of glass small and thick.

She calmed herself. Where would he keep the key? In the drawer of his writing-table, probably. She went to the table and pulled open the drawer. In it were a book with the horrifying title of *The Duchess of Sodom*, which she hastily pushed to the back, and a small silver-coloured key. She snatched up the key.

With a trembling hand she tried it in the lock of the cabinet. As she turned it she heard a bolt click, and a moment later the door opened.

She breathed deeply and waited until her hands stopped shaking.

Then she began to remove the boxes from the shelves.

CHAPTER FOUR
December

[I]

THE PILASTER CRASH was the society scandal of the year. The cheap newspapers reported every development breathlessly: the sale of the great Kensington mansions; the auctions of the paintings, antique furniture, and cases of port; the cancellation of Nick and Dotty's planned six-month honeymoon in Europe; and the modest suburban houses where the proud and mighty Pilasters now peeled potatoes for themselves and washed their own undergarments.

Hugh and Nora rented a small house with a garden in Chingford, a village nine miles from London. They left all their servants behind, but a muscular fourteen-year-old girl from a nearby farm came in the afternoons to scrub floors and wash windows. Nora, who had not done housework for twelve years, took it very badly, and shuffled about in a grubby apron, half-heartedly sweeping floors and preparing indigestible dinners, complaining constantly. The boys liked it better than London because they could play in the woods. Hugh travelled into the City every day by train and continued to go to the bank, where his work consisted of disposing of Pilasters' assets on behalf of the syndicate.

Each of the partners received a small monthly allowance from the bank. In theory they were not entitled to anything. But the syndicate members were not barbarians: they were bankers just like the Pilasters, and in their hearts they thought: *There but for the grace of God go I.* Besides, the co-operation of the partners was helpful in selling off the assets, and it was worth a small payment to retain their goodwill.

Hugh watched the progress of the civil war in Cordova with an anxious heart. The outcome would determine how much money the syndicate would lose. Hugh badly wanted them to make a profit. He wanted one day to be able to say that no one had lost money rescuing Pilasters Bank. But the possibility seemed remote.

At first the Miranda faction seemed set to win the war. By all accounts their attack was well planned and bloodily executed. President Garcia was forced to flee the capital and take refuge in the fortified city of Campanario, in the south, his home region. Hugh was dispirited. If the Mirandas won they would run Cordova like a private kingdom, and would never pay interest on loans made to the previous regime; and Cordovan bonds would be worthless for the foreseeable future.

But then came an unexpected development. Tonio's family, the Silvas, who for some years had been the mainstay of the small and ineffectual liberal opposition, joined in the fighting on the president's side, in return for promises of free elections and land reform when the president regained control. Hugh's hopes rose again.

The revitalized presidential army won a lot of popular support and fought the usurpers to a standstill. The forces were evenly balanced. So were the financial resources: the

Mirandas had spent their war chest on a fierce all-out initial assault. The north had nitrate mines and the south had silver, but neither side could get its exports financed or insured, since Pilasters was no longer in business and no other banks would take on a customer who might vanish tomorrow.

Both sides appealed to the British government for recognition, in the hope that it would help them get credit. Micky Miranda, still officially the Cordovan Minister in London, furiously lobbied Foreign Office officials, government ministers and members of Parliament, pressing for Papa Miranda to be recognized as the new president. But so far the Prime Minister, Lord Salisbury, refused to favour either side.

Then Tonio Silva arrived in London.

He turned up at Hugh's suburban home on Christmas Eve. Hugh was in the kitchen, giving the boys hot milk and buttered toast for breakfast. Nora was still getting dressed: she was going into London to do her Christmas shopping, although she would have very little money to spend. Hugh had agreed to stay at home and take care of the boys: there was nothing urgent for him to do at the bank today.

He answered the doorbell himself, an experience that reminded him of the old days with his mother in Folkestone. Tonio had grown a beard and moustache, no doubt to hide the scars of the beating he had been given by Micky's thugs twelve years ago; but Hugh instantly recognized the carrot-coloured hair and reckless grin. It was snowing, and there was a dusting of white on Tonio's hat and the shoulders of his coat.

Hugh took his old friend into the kitchen and gave him tea. 'How did you find me?' he asked.

'It wasn't easy,' Tonio replied. 'There was no one at your old house and the bank was closed. But I went to

545

Whitehaven House and saw your Aunt Augusta. She hasn't changed. She didn't know your address, but she remembered Chingford. The way she said the name, it sounded like a prison camp, like Van Diemen's Land.'

Hugh nodded. 'It's not so bad. The boys are fine. Nora finds it hard.'

'Augusta hasn't moved house.'

'No. She's more to blame than anyone else for the mess we're in. Yet she of all of them is the one who refuses to accept reality. She'll find out that there are worse places than Chingford.'

'Cordova, for instance,' said Tonio.

'How is it?'

'My brother was killed in the fighting.'

'I'm sorry.'

'The war has reached stalemate. Everything depends on the British government now. The side that wins recognition will be able to get credit, resupply its army, and overrun the opposition. That's why I'm here.'

'Have you been sent by President Garcia?'

'Better than that. I am now officially the Cordovan Minister in London. Miranda has been dismissed.'

'Splendid!' Hugh was pleased that at last Micky had been sacked. It had irked him to see a man who had stolen two million pounds from him walking around London, going to clubs and theatres and dinner parties as if nothing had happened.

Tonio added: 'I brought letters of accreditation with me and lodged them at the Foreign Office yesterday.'

'And you're hoping to persuade the Prime Minister to support your side.'

'Yes.'

Hugh looked at him quizzically. 'How?'

'Garcia is the president – Britain ought to support the legitimate government.'

That was a bit feeble, Hugh thought. 'We haven't so far.'

'I shall just tell the Prime Minister that you should.'

'Lord Salisbury is busy trying to keep the lid on a boiling cauldron in Ireland – he's got no time for a distant South American civil war.' Hugh did not mean to sound negative, but an idea was forming in his mind.

Tonio said rather irritably: 'Well, my job is to persuade Salisbury that he should pay attention to what is going on in South America, even if he does have other things on his mind.' But he could see the weakness of this approach, and after a moment he said: 'Well, all right. You're English, what do you think would engage his attention?'

Hugh said immediately: 'You could promise to protect British investors from loss.'

'How?'

'I'm not sure, I'm thinking aloud.' Hugh shifted his chair. Four-year-old Sol was building a castle of wooden blocks around his feet. It was odd to be deciding the future of a whole country here in the tiny kitchen of a cheap suburban house. 'British investors put two million pounds into the Santamaria Harbour Corporation – Pilasters Bank being the biggest contributor. All the directors of the corporation were members or associates of the Miranda family and I have no doubt the entire two million went straight into their war chest. We need to get it back.'

'But it's all been spent on weapons.'

'All right. But the Miranda family must have assets worth millions.'

'Indeed – they own the country's nitrate mines.'

'If your side won the war, could President Garcia hand

over the mines to the Santamaria Harbour Corporation, in compensation for the fraud? The bonds would be worth something then.'

Tonio said firmly: 'I have been told by the president that I can promise anything – *anything* – that will get the British to side with the government forces in Cordova.'

Hugh began to feel excited. Suddenly the prospect of paying off all the Pilasters' debts seemed closer. 'Let me think,' he said. 'We ought to lay the groundwork before you actually make your pitch to the Foreign Office. I believe I could persuade old Ben Greenbourne to put in a good word with Lord Salisbury, telling him he ought to support the British investor. But what about the Opposition in Parliament? We could go to see Dan Robinson, Maisie's brother – he's a Member of Parliament, and he's obsessed with bank failures. He approves of my rescue scheme for Pilasters and he wants it to work. He might make sure the Opposition supports us in the House of Commons.' He drummed his fingers on the kitchen table. 'This is beginning to look possible!'

'We should act fast,' Tonio said.

'We'll go into town right away. Dan Robinson lives with Maisie in south London. Greenbourne will be at his country house, but I can telephone to him from the bank.' Hugh stood up. 'Let me tell Nora.' He extricated his feet from Sol's wood-block castle and went out.

Nora was in the bedroom, putting on an elaborate hat with fur trimmings. 'I have to go into town,' Hugh said as he put on a collar and tie.

'Who's going to look after the boys, then?' she said.

'You, I hope.'

'No!' she screeched. 'I'm going shopping!'

'I'm sorry, Nora, but this is very important.'

'I'm important too!'

'Of course you are, but you can't have your way about this. I have to speak to Ben Greenbourne urgently.'

'I'm sick of this,' she said disgustedly. 'Sick of the house, sick of this boring village, sick of the children and sick of you. My father lives better than we do!' Nora's father had opened a pub, with a loan from Pilasters Bank, and was doing extremely well. 'I ought to go and live with him, and work as a barmaid,' she said. 'I'd have more fun and I'd be paid for doing drudgery!'

Hugh stared at her. Suddenly he knew he would never share her bed again. There was nothing left of his marriage. Nora hated him, and he despised her. 'Take your hat off, Nora,' he said. 'You're not going shopping today.' He put on his suit jacket and went out.

Tonio was waiting impatiently in the hall. Hugh kissed the boys, picked up his hat and coat, and opened the door. 'There's a train in a few minutes,' he said as they went out.

He put on his hat and shrugged into his coat as they hurried down the short garden path and out through the gate. It was snowing harder, and there was a layer an inch thick on the grass. Hugh's home was one of twenty or thirty identical houses built in a row on what had been a turnip field. They walked along a gravel road towards the village. 'We'll call on Robinson first,' Hugh said, planning their schedule. 'Then I can tell Greenbourne that the Opposition is already on our side. . . . Listen!'

'What?'

'That's our train. We'd better hurry.'

They quickened their pace. Fortunately the station was on the near side of the village. The train came into sight as they crossed a bridge over the line.

A man was leaning on the parapet, watching the approaching train. As they passed him he turned, and Hugh recognized him: it was Micky Miranda.

And he had a revolver in his hand.

After that everything happened very quickly.

Hugh cried out, but his shout was a whisper compared to the noise of the train. Micky pointed the gun at Tonio and fired at point-blank range. Tonio staggered and fell. Micky turned the gun on Hugh – but as he did so, steam and smoke from the engine billowed over the bridge in a dense cloud, and suddenly they were both blind. Hugh threw himself to the snowy ground. He heard the gun again, twice, but he felt nothing. He rolled sideways and got to his knees, peering into the fog.

The smoke began to clear. Hugh glimpsed a figure in the mist and rushed at him. Micky saw him and turned, but too late: Hugh cannoned into him. Micky fell and the gun flew from his hand and sailed in an arc over the parapet and down on to the railway line. Hugh fell on top of Micky and rolled clear.

They both struggled to their feet. Micky stooped to pick up his walking cane. Hugh rushed at him again and knocked him down, but Micky kept hold of the cane. As Micky scrambled to his feet again Hugh lashed out at him. But Hugh had not punched anyone for twenty years and he missed. Micky struck at him with the cane and hit his head. The blow hurt. Micky hit him again. The second blow maddened Hugh and he roared with rage, rushed at Micky and butted his face. They both staggered back, breathing hard.

Then there was a whistle from the station, indicating that the train was leaving, and panic showed on Micky's face. Hugh guessed that Micky had planned to escape by train, and could not afford to be stuck in Chingford for another hour so close to the scene of his crime. The guess was right: Micky turned and ran to the station.

Hugh gave chase.

Micky was no sprinter, having spent too many nights drinking in brothels; but Hugh had passed his adult life sitting behind a desk, and he was not in much better shape. Micky ran into the station as the train was pulling out. Hugh followed him, blowing hard. When they charged on to the platform a railwayman shouted: 'Oy! Where's your tickets?'

By way of reply Hugh yelled: 'Murder!'

Micky ran along the platform, trying to catch the receding rear end of the train. Hugh charged after him, doing his best to ignore the stabbing pain in his side. The railwayman joined in the chase. Micky caught up with the train, grabbed a handle and jumped on a step. Hugh dived after him, caught him by the ankle and lost his grip. The railwayman tripped over Hugh and went flying.

When Hugh got to his feet the train was out of reach. He stared after it in despair. He saw Micky open the door of the moving carriage and move gingerly from the step into the train, closing the door behind him.

The railwayman got up, brushing snow off his clothes, and said: 'What the 'ell was all that about?'

Hugh bent over, breathing like a leaky bellows, too weak to speak.

'A man has been shot,' he said when he caught his breath. As soon as he felt strong enough to move he walked back toward the station entrance, beckoning the railwayman to follow. He led the man to the bridge where Tonio lay.

Hugh knelt by the body. Tonio had been hit between the eyes, and there was not much left of his face. 'My God, what a mess,' said the railwayman. Hugh swallowed hard, fighting down nausea. He forced himself to slide his hand under Tonio's coat and feel for a heartbeat. As he had expected there was none. He remembered the mischievous boy with whom he had splashed around in the swimming-hole at Bishop's Wood twenty-four years ago, and he felt a wave of grief that pushed him close to tears.

Hugh's head was clearing, and he could see, with anguished clarity, how Micky had planned this. Micky had friends in the Foreign Office, as did every half-way competent diplomat. One of those friends must have whispered in his ear, perhaps at a reception or dinner party last night, that Tonio was in London. Tonio had lodged his letters of accreditation already, so Micky knew his days were numbered. But if Tonio were to die the situation would become muddled again. There would be no one in London to negotiate on behalf of President Garcia, and Micky would be the *de facto* Minister. It was Micky's only hope. But he had to act fast and take chances, for he had only a day or two.

How had Micky known where to find Tonio? Perhaps he had people following Tonio – or maybe Augusta had told him that Tonio had been there, asking where to find Hugh. Either way, he had followed Tonio to Chingford.

To seek out Hugh's house would have meant talking to too many people. However, he had known that Tonio had to come back to the railway station sooner or later. So he lurked near the station, planning to kill Tonio – and any witnesses to the murder – and escape by train.

Micky was a desperate man, and it was a fearfully risky scheme – but it had almost worked. He had needed to kill Hugh as well as Tonio, but the smoke from the engine had spoiled his aim. If things had gone according to plan no one would have recognized him. Chingford had neither telegraph nor telephone, and there was no means of transport faster than the train, so he would have been back in London before the crime could be reported. No doubt one of his employees would have given him an alibi, too.

But he had failed to kill Hugh. And – Hugh suddenly realized – technically Micky was no longer the Cordovan Minister, so he had lost his diplomatic immunity.

He could hang for this.

Hugh stood up. 'We must report the murder as soon as possible,' he said.

'There's a police station in Walthamstow, a few stops down the line.'

'When's the next train?'

The railwayman took a large watch from his waistcoat pocket. 'Forty-seven minutes,' he said.

'We should both get on it. You go to the police in Walthamstow and I'll go on to town and report it to Scotland Yard.'

'There's no one to mind the station. I'm on my own, being Christmas Eve.'

'I'm sure your employer would want you to do your public duty.'

'Right you are.' The man seemed grateful to be told what to do.

'We'd better put poor Silva somewhere. Is there a place in the station?'

'Only the waiting room.'

'We'd better carry him there and lock it up.' Hugh bent and took hold of the body under the arms. 'You take his legs.' They lifted Tonio and carried him into the station.

They laid him on a bench in the waiting room. Then they were not sure what to do. Hugh felt restive. He could not grieve – it was too soon. He wanted to catch the murderer, not mourn. He paced up and down, consulting his watch every few minutes, and rubbing the sore place on his head where Micky's cane had struck him. The railwayman sat on the opposite bench, staring at the body with fearful fascination. After a while Hugh sat beside him. They stayed like that, silent and watchful, sharing the cold room with the dead man, until the train came in.

[II]

MICKY MIRANDA was fleeing for his life.

His luck was running out. He had committed four murders in the last twenty-four years, and he had got away with the first three, but this time he had stumbled. Hugh Pilaster had seen him shoot Tonio Silva in broad daylight, and there was no way to escape the hangman but by leaving England.

Suddenly he was on the run, a fugitive in the city that had been his home for most of his life. He hurried through Liverpool Street railway station, avoiding the eyes of policemen, his heart racing and his breath coming in shallow gasps, and dived into a hansom cab.

He went straight to the office of the Gold Coast and Mexico Steamship Company.

The place was crowded, mainly with Latins. Some would be trying to return to Cordova, others trying to get relatives out, and some might just be asking for news. It was noisy and disorganized. Micky could not afford to wait for the riff-raff. He fought his way to the counter, using his cane indiscriminately on men and women to get through. His expensive clothes and upper-class arrogance got the attention of a clerk, and he said: 'I want to book passage to Cordova.'

'There's a war on in Cordova,' said the clerk.

Micky suppressed a sarcastic retort. 'You haven't suspended all sailings, I take it.'

'We're selling tickets to Lima, Peru. The ship will go on

to Palma if political conditions permit: the decision will be made when it reaches Lima.'

That would do. Micky mainly needed to get out of England. 'When is the next departure?'

'Four weeks from today.'

His heart sank. 'That's no good, I have to go sooner!'

'There's a ship leaving Southampton tonight, if you're in a hurry.'

Thank God! His luck had not quite run out just yet. 'Reserve me a stateroom – the best available.'

'Very good, sir. May I have the name?'

'Miranda.'

'Beg pardon, sir?'

The English were deaf when a foreign name was spoken. Micky was about to spell his name when he changed his mind. 'Andrews,' he said. 'M. R. Andrews.' It had occurred to him that the police might check passenger lists, looking for the name Miranda. Now they would not find it. He was grateful for the insane liberalism of Britain's laws, which permitted people to enter and leave the country without passports. It would not have been so easy in Cordova.

The clerk began to make out his ticket. Micky watched restlessly, rubbing the sore place on his face where Hugh Pilaster had butted him. He realized he had another problem. Scotland Yard could circulate his description to all port towns by cable. Damn the telegraph. Within an hour they would have local policemen checking all passengers. He needed some kind of disguise.

The clerk gave him his ticket and he paid with banknotes. He pushed impatiently through the crowd and went out into the snow, still worrying.

He hailed a hansom and directed it to the Cordovan Ministry, but then he had second thoughts. It was risky to go back there, and anyway he was short of time.

The police would be looking for a well-dressed man of forty, travelling alone. One way to get past them would be to appear as an older man with a companion. In fact, he could pretend to be an invalid, and be wheeled on board in a wheelchair. But for that he would need an accomplice. Who could he use? He was not sure he could trust any of his employees, especially now that he was no longer the Minister.

That left Edward.

'Drive to Hill Street,' he told the cabbie.

Edward had a small house in Mayfair. Unlike the other Pilasters, he rented his home, and he had not been obliged to move out yet because his rent was paid three months in advance.

Edward did not seem to care that Micky had destroyed Pilasters Bank and brought ruin to his family. He had only become more dependent on Micky. As for the rest of the Pilasters, Micky had not seen them since the crash.

Edward answered the door in a stained silk dressing-gown and took Micky up to his bedroom, where there was a fire. He was smoking a cigar and drinking whisky at eleven o'clock in the morning. The skin rash was all over his face now, and Micky had second thoughts about using him as an accomplice: the rash made him conspicuous. But there was no time to be choosy. Edward would have to do.

'I'm leaving the country,' Micky said.

Edward said: 'Oh, take me with you,' and burst into tears.

'What the devil is the matter with you?' Micky said unsympathetically.

'I'm dying,' Edward said. 'Let's go somewhere quiet and live together in peace until I'm gone.'

'You're not dying, you damn fool – you've only got a skin disease.'

'It's not a skin disease, it's syphilis.'

Micky gasped in horror. 'Jesus and Mary, I might have it too!'

'It's no wonder, the amount of time we've spent at Nellie's.'

'But April's girls are supposed to be clean!'

'Whores are never clean.'

Micky fought down panic. If he delayed in London to see a doctor he might die at the end of a rope. He had to leave the country today. But the ship went via Lisbon: he could see a doctor there in a few days' time. That would have to do. He might not have the disease at all: he was much healthier than Edward generally, and he always washed himself after sex, whereas Edward was not so fastidious.

But Edward was in no state to help smuggle him out of the country. Anyway, Micky was not going to take a terminal syphilis case back to Cordova with him. Still, he needed an accomplice. And there was only one candidate left: Augusta.

He was not as sure of her as he was of Edward. Edward had always been willing to do anything Micky asked. Augusta was independent. But she was his last chance.

He turned to go.

'Don't leave me,' Edward pleaded.

There was no time for sentiment. 'I can't take a dying man with me,' he snapped.

Edward looked up, and his face took on a malicious expression. 'If you don't . . .'

'Well?'

'I'll tell the police that you killed Peter Middleton, and Uncle Seth, and Solly Greenbourne.'

Augusta must have told him about Old Seth. Micky stared at Edward. He made a pathetic figure. How have I put up with him for so long, Micky wondered? He suddenly realized how happy he would be to leave him behind. 'Tell the police,' he said. 'They're already after me for killing Tonio Silva, and I might as well be hanged for four murders as for one.' He went out without looking back.

He let himself out of the house and got a hansom in Park Lane. 'Kensington Gore,' he told the cabbie. 'Whitehaven House.' On the way he worried about his health. He had none of the symptoms: no skin problems, no unexplained lumps on his genitals. But he would have to wait to be sure. Damn Edward to hell.

He also worried about Augusta. He had not seen her since the crash. Would she help him? He knew she had always struggled to control her sexual hunger for him; and on that one bizarre occasion she had actually yielded to her passion. In those days Micky had burned for her too. Since then Micky's fire had abated, but he felt that hers had grown hotter. He hoped so: he was going to ask her to run away with him.

Augusta's door was opened not by her butler but by a slovenly woman in an apron. Passing through the hall, Micky noticed that the place was not very clean. Augusta was in difficulties. So much the better: it would make her more inclined to go along with his plan.

However, she appeared her usual imperious self as she came into the drawing-room in a purple silk blouse with leg-of-mutton sleeves and a black flared skirt with a tiny pinched waist. She had been a breathtakingly beautiful young woman and now, at fifty-eight, she could still turn heads. He recalled the lust he had felt for her as a boy of sixteen, but there was none left. He would have to fake it.

She did not offer him her hand. 'Why have you come here?' she said coldly. 'You've brought ruin to me and my family.'

'I didn't intend to—'

'You must have known that your father was about to launch a civil war.'

'But I didn't realize that Cordovan bonds would become valueless because of the war,' he said. 'Did you?'

She hesitated. Obviously she had not.

A crack had opened in her armour and he tried to widen it. 'I wouldn't have done it if I'd known – I would have cut my own throat before harming you.' He could tell that she wanted to believe this.

But she said: 'You persuaded Edward to deceive his partners so that you could have your two million pounds.'

'I thought there was so much money in the bank that it could never be harmed.'

She looked away. 'So did I,' she said quietly.

He pressed his advantage. 'Anyway, it's all irrelevant now – I'm leaving England today, and I will probably never come back.'

She looked at him with sudden fear in her eyes, and he knew he had her. 'Why?' she said.

There was no time for beating about the bush. 'I have just shot and killed a man and the police are chasing me.'

She gasped and took his hand. 'Who?'

'Antonio Silva.'

She was excited as well as shocked. Her face coloured a little and her eyes became bright. 'Tonio! Why?'

'He was a threat to me. I've booked passage on a steamer leaving Southampton tonight.'

'So soon!'

'I have no choice.'

'And so you've come to say goodbye,' she said, and she looked downcast.

'No.'

She looked up at him. Was that hope in her eyes? He

hesitated, then took the plunge. 'I want you to come with me.'

Her eyes widened. She took a step back.

He kept hold of her hand. 'Having to leave – and so quickly – has made me realize something I should have admitted to myself a long time ago. I think you have always known it. I love you, Augusta.'

As he acted his part he watched her face, reading it the way a sailor reads the surface of the sea. For a moment she tried to put on a look of astonishment, but she abandoned it almost immediately. There was the hint of a gratified smile, then a faint blush of embarrassment that was almost maidenly; and then a calculating look that told him she was reckoning up what she had to gain and lose.

He saw she was still undecided.

He put his hand on her corseted waist and drew her gently towards him. She did not resist, but her face still wore that appraising look that told him she had not made up her mind.

When their faces were close and her breasts were touching the lapels of his coat, he said: 'I can't live without you, dear Augusta.'

He could feel her trembling beneath his touch. In a shaky voice she said: 'I'm old enough to be your mother.'

He spoke into her ear, brushing her face with his lips. 'But you aren't,' he said, making his voice almost a whisper. 'You're the most desirable woman I've ever met. I've longed for you all these years, you know that. Now . . .' He moved his hand up from her waist until he was almost touching her breast. 'Now I can hardly keep my hands under control. Augusta . . .' He paused.

'What?' she said.

He almost had her, but not quite. He had to play his last card.

'Now that I'm no longer Minister, I can divorce Rachel.'

'What are you saying?'

He whispered into her ear: 'Will you marry me?'

'Yes,' she said.

He kissed her.

[III]

APRIL TILSLEY burst into Maisie's office at the Female Hospital, dressed to the nines in scarlet silk and fox fur, carrying a newspaper and saying: 'Have you heard what's happened?'

Maisie stood up. 'April! What on earth is it?'

'Micky Miranda shot Tonio Silva!'

Maisie knew who Micky was, but it took her a moment to remember that Tonio had been one of that crowd of boys around Solly and Hugh when they were young. He had been a gambler in those days, she recalled, and April had been very sweet on him until she discovered that he always lost what little money he had in wagers. 'Micky *shot* him?' she said in amazement. 'Is he dead?'

'Yes. It's in the afternoon paper.'

'I wonder why?'

'It doesn't say. But it also says . . .' April hesitated. 'Sit down, Maisie.'

'Why? Tell me!'

'It says the police want to question him about three other murders – Peter Middleton, Seth Pilaster and . . . Solomon Greenbourne.'

Maisie sat down heavily. 'Solly!' she said, and she felt faint. 'Micky killed Solly? Oh, poor Solly.' She closed her eyes and buried her face in her hands.

'You need a sip of brandy,' April said. 'Where do you keep it?'

'We don't have any here,' Maisie said. She tried to pull herself together. 'Show me that paper.'

April handed her the newspaper.

Maisie read the first paragraph. It said the police were hunting for the former Cordovan Minister, Miguel Miranda, to question him about the murder of Antonio Silva.

April said: 'Poor Tonio. He was one of the nicest men I ever opened my legs for.'

Maisie read on. The police also wanted to question Miranda about the deaths of Peter Middleton, at Windfield School in 1866; Seth Pilaster, the Senior Partner of Pilasters Bank, in 1873; and Solomon Greenbourne, who was pushed under a speeding carriage in a side street off Piccadilly in July of 1879.

'And Seth Pilaster – Hugh's Uncle Seth?' Maisie said agitatedly. 'Why did he kill all these people?'

April said: 'The newspapers never tell you what you really want to know.'

The third paragraph jolted Maisie yet again. The shooting had taken place in north-east London, near Walthamstow, at a village called Chingford. Her heart missed a beat. 'Chingford!' she gasped.

'I've never heard of it—'

'It's where Hugh lives!'

'Hugh Pilaster? Are you still carrying a torch for him?'

'He must have been involved, don't you see? It can't be a coincidence! Oh, dear God, I hope he's all right.'

'I expect the paper would say if he had been hurt.'

'It only happened a few hours ago. They may not know.' Maisie could not bear this uncertainty. She stood up. 'I must find out if he's all right,' she said.

'How?'

She put on her hat and stuck a pin in it. 'I'll go to his house.'

'His wife won't like it.'

'His wife's a *paskudniak*.'

April laughed. 'What's that?'

'A shitbag.' Maisie put on her coat.

April stood up. 'My carriage is outside. I'll take you to the railway station.'

When they got into April's carriage they realized that neither of them knew which London terminus they should go to for a train to Chingford. Fortunately the coachman, who was also the doorman at Nellie's brothel, was able to tell them it was Liverpool Street.

When they got there Maisie thanked April perfunctorily and dashed into the station. It was packed with Christmas travellers and shoppers returning to their suburban homes. The air was full of smoke and dirt. People shouted greetings and farewells over the screech of steel brakes and the explosive exhalations of the steam engines. She fought her way to the booking office through a throng of women with armfuls of parcels, bowler-hatted clerks going home early, black-faced engineers and firemen, children and horses and dogs.

She had to wait fifteen minutes for a train. On the platform she watched a tearful farewell between two young lovers, and envied them.

The train puffed through the slums of Bethnal Green, the suburbs of Walthamstow and the snow-covered fields of Woodford, stopping every few minutes. Although it was twice as fast as a horse-drawn carriage it seemed slow to Maisie as she bit her fingernails and wondered if Hugh was all right.

When she got off the train at Chingford she was stopped

by the police and asked to step into the waiting-room. A detective asked her if she had been in the locality that morning. Obviously they were looking for witnesses to the murder. She told him she had never been to Chingford before. On impulse she said: 'Was anyone else hurt, other than Antonio Silva?'

'Two people received minor cuts and bruises in the fracas,' the detective replied.

'I'm worried about a friend of mine who knew Mr Silva. His name is Hugh Pilaster.'

'Mr Pilaster grappled with the assailant and was struck on the head,' the man said. 'His injuries are not serious.'

'Oh, thank God,' said Maisie. 'Can you direct me to his house?'

The detective told her where to go. 'Mr Pilaster was at Scotland Yard earlier in the day – whether he has returned yet, I couldn't say.'

Maisie wondered whether she should go back to London right away, now that she was fairly sure Hugh was all right. It would avoid a meeting with the ghastly Nora. But she would feel happier if she saw him. And she was not afraid of Nora. She set off for his house, trudging through two or three inches of snow.

Chingford was a brutal contrast to Kensington, she thought as she walked down the new street of cheap houses with their raw front gardens. Hugh would be stoical about his comedown, she guessed, but she was not so sure of Nora. The bitch had married Hugh for his money and she would not like being poor again.

Maisie could hear a child crying inside when she knocked on the door of Hugh's house. It was opened by a boy of about eleven years. 'You're Toby, aren't you?' Maisie said. 'I've come to see your father. My name is Mrs Greenbourne.'

'I'm afraid Father's not at home,' the boy said politely.

'When do you expect him back?'

'I don't know.'

Maisie felt let down. She had been looking forward to seeing Hugh. Disappointed, she said: 'Perhaps you would just say that I saw the newspaper and I called to make sure he was all right.'

'Very well, I'll tell him.'

There was no more to be said. She might as well go back to the station and wait for the next train into London. She turned away, disappointed. At least she had escaped an altercation with Nora.

Something in the boy's face bothered her: a look almost of fear. On impulse she turned back and said: 'Is your mother in?'

'No, I'm afraid she's not.'

That was odd. Hugh could no longer afford a governess. Maisie had a feeling that something was wrong. She said: 'Might I speak to whoever is looking after you?'

The boy hesitated. 'Actually, there isn't anybody here but me and my brothers.'

Maisie's intuition had been right. What was going on? How had three small boys been left totally alone? She hesitated to interfere, knowing she would catch hell from Nora Pilaster. On the other hand she could not simply walk away and leave Hugh's children to fend for themselves. 'I'm an old friend of your father . . . and mother,' she said.

'I saw you at Auntie Dotty's wedding,' said Toby.

'Ah, yes. Um . . . may I come in?'

Toby looked relieved. 'Yes, please do,' he said.

Maisie stepped inside. She followed the sound of the crying child to the kitchen at the back of the house. There was a four-year-old squatting on the floor bawling, and a six-year-old sitting on the kitchen table looking as if he was ready to burst into tears at any moment.

She picked up the youngest. She knew that he was named Solomon, after Solly Greenbourne, but they called him Sol. 'There, there,' she murmured. 'What's the matter?'

'I want my mama,' he said, and cried louder.

'Hush, hush,' Maisie murmured, rocking him. She felt dampness penetrate her clothing and she realized the little boy had wet himself. Looking around, she saw that the place was a mess. The table was covered with breadcrumbs and spilt milk, there were dirty dishes in the sink, and there was mud on the floor. It was cold, too: the fire had gone out. It almost looked as if the children had been abandoned.

'What's going on here?' she said to Toby.

'I gave them some lunch,' he said. 'I made bread-and-butter and cut some ham. I tried to make tea but I burned my hand on the kettle.' He was trying to be brave but he was on the brink of tears. 'Do you know where my father might be?'

'No, I don't.' The baby had asked for his mama, but the older boy had wanted his father, Maisie noted. 'What about your mother?'

Toby took an envelope from the mantelpiece and handed it to her. It was addressed simply: 'Hugh.'

'It's not sealed,' Toby said. 'I read it.'

Maisie opened it and took out a single sheet of paper. One word was written on it in large, angry capital letters:

GOODBYE

Maisie was horrified. How could a mother walk out on three small children – and leave them to fend for themselves? Nora had given birth to each of these boys, and held them to her breast as helpless babies. Maisie thought of the mothers in the Southwark Female Hospital. If one of them were given a three-bedroom house in Chingford she would think herself in heaven.

She put such thoughts out of her mind for the moment. 'Your father will be back tonight, I'm sure,' she said, praying it was true. She addressed the four-year-old in her arms. 'But we wouldn't want him to find the house a mess, would we?'

Sol shook his head solemnly.

'We're going to wash the dishes, clean the kitchen, light the fire and make some supper.' She looked at the six-year-old. 'Do you think that's a good idea, Samuel?'

Samuel nodded. 'I like buttered toast,' he added helpfully.

'Then that's what we'll have.'

Toby was not reassured. 'What time do you think Father will come home?'

'I'm not sure,' she said candidly. There was no point in lying: children always knew. 'But I tell you what. You can stay up until he gets here, no matter how late. How's that?'

The boy looked somewhat relieved. 'All right,' he said.

'Now, then. Toby, you're the strongest, you can bring in a bucket of coal. Samuel, I believe I can trust you to do a job properly, you can wipe the kitchen table with a rag. Sol, you can sweep up because – you're the smallest, so you're closer to the floor. Come on, boys, let's start work!'

[IV]

HUGH WAS impressed by the way Scotland Yard responded to his report. The case was assigned to Detective-Inspector Magridge, a sharp-faced man of about Hugh's age, meticulous and intelligent, the kind who would have made it to chief clerk in a bank. Within an hour he had circulated a description of Micky Miranda and set a watch on all the ports.

He also sent a detective-sergeant to interview Edward Pilaster, at Hugh's suggestion; and the man came back with the report that Miranda was leaving the country.

Edward had also said that Micky was implicated in the deaths of Peter Middleton, Seth Pilaster and Solomon Greenbourne. Hugh was shaken by the suggestion that Micky had killed Uncle Seth, but he told Magridge that he already suspected Micky of killing Peter and Solly.

The same detective was despatched to see Augusta. She was still living at Whitehaven House. With no money she could not hold out indefinitely, but so far she had succeeded in preventing the sale of the house or its contents.

A police constable assigned to check London steamship offices reported that a man answering the description but calling himself M. R. Andrews had booked passage on the *Aztec* sailing from Southampton tonight. The Southampton police were instructed to have men at the railway station and at the dockside.

The detective sent to see Augusta came back to report there was no answer when he rang and knocked at the door of Whitehaven House.

'I have a key,' Hugh said.

Magridge said: 'She's probably out – and I want the sergeant to go to the Cordovan Ministry. Why don't you check Whitehaven House yourself?'

Glad of something to do, Hugh took a cab to Kensington Gore. He rang and knocked, but there was no answer. The last of the servants had left, obviously. He let himself into the house.

The house was cold. Hiding was not Augusta's style, but he decided to search the rooms anyway, just in case. The ground floor was deserted. He went up to the first floor and checked her bedroom.

What he saw surprised him. The wardrobe doors were ajar, the drawers of the chest were open, and there were discarded clothes on the bed and chairs. This was not like Augusta: she was a tidy person with an ordered mind. At first he thought she had been robbed. Then another thought struck him.

He ran up two flights of stairs to the servants' floor. When he had lived here, seventeen years ago, the suitcases and trunks had been kept jam-packed into a big closet known as the box-room.

He found the door open. The room contained a few suitcases and no steamer trunk.

Augusta had run away.

He quickly checked all the other rooms of the house. As he expected, he saw no one. The servants' rooms and the guest bedrooms were already acquiring the musty air of disuse. When he looked into the room that had been Uncle Joseph's bedroom, he was surprised to see that it looked exactly as it always had, although the rest of the house had been redecorated several times. He was about to leave when his eye fell on the lacquered display cabinet that held Joseph's valuable collection of snuff-boxes.

The cabinet was empty.

Hugh frowned. He knew the snuff-boxes had not been lodged with the auctioneers: Augusta had so far prevented the removal of any of her possessions.

That meant she had taken them with her.

They were worth a hundred thousand pounds – she could live comfortably for the rest of her life on that money.

But they did not belong to her. They belonged to the syndicate.

He decided to go after her.

He ran down the stairs and out into the street. There was a cab stand a few yards along the road. The drivers were chatting in a group, stamping their feet to keep warm. Hugh ran up to them, saying: 'Did any of you drive Lady Whitehaven this afternoon?'

'Two of us did,' said a cabbie. 'One for her luggage!' The others chortled.

Hugh's deduction was confirmed. 'Where did you take her?'

'Waterloo Station, for the one o'clock boat train.'

The boat train went to Southampton – where Micky was sailing from. Those two had always been cronies. Micky smarmed all over her like a cad, kissing her hand and flattering her. Despite the eighteen years' difference in their ages, they made a plausible couple.

'But they missed the train,' the cabbie added.

'They?' Hugh said. 'There was someone with her?'

'An elderly chap in a wheelchair.'

Not Micky, evidently. Who, then? No one in the family was frail enough to use a wheelchair. 'They missed the train, you say. Do you know when the next boat train leaves?'

'At three.'

Hugh looked at his watch. It was two-thirty. He could catch it.

'Take me to Waterloo,' he said, and jumped into the cab.

He reached the station just in time to get a ticket and board the boat train.

It was a corridor train with interconnecting coaches, so he could walk along it. As it pulled out of the station and picked up speed through the tenements of south London, he set out to look for Augusta.

He did not have to look far. She was in the next coach.

With a quick glance he hurried past her compartment so that she would not see him.

Micky was not with her. He must have gone by an earlier train. The only other person in her compartment was an elderly man with a rug over his knees.

He went to the next coach and found a seat. There was not much point in confronting Augusta right away. She might not have the snuff-boxes with her – they could be in one of her cases in the luggage van. To speak to her now would serve only to forewarn her. Better to wait until the train arrived at Southampton. He would jump off, find a policeman, then challenge her as her bags were being unloaded.

Suppose she denied she had the snuff-boxes? He would insist that the police search her luggage. They were obliged to investigate a reported theft, and the more Augusta protested the more suspicious they would be.

Suppose she claimed the snuff-boxes were hers? It was hard to prove anything on the spot. If that happened, Hugh decided he would propose that the police take custody of the valuables while they investigated the contradictory claims.

He controlled his impatience as the white fields of Wimbledon sped by. A hundred thousand pounds was a big chunk of the money Pilasters Bank owed. He was not going to let Augusta steal it. The snuff-boxes also had symbolic importance. They stood for the family's determination to pay off its debts. If Augusta was allowed to make off with them, people would say the Pilasters were grabbing what they could, just like any ordinary embezzlers. The thought made Hugh angry.

It was still snowing when the train reached Southampton. Hugh was leaning out of the carriage window as the engine puffed into the station. There were uniformed policemen everywhere. That meant Micky had not yet been caught, Hugh inferred.

He jumped off while the train was still moving and got to the ticket barrier before anyone else. He spoke to a police inspector. 'I'm the Senior Partner of Pilasters Bank,' he said, giving the inspector his card. 'I know you're looking for a murderer, but there's a woman on this train who is carrying stolen property worth a hundred thousand pounds belonging to the bank. I believe she is planning to leave the country on the *Aztec* tonight, taking it with her.'

'What property would that be, Mr Pilaster?' said the inspector.

'A collection of jewelled snuff-boxes.'

'And the name of the woman?'

'She's the Dowager Countess of Whitehaven.'

The policeman raised his eyebrows. 'I do read the newspapers, sir. I take it this is all to do with the failure of the bank.'

Hugh nodded. 'Those snuff-boxes must be sold to help pay people who have lost their money.'

'Can you point out Lady Whitehaven to me?'

Hugh looked along the platform, peering through the falling snow. 'That's her, by the luggage van, in the big hat with birds' wings on it.' She was supervising the unloading of her bags.

The inspector nodded. 'Very well. Stay here with me at the ticket barrier. We'll detain her as she passes through.'

Hugh was tense as he watched the passengers stream off the train and out. Although he was fairly certain Micky was not on the train, nevertheless he scrutinized the face of every passenger.

Augusta was the last to leave. Three porters were

carrying her luggage. When she saw Hugh at the ticket barrier she turned pale.

The inspector was all politeness. 'Pardon me, Lady Whitehaven. May I have a word?'

Hugh had never seen Augusta so frightened, but she had not lost her queenly manner. 'I'm afraid I can't spare the time, officer,' she said coolly. 'I have to board a ship that is sailing tonight.'

'I guarantee the *Aztec* won't leave without you, my lady,' the inspector said smoothly. He glanced at the porters and said: 'You can put those down for a minute, lads.' He turned back to Augusta. 'Mr Pilaster here claims you have in your possession some very valuable snuff-boxes that belong to him. Is that so?'

She began to look less alarmed – which puzzled Hugh. It worried him, too: he was afraid she might have something up her sleeve. 'I don't see why I should answer such impertinent questions,' she said arrogantly.

'If you don't, I shall have to look through your bags.'

'Very well, I do have the snuff-boxes,' she said. 'But they belong to me. They were my husband's.'

The inspector turned to Hugh. 'What do you say to that, Mr Pilaster?'

'They were her husband's, but he left them to his son, Edward Pilaster; and Edward's possessions are forfeit to the bank. Lady Whitehaven is trying to steal them.'

The inspector said: 'I must ask you both to come to the police station while these allegations are investigated.'

Augusta looked panicky. 'But I can't miss my sailing!'

'In that case, the only thing I can suggest is that you leave the disputed property in the care of the police. It will be returned to you if your claims are verified.'

Augusta hesitated. Hugh knew it would break her heart to part with so much wealth. But surely she could see it

573

was inevitable? She had been caught red-handed and she was lucky she was not going to jail.

'Where are the snuff-boxes, my lady?' said the inspector.

Hugh waited.

Augusta pointed to a suitcase. 'They're all in there.'

'The key, please?'

Again she hesitated; again she gave in. She took out a small ring of luggage keys, selected one, and handed it over.

The inspector opened the case. It was full of shoe bags. Augusta pointed to one of the bags. The inspector opened it and drew out a light wooden cigar box. He lifted the lid to reveal numerous small objects carefully wrapped in paper. Selecting one at random, he unwrapped it. It was a small gold box inlaid with diamond chips in the design of a lizard.

Hugh let out a long sigh of relief.

The inspector looked at Hugh. 'Do you know how many there should be, sir?'

Everyone in the family did. 'Sixty-five,' said Hugh. 'One for every year of Uncle Joseph's life.'

'Would you like to count them?'

Augusta said: 'They're all there.'

Hugh counted them anyway. There were sixty-five. He began to feel the pleasure of victory.

The inspector took the box and passed it to another policeman. 'If you would like to go with Constable Neville to the police station, he will give you an official receipt for the goods, my lady.'

'Send it to the bank,' she said. 'May I go now?'

Hugh was uneasy. Augusta was disappointed, but not devastated. It was almost as if there was something else she was worried about, something more important to her than the snuff-boxes. And where was Micky Miranda?

The inspector bowed, and Augusta went out, followed by her three heavily laden porters.

'Thank you very much, inspector,' said Hugh. 'I'm only sorry you didn't catch Miranda as well.'

'We will, sir. He won't get aboard the *Aztec* unless he's learned how to fly.'

The guard from the luggage van came along the platform pushing a wheelchair. He stopped in front of Hugh and the inspector and said: 'Now what am I supposed to do with this?'

'What's the problem?' the inspector said patiently.

'That woman with all the luggage and the bird on her hat.'

'Lady Whitehaven, yes.'

'She was with an old gent at Waterloo. Puts him in a first-class compartment and then asks me to take the bath-chair in the luggage van. Glad to oblige, says I. Gets off at Southampton and pretends she don't know what I'm talking about. "You must have mistaken me for somebody else," she goes. "Not likely – there's only one hat like that," says I.'

Hugh said: 'That's right – the cabbie said she was with a man in a wheelchair . . . and there was an old fellow in the compartment with her.'

'There you are,' the guard said triumphantly.

The inspector suddenly lost his avuncular air and rounded on Hugh. 'Did you see the old man pass through the ticket barrier?'

'No, I didn't. And I looked at every passenger. Aunt Augusta was the last.' Then it hit him. 'Good God! Do you think it was Micky Miranda in disguise?'

'Yes, I do. But where is he now? Could he have got off at an earlier stop?'

The guard said: 'No – it's an express train, non-stop from Waterloo to Southampton.'

'Then we'll search the train. He must be on it still.'

But he was not.

[V]

THE *AZTEC* WAS festooned with coloured lanterns and paper streamers. The Christmas party was in full swing when Augusta boarded: a band played on the main deck, and passengers in evening dress drank champagne and danced with friends who had come to say goodbye.

A steward led Augusta up the grand staircase to a stateroom on an upper deck. She had spent all her cash on the best cabin available, thinking that with the snuff-boxes in her suitcase she need not worry about money. The room opened directly on to the deck. Inside it had a wide bed, a full-size wash-basin, comfortable chairs and electric lights. There were flowers on the dresser, a box of chocolates beside the bed and a bottle of champagne in a bucket of ice on the low table. Augusta was about to tell the steward to take the champagne away then changed her mind. She was beginning a new life: perhaps she would drink champagne from now on.

She was only just in time. She heard the traditional shout of 'All ashore that's going ashore!' even as the porters brought her luggage into the cabin. When they had gone she stepped on to the narrow deck, turning up her coat collar against the snow. She leaned against the rail and looked down. There was a sheer drop to the water, where a tug boat was already in position to ease the great liner out of the harbour into the sea. As she watched, the gangways were withdrawn one by one and the ropes cast off. The ship's foghorn sounded, a cheer went up from the crowd on the quay, and slowly, almost imperceptibly, the huge ship began to move.

Augusta returned to her cabin and closed the door. She undressed slowly and put on a silk nightgown and a matching robe. Then she summoned the steward and told him she would not require anything further tonight.

'Shall I wake you in the morning, my lady?'

'No, thank you. I'll ring.'

'Very good, m'lady.'

Augusta locked the door behind him.

Then she opened her trunk and let Micky out.

He staggered across the stateroom and fell on the bed. 'Jesus save me, I thought I was going to die,' he moaned.

'My poor darling, where does it hurt?'

'My legs.' She rubbed his calves. The muscles were knotted with cramp. She massaged his flesh with her fingertips, feeling the warmth of his skin through the cloth of his trousers. It was a long time since she had touched a man this way, and she felt a flush of heat rise at her throat.

She had often daydreamed about doing this, running away with Micky Miranda, both before and since the death of her husband. She had always been stopped by the thought of all she would lose – house, servants, dress allowance, social position, and family power. But the bank crash had taken all that away now, and she was free to give in to her desires.

'Water,' said Micky feebly.

She poured a glass from the pitcher beside the bed. He turned over and sat up to take it, then drank it all.

'Some more . . . Micky?'

He shook his head.

She took the glass from him.

'You lost the snuff-boxes,' he said. 'I heard the whole thing. That swine Hugh.'

'But you've got plenty of money,' she said. She pointed to the champagne in the ice bucket. 'We should drink this. We're out of England. You escaped!'

He was staring at her bosom. She realized that her nipples were hard with excitement, and he could see them poking through the silk of her nightwear. She wanted to say: *You can touch them if you like*, but she hesitated. There was plenty of time: they had all night. They had the whole voyage. They had the rest of their lives. But suddenly she could wait no longer. She felt guilty and ashamed, but she longed to hold his naked body in her arms, and the longing was stronger than the shame. She sat on the edge of the bed. She took his hand, drew it to her lips, and kissed it; then she pressed it to her breast.

He looked at her curiously for a moment. Then he began to stroke her breast through the silk. His touch was gentle. His fingertips brushed the sensitive nipple and she gasped with pleasure. He changed his grip and held her breast in his palm, lifting and moving it. Then he grasped her nipple between finger and thumb and squeezed. She closed her eyes. He pinched harder, so that it hurt. Then, suddenly, he twisted her nipple so viciously that she screamed and pulled away from him, standing up.

'You dumb cunt,' he sneered, getting off the bed.

'No!' she said. 'No!'

'You really thought I would marry you!'

'Yes—'

'You've got no money and no influence any more, the bank is bust, and you even lost the snuff-boxes. What would I want with you?'

She felt a pain in her chest, like a knife in her heart. 'You said you loved me. . . .'

'You're fifty-eight – my mother's age, for God's sake! You're old and wrinkled and mean and selfish, and I wouldn't fuck you if you were the last woman on earth!'

She felt faint. She tried not to cry but it was no good. Tears welled up in her eyes and she began to shake with sobs of despair. She was ruined. She had no home, no money and no friends, and the man she trusted had betrayed her. She turned away from him to hide her face: she did not want him to see her shame and grief. 'Please, stop,' she whispered.

'I'll stop,' he spat. 'I've got a cabin reserved on this ship and that's where I'm going.'

'But when we get to Cordova . . .'

'You're not going to Cordova. You can get off the ship at Lisbon and go back to England. I've no further use for you.'

Every word was like a blow and she backed away from him, holding her hands up in front of her as if to ward off his curses. She bumped against the cabin door. Desperate to get away from him, she opened it and backed out.

The freezing night air cleared her head suddenly. She realized she was behaving like a helpless girl, not a mature, capable woman. She had lost control of her life briefly, and it was time to seize it back again.

A man in evening dress walked past her, smoking a cigar. He stared at her nightclothes in astonishment but did not speak to her.

That gave her an idea.

She stepped back into the cabin and closed the door. Micky was straightening his tie in the mirror. 'There's someone coming,' she said urgently. 'A policeman!'

Micky's demeanour changed in a flash. The sneer was wiped off his face and replaced by a look of panic. 'Oh, my God,' he said.

Augusta was thinking quickly. 'We're still within British waters,' she said. 'You can be arrested and sent back on a coastguard cutter.' She had no idea whether this was true.

'I'll have to hide.' He climbed into the trunk. 'Close the front, quickly,' he said.

She shut him in the trunk.

Then she flipped the latch to lock it.

'That's better,' she said.

She sat on the bed, staring at the trunk. In her mind she went over and over their conversation. She had made herself vulnerable and he had wounded her. She thought of how he had caressed her. Only two other men had touched her breasts: Strang and Joseph. She thought of how he had twisted her nipple then spurned her with obscene words. As the minutes went by her rage cooled and became a dark, vicious yearning for revenge.

Micky's voice, muffled, came from inside the trunk. 'Augusta! What's happening?'

She made no reply.

He began to shout for help. She covered the trunk with blankets from the bed to deaden the sound.

After a while he stopped.

Thoughtfully, Augusta removed the luggage labels bearing her name from the trunk.

She heard cabin doors slam: passengers were heading for the dining-room. The ship began to pitch slightly in the swell as it steamed out into the English Channel. The evening passed quickly for Augusta as she sat on the bed brooding.

Passengers trickled back in twos and threes between

midnight and two o'clock. After that the band stopped playing and the ship became quiet but for the sounds of the engines and the sea.

Augusta stared obsessively at the trunk in which she had locked Micky. It had been carried up here on the back of a muscular porter. Augusta could not lift it, but she thought she could drag it. It had brass handles on the sides and leather straps top and bottom. She took hold of the leather strap on its top and pulled, tilting the trunk sideways. It tipped over and fell on its face. It made a loud bang. Micky began to shout again, and she covered the trunk with blankets once more. She waited to see if anyone would come to investigate the bang, but no one did. Micky stopped yelling.

She seized the strap again and pulled. It was very heavy, but she was able to move it a few inches at a time. After each tug she rested.

It took her ten minutes to drag the trunk to the cabin door. Then she put on her stockings, boots and fur coat, and opened the door.

There was no one around. The passengers were asleep, and if a crew member patrolled the decks she did not see him. The ship was lit by dim electric bulbs, and there were no stars.

She dragged the trunk through the cabin door and rested again.

After that it was a little easier, for the deck was slippery with snow. Ten minutes later she had the trunk up against the rail.

The next part was more difficult. Taking hold of the strap, she lifted one end of the trunk and tried to bring it upright. On her first try she dropped it. The sound it made when it hit the deck seemed very loud, but once again no one came to investigate: there were intermittent noises all the time on the ship, as its funnels belched smoke and its hull cleaved the waves.

The second time she made a more determined effort. She got down on one knee, seized the strap with both hands, and slowly heaved up. When she had the trunk tilted at a forty-five-degree angle Micky moved inside, his weight shifting to the bottom end, and suddenly it became easy to push the whole thing upright.

She tilted it again so that it was leaning on the rail.

The last part was the hardest of all. She bent down and took hold of the lower strap. She took a deep breath and lifted.

She was not taking the whole weight of the trunk, for the other end was resting on the rail; but still it took all her strength to lift the thing an inch off the deck, and then her cold fingers slipped and she let it fall back.

She was not going to be able to manage it.

She rested, feeling drained and numb. But she could not give up. She had struggled so hard to bring the trunk this far. She had to try again.

She bent down and seized the strap again.

Micky spoke again. 'Augusta, what are you doing?'

She answered in a low, clear voice. 'Remember how Peter Middleton died,' she said.

She paused. There was no sound from inside the trunk.

'You're going to die the same way,' she said.

'No, please, Augusta, my love,' he said.

'The water will be colder, and it will taste salty as it fills your lungs; but you'll know the terror he knew as death closes its fist over your heart.'

He began to shout. 'Help! Help! Someone, save me!'

Augusta grabbed the strap and lifted with all her strength. The bottom of the trunk came up off the deck. As

Micky realized what was happening his muffled shouts became louder and more terrified, sounding above the engines and the sea. Soon someone would come. Augusta gave another heave. She lifted the foot of the trunk to chest level and stopped, exhausted, feeling she could do no more. Frantic scrabbling sounds came from inside as Micky tried hopelessly to get out. She closed her eyes, clenched her jaw, and pushed. As she strained with all her might, she felt something give way in her back, and she cried out with pain, but she kept lifting. The bottom of the trunk was now higher than the top, and it slid forward on the rail several inches; but it stopped. Augusta's back was agony. Any moment now a passenger would be roused from a half-drunk sleep by Micky's cries. She knew she could only lift one more time. This had to be final. She gathered her strength, closed her eyes, gritted her teeth against the pain in her back, and heaved.

The trunk slid slowly forward on the rail then fell into space.

Micky screamed a long scream that died into the wind.

Augusta slumped forward, leaning on the rail to ease the agony in her back, and watched the big trunk fall slowly, tumbling end-over-end through the air with the snowflakes. It hit the water with a mighty splash and went under.

A moment later it surfaced. It would float for some time, Augusta realized. The pain in her back was excruciating, and she longed to lie down, but she stayed at the rail, watching the trunk bobbing on the swell. Then it disappeared from sight.

She heard a male voice beside her. 'I thought I heard someone crying for help,' it said worriedly.

Augusta composed herself rapidly and turned to see a polite young man in a silk dressing-gown and a scarf. 'It was me,' she told him, forcing a smile. 'I had a nightmare and woke myself up shouting. I came out here to clear my head.'

'Ah. Are you sure you're all right?'

'Quite sure. You're very kind.'

'Well. Good night, then.'

'Good night.'

He went back into his cabin.

Augusta looked down at the sea. In a moment she would stagger to her bed, but she wanted to look at the sea a little longer. The trunk would fill up slowly, she thought, as water squirted in through the narrow gaps. The level would rise up Micky's body inch by inch as he fought to open the trunk. When it covered his nose and mouth he would hold his breath for as long as he could. But in the end he would give a great involuntary gasp, and the cold salty sea would pour into his mouth and down his throat, filling his lungs. He would squirm and fight for a little longer, racked by pain and terror; and then his movements would become feeble and stop, everything would slowly turn black, and he would die.

[VI]

HUGH WAS desperately weary when at last his train pulled into Chingford station and he got off. Although he was looking forward to his bed, he stopped on the bridge over the line, at the spot where Micky had shot Tonio that morning. He took off his hat and stood there for a minute, bareheaded in the snow, remembering his friend as a boy and a man. Then he walked on.

He wondered how all this would affect the Foreign Office and their attitude to Cordova. Micky had so far evaded the police. But whether Micky was caught or not, Hugh could exploit the fact that he had witnessed the killing. Newspapers would love to publish his moment-by-moment account. The public would be outraged by a foreign diplomat committing murder in broad daylight, and Members of Parliament would probably demand some kind of rebuke. The fact that Micky was the murderer might well spoil Papa Miranda's chances of getting recognized by the British government. The Foreign Office might be persuaded to support the Silva family to punish the Mirandas – and to get compensation for British investors in the Santamaria Harbour Corporation.

The more he thought about it, the more optimistic he felt.

He hoped Nora would be asleep when he got home. He did not want to hear what a miserable day she had had, stuck in this remote village with no one to help her take care of three rowdy boys. He just wanted to slip between the sheets and close his eyes. Tomorrow he would think over the events of today and figure out where they left him and his bank.

He was disappointed to see a light on behind the curtains as he walked up the garden path. That meant she was still up. He let himself in with his key and went into the front room.

He was surprised to see the three boys, all in their pyjamas, sitting in a row on the sofa looking at an illustrated book.

And he was astonished to see Maisie in the middle, reading to them.

All three boys jumped up and ran to him. He hugged and kissed them one by one: Sol, the youngest; then Samuel; then eleven-year-old Toby. The younger two were simply overjoyed to see him, but there was something else in Toby's face. 'What is it, old man?' Hugh asked him. 'Something happened? Where's your mama?'

'She went shopping,' he said, and burst into tears.

Hugh put his arm around the boy and looked at Maisie.

'I got here around four o'clock,' she said. 'Nora must have gone out shortly after you.'

'She left them alone?'

Maisie nodded.

Hugh felt hot anger rise up inside him. The children had been alone here most of the day. Anything could have happened. 'How could she do that?' he said bitterly.

'There's a note.' Maisie handed him an envelope.

He opened it and read the one-word message: *GOODBYE*.

Maisie said: 'It wasn't sealed. Toby read it and showed it to me.'

'It's hard to believe,' Hugh said, but as soon as the words were out of his mouth he realized they were not true: it was all too easy to believe. Nora had always put her own wishes above everything else. Now she had abandoned her children. Hugh guessed she had gone to her father's pub.

And the note seemed to imply that she was not coming back.

He did not know what to feel.

His first duty was to the boys. It was important not to upset them any further. He set his own feelings aside for a moment. 'You boys are up very late,' he said. 'Time for bed. Let's go!'

He ushered them up the stairs. Samuel and Sol shared a room but Toby had his own bedroom. Hugh tucked the little ones in then went in to the eldest. He bent over the bed to kiss him.

'Mrs Greenbourne's a brick,' Toby said.

'I know,' Hugh said. 'She used to be married to my best friend, Solly. Then he died.'

'She's pretty, too.'

'Do you think so?'

'Yes. Is Mama coming back?'

That was the question Hugh had been afraid of. 'Of course she is,' he said.

'Really?'

Hugh sighed. 'To tell you the truth, old man, I don't know.'

'If she doesn't, will Mrs Greenbourne look after us?'

Trust a child to go right to the heart of the matter, Hugh thought. He evaded the question. 'She runs a hospital,' he said. 'She's got dozens of patients to take care of. I don't suppose she has time to look after boys as well. Now, no more questions. Goodnight.'

Toby looked unconvinced, but he let the matter drop. 'Goodnight, Father.'

Hugh blew out the candle and left the room, closing the door.

Maisie had made cocoa. 'I'm sure you'd prefer a brandy, but there doesn't seem to be any in the house.'

Hugh smiled. 'We in the lower middle classes can't afford to drink spirits. Cocoa is fine.'

Cups and a jug stood on a tray, but neither of them moved to it. They stood in the middle of the room looking at one another. Maisie said: 'I read about the shooting in the afternoon paper, and came here to see if you were all right. I found the children on their own, and gave them supper. Then we waited for you.' She smiled a resigned, accepting smile that said it was up to Hugh what happened next.

Suddenly he began to tremble. He leaned on the back of a chair for support. 'It's been quite a day,' he said shakily. 'I'm feeling a little odd.'

'Perhaps you ought to sit down.'

Suddenly he was overwhelmed by love for her. Instead of sitting, he threw his arms around her. 'Hug me hard,' he pleaded.

She squeezed his waist.

'I love you, Maisie,' he said. 'I've always loved you.'

'I know,' she said.

He looked into her eyes. They were full of tears, and as he watched one tear overflowed and trickled down her face. He kissed it away.

'After all these years,' he said. 'After all these years.'

'Make love to me tonight, Hugh,' she said.

He nodded. 'And every night, from now on.'

Then he kissed her again.

EPILOGUE

1892

From *The Times*:

DEATHS

On the 30th May, at his residence in Antibes, France, after
a long illness, the EARL OF WHITEHAVEN, formerly Senior
Partner of Pilasters Bank.

'Edward's dead,' Hugh said, looking up from the
newspaper.

Maisie sat beside him in the railway carriage, wearing a
summer dress in deep yellow with red spots and a little hat
with yellow taffeta ribbons. They were on their way to
Windfield School for Speech Day.

'He was a rotten swine, but his mother will miss him,'
she said.

Augusta and Edward had been living together in the
south of France for the last eighteen months. Despite what
they had done, the syndicate paid them the same allowance
as all the other Pilasters. They were both invalids: Edward
had terminal syphilis and Augusta had suffered a slipped
disc and spent most of her time in a wheelchair. Hugh had
heard that despite her illness she had become the
uncrowned queen of the English community in that part of
the world: matchmaker, arbitrator of disputes, organizer of
social events and promulgator of social rules.

'He loved his mother,' Hugh said.

She looked curiously at him. 'Why do you say that?'

'It's the only good thing I can think of to say about
him.'

She smiled fondly and kissed his nose.

The train chugged into Windfield Station and they got
out. It was the end of Toby's first year and Bertie's last
year at the school. The day was warm and the sun was
bright. Maisie opened her parasol – it was made of the

same spotted silk as her dress – and they walked to the school.

It had changed a lot in the twenty-six years since Hugh had left. His old headmaster, Dr Poleson, was long dead, and there was a statue of him in the quadrangle. The new head wielded the notorious cane they had always called the Striper, but he used it less frequently. The fourth-form dormitory was still in the old dairy by the stone-built chapel, but there was a new building with a school hall that could seat all the boys. The education was better, too: Toby and Bertie learned mathematics and geography as well as Latin and Greek.

They met Bertie outside the hall. He had been taller than Hugh for a year or two now. He was a solemn boy, hard-working and well-behaved: he did not get into trouble at school the way Hugh had. He had a lot of Rabinowicz ancestry, and he reminded Hugh of Maisie's brother Dan.

He kissed his mother and shook Hugh's hand. 'There's a bit of a ruckus,' he said. 'We haven't enough copies of the school song and the Lower Fourth are writing it out like billy-o. I must go and whip them faster. I'll meet you after the speeches.' He hurried off. Hugh watched him fondly, thinking nostalgically how important school seemed until you left.

They met Toby next. The small boys no longer had to wear top hats and frock-coats: Toby was dressed in a straw boater and a short jacket. 'Bertie says I can have tea with you in his study after speeches, if you don't mind, is it all right?'

'Of course,' Hugh laughed.

'Thanks, Father!' Toby ran off again.

In the school hall they were surprised to meet Ben Greenbourne, looking older and rather frail. Maisie, blunt as ever, said: 'Hello, what are you doing here?'

'My grandson is head boy,' he replied gruffly. 'I've come to hear his speech.'

Hugh was startled. Bertie was not Greenbourne's grandson, and the old man knew it. Was he softening in his old age?

'Sit down by me,' Greenbourne commanded. Hugh looked at Maisie. She shrugged and sat down, and Hugh followed suit.

'I hear you two are married,' Greenbourne said.

'Last month,' Hugh said. 'My first wife didn't contest the divorce.' Nora was living with a whisky salesman and it had taken Hugh's hired detective less than a week to get proof of adultery.

'I don't approve of divorce,' Greenbourne said crisply. Then he sighed. 'But I'm too old to tell people what to do. The century is almost over. The future belongs to you, I wish you the best.'

Hugh took Maisie's hand and squeezed it.

Greenbourne addressed Maisie. 'Will you send the boy to university?'

'I can't afford it,' Maisie said. 'It's been hard paying the school fees.'

'I'd be glad to pay,' Greenbourne said.

Maisie was surprised. 'It's kind of you,' she said.

'I should have been kinder years ago,' he replied. 'I always put you down as a fortune-hunter. It was one of my mistakes. If you were only after money you wouldn't have married young Pilaster here. I was wrong about you.'

'You did me no harm,' Maisie said.

'I was too harsh, all the same. I don't have many regrets, but that's one of them.'

The schoolboys began to file into the hall, the youngest sitting on the floor at the front and the older boys on chairs.

Maisie said to Greenbourne: 'Hugh has adopted Bertie legally now.'

The old man turned his sharp eyes on Hugh. 'I suppose you're the real father,' he said bluntly.

Hugh nodded.

'I should have guessed a long time ago. It doesn't matter. The boy thinks I'm his grandfather, and that gives me a responsibility.' He coughed in an embarrassed way and changed the subject. 'I hear the syndicate is going to pay a dividend.'

'That's right,' Hugh said. He had finally disposed of all the assets of Pilasters Bank, and the syndicate that had rescued the bank had made a small profit. 'All the members will get about five per cent on their investment.'

'Well done. I didn't think you'd manage it.'

'The new government in Cordova did it. They handed over the assets of the Miranda family to the Santamaria Harbour Corporation, and that made the bonds worth something again.'

'What happened to that chap Miranda? He was a bad lot.'

'Micky? His body was found in a steamer trunk washed up on a beach on the Isle of Wight. No one ever found out how it got there or why he was inside it.' Hugh had been concerned in the identification of the body: it had been important to establish that Micky was dead, so that Rachel could marry Dan Robinson at last.

A schoolboy came around handing out inky hand-written copies of the school song to all the parents and relatives.

'And you?' Greenbourne said to Hugh. 'What will you do when the syndicate is wound up?'

'I was planning to ask your advice about that,' Hugh said. 'I'd like to start a new bank.'

'How?'

'Float the shares on the stock market. Pilasters Limited. What do you think?'

'It's a bold idea, but then you always were original.' Greenbourne looked thoughtful for a moment. 'The funny thing is, the failure of your bank actually enhanced your reputation, in the end, because of the way you handled things. After all, who could be more reliable than a banker who manages to pay all his creditors even after he's crashed?'

'So . . . do you think it would work?'

'I'm sure of it. I might even put money into it myself.'

Hugh nodded gratefully. It was important that Greenbourne liked the idea. Everyone in the City sought his opinion, and his approval was worth a lot. Hugh had thought his plan would work, but Greenbourne had put the seal on his confidence.

Everyone stood up as the headmaster came in, followed by the housemasters, the guest speaker – a Liberal Member of Parliament – and Bertie, the head boy. They took their seats on the platform, then Bertie came to the lectern and said in a ringing voice: 'Let us sing the school song.'

Hugh caught Maisie's eye and she smiled proudly. The familiar notes of the introduction sounded on the piano, and then they all began to sing.

An hour later Hugh left them having tea in Bertie's study and slipped out through the squash court into Bishop's Wood.

It was hot, just like that day twenty-six years ago. The wood seemed the same, still and humid under the shade of the beeches and elms. He remembered the way to the swimming-hole and found it without difficulty.

He did not climb down the side of the quarry – he was

no longer agile enough. He sat on the rim and threw a stone into the pool. It broke the glassy stillness of the water and sent out ripples in perfect circles.

He was the only one left, except for Albert Cammel out in the Cape Colony. The others were all dead: Peter Middleton killed that day; Tonio shot by Micky two Christmases ago; Micky himself drowned in a steamer trunk; and now Edward, dead of syphilis and buried in a cemetery in France. It was almost as if something evil had come up out of the deep water that day in 1866 and entered their lives, bringing all the dark passions that had blighted their lives, hatred and greed and selfishness and cruelty, fomenting deceit, bankruptcy, disease and murder. But it was over now. The debts were paid. If there had been an evil spirit, it had returned to the bottom of the pond. And Hugh had survived.

He stood up. It was time to return to his family. He walked away, then took a last look back.

The ripples from the stone had disappeared, and the surface of the water was immaculately still once again.

KEN FOLLETT

The Third Twin

£6.99

A chilling story of hidden evil, set at the forefront of modern technology, *The Third Twin* is the heart-stopping new thriller from Ken Follett.

In the course of her work, beautiful scientist Jeannie Ferrami stumbles across a baffling mystery: Steve and Dan appear to be identical twins, but were born on different days to different mothers. A law student and a convicted murderer they seem a world apart, but when Steve is accused of a terrible crime, Jeannie must question just how different they really are.

As she begins to fall in love with Steve, Jeannie finds more than her professional future threatened. Her life is also now at risk. Together Steve and Jeannie will investigate the mystery, uncover all the secrets. But some secrets were meant to be left alone . . .

'Follett is a master storyteller'
The Times

KEN FOLLETT

Eye of the Needle

£6.99

His weapon is the stiletto, his codename: THE NEEDLE. He is Henry Faber, coldly professional, a killer, Germany's most feared deep-cover agent in Britain. His task: to discover the Allies' plans for D-Day, and get them to Germany at all costs. A task he ruthlessly carries through, until Storm Island and the woman called Lucy . . .

'An absolutely terrific thriller, so pulse-pounding, so ingenious in its plotting and so frighteningly realistic that you simply cannot stop reading'
Publishers' Weekly

'A tense, marvellously detailed suspense thriller built on a solid foundation of fact'
Sunday Times